Reasonable
DOUBT

This is a work of fiction. All of the characters, organizations, and events portrayed in this novel are either products of the author's imagination or are used fictitiously.

REASONABLE DOUBT. Copyright © 2008 by Mark Anthony. All rights reserved. Printed in the United States of America. For information, address St. Martin's Press, 175 Fifth Avenue, New York, N.Y. 10010.

www.stmartins.com

Book design by Jamie Kerner-Scott

Library of Congress Cataloging-in-Publication Data

Anthony, Mark, 1973–
    Reasonable doubt / Mark Anthony.—1st ed.
        p. cm.
    ISBN-13: 978-0-312-34080-3
    ISBN-10: 0-312-34080-X
    1. African Americans—Fiction. 2. Police—Crimes against—Fiction. I. Title.

PS3601.N556R43 2008
813'.6—dc22

2007042120

10 9 8 7 6 5 4 3 2

Reasonable
DOUBT

Mark Anthony

 St. Martin's Griffin ≈ New York

This book is dedicated to my sister Paula. You are the hardest worker that I know in one of the most important professions in life. I admire you and love you. Thanks for being the inspiration behind this book.

ACKNOWLEDGMENTS

As always I have to first thank God for giving me the gift to write. I thank my entire family for believing in me and always having my back. Monique Patterson and Kia DuPree at St. Martin's Press: Thanks for always making this writing process seem so easy and seamless. Shout-out to the whole staff at QBoro Books and Urban Books—we can't stop and we won't stop. And a shout-out to myself for following and living out my dreams in spite of the haters! To everyone who is unjustly serving mandatory minimum sentences, keep ya head up, keep the faith, and never stop fighting.

One

Whatchu think about shorty?" Snipes asked me as he placed a forkful of ketchup-drenched scrambled eggs in his mouth.

I was so tired and drained from not having slept in what felt like a week that I didn't even pay him any mind and I laid my head down on the restaurant table.

"Katrina! What the hell is wrong with you? You hear me talking to you, right?"

"What, Snipes? What?" I asked as I picked my head up off the table and wiped some cold out of my eyes.

"Shorty right there, our waitress! Whatchu think about her?"

"What are you talking about?" I asked as I stared at my pancakes and watched them get colder by the second.

"You think she sexy or what? I'm feeling her! Got damn, look at her ass! I think she's an Indian chick or Brazilian or some exotic shit like that. And you know you don't ever see no Indian chicks wit' ass like that!" Snipes said to me, blatantly disrespecting me, his girl.

I didn't respond as I continued to stare at my pancakes and wondered when the hell I was gonna be able to lay my ass down and get some real sleep.

"We gonna check into that hotel right down the block, the Days Inn. I'm gonna have us check in under the last name Rivers. A'ight?" Snipes stated.

I acknowledged him by slowly nodding my head three times.

"So you think she's sexy or what, ma'?"

"Yeah, she's a cute girl," I said with absolutely no emotion.

"I wantchu to get her to come back to the hotel and *chill* wit' us so we can do that threesome thing I been telling you that I wanted to do. That's our chick for the threesome right there. But you gotta kick it to her because it won't work if I talk to her. A'ight?" Snipes said with all seriousness. He got up and reached in his pants pocket. "Remember, we checking in under the last name Rivers, and we staying at the Days Inn. Give her the info and get her to come by," he added as he dropped a twenty-dollar bill on the table and sat back down.

"Snipes, we don't even know this broad. She's the damn IHOP waitress! What am I gonna say to her?" I asked, beginning to show some signs of aggravation and disgust.

"Katrina, come on, ma'! Kick it to her and don't fuck that shit up! I'ma wait at the door and watch you do your thing," Snipes said with a sinister look on his face, a face that was now my life's worst nightmare.

The sound of Snipes's chair scraping the floor as he pushed away from the table was a loud metal-grinding noise that did nothing for my headache. I watched him walk away from the table as his pants sagged off his ass and his loosely laced Timberlands made a thud with every step that he took.

I hate the sight of that sick motherfucker! I thought to myself as I looked at the waitress making her way over to my table.

"Is everything okay?" the Indian-looking waitress asked.

"Yeah, everything is fine. You can bring me the check," I replied as I thought about Snipes's selfish wish for a threesome.

"I have your check right here," the waitress said, looking into the pocket of her blue apron.

She placed the itemized bill on the table and prepared to walk away.

My heart started racing from nervousness but I could feel Snipes's stare burning a hole in my head.

"Umh, excuse me . . ."

"Yes?" the waitress asked as she quickly turned back to face me.

"Yeah, I was just trying to read your name tag. What is your name? Soraya?" I asked with a puzzled look on my face.

"Yes, it's Soraya, you pronounced it right," she said with a slight giggle.

"If you don't mind me asking, where are you from? Is that an Indian name?" I tried to muster up a smile.

"No, actually it's an Arabic name. My parents are from the Middle East."

"Oh, okay. Well, listen, my name is Katrina, and I know that I don't really know you, and I don't even know how to ask you this, but do you have a man . . . a boyfriend . . . are you married?" I said, stumbling over my words as my heart pounded and a nervous smile reappeared across my face.

Soraya smiled as she shook her head no and said that she didn't have a boyfriend.

"Like I said, Soraya, I know I don't really know you, and I know this may sound like the craziest thing you have ever heard, but I really think you are just so gorgeous, and I was wondering if you wouldn't mind hanging out with me and my boyfriend back at our hotel room when you get off from work later today? We're staying—"

Soraya cut me off in the middle of my sentence and laughed and shook her head, saying, "Oh no, no. I'm sorry. But I just, you know, I'm not like that, and I don't know who you are."

There was now this uncomfortable silence as I didn't know what the hell to say. It's not every day that I catch rejection from a woman that I'm trying to pick up for my man.

Soraya broke the silence as she took the twenty-dollar bill off the table and wiped the table with a damp cloth. "Do you need any change?"

"No, you can keep the change." I glanced at Snipes and watched him glare at me like he wanted to murder me or something.

"Look, Soraya, please just—"

Soraya cut me off and told me that she really was too busy and had to get back to work. And she quickly walked off. I honestly couldn't blame her for walking away as quickly as she had. She probably thought I was some kind of freak or something.

I glanced over in Snipes's direction and saw him violently push open the glass IHOP door in disgust and storm out of the restaurant with his arms and hands flailing.

I wasn't in the mood for his shit, not that morning I wasn't! I was thousands of miles away from my home. I hadn't seen or spoken to my family and friends in months, and I was beyond fed up with Snipes. I gathered myself and prepared to head out of the restaurant. I was wearing a nice pair of tight jeans and a wifebeater with some white high heels.

As I made it out of the restaurant, I could see Snipes already in the driver's seat of our luxury car, and he started the engine as I approached.

I opened the front passenger door and got in. There was silence and I could tell that Snipes was in one of his pissed-off moods *again*. I sat down but I didn't look at him. The only thing that I could think of was how in the hell had I ended up some three thousand miles away from New York City, in Tacoma, Washington, of all places?

The silence was killing me so I reached for the radio to turn it on and break the uneasiness. I was hoping to find a hip-hop or an R&B station.

"Turn that shit off!" Snipes immediately barked. "You fucked shit up with shorty and you gonna just sit down in my car like everything is everything?"

"Snipes, what do you want from me? She wasn't into that!" I yelled back.

He turned and grabbed my throat with his right hand and applied so much pressure that I thought he was gonna crush every bone in my neck. All of my air was cut off and I began scratching at him and flailing my arms trying to free myself of his grip.

"Let me tell you something! Don't you ever disrespect me like that again! That's the first got damn thing! And you fucked the shit up with shorty, otherwise she would be here in this car wit' our asses right now headed to the hotel! I don't need you causing me no more stress, Katrina! I got these niggas on my ass, I got the feds on my ass, I got this money to get, and I don't need no more bullshit to deal with!" Snipes violently slammed my head backward into the headrest before finally loosening his grip on my throat.

I coughed, desperately trying to suck air into my lungs. I massaged my throat with my right hand and hoped that the pain would quickly go away.

"I don't care who you dealing with, everybody has a price and everybody can be got and hustled if you spit game the right way. You remember that shit! And next time I don't wanna hear *she wasn't into that!* You make her get into it! You convince her to get into it!" Snipes chided as he put the car in drive.

I was still coughing, and I closed my eyes and held back my tears. I wanted to scream and end this nightmare that I was living. With my present circumstances, my dreams of studying to become a veterinarian weren't working out. I would have given anything to have turned the clock back to the start of my freshman year at the prestigious New York University. But unfortunately I couldn't turn back the hands of time. And, man, what a difference those past nine or ten months made.

Two

When we reached the parking lot of the Days Inn, Snipes turned the engine off and slumped down in his seat. I nervously bit my bottom lip and looked out the window at the overcast sky.

"We here." Snipes sounded as if he was looking in my direction.

"Okay," I replied, still looking out the window in the opposite direction. "Rivers, right?"

"Yeah, Rivers."

I had been through this numerous times before so I knew the routine. "Okay, I'll be right back." I gathered myself and pulled down the sun visor and looked in the mirror to see if I had any bruises on my neck. Fortunately there were none, but I still looked like a hot mess.

Since I was traveling with one of the U.S. Marshals' most wanted fugitives, I was instinctively suspicious of everyone and everything, so as I exited the car, I quickly looked around to see if anyone remotely ɔoked like a cop or a federal agent. Everything seemed cool so I made my way to the front desk of the hotel.

Making sure not to make direct eye contact with the lady at the front desk, I pretended to look at one of the road maps that I had grabbed when I first walked into the hotel lobby.

"Hello, I'd like to get a room."

"Oh, sure, do you have a reservation?" the attractive black chick with a long blond weave asked.

Still looking at the road map, I nonchalantly replied, "No, I don't have a reservation."

"Okay, that's no problem, I just need your name and I'll get you taken care of."

"Tiffany Rivers," I said while finally making eye contact.

The lady, who looked and sounded like she wanted to be white, began typing into her computer. "And, Ms. Rivers, I just need a credit card to cover any incidentals."

"What is the rate for the room?"

"It will be $49.99 a night."

"Miss, I am so sorry but there was some fraudulent activity on my credit card, and Visa will be sending me a replacement card soon, but until then I don't have any credit cards that I can use. Is it alright if I give you a two-hundred-dollar deposit for incidentals?"

"Two hundred dollars will be plenty. I am so sorry to hear about your credit card. That is just horrible," the lady said, moving some of the blond hair from in front of her face.

After typing some more into her computer, she gave me the keys to our room and I reluctantly headed back to get Snipes. Walking toward the car, I silently prayed for God to give me the courage to either call the cops, call my moms, or just flat-out escape from Snipes somehow and set myself free.

Katrina, you gotta leave this nigga and bounce, I told myself as I got closer to the car.

Katrina, you see this bitch-ass nigga Warren right here? This is what happens when motherfuckers snitch. They get earthed! I earthed his ass! Me! I did

this to his punk ass! And you can take this how you wanna take it, b
rina, word is bond, if you ever snake me or bitch up on me, I swear to God I
earth your whole fucking family! You make sure you remember that shit.

Snipes had spoken those words to me on the night that he had murdered his best friend in cold blood. He had murdered him, and then, as a scare tactic, he took me back to see the body. It was a sight that I will never forget, but his piercing and satanic threat about killing my family was something that stuck even deeper with me. And for good reason. Whenever I thought about leaving or escaping or calling the cops or calling my parents, I knew to do otherwise. I knew that Snipes was crazy enough and bold enough to actually carry out a hit on my family if I ever betrayed him in any way, and I guess that is one of the reasons why he was able to control me the way he did.

"I got the room, baby," I said, opening the driver's door.

Snipes got out and we made our way back to the hotel, entering through a side stairway entrance. We quickly made our way to the second floor and our room.

"Ahhhhh, shit, I'm tired like a moutherfucka," Snipes said as he fell out across the king-size bed as soon as we entered the room.

"You ain't say nothing but a word," I said as I began to strip out of my clothes so that I could take a shower and get in the bed and get some much needed sleep.

I went into the bathroom and turned on the shower.

"You wanna take a shower with me?" I asked, going to the bathroom door. I was trying to do and say anything that I possibly could to keep Snipes from snapping back into one of his fits of rage.

"Yeah, I'll be there in a minute." Snipes placed his loaded handgun and two bricks of cocaine that we were traveling with inside the drawer of the nightstand next to the bed. "I gotta move this shit before Sunday. We got what? Like four hundred dollars left?"

"We'll have less than that after we pay for this room and buy us some clothes, but don't worry, baby, you'll move it," I reassured him.

"Katrina, this is different though. I don't really know this city at all. I mean, I know the East Coast and I know the South, but out here it's a erent game. I'll fuck around and sell this shit to a fucking narc or ome shit."

I kissed Snipes on the lips and made my way to the bathroom and got in the shower.

Snipes took a while to join me and I could tell that he had a lot on his mind because he wasn't frisky with me at all. Usually just the sight of me naked would have his dick harder than Chinese arithmetic. But as they say, a man's dick can't do what his mind ain't into. And Snipes's mind was far from sex, or at least it appeared that way. A big part of me was glad though, because I was really not in the mood for having him banging my back out.

After the shower, we both got in the bed to get that much needed sleep that we had desperately been chasing. It was barely twelve noon but I knew that we would sleep like it was twelve midnight.

"When we get up, we'll go buy some gear and then bounce around to different clubs so I can see what's what," Snipes instructed as I lay with my head on the pillow staring at the ceiling.

In seconds we were both out like lights.

I didn't know how long we had been asleep but it felt like a long time, and out of nowhere I was suddenly awoken by Snipes's loud screams and pleas.

"Stopppp! No! No! Please, stop! Please!" Snipes screamed out loud in his sleep as he held up his hands and braced as if he was a boxer shielding off blows from his opponent.

"Snipes, Snipes! Wake up, baby, it's just a dream. Wake up!" I said as I shook him.

Snipes kept screaming and his screams seemed to get louder and I could see the tension in his muscles.

"Snipes!" I yelled, and shook him again. "You're dreaming, Snipes, it's just a dream, baby."

Snipes's eyes suddenly popped open and he sat up straight. He was breathing real heavy as he looked around trying to gather himself and figure out just what the hell was going on.

I also sat up and leaned over and hugged him. "You was just having another one of those wild dreams," I said, making sure not to insult his manhood by telling him that he was having another *nightmare.*

"It's okay," I reassured him as I caressed the muscles on his back.

"Fuck!" Snipes shouted as he flung the bedsheet off his legs and got up. He walked over to the window, wearing nothing but his boxers, and stared out at the view.

I had been through these nightmare episodes numerous times with Snipes. While I hated that I was living on the run with this hardened thug, who controlled me and made my life miserable, this huge part of me cared a whole lot about him. And I knew that he was troubled.

In fact Snipes had opened up to me some time ago and given me some insight into his background. This had opened my eyes and allowed me to see Snipes as a human being. A human being who, like most of us, had a whole lot of baggage from the past. Yeah, Snipes was lugging around a whole lot of emotional and mental baggage. I don't know if I was stupid, blind, naïve, dumb, or a combination of all of those adjectives, but knowing something about Snipes's baggage allowed me to overlook a lot of his ways and endure a lot of the pain from my being with him. Yeah, it was that, combined with this sick syndrome I would later learn I had, that allowed me to tolerate and endure all of the drama that I had been put through.

But if I left him, how would he cope? Who would he turn to? And most importantly, how would I be any different from the people in his past that had helped fill his hands and his mind with such heavy baggage?

As I lay in the bed and watched Snipes stare out the window in frustration due to his inability to control his recurring nightmares, I realized that Snipes was the way he was due to a lot of things that had happened to him that were out of his control, such as being a victim of child abuse, and I also knew that was probably the reason that I hated his guts, and loved him so much, all at the same damn time.

Three

Rewind . . . Approximately Ten Months Earlier . . . 1993

Coming from a small town in North Carolina, I had never in my life experienced anything like the fast life and pace of New York City. I had always craved the excitement of the fast life that living in the city had to offer. But in truth, I also knew that I was cut from a different cloth and could probably never make it on my own in New York or Chicago or any other big city. I'd always viewed myself as unassuming, unattractive, and boring, and it seemed to me that I would always be just an animal-loving country girl who could barely fit in down in North Carolina, much less New York City.

My college roommate, Candace, was from Philadelphia so she was used to the city life. Candace was cool and exactly what I needed to help keep me in check and serve as my guardian. For the entire first week that she and I hung together, she constantly had to remind me, as she would so eloquently put it, "Stop acting like you ain't never been nowhere before!" The thing was, I had never been *nowhere* before so I didn't know *how* to act or *how* to fit in.

I'll never forget one Friday morning that Candace and I left our dorm. I'll never forget it because that was the day I first encountered the man who would forever change and make a lasting impression on my life. It was the Friday after Labor Day and Candace and I were both on our way to our 1:00 P.M. African-American studies class. As we exited Rubin Residence Hall, on Fifth Avenue, Candace began to joke with me.

"Katrina, remember, act like you've been somewhere before. Don't be staring at people like you some damn tourist or some shit."

I laughed. "Nah, Candace, I'm just being me. See, us country folks, we speak to people when they walk pass us, we say, 'Hello, how you doing?' You know, we try to be polite, unlike y'all Philly and New York people, always trying to act all hard and always walking around with your guard up."

Before Candace could say anything else, we were both interrupted by a young, fine, dark-skinned brother who was trying to get our attention, more so my attention.

"Umh, excuse me, miss."

I heard him and I was sure that Candace heard him as well, but we both kept walking.

"Excuse me, miss, can I speak to you for a second?" This time, the guy had moved in close enough to make eye contact with me so I had to pay him some attention.

I don't know why but I immediately became nervous, but it was a butterflies-in-my-stomach kind of nervousness.

Candace in her hardened city way abruptly replied, "No, we can't talk right now, we're running late for our class."

The persistent dark chocolate, sexy-looking thing responded, "I was really trying to get your friend's attention. But if I need your permission to talk to her, that's cool, just let her know that I'll only take a minute of her time."

At that point both of us stopped. And I was finally able to look the guy in his face, and maybe I was just one horny bitch who hadn't had *any* in a while or something, I don't know, but my panties felt like they were getting wet just from looking at the chocolate Hershey's kiss that was now directly in front of me. *Yes, it was that serious for me.*

I laughed. "No, you don't need her permission to speak to me. I'm a big girl, I can speak for myself. . . . Candy, we have a few minutes. See, that's exactly what I'm talking about, you acting all rude and stuff." I smiled, looking in Candy's direction. Inside I was screaming with excitement and happy as hell that someone so cute had taken the time to try to get my attention.

"I'm Snipes." The guy extended his hand for a handshake. "And you are?"

"Oh, I'm sorry . . . Katrina. My name is Katrina." I reached out and grabbed hold of Snipes's firm right hand.

"And I take it that your bodyguard's name is Candy?" Snipes sarcastically asked while looking at Candy.

I was about to give him Candy's name but she quickly interjected, "Big Panties. . . . You wanna know my name? Everybody calls me Big Panties!" Candy replied with a matter-of-fact look on her face.

I couldn't help but laugh at Candy's remark, but at the same time I didn't wanna come across as immature or something.

"Big Panties, huh?" Snipes questioned with a smile on his face as he quickly nodded his head once. I couldn't help but notice that his teeth were perfectly aligned and sparkling white, which didn't help dry my panties at all.

"I'm not gonna hold y'all up, but I just wanted to introduce myself to you, Katrina. Actually I saw you two days ago and I tried to get your attention, but you dissed me and kept walking," Snipes explained.

"*Really?*" I asked, trying to sound surprised, which I was because I didn't remember having ever seen him before, much less him ever trying to talk to me. At that moment I was more *open* than anything, but I tried my best to hide it, even though my Kool-Aid smile had probably given me away.

"See, look at you smiling. You dissed me and you probably felt good about it, just crushed a brother's ego." Snipes stomped his right foot on the ground and grinded it like he was squishing a cockroach or something.

"Oh my God! That is so not true," I said, cheesing like there was no tomorrow.

"So, if you don't mind me asking, where's your accent from?" Snipes asked, switching up the pace just a bit.

"Accent? You the one with the accent," I snapped back.

"*Anyway!* Katrina, could you come on, we don't have all damn day!" Candace rudely interrupted.

A part of me wanted to tell Candace to just go ahead and that I would catch up to her. It wasn't really my style to just flat leave somebody like that, but from the time I had arrived at the NYU campus, and in fact my whole time in New York, I just felt like this outsider who was yearning for attention and trying to find herself. I knew I looked good, but in comparison to all of the other chicks that I would see walking around, I just felt like I wasn't measuring up and that I couldn't compete, which had been the story of my life and probably the reason I had battled low self-esteem throughout the years. Either I didn't have the body, or the clothes, or the personality. My whole style just seemed like it was missing something. So needless to say, I was really open when Snipes had spoken to me and I wanted to make sure that I capitalized on the opportunity, and that would have been the only reason I would have told Candace to bounce without me.

"It sounds like you're from North Carolina," Snipes correctly guessed, which impressed me. He was totally ignoring Candace, which was also good.

"I am! How did you know?"

"What part you from?"

"What the fuck is this? Twenty damn questions?" Candace asked with all kinds of attitude. "Katrina, we gotta go! Come on!"

"Ma', why you blockin' a nigga?" Snipes asked Candace, sounding like he was running out of patience.

So that Candace wouldn't lose it and cause an unnecessary confrontation, I told Snipes, "You know what? I do gotta go. It was nice meeting you though. But I know I'll see you around." I began to walk off with Candace. Inside, I was hoping that Snipes would ask me for my number or at least give me his.

"See, you doing it again, just crushing a brother's ego," Snipes said while again making that crushing movement with his foot.

"Big Panties, just give me two more minutes with your girl and I promise you I'll give her back to you," Snipes said as he followed behind us.

"*Whateva*. Katrina, I'll see you later on," Candace replied as I stopped and she continued down Fifth Avenue toward West Tenth Street.

As soon as Candace was outta earshot, Snipes asked, "What's up with your girl?"

"She's cool. She just got her ways about her," I replied, trying to stay neutral.

As we watched Candace walk off, Snipes jokingly replied, "I see why they call her Big Panties—she look like she got about a size sixty waist! Yo, why is it always the busted friend that be blocking on niggas?"

We both started laughing.

"Come on now, you can't be talking about my roommate like that," I said while continuing to laugh. "You know her waist ain't that big, and she ain't busted either."

There was a brief pause, then Snipes put on a serious face. "I know you gotta go, but *for real, for real* I had saw you walking with your girl for the past few days and I was hoping to see you alone so I could approach you. . . . I just, you know, I just wanted to introduce myself to you, find out where you was from, and . . ."

And? I said to myself as Snipes paused. I was eagerly waiting for his response.

"And, I wanted to ask you if I could take you out," Snipes said while finally finishing his thought.

I didn't want to appear too eager so I decided to change the pace a little bit.

"Snipes, is that your last name? A nickname? Or is it your real name?"

"That's what my people call me. My real name is Dwight Abrams. But ever since that movie *New Jack City* came out like two years ago, everybody has been calling me Snipes because they swear I look like Nino Brown."

"Like who?" I had never seen the movie *New Jack City*, but later on I would find out just how ironic it was that Snipes would say that people said he looked like the drug lord Nino Brown from the movie, as opposed to looking like the actor Wesley Snipes.

"I don't make the connection. How do you get from Dwight Abrams to Snipes from Nino Brown?" I said in a tongue-twisting way.

"Oh, my bad. You must not have seen the movie. Nino Brown was played by the actor Wesley Snipes."

"Oh, okay. Now I got you." I just couldn't believe how turned on I was getting just by talking to Snipes. It was like he had some type of voodoo spell on me or something crazy.

"So, Katrina, can I get your number and call you later on?" Snipes asked with his charming ass.

"Yeah, I can give you my number, as long as you ain't the stalker type that will be blowing up a sista's phone twenty-four–seven," I said with a smile.

I gave Snipes my number, and a part of me wanted to stand there and talk to him until I was blue in the face. But I knew that I was probably already ten minutes late for my class, so I began walking in that direction.

Snipes walked with me, then he and I both stopped as he extended his hand to me like a gentleman.

"It was nice meeting you," Snipes said, not letting go of my hand.

"You too," I said with a smile.

"Thanks for not crushing a brother's ego," Snipes joked while still holding my hand.

I laughed and didn't attempt to pull my hand from his. Part of me wanted to pull his ass close to me and press my body up against his and slob his ass down right there in front of everybody on Fifth Avenue.

"I know you gotta go, you probably late for your class now. But can I just be honest with you?"

I looked at him to sort of give him the go-ahead.

"I hope I'm not gonna scare you or anything, but I am just so attracted to you!" Snipes finally let go of my hand. "You got this sophisticated sexiness about you that is just crazy!"

I couldn't help but smile. "Is that so?" I continued to walk in the direction of my class, leaving Snipes behind.

"I'll call you later tonight."

I looked in his direction and nodded as I kept walking. I realized that I could not have cared less if I was late for class. In fact I didn't even want to go to class anymore. All I wanted to do was think about Snipes.

But can I just be honest with you? I hope I'm not gonna scare you or anything, but I am just so attracted to you!

That kept replaying over and over in my head. Maybe it was just game that Snipes was running on me and I was just some gullible chick from down South who was acting like *I had never been nowhere before.* Or maybe Snipes was just this genuinely charming good-looking guy that wanted to get to know me for all the right reasons.

At the time I didn't know what Snipes's true motives were, and to be honest, I didn't care. All I knew was that he looked good, he had approached me, he made me feel good about myself, and I wanted to get to know who the hell he was and what would become of our first encounter with each other.

Four

It wasn't until that following Monday that I spoke to Snipes again. The entire weekend I thought about him and hung around my dorm hoping like a fiend that he would call me. By Monday evening I was beginning to lose hope as I kind of figured to myself that everything had seemed too good to be true and it probably was.

He probably met some sexy chick later on that day and forgot about my ol' country ass. Or maybe he got a girl already and he's been chillin' with her and didn't have the time to call me.

Those thoughts kept running through my head. But it just didn't make sense to me that Snipes would have gone all out of his way to get my attention and then just not call a sista.

Finally at about eight thirty that night as I lay stretched out on my bed reading from my psychology textbook, the phone rang. I quickly maneuvered my body and reached for the phone hoping that it was Snipes, but I was truly figuring that it was probably my mother, who had made it a habit to call me just about every other night to see how I was making out.

"Hello," I said as I picked up the phone on its third ring.

"Hello, can I speak to Katrina?"

"Speaking."

"Katrina, what's up, ma'? Yo, getting in touch with you is like trying to get in touch with the president!"

"Snipes?"

"Yeah, it's me. What's up witchu?"

"What's up with me? I should be asking you that. I thought you was gonna call me later that night on Friday. I see you don't keep your word. That's not good." I made sure not to sound too serious as I was cheesing like the Kool-Aid character.

"I did call you that night. And I called you like three more times after that. Candace didn't tell you? I left my number for her to give to you and all that."

"She never gave me no message that you called. You sure you spoke with Candace?" I asked, while part of me was bugging out wondering why Candace hadn't left me the messages.

"Yeah, I'm sure I spoke to her! Yo, I know that's your girl and all, but on the real, that bitch is a fat-cock-blocking-ass bitch!"

"Come on, Snipes, you can't be calling my girl outta her name like that."

Snipes kept quiet and didn't say anything so I said, "Well, she ain't here right now but I'll find out what's what when I speak to her later tonight."

"A'ight, cool. But I'm glad that I gotchu now. Whatchu doing later?"

"I ain't got nothing planned. I'm just getting ready for this test that I got in the morning, but other than that I was just chillin'."

"Well, me and my mans and his girl are getting ready to go to the Shark Bar to get something to eat. You ever been there?"

Not only had I never been there, I was so naïve and clueless that I didn't even realize that the Shark Bar was more than just a bar, that it was a full-scale restaurant.

"Nah, I've never been there but I don't mind hanging out."

"A'ight, cool. You stay in Rubin, right?"

"Yeah."

"Look, I'm gonna be there at nine fifteen. I'll call you when I get there. And make sure that you answer the phone when I call," Snipes said with a bit of authority.

"Okay, so I'll see you later."

I hung up the phone and immediately ran to my closet. I didn't really have much of a wardrobe, but I knew that I looked my best whenever I wore tight jeans, high heels, and a nice top. Plus I figured that was a real neutral kind of outfit that would fit the dress code of most social establishments. I wanted to be at my best and I had about twenty minutes or so to kill, so I decided to take a quick shower before getting dressed. The showers were down the hall from my room so I scribbled a note that I left for Candace just in case she came back while I was in the shower and Snipes happened to call.

Needless to say, when I came back from the shower, Candace had returned to our dorm room and I sensed some real shade from her, but I couldn't understand what it was about.

"Hey, Candace," I said as I took off my bath towel and began putting lotion on my body.

Candace didn't say a word. She simply picked up the phone and began dialing.

"Candace, I said hello . . ."

Candace finally replied, saying, "Emh."

I shook my head and continued to get dressed and didn't say another word. I was learning that Candace was obviously a real moody bitch. In fact she had been in her little funk ever since Friday when I'd met Snipes. But moody or not, she had issues, because when she reached the person that she had dialed, she all of a sudden became bubbly and talkative but at the same time sounded kind of phony, like she was exaggerating the fact that she was talking to a good friend.

"Candace, I'm expecting a call, so if you get a beep, I need you to click over and answer the phone," I said in a stern tone.

Candace pretended she didn't hear me as she paid me no mind and kept on talking.

After I put on my jeans and my bra I walked right up to Candace so that she had no choice but to hear me. "Candace, I said that I'm expecting a call, so if you get a beep, I need you to click over and answer the phone!"

"Hold on a minute," Candace said to the person on the phone.

"You *need me* to click over?" Candace said in a mocking tone. "What *I need you* to do is watch your attitude! That's the first thing. And I also *need you* to get the hell outta my face while I'm on the phone! I already saw your little note, a'ight!" She sounded like the character Sheneneh from the Martin Lawrence sitcom.

Oh, no, this bitch didn't just come off like that! I said to myself.

"Sorry about that. . . . Yeah, that was my roommate. She all rude! I can't even have a decent conversation," Candace relayed on the line.

After I put on my heels and my top, I walked over to the phone and pressed the button near the dial pad to end Candace's call.

"Candace, I don't know what the hell your problem is, but I'm not in the mood for your childish bullshit! You haven't been giving me my messages all weekend long, and now you bugging out 'cause I asked you to click over if you hear a beep, and you got a problem with that!"

"Katrina, that was totally uncalled for and rude! And first of all, I did relay your messages. I might have *forgotten* to give you *certain* messages, and if I did, I'm sorry, but I'm not your personal answering service, so please let's not get it twisted!"

"Candace, I know you're not my personal answering service but, come on, you know there is a problem with the voice mail and until the school gets it fixed—"

I was interrupted by the ringing telephone. Candace and I both sort of lunged to answer it, but she beat me to it.

"Hello? . . . Who?" she asked with a bit of ghettoness.

"Oh. Yeah, hold on." Candace held out the phone for me.

"Hello," I said after snatching the phone from Candace.

"I see the blocker finally gave you the phone," Snipes joked.

I laughed, and immediately all of the frustration and tension that Candace had caused in me subsided.

"Yo, I'm downstairs. You ready?"

"Yeah, I'm ready. I'll be there in a minute."

I hung up the phone, put on some lipstick and my Gucci perfume, then I double-checked my appearance in my full-length mirror on my closet door.

"Candace, I'm going to the Shark Bar. I'll be back later tonight."

Candace didn't respond.

"Look. I'm sorry for hanging up on your call. That was wrong on my part."

Candace still didn't reply.

"If my mother calls, can you do me a favor and just tell her that I'm at the library or in the lounge studying . . . okay?"

Candace ignored that and replied with a frown, "The Shark Bar?"

"Yeah, what's wrong with that?"

"Nah, I'm just saying."

"You saying what?"

"That was that guy that we met the other day in front of the building, right?"

"Yeah. Why?"

"Katrina, I'm just saying be careful. That's all."

In my mind I just couldn't believe how much of a jealous hater Candace was.

"Candace, when I get back, we need to talk. 'Cause I know you been looking out for me and all, but it don't even sound like you trying to be fun with it anymore, it sounds like you really trying to cramp my style."

Candace laughed. "*Cramp your style?* Nah, not even. Look, Katrina, I was here on campus for that special summer program, you know that. And I seen Snipes around and he just seems like the crazy baller type that ain't about nothing. I always seen that dude with different chicks and all that. I'm just trying to look out for you so that you don't get caught out there. That's all."

I laughed as I opened the door to my room because to me it

seemed like Candace was just hating on Snipes. 'Cause if not, then why hadn't she ever mentioned any of that to me before?

"Candace, my parents were way overprotective when I was in their house, and now they're all the way down in Winston-Salem, North Carolina. I didn't come all the way up here to New York City to still be in nobody's prison. I gotta live a little. We'll talk when I get back." I closed the door and headed for the elevator with so much excited anticipation.

I was *going out* in New York City for the first time. I couldn't wait!

Five

I t took me an extra five minutes or so to make it to the lobby of my dorm because I took the stairs instead of the elevator. Before heading downstairs, I stopped off at the bathroom and went into one of the stalls and quickly downed three shot-size bottles of Bacardi dark that I had hidden inside my bag. I drank the Bacardi straight with no chaser, then quickly popped two Altoids into my mouth to mask any smell of alcohol on my breath.

See, I was basically a shy, introverted person. I had been that way most of my life. But I always envied people who were funny, outgoing, and could be the life of the party. My shyness had always prevented me from being noticed, and I always sort of played the background in social situations. The thing was, I knew that whenever I drank liquor, I would become *that person* that I always wanted to be. I would come out of my shell. All of my inhibitions would go away. I would become loose, loud, funny, and free-spirited as all of my social fears and anxieties would quickly fall by the wayside.

Some people are violent drunks, some people are sloppy drunks, but I was definitely a free-spirited, anything-goes kind of lush.

When I reached the front of my building, it took me a few minutes to recognize that Snipes was sitting inside an all-black Mercedes-Benz 190. I had vaguely remembered him standing in front of a Honda Accord on the day that he had first spoken to me, so I was sort of surprised to see him in such a nice car. Needless to say, a sista definitely wasn't complaining.

I walked as sexy as I could while approaching the passenger side of what looked like a brand-new Mercedes.

Snipes turned down the music as I got inside the car, which had that brand-new-car smell. I was gonna ask Snipes if it was his and if it was brand-new, but I didn't want to rub him the wrong way right out the gate. So I kept my mouth shut and let him speak first.

"Yo, you *really working* them jeans!" Snipes said with a sinister smile on his face.

I smiled back. "All my clothes were either dirty or wrinkled so I just grabbed these jeans and threw them on." Then I blew out some air softly as I tried to sit and relax.

Snipes put the idling car in drive and we took off down the street.

"I don't know if I told you, but my man and his girl are gonna roll with us."

"Yeah, you told me. It's all good. I ain't antisocial," I joked.

"They ain't too far. They at Hayden Hall, right near Washington Square Park."

I remained quiet. To break the silence Snipes pressed play on his tape deck and turned up a Kid Capri mix tape.

"Oh, I love this song! Turn that shit up!" I shouted as I could tell the liquor was starting to kick in just a little bit. I could feel that buzz that I was always searching for whenever I drank socially.

"Whatchu know about this?" Snipes said while turning up the volume to the remix version of Mary J. Blige's song "Love No Limit."

"Whaaat? This is my muthafuckin' *anthem* right here!" I shouted. Cursing was another thing that I did a lot of whenever I drank.

Feeling more relaxed and loose, I began looking in Snipes's direction as the *Rising To The Top* beat blared through the speakers. Then I began to sing and recite the lyrics to the song while I was also trying to subliminally send Snipes a hint by stressing particular parts of the song's lyrics, lyrics that in my mind I easily saw as applying to me and Snipes:

> *Baby, I'm in need of your love . . .*
> *Freely, completely, everything you want I'll be . . .*

I stopped singing the lyrics as Snipes looked at me, smiled, and re-marked, "Yo, I ain't know you was so animated. You seemed all shy and innocent when I met you the other day."

"There's a lot about me you don't know." I winked at Snipes, then immediately went right back to reciting part of the chorus of the song:

> *Don't you look no more*
> *Love without a limit.*

I didn't want to overdo it with the singing so I calmed down a bit and stopped reciting the song and just rocked my head and shoulders in rhythm with the beat. At that moment we were also just pulling up to Hayden Hall, where Snipes's friends were standing, chatting and wait-ing for us.

They immediately recognized the car and quickly made their way to the back passenger-side door and got in.

"What up, my nigga?" Snipes said as he reached his hand toward the backseat for a pound.

"My man. What's the deal?"

"Hey, Snipes," the young lady said as she scooted her body across the backseat and positioned herself directly behind the driver's seat. The young lady smelled and looked like a million dollars. In fact from when we had first pulled up to the curb and I noticed her, I couldn't help but notice how she had this stunning look about her. She reminded me a lot of the model Tyra Banks. She was tall like a model, and she was gorgeous and striking like a supermodel, only she had way more body than those skinny models on TV and in the magazines. I quickly began wondering if she was even a student at NYU.

"Alexis, this is my friend Katrina. Katrina, this is Alexis," Snipes introduced us.

Just as I was about to say hello, Snipes interrupted me, "And, Warren, this is Katrina. Katrina, this is Warren."

"Hello, nice to meet you both," I said with my body partially turned and my head facing the rear of the car. I couldn't help but notice again how gorgeous Alexis looked. She had these real defined cheekbones, and her features were just so knockout gorgeous. Her hair was jet-black, long and wavy, and I was trying to determine if it was a real expensive weave or if she in fact had Indian in her family.

"So, we going to the Shark Bar?" Alexis asked. Before giving anyone time to answer, she quickly asked, "So, Katrina, where you from? Do you go to NYU?"

I smiled. "Yeah, I go to NYU. Originally I'm from North Carolina. I never even been to New York before I started at NYU so this is my first time really going out in New York."

There was a brief silence.

"So what about you? Do you go to NYU?" I asked Alexis.

"Yeah, I'm a freshman. This is my first time in New York too, and I love it! New York is totally different than New Orleans."

"Oh, so you're from the South like me," I said.

At that moment Alexis's cell phone began to ring.

"Hello. . . . What? Come on, don't even say no stupid shit like that. . . . Yeah, whatever! I don't have time for games. I'll call you when I get back tonight if I get a chance to." Alexis hung up the phone.

"Bitch!" she shouted out. "I hate jealous-ass, broke-ass bitches!" Alexis continued to vent.

"What's up?" Warren asked.

Alexis didn't respond and just looked out the window of the car. I was shocked that she had a cell phone. You really had to be ballin' out of control to have one since most people only had pagers. What I couldn't figure out was, if that cell phone was Alexis's, where in the hell did she get the money to afford it?

Still feeling nice from the liquor and wanting to make a good first impression, I chimed right in to what Alexis had been saying.

"Alexis, you sound like you was talking to my fat-ass, jealous-ass roommate!" I knew that I was sounding two-faced by dissing Candace, but she wasn't there to hear me, and what she couldn't hear couldn't offend her, and besides, I was more concerned with fittin' in than I was about respecting Candace.

Snipes began laughing and telling everybody about Candace and her sixty-inch waistline and how she was such a cock-blocker. "Yo, and the bitch got the nerve to call herself Big Panties!" Snipes yelled into the car, to everyone's amusement. "Can you believe that bullshit?"

I was shocked that I was so quickly feeling comfortable and feeling like I really fit in with everybody, which was a good thing.

Before long we were pulling up to the Shark Bar, and after five minutes or so of looking for a parking spot we found one and quickly made our way inside the restaurant.

It was jam-packed, and as soon as we walked in, I noticed a bar to the left of us. I had never in my life seen so many cute guys, all who appeared to be ballers, all assembled in such a confined spot. As we walked in, all of the dudes at the bar seemed as if they turned their heads just to pay attention to us. But I quickly realized that most of the eyes had to be on Alexis and her sexy ass.

"I'll be right back. I'ma go put our name on the list," Alexis stated, sounding as if she had been to the spot before.

"A'ight, we'll be over here by the bar," Warren stated as he adjusted his shirt in an obvious and blatant attempt to show off his diamond-encrusted Presidential Rolex.

"Katrina, you can come with me," Alexis stated, and I followed her lead.

As Alexis and I snaked our way through the large crowd of people and attempted to reach the hostess, I commented, "Alexis, I can't believe that there are so many people in here this late on a Monday night!"

Alexis didn't respond and the two of us just kept walking. I had to quickly remind myself to stop acting so brand-new.

"Hi, how you doing, miss?" a cute guy said to Alexis as she accidentally brushed up against him in an attempt to get by.

Alexis didn't answer but rudely rolled her eyes and blew some air out of her lungs as if she was appalled and kept it moving.

"Oh, it's like that? A nigga can't even get a hello from chicks!" the guy said, his ego hurt.

"Hello," I said, as I was also accidentally brushing by the guy in the tight space. I was attempting to try to make sure that no heated words left the guy's mouth.

"Thank you, ma'!" the guy remarked emphatically in my direction with the sound of validation. "Your fuckin' friend is bad as hell, but her fucked-up attitude makes her look like shit!"

"Fuck you!" Alexis shouted in the guy's direction. "You don't know me! Who the fuck do you think you are!" Alexis added as she briefly caused a small scene. "And, Katrina, that's disrespectful on your part to even be speaking to that broke-ass nigga if you supposed to be up in here with Snipes."

Fortunately the guy didn't respond as Alexis and I finally reached the hostess. All eyes in that immediate area were on us, but I was glad that we were out of earshot from Snipes and Warren.

"Can I get a table for four?"

"Smoking or nonsmoking?" the hostess asked.

"It don't matter." Alexis was pretty as shit but I was quickly realizing that she also seemed to be ghetto as all hell with her attitude.

"Okay, it'll be about a thirty-minute wait. Just listen for your name."

"We'll be by the bar," Alexis replied as the two of us walked off and headed back in Snipes's direction.

"Katrina, I know you said you ain't been out before since you been here in New York, but I like you from what I see so far, so I gotta just tell you this for your own good," Alexis said. I waited to hear her out. "When you out in public with niggas like Snipes and Warren, you can't be speaking to no other dudes! I don't care if it's even just saying hello. The shit is disrespectful, that's the first thing, but the shit will also get your ass slapped and it'll get a nigga killed!"

We were just about back at the bar where Snipes and Warren were, so Alexis quickly wrapped up our conversation, which made me glad.

"Look, forget about that little incident. We here to enjoy ourselves and that's what we're gonna do, but we'll exchange numbers tonight and we'll talk. Okay?"

"Okay," I replied as we reached Snipes.

By that time, the Bacardi shots that I had drunk before leaving my dorm had worn off and I desperately needed a drink to calm my nerves.

Right on cue, Snipes asked what we were all drinking, and he ordered drinks for everyone. Alexis had a martini, but I knew that wouldn't be strong enough for me so I ordered a Hennessy and Coke. I quickly drank the Hennessy and Coke and I was soon ordering another one.

"Got damn! Katrina let me find out that you a lush!" Alexis said, laughing because I was already on my second drink while she was still sipping on her first martini.

I could have cared less about Alexis's comments as the drinks were starting to kick in. And before I knew it, I was downing one drink after the next, and in fifteen minutes I was past tipsy. I was actually drunk, but I was maintaining myself.

Dinner was like a quick blur. Maybe it seemed like a blur because I had been talking so much and flirting and having a good time. I'm not sure, but all I knew was that time had flown by.

Before long the four of us were back in the Mercedes-Benz and headed back toward the dorms. I don't know if it was the motion from the car or something I had eaten or the overindulgence of liquor, but everything appeared to be spinning around and I felt I was about to throw up my soul-food dinner.

I slumped in my seat and prayed that I didn't throw up inside

Snipes's car. Although I had been drunk the whole night, it had been a good type of drunk. It was a fun, life-of-the-party drunk so I was good, but I knew that if I threw up in his car, I would forever ruin my relationship with Snipes, Alexis, and Warren. And there would be no way that I could restore my credibility with them. I was sure that they would just look at me as a sloppy drunk.

Thankfully we reached Alexis's dorm, and she and Warren exited the car after saying their good-byes. Alexis came around to my side of the car and I rolled down the window as she handed me her phone number, which she had scribbled on a piece of paper.

"Call me, girl. Alright?"

"Okay, I'll give you a call tomorrow." I sat up and tried to play things like I was good. Meanwhile, do to my drunkenness, the street and everything in it were spinning around faster than a roulette wheel.

Snipes pulled off and headed toward my dorm.

"You gotta get up in the morning?" Snipes asked.

I nodded because I was feeling too horrible to speak. Snipes had reminded me of something that I didn't even wanna think about—that I had to get up for an 8:30 A.M. class.

When we reached the front of my building, I wanted to bolt out of the car and head straight to my bed. That feeling where everything seemed to be spinning had left me, but my head was pounding.

"I had a real good time," I said to Snipes, and extended my body toward his in an attempt to give him a hug and a good-night kiss so that I could get on with things and head inside.

Snipes reached over and met me halfway and gave me a quick kiss on the cheek. His car was double-parked but he said he was gonna leave it where it was and run up with me to my room.

"Snipes, I'll be fine," I said, running my hand down my face. I was feeling and looking like I had been to hell and back. "I'll call you tomorrow."

"Nah, I gotchu. I wanna walk you. It's all good."

I wasn't in the mood to argue, plus I figured that since Snipes was leaving his car double-parked, he wouldn't be able to stay long even if he wanted to.

We made our way into the building, signed the security guest book, and walked toward the elevator.

"Is your roommate here?"

"She's probably in the room." Vomit felt like it was right at the base of my throat and ready to exit.

The elevator opened up and Snipes and I got in.

I mustered up a smile as I said to Snipes, "You surprising me by walking me to my room like this. You don't seem like the chivalry type."

Snipes kept quiet.

We exited the elevator and began walking toward the room.

"Yo, hold up a minute." Snipes took me by the hand and pulled me close to him. "I just wanted to get a real kiss from you before the night was over."

"Snipes, no offense, but can we do this tomorrow? I mean I was drinking and—"

Snipes cut me off by forcefully pulling me toward him and thrusting his tongue down my throat. He was kissing me with such force that I couldn't really enjoy the kiss. It didn't feel real intimate or nothing close to it. Plus I was feeling subconsciously that my breath wasn't the freshest, not to mention that I thought I was going to throw up. In fact, Snipes's tongue felt like it was gagging me, so I was certain that I was about to hurl right into his mouth.

"Why you pulling away from me?" Snipes asked, all serious.

"It's nothing, really. I just would feel better doing this tomorrow."

"Tomorrow?" Snipes asked with a twisted look.

"Yeah, baby. Those drinks that I had tonight, they—"

"Come here real quick." Snipes led me toward an exit door that led to a stairwell.

"Snipes? What are you doing?"

When we entered the stairwell, Snipes closed the door, then he came toward me and began forcefully kissing me again.

"I didn't wanna do *this* in your hallway, and we can't go into your room," Snipes said, kissing me as he spoke.

I wanted to get the kiss over with so that I could hurry up and get in my bed, so I didn't resist and kissed Snipes back, trying my hardest to muster up a little bit of passion.

As we kissed, Snipes began feeling all over my body. He was palming my ass with one hand and massaging my breast with the other.

I definitely was not in the mood for making out, not at that moment, and especially not in the stairwell of my dorm.

"Snipes, listen." I pushed myself slightly away from him. "In the morning just come by my room and I'll skip my class and we can chill together alone and in the right environment."

It was as if Snipes hadn't heard a word that I said as he became more aggressive with his kissing. His hand was now completely under my shirt and he undid my bra and fondled my breasts, which were now exposed under my shirt.

"You was looking all sexy tonight and flirting with me and shit at the Shark Bar," Snipes said, simultaneously kissing my neck and breathing heavy. "Yeah, I wanted you all night long."

Wanted me? I thought. I wondered if I had said something while I was drunk that might have turned Snipes on or that might have come across as too flirty.

The next thing I knew, Snipes had unbuckled my belt and was quickly attempting to unbutton my jeans.

"Snipes, stop, come on! Not in here. I don't wanna do this right now!" I said in a loud and somewhat panicked whisper.

"Fuck that! I wantchu right now!"

My jeans had finally been unbuttoned and Snipes was trying to pull my pants down.

"Snipes!" I barked, raising my voice just a little. That drunken feeling had suddenly disappeared and I guess my adrenaline was starting to kick in.

"Don't fight me!" Snipes barked back as he kept kissing my neck and trying to pull my pants down.

I forcefully pushed Snipes away from me and attempted to make my way past him and into the hallway to get to my room.

Snipes swiftly grabbed my arm and took hold of the door that I had slightly opened and violently slammed it shut. He spun me around and pulled me toward him.

"Snipes, you *really* scaring me right now!"

"Just stop fighting me then!" He pushed me face-first against the wall and held me there with his left hand, while he reached his right hand around me and grabbed my unfastened belt buckle and yanked the belt from my pants.

Snipes then pressed his body against mine. My back was to his chest and he placed his forearm around my neck.

"Katrina, stop fuckin' fighting me!" Snipes began trying to pull down my tight jeans.

My heart was pounding with fear and my brain was racing, trying to get a grip on exactly what was happening and how the hell I was going to get away from him. My instincts told me to keep resisting Snipes and to try to get the hell out of that stairwell.

"Snipes, let's just wait on this," I pleaded as I tried to push away from the wall and free myself of his grip. Unfortunately, Snipes was too strong for me.

He now held me pressed against the wall with his left hand, and with his right he grabbed my jeans and, with the force of Mike Tyson, yanked them, pulling them halfway down and ripping them, exposing my bare ass.

"Oh my God! Snipes, why you doing this? You don't have to do this!"

"Shut the fuck up!" Snipes pulled some more at my jeans, until they were down at my ankles along with my panties.

"You got me all turned on and shit!" he grunted while massaging his dick through his pants.

I couldn't go through with this. I didn't know if this was rape, but I was definitely feeling like Snipes was violating me big-time. So I reached down and tried to pull up my pants.

Snipes then grabbed my belt from the floor and swung it, hitting me upside my head. As I grabbed my head in pain, Snipes grabbed my right arm and twisted it behind my back like a police officer getting ready to handcuff someone. He then grabbed my other arm and also pulled that behind my back. Before I knew what was what, Snipes had my wrists tied together tight with the belt.

Then I heard his pants being unbuckled, and the next thing I knew, Snipes was pushing my head down trying to get me to bend over. I stopped resisting Snipes. He was stronger than me and was obviously more than determined to get what he wanted, and I felt like I was fighting a losing battle. A battle that I didn't want to end up with me strangled to death or something crazy.

While I was slightly bent over with my arms behind my back and feeling humiliated, Snipes began trying to enter me doggy-style. Needless to say, my pussy wasn't the least bit wet, and Snipes wasn't exactly small. I could feel the tip of his dick ripping its way into my vagina.

"Got damn, your shit is tight, baby!" Snipes sounded as if he was actually enjoying the experience. With my lips and walls being torn by the friction from Snipes's dry dick penetrating me, my pussy felt like it was burning.

"Just don't fight me, baby," Snipes said as his dick made more headway into my pussy.

I wanted to scream from the pain, but for some weird reason I didn't want to yell and bring attention to what was going on in the stairwell.

Snipes had finally got the entire shaft of his dick up my pussy and began stroking and fucking me like I was lubricated, but unfortunately my pussy was drier than the Sahara Desert and it felt like it was on fire. And considering that I had only had sex once in my lifetime, my pussy wasn't ready for Snipes. Not with the way he was ripping into me anyway.

"Snipes, you're hurting me!" I felt like somebody was sticking a knife in my stomach.

Snipes simply pulled on the belt to make it tighter and to keep me from falling down, since I couldn't brace myself with my arms, and he began fucking me even harder.

Thank God my pussy finally started to moisten up just a bit. I was sure that Snipes could feel me getting somewhat looser as he started pumping his dick even faster. I wanted to scream so loud, but I clenched my teeth and endured being raped by the man who my *cockblocking* roommate said was crazy and had had reservations about.

"You like this dick?" Snipes asked as he raped me.

I kept quiet. I couldn't believe that he would ask me that. This had to be some kind of nightmare, I told myself. I would soon wake up and realize that I was only having a bad dream.

"Huh?" he said as he pumped his dick deep into me and waited for an answer.

"Katrina, you like this dick?"

I wanted to end the torture so I decided to just tell Snipes what he wanted to hear so that he would hopefully hurry up and bust his nut.

"Yes."

"Yeah. Say that again," Snipes demanded as he kept fucking.

"Yes, I like your dick!" I said through clenched teeth.

"Yeah, that's what I'm talking about!" Snipes said, sounding like he was smiling.

Those must have been the magic words because Snipes really began pumping his dick harder and faster than he'd been pumping it before. Then suddenly he stopped pumping and thrust himself into me one last time as he let out the biggest sigh and grunt and exhaled a mouthful of air. While he did this, he pulled really hard on the belt, causing the buckle to dig right into my skin. I wanted to scream from the tremendous pain.

I couldn't believe that Snipes had just raped me, and although I couldn't yet visually confirm it, I was sure that he had just come inside me. My pussy was now feeling soaked, and I knew that had to be from Snipes's semen.

Snipes finally loosened the belt from around my wrists and slowly slid his dick from me and pulled up his pants.

"Oh, shit! I forgot that I'm double-parked outside. I don't wanna get no fucking ticket!"

A ticket, I thought to myself. *This nigga is actually thinking about a parking ticket?*

At that point I had to wonder, just who in the world was Snipes?

"Katrina, I gotta go," Snipes had the *courtesy* of telling me. He didn't attempt to hug me or kiss me or anything. He simply adjusted his clothes and told me that he was "out," as he quickly vanished down the steps, leaving me standing there, sore and with my panties and my pants still bunched down around my ankles. All I could hear was the rhythmic echoing thud from Snipes's Timberland boots as he made his way down the stairwell and out of the building.

Six

My alcohol-induced headache suddenly returned and added to the disgust that I was feeling. I reached down and pulled up my panties and my jeans. I didn't bother to buckle my jeans or put on my belt. Rather, I just held my pants up with my right hand and gingerly walked toward my room with my zipper undone. I contemplated heading straight for the shower, which was just down the hall, but I didn't have a towel or soap or any of my toiletries. So I headed for my room and hoped like all hell that Candace was asleep.

When I reached my door, I paused before entering and pressed my ear against the door so I could hear what was going on inside. Although it was now a little after two in the morning, I could hear the television still on, and it made it hard to hear anything else, but I was almost sure that I faintly heard Candace running her mouth on the phone.

I sucked my teeth and sighed as I braced myself to enter my room.

As soon as I unlocked the door and stepped one foot in the room, I saw Candace looking at me. It was as if she had been waiting up for me or something.

Candace immediately paused in her conversation and directed her dramatized words toward me.

"Oh—my—God!" Candace said, stressing each word individually. "Katrina, what the hell happened to you? You look like a hot-ass mess!"

"Candace, not now, alright?!" I barked as I quickly made my way to my closet to grab a towel and my toiletries.

"Look, let me call you back tomorrow," Candace said to whoever she was talking to on the phone.

She then got up from her bed and walked over to me. "What do you mean not now? Look at you, girl. You look like shit! Where did you go? What happened to you?"

"Candace, can I breathe? Got damn!" I barked. I was not in the mood for her and her million questions. "Look, I had too much to drink, okay?"

"Katrina, I can tell that. I mean, you smell like a fucking distillery! And look at your pants. You sure you okay?"

I just ignored Candace. I wanted to hurry up and get in the bathroom and refresh myself so that I could go to sleep and end the horror that I was feeling. But Candace kept on yapping and I was two seconds from just slapping the shit out of her because I was so frustrated.

While Candace continued to question me, I reached in my drawer for a fresh pair of panties. I could feel Snipes's semen, which was still oozing out of my vagina, and I was just so thoroughly disgusted.

"And call your mother. She had to have called here about twenty times since you left."

I didn't say a word. I just made my way out of the room and down the hall to the showers.

To say that was one of the best showers that I have ever experienced would be an understatement. I turned the water on and made it as hot as I could humanly tolerate, then stood underneath the showerhead and let the water relax me.

Tears began to run down my face as I tried to figure out what exactly I had done to bring that rape on myself.

You shouldn't have been drinking like you was.

Why in the world did you wear them tight jeans, Katrina?

As I thought about what I had done wrong, I also contemplated if I should tell anyone exactly what had happened.

I lathered up my body, making sure that I concentrated on my vagina. Although I was sore, I vigorously rubbed soap between my legs and quickly rejected the thought of pregnancy. I reasoned with myself that there was no way that I could have gotten pregnant that quick.

Katrina, you ain't pregnant. Don't even think that. Just chill out. You'll be okay.

For the next five minutes that I showered, my thoughts went from fear of a venereal disease and pregnancy, to sadistic anger toward Snipes. Finally I turned off the water, prepared to get on with things. Normally my routine after a shower was to brush and floss my teeth and lotion my body, but I wasn't in the mood for following no routine. I simply dried off my body, wrapped the towel around myself, and went back to my room.

I headed straight to my bed. I pulled back the covers, removed my towel, and got in naked. As I lay curled in the fetal position, I forced myself not to shed a tear or get emotional, and I tried my best to fall asleep as quickly as I could.

Candace turned out the light and walked over to the television, and instead of turning it off, she turned the volume all the way down.

"Katrina, I know you trying to go to sleep and I know I ain't your mother or nothing. I'm just your roommate, I know that. And I know I have my ways about me where I can be really moody and bitchy, but I am just worried about you. Now I need you to sit up or turn over or something and just talk to me."

I sighed to express my disgust. I had just been violated in the worst way, and I already felt like I had done something wrong to deserve the rape, and I didn't need Candace talking to me like she was my parent or something.

"Talk about what, Candace?"

"Katrina, why are your pants ripped, why did you come in here smelling like an alcoholic, and why you coming across so distant?"

Again I sighed to show my disgust. "Candace, turn off the TV so I can get some sleep, please! I appreciate your concern but I'm good. Everything is good."

"Okay, whatever. But all I'm gonna say, Katrina, is leave that nigga alone!"

"Candace, go to sleep, alright? You don't even know Snipes. And if you ask me, I just think that you jealous and envious."

"Katrina, don't even go there. 'Cause I'm not trying to go there. I'm just—"

Turning over in my bed and sitting up, I finished Candace's sentence. "You're just wishing that you had somebody picking you up in a brand-new Benz, taking you out to eat at the Shark Bar, and spending money on drinks like it's nothing. And since you don't, you trying to cramp what I'm doing. You don't even know Snipes but yet you coming across like you grew up with him or something. Just mind your damn business!"

Candace put both of her palms up in the air and walked toward her bed. "Okay. Cool. I'm leaving it alone."

"Thank you! Now can you please turn off the TV so I can get some sleep?" I rudely said as I lay back down, curled into a fetal position, and pulled the covers over my head.

I couldn't begin to explain why I had just sort of defended Snipes. Nor could I explain why I hadn't used that opportunity to just tell Candace the real deal about what had happened with me and Snipes. Maybe I was just confused. Maybe I was still in shock. Or maybe it was my low self-esteem kicking in and telling me that I had gotten what I was worth and deserved. I didn't know what to think or make of my actions. But I do know that a big part of me felt like I was the one who was in the wrong and that Snipes had only done what he did because I had provoked him in some way.

As a sharp pain shot through my vagina and I clenched my teeth to keep from screaming, all I knew was that I would more than likely wake up in a few hours with a massive hangover. And the only thing that could be worse than waking up with a hangover was waking up with a hangover after having been raped.

Only thing was, as I tossed and turned before going to sleep, I just wasn't sure if I had been raped or if I was just inexperienced about a lot of things.

Oh, God, ouch! I screamed in my head as that sharp pain shot through my pussy once again.

Seven

The next morning I turned over and was groggy as all hell, and I looked and saw Candace getting ready for class. She looked as if she had already showered and was just about done putting her clothes on to head out the door. I glanced at the clock and realized that it was 8:15 A.M. and I had a class to go to at 8:30 A.M.

Sitting up on my bed, I asked, "Candace, why didn't you wake me up?"

Candace ignored me and continued to get ready to leave.

I sucked my teeth and lay back down. Who was I kidding? There was no way I could make it sitting through classes. Not with the way I was feeling. I pulled the covers over my head and attempted to go back to sleep so I could sleep off my hangover.

"I'm just minding my business," Candace sarcastically said as she walked out of the room and headed for her first class of the day.

I fell asleep for about a half an hour, and then the phone started ringing. I wasn't in the mood to talk to anyone and I wasn't in the mood to get up and look at the caller ID to see who was so persistent. But the sound of the telephone constantly ringing was driving me crazy and was only making my headache worse.

"Hello?" I said in a groggy voice as I picked up the phone.

"Katrina?"

"Yeah."

"Katrina, are you okay? You had me and your father worried sick about you. Didn't Candace tell you that we were trying to reach you last night?" my mother asked.

My mom was the last person that I wanted to speak to at that moment, but I had to pull myself up and try to come across as if everything were okay.

"Oh, yeah, Mom, she did tell me, but by the time I came back to my room it was so late that I figured I would just call you sometime today."

"Katrina, listen, you know it doesn't matter how late you call this house. You already know how I feel about you being up there in New York by yourself with no relatives or nothing. I get worried about you."

"Mom," I said with a sound of disgust.

"Katrina, I know you hate when I keep tabs on you, but you don't see things from my position," my mom explained in her usual overprotective-mother voice.

My mom and dad, whose first names were Patricia and James, treated me like I was precious refined gold. I knew that was partly because they had lost their first child when I was only two years old, so they were not trying to lose me or let anything happen to me in any way, shape, or form. One day my brother, who was three years older than me, had slipped out of my mother's sight, just being a typical five-year-old, and made his way to our swimming pool in our backyard. Unfortunately he couldn't swim and he drowned.

My mom forever beat herself up over his death, never forgiving herself for not paying attention to him before it happened. Our family life was never the same after that day. For years, my brother's death caused extreme stress on our family, and it nearly led my parents to get a divorce because the pain of the loss put so much emotional distance between them. And it also made them extremely overprotective of me.

"Mom, I'm gonna be fine. You gotta stop worrying about me. I was just studying and it's easier for me to concentrate in the study lounge as opposed to my room. I was just in the study lounge, that's all; I'm trying to get off to a good start." I couldn't believe how easily I was lying through my teeth. Nor could I understand why I couldn't bring myself to tell my mother the truth about what had transpired last night between me and Snipes.

"Okay, I'm just glad you're okay. You sound like you just woke up. Don't you have a class to go to?"

"Mom," I said with that same sound of disgust in my voice. "I got everything under control. Okay? I gotta go. Tell daddy that I said hello, and that I love him."

"Okay, I will."

Thankfully, my mother giggled and went along with what I had said. We ended the call by saying that we loved each other, and I contemplated getting up and making an attempt to get dressed. My mouth was as dry as a chalkboard and my stomach felt like I was bloated to no end.

I finally convinced myself to go to the bathroom and pee. When I reached the bathroom, I threw some water on my face, which helped me feel a little bit better but it wasn't enough to ward off the hangover.

As I made it out of the bathroom and back to my room, my heart practically dropped to my feet as I saw Snipes standing at my room door. He hadn't seen me yet and appeared to be listening closely to see if anyone was in the room.

I was frozen dead in my tracks like a deer in headlights.

Snipes knocked on the door three times, and when he got no answer, he reached for the marker attached to the small dry-erase board that Candace and I kept on the door for people to leave us messages if someone ever came to our room and we weren't there.

My heart began beating a little faster as I didn't know what Snipes actually wanted with me.

Ah, shit! I did tell him to come by my room in the morning, I thought to myself.

I slowly turned around, hoping that I could make it back down the hallway and into the bathroom without Snipes seeing me. I guess that my heart was racing from fear because I wasn't sure if Snipes was in the mood for round two of what he had initiated just hours ago with me.

I walked as fast as I could with my pink bunny slippers and robe, and I was right at the bathroom door when Snipes yelled out to me.

"Katrina!"

Keep walking, I begged myself.

"Yo, Katrina, is that you?" Snipes yelled out even louder. Only this time I could hear that thud from his Timberland boots quickly approaching me.

Katrina, he don't know it's you, just dip into the bathroom and stay there until he's gone. But what if he decides to come into the bathroom? Then what? I wasn't sure what to do, so I decided to just face the man who had raped me just hours ago.

I turned and saw Snipes quickly coming toward me.

When he confirmed that it was me, he had the audacity to plaster one of the biggest smiles across his face.

"Yo, what up?" Snipes asked as he came right up to me and planted a kiss on my cheek.

The kissed turned me off, but I wasn't as turned off as I figured I should be. I guess a small part of me wanted to give Snipes a chance to explain himself so I could hear from his mouth just what the hell he had been thinking when he violated me.

"I took a chance and stopped by to see if you was in your room."

I nodded my head but I didn't say anything.

"You okay?" Snipes asked with a small smiley smirk on his face.

I still didn't know exactly what to say or how to respond to his behaving like everything was normal between us. But I was smart enough to realize that Snipes had more than likely shown up at my room so early in order to assess the situation and enact some damage control if need be.

"Nah, I'm not really okay, and plus I feel like I got a hangover."

"A hangover?" Snipes began laughing. "You was drinking like a pro but it caught up to you and bit you in the ass." He grabbed my butt and squeezed it while continuing to laugh.

I quickly slapped Snipes's hand away from my ass as I started to make my way back to my room.

"What's up with that?"

I ignored Snipes and kept about my business.

"So you don't have classes today?" he asked, now trying to make everyday conversation.

"I told you I'm hungover and I'm not really in the mood today!" I said with an attitude.

We were just reaching my room and Snipes spoke up, "Okay, talk to me, Katrina. What's up?"

I unlocked my door and walked into my room. I didn't really want to let Snipes in, but I was like, *What the hell?* It wasn't like I had the power to physically prevent him from coming in.

"Snipes come on now," I said with a mixture of attitude and sarcasm.

"What? Talk to me." Snipes stood as I sat on my bed.

"Snipes, you practically raped me last night! What do you think is wrong with me?" I blurted out.

Snipes responded immediately, "What are you talking about? The whole sex thing?"

"Yeah, the whole sex thing!" I said sarcastically. "Snipes, don't play stupid." I got up and walked over to my closet. "This don't come from regular sex, Snipes!" I showed him my ripped jeans.

Snipes shook his head and smiled. "Yo, a'ight, look. Come here." He approached and gave me a hug. I wanted to pull away from him, but he seemed to be genuinely affectionate, the total opposite of his sadistic behavior the previous night.

"Katrina, I'm sorry for the way everything went down. I mean, I admit that I was a little rough with you, but trust me, I didn't rape you!" Snipes chuckled some more. "Oh, man, that is funny, but at the same time it's not funny. It's like it's not funny for you to feel all fucked up and shit like you got raped, but its funny that you could even think that."

I looked at Snipes like, *Whateva, nigga.*

"Katrina, sit down for a minute," Snipes requested.

I reluctantly sat down and he began explaining to me how back in the days when he was younger he always had low self-esteem when it came to women, and how when he became sexually active, he started hearing rumors that were started by girls that he had been with sexually, rumors that his shit was whack and that his sex was so lame and weak. And when he heard those rumors, it crushed his ego and made him always second-guess himself when it came to how he was performing sexually with a woman.

"So ever since I was like twenty years old, I've had this thing in my head that women only like sex and respect your sex game when it's rough and when the nigga is taking control and shit," Snipes explained as he held my hand in his.

I sighed and just looked at him.

"Katrina, on the real, I'm feeling you. And if I wasn't, I wouldn't be here right now. Matter of fact, if I had raped you, I wouldn't be contacting you the next day. Now, would I? Matter of fact, I wish you had called me last night and said something. I would have been back over here in a heartbeat. I wouldn't even have wanted you going to sleep with that in your head, thinking that you just got raped and shit. That's crazy!"

"Snipes look at me."

Snipes looked at me.

"Are you telling me the truth or are you just telling me what you think I wanna hear?"

"Baby, I'm telling you the truth. And that's easy because all I gotta do is just recap what happened last night and what I was thinking. I mean, you was looking sexy as you usually do, you was drinking and I was drinking, you was flirting with me and making my dick hard, which is a good thing, and I just really wanted you. And I know you was saying that we could wait until the next day, but you was just really turning me on and I knew your cock-blocking roommate was in the room, so it was just like one thing led to another and it was what it was." Snipes paused before adding, "But it definitely wasn't rape."

I kept quiet as Snipes looked at me trying to figure out what was going on in my head.

"Let's do this. Let's just start over. Tonight come hang out with us again and I'll make sure that the night starts off right and ends up right," Snipes offered.

He then reached in his pocket and pulled out a bankroll. He peeled off five one-hundred-dollar bills and handed them to me.

"You got Alexis's number, right? So why don't you just call her and ask her to go with you to get something new for yourself. Get a new outfit for tonight. We gonna go to this spot in Queens called Club Amazura. It's reggae night so it'll be bananas, and I promise you that you'll have a good time! Shabba Ranks and Super Cat and all them reggae niggas usually be chillin' up in the VIP area on reggae night. That's how hot the spot is. Word!"

I took in all that Snipes was saying. And I was trying my hardest to figure him out. He had this charming way about him that seemed irresistible to me. Then I had to think that maybe I had acted too flirtatious and had turned him on so much that he was ready to bust a nut on himself or something, and if so, then I could live with that. And I knew that I could be and should be woman enough to share the blame for exactly how things had gone down the previous night.

What also made me think was seeing all of the cash that Snipes had. Not from a gold-digging standpoint but from a logical standpoint, I told myself, Snipes couldn't be the rapist type. Because with the money that he seemed to have, I was sure that getting pussy wouldn't have been a problem for him, even if it meant that he would have to pay for it.

"Five hundred dollars? Snipes, I can't take this."

Snipes looked at me and smirked. He took the money from my hand and put it on my dresser.

"What do you do again?" I asked with genuine curiosity, being that I had never known what Snipes actually did for a living.

"I sell insurance."

I paused and bit my bottom lip to keep myself from laughing. "*You* sell insurance?"

"Word is bond! Well, I don't actually sell insurance myself per se; I have a company that has insurance agents who sell insurance for me."

"Oh, okay, so you're an entrepreneur, like an insurance broker?"

"Exactly!" Snipes responded with a smile on his face.

"I didn't mean to be sarcastic, it's just that you don't seem like the suit-and-tie type and I just couldn't picture you doing that."

"I feel you."

There was a lot that I didn't know about Snipes and I had a lot of questions that I wanted answered, so I kept on with the questions.

"So you go to NYU too? And how old are you?"

"Well, I'm twenty-four and I go to NYU but I'm not enrolled this semester. I've always put myself through college. I didn't wanna take out no student loans and all of that shit and I had nobody helping me, so I had to grind it out building my business and going to school at the same time. And when the business took off, I stopped going to school, but I'm gonna enroll again for the spring semester. I only need twenty more credits to get my degree. You feel me?"

I nodded my head as I listened to Snipes. It was funny because the hangover had disappeared and I had started feeling as if the cloud that was hanging over me during the previous night had lifted and moved on.

We continued to talk some more until Snipes said that he had to go take care of some things. So we slowly made our way to the door and into the hallway.

As I walked him to the elevator, he confirmed whether I was gonna hang out with him and Warren later that night.

"You talking about the club?" I asked.

Snipes nodded.

"Yeah, I definitely wanna go."

Snipes smiled and gave me a hug. "Okay, cool." He gave me a kiss on my forehead. "We'll probably bounce at like ten and get there at eleven."

I said okay and Snipes got on the elevator. As the elevator door was about to close, I stuck my foot in the door, causing it to open back up.

"What's wrong?" Snipes asked.

"I just wanna say, for the record, I've heard that some women do like it rough. But I'm new to this, so you gotta also know how to be gentle."

Snipes nodded and smirked as the elevator door closed.

Eight

Fifteen minutes after Snipes left, my phone rang and I picked it up.

"What's up, baby?"

"Snipes?" I said as a smile plastered across my face.

"Yeah, it's me. Yo, I miss you already. Let's go get something to eat, I don't wanna wait until tonight to see you."

"*Snipes,*" I whined. I had so much to do, but at the same time I didn't mind hanging out with him.

"You ever drank a mimosa?"

"A who?" I said with a chuckle.

Snipes laughed and explained that it was orange juice and champagne.

"Whoo, that sounds different," I said.

"Come downstairs, I know this little café spot that we can go to that sells them and I can read this poem that I wrote for you."

"Shut up," I said with a smile.

"Nah, I'm dead ass. That's my secret talent. I'm a poet and a writer on the low."

"Snipes, you are too much."

" 'How do I love thee? Let me count the ways,' " Snipes said in this funny Shakespeare-sounding voice while I began laughing.

"I love thee more than life—I love thee enough to make you my wife—I love thee like cooked food—I love thee 'cause she keeps me in a good mood . . ."

I couldn't help but laugh, and I cut Snipes off and told him that I was on my way down to meet him.

So I went downstairs and got in the car with Snipes and we drove off toward the FDR Drive. We soon crossed the Brooklyn Bridge and navigated our way to this quaint café in Brooklyn Heights.

"It's good, right?" Snipes asked as I sipped on the mimosa.

"Yeah, it's really good." After I sipped on the drink some more, I caught Snipes staring at me.

"What?" I asked, thinking that I had a booger in my nose or some food stuck in my teeth.

"Nothing, I just like looking into your eyes, that's the window to your soul."

"Really? And what Hallmark card did you get that out of?" I joked, then placed a piece of bacon in my mouth.

"That's not Hallmark, baby, I'm just deep like that when I wanna be." Snipes handed me a folded piece of paper. "This is what I wrote for you."

I unfolded the paper and saw lines of intricately neat handwriting.

"Oh, this is so sweet, you actually really did write me a poem." I hadn't even read the poem but just the thought of it was sweet, and no one had ever done anything like that for me before.

"Read it," Snipes instructed me with a smile, "it's really more of a letter than it is a poem."

I began reading:

Dear Katrina,

When I first saw you, my heart and my world stopped and I had to know who you were. You don't know it but I walked outside your dorm every day hoping that I would see you and each day that I saw you I didn't know what to say or how to approach you and that was when I knew that I would eventually fall in love with you. I have never been one who was at a loss for words when it came to meeting and talking to women. But the reason I was never at a loss for words is because with all of the women in the past I was always motivated by lust. But with you, right from the start it was love at first sight and I was motivated by love and I didn't want to say the wrong thing and screw things up. See the difference between lust and love is that with lust it's always about what someone can get at the expense of someone else. But with love it's always about what one can give to someone at the expense of oneself. Love is self-sacrificing. I knew that I loved you because from the moment that I saw you it was always and only about you and what I wanted to do for you at my expense. Katrina, I never open up like this with people because I don't want to be vulnerable to anyone, but I'm opening up like this with you because I want you to know that I care about you and I want you to be a part of my life for a long time to come, and if that makes me vulnerable then so be it. Please forgive me in advance for when I do stupid things because I have a whole lot to learn about life and about myself, but I promise you that if you give me the chance to be a part of your life, it will always be more about you than it is about me.

With Love,

Dwight, aka Snipes

"Snipes, this is really sweet." I got up to give him a hug and a kiss. "Thank you so much."

And before I could sit down, a gentleman walked over to me and asked if my name was Katrina.

"Yes, it is."

"Here, these are for you," the guy said to me, and like a skilled magician he pulled a dozen red roses from behind his back and handed them to me.

I don't know how Snipes had pulled that off or how his timing was so good, but it was smooth. The flowers were beautiful with the baby's breath and the glass vase, and they smelled good. I was so impressed, and it was the first time that anyone had ever given me flowers.

"Snipes, you gonna make me feel like I'm special or something."

"You are special, word, there's something different about you, word up, and that's from the heart," he replied.

"You are so smooth with it," I joked.

We eventually finished eating, then Snipes walked me back to his car so that I could put the flowers inside. And afterward he and I held hands and went for a walk.

"You ain't from New York so I know you probably never been to the Promenade before, have you?" Snipes asked.

"No, I haven't," I said as we walked.

"This is one of the best views in New York. See, right over there is the Statue of Liberty, and those two buildings right there, that's the Twin Towers, and that's the Brooklyn Bridge right over there," Snipes explained as we strolled along the Promenade like sightseeing tourists among the other New Yorkers who were also on the Promenade roller-skating, walking their dogs, reading, and just relaxing.

"This view is beautiful, I love the boats and the water," I said.

We walked closer to the edge of the Promenade, then just stopped and looked across the water and stared at the Manhattan skyline.

"My dream is to be bigger than Donald Trump one day. You see all them buildings over there?" Snipes asked.

I nodded.

"One day I'm gonna own all that shit. I wanna be one of the first black real estate tycoons."

"Really? So that's your dream?"

"Yeah, it's one of my dreams. I come out here a lot and just clear my head and think and when I wanna motivate myself. I look at that skyline and I get inspired, and to me it's just a matter of time before my real estate dream comes true. All I gotta do is learn that real estate game and then get in the game and go hard."

"You can do it. You can do whatever you put your mind to," I encouraged.

"Yeah, I know. And it's like I could start small and buy a bunch of houses and three- and six-family buildings, but I just always think big, and I want them skyscrapers and office buildings and shit. You feel me?"

"Yeah, I feel you. It'll happen for you."

Snipes and I talked for a little while longer, then we walked all the way to the end of the Promenade before turning around and walking back to the other end and to Snipes's car.

I didn't want our spontaneous date to end. It was so romantic and I felt like I was seeing a totally different side of Snipes. Just the night before I had seen a scary side of him, but at that moment I was basking in what I felt was the genuine side of Snipes and I loved everything that I was feeling, especially the warm and tingly feelings.

So Snipes drove me back to my dorm and told me that he had some moves to make but that he would see me later on.

"Okay," I said, then gave him a long, deep tongue kiss before departing his car and making my way up to my room. I was floating on cloud nine. And for hours, after situating the flowers on my desk, I just lay on my bed and thought about Snipes and the nice date that he had taken me on.

The only thing that interrupted my thoughts was when Alexis came through and scooped me up so that she and I could go shopping. And at eight in the evening, Alexis and I were just returning to my room from a day of shopping and getting our hair and nails and eyebrows done. I had thoroughly enjoyed myself and was finally getting a chance to really experience different things and places in New York.

I couldn't believe how quickly I had managed to spend the $500 that Snipes had given me. A part of me was feeling guilty considering that I had only purchased one outfit with the money. And actually it wasn't even a complete outfit. On Alexis's insistence I had bought a pair of $350 Versace "jeanlike" jeans. They were a pair of pants that resembled jeans but were made out of a wool material. I really did it up big and bought a pinkish, flamboyant color that really fit and hugged my ass. My hair and nails and eyebrows ran me another $100, which sucked up the remaining money. I decided to charge my top and my shoes on my credit card.

What the hell! I thought. *You only live once.*

Actually I was feeling guilty for having spent the money so quickly with so little to show for it, and I let Alexis in on my feelings. But she quickly squashed all of those feelings of irresponsibility.

"Oh, please! Katrina, you better learn to get up off of that guilty *responsibility* thing real quick." Alexis sat on Candace's bed, as she wasn't in the room at the time. "Warren and Snipes got dough, so it ain't nothing! As long as Snipes is tricking, you should be spending. Just do you!"

She continued, "You see that 850i BMW that I was driving you around in today? That's Warren's car, but he don't care about that. You see this phone, that nigga gives me the money for this shit. These New York niggas love them some Southern pussy! But with Warren and Snipes, they ain't just your average New York niggas that be frontin' like they got dough, Warren and Snipes they got money for real, and they *are* ballin'. And if Snipes is feeling you, then roll with that shit and don't fuck it up and you'll be good."

As I tried on my brand-new body-hugging $350 jeans and my new square-toe shoes with a stiletto heel, I asked Alexis, "So what exactly does Warren do?"

"What do you mean?"

"Like, is he in school? Is he working? Where does he get his money from?" I felt so naïve.

Alexis looked at me, then looked inside one of her bags and began rummaging through it. She retrieved the pair of Moschino jeans that she had purchased and began undressing so that she could try on her pants as well.

"Katrina, Warren and Snipes are both *ballers*. They get money!"

"Yeah, I know, but I'm always curious as to what people do when I meet them."

By this time Alexis had managed to get out of the tight jeans that she had been wearing all day and was standing in a red thong that had sequins on both sides.

"Katrina, they get they money how they get it," Alexis said in code. "One thing I can tell you is this: if you don't wanna have no issues with nobody, you gonna have to learn to keep your mouth shut and don't be asking questions about shit that don't need to be asked. Them niggas is getting money; you play your cards right and you'll be getting money too. Don't be worrying about shit and asking all kinds of stupid questions," Alexis continued as if she were schooling me.

I decided to switch subjects and just focus on the new clothes that we had purchased and anything else that I could find to talk about. I may not have been a girl with all the street smarts, but I was real perceptive at times and knew when to shut the hell up about something and change the subject.

"Girl, you must be in the gym every day. Your body is so tight!" I said to Alexis as I couldn't help but notice how toned her legs were. I was also a bit envious of her because she was the total perfect package.

"Actually I don't. I used to run track in high school, and ever since I started running track, my body just was always in shape." Alexis sat back down on Candace's bed and attempted to put on her jeans.

At that moment Candace walked into the room. She immediately drew this expression on her face like she wanted to kill. And I knew that it was because Alexis was sitting on her bed in a thong no less.

"Hey, Candace, this is my friend Alexis. Alexis, this is Candace," I said, hoping that Candace would be on her best behavior, especially with Alexis and her volatile ways.

Alexis immediately stood up and greeted Candace and apologetically said, "Candace, I'm sorry. Look at my country ass. I don't even know you and I got my ass cheeks all over your bed. I'm sorry about that, sweetie."

Alexis then wormed herself into the jeans she had been trying to squeeze into.

"That's okay, don't worry about it," Candace stated, to my shock and surprise. "I like those jeans. Are those Moschino jeans?" she asked, again shocking me with her politeness, and shocking me even more with her knowledge of fashion designers.

"Yeah, girl! Do you wear Moschino?" Alexis asked, seeming to get excited about the topic.

Candace laughed and playfully sucked her teeth. "Yeah, right, picture my broke ass spending two hundred dollars on some jeans."

We all laughed.

I knew that Candace had also noticed my Versace pants, but she didn't say anything about them. And I also knew that she knew that I couldn't afford pants like that on my own. I was wondering if she was hating on me again.

"Alexis, I know I've seen you around campus before. Were you here in the summertime?" Candace asked.

Alexis confirmed that she had been on campus since summer, then she and Candace and I made small talk. As I walked across the room to turn on the radio, Candace screamed and almost scared the shit outta me. "Oh my God! Katrina, look at your haircut! I love that! You didn't tell me you was gonna do that Halle Berry look to your hair."

I smiled a big Kool-Aid smile because Candace had just helped me confirm what I already knew—that my new Halle Berry look was off the chain!

"You really like it?" I asked.

"Yes! It's definitely the right look for you. It makes you look more grown-up. Matter of fact, you look completely different but in a good way," Candace explained.

I was beaming on the inside and was also glad that Candace and I were finally having a stress-free, non-drama-based conversation.

We all talked for a little while longer, but before we knew it, the time was approaching nine fifteen and we had to hurry so that we could leave and make it to the club in Queens by eleven.

"Candace we going to this club in Queens called Amazura. Do you wanna go?" Alexis asked Candace.

"Nah, I gotta get up in the morning so I'm not trying to hang out tonight. Maybe on a Friday or a Saturday. During the week is kind of rough for me," Candace said, sounding *nothing* like a young college student and more like a thirty-something woman that was married with children.

So Alexis and I quickly made our way out of the dorm and into the BMW. We were off to Queens to get our party on.

As soon as we crossed the Willamsburg Bridge, Alexis's phone began ringing and she asked me to pick it up since the BMW was a stick shift and she wasn't that skilled at driving the stick and speaking on the phone at the same time.

"Just press the green talk button," Alexis instructed while navigating the semicongested Brooklyn-Queens Expressway.

"Hello," I said while simultaneously pressing the talk button.

"Yo, hello, Alexis, listen. Some drama just went down and we can't make it to the club tonight but—"

I interrupted the panicked-sounding voice as I said, "This is Katrina, Alexis is driving, and who is this?"

"Oh, Katrina, this is Warren."

"Hey, Warren, is everything okay?"

"Nah, just all kinds of shit went down with the fucking police and shit! These muthafuckas, man!" Warren shouted into the phone like he'd lost his temper.

As Warren said that, that was when I remembered what Alexis had just told me a few hours ago about asking questions. *Keep your mouth shut and don't be asking questions about shit that don't need to be asked.*

So I made sure to keep my comments neutral.

"But you're okay though, right?" I asked.

"Yeah, I'm good."

"Is Snipes okay?" I asked out of genuine concern.

"Yeah, he good. Matter fact, he right here. Hold on a minute." Warren passed Snipes the phone.

"Hello," Snipes stated with a real raspy-sounding voice.

"Hey, baby," I said, not knowing where in the world that word *baby* had come from. "Warren told me that y'all can't make it tonight."

"Yeah, some shit came up, but listen. You wit' Alexis, right?"

"Yeah, she right here, we still on the Brooklyn-Queens Expressway," I replied, sounding as if I knew the New York streets by name like that.

"A'ight, just tell Alexis to meet us at my brother's house in Bed-Stuy. She knows where it is. Over on Halsey Street." Snipes's voice sounded raspier than ever.

"Okay, I'll tell her."

"And listen, I wantchu to spend the night with me tonight. I gotta bounce in the morning to Virginia. I'll be down there for a few days, maybe even a week, but I wanted to make sure I spent some time witchu before I bounced."

"Okay," I quickly answered, not even considering my class schedule for the next day.

When I hung up the phone, I relayed to Alexis everything that Snipes and Warren had told me. Alexis coolly went with the flow. Without asking any questions she simply turned up the volume on the radio and navigated us toward Halsey Street in Brooklyn.

When we reached Halsey, a street lined with connected brownstone buildings that reminded me of a more ghetto version of the house that the Cosbys lived in on *The Cosby Show,* I noticed a string of fancy cars double-parked toward the middle of the block.

"This is the block," Alexis stated as she pulled to the curb and parked the 850i.

We got out and walked toward a group of about fifteen guys who were standing in the middle of the street. They were all talking real loud, rolling dice, drinking, and smoking weed. And one by one Alexis began to introduce me to all of the thugged-out-looking dudes. She made sure that she introduced me as being "with Snipes," and that particular introduction seemed to get me all kinds of respect.

Snipes and Warren had not arrived yet, so Alexis took me into Snipes's brother's house and introduced me to his brother. Chase was the spitting image of Snipes, only he was about three inches taller and looked as if he weighed more than Snipes, about 230 pounds of all muscle, a jailhouse muscular look.

"So you the one that got my brother so wide open?" Chase asked. He appeared to be just as charming as Snipes as he offered us something to drink and something to eat.

I couldn't help but notice how immaculate the house was, and how enormous. He had shiny wood floors, plush-looking leather couches, and a big-screen television that was showing an old Mike Tyson fight.

"Yeah, I'm starving. You can get me some chicken wings," I replied to Chase, trying my hardest to make sure that I came out of my shell and displayed no signs of shyness.

"Okay, I gotchu. Alexis, what aboutchu? You want something?"

As Alexis sat on the couch and I looked at the pictures hanging on the wall, she replied with a smile, "You know me, Chase. You know what I want. You got some of them *thangs* for me?"

Chase smiled. "Them sticky green thangs? Yeah I gotchu, ma'."

Five minutes later Chase returned with a plate of chicken wings and hot sauce for me and handed Alexis two cigars and a clear plastic bag that looked like it had oregano in it.

"Katrina, you smoke weed?" Chase asked me.

I had never in my life smoked a *cigarette,* let alone smoked marijuana or even seen marijuana before for that matter.

"Nah, I don't smoke," I replied. Thankfully I wasn't feeling all flustered and nervous from his question.

I sat and watched Alexis and Chase roll a blunt, something that I had never seen before. Alexis seemed to be a pro at it. She had finished rolling hers and had it lit and in her mouth before Chase was done with his.

After Alexis inhaled, then slowly exhaled the weed smoke out of her mouth and nostrils, she said, "Katrina, one thing about me is, I *love* me some weed! I know you like to drink, but give me some weed any day over liquor. Word!"

I didn't say anything. I just sat and nodded and sucked on the bone of one of my chicken wings.

Alexis then passed me the blunt. "Here, hit this. And you ain't gonna have to be worrying about no hangovers and throwing up and shit like that," Alexis promised as I took hold of the weed.

I was game to try it but I didn't wanna make a fool of myself since I had never smoked before. And sure enough, on my first inhale I immediately began coughing up a lung as I felt a burning sensation ripping through my chest.

Chase and Alexis both chuckled before Alexis instructed me on exactly how to inhale the weed without killing myself.

As I sat and smoked, I realized I was getting introduced to a whole new world and a whole new way of life. This excited me because I wanted to be a part of something that wasn't so stale and mundane like my life in North Carolina. Yeah, I knew about the pitfalls of drinking and smoking weed, but I was eighteen years old and semi on my own and I just wanted to live a little.

Before long Snipes came through the door, and he had this uneasy, nervous, and disheveled look about him.

"Hey, baby," Snipes said, then kissed me on the cheek.

He was trying to act normal but wasn't his usual cocky and confident self. He hadn't yet commented on my new hairstyle or anything. He was more in a pacing mode as he went from the kitchen to the living room, then back to the kitchen, then upstairs, then back into the living room.

He sat down for about a minute before he and his brother and Warren went to another room to talk and smoke.

They emerged from the room about fifteen minutes later, and by that time the weed that I had just learned to smoke had kicked in and I was feeling extremely nice. I could quickly see where Alexis was coming from when she said that she preferred weed over booze, because it was a different kind of high compared to alcohol.

Snipes called me over to him and asked, "You still spending the night, right?"

"Yeah, but I ain't got nothing to sleep in."

Snipes told me not to worry about that. As he spoke, he continued to seem extremely nervous and out of his confident and cocky character until he finally joked, "Whatchu doing smoking weed? I didn't know you smoke."

"I didn't know either until I came here tonight," I said, laughing. I was laughing harder than necessary because I was suddenly feeling so good and free as a bird.

Snipes and I made more small talk for about fifteen minutes, and before long it was nearing midnight and the two of us made it to one of the bedrooms on the second floor of the brownstone.

After taking off my clothes, I put on one of Snipes's football jerseys, which was way oversize for me, but it made the perfect sleeping attire as it came down to my knees and fit real loose and comfortable.

Snipes took off his shirt, sneakers, and jeans and walked around in his boxers. That was my first time getting a look at his body, and I was instantly turned on. He had the hard-looking body of a lightweight champion boxer, complete with the six-pack and all.

Snipes sat on the bed, and as he reached for the remote control, I walked over and sat behind him and began massaging his shoulders as my titties pressed up against his back.

"You sure you okay?" I asked as I could feel the tension in his muscles.

Snipes let out a big sigh after inhaling. "Actually I'm stressed the fuck out like a muthafucka! But I'ma be a'ight though. Some things went down and I can't really talk about it witchu right now, but it ain't nothing for you to worry about."

"Okay." I continued massaging his shoulders. "If you ever need to talk, just let me know, no matter what it is, okay?"

Snipes nodded, then he got up and walked across the room and retrieved a small bottle of baby oil from off the dresser. As he walked back toward the bed, he said, "It's your turn now. Take off your shirt and let me massage *you*. You said you like that gentle shit, so let me show you that a nigga can be gentle."

I laughed as I definitely hadn't seen Snipes as the massage-giving type. But he impressed me because it showed that he had taken to heart what I had said to him earlier, and it made me think that maybe he was a sincere dude.

"I see you a fast learner," I joked as I took off the green-and-white New York Jets football jersey that I was wearing. I lay down on the bed on my stomach for my massage and playfully added, "But you still slipping 'cause you ain't even notice my new hairstyle!"

"Oh, shit! Nah, on the real, I noticed it as soon as I walked in! Word is bond!" Snipes laughed.

"Yeah, whateva! Just give me my massage. I'll forgive you if the massage is on point."

Snipes laughed and unexpectedly dripped the cold baby oil onto my back.

"*Ow!* That's cold!" I screamed, and laughed out loud. "See, that's strike one in your massage-skills category. You were supposed to rub that in your hands first and warm it up and then put it on my back."

"I got this. I got this. Just close your eyes and chill."

I did as he said and closed my eyes as he began to pour more baby oil all over my naked body. Then with his strong hands he began to massage my upper back like he was a pro. As he worked his hands back and forth across my muscles, he caused chills to run up and down my body.

"Hmmm, this feels soooo good, Snipes!" I moaned in enjoyment.

Snipes kept quiet as he focused on the task at hand.

He then began massaging my lower back and my waist, and he caused actual butterflies to flutter in my stomach. I was feeling so good and Snipes was definitely being the ultimate gentleman.

As he worked his way down my body, he skipped over my ass and began massaging my thighs instead. I was so turned on, it was like electricity was flowing through my body. I could tell that Snipes was also

I lay there and smiled as I felt like I was finally starting to truly live my life on *my* terms and not on my parents' terms. I also laughed as I wondered if Alexis or Chase or anyone else in the house had heard me screaming and hollering like I had lost my mind while me and Snipes were fucking. But even if they had heard me, it didn't matter because the multiple orgasms were definitely worth the embarrassment.

getting turned on because I could feel his dick getting hard as it pressed against my calves.

Snipes massaged my thighs, concentrating a lot on my inner thighs, and just to tease me he made sure that his hands kept brushing up against my pussy. He had me so turned on, my pussy was throbbing. It had only been about five minutes of massaging, but it felt like an hour's worth of foreplay. Especially in comparison to just twenty-four hours earlier when he had violated me in the stairwell of my dorm.

"Snipes, you are driving me *crazy*!" I said, stressing the word *crazy*, as Snipes began to concentrate on my ass. He rubbed and massaged on my butt checks as if they were dough that he was preparing to bake. My pussy was dripping wet. In fact if Snipes had pulled his boxers off and slipped his dick inside me, it would have just come with the territory because I was more than ready for him to serve me up some dick.

"Turn over on your back," Snipes said.

"Whew!" I yelled as I smiled and shook my body to acknowledge the chilling sensation that I was feeling. "This is what I'm talking about!" I was now on my back with my perky nipples staring straight up at Snipes's dark-chocolate frame.

Snipes wasted no time in spreading my legs, and to my complete shock he buried his face in between them. After spreading my lips apart with the thumb and index finger of his left hand, he began softly flicking his tongue across my clit, and I could not believe how good it felt.

I had been with only one other person in my lifetime, and that was a onetime, awkward-as-hell experience as the two of us were both virgins that didn't know a thing about sex. So I had never ever in my life been eaten out before. Up until now it had only been something that I fantasized about when I masturbated.

Snipes began to flick his tongue across my clit faster, and I squirmed in ecstasy and couldn't help but moan and yell how good his tongue felt.

"Oh my God! Snipes, your tongue feels soooo damn gooood! Damn!" I screamed out loud.

Snipes then began sucking on my clit as he simultaneously placed the middle finger of his right hand inside my pussy and began working it around.

"Oh, shit! Oh my God, Snipes!" I yelled as I began grabbing Snipes's head. "Don't stop! Don't stop!" I screamed louder than before. I was totally not caring if I was making too much noise.

Snipes didn't stop until I came. And it was the hardest and most powerful orgasm that I had ever had in my entire life!

My eyes were closed and my body had just finished twitching and I was still breathing hard from the powerful orgasm. Chills were running all through my body when Snipes grabbed hold of both of my ankles and lifted my legs up, placing my ankles on his shoulders he slid his dick inside me missionary style.

I was so wet and so ready for Snipes that I almost didn't feel him going inside me. But as he began working his dick like a porno star, I couldn't believe that I was about to cum again. But in a matter of twenty good strokes from Snipes, I was again yelling and screaming his name in sexual bliss.

Snipes must also have been real turned on because I could tell that he was about to cum as his strokes became more rapid.

"Make sure you pull out, okay, baby?" I said as Snipes fucked me.

Snipes had a determined look on his face and he nodded, and within seconds he pulled out and shot his hot cum all over my stomach as he let out a big sigh of release.

Snipes then plopped his body down next to mine and the two of us lay there with our chests heaving up and down as we tried to catch our breath.

"Now that's what the hell I'm talking about!" I said as I rolled over and hugged Snipes while I purposely smeared his cum across both of our bodies like it was lotion.

I knew that Snipes's ego had to be on cloud nine, but even if it was

on cloud nine, it was rightly so, because he had really just put it on me something special.

"I love you, babe," Snipes whispered to me while I hugged him.

"What did you just say?" I asked all cheerily. I knew what he had just said, but I wanted to confirm it.

"I said that I love you."

"Snipes, really?" I asked, sounding like an eager and happy little child. "Ohhh, you so sweet, I love you too." Then I asked in a puppy-dog voice, "You my baby?"

Snipes chuckled. "Yeah, I'm your baby."

I held on to him even tighter, then he added, "See, and I know whatchu like sexually." Snipes sat up in the dark room with only the streetlights and the light from the full moon peering in through the window.

Snipes then got up and explained that he had to jump in the shower and bounce.

"Tonight? Now?" I asked, confused, since he had totally come from left field.

"Yeah, but you can still chill and sleep here."

"No, I don't want you to leave tonight," I said in my baby-sounding, spoiled-brat voice. "I want you to get in the bed and hold me."

"I know. Trust me, I don't wanna bounce, but I gotta get going tonight. Just chill and sleep here and I'll call you in the morning when I get to VA." Snipes reached into a pocket of his pants that he had picked up off the floor and handed me two crisp hundred-dollar bills.

Snipes then walked out of the room butt-ass naked and headed for the bathroom to take a shower. I pulled back the covers on the king-size water bed and I got under them and cuddled in the fetal position, feeling better than I had ever felt in my life. I couldn't believe that Snipes had actually told me that he loved me.

I smiled as I lay in the bed and thought about taking a shower, but I didn't want to wash Snipes's scent off me nor his semen.

Nine

I t must have been about four or five o'clock in the morning when I turned over, slightly waking up. For a quick moment I got scared because I didn't realize where I was. I knew I wasn't at my home in North Carolina, and I knew that I wasn't in my dorm room at NYU. So I quickly sat up in a panic trying my hardest to figure out just where the hell I had fallen asleep.

Thankfully I remembered that I was still at Chase's house where I had spent the night. I quietly laughed to myself, then lay back down and thought about the good sex that Snipes and I had had. I giggled, because for the first time in my life I had experienced firsthand just what all the hype had been about when it came to having sex! After I'd lost my virginity, I swear I could never for the life of me understand what all the excitement was about when it came to sex.

As I lay there and tried to go back to sleep, I realized that Snipes must have already left for Virginia. I was a little disappointed because I didn't remember Snipes telling me good-bye before he'd left. I must have fallen asleep while he was taking his shower and he probably didn't want to wake me.

My bladder was full and I had to go to the bathroom and pee something terrible, but the bed was feeling really comfortable and I didn't feel like getting up. Besides that, I didn't feel too comfortable walking around an unfamiliar house to look for the bathroom. It was soon going to be morning, so I decided to just hold my pee and wait until everyone else was up before going to the bathroom.

I lay in the bed, still naked, and stared into space for the next fifteen minutes. And just as I was beginning to doze back off, I heard the loudest bangs coming from the floor below. And then I heard a whole bunch of noise and voices and footsteps.

What the hell is that? I thought to myself as I sat up in the bed and listened closer. My heart began beating a little faster from nervousness.

"NYPD! Don't anybody move!"

NYPD? I thought to myself.

"Y'all niggas better get the fuck up outta my house!" someone yelled. It sounded like Chase, but I wasn't sure. "Word! Fuck that! Y'all can't be running up in my shit like this!"

I could hear a barrage of footsteps coming up the stairs, so I quickly got outta the bed and scrambled around the unlit room looking for something to put on and cover up my exposed body.

Why the hell didn't I just go back to the dorm room when Snipes left? I thought to myself as I frantically searched for the football jersey that Snipes had given me.

Just as I located the jersey and was about to put it on, the bedroom door burst open and three police officers came charging in with their guns drawn and their flashlights shining.

I let out the loudest scream of both fear and shock and panic all combined into one.

"Get on the ground!" one of the police officers shouted at me.

I stood frozen like a deer in headlights as I desperately wanted to cover up my naked body.

Unfortunately the big, burly white officer didn't give me a second more to consider anything. He grabbed me by my wrist and forearm and with one powerful swooping twist and shove, spun me around and rammed my body to the floor face-first.

"I said get the fuck on the ground!" the officer shouted as his two-hundred-plus-pound weight came crashing into my ribs through his knee. I let out a yell of pain as the officer apparently didn't care that I was a harmless petite woman.

"Is anybody else in here with you?!" one of the other officers yelled as he looked in every closet and nook of the room.

"No, it's just me," I stated with my mouth pressed up against the hardwood floor and my heart beating rapidly. The wind was knocked out of me from the officer's knee still planted deep into my ribs and back.

I could hear other officers in other parts of the house yelling "Clear!" as they searched and ransacked the house.

"We have an arrest warrant for Dwight Abrams! Have you seen him?!" the third cop in the room shouted at me. I know the cops have authority, but I couldn't understand what all of their anger and hostility was about, nor could I understand why they didn't just ask me a question without shouting.

I was scared as hell but I kept my mouth shut.

"Snipes! You know who we're talking about! Now where the fuck is he?!" the cop that was holding me on the ground shouted.

"I don't know," I meekly replied.

At that point the cop grabbed my other arm and twisted it around my back and placed handcuffs on my wrists. The cuffs were so tight that they felt as if they were cutting into the bones of my wrists.

"Ahhhh! You're cutting me with those handcuffs!" I shouted out in pain. I could hear Chase and Warren arguing and yelling in other parts of the house. And of course I heard Alexis and her smart-ass foul mouth just cursing and swearing up a storm.

The cop finally picked me up off the floor and stood me in the corner of the room facing the wall butt-naked with my arms cuffed behind my back.

"Miss, is this your bag?" one of the officers asked as he rummaged through a bag that didn't look familiar to me.

I paused.

"Is it or isn't it?!" the cop screamed.

"Yes. I mean no. I don't know." I stuttered and stammered as I turned my head some more to get a better look at the bag that he was referring to. I winced in pain from the handcuffs and crossed my legs as I was about to piss on myself since I still hadn't gone to the bathroom.

"What do you do for a living, ma'am?"

"I go to school. I'm in college."

"So where did you get all of this money from and the money to afford this bag?" the cop asked as he emptied out the contents of a pricey Moschino Cheap & Chic bag onto the bed. The bag contained my regular purse that I had came to the house with that night and a knot of hundred-dollar bills that had a red rubber band around them.

I knew that Snipes must have bought the classy Moschino Cheap & Chic bag for me as a makeup gift and put that money and the bag in the room before he left so that I would wake up to it and be surprised, but I wasn't certain about that, and even if he had put it there for me, I definitely didn't know for sure why or where he had gotten the bag or the money from.

"This is about twenty-five hundred dollars! Where did you get it from?" the officer yelled as he came close up in my face with his hot breath that smelled like three-day-old cream cheese and coffee.

"I don't know?" I replied in all honesty.

"This is a fucking thousand-dollar bag! Lady, tell me something! Your parents rich or something? Don't insult my intelligence!" he screamed, looking at me with fierce anger and irritation.

One of the officers then tapped the shoulder of the officer who had been barking on me about the expensive bag and the money. When he had his attention, he held up the unfinished blunt that I had been smoking earlier.

"And I bet you don't know whose this is either?" the officer asked sarcastically as he turned me around so that my body was no longer facing the corner. He came up in my face and held the blunt right next to my eyes with his right hand, and he purposely brushed his left hand up against my pussy and left it there resting against my clit. Mind you, I was still handcuffed and naked with my hands behind my back.

My eyes immediately opened up real wide as I couldn't believe that the cop had just touched me like that and was not moving his hand.

I was scared as hell and didn't know what to say. I wasn't from the street. So I didn't know how to think fast enough to talk my way out of the predicament that I was in and make myself come across as credible. Not even remotely was I a street person. I had no idea what the consequences were for being in possession of a blunt. But between the blunt and a brand-new expensive bag that was full of money, things didn't look good. I knew that the cops could easily frame me or spin things like I was a drug dealer or something and falsely accuse me and lock me up. Or so at least I thought.

Being that I was so scared I didn't comment as the cop continued to touch my vagina, only now his hand was not just resting up against my clit; nah, the bitch had the nerve to actually be rubbing on my pussy. I felt so disgusted and horrified that it was unreal. He obviously knew that I was afraid, and he knew that no matter what, it would always be his word and the words of the other two cops that were in the room with him against my words.

I was just hoping like all hell that the cops didn't attempt to gang-rape me or anything like that, so that was another reason that I kept my mouth shut and just endured the violation and naked humiliation. But I was worried and petrified beyond belief, and I couldn't believe how fast my heart was beating as I just imagined what my mother and father would say if they found out. I was so afraid that I was on the verge of shedding a tear. But I fought as hard as I could to hold back my emotions because I didn't want to start crying and come across as weak, even though my tears would also have stemmed from anger.

The cop kept a straight face as he continued to hold the blunt to my face while playing with my pussy lips. It actually felt as if he was going to try to finger-fuck me! But fortunately one of the other cops that was in the room walked over to the cop and nudged him out of the way as he put the football jersey over my head and let it hang down and cover up my body.

Whew, I thought as my heart still pumped with fear.

I blew out the biggest sigh of relief. But as the sun was beginning to come up, I could not believe what was happening.

"We're placing you under arrest for the possession of a controlled substance," the officer that had put the football jersey on me said.

"You have the right to remain silent . . ."

I went blank and kind of numb as the cop read me my rights. I tuned him out and was so scared that I was about to pee on myself. I couldn't help but nervously move my body to keep from peeing, but I also did that just to calm my nerves.

"Oh my God. I can't believe this!" I said as the officer told me that I would be going to the Eighty-first Precinct and that I would be able to call anyone that I wanted to call when I got there.

"Are you serious? I'm getting arrested?" I asked in disbelief as I still wiggled and danced due to my nervousness and my bladder, which was bursting at the seams.

The cops just looked at me.

"Okay," I said in a defeated, nonresisting tone as I shook my head in disbelief.

Then as humbly as I could, I almost begged the officer to please loosen the handcuffs, which were still way too tight, and I also asked him if I could please use the bathroom so that I could take a desperately needed piss.

Thank God *that* particular officer had a heart as he joked that he'd rather I pissed here at the house as opposed to pissing all over the backseat of his patrol car. He escorted me to the bathroom and explained that he could loosen the cuffs slightly, but that I would have to keep them on while I used the bathroom, and that he wasn't trying to be a pervert or anything but that he had to watch me as I relieved myself.

"Okay," I humbly said again as the cop did loosen the cuffs a bit and escort me to the bathroom.

I sat on the toilet bowl embarrassed beyond belief and did my thing with the white cop staring right at me, looking as if he was getting some kind of cheap thrill.

"You weren't lying," the cop said. "That sounds like a Russian race-horse taking a piss!"

I tried to find humor in what the cop said, but there was no way I could make light of the situation I was in, which was being arrested inside a house in Bed-Stuy, Brooklyn, at a time when I was supposed to be asleep in my dorm room at one of the most prestigious schools in the nation. How the hell was I going to explain that?

The officer didn't take off the cuffs so I couldn't wipe myself after I had peed. Thankfully only a little bit of excess pee ran down my leg as the officer escorted me to the police car.

The officer did let me put on my shoes before we left for the police precinct. Although I looked like a fool, wearing stylish square-toe stilettos with no stockings and just a football jersey, I would rather have been dressed like that than to have been arrested and processed through the system in just my bare feet.

Ten

Alexis, this is so crazy!" I said as the two of us sat in a small holding cell at the Eighty-first Precinct station house. The holding cell had the worst stench of urine that I had ever smelled in my life! The two of us had just both been fingerprinted and our mug shots had been taken. I was scared as shit but I didn't want to show my fear to Alexis. She seemed calm and lackadaisical about the whole thing, viewing it as just a big inconvenience.

"Katrina, don't worry about this. All they found was a small amount of weed and that's it. They can't hold us too long for that," Alexis reasoned.

"I don't know, Alexis. I mean, when cops show up like that, they only do that for serious shit. Something is up." I shook my head in disgust and tried not to breathe in the horrible urine odor.

"Well, I mean, they were looking for Snipes, but that don't mean nothing. Warren already said that something went down earlier between him, Snipes, and the cops, so I know it probably had something to do with that."

"Katrina Easely!" a uniformed cop yelled as he came close to the bars of the holding pen that Alexis and I were in.

"Yes?" I said as I stood at attention. The cop had kind of startled me.

"Step to the gate and turn around," he ordered.

I did as he said and soon heard the cage being unlocked.

"Miss, put your arms behind your back, please," the cop instructed.

I did as I was told and soon felt handcuffs being placed on my wrists. The cage was relocked and I was escorted to a room where one detective was sitting down at a table.

"Have a seat, miss."

As I sat down, I was beyond nervous because from what I had seen on television I knew that the only time a person gets interrogated at a police station is when it involves crimes of a serious nature, and I could tell that I was about to be interrogated.

The cop began asking me a series of questions, mostly pertaining to Snipes and his whereabouts and the nature of our relationship.

Although I was scared as shit, I figured from the conversation that Alexis and I had had in my dorm room the day before, the best thing for me to do would be to not say anything.

"Officer, with all due respect, I really would rather not answer any questions right now," I said politely. I hadn't yet been allowed to call anyone, and I knew that my parents were the last people that I was gonna call, but I did know that I should probably try to arrange to speak to a lawyer ASAP. The thing was, how in the hell was I gonna get in contact with a lawyer, and furthermore, how was I gonna pay for one? I knew I was up shit creek without a paddle because I really had no one that I could reach out to for help. There was no way I was gonna call Candace, because I didn't want her to know anything about none of this that was going on.

The cop stared at me and smiled a sinister smile. Then he got up and walked around to my side of the table.

"Listen, Katrina, it's early in the fuckin' morning and I am not in the mood for no crap-ass bullshit! Answer my fuckin' questions, bitch!" he barked in my face.

My heart was racing as I wished like all hell that I was on my way to my African-American studies class instead of being screamed on by some stale-coffee-breath-smelling cop.

"Where is Snipes and how do you know him?" the cop screamed at me.

"Okay, listen. I don't know Snipes, I only know his brother Chase," I lied, and held my ground.

"You know Chase from where?"

"I met him in the club."

"What club!" the cop barked, still right in my face.

"A club in Queens called Amazura."

"When exactly did you meet him?"

"Like two weeks ago."

The cop finally backed off, then he sat back down and just stared at me as he sipped on his cup of coffee.

He was stone silent for about ten minutes straight. He stared at me and didn't say a word. Then he abruptly got up from his chair and left the room.

I sat in the cold, well-lit room by myself for about a half hour, and the only thing that I could do was pray to God that everything would work out okay and that they would let me go.

As I was saying a silent prayer, the detective reentered the room.

He calmly sat down and folded his hands and stared at me. This time he had no coffee.

"Katrina, what do you do? Do you work? Do you go to school?" the detective asked in a calm tone.

"I go to school at NYU."

"What are you studying at NYU?"

"I wanna be a veterinarian."

"Oh, really? So you go to NYU and you wanna be a vet. So you're obviously a smart young lady then."

"Well, I don't know. I mean that's the perception I guess."

"Katrina, you and I both know that you have to be extremely intelligent to get into NYU. You don't need nearly as much intelligence to be a lazy schmuck detective like me as you do to become a veterinarian." The white detective with salt-and-pepper hair laughed.

"I may not be as smart as you, Katrina, but I am good at what I do, and I have common fuckin' sense! And my common sense and my experience are telling me that you're not being straight up with me!" The detective was now turning red.

"What?"

"Alexis is in the other room saying that you date Snipes, and you're telling me that you don't know him! Chase is also in a room by himself, and he's saying that he just met you last night! What the fuck is the deal, Katrina?! You're in here on a goddamn drug charge and you're making this whole thing harder on yourself for no reason!"

At that point I was almost ready to start crying because I was so frustrated.

"Just tell me where Snipes is at!" the officer yelled.

I was scared as shit, but out of my love for Snipes I held my ground.

"I don't know where he is!" I shouted back as I trembled from fear and from being cold.

The cop shook his head and smirked. "So you don't know anything about what transpired last night in New Jersey?" the cop asked rhetorically. Then without giving me any time to answer, he got up from his chair and kicked it across the room and screamed, "A cop gets his head blown off by Snipes, the same guy that you're fucking and you tell me you don't know him! But yet your friends are telling me that you do know him! Again, I wasn't educated at NYU and I'm no rosy veterinarian, but I'm not a dummy, Katrina! Stop covering for Snipes and tell me where the fuck he is!"

I knew nothing at all about a police officer being shot, but things seemed real thick and I was scared as hell. I broke down and began crying as I shouted out, "Okay, okay! All I know is that he told me he was going to Virginia, but that's it. I don't know where at in Virginia or anything like that." I sobbed, and through my tears I begged the cop to believe me that I was now telling the truth.

Thankfully the cop relented and stopped the questioning. But unfortunately for me, the next twenty-four hours were pure torture. Alexis, Chase, and I ended up being taken to Central Booking in downtown Brooklyn, where Alexis and I were housed in holding pens with a bunch of other female prisoners.

The conditions at Central Booking were deplorable. It was dirty and disgusting and people were everywhere, prostitutes, drug abusers, you name it, they were in there, all packed in tight like we were on a slave ship or something. For twenty-four hours straight, I had to endure standing up in my stilettos with nothing else on but a damn football jersey! No panties, no bra, nothing! We were given disgusting peanut-butter-and-jelly sandwiches to eat. Sandwiches that I didn't even attempt to take a stab at because I knew they would make me sick. I was forced to pee in a toilet bowl that looked like it hadn't been cleaned in years, and I had to do that with absolutely no privacy in front of a crowd of about fifty women.

There were benches for the detainees to sit down on, but they were all filled with derelict-looking chicks, and I refused to sit or lie on that cold, disgusting floor like some of those dirty wenches had chosen to do. Or at least that's what I thought, but after the eighteen hours straight of just standing up on my feet in those heels, I couldn't take it anymore. No more seats were available on the benches, so I swallowed my pride and lay down on the cold, dirty floor and attempted to get a few hours of sleep. It was horrible, one of the worse experiences in my life.

Fortunately it was soon morning and I was allowed to speak to a lawyer that the city had provided for me. To my relief, the lawyer assured me that I was only going to be charged with a misdemeanor and not a felony, since it was such a small amount of marijuana. She explained that I would have to see the judge and that the judge would release me and that I should do my best to stay out of trouble.

After waiting another hour or so I was finally brought in to see the judge, and in literally a matter of seconds of standing before the judge

I was released. Just like that I was set free and allowed to walk out of the courthouse, which was situated above the underground holding pens that I had been in for the past twenty-something hours.

When I reached those Brooklyn streets, I wanted to run as fast and as far away from that Central Booking courthouse as I could. But I decided to wait for Alexis, who would, I was sure, be coming out right behind me in a couple of minutes since we had both been booked at the same time and were in the holding pens together.

As I waited for Alexis, I realized for the first time in my life just how precious freedom was. I had only been detained for a day, but that day felt like a year. And I vowed to never again let myself be caught up in a position where my freedom could be taken away from me.

I stood and counted $20, the $20 that the cops had let me keep from the $2,700 that they had confiscated from my purse. Those $2,700 along with the Moschino Cheap & Chic bag had been entered into a voucher system, and I was told that I would have to come back to the police station and pick up the bag and a check for the money at a later date.

Alexis finally emerged from the courthouse, looking disheveled and shaking her head and poppin' on Doublemint chewing gum. As she approached me, she said, "Can you believe this bullshit that they put us through? Here, you want a piece of gum?"

I blew out some air and shook my head. The two of us hastily headed for the subway station so that we could make our way back to NYU.

On the train, Alexis apologized for having told the cops that I was dating and fucking Snipes. She also told me that she was sure that this whole thing about Snipes shooting a cop was either a lie or just some big misunderstanding that would soon be cleared up.

I sat on the train and couldn't wait to get in my bed at the dorm. And I hoped that Alexis was right that this whole thing with Snipes would prove to be just one big misunderstanding that would soon be cleared up.

At the time though, the thing that I didn't know was that, when it came to Snipes and his background, there was just way too much to clear up and clean up to easily sweep things under the rug and have them *just* go away. Nah, with Snipes, legally, it was way past that.

As for me, my name was now in the *system*, and I was no longer just a shy, smart, naïve Southern girl who had come to New York to attend NYU. I was growing up quickly and learning what life in the big city was all about. But I had a man who said he loved me, and I knew that he could help navigate us through anything, and even if he couldn't, I was too blind with *love* to see it.

Eleven

It had been about three weeks since I had been arrested at Chase's house. And during those three weeks I had not spoken to or seen Snipes, but I was still obsessing over him. He had been in touch with Warren, so through Alexis and by way of Warren I knew that he was okay. A big part of me was worried about him, and I couldn't wait to speak to him so that I could try to get a grip on just exactly what was going on.

Warren began to stop by my dorm room every other day just to check up on me and see how I was doing, and I really got to know him and like him as a friend. He was so cool. The first day Warren came by my room he kind of surprised me because I didn't expect to see him. But the first time he came by and every time thereafter, he made sure that he was always on his cell phone with Alexis, and he would let me speak to her and say what's up to her. I never asked him why he did that, but I know he did it because he wanted to make sure that everything was on the up-and-up with him and me so that there could never be a question about anything happening that could be deemed inappropriate.

As I spoke to Alexis on Warren's cell phone, Warren walked over and turned on the television and began watching music videos as he stood in his baggy jeans, Timberland boots, and a stylish button-up shirt.

"So what's up withchu?" Warren asked after I hung up with Alexis and handed the phone back to him.

"Just trying to knock out this schoolwork, that's about it." I smiled as I sat down on my bed in the Indian position.

"Yo, this is my shit right here. Where's the remote, turn that up," Warren said.

I reached for the remote control and turned up the volume to the TV as it played Snoop Dogg's hit record "Nuthin' but a 'G' Thang."

Warren bopped his head to the song and began to recite the lyrics out loud.

Ain't nothin' but a G thang, baaaaaby!
Two loc'ed out Gs so we're craaaaazy!
Death Row is the label that paaaaays me!

"Yo, I love them Death Row niggas, the West Coast got this whole rap thing on lock," Warren exclaimed.

"You want something to drink?" I asked Warren after getting up from the bed and walking over to the small refrigerator that we had in our dorm room.

"Yeah, no doubt, whatever you got," he said, then continued to recite the lyrics to the song.

I handed him a small bottle of apple juice and also took one for myself.

Finally the song went off and Warren calmed down a bit and then picked up right where he had left off in the conversation.

"Oh, so you just bussing out your schoolwork? What are you taking in school?"

"Well, I didn't declare my major yet, but I know that I want to be a veterinarian."

"A veterinarian? Ain't those the people who don't eat meat? They got degrees in that shit now?"

When I heard that, I spit out my apple juice from laughing because Warren was dead serious.

"Nooo, silly, that's a *vegetarian*. I said I wanna be a veterinarian, you know, an animal doctor."

"Oh, a'ight, I feel you. So you wanna work with pit bulls and shit like that right?"

"Yeah, something like that." I chuckled.

Warren nodded, then finished his apple juice and put the bottle in my small garbage can.

"Well, I ain't gonna stay, I was just coming to check on you and make sure you were a'ight. I'm out, I'm gonna run by and see Alexis real quick, but if you need anything while, just shout me out, a'ight?" Warren instructed.

"Okay," I said, before asking how Snipes was doing.

"He doing lovely, and matter of fact he sent you something." Warren reached into his pocket and pulled out a huge bankroll. He had to have had about $10,000, all in hundred-dollar bills.

"Here." He handed me two crisp hundreds. "I'll be by later in the week to say what's up," he added before leaving.

I closed the door and placed the money in my pocket, and I couldn't help but laugh about Warren and the vegetarian-veterinarian comment he had made. He had a crazy sense of humor and was always so full of life, and I liked to be around him. But I liked being around Snipes much more and I missed him.

But during Snipes's absence I was able to buckle down and get caught up on my schoolwork and my studying, and I also reached out to several different animal hospitals to inquire about volunteering with them to gain experience, since I planned on opening up one in the future. Plus I just loved animals to no end, and since we couldn't have pets in our dorm, I figured volunteering at an animal hospital would be the next best thing.

"I took your advice," I said to my biology professor as I walked up to her at the end of my biology class.

"About volunteering?"

"Yes. I called three hospitals in the city and they all want me to come in so that they can meet me," I explained, sounding somewhat excited and eager.

"Katrina, that's good," Ms. Perkins said. I liked Ms. Perkins. She was a cool professor who always kept it real with me, and everybody else for that matter. She reminded me a lot of the actress who played Thelma from the TV show *Good Times*.

"Katrina, trust me, I have a daughter your age and she went down to Miami and all she wanted to do was stay on South Beach, go to the clubs, and all of that. She went boy crazy and started failing her classes, and I told her just like I told you a few weeks ago, it's that unstructured time that causes so many young people to get distracted, and it's better to be busy, but a constructive busy, and once you get constructive with your time, you'll see how quickly things turn around. So I'm so glad you followed up on that suggestion. Try not to pay these young men any attention. They'll want you even more when you get your degree. And they'll still be around. Trust me."

"You're right." I smiled and nodded. By this time all of the other students had finished piling out of the classroom and it was just me and Ms. Perkins left.

"Here." She handed me my paper.

"I got an A on this paper?" I said in a high-pitched tone, due to my surprise and excitement.

"Shhhhh, I graded yours first, I didn't finish grading any of the other papers, so don't say anything to the other students," she explained with a smile.

"Oh, okay, thank you." I leaned in and gave her a soft, quick hug.

"So this will erase that D that you got on that test the other week."

"You just made my day, Ms. Perkins."

"Katrina, you'll be fine. Just stop looking at yourself as an average student and don't get comfortable and the sky is the limit for you," she added before packing up her things and telling me that she would see me on Wednesday.

That A on that paper was clear and tangible proof of what I could do when I stayed focused and set my priorities straight.

Alexis and I still spent a lot of time together, but we weren't going out each and every night. Based on Candace's urging, I tried to relegate Friday, Saturday, and Sunday nights for hanging out, and all of the other nights during the week I remained focused on my schoolwork.

I had also been in touch with my mother and father, and I was able to assure them and put them at ease by telling them that I had been doing well in school and that I wasn't the least bit homesick. But I made damn sure that I never mentioned to them anything about my arrest, because I knew that if I told them about that, they would both have been on the next plane smoking out of North Carolina and heading to New York.

"So you're okay with money? Do you need anything at all?" my father asked during one of our telephone conversations.

"No, I'm good. I try not to spend too much money because everything is *so* expensive up here in New York," I said, knowing that the real reason that I didn't need any money was because I had retrieved and cashed that $2,700 check from the police department.

"Katrina, I'll wire you two hundred dollars in the morning. I don't want you up there with no money."

"No, Daddy, honestly, I'm okay. I mean you can send it if you want to, but I'm really okay with money right now."

"Well, your mother thinks I should go ahead and send it, so I'll wire it to you in the morning."

There was a brief pause, and then from out of nowhere, and I don't know what I was thinking, I said, "Daddy, can I tell you something?"

"Yeah, what is it, baby?"

"Well, I met this guy named Dwight, and I really like him and—"

My father immediately cut me off and practically jumped down my throat through the phone. "Look, Katrina, you are not up there to be chasing behind no guys! You're there to focus on your schoolwork! There will be plenty of time for guys and going out, but right now you need to be focused on getting your schoolwork done!"

"But, Daddy, I just—"

"Katrina, I know you're at that age where you want to meet guys and go out with them. And that's understandable, but what I'm telling you is—"

"Hello, Katrina?" My mother picked up another phone in the house and blurted herself into the conversation while rudely interrupting my father.

"Yeah, honey, Katrina is telling me about some guy that she met up there in New York, and I'm trying to explain to her that she doesn't need to be focusing on guys right now and that she needs to focus on getting her lessons done," my father said.

My mother chimed right in where my father left off, only she wanted to know more about the guy.

"Katrina, your father is right. I know you think we're old-fashioned and don't know much about nothing, but believe me, we have been there and done that so we know what is best for you. And who is this guy anyway? Where is he from? How did you meet him? How old is he?"

I sat on the other end of the line just shaking my head in frustration. I mean, I hadn't even uttered anything positive or negative about Snipes, I just merely mentioned that I met a guy that I liked, and to my parents it was like I had told them I was pregnant, dropping out of school, and planning on getting married.

My mother was actually silent and waiting for a response from me.

"Katrina?" my mother asked.

"Mom, I hear you, and I'm not trying to be rude, but can we just forget that I even mentioned anything about a guy?" I said with a bunch of aggravation in my voice.

"See, Katrina, you're taking this the wrong way and missing the point," my father stated as he and my mom continued to double-team me.

"Mom and Dad, please just hear me out. I hear what the both of you are saying. I hear it loud and clear. And I understand where both of you are coming from. Really I do. But can we just end this conversation here? I'm not trying to be disrespectful or anything like that, but I just don't even want to talk about it anymore right now," I said, annoyed.

My parents were both quiet, and before long we had all cordially said our good-byes.

"Ugggghhhh!" I screamed out in frustration and irritation after I hung up the phone.

Candace wasn't in the room at the time and I was glad, because her square ass would probably have sided with my parents.

I plopped myself on my bed and just lay there thinking about Snipes. And almost as if my thinking about him had willed him to call me, right on cue as I was remembering the strong orgasm that I had had with him, the phone rang and I picked it up.

"Hello."

"Katrina?"

"Snipes?" I recognized his voice. "Hi, baby! Where are you? I was getting so worried about you," I said as the biggest Kool-Aid smile appeared across my face.

"Yeah, I'm sorry, baby, for going AWOL like that. But I'm okay. You a'ight?"

"Yeah, of course I'm okay," I replied, still smiling because I was so happy to hear from him.

"That's good. You got the bag and that money I left you, right?"

"Yeah, I got that. I spent two hundred dollars of the money on my credit-card bill but I got the rest. Do you need it?" I asked in a rush.

"Nah, I'm good. That's for you. Spend it. You ain't gotta hold it."

"Oh, okay. Thank you."

There was some silence on the phone until I spoke up.

"So, baby, where are you?"

"I'm still in Virginia. I'm trying to get *my business* started down here too."

"What, with the insurance?"

"Nah, nah, something else. But I'll explain that to you when I see you."

"Okay," I replied, making sure that I wasn't overstepping my bounds by prying into his business.

"Listen, I can't stay on the phone that long, but I need you to do something for me."

"Okay, what's up?" I eagerly asked.

"Well, I need you to go by and see Warren later on. He has the keys to my Honda Accord. Get the Honda from him, and he's also gonna give you a suitcase with some of my clothes in it, and I wantchu to take the clothes and my car and come down to VA to see me."

"To *Virginia?*" I asked, confused.

"Yeah, I really need you to do this for me," Snipes stated convincingly.

"When though?"

"I wanted you to leave tonight."

"Tonight?" I asked with an even bigger reservation in my voice than before. "Snipes, but I got class all week," I said, realizing that it was only Monday.

"I know, I know. I wouldn't even ask you to do this for me but I really wanna see you," he stressed.

I sat and thought how ironic it was that my parents and I had just had a conversation about my essentially not losing focus due to male attention. But I was only human, not to mention that my hormones were racing.

"I really wanna see you too," I added.

"I would have just had Warren FedEx me the suitcase but there's gonna be some thangs in there and I'd rather just have somebody bring it to me directly."

See, this was a perfect example of my being naïve to the streets and to slang and the overall city life. At the time I had no idea that *thangs* was a street expression for "drugs." So it was like Snipes was, in his own way, being forthright with me and telling me that he wanted me to transport drugs for him from New York to Virginia. But I wouldn't find out until way later that I would be transporting drugs on that trip to Virginia. And my ignorance to everything kind of made Snipes think that I was a down-ass chick who was 'bout it and down for anything. But little did he know, or maybe he did know, that it was just my clueless-ness that made me agree to make the trip for him.

"Snipes, I never drove that far by myself before." I was now some-what eager to go, but I was a little jittery and apprehensive about the long ride.

"It's nothing. Just get on I-95 and take that all the way down until you get to I-64. You'll be here in like eight hours. I'm staying in Hamp-ton, Virginia, not too far from Norfolk."

Then Snipes instructed me to take some of the money that I was holding and buy a cell phone so that I would have it with me while I was traveling.

I agreed to Snipes's plan, and to his suggestion that I leave at like midnight to avoid all of the traffic delays I would have if I left in the morning or in the afternoon or during the early evening hours.

Before ending our conversation, I brought up something that had been weighing on my mind a whole lot during the past three weeks.

"Snipes, are you sure everything is okay? I mean, I know Warren had to tell you how the cops raided your brother's house looking for you. And when they locked me up for a misdemeanor marijuana charge, they questioned me about you like you was America's Most Wanted or something."

"What did they ask you?" Snipes questioned, concerned.

"They were just asking me how did I know you and where were you and shit like that."

"What did you tell them?"

"I didn't tell them nothing! I didn't know what was going on. So I kept my mouth shut."

"Good. Good. That's good." Then Snipes continued, "Look, it's nothing. They just saying that I shot a cop or some bullshit like that, but it's all bullshit, but when cops say you did this or did that, then it's always your word against their word, so I'm like let me just lay low for a while, get up some money and get the right lawyer and then just confront the shit head-on. You know what I mean? But, listen, when you come down here, I'll explain all of that to you. But don't worry about it. It's nothing," Snipes assured me.

We ended our conversation and I quickly went to my closet and reached into the jacket pocket where I had stashed the remaining money. I counted it out, and it was just under $2,500. I laid the money on the bed, then dialed Alexis on her cell phone and told her that I would be driving down to Virginia to see Snipes and that I needed her to quickly take me to get a cell phone and for her to have Warren call me as soon as possible.

Right after we hung up, Candace walked in the room and I had forgotten to remove the cash from my bed while I searched for some clothes to bring with me on the trip.

"Damn, girl! You hit the number or something?" Candace asked as she looked at all of the money sprawled out on the bed, mostly twenty-dollar bills.

Ah, shit, I cursed at myself. I didn't want Candace to see that I was holding so much cash.

I played it off by just laughing and not commenting. I scooped up the money and put it in my Moschino bag and continued to look for a couple of outfits to bring with me to Virginia.

"Well, I'm just saying, can a sista hold something?" Candace jokingly asked.

I knew what she was referring to, so I reached into my bag and pulled out three crisp twenty-dollar bills and gave them to Candace.

"Katrina, let me find out?"

"Let you find out what?" I asked, smiling.

"That you ballin' and you were trying to keep it hush all this time, while I was working my slave-wage work-study job."

At that point the phone rang.

"Hey, Warren," I said, quickly recognizing his voice.

I could tell that Candace was all up in my conversation, but I didn't look at her as I spoke.

"Yeah, I spoke to him not too long ago. I'm leaving tonight," I explained to Warren. "So what time you think you'll bring the car by? I'm getting ready to go with Alexis to get this phone, and I wanna make sure that I'm here when you come."

"Okay. . . . Yeah. . . . Okay, that's good. So I'll speak to you later on tonight." I hung up the phone.

"Where you going?" Candace immediately asked.

I sighed because something just didn't sit right with me knowing that Candace was all up in my conversation and because she knew too much of my business.

"Alright, Candace, here's the deal. But if my mother or father calls, you can't say nothing! Warren is bringing Snipes's car by tonight and I'm driving to Virginia to see him for a couple of days."

"Virginia?"

"Yes, Candace, Virginia!" I said with a tone like I was not in the mood for explaining anything.

"Well, when you leaving?"

"Tonight," I bluntly replied.

Candace didn't say anything, but I could tell she was itching to give me a lecture.

"Like I said, if my mother or father calls, you don't know nothing and you don't say nothing! I'm getting ready to go buy a cell phone, and I'll give you the number before I leave so if my mother or father calls or if something comes up and you need to contact me, then you can always get me on the cell phone."

The room was quiet for a minute and I had finally gathered three outfits, panties, a nightgown, and bras, and I began placing them inside a large duffel bag.

"Wait, wait, wait. Wait! Hold up! Here, Katrina, take this back." Candace sounded overdramatic as she attempted to hand me back the $60 that I had just given her.

"What?" I did not extend my hand to take the money back. "You can keep it."

"Nah. Take it back." Candace laid it on top of my duffel bag.

I couldn't understand why she was giving it back, but I didn't really care.

"Katrina, I know you don't wanna here this, but I'm giving you back that *drug money*."

"Whatever, Candace. Like I said, you don't have to give it back."

"Katrina, just answer this question for me. Did Snipes buy you that Moschino bag and give you all of that money?"

I ignored her and didn't answer the question.

"Katrina, come on now. He's driving a brand-new Benz. He's up in the clubs partying every night. Him and Warren both got flashy, high-end cars, and they got this whole campus on smash in terms of the women going crazy over them because of how they always profiling around campus. He's giving you cash like it's water. And he's in and out of town. Come on, Katrina. I'm not player hatin' or nothing like that. You should do you. By all means do you. But all I'm saying is you better be careful as hell, Katrina!"

I didn't catch an immediate attitude with Candace because she had some valid points. I knew, though, that had I told her about the night the cops raided Chase's house and I got arrested, she would really have had her mind made up. And the last thing I needed was her being so opinionated about something that she really was blind to and was stereotyping.

"Candace, Snipes has an insurance business," I explained.

"Yeah, and John Gotti owns a plumbing business," Candace sarcastically stated.

I didn't respond. I turned on the radio and finished packing and waited for Alexis to arrive so that I could get the cell phone and make my trip to Virginia to see my baby.

Twelve

aby, I ain't ever driving that late at night like that by myself again!"
I said in the cell phone as Snipes guided me from I-64 to the
Hampton Inn, where he was staying. "I almost dozed off at the
wheel like four or five times." It was like eight thirty Tuesday morning.
Snipes had apparently just woken up and sounded sexy with a Barry
White morning voice.

"I'm sorry, baby. I should've told you to just get some sleep and
come in the morning."

"It's okay," I quickly replied. "Hey, is this Hampton University?" I
asked as I exited the highway.

"Yeah, that's Hampton University. You should be able to see the hotel if you can see the university."

Hampton University had been one of the schools that I was real
close to choosing before I decided on New York University.

"Oh, okay, yeah, I'm pulling into the parking lot now. What room are you in?"

"I'm in room 215."

"Okay, I'll be right there." I pulled into a parking space. I couldn't wait to get to the room, take a shower, and then have Snipes *put it on me* like he had done the last time I'd seen him.

I parked the car and got out. I retrieved my duffel bag from the backseat, then made my way to the hotel entrance. As soon as I walked into the lobby, I realized that I had forgotten to get the suitcase that Warren had put inside the trunk for Snipes. I flung the duffel bag over my shoulder, turned back around, and marched back to the car to get it.

"Ms. Easely?" a white man called out to me as he and a white lady approached me.

Who the hell is that and how do they know my name?

"Ms. Easely, FBI. Can we have a word with you?" the white guy asked, as he was now right up on me showing me his credentials.

"FBI?" I stopped dead in my tracks.

"Are you Katrina Easely?" the female FBI agent asked.

My heart began beating as I nodded my head, but I didn't say anything.

"Katrina, we're looking for Dwight Abrams and we have reason to believe that you may be able to help us locate him," the female agent continued.

I remained silent and frowned, giving the agents a confused look.

"Katrina, where are you from?"

"North Carolina," I quickly blurted out as I decided not to go back to the car.

"Oh, really? Well, why does your car have New York plates?" the male agent asked me.

"Because that's not my car."

"Katrina, let's be straight up. The car you pulled into the parking lot with is registered to Dwight Abrams, but yet you claim you don't know where he is. Then you tell us you're from North Carolina, yet you're driving around with New York plates."

"Look, you asked me where I was from and I told you. I go to school in New York but I'm from North Carolina. What's with the million questions anyway?" Being arrested in New York had taught me that I didn't have to be so nervous just because I was being questioned by law enforcement.

The whole ride down to Virginia I had thought about what Candace had said about *drug money,* and although I didn't dismiss her opinion outright, seeing these FBI agents sort of cemented in my mind that *something* wasn't right. But at that moment my priorities told me or I guess I instinctively knew that I had to protect Snipes.

"So what's up, Katrina? You're telling us that you don't know where he is, yet you travel all the way down to Virginia in his car, after you told the NYPD that Dwight was in Virginia."

"I don't know what else to tell you. Yes, the car is registered to him, but, no, I don't know where he's at. I am traveling to North Carolina and I just decided to stop here in Hampton to get some rest and to check out some things at Hampton University, since I'm thinking about transferring to that school," I quickly lied, surprising even myself with how cool and fluid I was.

Just as I was done talking, my cell phone began to ring and I had a feeling that it was probably Snipes.

"Hello."

"Katrina, I'm just letting you know that your father called you last night at like midnight, and he just called you back. What do you want me to tell him if he calls again?" Candace asked.

"Candace, I'll call you back later, and when I do, I'm gonna need you to three-way me on a call with him, okay?"

Candace said okay, then I had to cut her short as she began to ask me where I was and had I made it safely to Virginia.

No sooner than I'd hung up from Candace, my cell phone rang again.

"Baby, where you at?" Snipes asked me.

"No, I'm not eating breakfast. I'll just eat something this afternoon after I go by the registrar's office," I said, attempting to not sound guarded.

"What?"

"No, I'm not hungry now. I'll call you back when I leave the school."

"Katrina, what's up?"

"Okay, so I'll call you later." I hung up. I was hoping that Snipes caught on and didn't try calling me back.

"Katrina, what room are you staying in?" the male agent asked.

"I didn't get a room yet. *My goodness! Anything else?*" I said, sounding as if I'd taken a page straight out of Alexis's notebook on rudeness.

"Yeah, do you mind if we take a look inside of your bag?" the female agent asked.

I unzipped the bag, and as the agents were looking inside it, I saw Snipes approaching the entrance door from inside the hotel. I looked at him and shook my head. Thankfully he stopped dead in his tracks and made his way back into the hotel without the agents seeing anything.

"Ms. Easely, we're sorry to inconvenience you. Here is my card. If you happen to hear from or see Dwight, can you give me a call or have him give me a call?" the male agent asked.

"I sure will," I said as I made my way into the hotel. I decided to play things safe and, instead of going to Snipes's room, actually get my own room.

After I checked in, I called Snipes's room repeatedly but I got no answer. In fact Snipes didn't call me on my cell phone until late that afternoon.

"Baby, where you at?" I eagerly and somewhat nervously asked Snipes.

"Where you at?" Snipes said, sounding like a parrot.

"Those white people said they were from the FBI, so I didn't wanna go to the room and I played things off and got my own room in the hotel."

"So you dolo right now?" Snipes asked, using his New York slang.

"What?" I didn't understand what Snipes was referring to by *dolo.*

"Are you alone?"

"Oh! Yes. Yeah. I'm alone. It's just me."

"Katrina, you *sure?*"

"Yes, baby. I'm alone."

Snipes was quiet and seemed to be breathing kind of heavy into the phone. After relaxing, he explained to me that he was glad that I'd been vague with the federal agents and not forthright. He also told me that he wanted me to immediately call a cab, take it to the airport, and rent a car. He said he would call me in about a half hour and that he was gonna have someone meet me to drop off some money to me and that he wanted me to then head straight back to New York.

"But, baby, I just got here," I said with a smile and some disbelief that Snipes wanted me to turn back around and go back to New York.

"Katrina, I know. And trust me, I wantchu to stay and chill wit' me, but I didn't expect this shit to come up," Snipes said, sounding frustrated.

"Baby, can we talk? I—"

"Katrina, not now, Okay? I just need you to do this for me. Don't ask me shit right now. I told you I would explain everything to you and I will, but right now I just need you to do this for me," Snipes barked. He totally caught me off guard with his unexpected change in demeanor.

"Just get the cab and go to Hertz Rent-a-Car, get a rental, and just wait there. And don't leave until you hear from me!" Snipes commanded, and hung up the phone.

The money that was dropped off to me at the rent-a-car place by one of Snipes's boys wasn't exactly a small amount. It was a little over $22,000. Snipes had instructed me to drop the money off with his brother Chase and told me he was gonna be heading back to New York the following week. When he got to New York, he promised, he would explain to me everything that had gone down and why I was transporting so much money for him.

Admittedly, I was a young, dumb, naïve small-town girl, but it didn't take a rocket scientist to help me realize what the hell was going on. All of the lightbulbs started turning on in my head, and my honest and authentic feeling was fear. How could I not be scared? The thing was, Snipes *needed* me, and I wanted to be there for him, so I didn't let the fear that I was feeling paralyze me and cause me to run from him. So I blocked out the fear, and what was weird is that I felt good about myself for doing so, and I knew that if I could just be there for Snipes, then he would also *wanna* be there for me and he would have a reason to be there for me.

Anyway, that next week eventually came, and Snipes did arrive back in New York, but he never did fully explain himself. And I think that Snipes could sense that I was feeling really uncomfortable. So to smooth things over and distract me, he took me on shopping sprees to Saks, Neiman Marcus, and Bloomingdale's. Snipes made sure that I had all of the hottest and latest designer shit like the DKNY sneakers. He went all out whenever we shopped—like with the DKNY sneakers, he bought me the red-and-white pair, the silver-and-white, and the black-and-white pair. Snipes even shocked me when he suggested that I buy some business suits, so he bought me a Tahari business suit and one by Parallel. And after each shopping spree Snipes would sex the hell out of me and leave my body and my mind thinking about nothing but pure ecstasy.

The shopping sprees became intoxicating to me because with the clothes and the money that Snipes was spending on me, it allowed me to blossom into someone that I had always wanted to be but always felt like I lacked something to be that. And as for the sex, it was like icing on the cake.

What was weird though was that Snipes would always fuck me either in my dorm room or at one of his men's cribs or at a hotel. He avoided taking me to wherever he slept, but I never questioned him on it because I was afraid that I would come across as nagging or nosy or a nuisance. Eventually though Snipes had me rent an apartment for him uptown in Harlem, where the lease was in my name and he allowed me to stay there rent-free. The apartment was off-the-hook, and Snipes laced the place with all kinds of toys and high-end furniture and electronics.

Before I knew what was what, I was spending most of my time either with Snipes or with Alexis, and I was becoming intoxicated by all of the material trappings that Snipes was affording me. At the same time I was genuinely getting closer to Snipes emotionally, like I was really getting past the obsession phase and was starting to catch feelings for him like I *loved-him*-loved him.

My schoolwork was suffering big-time. And by the time November rolled in, I had just about moved out of my dorm room and was holed up uptown with Snipes in Harlem daily. I was failing test after test, including midterm exams. I was missing class after class, and I was not handing in papers on time simply because I had become intoxicated and infatuated with Snipes and pleasing him became my number one priority. But in my mind I felt that I would be able to turn things around and rebound before it was time for final exams.

Although my schoolwork was suffering, I had become adept at lying and leading my parents to believe that everything was all good at school. And I knew that they were buying everything I was telling them, simply because their confidence and trust in me had begun to grow, which was funny because their confidence in me actually had every reason to fade if they had known the truth. But they didn't know the truth, and they had begun to trust me to the point where they finally relented and to my shock asked me if I was I still interested in "that boy" that I had mentioned to them some weeks back.

When I told them that I was indeed still interested in him, they almost floored me when they told me to ask Snipes if he would accompany me home for the Thanksgiving holiday so they could meet him.

"Mom, are you serious?" I asked with a huge smile on my face.

"Yes, I'm serious. Your father and I spoke about it and we just feel like if we extend that gesture, it would help you see that we can be flexible and that we aren't out to make your life miserable and, well, you know—"

"Mom, you don't have to explain no more," I said with the biggest smile on my face.

I was elated and shocked at the same time. I knew my parents would like Snipes once they met him, and I knew their actually meeting him would go a long way in their being able to give me that sense of freedom I so desperately needed.

I was just praying Snipes would agree to go to North Carolina.

I lay in my bed that night and just thought about how blissful Snipes made me feel and how thrilled I was about life and all that I was experiencing.

Thirteen

S o you think your pops will let me sleep in the same room as you?" Snipes asked me as I drove in his brand-new Honda Accord, which he had purchased a week ago. He had flat-out abandoned the Honda Accord I had driven to Virginia, but he'd never explained to me why he'd gotten rid of it, other than to say that he "just got tired of it." I would later find out that Snipes was a smart and calculating guy in that he loved high-end, flashy cars, but he also knew how and when not to be too flashy, and that was when the Honda Accord served him well.

I looked at Snipes with a comical smirk. "Come on now, let's not get crazy," I responded to his question.

We had reached Winston-Salem, North Carolina, and were just blocks away from my home.

"It's a big difference compared to Manhattan, right?" I asked Snipes.

He nodded in agreement, then added, "Yeah, but I bet I could get it poppin' down here."

I looked at him and didn't respond as we were pulling up to my mother's house.

"Snipes just be yourself and relax. Okay?"

"I'm good. You the one that sounds like you need to relax." He was absolutely right.

We had chosen to arrive on Thanksgiving Day, instead of the night before, and it turned out to be a huge mistake because we had gotten caught in traffic. It ended up taking us almost fourteen hours to get there instead of the ten hours it was supposed to take.

I was dressed in a regular-looking non-name-brand sweat suit, and Snipes was dressed in a pair of Karl Kani jeans, sneakers, and a hooded sweatshirt. He carried both of our bags as we approached the front door and rang the bell.

It was as if my mother had been waiting at the door or something because before I could lift my finger off the doorbell, she had flung open the front door and was waiting with open arms to hug me.

"Baby," my mother said as I could smell the aroma of soul food coming from the kitchen, "how was the ride?"

I shook my head as I pulled away from my mother. "Mom, you don't even wanna know. There were traffic jams everywhere!"

Then I plastered a big smile across my face. "Mom, this is Dwight, the one who I've been telling you about. And, Dwight, this is my mom."

She smiled and extended her hand to Snipes, who was still standing at the bottom step of my parents' front stoop.

Dwight gently placed our bags down and reached out and kindly took hold of my mother's hand. To my shock and to my mother's pleasant surprise, he kissed my mother's hand and then stated, "Nice to meet you Mrs. Easely. You're just as beautiful as your daughter."

When I saw my mother blushing, I wanted to pump my fist in the air because I knew that from that point on, Snipes was in there.

"Nice to meet you too," my mother said, smiling. "It's kind of cold so why don't y'all come on in."

We came into the living room of the house, and when I saw my father sitting on the couch watching the football game, I didn't know what to expect from him. I wasn't sure why he hadn't gotten up to greet us at the door when he heard my mother talking to us, and I just hoped that he wasn't on some ol' silent-treatment nonsense in an effort to intimidate Snipes.

"James, get up and speak to your daughter and her friend!" my mother said as she grabbed the remote control and looked as if she was about to turn off the game to get my father's attention.

"Oh, oh, I'm sorry, baby," my father said as he stood up from the couch. He was about six foot three and 240 pounds of back-in-the-day muscle, but he looked good for his age. In fact a lot of my friends used to say that my father reminded them a lot of the wrestler the Rock.

"Hey, baby-girl!" he said as he smothered me with a bear hug.

"Daddy, you're crushing me," I joked as I playfully pushed my father off me.

"Daddy, this is Dwight; Dwight, this is my father."

"How are you?" my father asked Snipes, gripping his hand. Then my father gave him one of those ghetto embraces.

"I'm doing okay. Nice to meet you," Snipes replied, seeming less confident than he had been with my mother. "Mr. Easely you have a nice home. I like the layout," Snipes chimed in, trying to break the ice.

My father took a lot of pride in his home so Snipes was right on point with his comment. That was all that was needed to break the ice as my father took it upon himself to take Snipes on a tour of our home.

As they slid off on their tour, I followed my mom into the kitchen and helped her with the food.

"So, Mom, what do you think?" I said, sounding all excited and more as if Snipes was my fiancé as opposed to my boyfriend.

"Well, he seems like a nice young man, Katrina. He's a good-looking fellow and I see why you like him. He's charming. Just let me and your father have a chance to get to know him."

* * *

Before long the table was set and my mother and I were trying to pry my father and Snipes away from the football game and into the dining room so that we could eat.

"Mrs. Easely, you should think about opening a soul-food restaurant. As good as this food looks, you would make a million dollars," Snipes said as we all sat down to eat. Snipes was pouring it on thick when it came to the compliments, and I was loving every minute of it.

"Dwight, since you're a male guest in our home, would you mind saying grace?" my father asked.

Snipes paused as we all sat at the table, and then he stated, "Mr. Easely, with all due respect, I would rather you say the grace. I have certain issues when it comes to God, and I wouldn't feel comfortable saying the grace."

Issues? What in the world was Snipes talking about? My mother was a religious nut so I was hoping nothing came of Snipes's comment.

My father simply nodded, then he asked all of us to bow our heads while he said grace.

In seconds we were digging into the food and passing plates to one another, and I could tell that my mother was tight and itching to ask Snipes about his God comment.

And sure enough, right on cue, my mom chimed in, "So, Dwight, what kind of *issues* is it that you have with God? Are you a Christian, if you don't mind me asking?"

I was hoping that the conversation wouldn't flow that way because I knew that the last two things that should ever be discussed among people were religion and politics.

"Well, I'm a nonbeliever," Snipes calmly replied as he placed a forkful of collard greens into his mouth.

The room got deathly quiet as my mother looked at me.

"Oh?" she said, now refocusing her eyes to look at her black-eyed peas.

"Well, yeah, it's like ever since I was small, I used to see things go on, especially with children, and I used to say to myself, 'If there really is a God, then why does so much bad stuff keep happening?' And to me there just can't be a God if He allows so much negativity. Like with child abuse for example, how can God let innocent children get beat and abused the way they do in some households?" Snipes coolly stated.

My father nodded his head and looked at my mother as if to say, *Change the subject.* And fortunately my mother left it alone by simply saying that she understood where Snipes was coming from and that she respected his beliefs.

"So, Dwight, what are you studying in school?" my father asked.

Snipes and I had already spoken beforehand and he was not going to mention that he was not presently in school.

"Business. I want to get my MBA," Snipes replied, trying to sound articulate.

My father was an assistant to an investment banker, so any talk of business was right up his alley.

"Oh, really?" my father stated with a smile.

"Actually, Daddy, Dwight even has his own insurance business," I added for good measure.

"Wow, that's impressive." My father asked Snipes about the business and how he was able to juggle going to school and running a business at the same time.

Snipes gave all of the right answers as he spoke about having the right team of managers in place to help him, and he also spoke about how he wanted to expand his business into a mortgage brokerage.

"Diversification! That's the name of the game!" my father shouted before putting some candied yams into his mouth. My father was obviously getting excited in his own weird way.

As I heard Snipes talk and interact with my parents, it was as if I was a spectator at times, but it was all good because Snipes was impressing me with what he spoke about and how articulate he sounded and how business-minded and smart he seemed.

Times like that, seeing him interact with my parents, made me not think so much about how he had issues going on with the law. His intelligence and his charisma were such that any potential problem that he was facing had to be of no major significance, as it seemed that someone so bright could never get into a situation that his brain couldn't get him out of.

Snipes continued to talk about his family and their Southern roots and his upbringing, and I was sure that my mom and dad would both approve of him. I knew that I would have to work on my mom to try to smooth over the whole Snipes-not-believing-in-God thing, but I was sure that one *issue* wouldn't cause my parents to disapprove of him.

And as it would later turn out, I was right. My parents both had nothing but good things to say about Snipes. He had successfully sold them on himself. And I figured that my road ahead with him would be much smoother since I now had my parents' approval.

Fourteen

bout a week after Thanksgiving, I decided to go to the library at my school to get caught up on some much needed studying. Final exams were fast approaching, and I had to ace every exam or I knew that I would probably be looking at a 2.0 grade point average if not lower.

I was done studying at around nine o'clock at night, and instead of heading to my dorm room I hopped on the A train and headed straight for the apartment that Snipes and I were sharing near City College in Harlem. It was a Friday night, and it was a rare Friday night that Snipes didn't wanna go out to pop champagne bottles while partying at some club. In fact, it was just rare that he didn't have a whole lot of hoopla going on or any people to see.

So I was planning on just spending the night with Snipes and watching movies or playing video games with him or something quiet like that. But as soon as I walked into the apartment, I got the feeling that it wasn't going to be a quiet night. Before I could get into the apartment good and lock the door behind me, Snipes was up in my face.

"Where the fuck was you at?" Snipes yelled. He had totally caught me off guard with his tone and question.

"Excuse me?" I said with a little bit of a neck-twisting attitude.

"I said where the fuck was you at!" Snipes barked again.

Snipes seemed dead serious, but I couldn't tell why he had an attitude.

Then from out of nowhere Snipes smacked me and mushed my face all with one swinging, open-hand slap.

"Bitch, what the fuck is wrong with you?! I'm not one of your little fucking friends! Where the fuck was you at?!" Snipes screamed as I went stumbling across the floor.

"Snipes, what the hell is wrong with you? Don't be putting your hands on me! Are you crazy or something?" I said, losing my temper.

Snipes looked at me as if I was a red bull's-eye target and he was a deranged bull. He charged at me and pushed with such force that when my body hit the wall, my head snapped back. I banged the back of my head into the wall and immediately fell to the ground.

"Ahhh!" I moaned as I rolled around in pain.

"It's fucking almost ten o'clock and I been calling your cell phone that I pay the bill for, and you can't pick up the phone or return my muthafuckin' calls?! And Alexis didn't know where you was at! That fat bitch Candace hadn't seen you either! And you walk up in here disrespecting me?!" Snipes shouted.

The wind had been knocked out of me when I hit the wall. I was still gasping for air trying to catch my breath, but at the same time I was heated. I couldn't believe what was happening. But with all of the drama I immediately went into fight mode.

I reached in my bag and retrieved my cell phone and threw it at Snipes with all of my force and might.

"Take your got damn cell phone! I don't want this shit! It's a cell phone, it ain't my leash! I was in the library and I had to turn the ringer off so that's why I didn't pick up when you called me!" I vented as the cell phone whizzed past Snipes's earlobe and smashed into the wall and shattered.

Snipes came up on me, and as he grabbed a fistful of my blouse, something scraped across my chest. I quickly found myself on the receiving end of about five right hooks to my face as Snipes held me up by my shirt with his left hand.

"The fuck is wrong wit' you, bitch?" Snipes yelled as he beat the shit out of me.

After a minute straight of being Snipes's punching bag, I wised up and realized that he was much more stronger than me. I didn't argue or fight back after that. And thankfully it proved to be a good move, because Snipes soon stopped hitting me and I was able to make my way to the bathroom where I locked the door.

As I leaned against the wall in the bathroom and tried to gather myself, Snipes just yelled and berated me as he menaced in the hallway outside the bathroom door.

I looked into the bathroom mirror and saw blood on my shirt. I lifted up my shirt and saw the gash on my chest and realized that it had to have come from the ring that Snipes was wearing since his fingernails were always kept low. I wanted to attend to that cut with some alcohol or hydrogen peroxide, but when I looked in the mirror and saw my face, I knew that I had much bigger concerns.

"Oh my God!" I said to myself in disbelief as I looked at the huge speed knot on my forehead. But what really got me and had me trippin' was my badly bruised and puffy left eye. I definitely looked like I had just went a few rounds with Mike Tyson or Hulk Hogan.

Snipes was still in the apartment yelling and cursing up a storm. I heard him talking out loud to himself and saying things like "That bitch knew I was hungry and she didn't give a fuck! And she better not be fucking with some other nigga or I will straight buss her red-bone ass!"

"My God!" I said as I looked at my face and listened to Snipes.

I was scared and didn't know what to think or do. So I just stayed inside the bathroom to wait out Snipes's fit of rage.

"That bitch gonna go and smash the damn cell phone! Can you believe this shit? She bought the shit with *my* money! I pay for the muthafucka and she just gonna be breaking up shit in my crib like that! What the hell is that?" Snipes carried on in his shouting tirade.

Soon after, I heard what sounded like the front door to the apartment slam. I waited for about ten more minutes as the whole apartment seemed to be quiet, other than the television, tuned to ESPN.

I was actually scared to come out of the bathroom because I didn't know what to expect, but I knew that I had to get the hell up out of that apartment as soon as I could. I waited five more minutes to be sure, then I quickly opened the bathroom door and walked out toward the kitchen.

I didn't see Snipes and I was kind of tempted to call out his name. But if he was home, I didn't want to arouse the deranged pit bull inside him again. I kept my mouth shut and looked for my purse and my bag. After I retrieved them, I quickly surveyed the apartment and got the hell up outta there as fast as I could. But I also made sure to grab a knife on the way out. I stuffed the knife in my bag and prayed that I wouldn't need to use it.

My head was pounding with the worst headache I'd ever had, and I was embarrassed to go out into the street and catch a train with a black eye and bruises because I knew that everyone I came across would be staring at me. And I definitely didn't wanna hear or see Candace. Facing her would be the equivalent of dealing with and facing my mother. Despite all of the pain and embarrassment, I felt that I would only be safe if I made it back to NYU and into my dorm room in spite of the blood, bruises, and the horrible-looking black eye. So that was where I headed for safety.

Fifteen

Katrina, either you calling the cops and that nigga is getting locked up tonight, or I'm calling some of my peoples from Philly to come out here and fuck his ass up! He can't be putting his hands on you like that!" Candace said with anger and conviction.

"Candace, I'll be alright. Let me just deal with it the way I wanna deal with it."

But Candace wasn't trying to hear any kind of cop-out talk from me, and she continued to insist that I either call the police or have some of her thug friends from Philly kick Snipes's ass for putting his hands on me.

Alexis was also in my room. I had called her and told her what happened, and she came over quickly to give me some support.

"I don't know, Katrina, I mean maybe he was just going through some shit or something," Alexis reasoned.

"So the hell what! I don't care what he was going through, he don't need to be beating on her like she's some punching bag or something," Candace retorted as she tended to my black eye. "Look at her eye! Katrina, your eye is closed shut like a damn boxer!"

I was just so confused and embarrassed at the same time, and I didn't really know how to respond to what had just happened to me. I had never been in that situation before. No guy had ever put his hands on me. I was still in shock.

"Katrina, you need to go to the hospital and get this eye checked out," Candace stated. "And while you're there, have them call the cops and file a police report or something! You can't just let Snipes do this to you with no consequences."

"I know. Trust me I know. But I think I'll be okay. Let me just get some sleep, and in the morning I'll figure out how to deal with this."

Candace shook her head and threw her hands up in the air. Alexis was more neutral and understanding of the predicament that I was in. She told me that she would check on me the first thing in the morning and that she would pick up a pair of sunglasses for me to cover up my eye.

"Alexis, sunglasses in December?" Candace asked as she shook her head again.

That night I didn't even bother to take a shower or brush my teeth or anything. I just changed into my sleeping clothes and got into the bed. Surprisingly, it was Candace who was hanging out. She was heading out to Hofstra University, on Long Island, New York, where she was supposed to be going to a AKA sorority party. She had been thinking about pledging AKA, so lately everything that she had been talking about was centered on the AKAs.

"You sure you gonna be alright?" Candace asked me as I got in the bed. "I won't go to this party if you need me to stay here with you."

"No, no, Candace, I'll be fine. Don't worry about me."

The truth was I was kind of wishing that Candace would stay with me and not go to the party, just in case Snipes called or dropped by my dorm room unexpectedly. I would feel a whole lot better with someone in the room with me while I interacted with him. At least I still had my knife for protection.

After Candace left I was all alone with my thoughts. And I desperately wanted to cry, but with one of my eyes closed shut, it actually hurt when I cried. So I just lay there with my thoughts, and I still could not believe that I had gotten my ass kicked by my man. That was something that was only supposed to happen to people that I didn't know, or to people in movies or on television or something like that. It definitely wasn't supposed to happen to me.

But the reality was that I had been battered, and just like other battered women I soon found myself justifying what had happened and Snipes's behavior. I began to beat myself up for not having checked my voice mail for his missed calls on the cell phone.

Katrina, all you had to do was just call him from the library and he would have been okay, I reasoned with myself.

I sucked my teeth and then I sort of hated myself for reaching for the telephone, but like an obsessive lover, that is exactly what I did, and I found myself dialing Snipes's cell phone number.

My heart raced as his phone began to ring.

"Hello," I meekly said to Snipes as he answered. Other than *love,* I had no real idea why I was calling him, but for some reason I felt the need to speak to him.

"Hello!" Snipes yelled into the phone, sounding real gruff. A whole bunch of noise and loud music was in the background so I could barely hear him.

"Hey, baby, it's me."

"Katrina?"

"Yeah, it's me."

"Oh, now you can fucking call a nigga, right?!" Snipes asked in a loud and sarcastic tone.

"I know, I should have called you earlier, and I'm just calling to tell you that—"

Snipes screamed into the phone, "Tell me what? Only now you

124 / Mark Anthony

calling me after all this time?! Yo, I'm in the strip club right now! I don't feel like talking about all that. I'll call you in the morning," Snipes stated loudly as I guess he was attempting to talk over the blaring and thumping sounds of music.

I just pictured some big-butt broad in stilettos, grinding on Snipes, giving him a lap dance. All while I sat in my dorm room with a package of ice held to my eye.

Snipes had hung up, not giving me the chance to say anything else. And I didn't know if I had just managed to tick him off more than I had pissed him off from earlier or what. At that point there was nothing that I could do, so I just hoped for the best and that Snipes would really call me in the morning like he said that he would, 'cause if he didn't call me, I knew that I would probably slip into depression.

Eventually I fell asleep and didn't wake up until the next morning around 5:00 A.M. when I heard Candace coming in from the party. She didn't know that she had woken me and I didn't say anything to her as she got in bed. I just lay there with my head still pounding with the headache from earlier.

For four hours I lay there in bed in silence, like I was in a trance. However, the ringing phone snapped me out of it.

"Hello," I said, sounding as if I was wide-awake, which I was at that point.

"Katrina, I'm just calling you like I said I would," Snipes said.

I have to admit that a big part of me was relieved that Snipes had kept his word and called me.

I could sense some tension so I tried to ease things by asking Snipes had he enjoyed himself at the strip club. And after I asked him that, I got nervous and hoped that he hadn't taken that question the wrong way.

"Nah, actually I didn't have a good time at all."

"Really?" I sat up in my bed.

"Yeah, I mean, after you called me, it was like I just started thinking, and I was like whoa! And it just hit me like, kid, yo, you wild out yesterday! And I wasn't feeling that. You kna'imean?" Snipes said as he blew a lot of air into the phone.

"Snipes, I just been thinking all night long, and all kind of thoughts been running through my head, and no matter what I think about, I still keep coming to the same conclusion that your ass was dead wrong for hitting me like that. I mean no matter what I said or did, you had no right to just wild out like that on me."

"Baby, I know. I know. You're right and I apologize right here, right now for that. I am sorry. On the real for real, I was wrong. I admit that and I'll make it up to you. I promise. Whatever you want, I gotchu," Snipes pleaded.

"Snipes, it's not about whatever I want. I mean, yeah, money and material things are nice and all that, but I don't want you to think that you can just buy your way out of situations. Like this is serious, Snipes! This is deep. How do I know this shit won't happen again?"

Snipes blew some more air into the phone and said, "You right. And I understand exactly where you coming from. I mean, last night I was at the strip club drinking straight shots of Henny one after another trying to drink until I felt a'ight. But I didn't feel a'ight. And I was like, 'What the fuck am I doing up in here?' It wasn't like the chicks in there were doing anything for me. You know?"

I didn't respond. I just listened to him and said, "Em-hmm."

There was silence on the phone for a few seconds, and that's when I saw Candace sitting up in her bed. Apparently she had been eaves-dropping on my conversation.

She began silently mouthing words and asking me was it Snipes on the phone.

I nodded to her. And she immediately got up out of her bed and began demanding that I give her the phone.

I told Snipes to hold on and covered up the phone with my hand so that I could talk to Candace without him hearing me.

"Candace, please just let me handle this!"

"Katrina, please do not disrespect yourself by talking to that nigga like everything is all good! I can't believe you!" Candace barked at me.

A big part of me knew that she was right, but at the same time she just didn't understand.

"Candace, let me just finish talking to him. Okay? Just chill for a minute!" I said, sounding as if Candace was irritating me. She shook her head and gathered up her things so that she could take a shower.

"Sorry about that," I said to Snipes as I resumed my conversation with him.

"Katrina, a'ight, here's the deal. Let me be straight up wit'chu. Now I ain't never in my life tell nobody this shit that I'm about to tell you, and I ain't trying to make no excuses or anything like that, but you was right when you said that this is deep."

"What do you mean?" I got up to look at my face in the mirror.

"Well, when we was at your mom's crib and I was saying what I said about not believing in God and all of that . . . ?"

"Right," I said eagerly.

"Where I got that from was when I was younger, in fact from as long as I can remember, my moms used to beat the shit out of me for the smallest things. Like you know how a kid could just be being a kid and be clumsy at times and spill milk or some shit?"

"Yes," I said quickly as I wanted Snipes to keep elaborating on what he was getting at.

"I remember one time, when I was like seven years old, and I had spilled a whole bowl of cereal that my moms had just poured for me. And I was trying my hardest to clean it up before she came back into the room and I was going to play it off like I had eaten everything. But before I could finish cleaning up the mess that I had made, my moms walked back into the kitchen and she flipped the fuck out. She got an extension cord and she lit my ass up for about an hour straight. I mean, she whipped me worse than a runaway slave. And the whole time she was beating me, she kept yelling at me and telling me how she couldn't stand me and how I 'look like, smell like, and act just like your no-good daddy!' And I was screaming and begging and pleading for her to stop, and she just kept on, and I think she would not have stopped until she either killed me or until I was unconscious. The only thing that made her stop was when I threw up and straight vomited on myself like a dog in the middle of the beating."

"Oh my God! Baby, are you serious?"

"I'm dead ass! And that was just one incident, but it was like that *all* the time."

"But what about your father? Did he ever try to step in and protect you?"

"Listen, I know I told your moms and pops about this rosy upbringing with my mother and father both being around. But the truth is, my pops didn't live with us and the dude was never around. It was just me and my brother, Chase. In fact Chase got that name from my moms always yelling at him, 'Boy, don't make me *chase* you!' Yup, it was just me and my younger brother always getting the shit beat out of us by my moms. And I used to pray to God every night for the shit to stop, but it never did stop. So in my mind I used to always be like there is no way that there's a God, because if there is one, then how in the hell did He let me and my brother live through those beatings and abuse and all that shit for so many years?"

"Wow! Baby, I am so sorry. I had no idea," I said with the deepest compassion.

"And then it was like at fourteen years old, me and Chase started getting bounced around from foster home to foster home after my moms got sick. And that whole foster-home system is the worst! Word! So after a while I stopped praying and I stopped believing in that God that never answered my prayers, and I just made a vow to myself that I was gonna get money and never be dependent on nobody but *myself*."

I was getting ready to speak and then Snipes added, "And while I'm at it, I might as well tell you everything. So when I was like sixteen, I caught a charge for assault and I had to do some time in the juvenile jail in the Bronx called Spofford. And when I was there, I had this psychologist chick who used to tell me that a lot of my aggression and anger stems from me subconsciously remembering and acting out shit from my childhood and what I went through when I was so powerless."

I sat on the line and just felt for Snipes. And I was like, how could I think of myself after he had just trusted me so much and opened up to me like he had done? The truth was, I had to be selfless at that point and I was willing to overlook what had transpired between Snipes and me because if what he was saying was true, then it really was not his fault for having put his hands on me the way he had. At least that's what I reasoned with myself.

"So, I'm not trying to make any excuses or anything, and I am really, truly sorry for hitting you yesterday. I was wrong and that should have never happened. It's just that I get these rages of anger and something comes over me that I just can't control at times."

I sighed into the phone and told Snipes that I understood and that I accepted his apology. A small part of me wanted to ask Snipes had he ever thought about getting help for his anger since it was him who had just said that he couldn't control it. Instead I decided to leave well enough alone, and we soon ended the conversation with plans to see each other later that day. And after I got off the phone, I just sat and blankly stared at the phone for about two minutes before deciding to get up.

At about two o'clock that afternoon, a white man showed up at my dorm room door with a bunch of shopping bags and boxes.

Snipes surprised me and had purchased clothes that would last throughout the winter and into the spring. He had also purchased me a new cell phone to replace the one that I'd broken, and he also had a $500 money order made out to me inside of a card.

The card read:

Baby, ever since I met you, it seems like that void and emptiness that I used to feel, it isn't there anymore. You are like a precious pearl to me and a pearl is something that should be treasured and not endangered in any way, shape, or form. I realize that I made a huge mistake yesterday and I also realize that I can't make up for my actions with money. But I just want these gifts to partly show how much I appreciate you, how much I value you, and since you are my pearl, I want these gifts to show how much I treasure you.

Again, I ask for your forgiveness and I apologize for what I did, from the bottom of my heart.

With lots of love . . . Snipes

The words in the card were so sweet and I just knew that they were from the bottom of his heart. And I did find it in my heart to forgive him. In fact I hooked up with him later that day and we ended up having some of the best damn makeup sex in the world, black eye, bruises, and all. We were straight slapping skins like two wild rabbits in heat. It was like fireworks were going off in my mind because the sex was so damn off the chain.

Alexis agreed with me that I was doing the right thing by forgiving him, but Candace thought that I was a fool and a grave statistic that was just waiting to happen.

The following week I ended up not going to class at all. My eye was still black, and I was still embarrassed to be seen in public with my face looking so bruised. So I skipped that week of classes and planned on just going to class the following week, during the week of finals, and hoping for the best.

Sixteen

B y the next weekend, my bruises and black eye were not completely gone, but I was healed up enough to face the public with a little confidence.

Snipes and Warren were planning on heading out of town Monday morning, so that Sunday night before they left, they thought that Alexis and I should go to this new hip-hop nightclub called the Tunnel. Sunday nights at the Tunnel in New York City, as Snipes and Warren so eloquently put it, *was the shit*. And just about anybody and everybody in and around New York City at the time made it their business to religiously go to the Tunnel on Sunday night.

I got dressed up in some of the new clothes that Snipes had bought for me, and I asked Candace if she wanted to go with us. Unfortunately, and I did understand where Candace was coming from this time, she had had a major attitude with me for forgiving Snipes so easily. In fact her lingering attitude caused her to basically stop speaking to me; other than an occasional hello and good-bye, Candace was as cold to me as a religious virgin. There had not been any conversations between her and me for that whole week, so when I asked her to hang out with us, she sort of just looked at me as if to say, *You have got to be smoking if you think I'm hanging out with you and your boxing-partner-crazy-ass boyfriend.*

Candace didn't faze me. I was determined to go out and have a good time and take my mind off some of the things that I had been dealing with lately.

At ten thirty we were all ready to go. Snipes surprised the hell out of me and Alexis when he pulled up in a brand-new all white Lexus GS 300 and blew the horn, motioning for us to get in his ride.

I bent over to get a better look and to confirm exactly who was in the car. After I took off my dark sunglasses, I confirmed that it was Snipes.

"Get in, y'all, hurry up!" Snipes yelled as he rolled down the power window and sat with a gangsta lean behind the wood-grain steering wheel.

Alexis and I rushed to the back passenger door and let ourselves in.

Warren was in the front passenger seat, and another of their boys was sitting in the backseat behind Snipes.

"Oh my God. Snipes, I am loving this car!" Alexis said in a high-pitched tone that sounded like she was about to cum on herself. "I want one of these for myself."

"This shit is hot, right?" Snipes gloated. "Baby, you like it?" he turned to the back and asked me.

"Of course," I said with a big smile. And I had to admit that it did feel good to always be riding in style and always have the best of everything. And it felt especially good to know that somebody with the ability to attract just about any woman he wanted had chosen to be with me.

Anyway, when we reached the Tunnel, the street was jam-packed with people and cars. All kinds of high-end cars were on the block. Snipes and Warren took note of each and every one of them.

"Look at them clown-ass herb-ass niggas with the convertible top down, as cold as it is out here. Them niggas is playing themselves," Snipes stated.

"Corny-ass niggas!" Warren added. "You can tell when cats is *really* getting money, because they don't do no stupid shit like that."

Snipes, Warren, and his boy, who they called Pit, continued to comment about how people were playing themselves by trying to make it seem like they had money, but Snipes was guilty of the exact same thing. He knew good and damn well that he wanted everybody to see him in his new Lexus just so he could boost his ego.

Pit, who was sitting next to me, jumped out of the Lexus and went to talk to one of the bouncers at the door. After about ten minutes he came back toward the car and motioned for us to all get out and make our way inside the club.

Snipes quickly found a spot for us to park, about three blocks away from the club, but it was okay. We made our way in the bitter cold to the entrance of the Tunnel, and as cold as it was, I was glad that arrangements had been made with the bouncer so that we could bypass that long-ass, triple-file line that snaked down the whole block.

Without getting frisked or anything, we were let into the club. The music was deafening as we tried to maneuver our way past the throngs of people, who were rammed together and right up on each other like sardines in a can.

"Y'all go do your thing. I gotta hook up with some more of my people. We'll be over by the bar," Snipes instructed me and Alexis.

We wasted no time and made our way to the dance floor and immediately began to dance up a storm. But Alexis was adamant about not dancing with any other guys.

To me, I was there to have fun and I was dancing with just about anybody that asked me to dance. I was actually surprised at how free and loose I was feeling, considering that I had not drunk or smoked anything.

"What's up witchu?" this light-skinned cutie politely screamed into my ear while he started dancing with me.

"I'm just partying and having a good time!" I screamed back over the loud music. I smiled at him and grooved with him as Funkmaster Flex kept playing smash hit after hit.

"Can I buy you a drink?" the guy asked me.

"No, that's alright! But thanks for asking," I replied.

I could sense Alexis looking at me so I turned to look at her, and sure enough, she was staring right at me. Once she had my eye, she quickly took her hand and waved it across her throat in a cutting fashion, signaling for me to stop dancing with the guy and to leave him alone.

I ignored her and kept on dancing and enjoying myself. To be honest, a part of me wanted to see if I was worthy enough for a guy to ask me for my number, but a bigger part of me wanted to see if I was worthy enough for a guy to get into an altercation over me. But I knew that I was playing with fire because I knew that Snipes would get upset with me if he caught me dancing with some random dude.

"What's your name?" the guy asked me.

"Katrina," I yelled back into his ear.

"I'm gonna call you Salt. You look like Salt from the rap group Salt-N-Pepa," the guy told me as I laughed. I had never heard that one before.

"My name is Derrick but everybody calls me D-Dot."

I nodded my head, and as the song was about to end, Derrick asked me for my number.

"I'm sorry, sweetie, I would but I'm here with somebody. I'm here with my man," I replied.

"Can I give you my number then?"

My ego felt like it was floating on thin air and I nodded yes and he gave me his business card.

The card said that he was an A&R executive at Bad Boy Records.

"We about to do major things in the music business!" Derrick exclaimed.

I nodded my head and smiled, mostly from the attention that I was receiving. As I put the card away, Derrick asked me would I call him.

"I probably will," I lied.

As a new record was being spun, Derrick began to walk off, but before he left me, he made it a point to say into my ear over the music, "Sweetheart, I hope that wasn't your man that did that to you."

I looked at Derrick with some shock, as I'd thought that my bruises were pretty much covered up with the shades that I was wearing, and considering that the club wasn't that well lit.

"Nah," I lied as I plastered a fake, nervous smile on my face.

"Okay, 'cause you too gorgeous for all that drama," Derrick stated as he walked off. "Call me."

I nodded my head, then I looked at Alexis. She came over to me and said, "I see you really trying to get your ass killed up in here tonight!"

"I'll be alright," I told Alexis as the two of us walked off toward the bar to get a drink.

The rest of the night went pretty smooth. Snipes never got wind of my friendly and somewhat flirtatious ways and how I had danced and mingled with other guys. In fact Alexis and I didn't even really see Snipes and Warren for most of the night. We bumped into them on two occasions, and each time they were congregated around the bar with a bunch of their friends, flashing money and jewelry and buying a ton of drinks. I definitely wouldn't have wanted to have been around them doing that all night long, so I was glad that I had enjoyed myself and let myself be loose and free.

When we finally left the club and after Snipes had dropped everybody else off and was ready to drop me off, he reminded me that he and Warren would be heading out of town in a few hours. He wanted some after-hours pussy but I was not really in the mood. It was already four in the morning and I desperately wanted to get some sleep as I'd planned on spending all Monday studying for my tests.

Snipes was quiet after I told him that I wasn't in the mood for sex.

My heart pounded a little as I hoped that he wasn't about to slip into one of his fits of rage.

He looked at me but didn't say anything, and I was trying my hardest to read through his silence and was getting more and more nervous by the second.

"When are you coming back?" I asked, trying to make last-minute small talk so that I could find an opportunity to exit the car.

Snipes looked straight ahead but didn't respond. Immediately I remembered back to what had happened to me that night in the stairwell.

"Baby?" I said, trying to get his attention.

"Yeah," Snipes responded as he finally broke out of his trance.

"What day you coming back?"

Snipes again went cold on me. I knew that I was going to be heading home for the winter break after my finals. I planned to talk to Snipes about visiting me in North Carolina during the break.

Yeah, talk about that, I nervously told myself.

But at that point his demeanor had made it clear that he had slipped into another one of his pissed-off moods, so I decided not to bring up that topic.

Fuck it. Just do it and get it over with, I told myself as I reached over to Snipes's crotch area and unzipped his jeans.

"I'll take care of you since I won't be seeing you for a minute," I said as I reached inside his pants and pulled out his dick, which looked like a king-size Snickers bar.

I looked up at him and he was no longer in that fucked-up mood. Like a spoiled little kid who had gotten his way, Snipes was now grinning from ear to ear as I prepared to go down on him.

I wasn't the best at giving head. It wasn't that I disliked it or anything, but I guess I was just not that confident in my skills due to a lack of practice.

Snipes was fully erect in no time, so I knew that I was doing something right. I had also heard that guys liked it when there were absolutely no teeth involved and when there was a lot of spit in a blow job. So I made sure that his dick was nice and wet and sloppy as I went to work on him.

"Your windows are tinted, right, baby?" I asked as I came up for some air.

"Yeah, yeah, don't worry about that! Just keep doing your thing,"

Snipes said as he immediately pushed my head back down toward his crotch.

I slurped and sucked and stroked his dick for what felt like an hour. He was taking forever to cum and I was hoping like hell that he would hurry up. If I knew it would take so long, I would have just went to the hotel with him like he'd originally suggested.

My jaw was so tired from my mouth being open that I thought I was going to get lockjaw or something. And my arm was feeling so numb from stroking his dick up and down that it felt like it was about to go to sleep on me or something.

Then finally without any warning whatsoever, Snipes shot his load right into my mouth. He had totally caught me off guard by not telling me or giving me any indication that he was about to cum. All I knew was that I felt this hot, slimy, snot-like shit in my mouth and I immediately spit it out as I almost gagged.

"Baby, why didn't you tell me you were about to cum?!" I asked as I wiped Snipes's cum from my face and mouth. I felt so disgusted and dirty that I think Snipes had just permanently turned me off from giving blow jobs.

"Whewwww!" Snipes exhaled loudly as he stroked his dick to get the full effect of his orgasm. "I'm sorry, baby. It was just feeling too damn good and I didn't want you to stop." Snipes began to laugh. "That's what I'm talking about! Now I can go in peace."

After wiping up his cum, I reached over to give Snipes a kiss, and I was about to tell him to have a safe trip and that I would see him after the winter break, but he abruptly stopped me.

"Nah, whoa, hol' up, chill!" He pushed me away from him. "I can give you a hug but I can't kiss you after that!" Snipes said, referring to his cum, which had landed in, on, and around my mouth.

"Baby, it's your cum!" I said in some disbelief. I mean, after all, I had wiped all of it off and spit it all out.

Snipes was doing a hell of a job of making me feel cheap as shit.

"I know, I know, but I'm just saying, baby," Snipes said with this stupid smirk and grin on his face that I wanted to slap right off.

"Whatever." I gathered my stuff and began exiting the car.

"I'll call you in the afternoon," Snipes said as I walked off without even thanking him for the night.

I made it up to my room and looked at Derrick's business card, wondering if I should call him. I thought about it and told myself that maybe I would, and I put the card back into my bag and got ready for bed. I decided I wouldn't call Derrick.

Snipes had this hold on me and this spell that was genuine, but at the same time it was cultlike and somewhat defied common sense. I saw all of the red flags, yet I ignored and justified them all.

Seventeen

My first final was at twelve noon, and then I was going to take another final at two thirty in the afternoon. So I decided to leave my room at nine thirty and go to the study hall so that I wouldn't be distracted. But just as I was about to walk out of my dorm room, the telephone rang. I contemplated answering it but decided against it and waited for it to stop ringing.

However, as soon as the phone had stopped ringing, it started right back, so I figured that it was urgent.

Against my better judgment I quickly ran from the door to the phone and picked it up.

"Hello."

"Yeah, hello, can I speak with Katrina?"

"Speaking." I tried to figure out the voice on the other end of the phone.

"Katrina, this is Chase," Snipes's brother said, sounding sort of panicked.

"What's up? You caught me just walking out the door. Is everything okay?" I asked since Chase had never called me before.

"Nah." He sucked his teeth and blew a bunch of air into the phone. "Snipes got locked up yesterday!"

Immediately my heart started beating fast with worry. "Get outta here! For what?"

"A'ight, I'll be straight up witchu, Katrina. Snipes didn't want me to tell you this, but I need you to help me out with this and I can't be lying to you about shit."

"No. Be straight up with me, please."

"He was in Virginia and the cops caught him with an illegal gun."

"Snipes?" I said, confused.

"Word is bond. But it's a bullshit charge that won't stick," Chase replied with confidence.

I was about to say something but he cut me off. "Katrina, this is the thing though, and you gotta follow me on this. Snipes used an alias when he got locked up, so we need you to do us this solid and go down to VA like right now and post bail for him before his prints come back."

"What?" I asked, confused. I was not following what Chase was saying to me. A fake name, prints, bail, Virginia. Everything he was saying just didn't seem real to me.

"Chase, you're serious?" I asked with a slight chuckle.

"Katrina, I'm dead ass! You know I don't call you. So if I'm calling you, it's on some real shit," Chase said convincingly.

"Why me and not you?"

"See, can't me, Warren, or any of his people go down there and handle this shit for him 'cause he using that alias and we don't want shit trippin' up on account of us. You kna'imean?"

"Okay, so when you say you need me to go to Virginia *like right now*, what exactly do you mean by *right now*? I got finals I have to take this week."

Chase sighed and mumbled under his breath before speaking. "Katrina, this caught everybody off guard. Word. I know you got school and all that, but Snipes specifically asked me to talk to you about this. He needs you right now."

I didn't actually know what he meant, and I couldn't understand his logic, and as he continued talking, he didn't really give me much of a choice.

"Katrina, his bail is fifty thousand. I got the fifty thousand with me at the crib right now. I'm gonna head to the city right now and scoop you up and take you to the airport and put you on the first plane going to Virginia."

"Chase, *right now*, as in *now* now?" I quickly tried to think of a way to get out of going to Virginia until after my finals were over at the end of the week.

"Yeah, we gotta bail him out today, if possible. Tomorrow might be too late. His prints will be back by then. Just wear some baggy clothes because what I have to do when I see you is tape a lot of this money to your body so you can get on the plane with it."

"What!" I whispered really loud into the phone.

"Yeah, you can't walk around with that kind of dough without the cops getting suspicious and checking shit out. But I'll hook you up when I get there. Let me bounce. I'll try to be there in about thirty minutes, but I might hit traffic. A'ight, so just chill in your dorm room till I get there, okay?"

I kept quiet and didn't respond, and Chase added before hanging up, "And, Katrina, on the real, good looking out on this. Snipes is gonna love you for this one!"

I sat there with the phone in my hand and stared at it for a few minutes. I got genuinely nervous and scared as I thought about how much of my parents' hard-earned money I was about to waste by missing my finals, which meant sure doom and definite failure in just about all, if not *all*, of my classes. Sadly, the decisions that I was making were proving that I cared more about Snipes and how he viewed me than anything or anyone else.

* * *

Chase did show up at my dorm. It took him a little over an hour to get there due to the congested Manhattan traffic. Thankfully though, when he got there, I was alone in my room and he quickly had me disrobe down to my panties and bra, and he taped wads of money to my thighs, my calves, my stomach, my ass, my back, and my upper arms using almost two full roles of masking tape. I looked like something straight out of some science fiction movie.

It was practically wintertime, so I wasn't too out of place when I put on some black, baggy jogging pants and a black, baggy hooded sweatshirt to help conceal the money that was taped to my body. I also threw on my three-quarter-length down winter coat, and I knew that there was absolutely no way that anyone would suspect that I was walking around with so much money on me.

Before long we were in Chase's Acura Legend and heading to La Guardia Airport in Queens.

"So repeat that back to me," Chase said.

"I wanna post bail for Randy Weeks, his date of birth is June tenth, 1971. And I think the arresting agency is the Virginia Beach Police Department, I don't have the booking number, the charge is criminal possession of a firearm, and the cash bail amount is fifty thousand dollars," I repeated like a parrot.

"What does Randy Weeks do for a living and where does he live?" Chase quizzed me.

"He owns an insurance company in Maryland and he resides in Maryland." I made sure to add, "And to the best of my knowledge he has never been arrested before."

Chase nodded with approval. After the quiz he made all kinds of small talk about nothing in particular. I could sense that most of his small talk was designed to keep me from asking questions about Snipes and the suspicions that were naturally forming in my mind.

What was weird was that as we made it to the departure terminal of the airport, I wasn't nervous at all. Although I had $50,000 strapped to my body like some kind of human mule, I didn't feel like I was doing anything wrong. So I suppose that my ignorance was the reason for my lack of fear.

As we were pulling to the curb of the US Airways departure terminal, Chase reached into his pocket and handed me ten crisp one-hundred-dollar bills. I was to use those for purchasing my airline ticket and for cab fare and for a hotel room, depending on whether Snipes wanted to book one.

"So you sure you good?" Chase asked as I prepared to get out of the Acura Legend and its plush leather seat.

"I'll be fine." I smiled as I reached over and gave Chase a hug and a kiss on the cheek.

"Call me if anything happens or if you ain't sure about something. Okay?"

"Okay," I replied in a determined tone, then ventured into the airport. I felt powerful and like I was *down*, and more important, I felt needed. I knew what I was doing and I blocked everything out of my mind and stayed focused on my task.

I was hoping that there was still room on the plane for me to purchase a ticket. Chase had said that he called the airline and they assured him that the flight wasn't going to be full, but for some reason I didn't believe that he had made any calls at all to check for seat availability.

Fortunately there was room on the flight and I purchased my ticket without a hassle. I made it past all of the security checkpoints without any hitches. Time seemed to be flying by, and before long the airline had begun boarding for my flight.

As I sat in my seat, I realized the flight was not going to be full. The seats next to mine were all empty, which was good, because I really wasn't in the mood to talk to some stranger. And if I needed to get up and go to the bathroom, I wouldn't have to jump over people and maneuver like a magician just to get through the cramped seats.

The main thing that ran through my head as the plane made its way to Virginia was how I was going to handle my failing at school. I loved Snipes and all, but I wondered if I was doing the right thing by focusing more on him and his needs than I was on myself and my own needs.

Before the plane began its final descent into Virginia, I made my way into the plane's tight and confined bathroom and did a quick magician trick where I took off all my clothes. I had left my coat at my seat so that it would be one less thing to cramp my space in the bathroom. Surprisingly it didn't take me too long to undress and remove all of the wads of money from my body and place them into a small, black plastic shopping bag that I had.

After the money was in the bag, I tried to get dressed as fast as I could, but apparently other passengers were becoming impatient with me as they began to knock on the bathroom door.

"Just a second!" I shouted as I quickly surveyed the bathroom and made sure that I didn't leave any money lying around. When I was sure that everything was good, I opened the door and almost got knocked over by this old, wrinkled white man who charged for the bathroom. I couldn't help but laugh. He looked to be about ninety years old and as if he was about to shit on himself at any second.

The man didn't say excuse me or anything as he barreled past me. He was trying to close the door so fast that he almost slammed my fingers in the door. The whole scene was funny to me and helped lighten my mood.

The plane ride seemed to be over before it had started, and we were soon taxiing into the gate. That had been the first time in my life that I had taken a plane with no luggage, so exiting was quick and painless. I didn't have to go to the baggage claim or anything like that. I headed straight out of the small Norfolk airport and hailed a cab.

By the time I made it to where Snipes was being housed, it was two in the afternoon and I was beginning to feel a bit tired and drained from the traveling. I called Chase and went over all of the details one more time so that I wouldn't screw anything up. Once I had everything down in my head, I felt confident and proceeded to try to spring Snipes.

For reasons that were never explained to me, there was delay after delay after delay, but finally, Snipes, aka Randy Weeks, was set free.

"Hi, baby!" I said excitedly as I got Snipes's attention.

He flashed a quick smile and then briskly headed in my direction. When he reached me, he gave me a hug and kissed me close to my earlobe.

"Thanks for this, baby," he said, then grabbed my hand and led me outside.

Snipes wasn't his normal self and I could tell that he had a lot on his mind. But his number one priority was getting out of Virginia as quickly as he could because he was certain that it was just a matter of hours, if not minutes, until his prints would come back from FBI headquarters.

The two of us headed straight to the airport, where we rented a car in my name and then hightailed it out of Virginia. Snipes was pissed at Chase for not telling me to use a fake identity when I posted bail for him. At the time I couldn't understand why he would get so upset about that because it appeared to me to be a minor detail.

Unfortunately, when Snipes's prints came back from the lab and the Virginia authorities realized that they had unknowingly released a criminal who was wanted in Newark, New Jersey, for the attempted murder of a police officer, as well as wanted in two states for drug trafficking, that minor detail that Chase had forgotten to fill me in on, well, it put me in the crosshairs of the feds' investigation of Snipes, which was now stepped up full throttle.

It was right around that time that I really started to get worried about my involvement with Snipes.

Eighteen

By about seven thirty that evening Snipes and I had reached Washington, D.C. Snipes wanted us to spend the night in a hotel while he contemplated what we should do next.

I desperately wanted to get back to New York so that I could take my last two finals. D.C. was only about a four-hour drive from New York, so I was hoping that even if we spent the night at a hotel, we would wake up at like six in the morning and leave for New York. That way I could still make it to my finals on time.

My finals were probably the last thing on Snipes's mind as was evident by what he instructed me to do as we navigated near Howard University.

"Yo, pull the car over there near that corner. I wantchu to cop some weed for me. A'ight?" Snipes asked.

Cop some weed for you? I asked myself. I didn't know the first thing about *copping* any weed, I didn't know what to say or how to say it, and

I also didn't know how in the world Snipes knew just where to cop his weed in this unfamiliar town.

"From who?" I asked, a hint of nervous uncertainty in my voice.

"From them cats right there!" Snipes pointed to a group of three guys who were standing in front of a 7-Eleven.

"You want me to buy some weed from them? Snipes, how do you even know that they're selling weed? And I ain't never buy no weed before! What do I say?" I asked Snipes with a bit of an attitude as I parked the car.

"Trust me, them niggas is hustling," Snipes confidently exclaimed. "Just walk inside the 7-Eleven like normal, and when you walk past them three dudes, all you gotta do is ask, 'Y'all got that chronic?' And when they respond asking you whatchu want, just tell them you want a fifty-dollar bag. A'ight?"

I wanted to hurry up and get the shit over with so we could continue on our way. So I agreed to execute Snipes's plan. I exited the car and my heart began to pound a mile a minute. I had *never* purchased any illegal drugs in my entire life so this was all new to me.

As I was walking toward the double-glass entrance doors of 7-Eleven, the thought of the crime I was about to do entered my mind. *What if there are cops around? What if these three guys are undercover cops?*

As I placed my hand on the door to open it, I could see one of the three guys looking in my direction. He was cute and was giving me that look as if he was checking me out in a sexual way. He had his hands inside his jacket pockets and gave this huddling look as if he was trying hard to keep warm.

Just ask him, Katrina! I silently urged myself.

"You got that chronic?" I asked sheepishly as I paused before walking into the store. Immediately I started thinking to myself that I must have sounded like a got damn fool!

"What's up, ma'?" the guy asked me as he had apparently heard me, and he quickly made his way inside the store where I was pretending to look for a particular flavor of Häagen-Dazs ice cream.

The cute, six-foot-four, brown-skinned guy walked right up behind me and asked how I was doing.

Without looking him in the face I stared at the ice cream cartons and repeated in a whisper so that the people around us wouldn't hear, "You got that chronic?"

I could tell that I caught the guy off guard as he was probably expecting that I was flirting with him as opposed to trying to cop some weed.

"Oh. Oh yeah, yeah, no doubt. I gotchu. You want nicks?" he asked.

I didn't have a clue what nicks were, so I hesitated. The guy looked at me, and my pause must have caused him to get suspicious.

"You from around here?" he asked me right at the same time I relayed to him that I wanted a $50 bag of weed.

He looked at me real hard as I pulled out a fifty-dollar bill and handed it to him.

"I'll see you on your way out," the guy said as he exited the aisle and made his way out of the store.

I wasn't really buying anything so I was practically walking out of the store right behind him. When I reached the front of the store, I decided to stand immediately past the entrance and I waited for the guy to come back over to me.

"I gotchu right near the base of the pay phone," the guy informed me.

I had no idea what in the world he was talking about so I didn't say anything. I just stood there in disbelief that I was actually attempting to buy weed for Snipes as he sat inside the rental watching everything go down.

"Ma', just go right there by the pay phone and you'll see it," the street hustler told me in basic instructional form.

I finally caught on and made my way to the pay phone, where I saw the fat bag of marijuana just sitting there waiting for me. I wasted no time in scooping it up and made my way back to the car and handed it to Snipes.

Whew! I thought to myself as I got into the car.

Snipes looked at the weed and smelled it. Then he asked me for $5 so he could go get the blunts that he had forgotten to tell me to get. As Snipes exited the car, I reclined the seat and just slumped back and exhaled a whole bunch of nervous energy and air from my lungs.

Snipes took a minute to come back to the car since he had apparently struck up a conversation with the guy who'd just sold me the weed. Snipes took a number from the guy, then made his way back to the car.

"You know him?" I asked out of curiosity.

"Nah, but I think I can build wit' the dude later," Snipes nonchalantly said as he reached for the radio and attempted to change stations.

Snipes directed me toward the Phoenix Park Hotel, which wasn't too far from the Capitol. The hotel was nice and we had a duplex suite with a living room and a TV downstairs and a spiral staircase that led up to a king-size bed and a nice bathroom and sitting area. Each of the rooms was named after some famous politician. Our room was named after President Ronald Reagan.

Snipes and I both had no luggage or clothes or anything other than the weed and the blunts and the cash that I had inside my Moschino bag. Snipes flopped on the couch and reached for the remote control as he asked me to hand him one of the blunts and the weed.

I reached in my bag, handed them to Snipes, and took a seat next to him.

"Baby, can we talk?" I asked. I had a million and one questions about his past and his present, both of which were quickly beginning to look bleak to me. I was starting to see the dropping of the veil that had been preventing me from seeing the real him.

"Definitely, boo!" Snipes reached and kissed me on my forehead. He knew what I wanted to talk about and knew that he had a bunch of things to explain that he had never taken the time to do. Like why was he implicated for shooting an undercover cop, and why was he traveling in Virginia with an unlicensed gun?

I felt a sense of relief knowing that a lot of misconceptions about the man who my heart was telling me I loved were finally about to be cleared up. He was going to clear everything up and allow me to see the bright future that lay ahead for the two of us. I snuggled close and put my arm around him and stretched my legs across his lap.

"Let me show you how to roll this," Snipes said, getting somewhat excited about smoking his weed.

Snipes explained and demonstrated the street art of slicing open a cigar and removing the tobacco and refilling it with marijuana.

"Here, take this." Snipes handed me a thin strip of the cigar paper. "You gotta moisten it by placing it between your lips and let your tongue wet the paper just a little bit though."

"Like this?" I asked, trying to make sure that I was doing it right.

"Yeah, just like that, but you gotta moisten the other side of the paper as well. A'ight, now lay the paper down and take some of this weed and spread it out evenly down the middle."

I smiled as I placed the weed on the paper and asked if I was doing it right.

"Yeah, you a pro at it," he said, gassing my head up. "Here, this is the hardest part, let me show you how to do it." Snipes delicately picked up the weed and the paper and held it between his thumbs, index fingers, and middle fingers and slowly and intricately rolled it and showed me the difference between rolling it just right and rolling it wrong.

And before I knew what was what, and before Snipes had opened up and talked to me about why the cops were looking for him and why he had used a false name when he was arrested and why he had been arrested at all, he was sparking up the blunt and he and I were both smoking weed inside the Reagan suite.

"How much more cash you got on you?" he asked as we both got high.

I coughed a bit before saying, "I got about three hundred dollars left."

"Yeah, we gotta get back to New York tomorrow," Snipes said, realizing that his cash position wasn't looking too good.

Good, I thought, realizing that I would probably be able to get to my finals.

"So come on, baby, tell me what happened. Why did you have to give the cops a fake name?" I was feeling really nice from the weed.

Snipes began kissing my neck and he spoke through his kisses. "Back in the days . . ." His words were cut off when his tongue went in my ear. "Like a year ago I caught a bullshit drug charge in B-More, and I didn't want that shit showing up." Snipes's hand was now inside my pants and he was playing with my pussy.

If it hadn't been for the weed, I would not have been in the mood for sex because I wanted Snipes to focus and just talk to me. I didn't know that *B-More* meant "Baltimore." And how in the hell was a drug charge a *bullshit* drug charge? Was it a misdemeanor possession charge like I had when I was in jail overnight?

"Snipes, baby, let's talk, sweetie."

"Okay. In a minute." He undressed me. Snipes was instantly aroused and I knew that talking was no longer on his mind. Snipes motioned for me to turn around so that he could do me from the back, doggy-style.

As he entered me, I was wondering what had happened to the lover who knew how to take his time and massage me and eat me out and get me to the point of multiple orgasms.

I didn't know where that lover had gone. While Snipes was inside me, stroking hard like he had done that night in the stairwell, it did feel good, but at that moment I didn't feel a connection with Snipes. It was like I was just this outlet for him to release his stress. But I made sure that I didn't complain. And I tried to get into it by rotating my ass and hips and moaning.

Unfortunately, before I could really get into it, Snipes was cumming.

"Baby! Not inside of me!" I screamed as Snipes was holding on to my hips for dear life and emptying his seed inside me.

Right then and there I vowed to either get on birth-control pills ASAP or start insisting that Snipes use a condom each and every time. Or else we wouldn't be sexing at all!

"Yo, I couldn't pull out! It was feelin' too good to pull out!" Snipes smiled, reaching over to kiss me.

I playfully threw my pants at him and told him that he wasn't gonna get any more unless he started playing by the rules.

Snipes laughed and walked off to go take a shower. His body looked so damn tight and good with a thin layer of sweat all over him. It made him look like some type of a chiseled Greek god or something.

When he finished his shower, he came back down the spiral staircase to where I was seated. As I prepared to also go take a shower, Snipes told me that he was going to the store across the street from the lobby of the hotel to buy us some toothbrushes and get some snacks and juice and some ice.

"The money is inside my bag," I said before disappearing upstairs.

Snipes was putting on the same clothes that he had on earlier when he commented that he would also buy us some deodorant.

Maybe a minute or so after I had gotten into the shower and was lathering up my body, I thought I heard someone come into the bathroom. I was in a stand-up shower that wasn't connected to the bathtub that was also in the large, plush bathroom.

Suddenly Snipes yanked open the door to the shower and I let out a startled yell.

"What the fuck is this?!" Snipes shouted as he reached into the shower and grabbed hold of my right arm, which was covered in soapy suds.

Snipes violently jerked my naked body out of the shower and onto the cold ceramic-tiled floor.

"What? What?" I shouted back. I had no idea what in the hell Snipes was talking about.

"This, bitch!" Snipes let go of my arm and mushed me in my face. My feet were wet and the floor was slippery, so I lost my balance and fell real hard and banged my face on the seat of the toilet bowl.

Pain instantly shot through me as I curled up on the cold floor and grabbed my mouth. My jaw felt like it had to be broken.

Snipes was mad as hell. Madder than I'd ever seen him before, and he was hyperventilating as he screamed at me, "Who the fuck is this nigga, Katrina?!"

I was in so much pain and my mouth was bleeding. It felt as if my teeth were loose. But my main concern was finding out what Snipes was so hot about.

"Answer me!" Snipes yelled as he reached down and grabbed my throat with one hand. Then with one enraged yell and thrust he stood me up on my feet with the hand that he was using to choke me.

With his other hand he pointed to the business card that Derrick, D-Dot, from Bad Boy Records had given me that night we had gone out to the Tunnel. Like a dummy I had never thrown the card in the garbage and had no idea why I had put it in my Moschino bag.

I was trying to talk and explain, but the force from Snipes's grip was preventing me from saying much. I began frantically waving my arms in the air and punching Snipes, trying to free myself.

Whack!

Snipes slapped me right across my face as he released his choking grip from my neck.

That open-hand slap was followed by a series of punches to my face, a face that had just healed from the last beating and still had some remnants of my previous black eye.

"Snipes, it's nothing!" I yelled as I tried to shield myself from getting hit.

"What the fuck was it doing in your bag for?! I bought you this bag and now you trying to play me?!" Snipes gave me two body shots, which knocked the wind out of me and doubled me over before sending me crashing to the floor.

"You cheating on me?! Huh?" Snipes yelled with the rage of a lion in his voice.

"No, baby, I'm not!" I frantically pleaded as I lifted my arms into the air and attempted to shield off the blows that Snipes was now throwing at my face.

The water was still running in the shower, so Snipes dragged me across the bathroom floor and toward the shower. He reached inside and grabbed the extendable showerhead. Then, holding a fistful of my hair with one hand so that I couldn't move, he held a steady stream of water to my face.

I was coughing and spitting out hot water that was running up my nose and into my mouth so fast that I couldn't breathe. Water was also quickly spilling all over the bathroom floor, causing a miniflood. As I tried to stand up, I lost my balance and fell to the floor again.

"Get the fuck up and tell me who this nigga is!" Snipes demanded.

I was beyond terrified because Snipes was madder than he had been when he beat me in the apartment in Harlem that night, and this time he sort of had legitimate cause to be upset.

I made it to my hands and knees and Snipes grabbed my hair again and made me look at him as he menacingly asked me, "Bitch, did you fuck that nigga?!"

"No, baby! No I swear to God! I just took his card!" I pleaded.

"If you lying to me, I'll kill you!" Snipes said in a convincing tone.

I begged Snipes to believe me. He finally relented and left me alone on the bathroom floor.

But to be honest, I wasn't sure if indeed he hadn't had every intention of killing me right then and there on that bathroom floor. Had I just gotten lucky and been saved by the bell? It did seem that way. The doorbell to our suite had rung; the maintenance people had come to investigate why water was leaking down into the suite below ours. When Snipes had heard the doorbell, it was like it had brought him out of a deadly trance.

Snipes had made it to the front door of the suite and thought up a quick excuse that appeased the maintenance people. Thankfully for me, he had snapped out of his rage long enough to think about what he was doing, and he left me alone upstairs in the bedroom. He stayed downstairs in the living room.

As I made it toward the bed to lie down, I reached for a towel. I was going to dry my body off, but when I glanced in the mirror and saw my bottom lip split right down the middle, I knew that the blood pouring from my lip needed the towel more than the water that was dripping from every part of my body. I made it to the bed and held the towel against my mouth and couldn't believe how terribly my throat was aching, as were my ribs and the bottom row of my teeth.

Again, Katrina? Again?! I thought.

In my head I was cursing myself out as I realized that I had screwed up by being disrespectful to Snipes. And I also realized that my disrespect, along with my newly inflicted bruises and split lip, was now more than likely going to keep me from taking any of my final exams.

Although finals were no longer my biggest concern, as I was more worried about facing my parents with my bruised and battered body. That Saturday, I was supposed to return to North Carolina for the winter break. It was Wednesday night and I knew that there was no way that my bruises would heal in less than seventy-two hours.

How am I going to go home like this? How am I going to explain my bruises to my parents? I was starting to worry my self sick trying to figure out an answer to those two questions.

Nineteen

At about eight thirty in the morning my cell phone rang and woke me up. I hadn't planned on sleeping for so long, but my body and my jaw were sore and all I wanted to do was lie down and stay in bed. Snipes hadn't slept in the same room with me so I had the whole bed to myself and I used every inch of it.

"Hello," I said as I grimaced in pain.

"Katrina, where's my brother?" Chase frantically asked.

"I'm not sure. I just woke up."

"Well, ain't he the fuck witchu?!" Chase barked.

I wanted to scream that I didn't know where Snipes was and that I didn't really give two shits where he was at.

"Yeah, but he didn't sleep with me last night. I—"

Snipes cut me off in midsentence as he had apparently heard the phone ringing and come upstairs. "Gimme that damn phone!" Snipes shouted as he snatched the phone from me. "Is this that nigga?!" He sounded as if he was picking up right from where he'd left off the night before.

I was in pain but I was feeling disgusted and aggravated and I was tired. I definitely wasn't in the mood for Snipes's jealous-ass bullshit.

"It's your brother!" I rudely shot back with a lot of attitude before making my way to the bathroom as I shook my head.

"Yo!" Snipes said into the phone. He paced back and forth as his brother spoke to him. He was nodding, then he stood still and paused as if he was listening intently.

Snipes had nothing on but his boxers, and he reeked of a mixture of Hennessy and weed. I wondered if he had stayed up all night long smoking weed and drinking from the wet bar in our suite.

"What?!" Snipes yelled into the phone. "Get the fuck outta here! Warren?" Snipes asked in disbelief. Then he paused and continued to listen even more intently.

"Well, how you know them niggas ain't just bluffing yo ass?" Snipes asked before pausing once again.

"Katrina, too?" Snipes said out loud as I wondered why my name was being mentioned. "Yeah, that had to be his ass 'cause who else knew that shit?"

"Shit!" Snipes hollered into the room. "Yeah, yeah. You probably right. A'ight, where you gonna be at? I'll hit you back in a few." Then Snipes paused. "A'ight, cool. If you hear anything else call me back." Snipes hung up.

"Baby, come here real quick," Snipes yelled to me from near the bed.

Baby? I said to myself as I couldn't believe that he had the audacity to actually call me baby.

I walked out of the bathroom and toward the bed. I was hoping like all hell that Snipes wasn't horny, because I was *definitely* not trying to be intimate.

"When the last time you spoke to Alexis?" Snipes asked, as if something heavy was on his mind.

"The other day like right before I left, why?" I could not believe that the man who had beaten my ass was just talking to me as if everything was everything.

"Did she say anything about Warren?"

"No. I mean she knew that you had gotten arrested and she was worried about Warren because he was down there with you. All she said was that she wanted him to come back up to New York, but that he had told her that he wouldn't be in New York for about another week."

Snipes sat quietly with his thoughts.

"What's wrong?" I asked as I looked at my face in the mirror.

Snipes blew out some air, then told me that he needed me to help him set up Warren.

Set him up? I thought that something didn't sound right, but I kept my mouth shut.

I looked at Snipes and waited.

"Yo, my brother just told me that the cops raided his crib *again* looking for me, right?"

I nodded, as I still couldn't believe that Snipes was talking to me so normally considering how bruised I looked. It hadn't probably even crossed his mind to tell me that he was sorry.

"So they arrest my brother and they holding my brother on some bullshit, and the DT is trying to get him to roll over on me, right? But my brother ain't gonna go for that shit that the police be kickin', right? And he knows to just keep his mouth closed and not say shit. So Chase tells me that while they interrogating him, the cops show him a signed affidavit from Warren just straight dry snitching on everybody. You believe this shit?" Snipes screamed.

I had never heard the term *dry snitching* so I didn't understand exactly what Snipes was talking about.

But Snipes continued, "Yo, the nigga even ratted on you about the work that you brought down to Virginia for me that time? Just straight dry snitching and shit."

"Dry snitching?" I said, confused.

"Yeah, if they ain't ask him about you and he pulled your name into it, then that's fucking dry snitching. That fucking bitch-ass nigga."

Okay, so I understood *dry snitching*, but *the work*? I was getting lost with all of the slang and I needed Snipes to speak straight. I was bruised and tired and getting drained from everything that was being said and from everything that was going on and that was happening to me.

Snipes sat me down, and through the horrible smell of liquor and weed on his breath, he explained to me how he and his brother had been forced to take care of themselves since they were young and that they ended up hustling and slinging crack. He also told me that he had been making money for quite some time now and that he was planning on getting out of the game and just going off to chill somewhere and to kick it, but that things had started getting real thick for him and the feds and the local police in like three states were investigating him, along with the state police.

"So it's like I can't get out the game now even if I wanted to!" Snipes said as he explained his dilemma.

"Now what about that cop thing in New Jersey?" I asked.

Snipes looked at me and contemplated his words before opening his mouth.

"Well, a'ight, this is the thing. I had a warrant that dated back to like '91. And the warrant wasn't no biggie, but the thing is, between '91 and now a lot of shit done went down, and when shit goes down, niggas be opening up their mouths and implicating me in all kinds of shit. So if the cops just knock me on a humble, then all kinds of other shit would start surfacing and I know that. So when this cop in Jersey pulled us over, I kind of panicked and opened up on the nigga and killed him!" Snipes said rather emphatically.

"Wow!" I got up from the bed and walked around. I didn't wanna believe what Snipes was telling me. But I was hearing it from his own mouth so it had to be true. I ran my hand down my face as my heart-beat picked up.

So this nigga is a drug dealer and a cop killer, I thought to myself.

"Damn, Snipes, why didn't you tell me any of this? You had me—"

"Katrina, don't come at me with that bullshit right now! A'ight? It is what it is! This nigga is ratting you out too! Remember that!"

"For what?"

Snipes looked at me and shook his head as if to say he was tired of my ignorance. "For the two kilos that you brought down to me in Virginia!" he said rather matter-of-factly. "And for that cash that you transported back to New York."

That was the first time that it really hit me that I had unknowingly transported cocaine for Snipes. But what scared the hell out of me was when I realized how close I had come to being caught in Snipes's car with the two kilos still in the trunk when the male and female federal agents had questioned me that day in the parking lot at the hotel. And it also explained why Snipes had chosen to just leave the car in the parking lot and buy a new one.

"Oh my God!" I grunted in disgust and disbelief. I held my face in my hands and couldn't believe what was happening to me. "I can't believe this."

"Well, believe it 'cause shit is real!" Snipes stated with commanding arrogance.

He then calmly but assertively told me that I wasn't gonna be going home for the holidays. And after he had made that clear to me, he schooled me to exactly how he was going to use me to help him reel in Warren, his best friend, so that he could assassinate him.

Man oh man, was I ready to bail out of this relationship. The problem was, it wasn't that easy to just walk away from a psychopath.

Twenty

Dance for me, baby," Snipes said to me as he sat in a chair watching television and downing a whole bottle of Bacardi with no chaser. He had his bare feet kicked up on a round table that was in our new hotel room.

"Dance for you?" Snipes had definitely caught me off guard with that one.

Snipes and I had checked out of the Phoenix Park Hotel in D.C. two days ago and traveled back to New York. He and I were holed up in the Holiday Inn near Kennedy Airport in Queens. I had checked us into the hotel under a fictitious name.

"Like dance, as in dance?" I asked, confused. I got up off the king-size bed and made my way toward the bathroom.

"Dance as in take off your clothes and shake dat ass for me!" Snipes said with a sinister smile on his face before he gulped down another glass of Bacardi.

"Oh, come on now." I closed the door to the bathroom and locked it.

I didn't actually have to use the bathroom, but for the past two days I had been pretending my stomach was upset and was constantly gassy and bothering me. The bathroom was my oasis. It was like my place of retreat to get away from him and his controlling behavior. Plus he had been either drunk or high for the past two and a half days straight, and I wasn't the least bit attracted to that type of drunkenness.

While in the bathroom, I would sit on the toilet and pray and contemplate my situation. I also purposely left the cell phone and its charger plugged into the outlet in the bathroom so I could make any necessary phone calls without Snipes knowing who I was talking to. To mask my voice while I spoke on the phone, I would constantly flush the toilet and run the shower water along with the water in the sink and talk real low so Snipes couldn't hear me.

I told him that I would be embarrassed if he heard my farts or any of my pushing and straining sounds while I was on the bowl.

"Don't tell me to come on!" Snipes barked. "When you finish taking that shit, I wantchu to come out here and give me dat lap dance!" he yelled through his drunkenness.

Looking at my bruised face and battered body in the bathroom mirror, I wondered if he was serious about me dancing for him. I didn't know how he could be serious considering that I looked like a straight hot mess.

Whatever, I thought to myself as I began to run the water to mask the phone call that I was about to make.

Before dialing Candace, I double checked that the bathroom door was locked, then I dialed the number to my dorm room and hoped that Candace was in the room and hadn't yet left to go home for the Christmas break.

"Hey, Candace," I whispered into the phone when she picked up.

"Yeah, this is Candace. Who is this?" Candace replied in her normal tone.

"Candace, it's me, Katrina," I whispered.

"Katrina?"

"Yeah."

"Girl, what the hell you whispering for, sounding like a damn pervert trying to do a prank sexual phone call?" Before I could answer, she asked, "Where the hell you been? You had me worried sick and your moms and pops been worried sick too! And the cops have been to our room like two times looking for you."

"Looking for me?" I asked nervously.

"Yeah, looking for you!" Candace replied rather matter-of-factly.

"Did they say why they were looking for me? What did you tell them?" I nervously whispered.

"I didn't tell them shit!" Candace shot back.

"Did my mother call the cops?"

"Katrina, I don't know if your moms called the cops or not. All I know is that the cops were here on Wednesday, and they were here again on Thursday."

"Katrina, hurry up and shit and get yo' ass out here and dance for me!" Snipes yelled from the other room, sounding like a drunken wino. I was hoping that Candace hadn't heard him. I started to panic because I wanted to talk more to Candace and be candid with her, but I knew that I had to hurry up and end the call. The last thing that I needed was for Snipes to hear me whispering on the phone, because he would whip my ass for sure if he caught me.

I breathed real heavy into the phone before whispering, "Okay, Candace, look, I can't stay on the phone, but just listen to everything that I'm about to tell you."

"Okay."

"Everything that you had been suspecting and telling me about Snipes is true. Don't start with the *I told you so*'s or anything like that. Just hear me out. I'm in a hotel with Snipes and he got me running around with him because the cops and the feds are looking for him. I'm kind of in a tough spot right now because he's been beating my ass."

"Katrina, where are you at right now?"

"In a hotel. And I'm whispering because Snipes is in the other room and I don't want him to hear me talking to you." My heart rate was really picking up.

"What hotel? Where exactly?"

I thought for a quick second as my heart pounded because I knew that Snipes would be looking for me to come out of the bathroom any second.

"Candace, I can't tell you that."

"Katrina, I swear to God I will hang up this phone on you right now! I'm tired of your naïve, dumb bullshit! You didn't listen to me when you should have. So just tell me what's up before you get yourself in some shit that you can't get out of! Where are you at, Katrina?!" Candace asked, annoyed.

"Candace, just call my mom and tell her that I'm okay and that I'll call her when I can and that I probably won't be coming home for the break. And make sure that you tell her and my father that I love them," I said really quickly as I instinctively knew that I had to get off the phone right at that moment.

"What? Katrina, you are—"

I cut Candace off and whispered nervously, "I can't talk no more, I gotta go. Bye."

A split second later Snipes was banging on the bathroom door.

"Katrina, open this fucking door!"

"Okay, one second, baby, I'm still on the toilet bowl."

"I don't give a fuck! Open up this got damn door before I break this shit down!" Snipes snarled.

My heart was pounding because I was wondering if he had heard me talking. I got up off the toilet bowl and flushed, then I put the phone down and unlocked the door.

Snipes pushed the door open real hard and forceful and surveyed the bathroom. "What the fuck is going on?"

My heart was now in my shoes. I knew for sure that he was about to hit me. I was almost instinctively ready to brace for the impact of his fist connecting with my face.

"You know I don't like you hearing me when I take a shit," I some-how managed the courage to say.

I could tell his wheels were spinning and he probably had heard me talking, but he had this look on his face that said he wasn't exactly sure what was going on.

"Take off your clothes and get in the shower!" he ordered.

A small sense of relief came over me because he hadn't questioned me about whether I had been on the phone.

"The shower?"

"Yeah, you got all this water running, you might as well wash that ass and then dance for me."

Inside I was cringing, but I knew that I had to go along with his re quest or else get smacked. So I undressed and got in the shower.

"Leave the shower curtain open," Snipes said as he retreated back to the room to fix himself another drink.

When he got back to the bathroom, he stood up against the wall gulping his liquor and watching the water bounce off my body.

"Yeah, this is what I'm talking about," Snipes said in between his guzzles. "Now lather up your ass and tits with soap. Make it real soapy. Just do your ass and tits!" Snipes sinisterly commanded me.

I obeyed. As he grabbed his crotch with his free hand, he looked as if he was getting turned on, as he usually did when he saw me naked. But he was definitely the only one getting turned on. Maybe under normal circumstances taking a shower for my man would have been erotic, but I was simply feeling humiliated, so getting turned on was out of the question.

"Yeah, yeah, just like that, just like that. Now get out, but don't dry yourself off and keep that soap on you."

My mind and my body were now on autopilot as I robotically obeyed every one of his commands.

The next thing I knew, I was parading around in our hotel room soaking the carpet with soap and water. And in an instant Snipes had me standing on top of the desk next to the television.

"Now dance, baby!" Snipes sipped his drink, then reached for some money and started throwing it at me.

"Do it like a Luke dancer!" he barked as I began to move my body to a rhythm that I was creating in my own head since no music was playing.

I danced for him for like ten minutes straight, while I hoped the whole time that I didn't slip off the desk from the wetness and bust my head open. Dancing naked for my man could easily have been a turn-on in a different situation, but I was totally turned off.

While I danced for him, he stroked his dick, though he hadn't ordered me to dance so that he could get turned on. I realized he ordered me to do that so he could get me nice and seasoned to go through with setting up Warren to be taken out. He wanted me to be used to following his commands.

I knew that because right after I finished dancing he told me to go dry off and then lie down. He wasn't interested in sexing me or doing anything sexual. Ten minutes after I had lain down on the bed, he told me to get up and get dressed.

Soon thereafter he and I walked out of the hotel and walked all the way to a pay phone on Rockaway Boulevard, which ran through the residential area in Queens known as South Ozone Park. I guess Snipes wanted to use a pay phone in an area that would confuse those trying to catch him if any calls to Warren or Alexis were being traced.

Just before making the call to Alexis, Snipes went over the plan with me again. I was to tell Alexis to relay to Warren that Snipes had been arrested yet again while he and I were hiding out, and that I needed Warren to bring like $10,000 in cash so that I could pay off one of Snipes's boys, a dude name Montuse, who was from Long Island. I was also to tell Alexis to tell Warren that I would be in a gray Dodge rental car at the Sunrise Executive motel, which was located on Sunrise Highway in Rockville Center on Long Island.

I did just as Snipes had told me. The only hard part was trying to evade all of the questions from Alexis as to where I had been and how come I hadn't called her and why exactly did I need the money and why didn't Snipes call?

"Alexis, aren't you the one who basically told me some time ago not to be worrying about a bunch of shit and asking all kinds of questions that I didn't need to ask?"

"Yeah, you right," Alexis said. "I'm just worried about my girl, that's all."

"Well, look. If you worried about me, then just make sure that Warren is here at eight o'clock tonight with that money, because when I see Snipes again, whenever that might be, I ain't trying to have that nigga kick my ass! You understand where I'm coming from?"

"Yeah, okay. I got it. Eight o'clock, right?"

"Yeah." I hung up the phone.

Snipes was paranoid that the calls to Warren and Alexis were being monitored, and he figured that the cops were probably on their way to our current pay phone location. So he and I scurried away from the pay phone and made our way back to the hotel.

It was now approaching four in the afternoon, and at the hotel Snipes revealed to me part of his plan to get at Warren. He told me that he would be waiting blocks away from the Sunrise Executive motel in our rental car. He knew that there was only one usual route to and from the motel if you were driving. So he would wait blocks away for Warren to come to the motel on a wild-goose chase and then leave. When he left, Snipes planned to follow and pounce on him at an opportune time.

"See, the feds and cops will be wit' that nigga when he comes to the motel. But they'll fall off and go their separate ways when they realize Warren showed up on false information," Snipes explained.

I was indifferent to everything that Snipes was saying. I had tuned out and resigned myself to the situation that I had let myself get tangled up in. But what was wild and what I wasn't too indifferent to hear was the last part of the plan, when he said, "And, Katrina, this is the thing. If you don't see shit, then you won't know shit if anybody ever asks you anything. So when we roll out in a couple of hours to ride on this nigga, I wantchu to roll wit' me, but I'm gonna have to have you ride in the trunk."

In the trunk? I thought to myself, and I instantly got petrified and for the first time wondered if Snipes was playing with a full deck. *You could be next, Katrina,* I thought, realizing that life probably meant nothing to Snipes if he could so easily plot to take out his man.

I looked at Snipes and didn't say a word. And right then and there I knew that there definitely was such a thing as a devil simply because Snipes had to be him. Only the devil could so calmly talk about killing his best friend and actually mean it. I continued to look at Snipes and didn't show any disrespectful movements with my body, but inside I was shaking my head and saying to myself, *You sick psychopath bastard. What the hell is wrong with you?*

Like Snipes, for the first time in my life I had begun to question if there was a God, because if there was a God, then how come He hadn't answered my prayers yet and gotten me out of this situation? A situation that I had admittedly gotten myself into. And not only that, but how come this so-called God was allowing things to go from bad to worse?

Twenty-one

Snipes and I were in our hotel room waiting for the time to pass so that he could "ride" on Warren. But the moment we'd returned to the hotel room and taken off our coats, Snipes had headed straight for his liquor bottle and begun guzzling nonstop. I realized that Snipes had major troubles to deal with, and deep down inside I knew that he was probably scared and didn't know how to handle any of his problems, so he got drunk to medicate his feelings. Not to mention that most people, even the most crazed psychopaths, would probably have to be drunk to carry out a hit on their best friend.

As for me, I had never wanted to speak to or hear from my mom more than I did now. I think it was my overwhelming desire to speak to my mom that was causing my head to hurt. As each minute passed, my head would hurt more and more. I had had bad headaches before, but never anything like the headache that I was feeling. I felt really nauseous, so I made my way to the bathroom yet again, but this time I went because I felt I was gonna throw up and I would rather do that in the toilet versus on the carpet in our room.

"You gotta shit again?" Snipes asked with a hint of laughter.

I shook my head no and pointed to my stomach and told him that I felt like I had to throw up, then I locked the door.

I knelt at the toilet bowl as if it was some kind of porcelain god that I was worshiping and paying homage to. But I was far from worship mode. I was hyperventilating on a small scale as I thought about what was about to go down with Snipes setting up Warren for murder.

Whatever you do, Katrina, do not get inside that trunk! I adamantly warned myself. My thoughts caused me to hyperventilate harder and harder.

I heard the sounds from the television in the other room, but before long my thoughts were as loud as a siren inside my head and I didn't even hear the television anymore.

Katrina, that nigga is gonna kill you if you let him put you inside that trunk. Girl, that trunk will be your casket!

I couldn't take those types of thoughts anymore, and somehow I mustered up the courage to reach out to my mother to tell her what was going on and what a predicament I was in.

Katrina, just call 911! Call them right now and you can speak to your mother later! a voice inside my head pleaded with me.

I knew that voice was right. I slowly got up and, with my heart pounding so hard and my palms sweaty, made my way toward the cell phone.

Shit! I said to myself as I realized that the cell phone wasn't in the bathroom. I instantly began cursing myself because I *thought* that I had taken the phone into the other room without thinking.

Breathe, Katrina. Just breathe, I told myself as I tried to calm down.

I realized that the feelings of regurgitation had subsided and I needed to just gather myself, control my breathing, and face Snipes and let him know that I was not gonna get inside that car trunk under any circumstances.

Never let your abductor take you to another location because your chances of surviving are slim to none. That ran through my head and I think I had heard it on some talk show before, I wasn't sure, but I knew that it was a sound and accurate theory.

I didn't take the phone from outta here. I know I left it in here, I said to myself as I started panicking and going crazy looking for the phone. There weren't too many places to look, but I looked under towels, inside the shower, behind the toilet bowl, everywhere, and I couldn't find it.

I stood still for a moment and finally convinced myself to calm down as I was just about ready to exit the bathroom. As I put my hand on the door knob and twisted it, it felt as if someone was on the other side of the door and twisting the knob at the same time.

"Snipes?" I said as I pulled the door open.

Snipes was standing right at the door and kind of startled me.

"The phone ain't in there if that's whatchu went in there for!" Snipes had caught me totally off guard. And right then and there I was prepared to get beat.

"What?" I asked with a confused look on my grill. I was desperately hoping that I was a good enough actress to play things off.

Snipes stared real hard at me but didn't say anything.

Katrina, get the hell out of this hotel room and just run or this nigga will kill you! I pleaded with myself. *Just run as fast as you can downstairs to the lobby and tell somebody to call the cops!*

"We outta here in a few," Snipes said as he walked back toward the bed and plopped his body down.

"Snipes, I'm not getting inside no trunk!" I blurted out.

Snipes kept quiet and began flipping through cable channels with the remote control.

I stood exactly where I was and waited for him to respond. I knew that he had heard what I said. But after two minutes with me standing just feet from the entry door to our room, I took that as my cue to just bolt and get help.

Without any more hesitation I ran for the door, snatched it open, and ran as fast as I could down the long hotel hallway. Halfway toward the exit sign, I turned and looked over my shoulder and saw Snipes come bursting out of our room, chasing me with no shoes on.

"Katrina!" he yelled.

I didn't answer and kept on running, and I made it to the exit door and pushed it open and ran straight for the stairs. As I made it down one flight of stairs, I could hear Snipes as he forcefully pushed open the stairwell door, the sound of the door banging into the wall echoing throughout the narrow, dimly lit stairwell.

Hurry up, Katrina! Run. Run. I was running as fast as I could and breathing hard.

"Katrina!" Snipes yelled angrily.

I had made it down another flight of stairs so I figured and hoped that I only had three more to go.

"Katrina, get over here! I'ma fuck you up when I catch you!"

At that point I knew that I could not stop running, and I finally made it down to the last flight of stairs. Snipes was right on my tail as I pushed open the emergency exit door. The alarm sounded. It was ringing loud, so loud that it was almost deafening. I was glad that it started to ring because I figured that it would attract attention to us. After I exited the door, I realized I was in the side parking lot of the hotel.

"Help me! Somebody help me!" I yelled as I ran, hoping that I was running in the right direction to the front lobby.

"Shut the fuck up!" Snipes yelled as he pushed me from behind and made me lose my balance. I fell to the ground.

"Bitch, what the hell is wrong with you?!" Snipes screamed as he reached down and slapped me across the face.

Although I had skinned up my knees and hands and didn't have a coat on despite the cold, none of that mattered as I got to my feet as quickly as I could and prepared to do battle with Snipes.

I balled up both of my hands and began throwing punches with both fists as fast as I could. I knew that Snipes didn't expect that from me. I surprised him as I connected right-hand punches to his face.

"Help me! Call the police! He's trying to kill me!" I yelled to a couple that was walking by in the parking lot.

Snipes was getting desperate and rushed me and tackled me to the ground.

Another couple was walking by and I pleaded with them to help me, but like the first couple, they just kept on walking right past me.

"She's okay! Everything is okay!" Snipes yelled to the people that were walking by and watching what was going on.

"No, I'm not!" I screamed.

My screams were immediately silenced as Snipes lay on top of me and gripped my throat with his right hand. His grip was so tight that I could not get an ounce of air, and I instantly panicked and feared the worst as my eyeballs bulged out of my sockets.

Snipes's body was positioned to shield his hand from the public so no one could see that he was choking me as he lay on my stomach. He leaned forward and put his mouth right near my ear. I was sure that from the opposite view it must've looked as if he was trying to make love to me and kiss my ear or neck.

"The hell is wrong with you! I'll kill you! Do you know that? I'll kill you!" Snipes loudly whispered into my ear in a threatening tone. He would not loosen the grip that he had on my neck.

"Everything is cool, y'all can keep walking!" Snipes yelled at the people passing by. I kicked my legs in the air like scissors opening and closing, hoping that one of the men in the parking lot would muster up the courage to confront Snipes for his apparent physical abuse.

My eyes were wide-open and still bulging out of their sockets as I lay on the cold ground being choked. I was looking up at the moon and the stars, and again I wondered where in the hell was that God that was supposed to prevent things like this from happening to me? More immediately though, I couldn't understand why no living and breathing human being was coming to my aid.

I was trying my hardest to make a sound, but my voice box was being crushed by Snipes. I had the fingernails of both of my hands dug as deep as I could into Snipes right hand, and I was desperately trying to get him to loosen his grip from my neck. But unfortunately Snipes's grip around my neck was only getting tighter and tighter.

I was beyond nervous as I was sure that I was facing death. Just like I thought, Snipes wanted me dead just as he wanted Warren dead because we were too close to him and therefore we both posed threats to his freedom and his ability to evade the law.

See, he would have killed you had you let him put you into that trunk. Katrina, don't die right here in this parking lot, I said to myself as I suddenly saw images of my mom and dad and my deceased brother. I also saw images of my first boyfriend and images of many of my high school friends from North Carolina. Then I saw an image of my roommate, Candace, sleeping in her bed.

Those images were my last, and I knew that I was seeing my life flash before me as a person does before passing into another life. My legs stopped kicking and I loosened my fingernails from Snipe's hand as my entire body went limp. I passed into unconsciousness.

Twenty-two

When I opened my eyes, it took me a minute or two to realize that I had passed out and had just regained consciousness. It was dark and I was shivering from being so cold. I had no idea where I was. My first thoughts were focused on trying to figure out if I was still alive or dead. But with something tied and stuffed into my mouth that felt like a sock, it confirmed to me that I was still very much alive.

When I felt around, I realized how confined the space was that I was in and I started to panic. I listened for a while, then I realized that I had to be inside the trunk of a car. I was happy to still be alive, but I knew that I had to get out of that car. And I immediately started to panic because I didn't want that trunk to be my casket and my grave.

I couldn't move around much. I was balled up into the fetal position and couldn't fully extend my arms and legs, nor could I yell for help. Everything was so quiet and still, and I wondered just where the heck the car was parked.

Lord, if you're real, please help me get out of this situation! I pleaded as my body was trembling uncontrollably from the cold and the fear.

The quietness continued for about another fifteen minutes. That quietness was followed by footsteps, reminiscent of the thud-sounding walk that Snipes made every time he wore his Timberland boots loosely laced. Then I heard the car door opening and the engine being started.

I began yelling as loudly as I could. But with the sock stuffed inside my mouth, my yells sounded more like humming. So I hummed as loud as I could and also began frantically feeling and kicking as best I could. I was feeling for and aiming to push out or kick out the car's taillights so that I could get some fresh air in the trunk, but more important, I wanted to get the attention of the cars that would hopefully be behind us in traffic.

As we drove, I felt each and every bump that we hit in the road. Each bump made me feel as if I was getting hit with an aluminum baseball bat. With the pain from the bumpy ride, along with my cold and shivering body, and my inability to move in the way I wanted to move, I just gave in and didn't try to fight anymore. I stopped humming and resigned myself to whatever was going to happen to me, even if it meant death.

I wanted to scream and tell Snipes to just kill me. He was treating me worse than someone would treat a dog. I felt humiliated, frustrated, scared, used, and death really seemed like my best option.

The car's bumpy ride finally smoothed out, and it began to feel as if we were riding on a superhighway because there were no stop-and-go movements or any slowing down. I just wished the car would hurry up and take us wherever we were going.

Finally after about fifteen more minutes of driving, the car stopped. The engine sat idling but the car did not move. I felt I was going to pass out from the loss of body heat, that's just how cold I was feeling. As the car sat idling for what felt like thirty minutes, I decided to just take my mind elsewhere.

I thought about how elated and relieved I was going to feel once I got free of Snipes's grip and was in the comfort of my father's arms. I also thought about how I was going to focus strictly and solely on my schoolwork the next semester. I didn't want to think about the word *party* or hanging out for the next four years until I was completely finished with college. In fact Snipes had me rethinking the whole dating thing as well.

"Hmmmmmm! Ugggghhhhhh!" I yelled as I'd grown tired of dealing with my thoughts and wanted out of that trunk.

"Ugggghhhhh! Ugggghhhhh!" I vented as I kicked at the trunk. I knew that the car was quiet enough for Snipes to hear me. And when I heard the car's radio turned on and the volume turned up, I knew that Snipes had purposely done that to drown out my groaning.

Now in addition to my cold and trembling body, I had to deal with loud music being pumped directly into my ear. And with the music drowning out everything, I could no longer even really tell if we were moving or still sitting idle.

God, you can't be real. You can't be real if you're letting me go through this! I complained.

After about an hour or so, I still hadn't gotten any relief from God. He hadn't come to my rescue and I was certain that I was going to lose all of my fingers and toes to frostbite. The car had moved and stopped and started and stopped so many times during that past hour or so that I'd lost track of the number of times.

Suddenly I heard a thud sound as if the trunk had been released. I wanted to lift my legs to check to see if the trunk had in fact been released, but I was way to frozen to move any part of my body.

The trunk was lifted open and I saw Snipes standing over me, looking. I was shivering uncontrollably and had no energy to even try to talk or yell through the sock. With all of my might I reached out my hand to Snipes, and I desperately hoped that he had an ounce of compassion somewhere inside his evil mind.

Snipes grabbed hold of my hand and reached into the trunk and lifted me out of the car. I could barely stand up and my knees were buckling as I held on to him. I wondered, how could he have done that to me and left me inside that cold-ass trunk like that?

I was still shivering uncontrollably, and I think part of my shivering derived from my nerves. I was scared as hell and didn't know what was going on or what was about to happen.

Snipes loosened whatever had been holding the sock in place in my mouth.

"Get in the car, baby," Snipes said to me as he opened the front passenger door for me to hop in.

I got in the car with no coat on. I only had on a short-sleeve shirt and a pair of jeans and some sneakers. I had left my coat back at the hotel. Thankfully the inside of the car and the seats felt a whole lot warmer than it had felt inside that trunk.

Snipes made his way around to the other side of the car and into the driver's seat. As he got in, I didn't care if he beat me, slapped me, or killed me, as I gave him one of the most evil looks that I could muster up.

"How ccccould gewooh dooo thaaat ta me?!" I tried my hardest to angrily say through my frozenness, shivering, and chattering.

"It's a'ight, baby! It's a'ight. I'm sorry. Everything is good now," Snipes said nonchalantly as he turned on the car's heat full blast and fully opened up all the vents so that the heat could rapidly fill up the car.

I rubbed my exposed arms to warm them up. I had goose bumps all over my arms.

"Here, take my jacket." Snipes handed me his jacket.

I slapped the jacket out of his hand and it landed down near the brake pedal. I barked at him that I didn't want his fucking jacket touching me.

"Baby, I said that I'm sorry!" Snipes looked at me as if I'd disrespected him. He didn't seem to have that look of Satan that he gets whenever he beats me. But at the same time he did have that look as if to say that I was pressing my luck.

The heat was finally penetrating my body to the point where I was beginning to feel warm and I was able to relax my position somewhat.

"I need to call home!" I defiantly said to Snipes.

Snipes didn't look at me nor respond.

"Snipes, I said that I need to call my house!"

Snipes still didn't respond and reached and turned on the radio. Before I could say anything else, Snipes was bopping his head to music.

"Snipes!" I yelled over the loud music.

Snipes calmly looked at me and lowered the music, then told me I was going to be traveling with him to Ohio in a few days. Then he turned the volume of the music back up.

I ignored his words and defiantly responded by turning the music back down before yelling, "Snipes, pull over or give me the cell phone or something! I need to call my house!"

Snipes just looked straight ahead and began nodding his head to the sound of the music that was now not that audible. He continued to ignore me as he maneuvered the car into what appeared to be a quiet residential neighborhood that I would later find out was called Rosedale, Queens. Snipes then reached and turned off the car's headlights as he drove.

There was silence for a while as I said nothing and he said nothing.

My stomach was growling and I was starving and beyond aggravated. Snipes continued to drive with no lights on, and we soon approached what appeared to be a dead-end-looking street. The street wasn't actually a dead end but looked drastically different from the nice blocks and houses that surrounded it. In fact the street reminded me of a country part of North Carolina, with swampy-looking water all around and tall weeds reminiscent of cornfields.

"You wanna call home?" Snipes asked me as we parked the car real close to the cornfield-looking weeds.

I didn't respond as I didn't know what Snipes was up to. Instinctively my heart rate began to pick up.

"Get outta the car, I wanna show you something," Snipes coolly said as he turned off the ignition and prepared to exit. I stayed put and didn't move.

"Katrina, come on!" Snipes commanded.

I still didn't move an inch as I ignored him.

"Get the fuck outta the car, Katrina!" Snipes yelled.

Although my heart rate had picked up and I was somewhat nervous about what was about to happen, something had come over me that told me not to be afraid and to stand up to Snipes.

"If I have to come around there, Katrina, I will—"

"You'll what? Fuck me up?!" I yelled at Snipes. "You can hit on me and beat my ass! So what? Does that make you feel like you a man 'cause you can do that?!"

Snipes looked furious.

It wasn't that he had intimidated me, it was more that I was not in the mood for his shit, so I yelled, "Fine, I'll get out the car!" I got out and marched right up to Snipes's face to see what he was going to do. If he was going to hit me, then I wanted him to hurry up and hit me and get it over with.

Snipes snatched me by the back of my biceps and led me about thirty yards into the swampy weeds. I didn't say a word as I noncompliantly walked alongside him.

As we walked, the weeds were getting higher and higher and it was becoming harder and harder for me to see where I was going. I knew that had this been summertime, those bushes and weeds would have been full of all types of bugs and mosquitoes, but there weren't any bugs or mosquitoes around because it was so cold. Yet, in spite of the cold weather, what was weird was that I kept swatting at huge horse flies, and it was sickening and annoying.

I tried to yank my arm free of Snipes so that I could turn around and go back the way in which we had come. I had no idea where Snipes was marching me off to and I had had enough. So as I pulled away from him and prepared to turn, I stumbled on something that felt like a rock but was too plump to be one. I almost tripped and fell over it, but Snipes grabbed me and prevented me from falling.

But he didn't prevent my seeing something that would forever scar and damage my mind.

"Ahh shit! Oh, God, no," I screamed as I saw Alexis laying faceup with half of her head blown off!

Although she was dead and mutilated, she had one eye open and appeared to be looking right up at me.

"Oh my God!" I gasped, and held one hand over my mouth and the other over my stomach. I was scared stiff as a streetlight shined light right on top of Alexis's dead body.

"You see that?!" Snipes yelled as he grabbed the back of my head and forcibly aimed it at Alexis's body so that I couldn't help but see it.

Then Snipes violently turned my head to the right and pointed it down even farther as if trying to push my head into the swampy ground.

"Ahhh!" I yelled, and grabbed my heart.

Immediately, I was grossed out a second time and wanted to run and puke somewhere. But I couldn't run because Snipes gripped the back of my head so tight and forced me to look down at Warren.

Warren looked as if he had been shot in one temple and the bullet had exited through his other temple. His tongue had been cut out of his mouth and was dangling near his neck.

Snipes held tight to my head with one hand while he simultaneously held my arm with his other hand. Then he barked, "Katrina, you see this bitch-ass nigga Warren right here? This is what happens when motherfuckers snitch! They get earthed! I earthed his ass! Me! Dwight 'Snipes' muthafuckin' Abrams! I did this to his punk ass! And you can take this how you wanna take it, but, Katrina, word is bond, if you ever snake me or bitch up on me, I swear to God that I will earth your whole fucking family! You make sure you remember that shit!" Snipes mushed my head closer to the dead bodies one last time for good measure.

Then he turned and walked back toward the car.

"Come on!" he yelled at me.

I was in shock but I followed behind Snipes. Actually I was beyond shock. I was so scared that I thought I was going to have a nervous breakdown or something. I got inside the car with Snipes and was crying and sobbing, and Snipes stared at me before quickly speeding off.

"What the fuck you crying for? Stop all that shit and wipe your motherfucking face," Snipes ordered.

As I wiped my tears with the palm of my right hand, all I knew and could think of was that I was in some deep, deep shit with this nigga, because if he was crazy enough to murder Warren and Alexis, then he was capable of just about anything.

Snipes had scared me like I didn't know was humanly possible. And I don't remember much else of what happened during the rest of that night. I did not ask or demand to call home anymore. After making me witness such a grotesque and gruesome sight, Snipes had got me in line better than the best basic-training drill sergeant ever could have! Only I wasn't training for no military. I was in training to go on the run with a violent, murderous, thugged-out criminal.

Twenty-three

A lot had transpired since the night Snipes had taken me to see Warren's and Alexis's dead bodies. Snipes was still on the run and I was running right along with him. I was still scared and worried and I constantly looked over my shoulder. Every day I wondered if Snipes would kill me.

However, in between my looking over my shoulder and our being on the run, some good times were mixed in when Snipes would surprise me and make me feel like a queen.

"Baby, wake up," Snipes said as I was in a deep sleep on our hotel bed.

I opened my eyes and yawned and asked Snipes what was wrong.

"Nothing's wrong." He reached over me and took hold of my legs and my back and held me in his arms. "I know you're tired, but I got a surprise for you."

Snipes walked me toward the bathroom. Then I saw the bathtub filled with bubbles and four candles around the tub, rose petals on the floor, and a bowl of fresh fruit and a glass of orange juice.

"Oh my God, Snipes, this is so nice." I kissed him on his cheek and hugged his neck while he still held me in his arms. "When did you have time to do all of this?"

"Don't worry about all of that, it's a surprise and I can't give away my secrets. I know we been scrambling lately, and I wanted you to have some time to relax and just chill." Snipes put me down and I immediately went to the tub and tested the water temperature and it was perfect.

"The water is good," I said with a big smile, and I began to undress and then got in the water.

"Here you go." Snipes handed me the bowl of fruit and placed the glass of juice on the edge of the tub. He then turned out the lights so that the only light was from the candles.

"Snipes, this is so nice, thank you." I bit into a strawberry.

Snipes nodded and before walking out of the bathroom came over and kissed me on my forehead. "Look at this." He showed me a clear bag with a nail file, nail clipper, nail-polish remover, and a bottle of red nail polish.

"You trust me?" he asked.

I burst out laughing because the gesture was just so sweet.

"Yeah, I trust you," I said, smiling.

"Okay, so when you done, we gonna watch a movie on HBO and I'll give you a pedicure and a manicure."

I nodded and closed my eyes and just relaxed my body so that I could enjoy the tranquillity of the bubble bath.

The federal authorities had greatly stepped up their measures to find and arrest Snipes. By now he was on the U.S. Marshals' ten most wanted list. What was weird was, as Snipes and I read the different newspaper accounts on him, about how he was this great menace to society, and how he was assumed to be armed and dangerous, I found myself bonding more and more with him. I started to feel like I had to be there for Snipes, and if I wasn't, then that would surely lead to his demise. It was like I didn't want to betray him, and even though I missed being home and missed everyday normalcy, the bottom line was that my fear of betraying Snipes became a bigger motivator than my longing to return home.

I can't deny how I felt. Of course, whenever he would hit or yell at me, at those times I would hate his guts and hate the ground that he walked on and I didn't wanna be around him. I saw the softer side of Snipes, and it was in direct contrast with the way the media was portraying him. Or at least that's what I managed to convince myself. And I knew that my parents or no one else would understand.

They wouldn't understand because they didn't see how Snipes held me close when we spent hours watching movies together or when we went to sleep every night or how he would whisper in my ear and tell me he loved me when we were having sex. Nor did they see the foot rubs and the full-body massages that he would give to me or how he would feed me fruit while I soaked my body in the bubble baths that he would run for me.

Of course, I didn't like the conditions that I was now forced to live under. No adult likes being told what to do and when to do it, and I did initially resent that Snipes controlled me to the point where I couldn't call certain people unless he approved of it first, and I especially hated that he had isolated me from my parents.

I had only contacted my mom one time since December 1993 to tell her that I was alright and to tell her that I needed her to wire me some money. My mom had thought she was wiring me money to purchase a ticket to come home, but in reality the money was for Snipes and me when our funds had gotten extremely low and we were hungry and desperate. It had been five months since my mom had wired me the money, and I knew she was worried sick about me.

However, throughout all of the abuse and the sweet talks and the making up and the makeup sex, I came to see myself as someone that

Snipes "needed." I was convinced that Snipes *needed* me by his side, and without me he would be wrongly vilified and betrayed by the government, similar to how his so-called best friend, Warren, had betrayed him by ratting on him.

I was so convinced that Snipes *needed* me that I didn't think twice about putting apartment leases in my name as the two of us bounced from state to state. Nor did I think twice about putting a car and car insurance in my name for Snipes.

He was in a tough position since he had been on top of the world from a baller standpoint, but after Warren had ratted him out and his brother, Chase, had been arrested, Snipes had no way of retrieving the large amounts of money that he had stashed in several places in New York. Nor could he retrieve many of the luxury cars and other high-end items that he had accumulated during the years that he was hustling.

He knew for sure that if he returned to retrieve any of his money, cars, or jewelry, the feds would be waiting to arrest him.

So in essence Snipes had taken a hard, rapid fall and was quickly being squeezed on both sides. He was being squeezed by law enforcement and by his cash being cut off.

The one thing Snipes had going for him was that over the years he had been hustling, he'd met a lot of other hustlers, particularly those who had found abundant street success by relocating to other states and transplanting their New York street smarts in small towns.

After Snipes and I left New York, we ended up in Cleveland, Ohio. We had no money and we were driving around in a rental car that was way overdue and needed to be returned before it was reported stolen.

The little money that we did have was spent on our hotel room, food, and gas. But Snipes had decided to go to Cleveland because he had some old homeys from New York who had it on and poppin' out there.

Within days of our arrival in Cleveland, Snipes had hooked up with some of his old homeys. And since he was trying not to let me out of his

sight for fear that I would abandon him, I saw firsthand how he operated and I heard just about all that he discussed.

Snipes agreed to sell drugs hand to hand for his former right-hand
man Papoose. Snipes hated to go hand to hand but he needed to get
up some money. He had no other choice but to get on his grind and
get up some dough.

"That nigga is really trying to play me!" Snipes barked at me on our
way back to our hotel, referring to his man Papoose.

I had learned to limit my comments so that I wouldn't mistakenly
say the wrong thing and send Snipes off on one of his rampages.

"What do you mean?" I asked Snipes as I looked straight ahead and
wondered how my mom and dad were doing.

"The nigga knows how I get down. He knows my stats in New York.
And the nigga gonna offer to front me a g-pack?!" Snipes vented.
"And the nigga only giving me forty cent at that! Yo, Katrina, you
don't understand. This nigga used to be on my dick and now he trying
to play me!"

Snipes explained that a g-pack was a package of drugs with a street
value of $1,000. Papoose was willing to let Snipes keep $400 of the
$1,000 once the drugs were sold.

"Katrina, this is what I do! I hustle in a major way! I'm past that
hand-to-hand grindin' bullshit! But this nigga think I'm stupid. He
knows how I get down, and he knows I can move weight, and I'm just
asking the nigga to let me hold a quarter of a key. Not even a whole
kilo. Just a fucking quarter! And this nigga is frontin' like I can't move
the shit!" Snipes yelled.

"He probably just don't trust you," I instinctively said. And then on
the inside I cringed as I hoped that I hadn't said the wrong thing.

Snipes said that with Papoose it had nothing at all to do with trust
and that Papoose was just like everybody else that was mounting up
against him in order to see him fall. He convincingly told me that I was
the only one that he could really count on to have his back. And when
he said things like that, it made me feel really good.

It also made it easier for me to go along with Snipes's plan, which was to hustle for two days and for me to do the hand-to-hand thing with him. I mean, I wasn't the one physically selling the drugs on the block. That was Snipes's job, but I was right there on the block with him. He told me that after the two days that he was gonna surprise Papoose and rob him.

True to his word, two days later Snipes had knocked off the g-pack and had the $400 in his pocket when he went to see Papoose.

"You got my back on this?" Snipes asked me as I sat in the driver's seat of the car.

I nodded yes.

"Okay, cool. When I come back, you gotta be ready to bounce, so keep this shit running!"

Snipes got out of the car and closed the door and made his way into an apartment above a small convenience store. He was supposed to give Papoose his $600 from the g-pack and to be *re-ing up*—getting more drugs to sell from Papoose. Snipes's true intention was to rob Papoose, to keep the entire $1,000 from that g-pack and take whatever other drugs and cash that he could.

As I sat with the car's engine running, I thought of just driving off and leaving Snipes hung out to dry.

You can't do that, Katrina. Then you would be just like the other people who turned their back on Snipes.

My heart was racing as I wondered if I drove off and left, just how quick would I be able to make it to my mother's house in North Carolina? But then I also wondered that if by leaving I would be setting myself up for a lifelong game of cat and mouse with Snipes. In the end, I couldn't bring myself to betray him and leave him stranded like that. God forbid that I left him and he ended up getting killed by Papoose. I would probably never be able to forgive myself.

After about ten minutes, Snipes came racing toward the driver's side of the car. Actually he was hobbling as he ran.

"Hurry up, drive! Drive! Drive!" Snipes yelled at me before even closing the car door on the passenger side.

My heart began pounding, and without even looking in my side-view or rearview mirrors, I mashed down my foot on the gas pedal and pulled off with screeching tires and all. We were on a congested street that reminded me a lot of Harlem, and onlookers and thugs were everywhere.

"Ahhh, shit!" Snipes yelled as he grimaced in pain.

"What's wrong?" I nervously maneuvered the car without a clue as to where I was driving to. My first thought was that Snipes had been shot.

"Hugggh!" Snipes grunted as he tried to direct me in what he thought was the direction of the highway.

Then he explained that he had fallen down the steps when he was running to get out of the apartment and that it felt like he had twisted and sprained his ankle.

"Gotdamit! I hope this shit ain't broke!" Snipes exclaimed. "Fuck!"

Fortunately for the two of us, Snipes's ankle wasn't broken, but we still had to nurse his badly sprained ankle as the two of us never even went back to check out of the hotel that we had been staying in. Instead we made our way back to Washington, D.C., so that Snipes could see if he could move the drugs that he had stolen from Papoose.

"Yo, you believe that the bitch-ass nigga had that quarter of a kilo for me when I got there? But the nigga had to be frontin' 'cause he didn't offer it to me until I had my gat in his mouth!" Snipes explained through his grimacing.

In addition to the quarter of a kilo and the $1,000 from the g-pack, he thought he also had about another $2,500 in cash from robbing Papoose.

"Niggas can't fuck wit' the kid!" Snipes exclaimed, displaying a great sense of pride although he was in a hell of a lot of pain from his ankle.

* * *

We managed to live off the newfound cash for about a month, and just as that was running out, Snipes made a windfall of even more money. During that month, he had flipped the quarter of a kilo into a half kilo, and from that he was able to flip it into a whole kilo, and once he sold that, we had some cash to hold us for what I thought would be a good minute. We had more than $20,000, but unfortunately it didn't last too long.

It didn't last long because Snipes had the biggest ego in the world. To him nobody could outhustle him. Nobody was better or tougher than him, and he was not gonna be outshone by anyone. So he immediately had *me* purchase a used 3-Series BMW so that we could get around, and more important, so that he could floss and look like a baller.

That soon became the pattern. Snipes would hustle and get money for us, and we would live it up buying all kinds of clothes and going to strip clubs and nightclubs spending all kinds of money on drinks and wasteful things, just living for the moment. And when he thought that the car that we were driving was getting too *hot*, we would ditch it and buy another one. Snipes always overspent and enjoyed every minute of every dime that he was spending. And when we were broke, he would always stress out, and that was usually when the physical abuse would resurface. Needless to say, I was all for him getting money, and I did whatever I had to do within reason to help him get it.

And really, anything and everything was in reason. Like when we left D.C. after flipping the cocaine, Snipes suggested that we travel all the way to Houston, Texas, and get an apartment so that he could get some money down there. Well, that too was within reason for me.

And soon another pattern emerged. Snipes and I would go to a new city, set ourselves up in an apartment that was in my name, and Snipes would begin to get "connected" with the ballers in that area. But before long he was sure to snake and cross somebody in some way, and so we would have to bounce up outta that city. It didn't take long before we had the feds and thugs from multiple states hot on our tails and hip to our MO. A couple of times, just by sheer luck and good timing, we barely missed getting caught in massive police raids.

The drama and the constant hustling was nonstop and I wasn't built for it. But when I was around Snipes and he wasn't abusing me, I felt safe. Therefore, I was willing to stick it out with him and ride for as long as I had to.

Twenty-four

A fter Snipes and I bought outfits for ourselves, we were down to about $150, and from that $150 we had expenses to pay. I wasn't too worried though because Snipes had two bricks of cocaine, and as soon as he found a buyer, we would be sitting on more than $40,000. The thing was, finding a buyer proved to be harder than the both of us expected.

We had no luck at two nightclubs we visited. At around twelve midnight Snipes and I headed over to this strip club called Déjà-Vu, where Snipes and I made our way to the bar. I was wearing my trademark tight jeans and high-heel shoes along with a backless top. Snipes was wearing an all-white linen suit that looked real nice on him in the way it contrasted with his dark skin.

"Let me get a Baileys on the rocks!" I shouted over the loud music. I had become a pro at ordering drinks.

The bartender nodded her head and then pointed to Snipes. He ordered Grey Goose vodka and orange juice.

Now we're down to $140. I pulled a twenty-dollar bill from our declining bankroll and handed it to the bartender.

"Yo, let me get fifty singles!" Snipes shouted to the bartender, then he asked me for $50.

"Baby, we don't even have two hundred dollars left!" I said with a whole bunch of concern.

Our drinks arrived and Snipes handed the lady $50 to convert into singles, and she told him that she would be right back.

"A'ight, no doubt," Snipes said nonchalantly as he downed his drink in one big gulp.

The bartender returned with the singles and with my change from the first round of drinks, and Snipes immediately ordered another Grey Goose.

"In a few days we'll be up in here spending about two grand buying out the bar!" Snipes shouted to me as he turned and threw a handful of dollar bills at one of the dancers as she danced on the stage.

What the hell are you doing? I wanted to scream. I could not believe that he was literally throwing away money that we desperately needed for essentials like food.

The voluptuous dancer smiled at Snipes. She was practically butt-ass naked in her prostitute-red patent-leather stilettos and matching red thong. She bent down and picked up the money that Snipes had thrown at her and blew him a kiss. It looked as if it was about $7 or $8 that he had thrown at her, but I was looking at that as two meals at Burger King. And I would be lying if I said that I wasn't getting jealous of the attention that Snipes was paying to the stripper.

Snipes's second drink arrived and he wasted no time downing it quicker than he had downed the first one.

And before I could blink, the sexy stripper had made her way off the stage and was up in Snipes's face dancing provocatively and seductively. Snipes whispered something into her ear, and she smiled and turned around so that her ass was now smack dead center on Snipes's dick.

I felt so uncomfortable and disrespected as the dancer looked in my face while she grinded on my man. She didn't stop as long as he was stuffing her G-string with dollar bills. He was really doing a good job of pissing me off. He had disrespected me in the past in similar ways, but for some reason I was feeling more disrespected than ever before. I mean, here I was running across the country trying to avoid the cops with this dude, and instead of his embracing that kind of loyalty, he was just trampling all over it and throwing shit up in my face.

I turned and faced the bar because I no longer wanted to look at Snipes in the face of the stripper, nor did I want to watch him handing over the little money that we did have to some big-butt, ho-ass stripper.

Fuck it! If he didn't care, then why should I?

"Let me get an order of buffalo wings!" I shouted to the waitress who was standing next to the bartender. *I might as well eat now because we'll probably leave here broke.*

I surveyed the club and looked at all of the men, who seemed as if they were in heaven watching all of the naked and half-naked women. The music was so loud that I could barely hear myself think.

"Yo, Katrina, I'll be right back!" Snipes yelled as he smiled and walked off with the stripper.

I shook my head and couldn't believe that Snipes was probably on his way to get a private lap dance. And for all I knew he could have been on his way to get his dick sucked or to get some pussy.

"How you doing, ma'?" some guy asked me as he stood right where Snipes had just been standing. It was as if he was a vulture just waiting for Snipes to leave so that he could swoop in for the kill.

I looked at him, and he was cute and attractive, but I had long since learned how to interact with guys on a level that would never disrespect Snipes and one that would let the guy know where I stood right away.

"Please." I shook my head and paid the guy no mind.

"Oh, it's like that?" The guy obviously felt that I had dissed him.

"Look, I'm spoken for, okay?"

"It's all good! I was just saying hello. I wish my wife was more like you and was willing to come with me to the strip club every now and then."

Your wife? I thought to myself.

"Stop please. Just stop!" I pleaded to the guy and hoped that he had gotten the hint that I was now disgusted by his mere presence. "So lame!" I said under my breath as I realized that I had unknowingly adopted that same sassy attitude that Alexis had had when she was alive and we would go out with Snipes and Warren.

The guy looked at me and didn't say anything more. He quietly slid off to another part of the club.

Before long I saw Snipes walking back in my direction hand in hand with a new stripper! My wings arrived at the same time that Snipes walked up next to me.

"Katrina, what the fuck?! Why you spending money on food if you saying that we don't have that much dough left?!" Snipes barked with that look he gets when he drinks.

I didn't say anything and just looked at him while the stripper made her way behind the bar and up onto the stage to work one of the poles.

I bit into one of the buffalo wings, and then out of nowhere Snipes started rambling on about how hot it would be if I was a dancer.

I looked at him as if he was crazy.

"Word is bond, your body is a'ight and dudes will throw money at *anything* up in a strip club," Snipes said as he quickly ordered another drink.

Gee, thanks, I wanted to respond, but I suddenly had the most queasy feeling come over me like I was gonna throw up or something.

Instantly I held my hand to my mouth and my other hand on my stomach.

"I'll be right back," I mumbled to Snipes as I quickly made my way to the bathroom.

Thankfully, no one was in the stall because no sooner had I burst open the door, I was vomiting all over the place. Like out of nowhere I had gotten sick. I knew that it couldn't have been from the drink because I had only sipped on it. One drink wouldn't have done that to me. And I had barely eaten one of the buffalo wings, so I knew that it couldn't have been that.

Thirty seconds later I was heaving again.

I can't believe this! I thought as my stomach began feeling even worse. I made my way to the sink and washed out my mouth with water before splashing some all over my face.

I knew that I had to get to a bed and lie down. So I made my way back out to where Snipes was sitting and let him know that I wasn't feeling well. I wanted to go.

"But we just got here!" Snipes barked.

"I know but I'm throwing up all over the place and I'm sick!" I shot back.

"You come up in here spending my money on dumb shit like them buffalo wings! That's probably what made you sick. But that's your fucking fault! Nobody told you to eat that shit! We gotta get this money and I can't leave right now. Just chill over there in the corner some-where," Snipes commanded with no sympathy whatsoever.

I wasn't gonna argue with him because he had that look he gets when he beats me, and I didn't wanna be getting my ass beat while I was feeling sick. So I made my way over to a somewhat isolated part of the club and put my head down on a table while I sat in a cushioned folding chair.

Snipes continued to mingle and flirt with the dancers while also try-ing to meet a contact so that he could move the drugs that he had stashed at the hotel. While he mingled about the club, something hit me like a revelation! *Was I pregnant?* I quickly picked my head off the table and my heart started racing. I remembered back when I was in high school and one of my friends had gotten pregnant, and she would throw up all the time during our lunch period because smells of cer-tain foods would cause her to hurl.

With all of the running around and hopping from state to state, I couldn't remember the last time that I'd had my period.

Maybe you didn't have it because you were stressed out, I reasoned.

I quickly realized I could indeed be pregnant, since it had to have been five months or better since my last period. *But my stomach ain't even showing*, I thought.

With so much drama and running around, I wasn't certain how long it had been since my last period, but it had been sometime during the winter.

I quickly stood up from the chair and my adrenaline started pumping. Some of the queasy feelings disappeared as I wondered what the hell I would do if I was pregnant, and more important, what would Snipes's reaction be?

I needed that stress like I needed a hole in my head! It seemed like when things couldn't have gotten any worse, they somehow found a way to get worse. But as I thought and thought and thought about what to do, I realized I had to quickly take action. So I decided to take a page out of Snipes's handbook of deceptive charm.

Later on that night at like two in the morning, I found Snipes isolated in the club, and he seemed perturbed because he hadn't had any luck in finding a drug connection. I told him not to worry and that I had thought about what he had said, and that I was willing to dance at any strip club so that we could get up some money to live on.

"You dead ass?" Snipes asked with a huge smile as his mood seemed to brighten quickly.

"Yeah, I'll hold us down for a minute," I said with a fake smile. I was trying my hardest to get on his good side so that I could make my move and deal with the pregnancy.

"I already got the heels and I can throw on a thong and I'm good!" I said, trying my hardest to come out of character and sound as ghetto and as animated as possible.

Snipes was buying everything that I was telling him, and he was in the best of moods by the time we left the club. And although we had less than $100 to our name, Snipes didn't seem to mind because he now had me to count on to shake my ass for some cash. But had I not offered to strip and make money for us, I knew I would probably have got my ass blamed and beat for our lack of funds.

Instead, when Snipes and I left the club and made it to our room at the Days Inn, he was still on cloud nine, and I was sure he was horny from seeing all of the half-naked women at the strip club.

He sexed me that night like he had never done before. The liquor he had drunk made him take longer to cum, but that was okay because I wanted him to keep sexing me. I wanted to enjoy and savor the experience because, although I was as nervous as hell about what was gonna happen with the pregnancy and all, I knew that that night would probably be the last time that I would ever make love to Snipes.

I still had my deceptive charm going and was laying it on thick as I told Snipes how good he made me feel and how I had never cum as hard as I had that night. Snipes was sucking it all up and I was continually stroking his ego.

But with the lovemaking, I had also been trying to rock his ass to sleep so that I could make my move. Unfortunately Snipes wasn't going to sleep, he was just lying in the bed wide awake and preparing for round two of our lovemaking.

Now, Katrina. Just do it! I urged myself.

Without hesitation I got up from the bed and I reached for my jeans and purposely put them on with no panties.

"Why you getting up?" Snipes asked.

"I'm just gonna run downstairs and get some ice and something to drink," I said as I slipped on my flip-flops. "Throw me your shirt," I said, hoping to keep him from asking any questions and hoping that his suspicions were not aroused.

Snipes did exactly as I told him, and he threw me his short-sleeve, buttoned-down, white linen shirt.

As I put it on and buttoned it, I said with the realest-looking fake smile on my face, "When I come back, I'm gonna give you a lap dance so I can get ready for the strip clubs."

"A'ight," Snipes said as he watched me walk out the door.

As I walked out of the hotel room, I realized that this was the first time in months that I had not been within eyesight of Snipes. My heart was pounding as I tried to hurry up.

As I rushed to the car, I frantically searched my pants pockets for the car keys.

"*Shit!*" I yelled as I realized that I had left the keys up in the hotel room. I knew that there was no way that I could go back for them.

A voice inside of me kept screaming, *Run, Katrina.*

It was a little past four in the morning and nothing was open and there looked to be not a soul in sight as I made it to the parking lot of the hotel.

Then a voice told me to call the police, but I didn't want to do it out of fear that if I did call, it would make things bad on Snipes. But I knew that it would only be about two more minutes before he would be coming to look for me if I didn't return to the room.

So without any more hesitation, I started running as fast as I could in my flip-flops. I ran in the direction with the most lights. The hotel was located on a busy street called Tacoma Way, which had a bunch of stores and gas stations and things of that nature, but at night things looked deserted.

I ran and ran even though it was laborious. My breathing wasn't controlled because of my nervousness. Not to mention that it is hard as hell to run in a pair of flip-flops.

Cars would drive by, and each time I looked and saw headlights coming I hoped it wasn't the headlights from a BMW with Snipes inside.

I was beyond out of breath and I felt like I wouldn't have any luck finding an open store. So something inside me told me to hide. I quickly looked for a place and ran behind the next row of stores where I saw a big green Dumpster and ducked behind it.

My chest was heaving up and down rapidly as I knelt to catch my breath. I started praying to God that I would be okay, then I tried to convince myself to just stay right there until the sun rose and stores opened up. And that is just what I did. I sat down next to the Dumpster and waited and waited and waited.

My stomach growled. I only had $2 on me. I wondered if I was in fact pregnant, and if so, had I harmed the baby by the way I had been living during the past months. I was not eating regularly, and when I did eat, all I ate was junk food. I hadn't eaten any vegetables or anything healthy in months.

You'll be okay, I told myself as I was just happy like all hell that I had finally drummed up the courage for what I suspected would be my baby's sake to get away from Snipes and get some help and get to a doctor.

Just as the sun was coming up, I heard a car slowly driving by. My heart just about jumped out of my chest when I realized that the car didn't have any lights on.

Katrina that's him! Oh my God! I thought that I was gonna die for sure.

Although I couldn't physically see the car, I could tell that it had just stopped.

My palms were sweaty and I was beyond fearful. *Be still.*

Then I heard the car door open and someone got out.

"Katrina!" Snipes yelled.

I tried everything I could to keep from yelling out in fear and to keep myself from making any sounds. I could hear Snipes on the other side of the Dumpster, and I just knew that I was about to die.

Okay, okay, okay, just relax, I told myself as I sat trembling.

Then I heard the loudest *boom* that I had ever heard in my life. Followed by Snipes yelling, "Fuck!"

The boom was the sound of a gun. Then I heard Snipes's footsteps and the sound of the car peeling off. Apparently out of frustration Snipes had fired a shot into the air before leaving.

I thanked God that he hadn't seen me because I was sure that that bullet would have been put in my head. There was absolutely no doubt in my mind.

I was beyond scared but I knew I could wait no longer. I had to get up and run. And that is exactly what I did, only instead of running on the main road I found my way to the back residential streets. Then I ran to the first house that I saw that looked welcoming.

204 / **Mark Anthony**

I made it up the steps of the front door to a house that looked like the one the Brady Bunch family grew up in. I began frantically ringing the bell. After about two minutes of waiting, a white lady who looked to be in her fifties answered the door and asked me if she could help me. It was now barely approaching six o'clock in the morning.

I was still breathing rapidly and I knew that I looked really disheveled. I didn't know what to say to the lady so I just blurted out words.

"Hi, miss, listen, I know you don't know me," I said with my hands up in the air to show that I meant no harm, "but I am pregnant, and I just ran away from my abusive boyfriend, and I am so scared right now that he's gonna find me. Can you *pleaaase* let me use your phone? I just wanna call my parents so that they can help me. I promise I'll be in and out. I'm so sorry to bother you this early." My heart pounded and I looked over my shoulder to make sure that Snipes was nowhere around.

Only by the grace of God did that lady decide to trust me. She looked me up and down, and I think she sensed my sincerity because she hastily opened up the door, still in her robe, and ushered me into her house.

"I appreciate this so much. Thank you. Really." I told the lady not to worry, that I would just have to make one collect call.

"It's okay, it's okay. Call whoever you have to call. Don't worry about it," she said.

Without any more hesitation I began dialing the 336 area code and my house. It was just reaching six o'clock in the morning on June 18, 1994, but that was on the West Coast. Thousands of miles away on the East Coast in Winston-Salem, North Carolina, it was approaching nine o'clock in the morning.

It was a Saturday, so it was safe to say that everyone in my mom's house was probably still asleep, which I confirmed when my father picked up the phone in a groggy, sleepy voice.

"Hello," he grumbled in his tired voice.

"Daddy? It's me, Katrina." And after those few words I burst into a ball of tears as I could tell that my father had quickly woken up and was desperately trying to calm me down so that he could figure out if I was okay and just where the hell I had been all this time.

Twenty-five

B aby, where are you?" my father asked desperately as I could also hear him trying to wake up my mother.

"In Tacoma. I'm in Tacoma," I said as I tried to gather myself.

"Katrina, thank God you're alive! We've been worried sick about you."

"I wanna come home," I replied through my tears.

"Katrina, oh my goodness. Lord, thank you!" my mother shouted into the phone as she had picked up another phone in the house.

"Katrina, where is that boy?! Is he with you?" my father asked, and I immediately knew that he was talking about Snipes.

"No, I'm by myself. Daddy, I got like two dollars to my name and I—"

My mother cut me off and she told me that she would wire me some money to get home. And then she started questioning me about the last time she had wired me some money, money that, unbeknownst to her, I lied to her about and ended up spending on Snipes and myself.

My father cut my mother off and told her not to worry about that right now, and he also told me that bounty hunters had been to the house on several occasions looking for Snipes.

"Really?" I said as I felt horrible, realizing that I must have caused all kinds of worry, drama, and grief for my parents.

I spoke to my parents a little while longer, and I know that the white lady that had opened her home to me so that I could use the phone was probably trying to figure out what the hell was going on. But she was extremely nice and uncommonly trusting. She told me where the nearest Western Union locations were and also offered to drive me there.

When I hung up, she offered me food and wanted to know if there was anything more that she could do for me.

At that moment I knew God had to have directed me to that house. Of all the houses on that street, the lady who opened the door had to have been an angel sent by God, because without her I don't know what I would have done.

"No, young lady, you need to eat something. Let me just fix you something, anything," she said. "Can I make you some toast?"

"Okay," I said, too on edge to smile.

"You want raisin toast or regular toast?"

"Raisin toast is fine."

The lady popped the bread into the toaster and then said, "My son-in-law is a police officer, do you want me to call him?"

"Oh, no, definitely not. I don't want to get the police involved, I'll just deal with it when I get home. But if you don't mind, could you please take me to a Western Union?"

The lady reached for butter and jelly and placed it on the table in front of me. "I most certainly can."

The toast was ready and she placed it in front of me with a carton of orange juice and told me that when I was done, she would grab her car keys and take me to a Western Union.

Not only did she take me to the Western Union, she also offered to drive me to the airport, which was some twenty miles from where she lived.

My parents had immediately called all of the major airlines and looked for flights that were leaving from Seattle for North Carolina. After about thirty minutes they had called me back at the lady's house to let me know that they had booked a flight in my name on their credit card, and that the flight would be leaving at twelve noon West Coast time.

I had about five hours to spare before my flight left, and during that time the lady, who told me her name was Mrs. Boston, chilled with me and took me to a fast-food restaurant to get something else to eat.

While I didn't quite open up to her and tell her *everything* that I had been through, I did tell her that I was in an abusive relationship, one that had me confused.

Mrs. Boston didn't pass judgment on me in any way. She even waited with me in the airline passenger terminal until my flight began boarding, just in case Snipes had got smart and called around to different airlines to see if I had booked a flight. After exchanging phone numbers with the lady, who told me that she wanted me to call her as soon as I got home, I boarded the flight, happy to be on my way to North Carolina to see my parents and get my life back on track. Hopefully, I wasn't pregnant and I would be able to go back to school during the upcoming fall semester.

Being on the run was now over and the nightmare had ended.

The nightmare had ended.

Twenty-six

Aside from my throwing up twice on the airplane, my flight back to North Carolina was pretty smooth. I was exhausted and tried my best to sleep most of the way, but I couldn't sleep. I had too many thoughts running through my head.

I wondered what Snipes was thinking and doing and how he would make out. I also wondered if he would come looking for me. Would he try to make good on his threat to kill my entire family? I was so stressed out. But I knew that when I got home, the best thing to do would be to come clean with all that had transpired and all that Snipes had put me through, including the threats that he had made.

When I got off the plane and made my way to the terminal, my mother was the first person I saw. She was right in front of others at the exit ramp that led from the plane and into the airport.

When she saw me, she practically tackled me like a football player as she hugged me tighter than I had ever been hugged in my life. My father and his brother were standing not too far off, and they also came up to me with looks on their faces that showed that they were relieved beyond belief.

The four of us hugged and embraced and no one wanted to let go. During the embrace my mother couldn't stop crying and saying how happy she was to see me. My father kept asking a bunch of rapid-fire, nervous questions—if I was alright, if I had been hurt, what happened, and how come I had never called? Soon enough we were each crying except for my uncle. We decided to make our way home before we became one big snot-slobbering mess.

"Katrina, you look like you lost about twenty pounds, baby, you sure you okay?" my mom asked.

"Mom, it's just the stress that caused me to lose all that weight, stress and not eating on a routine basis."

"Oh, thank you, Jesus! Katrina, you just don't know how worried we were about you," my mom added.

We didn't live too far from the airport, so with all of the questions my parents were throwing at me, time flew by. We reached home in no time. As we were pulling into my parents' driveway, I felt the greatest sense of relief, but also an overwhelming fear. I knew I had to share it with my parents.

"When we get inside, I'll tell y'all everything that happened from the time I met Dwight, up until now. But just understand that what I tell you may not be all that easy to listen to," I warned.

My father told me that they didn't know what to make of the fact that I either didn't or wouldn't or couldn't call them, but from what my roommate had told them and the bounty hunters along with numerous other investigators, who had stopped by the house, my father was able to piece together a story that was probably similar to the one that I was getting ready to tell him.

He was furious at himself for not having picked up any signs that Snipes was this big criminal when he'd visited for Thanksgiving dinner. My father made it clear that had he picked up any hints of Snipes's criminal ways, he would have shut down our relationship in a heartbeat.

Then my mom chimed in and I know she had probably been wanting to vent at me from the time she had spoken to me on the phone at that lady's house.

"Katrina, what in the world would make you want to even be interested in a guy like that?! Didn't you know what he was into?!" my mom asked, a bit of anger resonating in her voice.

"Mom, but see, the thing was—"

My father cut me off as he wanted me to tell him everything that had happened from the beginning.

So I began to break down everything that I had been through from meeting Snipes and his charming ways, to the time that he forced himself on me in the staircase, to the times that he had beaten me. I even told them about the time that I had been arrested at his house. I left out no details. There was no sense in covering up anything at this point.

I couldn't help but break down and start boohooing as I told them in intricate detail how Snipes had locked me in the trunk of the rental car and how he had taken me to see both Warren's and Alexis's murdered bodies and how he had threatened to do the same to my family if I didn't do as he said.

Through my tears I explained to them how sorry I was for having let them down and for having scared them the way I had. Then I begged them for their forgiveness. I had kept them in the dark mainly because I was fearful for my life and fearful that Snipes would make good on his promise to harm them.

My mother and my father and my uncle sat stunned and in silence as I talked. And when I was done, they continued to look at each other baffled and bewildered. I could see the confusion and concern on each of their faces.

My father shook his head, then for the first time in my life I heard him curse, as he got up and walked out of the room and swore that he would kill Snipes's "motherfucking ass!" My father was beyond livid as he told my uncle to get ready to fly out with him to Washington so that they could find Snipes and "whup his ass!"

I had never in my life heard my father talk like that, so I knew that he had reached his boiling point and was talking from deep-rooted anger that had probably been building up inside him ever since I had vanished with Snipes.

My mom was also livid and upset but proved to be the voice of reason as she went for the phone and asked my father for a bounty hunter's card. She thought that it was best that she and my father do as the bounty hunter had said, which was for them to contact him as soon as they had heard from me or made contact with me. And that is what they intended to do.

I was waiting for the right time to drop the other bomb on my parents, which was that I thought I was pregnant, but there never seemed to be a good time to deliver that news, so I kept it to myself.

As my mother dialed the bounty hunter's number, she yelled for me to hurry up and change my clothes. She wanted me to get out of Snipes's white linen shirt, which I was still wearing, and take a shower. Anything related to Snipes or anything spoken about Snipes brought a bad spirit into the house as far as my moms and pops were concerned. That I was wearing his shirt thoroughly disgusted them. Secretly, as I would never tell my parents this, I actually liked keeping on Snipes's shirt because it had his scent on it and kept the good thoughts about him fresh in my mind. I still loved him despite everything, and feelings are hard to control.

It was fast approaching eleven o'clock in the evening, so I made my way to my room to get some clothes to change into. As I walked into the room, this unreal sense of déjà vu came over me like I had been through this exact same experience before. Of course, I had been in my room before, but all of the circumstances surrounding the day's events, leading up to the moment I went into my room, felt like I had lived them before.

"No. That can't be! There's no way!" I heard my mother yelling from downstairs. The TV in the living room was on so it was kind of drowning out what was going on downstairs. I quickly ran to the top of the steps so I could listen better to what my mother was talking about.

I knew that she was on the phone because I heard her tell my father to pick up the phone in the kitchen. I tiptoed into my parents' room and carefully picked up their phone so I could hear the conversation with the bounty hunter.

"Mr. Easely," a male voice on the other end of the phone said, "I was explaining to your wife that we will definitely take any information that your daughter can provide to us on Mr. Abrams and where he might be."

"Um-uh," my father said into the phone to acknowledge that he was listening.

The man continued, "But it seems like you may have a much bigger problem to deal with other than helping us locate Mr. Abrams."

My father was silent on the phone, and before the man could even finish what he was saying, I heard my mother interrupt, "Lord Jesus, tell me that this ain't true! Tell me it ain't true!"

"It seems as though your daughter has been indicted on a number of federal criminal charges, and you might—"

"What?!" my father yelled into the phone. "But she didn't do anything illegal!" my father growled as my heart beat like it had never beat before in all of the time and all of the things that I had been through with Snipes.

"James, like I was saying—"

My father cut him off again. "What do you mean it 'seems like' she has been indicted? Has she or hasn't she?!"

My heart was racing and I thought about hanging up the phone, but I didn't want my mother and father to know that I had been eavesdropping so I held on the line.

"James the only thing that I can tell you is that you might want to contact a lawyer as soon as possible and get legal advice from an attorney and have your attorney look into the validity of the indictment," the man said as calmly as possible.

"Patricia, can you believe this shit?" my father asked my mother, and again I had heard him curse.

"This is unbelievable! It's like a nightmare that won't end or a movie or something!" my mom said as she sighed into the phone.

My father told the man that he would touch base with him after he'd spoken with an attorney. I too hung up the phone.

Although I desperately needed a shower, it was not my biggest concern. I was now more concerned with finding out if in fact there was a criminal indictment against me, and if so, just what did this indictment mean and just exactly how would it affect me.

Twenty-seven

At eleven thirty the following Monday morning my parents and I went to see a prominent Winston-Salem criminal attorney. Just to sit down and consult with the attorney for one hour was $400. At $400 an hour, we had to talk fast and hope that he'd listen quickly so that we wouldn't go over our one-hour limit.

During the consultation my parents gave the attorney a brief summary of what had transpired between Snipes and me. Then I was allowed to talk, at which time I gave the blow-by-blow, intricate details. I told him *everything* that had gone down from the day I'd met Snipes up until the present moment.

The attorney was a distinguished-looking black man who stood about six foot three. He had brown skin like the complexion of LL Cool J and slightly graying hair. As we sat in the high-quality leather chairs and the attorney, Mr. Hightower, sat behind his beautiful desk with his dark blue pinstripe suit with matching suspenders, he began to give us his assessment based on what we had told him.

"Okay, the first thing that we would have to determine is if in fact there is an indictment against Katrina. And if so, we would need to find out the particulars of the indictment. But if the bounty hunter is telling you this, then he is getting it from somewhere, and I would suspect that the indictment probably does exist."

"But, Mr. Hightower, how could that be if—," my mother tried to interject, but she was quickly cut off by the attorney.

"Mrs. Easely, trust me when I say I understand your concerns and your plight. But what you have to understand is that the federal government has numerous resources, tools, and laws at their disposal to fight crime, and one of those resources, which I guess more accurately should be described as laws, one of those laws is called conspiracy to commit a crime." The lawyer paused to ask me a question. But before doing so, he looked at all of his notes from earlier while we were talking to him.

"Now, Katrina and Mr. and Mrs. Easely, in all due respect I just have to state this and then ask a question, so please don't take offense to it. There is something called attorney-client privilege, which basically means that *whatever* we discuss strictly stays between us, and no one can force either of us to divulge anything that is discussed between us. Now the reason I say that is because, Katrina, I want you to know that after I check into the indictment, and if there is an indictment, that the only way that I would be able to help you to the best of my ability is if you tell me anything and everything that you know as it relates to your involvement with Snipes. Don't hold back anything in an attempt to protect someone or in an attempt to protect yourself. I'll need to know *everything*. Do you understand that?"

I nodded and told him that, yes, I did understand, and I also said that I had told him all that there was to know.

Then Mr. Hightower explained that under the conspiracy law, the government could hold me criminally accountable for everything that had transpired after the time that I realized that Snipes was into illegal activities. From that point all the way up until I withdrew myself from

Snipes's circle and his organization, I could be held criminally responsible.

Then the lawyer began to press me as to when I first had any inkling that Snipes was into something illegal. I told him Snipes's story about his insurance business, which I believed for quite some time. "It probably was about two months or so after I'd met him that I realized that he was a drug dealer," I said.

After a bunch of other talk between my parents and me and the attorney, the attorney began to cut things short.

"Alright, well, I think I have enough information to get started. But if I can be quite frank with you, we are talking about a guy who is wanted by the DEA and the FBI. Several state and local police organizations are looking for him, and he is one of the U.S. Marshals' most wanted fugitives. There is probably videotaped evidence and personal sworn affidavits from other criminals that will corroborate the indictment that they may have against you, Katrina." The attorney paused before continuing, "I say that because the government has a ninety-eight percent conviction rate against those that they prosecute, and in all likelihood and without holding any punches, Katrina, you will more than likely have to do some jail time if this indictment is indeed true."

When the lawyer said those words, I just gasped and put my head down and instinctively cradled my stomach.

My mother looked as if she was about to cry or have a nervous breakdown. Then my father stood up and said, "Mr. Hightower, look, we ain't rich or anything like that, but I will pay whatever it is that I have to pay in order to help my daughter fight these charges because she really didn't do anything wrong!"

My father paused, then said, "How much is your retainer? Ten thousand? I'll bring a certified check by your office in the morning to pay that."

My heart was just melting away as I looked at my father and saw how desperate he looked and was sounding, and it was all a result of my stupidity. I mean, I had already wasted about $30,000 of my parents' money on a year's worth of tuition in which I flunked out one semester by not showing up for the tests and finals, and then the other semester I didn't show up at all because I was on the run. And now my parents would have to shell out more money for me to pay a lawyer to help get my ass out of a sling? I couldn't believe it. It seemed unreal but it was getting more and more real by the minute.

"Mr. Hightower, just tell me how we can overcome that ninety-eight percent conviction rate, that's all that I want to hear," my father said as we probably only had about ten minutes left of our one-hour consultation.

The lawyer stood up and sighed, and he seemed to be thinking as he held his hands together and walked around the room as if he were in a courtroom pleading his case to a jury.

He explained to us the Stockholm syndrome, where someone is held against his will, and as a strategy to keep his captor happy in order to stay alive, the captive develops this obsessive identification with the likes and dislikes of the captor. This warps the captive's own psyche in such a way that the abducted person comes to sympathize with his abductor. He starts to almost subconsciously but emotionally bond with his abductor. Mr. Hightower restated that the person being held against his will does this as a survival technique. And against all common sense, the person who has been abducted will go as far as to look at those in authority, like police officers and relatives, who are trying to rescue the captive or come after the abductor, as the bad guys looking to do harm to the abductor. The lawyer explained that when the abductor does kind things like buys a gift for those abducted or gives them food or protects them in some way, it intensifies that dysfunctional bond that exists.

Oh! My! God! I thought to myself as I sat and listened to the lawyer speak. I was in awe because I realized that he was describing my actions and my mental process down to a T. In fact he sounded more like a psychologist than a lawyer at that point.

"Yes, the Stockholm syndrome, along with the battered-spouse syndrome, are definitely defenses that we could raise, along with others, and the jury may or may not buy it. But I am sure that I could convince them to the point where reasonable doubt would be present in the minds of the jury. And in all honesty, I would recommend that Katrina receive some kind of psychological counseling, because she just might have been a victim of these two syndromes, and it would bolster the credibility of her psychological state if she seeks mental help now, way before any court proceedings. In any case, to use a defense such as this you would be talking about calling in expert witnesses to testify, and things of that nature could get quite costly and expensive. You could easily be looking at upwards of one hundred thousand dollars in legal fees," the lawyer said nonchalantly as he filled himself a cup of water from the watercooler.

Wow! I told myself.

The lawyer then told my parents that he would love to take on the case and that they should think it over. He reminded them that plea bargaining and not going to trial was always an option, and that depending on the indictment, they would probably be looking at around $15,000 in legal fees if we decided to take a plea versus going to trial.

"But let me look into the indictment and then I will follow up with you, and we can take it from there in terms of contacting the authorities and seeing how to best proceed. With something like this we will want to move quick before there is an arrest, so I'll be back in touch with you guys before the end of the day."

And with that we left the lawyer's office in a somber mood and went home and evaluated our options.

My parents were more than good to me, and they never came down on me with "I told you so" and "You should have listened to me."

I was grateful for that, but it made me feel even more horrible about all of the drama I was now bringing into their lives. I was really a mess when I sat at the top of the steps that led to my bedroom and heard my parents discussing things that I had never heard them talk about before. Apparently, my mom had been sick within the past year with something that their medical insurance didn't cover. To avoid being up to their necks in debt and medical bills, my parents had taken out a second mortgage on their home to pay off the medical bills. I couldn't believe I'd missed out on so many changes in their lives.

"We really don't have many options," my mother said to my father in a dejected and somber tone.

My father contemplated asking his brother to loan him the $100,000 to cover my legal fees, but then they quickly decided against that, realizing that they would have no viable way of ever paying him back other than to possibly sell the house.

All kinds of thoughts were running through my mind, but I knew that there was no way I could now spring the possible pregnancy on my mother and father. I decided to keep that a secret for now.

I desperately wished that I could turn back the hands of time. At least so I could secretly stash some of the money that Snipes had lavishly flaunted in front of me, money that was straight wasted on fast living. If I had known that I would need it in the future for a defense fund, then I would most definitely have done that.

Twenty-eight

L ater that Monday afternoon Mr. Hightower called the house and confirmed that I had been indicted. Not only had I been indicted on federal conspiracy charges, but the indictment included money-laundering charges, as well as charges of lying to federal officials.

My mother, my father, and I listened as the phone was on speaker mode. Mr. Hightower rambled on and on about different technical legal jargon, but I had tuned him out the moment he said he was calling to confirm the indictment.

The mood in my mom's house was reminiscent of a funeral parlor. All of us were quiet and deep in our thoughts. The defeated looks on our faces told the story. My mom broke down and cried, while my father pretty much turned his thoughts into anger. I basically went numb and don't remember much of what else happened for the remainder of the day.

On Tuesday morning, June 21, 1994, my parents sat me down and explained how they would be willing to give their right leg for me, and that they wanted nothing but the best legal counsel for me, but they simply couldn't afford Mr. Hightower.

It broke my heart and made me feel like shit to see my father, a grown, strong man's man, shedding a tear as he told me that if he had it to give me, he would. But he simply didn't have it.

Later that day, the three of us went to see another attorney, a white man, who, like Mr. Hightower, was a criminal attorney. But right from the gate, I could tell that this new attorney, Mr. Pittershawn, was going to be a problem. The level of competence and confidence didn't seem to be there like it was with Mr. Hightower, nor did the level of compassion. It was like he could not have cared less when we mentioned to him things like the Stockholm syndrome and the battered woman syndrome. The only word that kept coming out of his mouth was *plea*. He must have said the word *plea* at least one hundred times while we were in his office, and it was getting extremely frustrating because I knew that to cop a plea would basically mean that I would have to admit guilt, and something inside me didn't feel good about doing that.

Since all we could really afford was an attorney with Mr. Pittershawn's level of expertise, we had to trust the advice that he was giving us.

Mr. Pittershawn explained that he would accompany us to turn myself in to the authorities, and that they would more than likely set a bail at an amount that we wouldn't be able to afford.

"Wow!" my father said as he shook his head. "So you mean to tell me that once Katrina turns herself in she's gonna be locked up behind bars?"

Mr. Pittershawn nodded.

"So if we can't afford to post the bail, then how long would we be looking at before Katrina could come home?" my father asked, looking both angry and dejected, while my mom just cried as she quietly listened.

"Well, Mr. Easely, I really cannot answer that right now. If Katrina takes a plea, she will be admitting guilt to a crime or to possibly more than one crime, and with that comes a sentence, and that sentence will determine how much jail time Katrina would be facing."

"But she didn't commit a got damn crime!" my father yelled as he got up from his seat and banged his fist on the back of his chair.

Then my mother chimed in through her tears, "This is ridiculous. I mean, you have people out there murdering and killing people and raping and robbing people! Those are the criminals! Not my daughter! My daughter didn't do anything wrong! The only thing she is guilty of is having met and befriended the wrong person. That's it!"

Mr. Pittershawn finally showed a bit of emotion as he stood up from behind his desk and told my parents that he understood how they felt, and while he sympathized with them, the fact remained that the law was the law and there was little any of us could do about it.

My father exhaled visibly.

"So what we'll do is make arrangements with the authorities to bring in Katrina one day this week, where she will be processed, and in the interim I will contact the prosecutor who will be handling this case and see if we can work out a favorable plea deal," Mr. Pittershawn said.

Then finally he offered up some hope as he explained that the thing we had going in our favor was that Snipes was akin to a kingpin, and a dangerous man, and it was really *him* the government wanted. They didn't really *want* me, he explained. But the government would probably be willing to spring me loose if I could help them get to Snipes.

Whew! I thought to myself. *Why in the hell did it take you this long to tell us that?* I wanted to ask, but I kept my mouth shut.

"So we enter into some kind of plea negotiations because it's really Snipes that they want. And Katrina can help them get to Snipes," my father said. "I think we're all on board with that, but tell me, in your expert opinion, since you know the law and we obviously do not, what is a best-case and a worst-case scenario?"

"Best case is, they'll have Katrina plead guilty to one of the lesser charges, and since this is her first offense, she would walk with probation as long as she would be willing to cooperate fully, which would mean testifying against Snipes and others within his organization," the lawyer explained.

"And worst case?" my father asked.

"Worst case, with her cooperation, I would say twenty-four months."

"Really?" I said in astonishment as I couldn't even begin to fathom the idea of me doing two years in prison. There would just be no way. I wasn't built for it.

Twenty-nine

I was so totally on pins and needles that I couldn't eat or drink anything. The next day I was scheduled to turn myself in to the authorities and face my indictment.

Throughout the day the telephone in my mother's house kept ringing, and each time the person on the other end would hang up whenever somebody answered.

"I know it's you! You motherfucking bastard! If you got some balls, then bring your black ass to North Carolina!" my father would shout in vain to who we all suspected was Snipes on the line.

"Honey, hang up the phone!" my mother said to my father.

The tension in the house was already so thick that you could cut it with a knife, so all of the harassing prank calls weren't making things any better.

In addition to all of that, that Sunday morning I had also finally decided to come clean to my parents about my possible pregnancy. My mom went to the local drugstore to buy me an EPT, and sure enough, the test turned up positive.

"Katrina, was there any way at all you could have used protection?!" my mother asked, sounding really exacerbated as she fought back tears.

My father had thrown up his hands and just walked out of the room as if he had thrown in the towel and given up.

One of my worst fears had been confirmed. I now knew that I had been impregnated by a man who was wanted and on the run, the same man who I was now supposed to totally turn my back on and tell the authorities everything that I knew about so that they could lock him away for the rest of his natural life.

Whoa! Helping to rat out my future baby's father, now that was a heavy task for me, but I didn't believe in abortion and knew that fully cooperating and snitching on Snipes was my only option. But I also knew that it wasn't going to be easy.

The phone began ringing almost on cue right after my father had thrown up his hands and walked out of the room. It rang like five times and nobody answered it. And then the phone began to ring again and still no one in my house made a move to answer it. I think everyone was still in shock from the result of the pregnancy test.

As the phone began ringing for the third time in a row, I decided to break the mute mood that was in the room and walked over to the phone.

"Hello?" It seemed really weird and somewhat surreal to be answering the phone in my own home simply because I honestly never thought that I would make it back home.

The person on the other end didn't respond. My brain instantly wondered if Snipes was on the other end, and then I wanted to curse myself for having answered the phone in the first place.

"Hellloooo?" I said sarcastically.

There was still some more silence, but then a raspy voice on the other end said, "Katrina, see how you did a nigga dirty?! If you rat on me, trust me, I will have you and your family touched!" Then the person on the other end hung up. I was sure that it was Snipes.

"Katrina, who was that?" my mother asked.

I was nervous but my instinct to still protect Snipes kicked in, and I lied and told my mother that the person never said anything.

The somber night carried on, and it seemed as if the day and the bleak mood would never end. My mother and father had no answers about what to consider or how to proceed with the new revelation that I was pregnant. The only thing that I knew to do was pray.

That I had made it home and away from Snipes had given me a newfound hope in the Lord. So since I'd been home, I'd made it a point to pray every day about my circumstances and everything that was impending.

That same night, I went into the bathroom and closed the door and poured out my heart to God. With the baby fresh on my mind and with me having to give up my freedom the next day, I had a whole lot to pray about to the Lord. That night I prayed harder and longer than I had ever prayed before in my life. Only this time it seemed as if God was silent and not answering. Usually after I poured out my heart to God, I would be still and listen to that voice inside me. That inner voice was God, and He would always reassure me or confirm that things would be alright, but this time I didn't get that confirmation. All I got was dead silence.

On Monday afternoon, June 27, 1994, I was escorted by my lawyer to turn myself in to the FBI. Everything about the experience was surreal and unbelievable.

I was frisked and fingerprinted. My mug shots were taken. I was basically processed and treated like a criminal. My parents were right there with me, and I could tell that with each action that I had to perform, a little piece of their hearts broke off. My father couldn't bear to look when I was being fingerprinted, and my mom shed tears as my mug shots were being snapped.

Thankfully, the people who booked me at the FBI were nice and cordial, making it a bit less humiliating. The entire process reminded me of what I had gone through when I was arrested in New York.

But the big difference was that in New York my arrest had been more like an inconvenience, and in twenty-four hours I was released. This time around, however, a lot longer than twenty-four hours would pass before I would ever taste my freedom again. With each hour that passed, I got more and more nervous about the prospect of regaining my freedom.

Thirty

On Wednesday morning, June 29, 1994, I was feeling extremely sick. At first I thought it was my nerves, since I was preparing to see the judge in about an hour or so. But I quickly realized that my sickness was due to the pregnancy. I was experiencing morning sickness again. I felt I was gonna throw up at any minute. And then the reality of my situation kicked in and hit me in the face like a ton of bricks.

I would have given anything to be able to lie in my own bed and rest and deal with my morning sickness. In fact, I needed to see a gynecologist as soon as I could. After all, I still didn't know exactly how many months pregnant I was, and for the baby's sake, the quicker I could get prenatal care the better off I and the baby would be. Unfortunately, the judicial system didn't think the way I thought, and my pregnancy or my morning sickness was not a high priority on their list of things to take care of.

Before long the correction officers came to my cell to take me to see the judge. I didn't know what to expect as the two male correction officers told me that they had to handcuff me before escorting me.

"Can you handcuff me in front of my body instead of behind my back?" I asked. I explained that I was having morning sickness and felt I would probably throw up at any minute, and if I did, I would like to have the use of my hands.

"Sorry, sweetheart, but we got rules that we have to follow," one of the officers said to me as he put the cuffs on tight as hell and led me by my arm.

They walked me into a courtroom that was half-full with spectators and what I suspected were family members of other criminals and inmates. I was led to where my attorney was standing, but I could only focus on my mother and father, who were seated in the front row. My mother began weeping as soon as she saw me come into the courtroom wearing handcuffs.

At that point I really knew I had let both of my parents down. There was no way they could have envisioned this when they sent me off to NYU. But this is where my bad decisions had landed me.

"I can't believe this is happening," I said to my lawyer.

"Don't be nervous at all," he explained. "This is just your initial appearance, like I explained to you. This is just the real technical part. Nothing to worry about here, I'll do the talking, and if you have to talk, either I or the judge will guide you."

Then the judge, my attorney, and some white lady began talking, and before long the judge began talking directly to me. I immediately took offense to the first words out of his mouth, as he said I had been arrested not too long ago on a minor drug-possession charge, and it appeared I had an "escalating pattern of criminal behavior." He also said it seemed I was lax as to the seriousness of illegal activities, which was something that I really needed to consider.

What the hell are you talking about? I wanted to scream. *Motherfucker, you don't even know me! I'm a college student, not a criminal!*

I held my cool as the judge explained all of my rights. He also read out loud the full indictment against me, along with the affidavits and other documents that had been filed, including my school attendance records, which showed that on the days that I was heading out of town doing things for Snipes, or with Snipes, I had been absent from all of my expensive NYU classes. The police report from my New York misdemeanor drug-possession charge was also included.

I stood there shaking my head as I could not believe that the smallest and the most detailed of things had been included in signed affidavits. Warren had basically dropped dime on every intricacy of my relationship with Snipes. In the affidavit he told how I *knowingly* transported drugs out of state for Snipes as well as transported cash back to New York for him. He also chronicled how much cash Snipes gave me, how I stayed with Snipes in the apartment in Harlem, and how Snipes would give me money to buy clothes. The affidavit went on and on and on and on. The kicker was, Warren swore that after I had been arrested in New York on the misdemeanor charge, from then on I undoubtedly knew that Snipes headed a criminal enterprise and that I still willingly participated.

The sworn statements from the FBI agents who had questioned me in the hotel parking lot in Virginia were also included. That was damaging because it clearly showed that I had knowingly and willingly lied to federal authorities, and it also corroborated Warren's statements by pinpointing the days and the mode of transportation when I had *unknowingly* transported kilos of cocaine to Virginia in a vehicle that was registered to Snipes.

"I can't believe this," I whispered in my lawyer's ear. "Warren is dead and—"

My lawyer cut me off and told me to just listen and not to worry.

It was easy for him not to worry because the accusations weren't being made against him.

Say something! I wanted to scream at my lawyer. *Talk about the beatings that Snipes gave me. Tell them that I didn't know drugs were in the car! Say something, asshole!*

The judge then explained that since my alleged offenses had

occurred in New York and in districts outside North Carolina, my prosecution should be transferred to another district. But he then informed me that based on my attorney's discussions with the prosecution from the district that we were in and in the district in New York and my pending guilty plea, consent to transfer prosecution to North Carolina had been granted, and he asked me if I understood.

"What the hell is he talking about?" I whispered to my attorney.

"Yes, Your Honor, she understands," my lawyer spoke up for me.

I wanted to kick him in his balls because that was not what I had said, and things were moving so quickly and I didn't understand what the hell was happening, and it was getting extremely frustrating. Not to mention I felt like I really had to throw up due to the morning sickness.

The prosecutor then explained to the judge that she had been informed by my counsel that I was prepared to enter into plea discussions, and therefore she asked that arraignment be set for one week from the current date.

"Mr. Pittershawn, can you please let me know what all of this means?!" I asked sternly. This time I wasn't whispering.

"This is what we spoke about in my office with your parents," he briefly said.

Oh, gee, thanks! That really clears up the confusion, I wanted to say.

The judge then stated that my bail had been set at half a million dollars, and he asked if I was prepared to post bail.

"No, she's not, Your Honor."

Soon after that I heard the judge's gavel being tapped, and he said a few more words that I didn't understand.

I looked back at my mom and she had stopped crying. Then I looked at my dad, and he nodded to me but showed no emotion. Then, like a flash, things were over and people began milling around. A court officer came up to me and grabbed me by my arm and began leading me off to the same two correction officers that had escorted me into the courtroom.

"I'll be by on Friday to discuss some things with you," my lawyer said

as he briskly stuffed papers into his leather briefcase and prepared to leave the courtroom.

I tried to turn to see if he had stopped to speak to my parents, but I was instructed to keep walking. Actually I was told, *"Hurry your ass up and walk!"*

Later that night as I sat in my cell, I heard that *voice* again. It had come back to me to tell me, *The sun always comes out after the storm.*

And what does that mean? I asked the voice.

I sat there and waited and waited for the voice to explain what it meant. I got no answer and soon the lights were out. I silently hoped that the hours would quickly pass by so that I could regain my freedom. I thought about my baby before I went to sleep and wondered who the baby would look like and what it would feel like to be called Mommy. I was definitely beginning to develop an emotional connection with my baby.

I also thought about Snipes. I wondered if he was okay, and for some odd reason I still had to block out the thought that I had betrayed Snipes by abandoning him. But more important, I wondered if Snipes would make good on his promise to harm my family. After all, I had seen firsthand what he had done to Warren and Alexis.

Thirty-one

"Daddy, I just want this whole thing to end so I can come home and get on with my life," I said to my father over the phone, expressing how unhappy I was with Mr. Pittershawn.

"Baby, I know it's frustrating. And believe me, we want you home too, but we have to be patient and let things just run their course. We'll enter the plea on Wednesday, and you should be home, Lord willing, this week if everything goes the way we all think it will."

It was Friday, July 1, when I spoke to my father. My lawyer was supposed to come by to see me, but he explained to my parents that he wouldn't be able to see me until that following Tuesday, being that Monday was July the Fourth.

"See, Daddy, that's exactly what I mean. It's like my case is not a priority to him!" I vented. "Oh, hold on a minute." I spit into a stack of napkins. Lately I had been throwing up a lot, and I would usually spit a few times before I threw up, so I knew what was about to come.

My father told me not to look at it that way. He tried to lift my spirits by explaining that Mr. Pittershawn and the prosecutors had been speaking, and that my case was pretty simple and that reaching an equitable agreement wouldn't be a problem. He also told me that according to the lawyer, there was really nothing for the lawyer to discuss with me at this stage since everything was just a matter of procedure.

"Baby girl, they don't want to lock you up. They want to lock up Snipes. Just remember that, okay? Don't worry, because when you worry, it upsets Patricia, and with her blood pressure and all, she don't need to be worrying and running it up."

I just hoped he was right. I guess I just wanted to hurry up and get the assurances that I would be handed probation and allowed to continue with my life like the lawyer said I would.

When I hung up from my father, I sat and thought about everything. What was it that really had me sitting in jail? What was it about me that allowed me to make such horrible decisions and get so wrapped up in a person like Snipes? Or was all of this a part of God's much bigger plan that would later be revealed to me?

One thing that I quickly learned to hate about being locked up was that time seemed to drag. Seconds would feel like hours, and days would feel like years. And I knew that I couldn't take much more of this being-locked-up shit.

The holiday weekend was coming and I was not looking forward to spending it locked up. Unfortunately, there was not a damn thing I could do about speeding up time. The only thing that I could do to speed things up was sleep. Sleeping seemed to be my answer to not consciously thinking or dealing with what I was facing, so I found myself trying to sleep as much as I possibly could.

That Friday night I went to sleep around eight thirty. I had the weirdest and wildest dream. I felt like I was paralyzed in the dream. I remember trying to consciously wake up so that the dream could end, but no matter how hard I tried, I just couldn't.

In the dream I had run away from the hotel room that Snipes and I were sharing, but we were in a city that the two of us had never been to,

Las Vegas. As I ran from Snipes, he started chasing me in just his boxer shorts and his wifebeater, and I was running full speed until I reached this open hotel room that wasn't our room, but I ran inside it anyway. I shut the door behind me and hoped that Snipes hadn't seen me run inside. I ran into the bathroom and I peeked from behind the bathroom door, then all of a sudden Snipes kicked in the main door to the hotel room and began calling out my name.

"Katrina! Where you at, Katrina?!"

My heart was pounding a mile a minute, and this is when I was trying to wake myself from the dream because Snipes had a gun in his hand and I knew he was gonna come inside the bathroom to kill me. But I could not move. I was frozen stiff.

"Katrina, I know you in here, bitch!" Snipes yelled again in the dream as I continued to peek from behind the bathroom door.

I felt as if I was going to pee on myself from the fear.

"Why you running from me, girl?!" Snipes asked in the dream.

Then from out of nowhere two black guys came into the hotel room.

"There go that bitch-ass nigga!" the taller of the two guys said as he raised his gun and began firing at Snipes.

The bullets hit Snipes right in his torso, and he spun around and fell to the ground. The gunmen both walked up to him and stood over him and opened fired on him.

In the dream I tried my hardest to scream but couldn't. I saw bullets entering Snipes's body at a rapid pace, and I heard him grunting in pain as each bullet entered, leaving huge holes in his flesh.

"Stupid mothafucka!" the other guy yelled at Snipes as he shot him one last time before checking his pockets and robbing him of his money. The two gunmen then quickly ran out of the room after rolling Snipes onto his back so that they could see his face and make sure that he was dead. When I was sure that the gunmen were gone, I ran out of the bathroom, scared. I wanted to run out of the hotel room altogether, but for some reason I couldn't just leave Snipes like that, so I ran over to him.

"Why you run from me, baby?" Snipes whispered as he coughed up blood. Surprisingly, he was still alive.

I started crying and told Snipes that I was sorry and that I was gonna go and call for help.

"No, don't leave me, Katrina!" he struggled to say as he reached out and tried to grab my hand.

"I'm not gonna leave you," I said through my tears. "I just wanna go and call an ambulance."

Snipes gripped my hand a bit tighter, but I could tell that he had no strength left in his body.

"No, don't leave me. You see what they did to me? If you hadn't left me . . ." As Snipes said those final words, he completely loosened his grip and his hand fell to the floor. His whole body went limp and his eyeballs rolled into the back of his head.

"Snipes! Baby, wake up, baby! I'm gonna call for help!" I desperately pleaded as I knelt down and shook his body. While my heart raced fast, I stood up and tried to locate the phone. I tripped over Snipes's body and landed right next to him. I was now face-to-face with his dead, bullet-riddled body, and I watched in horror as blood slowly seeped out of the corner of his mouth. I screamed hysterically as I quickly tried to get to my feet.

"Ohhhh!" I yelled, and gasped as I quickly sat up. I looked around my cell wide-eyed as my heart pounded and jumped out of my chest.

It took me a while to realize where I was. But it took me even longer to realize that it was *just* a dream. My hands instantly went to hold my belly. It wasn't hurting nor was I feeling nauseous, but for some reason I held it tight.

It was just a dream, Katrina.

That was what I told myself. But because of the realness of the dream, I was so spooked that I could not go back to sleep. And each time I tried to close my eyes, that picture of Snipes's bloody body kept reappearing in my mind.

Thirty-two

The following Monday morning, on the Fourth of July, when I phoned my father, he seemed upbeat, but I could tell that he wasn't his normal self, and it didn't take long for him to relay what was on his mind.

"So I take it that you haven't spoken to Mr. Pittershawn?"

"No. Why?" I asked nervously, anticipating the worst.

"Well, he called us over the weekend and let us know that he'd been contacted by the state police. They have information on Snipes."

"They caught up with him?" I asked in a high-pitched tone that masked some disappointment. A part of me didn't want them to find him.

"Well, actually they found him dead in a Las Vegas hotel room—"

"What?!" I yelled, cutting off my father as my heart dropped to my feet. "Daddy, are you serious?" My body began to shake uncontrollably.

"They say it was a drug deal gone bad. From the looks of things, that is what they are theorizing at this point."

"When did this happen?" I instinctively held my stomach.

"From what they gather, he's been dead since Thursday night."

I wanted to drop the phone because I couldn't believe it had been the day after Snipes had been killed that I had the dream he'd been killed.

"God showed me that in a dream the other night," I said blankly and softly.

"What?"

"Or maybe that was Snipes's spirit talking to mines," I said even softer.

"What are you talking about?"

I explained to my father about the dream that I had had on Friday night, especially the words that Snipes spoke to me in the dream.

"Daddy, that's not a coincidence," I said as my heart began beating rapidly.

Before my father could say anything, I heard that little voice inside me say again, *The sun always comes out after the storm.*

"No, it's not a coincidence at all," my father confirmed.

I wasn't sure what to think about the news about Snipes. In fact, I was too numb to think. A part of me was mad at Snipes. I was mad because I saw it like it wasn't fair how he popped into my life and caused so much drama and destruction and then he up and got killed. He would never have to deal with any consequences of his actions, or even be around in any way, shape, or form for his baby. It was like getting killed was the easy way out. However, I was also comforted that my parents and my family would be much safer now that Snipes was out of the picture. But I could sense that even with Snipes gone, I personally wouldn't be any safer.

And the knowledge of his death didn't make me feel any sense of relief either.

Thirty-three

T he day before my next scheduled court appearance, my lawyer showed up to speak to me. And right off the bat I didn't like the nervous, unsure vibe that I was getting from him as we sat in a small closet-like conference room.

"So, Katrina, we're in the homestretch right now," Mr. Pittershawn said with a half smile as he reached into his briefcase and pulled out some papers and handed them to me. "This is the plea agreement that we were able to work out. Read it over and sign it, and I'll answer any questions that you may have."

I slowly read the agreement, and as the words began to look familiar, I tried to read faster to get to the point that covered the *agreement*. I read and read as fast as I could, but I only seemed to be reading language that looked similar to that in the indictment.

"*This* is the plea agreement?" I asked, confused.

"Yes," Mr. Pittershawn nonchalantly answered as he sat across from me.

"But this just seems like wording that was in my indictment. I thought it would talk about me getting probation and things like that."

Mr. Pittershawn sighed. "Well, this is what the prosecutor is putting on the table as of early this morning."

"I don't know about this?" I said instinctively. I could tell that something wasn't right.

"Well, Katrina, after your guilty plea, then what will happen is the sentencing will be set by the sentencing guidelines and—"

I cut Mr. Pittershawn off and told him that I didn't need him talking all technical to me and that I needed him to be straight up with me. I was shocked that I was so ticked off, but then again I allowed myself to be ticked off because, after all, this was my life. So I had a right to be ticked off and demanding. The man who was supposed to be stepping up to the plate and protecting my life just wasn't cutting it.

"Did you speak to my parents about this? What exactly does this mean? Are you sure I should sign *this* agreement? I'm scared! This just doesn't seem right to me," I vented, rapid-fire.

There was silence as I sat behind steel bars and spoke to my attorney, who was fidgeting in his chair.

"Yes, I spoke to your parents, and I told them the same thing that I'll tell you."

"And that is?" I asked sarcastically but attentively.

"I'm scared of this. It scares the shit out of me."

"What the fuck?!" I yelled. *"You're my lawyer and you're telling me that you're scared?"*

I closed my eyes and bowed my head and blew out some air. Without making eye contact, I asked, "Okay, so basically then, realistically, I'm looking at the worst-case twenty-four-month scenario?" I tried my hardest to make sense of everything that was going on.

All I wanted was to know the reality of my situation, exactly what I was facing, so that I could deal with it and not be in for some kind of emotional letdown.

"Yeah, it's definitely a worst-case scenario *now*," he said.

"So are you sure I should sign this agreement since its not really guaranteeing anything with the way it reads?"

Mr. Pittershawn nodded, and with much frustration and no more hesitation, I quickly John Hancocked the agreement, hoping that I was doing the right thing. I slid the signed papers to my lawyer and remained silent.

He rubbed his head and informed me that tomorrow's day in court would be pretty straightforward. I would enter my guilty plea, then we would discuss the terms of the agreement with the judge and the prosecutor.

"And then?" I eagerly asked. But before my lawyer could answer, I spoke up in frustration, "Why does it feel like I have to pull shit outta you? I already told you just be straight up with me!"

Mr. Pittershawn blew out some air before saying, "Katrina, I am being straight up with you. What is it that you want to hear?"

I shook my head. "Okay, and after we discuss the terms of the agreement with the judge and the prosecutor, what happens after that?"

"And then we hope for the best," Mr. Pittershawn replied nonchalantly.

At the sound of those words I just dropped my head and began mentally trying to come to grips with having to do twenty-four months in jail. I would be lying if I said that I wasn't starting to have a minor nervous breakdown and a panic attack all in one. I was stressing out because I hadn't done anything that warranted two years of jail time. And now with a terrified, unconfident, and incompetent lawyer, I knew that I was gonna more than likely be screwed with no Vaseline.

"Katrina, what you have to understand is that Snipes was the kingpin and that was our bargaining chip. We're plea-*bargaining*, with an emphasis on the word *bargain*. We help the government get what they want, and in return they bend and help us with what we want. It would be a *bargain* for them to give you up and let you go free if they could get a hardened and violent criminal on the level of Snipes's caliber. They would easily trade a first-time nonviolent offender such as yourself for a violent career criminal such as Dwight Abrams. But as of last week when he was found dead, he basically became useless to them in their prosecutorial efforts. Snipes was our ace in the hole. And now if they can't get the kingpin, I am sure that their thinking is, 'Well, let's get the queen bee instead.'" Mr. Pittershawn was finally speaking in a way in which I could understand.

Tears began forming in my eyes as I started crying and pouring out my heart to him.

"But I'm not a criminal, and I wasn't the *queen* of no criminal enterprise. At best, I was a good girl gone bad because of some bad decisions I'd made." I paused and wiped tears from my eyes before continuing.

"It's not fair! For real, Mr. Pittershawn, this shit ain't fair! I didn't benefit from the life that Snipes led! Okay, yeah, he gave me a couple of dollars here and there, and he bought me nice clothes and shoes and bags, but that's it! At the end of the day, I was the victim, not a queen bee! What queen bee do you know that constantly gets her ass whupped? He controlled me with fear and intimidation! My only crime was befriending him, but how could I be faulted for that? I was just a freshman in college, I was a good girl and I didn't know any better. I'm a small-town girl that was thrown into a big city and I—"

Mr. Pittershawn stood up and cut me off in midsentence, "Katrina, I understand you and I believe you. Believe me I do. But at this point we just have to hope for the best, and everything will work out."

With those words, the prison guard stuck his head into the tiny conference room and told us that our time was up. My lawyer then made his way out to take care of other business.

I stood up to be escorted back to my cell. As I walked back, I wondered, what in the hell was it that I had just signed? Mr. Pittershawn's words had given me a headache as they kept replaying in my mind over and over.

If they can't get the kingpin, I am sure that their thinking is, "Well, let's get the queen bee instead."

Thirty-four

On Wednesday morning, I made my way to the courtroom, where I saw my mother and father along with my uncle. They were already seated in the front row of the pretty empty courtroom. I was led over to the defense table, where my lawyer and junior attorney who worked for Mr. Pittershawn were seated.

I saw the prosecutor seated at her table with an unreadable poker face. I also noticed a young, black, female court reporter that looked as if she could have been my college schoolmate. For some reason, I noticed every detail inside the modern-looking, newly renovated courtroom.

My eyes were soon fixed outside through the window, and I noticed that it appeared to be extremely bright and sunny, and from the looks of the tree leaves slightly swaying in the wind, I figured there was also a slight breeze. It appeared to be a picture-perfect day.

I wished that I felt picture-perfect, but I was a ball of nerves. Both of my hands were shaking and I felt cold as if I were outside on a winter day with no coat.

As I sat next to my lawyer, he explained how things would work. He informed me that the judge was going to go over a bunch of things with me to make sure that I understood everything and was in agreement.

"It shouldn't take long at all. You'll be fine, Katrina," my lawyer said. Thank God he was finally exhibiting some confidence because that made me feel a whole lot more relieved.

I had my head down on the defense table and was praying, but I was soon interrupted by the booming, deep Barry White type of voice of a court officer as he instructed everyone to rise for the Honorable Judge Gerald. Judge Gerald was the same judge from my initial court appearance.

I stood and my lawyer grabbed my hand. He assured me again that things would be okay and that I didn't need to be nervous. Again his confidence seemed to do wonders for me and my cold, clammy hands.

A lady spoke and I tilted my head down, silently praying and hoping. Then I repeatedly said the name Jesus, over and over and over. I tuned out and wasn't paying attention to anything that the prosecutor or the judge or anyone else was saying. I wanted to totally concentrate and try my hardest to connect with God so that He would pull me through and I could get on with the rest of my life.

My prayer was interrupted as I had to raise my right hand and be placed under oath. Then the judge addressed me by my full name and told me something about perjury and making false statements and the government's right to use against me any statements that I gave under oath.

Then he asked me if I understood that I had the right to plead not guilty.

"Yes, Your Honor, I understand that," I said in the most articulate and polite voice that I could muster up through my nervousness.

Then he asked me if I understood that I had the right to a jury trial.

"Yes, Your Honor, I understand that."

Then he informed me that I had the right to be represented by counsel of my choice, and if necessary, I could have the court appoint counsel at trial and at every stage of the proceedings if I chose to go that judicial route. The judge went on and on explaining to me that at trial I would have the right to confront and cross-examine adverse witnesses, and he explained more about the judicial process and my overall rights.

"Now, Ms. Easely, you understand that you would be voluntarily waiving these trial rights if the court accepts from you a plea of guilty?"

"Yes, Your Honor, I understand that as well." My heart began beating rapidly and my stomach felt funny.

The judge then made sure that I was aware of the charges against me in the plea agreement. And I quickly told him that I was aware.

I had been indicted for a number of things, but under the plea agreement the government would waive their right to prosecute me for all of the offenses as long as I pled guilty to the charges of criminal possession of a controlled substance and lying to a federal agent.

After I answered the judge, he looked through some papers and seemed a bit fidgety and uneasy or a bit uncertain about something. Then he took off his glasses and held them in his right hand. He looked at me and resumed talking. He explained to me the maximum penalty for the crimes that I was admitting to as well as the mandatory minimum penalty.

This is when my heart really began pounding and I looked dead at my lawyer, but he would not look at me. All I knew was that the judge was *not* talking about no probation to twenty-four months' jail time. Nah, his numbers were a hell of a lot higher! He was talking *football numbers* in the range of twenty-five years to life!

I didn't want to be rude to the judge, so I turned my head back in his direction and nervously continued to pay attention to him as he spoke.

The judge rambled on and on, speaking and explaining something about the court's obligation to stick to and apply the sentencing guidelines. Then as he also explained the court's discretion to depart from the sentencing guidelines under some circumstances, I felt a bit more at ease.

Finally the judge said something that my lawyer had explained to both me and my parents. Under the circumstances of me being a first-time nonviolent offender, the judge could use his discretion and his legal power and not sentence me under the sentencing guidelines, but rather just give me a slap on the wrist with probation or at worst twenty-four months.

"And, Ms. Easely, you also understand that under the terms of your plea agreement that you are voluntarily waiving your right to appeal or to collaterally attack the sentence?" the judge asked me in a firm and stern tone.

I didn't answer his question because that had never been explained to me, and I wasn't exactly sure what the judge meant. I immediately looked at my lawyer, and he nodded, indicating that it was okay to answer the judge with a *Yes, I understand.*

"Ms. Easely?" the judge called in a tone that said he didn't have all day for me to answer.

"What is he talking about?" I whispered into Mr. Pittershawn's ear.

"It's okay to waive those rights. It's just like the other rights that you waived by entering a plea agreement. It's pretty much standard procedure," he explained. But I still couldn't grasp what was happening.

Katrina! that voice inside me yelled to get my attention.

"Ms. Easely, do you understand?" the judge demanded.

Katrina! the voice called out to me, and I desperately wanted to answer it but there was no time.

"Y-yes, Y-yyour H-honor, I understand," I softly replied.

I turned and looked at my parents, and my father looked pissed off as hell. I could tell he wanted to say something, but he seemed to be holding his tongue.

The judge then addressed the prosecutor and then my attorney, and they exchanged a bunch of legal talk that I didn't understand. I figured I might as well go back to praying because it appeared as if things were just about wrapping up.

Katrina, this is gonna all be over in a few minutes and you'll be going home, I told myself, trying my best to stay positive. I was still nervous, so I tried to think of anything that would take my mind off the stress at hand. And all I could think about was how I was going to have my mother cook some pork ribs and drown them in barbecue sauce, along with collard greens, black-eyed peas, rice, corn bread, and sweet potato pie.

Just pig out when you get home, girl, because this nightmare will finally be over, I told myself as I chuckled.

Then the judge spoke and got my attention.

He told me that the court had decided to accept my plea of guilty under the terms of the plea agreement.

Okay, good, I thought as my anxiety subsided.

Then he mouthed words that I would never forget and that would always ring in my mind.

"Ms. Easely, I've seen numerous men and women such as yourself come into my courtroom after having had a prior brush with the law, no matter how big or small. And the fact still remains that laws are designed to serve as deterrents for certain behaviors. And in your case, after your arrest in Brooklyn, New York, which was not that long ago, you obviously still found no restraints for your activities, and it seems as if that minor arrest didn't deter you from your future involvement with the same world of controlled substances. In fact, if anything, it seems as if that minor arrest taught you to try to be smarter and wiser and try to outwit the law by consciously lying to federal agents. It appears that if your behavior is not curbed and the laws are not enforced, that you will only repeat your *escalating pattern of criminal behavior.* And I am afraid that the consequences to society might be grave and irreversible if your pattern of criminal behavior were to escalate. Ms. Easely, with those factors in mind, along with your admission of guilt to the violation of Title 21, Section 812, criminal possession of two hundred ounces of cocaine, a controlled substance, and in accordance with the federal sentencing guidelines, I hereby inform the court that you start serving immediately a minimum sentence of no less than twenty-fours years in a United States federal penitentiary. . . ."

The judge said something else about me serving an additional year for lying to federal authorities, but my head instantly started ringing and my hands began violently shaking as I looked at my lawyer and asked him to explain what was going on.

"Mr. Pittershawn!" I yelled since it seemed like I could not get his attention.

I then heard my father and my uncle yelling and cursing in the background, and my mother was wailing as the judge repeatedly slammed his gavel down and tried to get them to be quiet.

Two court officers approached me and attempted to put handcuffs on me, but I violently swung my arms free and screamed for them to get off me.

"I didn't do anything!" I yelled hysterically in the courtroom.

The judge continued to slam down his gavel, while my lawyer quickly packed up his things.

"Get off of meeeeee!!!" I screamed at the court officers as one of them was able to place one of my wrists inside the handcuffs.

I then looked at the white female prosecutor who had had the poker face all during the proceeding, and she stood and stared at me. And while she stared at me, I was one hundred percent certain that I saw that white bitch smiling like something was comical!

Such rage ran through my body when I saw her smiling that I instantly started screaming like I was being attacked or gang-raped or something. I remember pushing past one of the court officers and charging at the prosecutor, but I was violently yanked to the ground by the court officer who was holding the other end of the handcuff that was on one of my wrists.

There was a bunch of commotion inside the courtroom that I couldn't make out, nor was I trying to make sense of any of it. I was simply trying to get my hands on someone so that I could kill somebody for doing me so unjustly.

Then for some strange reason my mind thought back to the night in the stairwell of my college dorm when Snipes was forcing himself inside me. I remembered my hands being tied behind my back with the leather belt and the burning and tearing sensation that I felt from Snipes ripping into my vagina.

My heart was pounding incredibly fast as I lay on the dusty courtroom floor fighting off the court officers and screaming and hyperventilating. And then suddenly I didn't remember a thing as right there on the courtroom floor I blacked out in defeat.

Physically, mentally, and emotionally, I was defeated.

Thirty-five

T he best way to describe my mental state during the weeks that followed is to say that I was *extremely* suicidal. I was also depressed, angry, bitter, sad, and confused. Although I wanted to eat, I simply
could not bring myself to eat anything and I was losing an awful
amount of weight. Realizing that I was nineteen years old and that I
would not be getting out of prison until I was in my forties, well, I think
it is safe to say that a thought like that would take away just about anyone's appetite, especially someone who had been railroaded by an incompetent lawyer.

The bright green prison pants and bright green prison shirts that I
had been issued when I first arrived about six weeks earlier barely
stayed on my body, sagging and drooping due to my weight loss.

Although I couldn't believe it, the reality was that I had been shipped
off to a federal prison for women in West Virginia. That is where I, inmate number 63284-910, would begin serving my twenty-five-year term.

Not a minute of the day went by when I did not think about my freedom, think about Snipes, think about the baby that I was carrying, and think about all of the things that had led up to my ending up caged like some damn animal.

Immediately upon my arrival at the prison, I went into a shell of my own world. I wouldn't let anyone into it either. I had no plans on ever letting anyone into my world, which meant that I planned on staying to myself for the duration of my bid. It was gonna be just me and my baby, and in some respects it was good because it allowed me to bond with the baby, as I would just talk to my baby as if the baby were born and could talk back.

"Mommy is so stressed out," I said, talking out loud.

"You don't even care, do you?" I added with a smile.

Of course there would be no answer, but in my head I would hear the baby talking back to me.

"Yeah, I know I gotta eat better, you getting bigger and my stomach is getting bigger, but I ain't eating the way I should be because I just be so depressed that I can't eat anything. Mommy is confused, Mommy is scared, and you're gonna be Mommy's first baby so I don't even know what to expect." I paused, feeling myself tearing up.

"You think I'll be a good mommy?" I asked. And right after I asked that question, I felt the baby kick for the first time.

"Oh my God!" I screamed out loud. "You answered me." I couldn't believe that I had felt the baby kick for the first time, and I definitely took that as a sign from God that things would be okay.

"Do that again," I said as I rubbed my stomach, and sure enough, the baby kicked again.

And instantly I teared up again because the connection between me and my baby was real, and it had just gotten so much stronger because I knew that I could communicate with my baby. And I felt horrible for even having contemplated aborting my baby. I had always been against abortion, and I never even wanted to consider it an option, but with the stress and the uncertainty of life behind bars, I have to admit that I did think about aborting my child because I didn't think I had the courage to endure it.

But those kicks from the baby helped to cement in my mind that there was no way in the world that I could abort my precious baby.

My parents had been to see me every weekend for the past six weeks, but I was trying my best to figure out a way to make them stop coming. I had already done enough to ruin their lives, and I had been more than a big enough burden on them. So to have them missing work and spending money traveling to West Virginia to see me, and spending money on me in general, well, I couldn't allow it to continue.

Besides, whenever my parents would come to see me or whenever I would talk to them on the phone, all they would talk about was my case and what they had done, what they should have done, and what they would now try to do to get me out of my predicament.

As for me, I just wanted to deal with reality, and the reality was that I had literally signed off on allowing the government to railroad me—I had waived my rights to appeal my case and my sentence. So I knew that my parents could talk all the talk that they wanted to talk, and even if they had the money to pay the best lawyer in the world, which they didn't, no matter what, my black ass was gonna be stuck in prison for the next quarter century. That was my reality. And with no possibility of parole, I knew that I would not be a free woman again until sometime during the year 2019.

I realized that I was at my lowest point the night I thought about purposely killing my baby, for two reasons. The first reason was so I would get sent to a hospital and could possibly escape while I was being transported. And the second reason that I insanely rationalized was that if I killed my baby, then I would be a murderer, and at least then my twenty-five-year sentence would be justified.

But the thought of harming my baby stayed with me throughout the night and the next morning.

If you could just get your hands on a wire hanger or something like that, that would be all that you'd need. I was truly beginning to go stir-crazy.

Thank God, as I sat with my insane thoughts of murdering my baby, out of the blue I was told by one of the guards that I had a visitor. That was a complete shock to me because it wasn't the weekend, so I had really not been expecting anybody to come see me.

Escorted by a corrections officer, I made my way to the visiting area and scanned the room looking for someone I knew. Finally I saw my college roommate, Candace! My eyes got wide and I didn't know what to think as I walked over to her and prepared to sit down.

"Hey, girrrl!" Candace said with tons of compassion. She hugged me and then just stared at me. She looked at me for about thirty seconds straight without saying a word, but her look showed me that she cared about me.

As we sat down, Candace would not look me in the face. She bowed her head as if she were looking at the floor and seemed to be in deep thought.

I didn't know what to say, and I still didn't know what to think. I mean, for the entire time that I had been locked up in West Virginia, I hadn't held one conversation with anybody, not one. Not with the guards, not with the other inmates, nobody other than my mother and father. And even with my mother and father most of my talk with them was limited to terse one-word answers.

But as I sat across from Candace, I finally started to *feel* again. I didn't feel much, but I felt some hope or something stir up inside me. Yet I still didn't know what to say to her.

Candace finally lifted her head, but she immediately covered her face with her left hand and began slightly stroking her face with it.

Finally Candace removed her hand from her face and I could see how watery her eyes were and I knew that she had been holding back tears.

"Katrina, I just wanna say that *I love you soooo* much!" Candace's voice cracked as she attempted to emphasize her words. Then she blew out some air and shook her head but did not look me in my face.

What had been really weird was that with all of the emotions that I had gone through since arriving at prison, I had never allowed myself to cry. In fact it was like I had refused to cry. I had been depressed and suicidal, but part of me felt I had been so wronged, and therefore I guess I was just too mad to cry, a genuine, get-it-all-out-of-your-system-and-grieve-this-whole-experience kind of cry.

But when I heard the authenticity in Candace's words, with her voice cracking and her telling me that she loved me, something inside me unlocked, and for the first time since I had come to West Virginia to do my time, the tears began to fall from my eyes like a river.

"I love you too, Candace," I said as I wiped my tears with my right hand. "You surprised me." Then for the first time since I'd been in prison, I cracked a partial smile and just looked at Candace and how good she looked.

She appeared to have lost a *whole* lot of weight. In fact she looked to have gone from a size 18 to a size 10! Candace also had a short haircut that was similar to the way the singer Toni Braxton used to wear her hair.

"You look good, Candace," I said, starting to gather myself.

"Girl, please." Candace smiled and just looked at me.

There was some awkward silence on both our parts, but more so from me because I knew that I felt way more uncomfortable than Candace.

"So you must have spoken to my mom," I said to Candace.

"Yeah, I did." Candace sighed. "Katrina, look, I can't even begin to imagine what you are dealing with, and I want you to know that when I said that I love you, I *really* meant that. I mean I know that we only met each other last September, and we were really only rooming together for like three or four months, and we have had our little minor issues here and there, but for real I love you and I care about you, Katrina! I really do. And I also want you to know that I'm not gonna judge you or speak down to you or anything like that. The only thing I'm gonna do, and I promise you this, is I'm gonna be here for you. Just know that no matter what, I got you. You can call me whenever you want, you can write me all the time, and I'll see you as much as I possibly can. And I'm not just saying that to say it. I mean it!"

I blew out some air and then thanked Candace for her words. I paused before continuing, and the tears began to fall from my eyes again.

"Candace, I'm just angry, I'm confused, I'm bitter, I'm sad, and I really feel suicidal!" I guess my tears made her tears begin to fall. "I didn't even do anything wrong, Candace! Nothing! It's just so not fair that I'm locked up like this!" I said in a loud, angry whisper as I pointed to the room walls and pulled on my prison-issue garb.

"I know. You're absolutely right, Katrina." Candace nodded. "But you know what? You also have the right to feel any type of emotions that you need to feel. And like I said, I know that I can't even begin to imagine what it is that you are dealing with. I just can't." She shook her head. "But there was one thing my pastor said this past Sunday at church, and I think it makes so much sense. He was quoting Dr. Martin Luther King Jr. and he said, 'Truth that is crushed to the ground will always rise again!' And, Katrina, you will rise from this. I promise you," Candace said with so much conviction.

"Candace, but I don't even have a shot at parole! This is it for me for the next twenty-five years!" I said in despair and defeat as I tugged on my prison shirt.

"Fuck that, Katrina! You know what you have?" Candace asked rhetorically. "You have hope and you have faith! And as long as you don't let go of those two things, then you will be okay. You're gonna get outta here because you don't deserve to be here! The *truth* is you didn't do anything wrong to put you here! You are truth, Katrina, and truth that is crushed to the ground will always rise again! Remember that."

I mentally filed that saying into my brain as I wanted to remember exactly what Candace had said.

Candace's coming to see me was just what I needed. And while Candace spoke to me, that little voice inside me returned and told me that God had sent Candace to see me to lift my spirits. And then the voice reminded me once again, *The sun always comes out after the storm.*

"You don't know what you did for me by coming to see me, Candace," I told her as I knew that we would soon have to wrap up her visit.

But before she left, and although she never asked me to recap anything, I made sure that I filled her in on how right she had been about Snipes. I told her about the time that I had gotten arrested at his brother's house and how that minor arrest had come back to haunt me in my indictment and in the judge's decision to send me away for so long. I told her how Snipes had killed Warren and Alexis and then taken me to see their dead bodies. I told her about all of the beatings and the hell that I had lived through for the six months that I was on the run with Snipes. One thing that I was sure to tell her was that the short-lived money that Snipes had given me here and there, the clothes, the bags, the parties, the drinking, and all of that were definitely not worth it. Not one bit!

Candace listened in disbelief and anger. She told me that a lot of what I was telling her, my mom had already filled her in on. And Candace was so angry at herself for not having done more to shield me from Snipes. She was extremely pissed off that she had allowed me to let Snipes off the hook that first time he had beaten me, because had I not, my relationship with him could have played itself out in an entirely different way.

Visiting hours were up and Candace promised me that she would come back and see me in two weeks. While we both didn't want the visit to end, I think we were both elated that the visit had indeed ended on a positive note with me informing Candace about my pregnancy.

"Can't you tell?" I asked her as I pressed my baggy shirt up against my stomach to reveal my round belly. My stomach had started to show as of late.

"Katrina?" Candace gasped as she held her hand over her mouth. "Call me and fill me in," she continued as the corrections officer politely escorted her out.

"Okay," I yelled back.

"And you know I'm the godmother, the auntie, all of that!" Candace yelled with her somewhat ghetto Philadelphia accent.

"Okay," I yelled back, and smiled.

I couldn't believe how much my spirits had been lifted. It was scary thinking that just hours earlier I had seriously considered murdering my baby.

I held my growing stomach and realized that there was no way on God's green earth that I could *ever* harm the innocent, precious life that was growing inside me. Right then and there I decided that my life was not over. If anything, I had a baby to look forward to giving birth to and raising. My baby had no control over who his or her daddy was, nor did my baby have any control over my being in prison. But at the end of the day none of that mattered. The only thing that mattered was that I had a baby to live for!

Thirty-six

I t was September and it had been about one month since Candace had come to visit me. As I lay in my bed contemplating many different things, I couldn't help but realize how ironic it was that Candace was now in her sophomore year at New York University, while I was entering my third trimester of pregnancy and locked behind bars in a West Virginia federal prison. What a difference a year had made.

Yeah, it had been one year, almost to the day, since I had met Snipes, and so much was different. A year ago I had thought I'd met Prince Charming and was wondering how I'd come to be so lucky to meet a man such as Snipes. But now Snipes, the ex-hustler, ex-murderer, and ex-fugitive, was dead, and I was more than six months pregnant with his baby. I figured that I was actually seven months but I was not certain.

Since I'd been in custody, I had only been to see the doctor twice. The first time was for a physical exam that was mandatory for all inmates, and the second time was when I was examined by a gynecologist who had given me a sonogram and prescribed me some big-ass horse pills that I was supposed to take every day. Other than that, I had had no prenatal care.

I figured that once I got closer to my ninth month I would be taken to see the doctor more regularly to ensure that everything was going smoothly. But that didn't happen. There was only one sonogram check, and even then they didn't give me the pictures to keep. I was given no expected delivery date, nor was I told what the sex of my baby would be, none of that mushy stuff that makes pregnancy exciting. I was just treated like a criminal who had some sort of abnormal growth in her stomach.

My mother and father both raised as much hell as they could for the prison system to get me more medical treatment, but their pleas and cries fell on deaf ears. I was now property of the federal government, and the government made it clear that they were going to spend the least amount of money possible to care for my ass, no matter how many months pregnant I was.

Fortunately for me, I had begun to mingle more with the other inmates, and I was slowly but surely regaining my sanity and coming out of the depression that I had been in since I had been sentenced. And as my mental state got stronger, my appetite started to come back and I began eating a lot more. I still didn't look huge like a lot of pregnant women can look, but I was putting on more weight and my belly was getting rounder with each passing day.

As the months slowly crept by and I got closer and closer to giving birth, my mom decided to take a leave of absence from her job so that she could be closer to me when I gave birth.

On November 1, 1994, against my wishes, my mom headed to West Virginia and stayed in a hotel not far from the prison. We both figured that I would more than likely be giving birth during November, and more than likely before Thanksgiving Day. She didn't want to take any chances that she would miss the delivery of her first grandchild.

From the day that I had been sentenced by the judge, my mother and father had been on a tiring, nonstop, and financially draining mission to help me regain my freedom. They were constantly meeting with a lawyer or talking with a lawyer over the phone in regards to my case. And now with my mom taking time off work to be with me, I felt horrible for all of the heartache and trouble that I was putting them through, and I begged my mom to head back to North Carolina and assured her that I would be okay. But unfortunately she was not trying to hear that and insisted on being there for me.

On November 14, 1994, I began to have what felt like the worst cramps in the world. It was in the middle of the night so I decided to see if I could wait it out and see if the cramps would go away, and if they did go away, then my plan was to try to convince whoever I had to convince to take me to a hospital to get checked out. But the cramping pains only seemed to intensify and get worse as the minutes passed.

"Ahhh!" I screamed as the sharp pain ripped through my stomach and my back. The pain reminded me of the cramps that I got with my period, only this cramping pain was one hundred times worse than those.

I got up out of my bed and got the attention of one of the corrections officers.

"What's the problem?" the husky female CO asked.

"I think my baby is ready," I said, wincing, as just at that moment another sharp pain hit me.

"Come again?!" The CO was obviously irritated that I had interrupted her nap time.

"I think I'm going into labor."

"Motherfucker!" the husky white lady belted out. "Why on my shift?! I got shit to do and I can't get stuck here in the morning." She groaned and complained.

"I'm sorry, but please can you call somebody?" I desperately wanted to lie or sit down as soon as I could.

"Ah, shit! Alright. Just relax and wait here," the guard instructed as she walked off.

Since my arrival at the prison I had been moved from the dormitory-style setup and was now sharing a cell with just one other inmate, named Shirley. Everyone called her Big Shirley because she looked just like the waitress Shirley from the old TV show *What's Happening!!* and because another, petite inmate was also named Shirley and thus nicknamed Little Shirley.

"Girl, you okay?" Big Shirley asked me.

"Nah, I think I'm going into labor." I held on to my stomach.

Shirley immediately got up out of her bed and came to my aide.

"Well, girl, what the hell you doing standing up? You trying to have that baby here in this damn cell?" She took hold of my hand and led me back to my bed. "Don't you know that with you standing up and shit that gravity will make that baby pop out quicker?"

I couldn't help but let out a slight laugh.

But my laugh was quickly replaced by another sharp pain.

"Ahhh! Shiiitt!" I winced as that pain was definitely much more excruciating than the other bursts of pain.

"Oh, Lord, Katrina, please don't have this baby up in here, please just hold up a minute and we gon' get you to a hospital, baby," Shirley said in her motherly tone. Shirley was in fact old enough to be my mother. She was fifty-one and was doing a life sentence for the murder of an IRS agent. She had been in prison for thirteen years. She admitted to me that she had killed the IRS agent, who had been investigating her for a tax scam that she had been running for years.

"Mothafuckas, this girl is having a baby! What the fuck are you talking about over there? Just call the damn medics and get her to a fucking hospital!" Big Shirley screamed at the corrections officers who had began to congregate not too far from my cell.

Everyone respected Big Shirley, all of the inmates and all of the corrections officers. And as if Big Shirley was their boss or something, the corrections officers came to my aid before long.

My cell was unlocked and I was quickly escorted to the infirmary. There, after being frisked yet again, I was examined by one of the doctors as the burly, white female corrections officer looked on.

The doctor asked me to undress and to lie on the bed so that he could examine me. I did as the doctor told me, but I immediately wished that the corrections officer would leave the room and give me some damn privacy.

I was soon undressed and lying on the bed with my legs in the air in stirrups as the doctor asked me a bunch of questions. He then put on some latex gloves and, without warning, inserted his fingers inside me.

The corrections officer was all up in my business and was glaring harder between my legs than the doctor.

"Excuse me," I said, trying to get the corrections officer's attention. Both her and the doctor looked up at me.

"Nah, I was trying to get her attention," I said to the doctor.

"Yes," the CO replied.

"Is there any way that you can contact my mother and let her know what's going on?" I asked as politely as I could.

"What?!" the corrections officer responded with more attitude as I had apparently pissed her off once again.

"Please!" I said as I winced in pain from the contractions and from the doctor's probing hands.

"I don't know. We'll see." The corrections officer walked toward another part of the room.

This is not, I think, how any mom would ever envision her baby being born. I'm sure that most would picture themselves surrounded by a support group that would include the baby's father, a girlfriend, and family members. But for me, the only person in my corner was an arrogant-ass, could-not-care-less, fat-ass corrections officer.

"You know, you women come in here after getting knocked up after being on some crack binge, or 'cause you was out shaking your ass in some strip club, and most of the time you have no idea who the father is, and then you want to snap your fingers and demand this and demand that!" the corrections officer had the nerve to say to me as she walked back toward my side of the room. But she was sure not to look me in the face.

"Excuse me?!"

The corrections officer would not repeat what she'd said and still did not dare to look at me.

At that point I felt all of the anger and rage that had been stored up inside me from the time I had been sentenced. All of the furious rage and anger was boiling over, and I was ready to take it out on the corrections officer.

I immediately grabbed on to the hospital-bed railings and attempted to lift up my body as best as I could with my big belly. A contraction had shot through me, but I didn't care as I tried my best to brush through the pain.

"Bitch, you don't know the half of what I've been through and what got me here to this point! I didn't ask for this shit!" I barked at the corrections officer as I was now trying to get off the bed so I could punch her dead in her face.

"Miss, please just calm down and don't move! Just lay back down," the doctor yelled.

"Lay down on that gurney or you'll be delivering that crack baby by your got damn self in the fucking hole!" the corrections officer threatened as she looked at me with a deathly stare.

I bit my lip and thought about how powerless I was, and as tears began to well up in my eyes, I knew that it was best that I not fight a battle that I could not win.

Inside I was still raging and screaming and I wanted to rip that corrections officer's head off. I could not understand how someone, especially another woman, could be so insensitive to a pregnant human being.

"Okay," the doctor said as he stood up and smiled a half smile. He had obviously spoken up in an attempt to ease the tension in the room.

"It looks like your baby is definitely ready to make its entrance into the world today. You're just about five centimeters dilated, which means that we need to get you over to the hospital where they are better equipped at handling the delivery of your baby."

"Oh, God, no!" the corrections officer said as she dropped her head into her hands and shook her head. Under her breath she mumbled, "Now I have to go with the medics to transport this bitch to the hospital?!"

"What the fuck is your problem?!" I yelled at the CO. I couldn't take her verbal abuse anymore.

"You and your crack baby are my problem!" she shot back as she walked over to me and got in my face. A few hairs were growing out of her chin, which made it look like if she didn't shave, she would be capable of growing a full goatee. She blew her hot-ass breath in my face and waited for me to respond.

"You know what? You can put me in the hole and I *will* deliver this baby on my own. But I tell you one thing, and that is you are not gonna disrespect me or my baby like that again! You say one more word and I swear on my life and on the life of my baby that I will fuck you up! You fucking bitch!"

The CO just looked at me and blew some more of her hot-ass breath in my face as we stared each other down, then she hollered for other corrections officers to come to the room.

Two male COs came into the room and, without regard for my nakedness, asked what was the problem.

"We got a live one! Right there!" the lady CO said to the two male COs. "Looks like she wants to *fuck* me up!" the CO added mockingly, then explained that she just wanted the two other correction officers to act as witnesses as she handcuffed me.

Then she grabbed me by my shoulder and yanked me up and began placing handcuffs on me! And she forced my hands behind my back at that!

"Let's see you fuck me up now with those handcuffs behind your back!" the corrections officer said as she laughed.

I was extremely physically uncomfortable and I felt so victimized and pitiful, and I knew not to respond. I was on the verge of letting out tears of anger, but I didn't want to give her the satisfaction of knowing that she had succeeded in breaking me down.

Thankfully the doctor spoke up and asked the corrections officer if my arms could be placed in front of my body instead of behind my back. He said it would help the blood flow better to my abdominal area.

The CO gave the doctor a look that said, *You have got to be kidding me.* But fortunately she relented and sat me back up and took off the cuffs and repositioned my arms in front of me, but my wrists were still cuffed. Only now my hands were around my stomach, waist, and vaginal area.

"We don't want nothing happening to the crack baby, no, no, no, we can't have that," she said comedically.

With my hands now cuffed, the corrections officers walked off and congregated near the entrance door of the room that I was in.

"Here, read this." The doctor handed me an index card and a small, eraserless pencil.

I began to read the card and he said, "Just look at that clock, and whenever you have a contraction, I need you to write down the exact time on the clock."

The index card read, *I will call your mother for you. Write down the telephone number on this card.*

I wanted to let out the biggest sigh of relief because I felt like at least *someone* with a human heart and spirit was in my corner.

I quickly wrote down my phone number in North Carolina because I knew that my father would be there and would relay the information to my mother.

"Thank you sooo much!" I whispered to the doctor as I handed him back the index card.

"Uh, excuse me. What is that, sir?!" the CO asked the doctor as she spied on what we were doing. "Oh, no! She can not have any sharp objects like that."

The doctor played it cool and told the CO that he was going to have me keep track of my contractions, but with the handcuffs on it would be difficult for me to write.

"Well, those handcuffs ain't coming off, so the bitch better use her brain to keep track of the contractions!" the CO stated with all kinds of satisfaction just oozing out of her voice.

"Not a problem," the doctor said, nodding. Then he whispered to me, "I'll take care of this for you. Just relax and everything will be okay. Don't be nervous or anxious, alright?"

"Okay, thank you so much. Really," I said, so that the doctor would know that I didn't take his graciousness for granted.

I don't know if there is such a thing as inward tears. But as I sat there naked on the gurney with my belly big as hell and my baby ready to enter the world and with painful contractions ripping through my body, I couldn't help but cry. I think I would have been okay, but the mere sight of those handcuffs around my wrists as I lay in the most vulnerable and helpless position a woman could be in, that went a long way in almost taking me mentally over the edge.

The corrections officer had succeeded in breaking me down a bit, but I was determined not to let the sight of the handcuffs break my will. I had a will that was as strong and determined as anything. But I knew that if I let those tears roll down my face or if I continued to look at those handcuffs on my wrists, my will to press on would probably be broken.

So the best thing for me was to lie in silence with my eyes closed. And with my eyes closed I caused the tears to back up and roll onto my soul instead of letting them roll down my face.

You'll get through this, I told myself as I lay helpless. *It'll be difficult as hell, but you'll get through it.*

I convinced myself that I would get through the pregnancy and the delivery with my mental still intact. If for nothing else, I knew that I would make it through for my baby's sake.

With my eyes closed and my soul being watered by my tears, I heard that little voice inside me once again. Only this time it addressed me by my name as it said, *Katrina, just remember, the sun always comes out after the storm.*

Thirty-seven

I had to wait for several U.S. federal marshals to arrive so that they could transport me under heavy guard to the hospital that was located about twenty minutes or so from the prison in West Virginia. When I arrived at the hospital, I was thankful to see my mom there. My father had called my mom and told her what the doctor in the infirmary had said.

My water had broken and I was now seven centimeters dilated. The doctors told me that I would have to be ten centimeters dilated before I would be ready to deliver the baby. All I knew was that I could not care less about math and centimeters and inches and all of that. The only thing that I could concentrate on was the extremely intense pain that the labor and contractions were putting me through.

My mother tried to be as helpful as possible as she continually stroked my hair and fed me ice chips and told me to relax and to concentrate on breathing easily.

"Mom, I can't concentrate on anything but this pain!" I screamed.

"You'll be okay," my mother said as she did her best to keep her cool.

My mom had just had a screaming match with the marshals, who under the urging of the corrections officers from the prison had decided to keep me handcuffed.

"She's not an animal! You would never do this to an animal, and if she was white, there is no way in the world she would be handcuffed like this!" my mom screamed like I had never seen her scream.

"Test me if you want to, but I'll tell you one thing, if those handcuffs are not off of her within the next fifteen minutes, I swear to God that I will own this hospital!" my mother threatened. Then she bent over to whisper in my ear that she was going to run out and buy a disposable camera so that she could document what they were doing to me.

Within ten minutes my mother was back with the disposable camera, and as soon as she began snapping pictures, it was like magic, and the handcuffs came off my wrists and the apologies from the hospital staff and the marshals began to flow nonstop. Suddenly I was being given the best care as all types of monitors were hooked up to me.

After my mom had straightened things out and calmed down, and after I was finally given a room of my own that the hospital called a birthing center, my mother told me between contractions that she and my father didn't want to tell me anything prematurely, but there seemed to be a good chance that I would have my sentence reversed or reduced on appeal.

"What?" I asked through my pain.

"Your father and I spoke to a top criminal defense attorney, and he told us that he could represent us in filing a notice of appeal of the sentence as excessive."

"But I waived my rights to appeal," I replied, making sure not to get my hopes up.

"Yeah, but, baby, he was explaining to us that with the way things transpired in the courtroom, more than likely you did not validly waive your right to appeal, and if the appellate court were to agree, then there stands a good chance that your sentence could be reduced."

My mom had all kinds of confidence in her words, and if she was that confident, I felt I needed to be just as confident, because I knew there was no way that my parents would allow me to be taken on an emotional roller coaster of false hope.

"Ahhh! My God! Mom, I think I need something for this pain! I can't take it anymore," I screamed.

In truth, the thought of possibly ending my nightmare on appeal was more than enough to help take away my labor pains. That was all that I tried to think about as my mother stroked my hair and relayed the reasons why the lawyer felt that I had a good shot on appeal.

Eventually the moment of truth arrived and my baby was not waiting any longer. I had dilated ten centimeters, and in what felt like a flash I was moved from the birthing room into the hospital's delivery room, where there were three nurses, a doctor, and two U.S. marshals strapped with guns and all. My mother was told that she would not be allowed in the room while I gave birth, but that she could rejoin me in the birthing room after I had delivered the baby.

All sorts of wild thoughts ran through my head as I knew that I was about to become a mommy for real. I thought about Snipes and wondered if his spirit knew what was taking place. I wondered how life would be now with a baby. I also wondered just how much stress this baby would put on my mother and father, who had vowed to raise the baby for me. I felt extremely guilty about that because they had already raised their kids and now here I was giving them another baby to care for. But the biggest thing I realized, as I lay with my legs up in the air and the nurses and doctors yelling for me to push, is that I was as scared as I don't know what!

I was scared that I would never get to really *know* my baby. I was scared that my baby would never have any respect for me. I was scared of what would happen to my baby if my mother or father were no longer around or were incapacitated in some way.

"Push, Katrina, you're almost there!" the doctor yelled to me as the male marshal was all up in my coochie probably getting his first and last glimpse ever of black pussy.

I pushed as hard as I could and it felt like I was taking the biggest dump of my life! And then like magic I heard the doctor yell to me that I had a baby girl. And after a brief pause I heard my daughter crying.

"Oh my God! I can't believe it!" I said as I looked over at my daughter, who had a head full of hair. She just looked so beautiful and peaceful, and I just couldn't help but cry as tears of joy began to pour out of my eyes.

"Congratulations, Katrina," all of the nurses said to me one by one.

"Thank you," I said to them and to the doctor. Then I asked one of the nurses if I could hold my baby.

She placed a bracelet on my wrist and one on my daughter's ankle, and she told me that they were going to clean me up and also clean up the baby and that they would bring her to me in a few minutes.

"Okay," I said, wiping tears from my eyes.

"What's her name?" one of the nurses asked me.

Then it hit me that I had never once considered any girl names, or any boy names for that matter. I can't say I know why I never thought of any baby names other than to say that jail sometimes has a person focused on things that are more of a priority.

"Paris," I blurted out.

"Wow, I like that," the nurse responded.

I didn't know where that name had come from, but I did know that each night as I lay in my bed at the prison, I would take my mind on trips to places and cities that I had never before been. It was one of my coping mechanisms. And for some reason the city of Paris would always enter my mind.

I had been back in the birthing room with my mom for about two minutes when the nurse brought my daughter to me.

"Hey, Paris, there's Mommy!" the nurse said in a baby voice as she handed my daughter to me.

Paris was wrapped in a little white blanket and her eyes were as wide as the moon as she looked up at me and gave me a look that said she felt safe.

"Katrina, look how gorgeous she is!" my mom said, telling me that Paris looked just like I did when I was born. Which I found hard to believe because when I looked at Paris, all I could see was a strong resemblance to Snipes.

"Was I this light too?" I asked, referring to Paris's extremely light skin color.

My mother nodded yes.

"You okay, booobie-boo? You hungry?" I asked Paris as I looked right into her eyes. "Mom, should I feed her now?"

My mother told me to wait on the direction of the nurses.

It was only approaching noontime, but it felt like the day had been so long, and that was because I had been up since the middle of the night with my labor pains.

"Fifteen more minutes, Miss Easely," one of the marshals said to me as he stuck his head inside the birthing room.

Fifteen minutes for what? I thought as I wanted to scream, *Fuck you!*

"They probably want me to leave," my mother said.

I felt rage and anger starting to build up in me again, but I knew I had to check myself because I didn't want my daughter to be around that type of negative energy. But it irked me that the marshal wouldn't even say anything like congratulations or ask me if I was okay. All he was worried about was doing his job like a fucking idiot robot or something.

My mother asked if she could hold Paris, and although I didn't want to let her go, I also didn't want to be selfish, so I handed her off to her grandmother.

"Ohhh, she is so cute!" my mother said as she gazed at Paris. Then she pressed Paris up against her body and hugged her. "I feel her little heart just beating so fast," my mother said as Paris began to cry. "Oh, *excuse me.* You attached to your mommy already?" my mother playfully asked Paris as she handed her back to me, and almost on cue Paris stopped crying.

"Oh my God, she is spoiled already!" I said to my mother as we both began laughing.

Then my mother told me that she would be right back after she went to a pay phone and called my father and let him know that he was a granddad.

So it was just me and Paris Shanice Easely sitting up together, staring at each other.

"Why you cause Mommy all of those labor pains?" I playfully asked Paris.

She didn't answer and I looked at her and playfully told her that she was the cutest thing in the world. And I still couldn't believe how much she looked like her father. Apparently Snipes's genes were as strong as his personality and his will.

"You hungry?" I asked as I put my pinkie toward her mouth. Instinctively she began forcefully sucking on my finger. "Wow, you really are hungry."

I knew that I would not be able to even consider breast-feeding Paris due to my prison sentence, but I wanted to breast-feed my baby at least a few times before I was sent back to jail. I had read up on breast-feeding from some books that were in the prison library, and I wanted to experience it because everything that I had ever read said that a mother's milk was the best thing for a baby's health, and it was also the ideal way for a baby and a mother to bond.

So right there I pulled back my hospital gown so that my left breast was exposed. Then I positioned Paris so that her mouth could get to my nipple and she would be comfortable.

"You comfortable?" I asked Paris as I held her in my left hand and placed my nipple into her mouth by lifting my left breast with my right hand.

Before long Paris had latched onto my nipple and was sucking so hard it almost felt like she had teeth.

"You trying to kill Mommy?" I jokingly asked her.

In truth I didn't care how painful her sucking was because I knew that the pain would subside as I got used to her nursing. I was just happy that she was happy and getting her nourishment directly from me.

Paris was making the cutest and the loudest sucking sounds as she just drank away. She looked so cute and peaceful as she closed her eyes and seemed to be in heaven as she clutched me, her mommy.

"Miss Easely, that will be all for today!" one of the marshals said as both of them came into my room.

"I'm feeding my baby! Can I get some privacy?!" I tried to cover up my chest.

"You have to give us this baby, Miss Easely."

"What are you talking about? And what do you mean by *this* baby? I just gave birth to her!" I pleaded as the marshal stood over me with his arms extended, waiting on me to hand over the baby.

"Miss Easely, please hand us the baby, otherwise we will have to remove her from you forcefully, and that wouldn't be the best thing for the baby," the marshal sternly warned.

"But I'm saying they told me I have two days. Plus she's eating right now and I just don't understand."

But the marshals weren't trying to hear anything as I asked them to at least wait until my *camera-toting* mom came back to my room. I made sure, though, not to mention the camera.

"Miss Easely, hand us the baby right now!" the taller marshal yelled at me.

Paris was still eating and she was obviously hungry as her sucking was loud. There was just no way that I could part with Paris at that moment so I was not budging.

Unfortunately the next thing that I knew, Paris was being forcibly taken from me and she instantly began crying.

"Give me my baby!" I yelled as I attempted to get up out of my bed.

The marshal who was holding Paris began to walk off with her, and the other marshal must have thought I was a dude or something because while he placed one of his hands on his holstered gun, with the other hand he pushed me so hard back onto the bed that my head snapped back. Then he grabbed my right wrist as I yelled for him to get off me. He didn't listen and quickly handcuffed me to the bed's railing.

"Why are you cuffing me?" I screamed while trying to rip my wrist off to get free of the cuff, which was on way too tight. I knew that I could break my wrist as hard as I was yanking, but I didn't care. I was ready to kill like a bear protecting her cub.

The marshal then made his way to the other side of the bed and grabbed hold of me and cuffed my left wrist as I screamed for my baby and for my freedom.

"Get off of me!" I yelled.

"Calm down!" the marshal barked at me.

"Nooooo!" I yelled. "I want my baby! Give me my babyyyyy!" I screamed in a loud rage that was even scaring me.

Unfortunately my screams fell on deaf ears. I continued to violently yank both my wrists trying to break free of the handcuffs. I even started kicking the bed rails with my bare feet.

"Give me my baby! She's hungry!" I growled.

I was seeing red and breathing fire as I lay hyperventilating. I was trying my hardest but couldn't think of a solution.

As I sat there and looked down at my chest, I saw my left tittie exposed with my breast milk running out of it. I also saw both of my wrists cuffed to the side rails of the bed, and blood coming from the bottom of my right foot as a result of my kicking the railing.

I was defeated, and there was nothing I could do about it.

They had won.

They had just stripped my baby from me. And my baby was the only hope that I had left to sustain me. My baby was fueling my will to go on.

But the cuffs on my hands were a reminder that the system had me. The blood on my foot and the breast milk leaking from my chest were reminders that I had been broken down by the system. Violently stripping me of my baby, the system had broken my will.

As I lay there, I realized that there was no more fight left in me. My whole existence was now crushed and numb. There was no way that I could continue.

No will. No way.

Thirty-eight

The days that followed the birth of my daughter were really fuzzy to me as I slipped back into the depression that I had been in when I first arrived at the prison. I was only allowed to spend two days at the hospital, then I was transported back to prison under heavy guard by the U.S. marshals. I had spent the entire rest of my hospital stay handcuffed to my bed, unable to hold or touch my baby. Not to let me hold her and touch her was like torture and cruel and unusual punishment. But, hey, what was I gonna do besides go crazy?

The nurses would bring Paris in, in this little baby crib on wheels that they would roll right up to my bed and just leave her there. And all I was allowed to do was stare at her as she stared back. When she would cry, I would feel so helpless because I could do nothing at all about it. I couldn't feed her, I couldn't comfort her, nothing.

I was so desperate that I begged the nurses to let me change one of my daughter's diapers. Although the nurses felt my pain, their hands were tied just as much as mine, and they could do nothing with the marshals standing in my room and staring at me the entire time to keep me in line.

My mom, who was given custody of my daughter by me, was not allowed to visit me or be with me after she had run downstairs to a pay phone to call my father.

I would later find out that the cracker-bitch corrections officer who I had had words with had thrown all kinds of hate and salt on my game. She had made this big stink about how I had *threatened* her at the infirmary, and how she thought that I would act on those threats and blah, blah, blah. But her boss bought everything that she said hook, line, and sinker, and her boss ordered me handcuffed to the bed at the hospital and disallowed me any visitors.

When I got back to the prison, Big Shirley did her best to bring me out of my depression, but there were no words that she could have used to make me feel any better. All I did was work my menial job of keeping the library clean and think about my baby and how I so desperately wanted to see her and be a mom to her.

On days when I would call home, it would absolutely crush me to hear Paris in the background crying. It got to the point where I dreaded to call home because each time I did the emotional pain would intensify.

In between my calls home and my job at the library, I had to deal with the everyday prison bullshit and the cattiness that the other prisoners brought my way. Like, a few days after Paris had gone home, I was in the mess hall and I hated the food and I still had no appetite, and it was written all over my sulking face that I was depressed and going through some things.

"That spot is taken," one of the inmates said to me as I sat down with my tray of food in my usual spot.

I looked at the girl. I didn't know her personally but I knew of her; she was from Miami but her nickname was Brooklyn. She was a dark-skinned lesbian with a low, boy-style haircut.

I didn't say anything and simply got up and moved to the adjacent table.

"That spot is taken too," Brooklyn said as some of the other inmates began chuckling at me.

Other than being beaten by Snipes, I had never been in a fight in my life, but I was in no mood for bullshit and I didn't wanna bear the brunt of Brooklyn's jokes and her little games.

"Brooklyn, I'm not in the mood for your bullshit," I barked, and I know that I totally caught her off guard as the other inmates began laughing and instigating like school-yard children.

"Uh-oh, Booklyn she trying to clown you," one of the other inmates said to me.

Brooklyn kept quiet and I didn't look in her direction. And then I heard her ask me where I was from.

"Brooklyn, knock it off, alright? Don't worry about where I'm from, you don't know me and I don't wanna know you. Let's just leave it at that," I said, clearly not in the mood to be bothered.

"Damn, that bitch is touchy," one of the other inmates said.

"You miss your little *pooch* that you popped outta your pussy the other day? Is that what's wrong with the little boobie-boo?" Brooklyn said to me, mocking me in a little baby voice as she pinched me on my cheek.

I instantly lost it and slapped her hand away from my face and pushed her backward. I got up from my seat and charged her and began punching her.

"Don't you ever disrespect my daughter! I don't care who you are!" I screamed. I had clearly caught Brooklyn off guard and she lost her balance and nearly fell to the ground.

All of the other inmates jeered and yelled in excited anticipation of a good fight.

Whack!

Brooklyn punched the shit outta me after she regained her balance, then she charged straight for my throat, and as she choked me, she put a sharp object to my throat. I couldn't see it but I was sure that it was a homemade shank.

"Pull some shit like that again and I will murder your ass up in here," Brooklyn threatened me, growling those words into my ear as the other inmates warned her that the corrections officers were quickly closing in.

Brooklyn loosened her grip on me and handed her shank to another inmate.

"She was just agreeing to be my bitch," Brooklyn said to the corrections officers, who asked if was I okay and what was going on.

"I'm okay, everything is alright," I said as my heart pounded and I felt jittery and on edge. I didn't even bother to sit back down and walked off to another part of the mess hall. I wanted to cry my eyes out like a baby.

Don't let it get you, Katrina, I said to myself as I calmed down and stood with a blank look on my face.

The only thing that got me through that period of my incarceration, which was by far my roughest stretch, was the great chance that my sentence would be reversed on appeal, which provided me with so much hope.

"Katrina, you're coming home in six months, don't even think about anything else but that," my father would assure me each time I called home. "Your case is a slam dunk because there is already a precedent case that is very similar to yours that won on appeal!"

"Daddy, I hope so. I just wanna come home so bad! You just don't know," I would respond.

"You are coming home, Katrina! I'm paying one of the top lawyers in this area, and his track record alone speaks for what he can get done."

My father explained that he had done what he had to do to come up with the money to pay for this new attorney to represent me on direct appeal.

Right after I had been sentenced, my mother and father felt horrible about their decision to go with Mr. Pittershawn instead of their first choice. So to file the notice of appeal, my father hired a new, very competent attorney, but he was also a very expensive attorney. His fee just to file the notice of appeal was almost three grand, but my father no longer wanted to skimp on expenses and paid the fee so that the notice could be filed within the proper time limits.

The notice of appeal was filed on time by my new attorney, and the court had subsequently set March 1995 as the date that the appellant brief or my written argument was due. My new attorney would also prepare my appellant brief.

Although I had waived my right to appeal in my plea agreement, the new lawyer explained to my father that in no way, shape, or form had I waived my right to claims of ineffective counsel, which meant in plain English that since my first lawyer, Mr. Pittershawn, was so incompetent and lacked a backbone, he had put me at a disadvantage right from the gate. If I could now prove that to the appellate court, then I stood a good chance of not only having my appeal granted but actually winning my appeal.

"Baby, not *if* you win on appeal, but *when* you win on appeal," my father said to me. "The lawyer explained to me that the court will more than likely grant you a resentencing. And by the time the appeal process is completed, you will have already served a year in jail, and he was saying that he can't see them giving you more jail time over that one year that you'll already have served. He was drawing that conclusion based on the fact that you were not convicted on violent charges and considering the fact that you have a newborn baby." My father then paused. "Katrina, he's good. I'm telling you he is good, baby!"

Like I said, the chance of getting out on appeal was now the only thing providing me with hope. So every day, literally every day, for an hour straight, I would get on my hands and knees in my cell and pray as hard as I could. I would beg God to no end to please let me get off on appeal and go home and be with my baby. I figured that during the six months or so while I waited for a decision on my appeal, I would accumulate so much prayer time with God that He would by default have to get me off on appeal.

"Girl, with the way you praying like that every day, not only will you get up outta here on appeal, but I think you're gonna be speaking in tongues real soon!" Big Shirley would tease me. "I ain't never seen nobody pray as much as you pray!"

"Shirley, this is all I got. Jesus will get me outta here. Watch! And if he can't get me outta here, then I'm fucked! But I know one thing, and that's that there is nothing that is too hard for God! Nothing!" I added with heartfelt conviction.

Thirty-nine

Paris had just turned eight months; Candace had finished her sophomore year at NYU and was preparing to enter her junior year; while I had just eclipsed my one-year prison anniversary. But I was still very much prayerful and hopeful that I would be coming home in a matter of weeks if not days.

Two months had passed since all of my appeal briefs had been written and my attorney had conducted an oral argument before the judges of the appellate court. Now all I had to do was sit back and wait for the judge who was assigned to my case to write an opinion stating the court's decision and the reason for it. And wait I did.

I was antsy because I knew that I could at anytime get the news about the court's decision. My new attorney had told me that the word that we did not want to hear was *affirmed*.

"Katrina, if we hear that word, then we are dead in the water. But I doubt that we'll hear it, and I also doubt that there will be a reversal in your conviction. So like I said from the outset, what we are hoping for and banking on is for the judgment to be modified in some way. We got a good shot at that." My attorney spoke confidently and authoritatively.

I had informed my lawyer of how much I had been praying, so he reminded me to be specific in my prayers and to make sure that I asked God to not let the word *affirmed* show up in the court's opinion.

Those two months waiting for the judge to write his opinion were absolutely nerve-racking. My lawyer told me that it normally took about thirty days to three months for a decision to be issued, but he also warned that it could take as long as six months.

I had been in jail for more than a year, so I figured that a few more weeks wouldn't kill me. And I decided to make the most of my time by thinking about all of the things that I was going to do with Paris once I got home. Those types of thoughts made the days go faster. As did thoughts like knowing I would be home to see Paris take her first steps and hear her speak her first words.

Although I knew the decision might not go in my favor, I simply refused to let myself think in those negative terms. I firmly believed that whatever a person thought about the most was what would eventually manifest in their lives. So if my only thoughts were about freedom and a favorable court decision, then I knew that that would be the outcome. There was no way that things could be any different, especially when I factored in how much I had been praying.

September 1995 rolled in, and it had been four months and I still hadn't heard anything from the appellate court, but my instincts told me that it had to be any day now, and that there was no way I would have to wait another two months.

My instincts proved correct as one of the corrections officers approached my cell to tell me that I had a visitor.

I had just recently spoken to Candace and she was in school, so I knew that it wasn't her coming to visit me, and I also knew that it wasn't my parents, who were at home and had their hands full with Paris.

"That has to be my lawyer," I said to Big Shirley as I made my way out of my cell, but only after making sure that I had run my hand across my daughter's picture and looked up toward the ceiling and said a short, quick prayer.

I approached the visiting room in a normal, calm pace, but my heart was beating a mile a minute and my mouth was turning white and pasty.

My nervousness quickly subsided when I saw my lawyer smile once he'd recognized me.

Whew, I said to myself as I blew out some air and smiled a huge smile of relief.

"You're smiling," I said sheepishly to my lawyer as I smiled at him and stared at his face, trying my best to read his mind.

"Yes, I am, Katrina. I'm smiling because I have the judge's decision." He reached down into his briefcase.

Thank you, God! Thank you! I said silently to myself as I closed my eyes, bowed my head, and placed the fingertips of my left hand to my forehead.

"Here's the judge's written response, Katrina. I want *you* to read it, and then I'll explain it," my lawyer told me as I opened my eyes and looked at him.

I looked down at the report and my heart rate picked up as I noticed that the smile on my lawyer's face had disappeared. I knew that I only had to ask one question of my lawyer, who always insisted that I call him by his first name, Rick.

My hands began to tremble as I picked up the bound pieces of paper that contained the keys to my future.

"Rick, I don't have to read this. Just tell me if the A-word is in here or not." I looked into his face with fear, seriousness, concern, and optimism, all wrapped up in the same look.

Rick paused. He was an attractive and distinguished white man who looked a lot like the actor Tom Selleck.

Two wrinkles formed across Rick's forehead as he squinted and frowned and shifted in his chair and blew out some air before he spoke.

"Katrina, your case was affirmed."

"Noooooo! Rick, noooo!" I said in a loud whisper. I didn't want to be too loud or dramatic with my voice, but I couldn't help my body language from being dramatic. I fell backward in my chair, and as if my spine were made of spaghetti, I slumped low in the chair until my entire body slid completely off the chair and I fell to the floor.

I sobbed uncontrollably as I thought about my daughter and not being reunited with her.

"Is everything okay?" one of the COs asked with much concern as he ran over to where I was lying on the floor.

"Katrina. Katrina, listen to me," my lawyer said as he knelt down on one knee to console me.

My head was plopped face-first into the dirty, dusty floor, and my body was stretched out on the floor with part of my legs underneath the table.

"Miss, you're gonna have to get up!" the CO barked.

As I cried and sniffled and groaned, I felt Rick's hand caress my head, and he knelt down right beside me on the floor and pressed his face practically on my face and held me and told me that he was sorry.

"Katrina, I'm sorry. I did all I could do and then some! But we'll get through this, Katrina. I believe in you, and I believe enough in you to dedicate all of my time and energy free of charge in helping you!" Rick passionately spoke into my ear. And I could tell that he meant and felt every word that he said to me.

"Sit up, Katrina," Rick said to me as he told the CO to just give us one minute.

"Katrina, I know I told you that if your case was affirmed, we would be dead in the water. But I shouldn't have told you that. We still got a shot to get you outta here, and we will get you outta here," Rick said as I began to rise to my feet with tears and snot still streaming down my face.

I had no strength in my body as I shook my head, and I just could not understand why my life had been cursed the way it had.

"Why were you smiling when I first looked at you? Why me, Rick? What did I do to deserve this? Why can't I just be with my daughter?" I asked through my tears.

Rick blew out some more air, then I saw his eyes well up and he shed a tear. "You did nothing to deserve this, Katrina. Nothing at all." The single tear slid down his face.

Then there was a brief pause.

After he was done thinking, Rick said, "Katrina, I smiled when you saw me because I believe in you and because I know that *now it's on.* Now it's time to show what we are made of. Right now we can either fold up and die, or we can roll up our sleeves and get busy and start fighting. And I smiled because I'm ready to fight! I love a good fight, and, Katrina, we are getting ready to fight like you couldn't imagine! I believe in our judicial system, Katrina. And I know right now it is probably hard for you to have any faith in it, but it is the best judicial system on the face of the earth. It's not perfect, but it's the best that's out there. And there are measures that we can take to right wrongs like this. In your case we only have one more measure that we can take, but I promise you we'll do what we have to do to get it done."

"Rick, it's not your fault," I said through my tears, which were starting to slow down after hearing how passionate Rick sounded. "I know you did all you could do. Believe me I do. These are just the cards that I was dealt." I shook my head. "You know what? I could do the time if it were just me. But it's not just me. My daughter and my family are being punished right along with me. It's like they have to do time with me. Man! When I think about Paris, it is just devastating to think about not being able to be there for her. That's what's gonna make this so hard for me to swallow." I exhaled and shook my head again.

I could have been mad at God and blamed Him and questioned Him as to why He hadn't answered my prayers, but I decided not to do that. Instead I decided to trust Him even more.

Rick was quiet for a moment and so was I.

Then I said, "Rick, my friend Candace was telling me how God works in the midnight hour. Matter of fact, it seems like lately every time I speak to her she reminds me, 'Late in the midnight hour, God is gonna turn things around for you.'"

"Your friend is right, Katrina. I believe that."

It took a long time for me to regain my composure. Rick told me he hadn't yet spoken to my parents about the court's decision because he wanted to speak with me first. He also explained that the appellate court had ruled that since I had the mental capacity, and the financial means, however limited, to independently select my own attorney and I hadn't had one appointed by the government, it was in essence my lack of due diligence in checking out the qualifications of my attorney that ultimately led me to trust his advice. Therefore, they could not modify the judgment in my case and had no other choice but to affirm my case.

I was getting ready to respond to what Rick had been saying, but Rick cut me off.

"Katrina, I know what you're about to say. But it makes no sense in griping about what we cannot control. This decision is in the past now, and we cannot control the past. But what we can control is what we do from this point forward. You understand me?"

I nodded.

"Now it may take some time, but we will get you home to your daughter," Rick said as I gave him a blank look.

"Let me ask you this, and I need you to be perfectly honest with me. *Katrina, do you trust me?*"

"Rick, of course I trust you," I calmly replied.

"Do you trust me with your life?"

"Yes." I smiled a small, uncomfortable smile.

"I ask you that because there are gonna be some real bleak and miserable days for you as we move forward. And the reality is, it may take us four years or more to get you outta here but—"

"Rick, I can't do four more years in here! I just can't!"

"Katrina, you don't have a choice. Now either you can lie down and die right now or you can fight! The choice is yours. But I can tell you this. Without you fighting as hard as you can fight, then we don't stand a shot in hell," Rick said bluntly.

"So what do we do? I mean, what are my chances of getting out now? Rick, I'm not doubting you or anything like that, but you just have to see things from my end and know what the torture is like to have your hopes inflated only to have the air popped like a balloon, and then your hopes just come crashing to the ground. That's the part that emotionally makes me consider just laying down and dying."

"It's rough, Katrina, I know that. And I understand your situation is one hundred times tougher than anything I could imagine or endure. But you still gotta start fighting from right now. And you can't stop swinging and kicking and scratching and clawing and believing, not until we get you outta here."

I looked at Rick and nodded.

Rick explained that my only other shot at regaining my freedom was to have my crime pardoned by the president of the United States.

At first I thought that he was joking, but I quickly realized that he was dead serious as he detailed how he would apply for a presidential pardon. He would file an application with the Office of the Pardon Attorney, and the pardon attorney would review the details and the merits of my application and would in turn make a recommendation to the president. The president would base his decision heavily on the recommendation of the pardon attorney.

"So President Bill Clinton would have to forgive me in order for me to get out? What are the chances of that?" I asked with tremendous doubt in my voice.

"You have a ten percent chance." Rick said that only ten percent of the pardon applications that are filed actually result in a presidential pardon.

I shook my head in defeat as I knew that to get my hopes up for a presidential pardon was only asking to be severely disappointed in the end.

"Wow," I said as I could not come to grips with such a long shot.

"Do you trust me, Katrina?" Rick asked again.

I looked at him and nodded and told him yes.

And right then and there, Rick literally rolled up his sleeves and began outlining on paper his plan to get me presidential clemency.

"The main problem and obstacle that we face right now, Katrina, is that no one knows you. And we have to have some political allies on our side. And what I mean by that is, before we can even think about filing an application for pardon, we first need to get the world to know how outrageous it is that you, a nonviolent offender, were sentenced to twenty-five years in prison! This is where the fight is. We have to organize thousands and hundreds of thousands of people to sign petitions on your behalf. We have to get tons of media attention to publicize your case. We have to get congressmen to rally behind you, and when we do all of that and begin building momentum, I will approach the NAACP and the Urban League and request that they step in and assist in the filing of your application for pardon. And if we execute that plan, then we will be in a great position to be a part of that ten percent who receive the presidential pardon."

Rick finally came up for some air and paused and looked at me. I know that he was trying to figure out what I was thinking, but he couldn't, so he asked me.

"And you're willing to help me do this free of charge? Why?" I asked.

Rick paused and thought before he spoke.

"Katrina, this isn't about money. It's about what happened to you at the hands of our judicial system. It is about right and wrong and about fairness and justice. It's about the human spirit. And I know that you pray a lot, and I am not big into the Bible, but there was one thing that is mentioned in the Bible that always stood out to me, and that is where it says that *the letter kills but the spirit gives life*. Do you understand what that means?"

I shook my head no.

"It means that if you follow things by the letter of what is detailed and not by the intent that is supposed to be conveyed, then it can and very often does have devastating effects. With you, for example, the *letter* of the law says that you are supposed to be sentenced to twenty-five years in jail. But the *spirit* of the law was never designed to lock away nonviolent, abused, and battered women such as yourself whose only mistake was falling for the manipulative words of a man that they thought they loved. Katrina, the letter of the law is killing you, it is killing your spirit, and it is killing your relationship with your family and all of your loved ones. My job as a lawyer now in this particular case is to do all that I can to make sure that our judicial system interprets the spirit of the law and not the letter of the law as it concerns you. And if I can get them to do that, I will be helping to give life to you, and life to all of those that your spirit will touch. Katrina, it is about giving life to your spirit, a spirit that the letter of the law is trying to kill. There is no way I can charge you for something like that. My spirit wouldn't allow me to charge you." Rick paused and looked at me.

My eyes welled up again, and two tears ran down either side of my cheeks.

"Thank you, Rick. Thank you so much!" I leaned over and hugged him.

Rick got it. He had articulated to me exactly what I had been experiencing ever since I'd been sentenced, something that even I didn't know how to articulate. And that was that my spirit had been killed by the laws of this country simply because the spirit of those laws had not been considered.

Finally, at least in Rick anyway, someone understood and was now going to help me articulate to the world, and most important to the president of the United States, that, yes, I had made bad choices, and, yes, I had made mistakes, but the spirit of the law needed to be considered, and when considered, my sentence had to be viewed as unfair. Those with a heart and a soul could quietly sit and ask themselves, *Is it fair?* And I am sure that the little voice inside of them would say no—no, it is totally unfair.

That was what we needed to get people and ultimately the president to see and feel and understand.

I trusted Rick to help me get that done.

But I would be lying if I said that I wasn't still extremely scared about my chances of being freed.

In fact I was terrified about my slim chances!

When I sat in my cell that night after I had learned that my appeal had been denied, I had to tell myself that it was okay to be scared as long as I didn't let that fear control me and immobilize me.

This entire ordeal had happened to me for a reason, and I was getting a small glimpse as to maybe why God had *chosen me* to go through this nightmarish experience. He had chosen me because He knew that I would be strong enough and have enough faith to endure the experience, and because He knew that by me going through this experience, whether I ever regained my freedom or not, I would become a voice for all of those thousands and hundreds of thousands of individuals who, like me, had been *victims of the letter of the law* and how the laws are interpreted instead of having their cases and sentences looked at and interpreted through the lens of the spirit of the law.

Forty

F or anyone who thinks there is no such thing as hell on earth, I am living proof that it definitely exists. I say that because nothing in this world or in the afterworld could be as mentally and emotionally torturous as having to spend all of your daughter's primary developmental years locked behind prison walls.

By the time my daughter's fifth birthday arrived, I had done more than five years in prison. I was still fighting to be released. But as I fought for my freedom, I had missed my daughter's first steps, her first words, and her first day of kindergarten. If my pardon application was denied, I knew that I would surely and completely miss out on my daughter's entire life.

The week before my daughter's fifth birthday, I called my parents' house. It was about 7:00 P.M. on a Wednesday night, and my mom answered the phone but she didn't sound like her usual self.

"Katrina, I'm just so tired and drained," my mom explained after I asked why she sounded so somber. "It's not easy, Katrina." My mother sighed. "Now that Paris is in school, it put an extra strain on things and I just don't know."

"I don't understand."

"Katrina, I know you don't understand, and that's because day in and day out you're not dealing with the day to day of raising a five-year-old. Putting her to bed, bathing her, and getting her up in the morning and getting her to school on time, and then she needs so much attention, it's tough with the demands from my job and all—"

I cut my mother off and immediately began to get defensive. "Mom, she is five years old! How hard could it be?!" I asked rather disrespectfully.

"How hard can it be? Katrina, do you have any idea what it is like for me and your father day in and day out putting in the extra hours of overtime to try and pay off this debt that we got ourselves into with legal bills? And then to come home and put in hours trying to do whatever we can do to help fight and get you out of prison? And then on top of that we have to try and do our best to raise Paris. It just leaves us no time for ourselves or for each other."

I didn't say a word because I was so frustrated and knew that I would definitely say the wrong thing. Admittedly I was probably clueless as to the amount of work and energy it took for my parents to do what they were doing for me and to raise my daughter. However, I was sure that my parents were clueless as to the torture that I endured from not being there for my daughter. And on top of that, I still had to deal with the everyday harsh realities of prison life—the dykes, the fights, the racist COs, the bad food, the troublemaking inmates, and all of that.

"Well, Mom, I'm still trying to adjust to being transferred to this prison in Connecticut. At least when I was in West Virginia, I had a support system and I had developed bonds in there, and now all of that has been taken away from me. Mom, it's hard on me too! I didn't ask to be here, and you know I would do anything to get out of here and relieve you and Daddy of this stress that I'm causing," I replied desperately.

My mother blew out some more air, but she didn't respond.

"Where's Paris?"

"She's in there watching *Power Rangers* or something like that." My mom yelled for Paris to come to the phone.

"Yes?" I heard Paris screaming from the other room.

"Your mom is on the phone. Come here, okay?"

In seconds Paris came to the phone and began talking a mile a minute and wouldn't pause to let me get a word in.

"And Miss Patterson said that we can have my birthday party in the classroom, and we can have ice cream and cake and balloons and candy and whatever we want," Paris gloated.

"Really, sweetie?" I asked as my heart just melted to hear her voice and to realize that she was getting so smart.

"Yeah, and, Mommy, I want you to come to my birthday party, okay, Mommy?"

"Paris baby, I would love to come to your party, but you know that Mommy can't come. Remember what I told you?" I asked as my heart sank.

"But it's not fair! All of the other kid's mommy and daddy come to their birthday party!"

I knew that I would be in tears soon if I didn't think of something quick to say that would pacify Paris.

"Yeah, but that's why you're gonna have *two* birthday parties, one at school and then one here with me when you come to see Mommy next weekend. And I bet you none of your friends will be that lucky!" I said, hoping to clean things up with my conscience and with Paris.

"Two parties? Yeah! Mommy, you're the best!" Paris said with her sweet little voice.

And then she asked me would I be able to read her a bedtime story later on.

"We'll see, sweetie. I'll try my best, okay?" I said, but in actuality I knew that I would not be able to call her back and read her a bedtime story because of the time restrictions that the prison had on using the phones.

"Okay."

"Paris, I love you," I stressed.

"I love you too."

We then both playfully said, "Muah!" This was the symbolic sound that we had made up to show that we were giving each other a kiss.

"Put Grandma back on the phone, okay, sweetie?"

"Okay."

"And, Paris, make sure you're good in school and listen to your teacher."

"Okay, Mommy."

"Hello," my mom said as she took the phone.

"Mom, that girl is getting so big and she's talking so good." I beamed with pride.

"Yeah, and she is looking more and more like you every day."

I had asked to speak to my father, but he was not home. He was still at work, but my mother wanted me to know that he had been making real big strides on my behalf.

Every time I called home my mom told me about some new politician or celebrity that my father had contacted and got on board to help support my legal cause. This call home was no different, only my mom shocked me with her latest report.

"Girl, your father done broke through and he got Jessie Jackson's ear!" My mom now seemed to be smiling, and that sense of exasperation that she'd had when she first picked up the phone seemed to have disappeared.

"No way!" I said in disbelief. "Jessie Jackson?"

"Jessie Jackson!" my mom replied nonchalantly but confidently.

"Whoa!" I knew how potentially big that news could be.

"And you know what?"

"What?"

"Jessie Jackson is Bill Clinton's spiritual adviser!"

I knew why my mom had emphasized that point. If Jessie Jackson was that close to Bill Clinton, then he could make a direct appeal on my behalf to the president if he believed in my case enough to take a personal interest.

My mom told me that we would talk about it more when they all came to see me the following week.

So I got off the phone with mixed emotions that night. On one hand I felt extremely gratified about the potential of a heavyweight such as the Reverend Jessie Jackson taking up my case and helping to galvanize support for me. But on the other hand, I knew that I was at the end of my rope on a lot of fronts. I could hear in my mom's voice how my whole ordeal was finally starting to wear her down physically and mentally, and I felt that if my pardon application was denied, in time the many visits from my family would end.

It would also be only a matter of time before just about everyone else, including my daughter and Candace, would abandon me. They would abandon me not because they didn't love me or care about me, but more so because of the natural progression of their lives and the normal ups and downs that life takes. And unfortunately, during that normal course of life, people grow tired and weary, and they also grow apart, and I knew that the prison walls would eventually place too much distance between me and *life* to keep the bonds strong between me and my loved ones.

My emotions were mixed, but instead of thinking about the negative I wanted to focus on all of the positive things that had been transpiring. I lay in my bed that night thinking about all that had happened since my first appeal had been denied.

Since that time my lawyer, Rick, had stayed true to his word. He orchestrated all of our efforts so that those that had been willing to help me would be working in the most effective way.

For example, one of the first things he did was to have Candace organize other students at NYU to get signatures for my petition. He felt that would be one of the most important and effective ways that Candace could help me. And, boy, did Candace ever come through for me. By the time Candace graduated from NYU in the spring of 1997, she had a committee of students that she had organized. They accumulated just over two hundred thousand signatures on my behalf! Rick had photocopies of all of the signatures, which he was going to submit along with my pardon application.

My mom and dad had placed phone calls and written numerous letters on my behalf to congress, to senators, to local politicians, and to numerous civil rights leaders. Once they had garnered the initial interest of any of those individuals, they would try to persuade them to personally write a letter on my behalf and send it directly to Rick.

My parents' tenacity paid off, because before long they had gained the support of numerous bigwigs such as Senator Chuck Schumer from New York, Congressman Charles Rangel, also from New York, the former mayor of New York, David Dinkins, the Reverend Al Sharpton, and the Reverend Jessie Jackson just to name a few.

My mom had also garnered a bunch of support from a group called Families Against Mandatory Minimums, or FAMM. FAMM helped a great deal in grassroots efforts to get the word out about my case by littering various urban and suburban mall parking lots with informational flyers and brochures that detailed my case and urged individuals to call their government officials on my behalf and to sign petitions on my behalf.

Out of Rick's own pocket and for four years straight he paid one of the best publicists that money could buy to help publicize my ordeal. And, man oh man, was his money well spent. The publicist managed to get my entire ordeal, including all of the ups and downs but most important the *facts*, published in many well-known newspapers and magazines such as the *Washington Post, New York Daily News*, the *New York Times, L.A. Times, USA Today, Ebony, Jet, Essence, Upscale*, and *Vibe*, to name just a few.

What was bugged was that as the publicity for my case began to build momentum, I was starting to get famous! Suddenly I bagan to receive hundreds and thousands of letters from people from all across the country. All were either expressing their support for me and their outrage at my sentence, or they were telling me how they knew of other women that were in my same shoes. I even got some weird letters like marriage proposals from men across the country, men of all different races, ages, and nationalities. Yes, marriage proposals! But, hey, I wasn't complaining. I was taking the good with the bad.

These numerous letters of support and the momentum that I was building allowed me to press on and helped the time to pass faster. I am not sure it would have passed fast at all had I not been kept busy and preoccupied with the efforts to build support for my case.

Yet, as time went on, I was always nervous and fearful of one thing, and I always tried to block it out of my mind. *What if all of the work that was being done on my behalf was being done in vain?* What if Bill Clinton eventually decided not to pardon me? If that were to happen, then I knew that all of the letters would stop and all of the magazines and newspapers and television and news shows would no longer care about me.

I knew that was *more* than just a possibility; in fact, it had a ninety percent chance of coming to fruition. While I blocked out the thoughts of failure, I also prepped myself for a huge, devastating letdown that I would have to swallow and endure for close to another twenty years if this didn't work.

At the end of the day, I did trust Rick and felt good about my chances. He had kept his word so far, so I had no reason to doubt him. The only time I did doubt him was when he felt that it was best not to submit the pardon application before the end of Bill Clinton's first term.

Rick had insisted that it would be a huge mistake and that the application would get turned down simply because we didn't yet have enough momentum. But I was worried that if Clinton lost the election to a Republican, I would be in trouble because a Republican president would more than likely not pardon me no matter how much merit my case had. However, once Rick explained to me that I could get turned down by a Democratic president if I didn't play the game the right way, I decided to listen to him because I realized that we only had one shot to get it right, and if we blew it, I would have no other recourse. So needless to say, I decided it was best not to be hasty.

In November 1999, Rick informed me that we had built more than enough momentum and he would file my pardon application in two months. To my great relief I knew that the moment of truth was finally arriving soon. All of our hard work would be coming to a head.

Clinton only had one more year left on his second term in office, and I didn't want to take the chance of his being replaced by another Democratic president or of possibly submitting the application too late for him to decide before his term was up.

So, as I prepared for my daughter's fifth birthday, I knew that I only had two more months to wait for the application to be filed, and then I could only wait and hope for a favorable ruling from President Clinton before he left office.

The weekend of Paris's birthday, she came up to Connecticut with my parents to visit me. Candace had also come as well, along with her fiancé. We planned to have a little impromptu birthday party for Paris, and we did.

Thanks to all of the press that my case had been receiving, I had begun to experience both hate and love from the inmates as well as the corrections officers. By that I mean some inmates and COs were jealous of my good chance of being pardoned, so they would go out of their way to make my life miserable by doing stupid shit like stealing my mail and trying to provoke me into fights over trivial nonsense. But then some inmates and COs bonded with me and felt for my plight. They were rooting for me and were in my corner. Many of them went out of their way to help me and to be accommodating in any way that they could.

A CO named Dickinson would talk to me every day and treat me like a human being. Every day she had nothing but encouraging words for me.

"Ms. Dickinson, I ain't never heard you raise your voice or curse or any of that, and you always so nice," I said.

"That's because I'm too blessed to be stressed," she said, laughing.

"Well, I appreciate you for always showing me nothing but respect."

"Katrina, you always hear me talking about God and praising the Lord and all of that, so how could I do that and then turn around and disrespect you or anyone else that's in here. That would be so hypocritical. And besides, everyone in here has value and is loved by God, and I feel that part of my job is to just let all of y'all know that y'all have value. Especially you, baby."

Just the way she called me baby, it just resonated with my soul and made me feel so good, and I smiled to let her know that I was happy.

"You smiling, but it's true." She leaned in and whispered to me, "Like I been telling you, I been praying every day for you and you're gonna be just fine, Katrina. The only thing that I want you to promise me is that when you go on and do big things with your life, you'll stay just as sweet and humble as you are right now."

"Okay," I said with a smile.

Ms. Dickinson was a Christian, and although she never tried to spiritually *mug* me, she would always share her different testimonies and tell me encouraging things like that she was praying for me and how the people in her church were also praying for me.

I really appreciated her for that. She never tried to use her position of authority to force her religion on me. We respected each other, and therefore I felt comfortable asking her if she could in any way accommodate my mom, my dad, Candace, Candace's fiancé, and Paris in a private room for Paris's birthday party.

"I tell you what. Not only will I accommodate that for you, but I'll even bring my six-year-old daughter to the party," she told me.

"Oh my God, thank you, my daughter will love that."

"And the balloons and party favors and the cake, all of that is on me, that'll be my gift."

"Oh, Ms. Dickinson, that is so sweet of you. Thank you so much. You gonna have me in tears up in here," I said, genuinely moved to cry in response to her genuine kindness.

I was thrilled, overjoyed, and blown away by her compassion. And on the day of Paris's party, the tears would not stop flowing from my eyes when I saw how happy Paris was at her party and how she interacted so well with Ms. Dickinson's daughter.

I was so thankful to God because I knew that He had not only heard my prayers, but He had answered my request to be a part of my daughter's life and to be there for her and to have her feel like I was *really* her mommy.

Paris's birthday party went off without a hitch, and we did all of the traditional things that are done at a kiddie birthday party. We sang "Happy Birthday" to Paris. She made a wish and blew out her candles. She opened her presents and played games as well as ate cake and ice cream.

The only thing that broke my heart was to know that Paris was going to leave when the party was over and I would not be able to leave with her. In fact, every time that she left after visiting me, I didn't know if I would make it. It was just so hard emotionally. It was almost as hard on me as it had been when she was first born and the marshals literally snatched her from my bosom as she drank my breast milk.

But as Paris prepared to leave that day of her party, I walked over to the corner of the room and sat in a chair and just meditated. And as I meditated, I silently told God that I didn't think that I would be able to make it through many more of Paris's visits and not be able to leave with her.

God, it is just too hard! I lamented. *God, I can't do this for another twenty years. I mean, I thank you for this wonderful party today, but, God, please, I can't do it for much longer. I won't make it.*

"Mommy, what are you doing?" Paris came up to me and sat on my lap.

I paused because I felt a tear in my eye.

"I'm talking to God, sweetie," I said as a tear ran down my face.

"Mommy, why are you crying?"

"Because Mommy wants to come home with you but she can't." The tears fell a bit faster.

"Don't cry, Mommy."

I looked at her and smiled.

"Mommy, I'm a big girl and I don't cry," Paris said in her sweet little voice. She had clown paint on her face and looked too cute.

I continued to smile at her.

"Rachel was laughing at me because she said you couldn't come to my party because you are in jail. But I didn't cry when she said that."

Those words caught me off guard and almost crushed me because I knew that Rachel was a little girl in Paris's class. Paris always spoke about Rachel in good terms. But knowing how cruel kids could be toward each other, I instinctively knew that Rachel had probably been taunting and teasing Paris about my incarceration, which Rachel had probably known about from her parents. Due to all of my publicity, her parents probably told her that Paris's mom was in jail. I wondered if the other kids had also teased or taunted Paris.

"Oh, sweetie, she shouldn't have said that to you!" I said, gasping. "Did any of the other kids say something like that?" I asked protectively.

"Yeah, they were all laughing at me and saying that my mommy is a jailbird!" Paris pouted her lips and clenched her little fists.

My heart sank to the soles of my feet when I heard her say that. I was on the verge of crying again, but I knew that I had to be strong. I was about to explain how kids can be cruel to each other and tell Paris once again how much I loved her and why I was in jail. But fortunately Paris spoke up, saying words that melted my heart and made me want to hug her so tight and never let go because I knew how much she loved me.

"But, Mommy, I didn't cry when they said those bad things because I know you are in jail and jail is for bad people, but I know you are not a bad person, Mommy."

"That's right, sweetie! Mommy is not a bad person. You are so right!" I hugged her. I wanted to say more but I knew that there was no need to, because in her own little five-year-old mind she *got it*. She understood fully at her age what was going on with her mommy.

"I love you, Mommy." Paris hugged me.

"I love you too, baby!" I held her as tight as I could.

Before long I had said my good-byes to everyone and made my way back to my cell. For the entire rest of the night I kept hearing Paris say, *Jail is for bad people and you are not a bad person.*

She's right, God, I thought before I went to sleep. *She is so right.*

I sat quietly for a minute and then thanked God for allowing Paris to understand in her own way exactly what was going on. Before I fell asleep I said to God, *Please, God, please. You know how much I can handle. And You know I can't handle much more. Please take me home. Please.*

Forty-one

Many of the inmates that I'd come to know during what was now my *six*-year prison stay were your everyday, average people who came from all backgrounds and all walks of life.

One young black inmate named Paula Parker, nicknamed PP, was pretty and petite, and she was highly educated, with a master's degree, and looked like she could be your sister. Paula had struggled with a gambling addiction that led her to devise a mail order scheme to support her gambling, and she got caught and sentenced on a federal level since the U.S. Postal Service is governed by the federal government.

This other inmate who I bonded with really well was Cecilia Carlson, who everyone called CC. CC always jokingly referred to herself as "Kentucky-trailer-park white trash." She was in prison on federal kidnapping charges, and the funny thing is that my path and CC's path would probably never have crossed during everyday life had we not been in prison. CC kept me and all of the other inmates laughing nonstop throughout the day with her jokes, impersonations, and wittiness. She was just naturally funny, and I would always tell her that when she was released she had better become a comedian and get her own television sitcom, and I meant it because that's just how talented she was.

Another cool inmate was this black girl named Tamia Simpson, nicknamed Me-Me. Me-Me was reserved and quiet like I was, and she stayed talking about her kids and how much she missed them. Although she was reserved and quiet, she still had this swagger to her that let everyone know that she was hard and wouldn't hesitate to beat someone down. Me-Me was serving time on drug-related charges. But what was impressive about her was that she was a published author who wrote fiction books about street life. I read all of her books and she was definitely talented, and I would always tell her how inspiring she was to be locked up but yet have her books on bookstore shelves all across the country.

Yup, PP, CC, and Me-Me were three of the coolest inmates that I had met, but there were so many others. What I found interesting was that each inmate did her time differently. Some remained closed and to themselves throughout their entire prison stay. Some watched trash-talk television shows all day long. Some inmates found God or some sort of religion that kept them preoccupied. Some inmates lived simply to make the other inmates' lives a living hell and harassed people all the time. Some were fitness freaks and just worked out all day long. Some inmates stayed on the phone as long as the COs allowed. And still other inmates tried to control people and relatives who were on the outside living in the free world.

As for me, I found reading to be the best way to pass my time. During my six years I would estimate that I easily read close to four or five hundred books. I had never known that I enjoyed reading so much, but I took to it easily. I enjoyed all types of novels as well as nonfiction. I read the newspaper daily and just about any magazine that I could get my hands on.

But even with all of the reading, I tried to stay aware of things.

Something about prison life robs you of everything that people freely experience and know about on the outside world.

For example, during my six years in jail, Puff Daddy had emerged from being just this new face on the record scene to being a superstar mogul and boyfriend of J.Lo, who was about to face trial for the Club New York shooting with his protégé, Shyne. The Notorious B.I.G. had risen from a relatively unknown low-level Brooklyn drug dealer to an international rap superstar who had been murdered. Superstar Tupac Shakur had been killed and was a distant memory. Jay-Z had emerged as one of the hottest and most prolific rappers ever. Murder Inc. was rising on the charts while Death Row Records was becoming a faint recollection. Arsenio Hall was no longer this big name; in fact, he was no longer even on television. Mike Tyson was no longer this powerful, feared boxer who knocked everyone out in the first round. Instead, he had been to jail for rape, had gotten out of prison and fought Evander Holyfield and chomped part of his ear off, and no one was even talking anymore about the washed-up has-been who could have been one of the greatest boxers ever. Technology was the hugest change of all. The Internet and e-mail were now an everyday part of people's lives. Cell phones, which when I first went to college were reserved for big ballers, were now nothing special and everyone had one. The O. J. Simpson murders and his trial had come and gone and were now a faraway memory. Michael Jordan had retired from basketball, taken a shot at baseball, returned to the NBA and won multiple championships, and had retired again.

On a more personal note, Candace had not only graduated from NYU but she had gone on to graduate school and earned her MBA. She was now married, making six figures a year, and had a son. My parents, who had planned on being retired at this stage in their lives, were still working as hard as ever to take care of my six-year-old daughter.

If my pardon application was denied, then I could only imagine what other countless things would transpire in the world and in the lives of people that I would miss out on and never really capture the essence of.

Fortunately for me, earlier in the year of 2000, the Urban League Legal Defense team, along with my attorney, Rick, had filed my pardon application with the office of the U.S. pardon attorney. My entire defense team felt that I had a good shot at my pardon, but no one wanted to take anything for granted.

So with Bill Clinton's final presidential term quickly coming to a close, everyone who was supporting me stepped up their efforts bigtime to bring more light to my case and to rally more support behind me. ABC's *Nightline* and the A&E cable channel even interviewed me and broadcast profiles on my case. Jessie Jackson, one of the most outspoken African-American leaders, made a personal plea on my behalf to the president. At times, all the attention that my case was receiving seemed surreal to me. At times I would feel numb and have to pinch myself because I couldn't believe that so many people were in my corner, rallying behind me, and even cared for that matter.

But the biggest thing to happen was that Oprah Winfrey had caught wind of my case, and she agreed to come to the federal prison in Connecticut to interview me. No disrespect to the president, but to me, Oprah was bigger than Bill Clinton. And needless to say, after I had appeared on *Oprah,* my case was galvanized in the media.

With all of the national media attention, I was optimistic as was everyone else around me. But for sure the president had a lot more bigger fish than me on his plate to fry, as other pardon applications were from more well-connected individuals. He had to deal with personal scandals and with world issues and all of the everyday demanding things that world leaders deal with. And despite all of the media attention, after my pardon application was filed in January of 2000, President Clinton had still not pardoned me and only had about thirty more days left in office.

The president ain't thinking about you, Katrina, I told myself. *He probably never even seen your application.*

I didn't want to lose hope and I wanted to stay positive, but my thoughts were constantly worried. And I would be lying if I said that I didn't start to believe that all of the support that I had received and all of the work that had been done on my behalf was about to go to waste.

When I called home to check on my daughter, I made sure to tell my dad to relay to all of the people in my corner like Rick and Candace who had been supporting me all of these years that I wasn't going to speak to anyone until either *after* a decision had been made by Bill Clinton or he had left office, whichever came first.

My father and my mother could not understand my rationale, and I didn't really care if they understood it. I felt like I needed to totally isolate myself from everyone other than my daughter so that I could pray to God. I didn't want my emotions to be swayed in any one direction, and I knew that if I spoke to people like Rick and Candace, I would get more anxious about coming home. What I wanted was to remain neutral and prayerful about everything, in case things didn't go my way.

My father told me that they had heard from the Office of the Pardon Attorney, but the pardon attorney had informed them only that *there were no guarantees that the president would even rule on my application.*

News like that wasn't helpful at all. It did nothing but cause all kinds of mixed emotions to run through my mind and my body. So I even told my father and my mother that when I called, they should simply hand the phone off to my daughter. I didn't want them mentioning anything to me about my application status.

However, with Christmas quickly approaching, even just speaking to my daughter proved difficult. On December 21, my daughter cried to no end as she asked me if I was going to be home to help her open her Christmas presents. Since I didn't want to get her hopes up to only disappoint her, I told her no.

"But that's not fair, Mommy! That's the *only* thing that I asked Santa Claus for. And I've been good, Mommy!" Paris vented.

"Okay, honey. I understand" was all I could say before I began shedding tears on the phone. I didn't want to let Paris know that I was crying, so I simply told her to be good and that I loved her and that I had to go.

When I went into my cell, I prayed unceasingly to God. I prayed so hard that my body trembled and sweat began pouring off my body. I prayed until the morning, nonstop, pouring out everything that was inside me for God to hear. I no longer shared a cell with anyone like I had done with Big Shirley in West Virginia. So I was free to do whatever I wanted in my cell with some level of privacy.

"I will never leave you nor will I forsake you—the Lord is my helper and I will not fear what man shall do to me." Those were the words from the Bible that I had memorized, and I continually chanted those words out loud and in my head throughout the night while I prayed.

When those words weren't enough for me, I would recite out loud the verse from the book of Matthew that focused on faith: "If you have faith as small as a mustard seed, you shall say to this mountain 'move,' and it will move, and nothing will be impossible for you."

Later that afternoon, December 22, many of the other inmates began to ask me what was wrong because I looked so disheveled and like I hadn't slept in days. When I replied that nothing was wrong, they wanted to know if my somber, drained mood was because my pardon application had been denied.

"Nah, I was just up all night and all morning praying and I didn't get any sleep," I said to one of the white inmates, named Collard.

Collard began laughing at me and snickering with some of the other inmates.

"You didn't hear?" Collard said.

"Hear what?" I asked as my heart began beating.

Collard told me that five of the women that were locked down with us in Connecticut had had their pardon applications denied.

"You see where praying got them, right?" she said, laughing.

"Who got denied?" I asked as my mouth instantly got dry and pasty.

"I don't know. Everybody! I think your name was on that list too."

I immediately ran off to the phone to call home. But I got no answer.

Then I called Rick's office, but he wasn't there. His secretary said that she couldn't give me any answers about my case, which I found strange. She was always Rick's eyes, ears, and mouthpiece, and she always gave me whatever answers I was looking for whenever Rick wasn't around.

Finally I called Candace and she picked up.

"Candace, *my application was denied?*" I immediately blurted into the phone.

"What? I didn't hear that. Where did you hear that?" Candace urgently asked.

"No. I'm asking you," I said, feeling like I was about to crap my pants. "That's what the other inmates are saying. Is it true, Candace? I tried to call home and I got no answer, and then I called Rick, and his secretary won't tell me anything, but I think she is just stalling and bullshitting me."

"Katrina, calm down, girl," Candace said calmly. She told me that she hadn't heard anything but that she would call around to see what was what and for me to call her back in a couple of hours.

From that point on I couldn't eat or drink anything. Later in the day when I saw a couple of inmates who had in fact had their pardon applications denied, I almost puked on myself with worry.

Then when I called Candace back, two times I got nothing but her voice mail.

Shit. She's ducking me too now! I said to myself as I decided to just go back to my cell and be alone with my thoughts.

I couldn't bring myself to even look at my daughter's picture or any of my other pictures because it was way too painful. I simply got on my bed and lay there numb and staring at the ceiling, not allowing myself to think about anything. I was hoping the rest of the day would zoom by with no visitors. I knew Rick, Candace, and everyone else were probably on their way to see me so they could tell me in person my application had been denied.

Yeah, and then I'll probably never ever see or hear from them again, I thought.

At that point I started doing something I had promised myself I would never do, and that was think hateful things toward Snipes.

I tried hard not to, but as I lay there staring at the ceiling, I cursed Snipes to no end and desperately hoped that he was somewhere burning in hell! I threw punches and kicks in the air as I remembered the beatings and the times he had choked and threatened me. And then as I saw the picture flash in my mind of Alexis's and Warren's dead bodies, I screamed, "You sick bastard motherfuckerrrrrrr!"

In minutes a CO was standing at my cell asking me if everything was okay.

"Just leave me alone, please!" I barked.

The CO looked around my cell, then strode off.

I exhaled air from my lungs and returned to staring at the ceiling, and before I knew it I was out like a light. My body had slipped back into depression. I knew that because it was the only way that I could have slept straight through until the next morning.

The next morning as I was heading toward breakfast I got ambushed by what seemed like a tornado of inmates rushing and running toward me screaming my name.

"Katrina! Katrina! Girl, you got a reprieve!" I thought I heard one of the voices from out of the throng of voices screaming at me.

"What?" I yelled as I tried to make sense of what was being said.

"You got a reprieve! You're going home!" they continued to scream as they ushered me, actually more like rushed me, toward the television that was not too far from the mess hall.

"What are y'all talking about?!" I shouted, a bit annoyed, hoping that this wasn't some kind of cruel joke they were playing on me.

As I made it in front of the nineteen-inch color television that hung from the ceiling, the other inmates informed me that the cable channel C-SPAN had a list of names, being scrolled across the bottom of the television screen, of all the people President Clinton had either outright pardoned or given a reprieve—a lessening of the penalty for the crime.

"Y'all saw my name?" I asked in disbelief. My heart started pounding and again I desperately hoped that this wasn't some kind of cruel-ass joke!

"Yes, just watch!" they all shouted at me.

I looked at the television with intense anticipation. My heart was racing as names scrolled across the bottom of the television screen. My name did not come up, and before long a preview of an upcoming C-SPAN special appeared on the screen, which interrupted the flow of scrolling names. My heart couldn't stop racing and I had never felt it pound the way it was pounding. My chest was visibly rising and falling, and thoughts of my daughter raced through my mind. To calm down I paced back and forth and just closed my eyes and pictured my daughter.

After the preview was done and C-SPAN was back to its original program, I opened my eyes and saw about fifteen names scroll across the bottom of the screen. In clear bold letters it said, "The following persons have been issued a federal reprieve by President Bill Clinton."

Then after the fifteenth name or so had scrolled across the screen, I saw my name, KATRINA EASELY, crawling across the screen in big bold letters.

"See, there it is! I told you! I told you!" one of the inmates shouted at me.

I dropped to my knees and held my outstretched arms and hands up toward the ceiling and let out the loudest scream imaginable.

"AHHHHHHHHHHHHHHHH!!!!!!!!!! I'M GOING HOME!"

And just like that, my nightmare ended.

The nightmare had started seven years earlier, on the day I'd met Dwight "Snipes" Abrams at New York University when I was just eighteen years old. A nightmare full of the most dreadful years of my life, spent behind bars and locked away from life, my loved ones, and my precious daughter. A nightmare that, at twenty-five years old, I could finally say was over.

"Paris, Santa Claus is real! Mommy is coming home!" I shouted to my daughter, even though I knew that she was miles away and couldn't hear me.

Yeah, Santa Claus was definitely real. Christmas had arrived two days early for me, and with it came the best present imaginable. My freedom!

Epilogue

I realize that there is no way to get back the years that I spent in prison. And that realization caused much unsettled anger and resentment to build up inside me. I carried that anger and resentment around for more than five years *after* my release from prison.

Yeah, I now had full access to my daughter, to my family, to my lawyer, Rick, and to my best friend, Candace. Yet it still seemed like something was constantly weighing me down and not allowing me to release that anger and resentment. It was like I was still in prison. Only this prison was *the prison of my mind.*

Within five years of my release from prison, I had returned to college and earned my degree. I had met a man who I knew was bound to be my soul mate. I had started a gratifying career working for Rick's law firm as a paralegal. And even with those positive things going on in my life, I still wasn't able to release the anger and resentment. I was still in a sort of prison.

I thought that working with female inmates in the federal prisons would help me to see how blessed and fortunate I was, and maybe *that* would be the thing to help me release the anger and resentment that I was holding on to, but it wasn't the thing that I needed.

I had accepted that I had made bad decisions, but this big part of me was still mad and bitter at the world and wanted to blame my loss of years on any- and everybody and on any- and everything.

When my daughter graduated from the sixth grade, I decided to take a trip with her to New York. I told her that the trip was going to be her graduation present, but what I hadn't told her was that she and I would also use that trip to visit her father's grave for the first time.

In June, Paris and I headed to New York City, where I took her to Montefiore Cemetery, in Queens, New York. On an overcast day with a slight drizzle, Paris and I both walked up to the tombstone of Dwight Abrams and placed flowers on his grave. Paris and I then knelt down and prayed together, and when we were done, I told Paris that I would give her some privacy so that she could spend some time with her father and *talk* to him.

I had told Paris everything about her father, but I made sure that I wasn't detailed when I didn't have to be. For example, I told her things like *Me and your father had our problems in the past.* To me that was better than telling her that Snipes used to beat me. I also told her that he had been in trouble with the police and why. And I made sure that I explained it in a way that didn't demonize Snipes but rather educated her against the ills of doing wrong and about the importance of doing right. I wanted to be the one who Paris heard everything from, and the last thing that I wanted was for her to one day hear negative things or false things about her father that could lead to her own low self-image.

When Paris had finished *talking* to her father, she returned to where I was standing and I could tell that she had shed some tears. I gave her a hug and held her before stroking her hair for a few minutes.

"Give Mommy a few minutes to *talk* with your father. Okay?"

"Okay," she replied.

Paris stayed put and I walked the twenty yards or so over to Snipes's grave. I knelt down, and at first I didn't know exactly what to say, but I knew that there was something that I *had* to say. There was no need to be long-winded, so I kept it short and simple.

"Snipes, I *forgive you* for everything negative that we ever experienced, both together and individually. And I want you to know that I never have and I never will *dishonor* you or dishonor your name, or dishonor your memory in front of your daughter. I'll always tell her the truth, but never in a way that will disrespect you."

Then I paused for a few minutes before continuing, "I made it, Snipes. I made it despite all that you put me through and took me through. I made it!" I stressed, and I could feel myself about to well up, so I calmed down a bit and checked my emotions.

"I made it because I was stronger than you were, and I made it because I had to make it for Paris, your daughter." I paused again. "Snipes, *we* have a beautiful daughter. She's so beautiful. You'll see her one day. I pray that you will."

I blew out some air. I stood and took about two minutes to gather myself, then I walked back over to Paris, smiling.

"Mommy, why are you smiling?"

I looked at Paris and paused before responding. I knew she was too young to really understand, so I tried my best to keep my response to her as short and as simple as possible.

"Paris, you'll understand this better when you get older. But I'm smiling because . . . well, how should I say this? I'm smiling because it just hit me *that a person can never ever truly be free until they are able to forgive from the heart. And Mommy finally, finally has her freedom.*"

READING GROUP GUIDE

The following discussion questions are intended to enhance your group's reading of Mark Anthony's *Reasonable Doubt*. It is our hope that this reading guide will stimulate insightful discussion and broaden your group's reading experience.

1) Snipes was very cunning, and he was also a good manipulator. With that in mind, do you think that his intentions toward Katrina from the outset were purely selfish in nature or on some level did Snipes genuinely care for and love Katrina?

2) Katrina had been pretty much sheltered growing up in North Carolina, then she was thrust into a big city like New York. Do you think it was her lack of life experience that ultimately made her miss many of the warning signs related to Snipes's character and his criminal dealings?

3) Many women are attracted to "bad boys." Once Katrina realized that Snipes was a "bad boy," do you think that caused her to become more intrigued and infatuated by Snipes?

4) Snipes obviously used fear, abuse, and pressure tactics to control Katrina. His actions escalated from things like date rape and fistfights to him locking her in the trunk of a car and showing Katrina the body of his best friend who he had murdered. With those things in mind, was it only the fear and the abuse that made Katrina stay with Snipes and never try to flee from his control or do you think there was something else that compelled her to act and behave the way she did when it came to her "loyalty" to Snipes?

5) Many women are currently incarcerated due to their relationships with men who are involved in criminal activities. The law basically says that from the time that a person becomes aware of another person's criminal activity they either must withdraw totally from being in that person's company or report that person's activities to law enforcement officials. If they fail to do either one of those things or both, then they can be charged as a co-conspirator from the time commencing with when they became aware of the person's criminal activity. Considering how a woman's emotions can get wrapped up in a man when she really loves him, do you think laws such as these are fair and practical? And if not, then what would be a healthier and more just alternative?

6) To what extent, if any, should "outsiders," such as Katrina's parents and, at the time, Katrina's roommate, Candace, have gotten involved in order to protect Katrina from Snipes and his predatory nature?

7) Katrina's first lawyer obviously did not advise her properly, and many in some circles would say that she got "railroaded" by her first attorney. Although Katrina pleaded guilty and entered into a plea agreement, do you think that her attorney should ultimately bear all of the blame for her agreeing to go along with what he had advised her and

her parents to do? Or do you think that Katrina and her family should have merely listened to the advice and the counsel of her attorney, but then she should have ultimately been the one to make the decision on how she moved forward based on her "gut" feelings combined with the advice of her first lawyer?

8) Do you think that all mandatory minimum sentences should be abolished from the law? If no, why not? If yes, how would individuals then be able to safeguard against the biases of a judge who sentences them, and how would society be able to ensure that the punishments for crimes are commensurate with the crimes committed?

9) As she gets older and ultimately matures into adulthood, how do you think Katrina's daughter, Paris, will be affected by the actions of her father that led to him being killed and to her mother being incarcerated for her involvement in his crimes?

10) How do you think Katrina's life will ultimately turn out? Do you think that all that she had to endure happened for a reason? If so, what do you think that reason is, and, ultimately, what could Katrina do in order to turn all of the negative things that she experienced into positive things?

CONTENTS

Illustrations follow page 244.

PREFACE

If, as the Chinese say, a journey of a thousand miles begins with a single step, this book had its origin in the now dimly remembered crisis over the islands of Quemoy and Matsu in 1958. In August of that year Mao Zedong had ordered the bombardment of these two outposts occupied by the Chinese Nationalists, and there was fear the Eisenhower administration might be drawn into war with Peking because of the Mutual Security Treaty between Taiwan and the United States. I was about to begin my sophomore year at Harvard, and the controversy over the "offshore islands" impelled me to attend a lecture by Professor John K. Fairbank. Fairbank, a tall, spare man with a passionate commitment to the study of China and a dry, ironic wit, told the audience that China had 800 million people and an ancient history —and therefore it was a country to be taken seriously.

On the surface this seemed a simplistic thesis, but as Fairbank expounded it, I began to appreciate that here was the oldest nation on earth, with the largest number of people, and I knew nothing about it. I decided to sit in on Social Sciences 111, an introduction to the history of China, Japan, and Southeast Asia then taught by Fairbank and Edwin O. Reischauer (three years later, President Kennedy named Reischauer as his ambassador to Tokyo). It turned out to be the beginning of a romance that has lasted over two decades; I was infatuated with China. I still couldn't pronounce Chinese names correctly. But when we read Edgar Snow's account of the Communists' epic Long March in the 1930s, *Red Star Over China*, I instinctively felt attracted to Mao and his followers for the hope and idealism they offered China after the misery and corruption of the Kuomintang period.

The next spring, when final exam time came, I enclosed a stamped, self-addressed postcard with my blue test booklet, in keeping with Harvard practice. The card came back with a summons to report to Fairbank's office. What had I done wrong? I wondered as I walked to Widener Library at the appointed hour.

"You wrote a wonderful exam," Fairbank said, to my relief. "Have you considered Chinese studies as a career? You ought to begin studying Chinese."

I was flattered. I didn't yet know that Fairbank, the proselytizer, tried this routine out on almost anyone eccentric enough to show an interest in his field. And so that summer I did start studying Chinese. It was still such an obscure subject that the next fall when I asked for Chinese tapes at the Harvard languages laboratory the matronly looking woman behind the desk peered at me over the top of her glasses as if I had stumbled into the wrong church. "Chinese? Chinese?" she repeated. "Isn't Chinese a dead language?"

But each new course I took drew me deeper. I wrote my senior thesis on an unlikely group of American missionaries in north China who at the beginning of World War Two cooperated with the Communists, also attracted by their ideals and reform-minded policies. When I graduated in 1961, I journeyed to Taiwan on a Fulbright Fellowship to try to improve my spoken Chinese. There I lived with a Chinese family, discovered the joys of real Chinese food, and began to learn about how the Chinese social universe differs from ours. Later I went back to Harvard for five years for graduate work in Chinese history and then returned to Taiwan again in 1967 to do research on my doctoral dissertation.

By now, however, it was the height of the American war in Vietnam, and a life spent re-creating the past in musty library stacks had come to seem irrelevant. I wanted to get to China, to experience it first hand. So when I was offered a job as a stringer, or part-time reporter, in Taiwan for *The New York Times,* I happily accepted. I dreamed of being the first American correspondent to live in Peking after 1949.

It took me ten years to get there. There were two mandatory years learning the craft of journalism at *The Times* in New York and then a series of assignments in Asia—in Vietnam, Japan, and Hong Kong—waiting for China to open its doors to U.S. news organizations. When Jimmy Carter finally normalized U.S. relations with China in December 1978, I was ready to go to Peking, though unfortunately it meant leaving my wife, Barbara, who was pregnant, and our three-year-old son, Ethan, in Hong Kong. Peking had an acute housing shortage, and the government warned me that the only accommodation they could offer for at least the next year was a single hotel room, hardly enough space to both live in with my family and do my work.

As a police state, China poses special problems for a journalist. Many of the most significant insights I gained, or the most poignant anecdotes I heard, came from people I cannot name or portray in detail because of the reprisals they would face. Wherever possible, I have identified the people I knew, and wherever a full three-syllable Chinese name appears, like that of the sculptor Wang Keping, it is the name of the actual person. But where I felt it necessary to camouflage identities, I have either left my informants anonymous or given them only a fictional first or last name, like Lihua, the young petitioner in Chapter 5, or Bing, in Chapter 10. In several cases, I have altered minor details of my friends' lives to protect them—placing them in a different city or giving them a new occupation. But all their comments and quotations are genuine, and none of the characters are composites.

This book is intended for general readers, and I hope that specialists will forgive a few conventions I have chosen to make it easier for the ordinary reader. Instead of the usual Chinese nomenclature for their education system —junior middle school and senior middle school—I have opted for the more familiar terms junior and senior high school. I have followed *The New York Times*'s policy of adopting the Communists' *pinyin* system for transcribing Chinese names except for a few well-known places. The capital of China thus remains Peking, rather than the *pinyin* version, Beijing. Similarly, in keeping with *The Times*'s format, I have retained the traditional spelling for places and people outside the mainland, like Hong Kong (which would become Xiang Gang in *pinyin*), and the Nationalist leaders like Chiang Kai-shek and his son, Chiang Ching-kuo. The *pinyin* system presents a few special tasks for the English-speaking reader: Q is pronounced like the ch in chicken, x like the s in she, zh like the j in Joe, and c is like the ts in hats.

I alone am responsible for the judgments in this book, but my obligations to others who helped me on my journey are manifold. I owe a primary debt to Jan Wong, my assistant in Peking, for her guidance, enthusiasm, and generous introductions to her Chinese friends. Jan appears by name on a number of pages, but her real contributions are immeasurable. I am deeply grateful to my editors at *The New York Times*, A. M. Rosenthal and Seymour Topping, who encouraged and sustained this enterprise. John Fairbank at Harvard, who introduced me to China, has been a wise counselor for many years. To him and to several other academic specialists I am indebted for their useful suggestions: Merle Goldman at Boston University, Nicholas Lardy at Yale, and Jerome Alan Cohen, formerly of the Harvard Law School and now of New York. I want to express thanks to two sage Chinese friends in Hong Kong who instructed me in the arcane art of China-watching, Vincent Lo and Sydney Liu; to my journalistic colleagues in Peking, Michael Parks, Victoria Graham, and Liu Heunghsing, for their timely assistance; to friends in the diplomatic corps who shared their knowledge and time, Roger Garside of the British Embassy, and Charles Sylvester, Christopher Szymanski, and William McCahill of the U.S. mission; to the research staff of *The New York Times* for their prompt and resourceful aid, Barbara Oliver, Donna Anderson, and Judith Greenfeld; to others in Peking who contributed generously, Eileen Wu and Janet Yang; and not least to Charles Chu of Connecticut College, who graciously provided the handsome calligraphy that decorates the book.

Roger Jellinek, my main editor, has been an imaginative, patient, and invaluable guide. I also want to express special acknowledgment to my other editor, Fredrica S. Friedman, for her constant encouragement and judicious improvements. And I have a particular debt to my wife, Barbara, for her forbearance and support, and to those Chinese who cannot be named but who made this book possible.

F.B.
Wellesley, Massachusetts
February 1, 1982

Clawed by the Tiger

INTRODUCTION

It was a cold, overcast day in January 1980 when I arrived at the cavernous Shanghai railroad station for the overnight express train to Peking. A blue-uniformed woman conductor with short pigtails poking out from under her round cap was waiting beside the door to my car. In what had seemed a routine transaction, I had purchased my ticket the day before in an office of the China Travel Service, the state-run tourist agency. At least the middle-aged clerk at the counter had not evinced any particular interest in me—I just presented my green travel pass from the Public Security Bureau, China's police, and paid for my passage. That struck me as a good omen. I had chosen to make the trip by train, a twenty-hour ride, rather than by plane, a mere two hours' flight, in hopes of encountering some Chinese who might be willing to ignore the official regulations against talking to a foreigner away from the prying eyes of neighbors or office mates. It was a tactic other Westerners in China had sometimes used with success.

But when I approached the green and yellow train, the conductor's broad face broke into an immense smile. "Welcome to our train," she said almost too eagerly. "You are the American reporter, are you not?"

It was more a statement of fact than a question. As I stood with my suitcase in my hand, I might as well have been naked. My hopes continued to fade as the conductor, a stocky woman in her late twenties, whose bulk was magnified by the layers of sweaters and padded underwear she had stuffed under her uniform, began walking down the car corridor. Through a crack in my compartment door, I could hear her stopping to announce to the other passengers in her booming voice:

"We have a foreigner on board. He is an American journalist. He speaks Chinese. He speaks very good Chinese." That was the alert, I calculated.

Then she returned to minister to me. "Please let me know if there is anything I can do to serve you. My name is Ding." An appropriate appellation, for in Chinese *ding* means solid, like nails, and she struck me as a rare cross between a Marine drill sergeant and a cheerful, overweight waitress.

Mustering the remains of my courage, I asked Ding how she was so well informed about me. "The responsible comrades notify us who the passengers are, so we can make preparations," she replied.

Ding's preparations included making sure that I had the four-berth compartment all to myself, a comfortable but to me disappointing way to travel. Still, I thought, I might meet someone in the dining car. What time was lunch? I asked Ding.

"I will call you after the other passengers are finished," she answered. "It will be more convenient for you, it won't be so crowded."

Indeed, when she finally did summon me, there were only two Chinese left in the dining car, and they were finishing their soup, the last course in a Chinese meal. When they saw me, they hastily gulped down the final sips and departed. I felt like the plague. As the train crossed the rice fields of the Yangtze River Valley, dry and brown in the weak winter afternoon, the long trip appeared a mistake.

Several hours later when we stopped in Nanjing, the old capital of Chiang Kai-shek's Nationalists, I got out to stretch my legs. Ding was already on the platform, a bucket and mop in her hands, to wash down the outside of our car. She was the model of discipline. Another passenger, a dignified man with only a thin patch of white hair left on his head, who appeared to be in his seventies, was also taking some exercise. In the most innocent gambit I could think of, I asked if he was going to Peking.

The answer came back in flawless English. "Yes, are you?" Again I was caught off guard. "Where did you learn such good English?" I continued, growing bolder.

"At Harvard. I went to Harvard Medical School and lived in Cambridge, before Liberation in 1949," the stranger explained. By chance, I went to Harvard also, and Cambridge is my hometown. When the time came to reboard the train, the doctor volunteered to sit with me.

"You are the first American I have talked to since 1949," he said. He had tucked his hands up inside the long sleeves of his padded brown jacket with a high mandarin collar against the cold, an old Chinese gesture. "Until recently I wouldn't have dared to be seen with you, but I think it may be all right now," he said. Then, as afternoon turned into evening, he recounted the story of his past thirty years.

Like many of his friends studying abroad, he had returned to China in 1949 because he felt himself a patriot and wanted to take part in rebuilding China. "I was not a Communist," the doctor said, "but I admired what they were trying to do. Old China was so backward, so poor, and so corrupt, there

4

were beggars who starved to death in the streets every day." The early 1950s were a time of optimism—under Communist guidance, new factories were built, land in the countryside was collectivized, and China proved its strength by fighting the United States to a standstill in Korea.

But the doctor's life changed in 1957 with the Hundred Flowers campaign, the time when Mao Zedong encouraged greater freedom of expression and invited intellectuals like him to criticize the Party's shortcomings in the belief that the overwhelming majority of Chinese now accepted Communist rule.

"I took Mao at his word, I thought he was sincere," the physician recalled. When the Shanghai city government asked him to a large meeting to express his views, he recommended that the Communists ought to remove the largely uneducated former peasants turned guerrilla warriors whom they had installed as Party secretaries to run the country's hospitals. Instead, he urged, hospitals should be left to the charge of professional doctors. But a few weeks later Mao reversed his policy and instituted the Anti-Rightist campaign.

"They did what they call 'putting a cap' on me, I was labeled a rightist." The doctor was taken to a struggle session, a mass meeting where the victim is shouted at, insulted, and often beaten by dozens of people until he finally confesses his supposed crimes. "They called it a 'self-help meeting,' to help me improve my attitude," he continued in a simple matter-of-fact tone devoid of self-pity. After a month of this treatment, he was arrested, imprisoned, and eventually sent to a labor reform camp in the mountains several days' bus ride from Shanghai, where he worked breaking rocks in a quarry.

He got out of the labor camp just in time to be assailed again in the Cultural Revolution. Mao launched this adventure in 1966 both to oust his adversaries in the Party hierarchy and to prevent the country from slipping back into what the Great Helmsman feared were the soft, corrupt ways of pre-1949 China. The doctor was arrested once more—his old label of rightist made him a handy target for eager radicals in his hospital. They incarcerated him in a basement room in the hospital where autopsies were performed and beat him with wooden boards every day for several months. This time his label was also extended to his family. His wife, a doctor herself, was prohibited from practicing medicine and made to sweep the floors and clean the toilets in her clinic. His son, a brilliant medical school student who had passed the college entrance exams with nearly the highest marks in China, was shipped off to labor as a peasant in a village in the far northeast. His teen-age daughter was expelled from her junior high school, since she was the offspring of a reactionary, and assigned to work in an automobile garage.

After Mao's death and the overthrow of the radical Gang of Four, including Mao's termagant widow, Jiang Qing, in 1976, the doctor had been restored to a position of authority in his hospital. But he was still surrounded by his former tormentors, with whom he had to work daily. "It's funny, some of them now fall asleep at political study sessions from boredom," he said of his accusers. "For all of us, the revolution is over. What is left is cynicism. It is very sad for China."

This episode on the train was typical of my experience in China. There seemed to be two Chinas: one the official version, with a cast of people like the conductor, cardboard cutouts from the *People's Daily*, the Communist Party newspaper, always smiling, selfless, and dedicated to the cause. The other China was partially hidden, an inner universe whose one billion inhabitants had gone through three decades of cataclysmic change, sometimes for the better, but often, like the doctor's trauma, involving brutality, waste, and terrible personal suffering. The tragic concatenation of one political campaign after another—land reform in the early 1950s, the Hundred Flowers Campaign, the Great Leap Forward in 1958 with its resulting food shortages, the Cultural Revolution in the late 1960s, and the continued factional battles in the 1970s—had left a legacy of popular apathy and disillusionment. Gone were the idealism, the drive, the almost religious fervor which marked the Communists' early years.

The official China was the one I had read about in the often breathless accounts of Western visitors who had spent a few weeks in China. Traveling on the invisible dotted line of a few dozen cities and communes that is the authorized itinerary for almost all foreigners in China, they had returned to assure the world that China had really ended crime, inflation, and unemployment. China was the country where a tourist who left a used razor blade or an expended ball-point pen in his wastebasket would have it miraculously returned to him at the next city he visited. China was also the remarkable land where millions of urban high school graduates, following Chairman Mao Zedong's call, happily went off to work for the rest of their lives as peasants in the villages, like Boy Scouts, some Americans said. I remembered Jerry Rubin stopping in my office in Hong Kong, where I reported on China for four years for *The New York Times* before American news organizations were permitted to open bureaus in Peking in 1979, after the normalization of Sino–American relations. The former Yippie leader had just spent several weeks touring China and he enthused over what he said was "the spirit of real love the people all have for each other. You can see it in their eyes." They weren't concerned for themselves or money, like materialistic Americans. I asked him if he had any doubts about what he had seen. Yes, he admitted, he had wondered, briefly. "One day as I was riding on a bus, I said to myself, either everyone is telling the truth or everyone is pulling my leg. It came to me that everyone must be telling the truth."

Americans would not suspend their critical judgment like this in analyzing the Soviet Union—we had learned what Stalin was like; we had read Solzhe-

6

nitsyn. But we gave China the benefit of the doubt. It seemed to me that China cast a kind of magic spell over Americans and other Westerners. There was nothing new in this. It had been going on since the French Philosophes of the eighteenth century, who imagined that the ancient sage Confucius had created a perfectly harmonious government which China was still following. In the late nineteenth century, when a current of missionary zeal swept churches and college campuses in the United States, Americans dreamed of converting China to Christianity and "saving" China in a single generation. At the turn of the century, as Americans became terrified by the specter of what was then called overproduction, a new image arose—that of the fabulous China market, the 400 million customers who would buy up the excess of American manufacturers. During World War Two, when we were fighting Japan, we looked to Chiang Kai-shek as a valiant democrat leading China into the free world. All these images were more the projection of our own myths than a hard look at reality. Indeed, they contained a measure of cultural condescension, an unwillingness to look at things from the Chinese perspective.

But the longer I lived in Peking, the more the other dimension came into view—the hardships, the absurdities, the stratagems of daily life. Gradually over the twenty months I lived there, I formed genuine friendships with a number of Chinese and they initiated me into this human quotient, the myriad ways Chinese had invented to ignore, evade, resist, or confound the revolution that Mao had thrust on them. In short, to survive.

In the process, I had to unlearn many of what I took to be facts about China. The 38 million members of the Communist Party, I had presumed, must be stalwart adherents of the revolution. So I was not prepared for an energetic, candid, middle-aged Party member who was chairman of her local street committee, the lowest level of government organization. One evening when I stopped by her fifth-floor walk-up apartment, I found she was reading the Bible. I was incredulous. By its own regulations, the Communist Party is devoted to atheism, at least when it was not worshiping Mao. When I asked if she was not afraid of getting in trouble, she laughed and awkwardly practiced crossing herself. She explained that recently a forty-five-year-old man had knocked on her door, claiming to be a friend of a woman she knew. He wondered if she believed in God or had read the Bible. It was a very dangerous act, but she was impressed with his sincerity and intrigued by what he had to say. He had spent ten years in prison because of his Christian belief and was unable to get a job.

"If there is a god, why has he let you be treated so cruelly?" she asked.

"You don't understand," he replied. Actually, he claimed, he had been very lucky. "God gave me a wonderful wife. When I was in prison, the police demanded that she divorce me to show she did not share my ideas, but she

7

refused. Now I can't get a job, but though she is only a factory worker, she supports both of us."

In the end, my friend accepted his offering of a Chinese-language Bible that had been printed in Hong Kong and smuggled into the mainland. She was reading it with evident interest. "You don't know it," she advised me. "But Christianity is spreading rapidly in China because people are so disillusioned with communism." If she had been a political dissident, I would have been doubtful. But she was the neighborhood Party boss.

With Mao's commitment to revolution, I had assumed China would offer great social mobility, the chance for people to get ahead. But in many ways, I discovered, China was more conservative and hierarchical than the United States, Japan, or Western Europe. Only 3 percent of China's young people can go to college, one of the major routes to success. By comparison, 35 percent of Americans go to university. Chinese can't pick their own job, they must wait till they are assigned work by the state, and once given a job, it is very difficult to arrange a transfer. China's peasants probably have less chance to escape their bondage to toil than their ancestors did before 1949 because of the restrictions the Communists have erected against people leaving the countryside.

A hustling, fast-talking youthful official in a foreign trade corporation who had recently returned from his first trip to the United States said the most impressive thing in America to him was its sense of opportunity.

"Even an elevator operator can start his own business and become a millionaire if he works hard and saves his money," the official commented over lunch in the Peking Hotel where I lived and worked for the first year I was in China.

In a joking riposte, I suggested the opposite might happen in China—the ex-millionaire capitalist would be turned into an elevator operator. For a moment my companion stared at me in silence and I was afraid he had construed my remark as a slur on China.

"No," he finally said. "In China they wouldn't let a millionaire be an elevator operator. That is a job for someone who works for the Public Security Ministry, to keep track of who goes in and out of buildings. The millionaire would be forced to clean toilets."

Mao demanded a strong belief in equality. So I was surprised to find that the Party itself is divided into twenty-four grades, and that in a supposedly classless society the children and grandchildren of people who were branded as landlords in 1949 are still stuck with the stigma, barring them from joining the Party or the army, or sharing in benefits like cooperative health insurance in the countryside. I was also startled to discover that some of my new Chinese friends had servants, affectionately and euphemistically dubbed

8

"aunties." I hadn't realized that Party officials have their own exclusive network of markets, bookshops, hospitals, and resorts which provides them with food and services unavailable to the "masses." Many of these privileges are carefully sheltered behind official secrecy to preserve the appearance of equality. Only at the end of my tour in China was I able to find out where Hua Guofeng, then still Chairman of the Communist Party, lived. A friend whose father was a general in the People's Liberation Army volunteered to drive with me there. Hua's residence turned out to be a large, forbidding compound in the northwest section of the city, measuring four hundred yards long by three hundred yards wide, set behind twenty-five-foot-high gray concrete walls that were topped with slits for guns. Chinese called it simply "Building Number Eight," since they said it had cost eight million yuan, or $5.3 million, to construct, an extraordinary sum of money for China.*

Chinese industry has grown at the impressive pace of almost 10 percent a year since 1950, I knew from reading Peking's statistical claims, so I was constantly struck by reports of bungling and incompetence by the country's economic managers. In 1981, the New China News Agency disclosed, the Ministry of Petroleum had wasted several billion dollars on building a cross-country pipeline for natural gas from Sichuan province to the industrialized region of China along the middle and lower reaches of the Yangtze River. Senior officials of the ministry had deliberately inflated Sichuan's gas reserves, ignoring protests from lower-level technicians, in order to get the appropriations to build the pipeline. Then when the promised gas failed to materialize, the project had to be scrapped.

That Peking maintained its control through a large police ministry, supported by a sophisticated system of agencies like the street committees, was no secret. But it took a personal encounter to learn just how pervasive the police could be. One evening when I went out for a walk from the Peking Hotel, I noticed a tiny figure of a woman in the shadows. It was a bitterly cold February night, and she was bundled in a black overcoat, with a yellow scarf over her head and a cotton surgical mask covering her face, the kind many Chinese wear to help keep out Peking's cold and dust. As I walked, I sensed she was keeping pace with me and, after fifty feet, was approaching me.

"Where are you going?" she asked. It was an unexpectedly bold opening for a Chinese.

"For a walk," I replied.

*At the official exchange rate set by Peking in 1981 $1 is worth 1.50 yuan. But most diplomats and foreign businessmen calculate that the real value of the Chinese currency is only about half that. Peking has conceded as much by allowing Chinese factories which export their goods to sell them at a lower exchange rate; otherwise they would be priced too high for the world market. In the interest of simplicity, I have stuck with the official rate.

"May I walk with you?"

"Yes," I replied, "but aren't you afraid of being seen with a foreigner?"

No, she responded. Then, through her mask, with only her small eyes showing, she began pouring out a tale of trouble which was only half comprehensible. She seemed nervous, or feverish, it was impossible to tell which.

She was twenty-three years old, she related, and had been sent to work in the countryside after she finished junior high school as part of Mao's utopian program to rusticate urban youth. Life had proved harsh in the village where she had been settled, and she had finally resolved to come back, illegally, to Peking. Her father was retired, and the family had little money. She couldn't get a job, because she was in the city without proper identification papers. As she talked, she took my hand, another unlikely gesture for a Chinese. Was she a prostitute? I began to wonder. It was then that I realized someone else was following us, a young man in a blue jacket, with crew-cut hair and sunglasses, though the night was dark and there were only a few faint street-lights. Ostentatiously, he would walk a few steps behind us, then trot to the front, then back again. Finally he pushed directly in front, blocking our path on the sidewalk. Were they working as a team? the thought flashed through my head; had I been set up in a Chinese gang mugging?

"Who are you?" he demanded of me.

I returned the question.

"What are you doing with her, what is your relationship?" he continued, without identifying himself. We were friends, I told him. By now two more men, in their forties, had joined us, one of them in the blue uniform of the Public Security Bureau, China's police, with a high fur cap on his head. My anxieties about being robbed vanished, but other fears took their place.

The uniformed policeman grabbed my new acquaintance by the arm and shoved her up against a storefront wall. "How did you meet?" he began interrogating her. "What is your work unit?" By then half a dozen more police, some in uniform, some in plainclothes, had appeared out of the night and surrounded me. "Go home, get out of there," they ordered me.

A typical American, I felt compelled to try to protect the woman, whoever she was, and the journalist in me wanted to know exactly who she was. So when the police began marching her back down the street toward the Peking Hotel, I followed to see where they would go. This time two police pushed me against the wall.

"What did we do wrong?" I asked. "Can't a foreigner talk to a Chinese?"

At first they just glowered at me, the interfering foreigner. Finally the younger of the pair, who was in his early twenties and had a strong smell of garlic on his breath, answered with bureaucratic ambiguity. "It is okay to talk in the daytime, but not at night," he said. By then, the woman had been led around a corner and was out of sight. I had to admit defeat.

Despite the pervasiveness of the police network, however, I also learned it had its holes. In Zhengzhou, the nondescript capital of Henan province, on the north China plain, a group of robbers armed with AK-47 automatic rifles held up the main office of the People's Bank, killing one of the guards and escaping with the equivalent of more than $150,000. An American married to a Chinese woman from Henan told me that the thieves had become local folk heroes for their daring. Defying an intense police search for them, they put up wall posters around the city on black paper: "You can dig up all of Henan province to a depth of three feet, but you will never find us."

In the aftermath of the Cultural Revolution, there was a growth of white-collar crime, too, corruption in the ranks of the Party. A fifty-eight-year-old woman cashier in a county coal company in the far northeast of China, named Wang Shouxin, was accused in the press of being the ringleader in a syndicate of officials which embezzled $320,000. Wang was said to have lavished furs, television sets, record players, tape recorders, electric fans, and eiderdown quilts on more than two hundred people who participated in the scheme.

When I tried to puzzle out how such anomalies as crime and corruption could exist, given the size of China's police apparatus and the earlier reputa-tion of the Party for selflessness, a graduate student friend laughed at my naïveté. In China, she said, everyone had to devise his own method for dealing with the omnipresence of authority. Her technique was daydream-ing. That was how she had learned to speak almost flawless English. Because her father was condemned as a counterrevolutionary during the Cultural Revolution, she had been forced to drop out of school and never went beyond the sixth grade.

"But I got an English textbook and went through it in two months on my own," she said as we drove around Peking in *The Times*'s office car, a tan Honda, one of the best ways to talk to a Chinese without being observed. "Then I just daydreamed long conversations in English with myself. I could even speak it out loud, no one else understood." Eventually, in 1978, after the radicals' downfall, her father was rehabilitated and she was able to use her ability in English to win admission to a graduate school.

This penchant for inventiveness, born of necessity, had spawned an entire counter economy, what the Chinese call "going through the back door." They used the back door to break through the restraints placed on them by the cranky bureaucracy and the cumbersome centrally planned economy. A young journalist at the New China News Agency who favored well-tailored Mao suits explained how this worked. When his neighborhood market ran out of bean curd, a cheese-like food rich in protein made from pressed soybeans, his parents sent his sister to shop. She had former schoolmates who worked in the market and would pull out reserves they had hidden under the counter. That was her back door. He himself would have been shipped off to the countryside after he finished high school as part of Mao's rustication program except that his father, a general, had a former comrade-in-arms from the Communists' guerrilla days who had become a senior official in the press agency. The colleague arranged a job for him there. Later, in exchange, his father was able to secure a comfortable post in the army for the official's daughter. One day my friend pulled back the sleeve on his blue jacket to show me a new Chinese-made wristwatch. His father had been given it by the factory as a so-called trial product, a disguised way of distributing scarce items to favored officials or relatives. His family also had a trial television set and refrigerator at home, two real luxuries in China. The system of trial goods had become so widespread, he added, that some people jokingly wondered if they could get trial cremations, since China's cemeteries and crematoria have long waiting lists. My friend had applied to get an exit visa and passport so he could go abroad to study in the United States. He didn't expect any trouble getting them; he had a back door in the Public Security Ministry, his uncle.

This counterpoint of the two Chinas, the formal system and the eccentric, often-anguished human dimension, was much like what my colleague on *The New York Times,* Hedrick Smith, had found in the Soviet Union and portrayed brilliantly in his book, *The Russians.* That was not a coincidence, the doctor on the train from Shanghai suggested. He had read Smith's book in Chinese translation. Peking had printed it in installments in one of the confidential bulletins circulated to officials and then often illegally passed on to their friends. The government presumably calculated it would show how bad conditions were in the Soviet Union. But the doctor had another perspective. Actually, he said, much the same book could be written about China. Nothing he read had surprised him. It was all too familiar. Both countries were run by powerful bureaucracies that stifled individual initiative and often gummed up the economy. But there was a significant difference between Russia and China, he pointed out—it lies in the history of the two peoples. China was the only survivor of the world's great early civilizations: Egypt, Mesopotamia, Greece, and Rome. That gives China a language, culture, and state structure that date back over two thousand years. It also makes history a palpable force, not just something written down in textbooks for schoolboys to read about. Mao often liked to compare himself to the first Emperor of the Chin dynasty, Chin Shi Huang, who unified China in 221 B.C., built the Great Wall, and ruthlessly burned all heterodox books. Ronald Reagan thinks his style of government compares with that of Eisenhower. But no American President would be likely to reach back to Julius Caesar or Hannibal for inspiration. The very Chinese name for their country, Zhong Guo, is redolent of the antiquity and the pride Chinese feel about themselves.

It means "central country," the seat of civilization at the middle of the known world.

Customs spawned over these two millennia have not easily withered with the advent of communism, an import from the West. When the doctor and I went to the dining car for supper, ignoring a look of displeasure from the conductor, he noted one simple but profound difference between Chinese and Westerners. We order our own separate food from the menu and eat from our own individual plates. Chinese order their meals together and then share the dishes, each person eating with chopsticks from the same plates and bowls in the middle of the table. We are oriented to the individual, to satisfying and gratifying his needs, catering to his tastes, and we feel this is legitimate. But the Chinese has his center of gravity in his group or his family. A Chinese scientist who visited the United States and stayed with an American family told me afterward that he had been surprised to find the children all had their own rooms. He felt it was unnatural sleeping in a bed by himself, so accustomed was he to having his entire family together. To spend the night in a room alone actually made him nervous. He could not imagine how some Americans managed to live in a whole house by themselves.

The primacy of the group in China has political repercussions. It makes it easier for Chinese to adjust to pressures to conform and to accept authority —"The tall tree is crushed by the wind" is an old proverb. But many Chinese still try to develop their own personal lives free from the official trammels, I found. The government is puritanical and frowns on even kissing and dancing. But most young people I met admitted they had slept with their spouses before getting married. A nurse told me that her hospital made money by quietly performing abortions on unmarried women without reporting them to their work units, as many clinics would. That would have ruined the women's reputations. Chinese go through many of the same life crises as Americans. A precocious teen-age girl complained bitterly to me that her parents didn't understand her. A thirty-year-old woman charged that her husband was interested only in his career and was insensitive to her. When he came home at night, all he wanted was for her to cook for him and make love with him before he fell asleep. She wanted to grow, to expand, to travel abroad if possible, to go back to graduate school. It was like a classic thirties passage in Gail Sheehy's popular book *Passages.* She ended up having an affair with another man.

The Chinese preference for the group over the individual may have grown out of the country's economic conditions. From early times the Chinese planted rice in irrigated fields, a type of agriculture which calls for intensive cultivation by large numbers of strong backs and in turn produces high yields that can support a bigger population than Western farming did until the last century. The result is everywhere visible. As our train crossed the flat countryside north of Nanjing, we could see whole villages of small mud-walled houses at half-mile intervals. In the American Middle West there would be only the farmstead and clump of trees of a single family in the same area. This density of people on the land has subtly conditioned the minds of centuries of Chinese.

Geography and history have also left a legacy of harsh facts for China. In total area China is only slightly larger than the United States (3.7 million square miles to 3.6 million square miles), stretching 2,500 miles from the Pamir Mountains in the west to the Pacific Ocean in the east, and 2,000 miles from the Amur River in the north, on the border of the Soviet Far East, to Vietnam in the south. But much of this territory, particularly around the periphery, is uninhabitable mountains and desert, like the vast 10,000-foot Tibetan plateau and the Taklamakan desert in Xinjiang, the most utterly desolate region in the world. Only one tenth of China's land, in fact, is cultivable, a scant quarter of an acre per person. On this, China must feed a population of one billion people, almost a fourth of the world's total, more than the total number of inhabitants of the United States, the Soviet Union, and Western Europe combined.

These bare statements of geography and demography do not really convey the sense of crowding, the ubiquitous swarm of people that overwhelms a Westerner on his first exposure to China, what the Communists with simple truth call "the masses." Invariably, Chinese who travel to the United States have the opposite impression. "The first thing I noticed about New York," a Chinese journalist told me, "was that there never seem to be any people on the street." For whoever governs China, this sheer bulk of population makes the country almost unmanageable.

Traditionally, the Chinese themselves were confined to a square-shaped segment in the east and central part of the country, roughly half the size of the continental United States. The vast outer zone was sparsely populated by separate ethnic groups who today have come under Chinese Communist rule: the Manchus in the northeast, the Mongols, the Moslem Uighurs in Xinjiang, the Tibetans, the Zhuang, and the Dai, cousins of the natives of Thailand, in the south. Climatically, the great divide in China was between the cold, dry wheat-growing north and the moist rice land of the south. These regions separated at a line halfway between the Yellow River and the Yangtze, on the 33rd parallel. In comparative terms, China lies somewhat south of both the United States and Europe. Peking, in north China, just inside the Great Wall, is on the same latitude as Philadelphia and Madrid; Shanghai, in central China, corresponds to New Orleans and Suez; Canton, in the south, to Havana and Calcutta.

With hard work and improved organization, the Communists have succeeded in doubling China's grain production since 1949. But with peace and good public health work, the population has also nearly doubled at the same time. It took over 4,000 years of recorded history for China to reach its first 500 million people, but a mere three decades more to swell to one billion. In the 1950s and 1960s, as China experienced a baby boom, Mao dismissed warnings about the danger of overpopulation as bourgeois claptrap and purged China's most respected economist for his temerity in urging the necessity of birth control. The more people, the greater the value of production, Mao argued, following Marxist orthodoxy. In the long run, that miscalculation may prove the Communists' most calamitous error. For recent Western studies show that food consumption per capita is actually only about what it was in the mid-1950s and, more surprisingly, no better than in the 1930s, before World War Two. These studies suggest that the average daily calorie supply in China is between 2,000 and 2,100 per person. Two thousand calories a day is the level of India, 2,100 is the norm in Pakistan. Americans eat an average of 3,240 calories a day. But what makes these figures worse is that three fourths of the protein in the Chinese diet and five sixths of the calories are derived from food grains like rice, wheat, and corn, rather than from other richer and more varied sources like meat, fish, eggs, vegetables, or sugar. In Asia only Bangladesh and Laos approach these proportions. Uneven distribution has compounded this shortage of food. A Communist periodical in Hong Kong disclosed in 1978, while I was based there, that the annual grain ration of 200 million Chinese peasants was less than 330 pounds a year. "That is to say," the journal said, "they are living in a state of semistarvation."

Here was another of those paradoxes, or to use one of Mao's favorite terms, contradictions. Because China has launched an intercontinental ballistic missile and exploded hydrogen bombs, because it has a sophisticated art and literature, it is easy to forget that China is still a poor country, that in some ways it belongs to the third world, not to the superpower category. I was constantly struck by these contrasts. Chinese industry now turns out over two million television sets a year; but in Sichuan province, in the southwest, I saw four teen-age girls hitched to a cart, like oxen, pulling hundreds of pounds of steel reinforcing rods up a steep hill. I had dinner one night with a Chinese pilot who had trained to be an astronaut. But his family lived in a house without a toilet or running water. They had to use a public lavatory, with an open hole to squat over, that was a hundred feet from their house. The stench instinctively made me hold my nose. Peking University is one of China's two most prestigious colleges. But because of the penurious budget for education, the school cafeteria has no tables, chairs, or even bowls or chopsticks. The students must bring their own utensils and then take the food back to their dormitories to eat, a situation that has led to occasional campus protests.

The most important contrast is that between the large cities and the countryside, where live 800 million Chinese, one third of all the world's farmers. Parts of rural China seem stuck in another century. A Chinese professor who at the end of the Cultural Revolution was sent to Anhui province, in central China, not far from where we saw the mud-walled villages from the train, described what it was like to live there. Everything was made from mud, he recalled: the floors, the walls, even the beds and the stools the peasants sat on were constructed from pounded earth. The villagers had no wood for fuel —all the trees in the region had long ago been chopped down—so the women and children gathered grass and wheat stalks, depriving the earth of valuable natural nutrients. During the year the professor was there, he ate no meat, and the family he was quartered with had no matches, no soap, and most of the time no cooking oil, an essential part of the Chinese diet. A wrinkled seventy-year-old woman neighbor said to him admiringly one day, "Even the hair on your legs is bigger than the hair raised on ours."

The Communists have largely abolished the brutal poverty and starvation which afflicted China before 1949, a significant achievement. The clearest indication is that the average life expectancy has jumped from thirty-two years before Liberation in 1949 to sixty-four years now, a phenomenal improvement matched by only a few other developing countries. But there is still great disparity, though it is often obscured from foreigners in comparatively comfortable Peking.

My wife, Barbara, discovered this when she went on a visit with an Australian friend, Sue Walker, to Xian, 600 miles southwest of Peking, once the ancient capital of China in the Han and Tang dynasties when it was known as Changan. At the recommendation of their guide from the China Travel Service, they went out to dinner to the May First Restaurant, one of the city's main eateries. From the time they sat down on low stools at a plain wooden table covered with dirty dishes, leftover scraps of food, and puddles of grease, the atmosphere made them uneasy. There were flies buzzing around the table, and the concrete floor was littered with bits of bone and gristle shoved off the table by previous customers who had cleared a space for themselves at which to dine. A waitress wearing a dirty white smock and cap informed them brusquely that the only thing left to eat was *baozi,* a kind of steamed roll filled with chopped cabbage and bits of meat. As they waited for the food to arrive, eight other customers, all men dressed in patched and faded blue clothes, pulled up their stools in a semicircle around their table to watch. Some of them were picking their teeth. "We got the feeling we were the nightly entertainment," Barbara said after she came back to Peking.

Finally the food came, along with a bowl of greasy chicken broth with small pieces of coriander floating in it, the only thing the restaurant had to drink. After the two women ate all they could and were about to leave, "suddenly a dirty, weathered hand appeared on the table, palm up. Almost before we realized that the hand belonged to a disheveled old beggar dressed in rags, a waitress spotted him and shooed him away." He moved a few paces off, then squatted down on his haunches to watch for another opportunity.

It soon came. Barbara's friend decided it was best to leave and went over to the cashier's table to pay but left her silk Chinese-style jacket draped over her stool. As she got up, the beggar who had been eying them leapt onto the table, while another beggar, just as dirty and ragged, appeared from the opposite direction.

"They began fighting over what was left of the food," Barbara related. "The first man grabbed three of the steamed rolls, clenching them so tightly the juice ran down his sleeve. The other grabbed for a bowl of soup, splashing it all over Sue's jacket. The whole time they were yelling and flailing at each other. Finally the waitresses and some of the other customers managed to pull them apart. But they kept their loot."

As the restaurant staff urged Barbara and her friend to leave, out of evident embarrassment, they saw the two beggars jump for another table that had just been vacated by a Chinese.

None of these experiences moved me as deeply, however, as did the accounts our Chinese friends told about the persecution they had undergone during the political campaigns of the past thirty years, particularly the most tumultuous of all, the Cultural Revolution. A young girl recounted how her family was banished from their home in Peking to a remote mountain village and she had to watch as her mother was clubbed to death with iron bars and her father beaten senseless because they were accused of being reactionaries. A woman in her twenties recalled how she felt when as a teen-ager in 1966 she willingly denounced her father as a counterrevolutionary at a mass meeting in front of her parents—it was all for the glory of Chairman Mao, she believed at the time. A Chinese surgeon told me how his father, a respected engineer, and his mother had been tortured to death and he himself exiled to a kind of Chinese Siberia in Xinjiang province in the far northwest, all on suspicion they were American spies.

The official Chinese press itself has limned the dimensions of the disaster brought on by the Cultural Revolution. According to the *People's Daily,* 100 million people suffered from political harassment during the decade from 1966 to Mao's death in 1976. Three reporters from the New China News Agency recounted an incident in Shanghai that more than any other episode illustrates to me the brutalization of the spirit at the time. On May 1, 1968, by their account, a contingent of government officials went to the Shanghai home of the mother of a young woman named Lin Zhao, who had been jailed for keeping a diary critical of the Party. The officials told Lin's mother that her daughter had been executed three days earlier as a counterrevolutionary.

But the money spent on the execution had been a waste, the officials added sardonically, and they demanded that the mother pay five fen—a little more than three cents—to cover the cost of the bullet they had put through the back of her daughter's head.

Almost all the Chinese I met had been compelled to throw away valued books, records, or paintings to placate bands of fanatic Red Guards who ransacked their homes looking for decadent "bourgeois" or "feudal" culture. Most of China's leading writers, musicians, and artists were imprisoned or forced to stop their creative work for over a decade. For some it was worse. Lao She, the brilliant author of the poignant novel known as *Rickshaw Boy* in the West, about the tragic life of a rickshaw puller in Peking before 1949, was forced head-down into the bottom of a muddy lake by a band of Red Guards till he drowned.

Looking back on the Cultural Revolution, Liao Mosha, a distinguished seventy-five-year-old Communist Party writer who himself had his teeth knocked out by Red Guards and was imprisoned for thirteen years, wrote in 1981, "When we old comrades get together we often talk about the books we miss, books that have been forbidden, books that have been destroyed, books, carefully collected in libraries, that have been stolen, books that have perished. The 'Great Cultural Revolution' was the great revolution that sent culture to its death."

Ironically, the Cultural Revolution was also a disaster for the Red Guards themselves, for young people between the ages of fifteen and thirty-five. Many were thrown out of school as Mao ordered the nation's colleges closed and the curriculum shortened and simplified. Standards slipped when tests were abolished. Eighteen million urban teen-agers, one out of every ten people in the cities, were shipped off to the countryside in another of Mao's experiments. All of these changes resulted in over 100 million young people, by government count, ending up illiterate and many jobs being filled with people who had little or no training because of Mao's disdain for expertise. An architect pointed with shame to the Telecommunications Building, a hulking, Soviet-style edifice topped by a pointed tower at the western end of the Avenue of Eternal Tranquility in Peking. From the street it seemed to have no front door. The reason, my friend explained, was that young, untrained architectural students had been used to design the building at a time when older, more qualified builders were under political attack and by mistake they put the door at the rear of the building. A surgeon told me with anguish that most of the younger doctors on his staff couldn't be trusted to operate because they barely knew the difference between a vein and an artery. A first-year student at the Peking Foreign Languages Institute complained that his English teacher, who graduated from the same school in 1976, when Mao's Cultural Revolution reforms were in effect, didn't know as much English as he did. The legacy of Mao's utopian venture was a generation of lost and frustrated youth.

But ultimately the most corrosive effect was on the Communist Party itself. In the 1950s, Chinese friends assured me, most people had a genuine enthusiasm for the Communists. They had stamped out inflation and corruption and helped China "stand up," in Mao's phrase, for the first time in over one hundred years. No more. A middle-aged Party member, a short combative man with a square jaw, recalled how when he first joined the Party as a twenty-year-old he had written many letters volunteering to be sent to work in Hainan, the backward, jungle-covered island in the South China Sea. "I wanted to go to the poorest, hardest area to build a new China. My friends all had the same ideals," he said. "Now, no one would write such a letter."

One of the most chilling comments I heard came from a sixteen-year-old high school student, a lithe, intelligent girl who had a secret passion for trying on makeup and fashionable clothes when she wasn't in school.

"The Cultural Revolution actually was a good thing," she told me one day during a walk around the North Ocean Park in Peking, where China's emperors and their consorts used to stroll. "In the 1950s the Chinese were very naïve. They believed in the Communists, like my mother. Whatever the Communists said, she thought, that's great." Her mother is a high school teacher.

"Then in the Cultural Revolution, they locked her up for a year and a half because her father was a well-known scholar, what they derided as a 'bourgeois authority.' Some Red Guards in her school made her kneel on broken glass in front of all the students. For an intellectual, it was the worst thing that can happen—humiliation. She was disillusioned. With the Cultural Revolution, she saw through the Communists."

A balding archaeologist tried to put China's experience in perspective: "It may be presumptuous to say it, but what China has been through is like the holocaust," he remarked. There were no gas ovens, of course, no genocidal plan to eliminate an entire race. But there are horrifying parallels. Many people, like the doctor on the train or the teacher, were persecuted, arrested, tortured, or killed because of their class background, not for what they did, but for what they were said to be. Moreover, the destruction in lives, in lost education, in ruined books and art, in mismanaged factories and wasted resources as the country's population spiraled out of control was so staggering that it defies the Western imagination. What made it even more painful was that it began with a noble purpose—Mao launched his campaigns to eliminate poverty, bureaucracy, and class differences. But enthrall to his vision, his great if not final solution, he lost sight of the people who were forced to implement his dictates.

There was another similarity to the holocaust. Chinese who came through the cataclysms of the past thirty years seemed to me like survivors; they were chastened and cynical and numb. When I asked friends how they had coped with their personal tragedies, they often answered, *"Ma-mu-le"* (I was numbed). "Surviving" was also a word they frequently used. It reminded me of a passage in the most daring and dramatic of all the posters that have been affixed to China's walls in recent years, an epic 20,000 word broadside written on sixty-seven sheets of newsprint strung out for one hundred yards in downtown Canton in 1974. It was penned by three former Red Guards who combined their surnames into a single pen name, Li Yizhe. The Communist regime had degenerated into a "feudal fascist autocracy," they charged. They were soon arrested, then released after the downfall of the radicals in 1976 when Deng Xiaoping, Mao's successor as China's paramount leader, offered what seemed like greater freedom of expression. But in late 1980, shortly before I left China, they were rearrested as Peking clamped down again.

"We are survivors," the three men had written. "We were once bitten by the tiger but it failed to grind us small enough to swallow. Its claws left scars on our faces, so we are not handsome." They spoke for the many Chinese I met who had all been clawed by the tiger.

PART
1

CONNECTIONS

—

I.

Foreign Devils

洋 鬼 子

HOSTMANSHIP

"Is it not a pleasure to have friends come from afar?"
Confucius, *in the opening passage of the* Analects

My four-year-old son, Ethan, and I were walking down the Avenue of Eternal Tranquility outside the Peking Hotel on a blustery fall afternoon when I noticed a bespectacled man in his fifties, dressed in a shabby gray overcoat, staring at us. I had long since become accustomed to the Chinese habit of gawking at foreigners. They gathered in front of the Peking Hotel, where I lived and worked for the first year I was stationed in China, and surrounded any Westerner who emerged. It was always friendly, simple curiosity, never menacing. And Ethan was a special marvel, with long blond hair trimmed in a Buster Brown cut and the build of a miniature fullback.

This spectator was so intense that he began to follow us, a few steps off to the left, never taking his eyes off us. He was still staring at us when, with a loud thwack, he walked straight into a tree. His horn-rimmed glasses split neatly in two over the bridge of his nose, the two halves dropping to the pavement and smashing. He was stunned by the blow, bouncing off a few feet before falling to the ground. A trickle of blood flowed from a gash on his forehead. I went over to try to help him, but he looked up at me and smiled. Where an American would have cursed or cried out in anger, he smiled.

As much as any other during my twenty months in China, this tragicomic encounter illustrated how bizarre foreigners seem to Chinese, how exotic Westerners are in Chinese eyes. For in a land of people who all have straight dark hair, our hair is not hair color at all, but yellow, brown, even red, curly, not straight, like old Chinese paintings of demons. Our bodies are too fat and covered with horrible fuzz, like animals; Chinese have smooth, hairless skin.

In a country where history weighs heavily, we foreigners have too much bouncing vitality and always try to get things accomplished too quickly. Perhaps because of our richer diet, we have energy to waste that Chinese prefer to conserve for the long haul. If we move in allegro, Chinese are keyed in adagio. We are too frank; we can quarrel in public and then make up later without fear of losing face and causing permanent enmity.

The gap between Chinese and foreigners is almost unbridgeable. Every Monday through Saturday I sat in *The Times*'s office—an ordinary hotel room supplemented by three filing cabinets, a bookcase, and a typewriter—with my Chinese assistant, Wu Qianwei. Lanky and angular, with an incorrigible cowlick and heavy Coke-bottle glasses, he was assigned to me by the Diplomatic Services Bureau, the government agency which provides foreign diplomats and journalists with everything from housing to maids and chauffeurs. But despite our constant physical proximity and a certain slow warmth that developed between us, Wu still referred to me, when he was talking to other Chinese in the room or over the phone, as the *wai-guo-ren,* literally, the "external country person," the foreigner. When I lived in Taiwan for three years as a graduate student and later as a part-time correspondent for *The Times,* the neighborhood children always shouted, *"Yang-gui-zi"* (Foreign devil), when I walked in and out of the house.

China's greatest twentieth-century writer, Lu Xun, observed, "Throughout the ages, the Chinese have had only two ways of looking at foreigners, up to them as superior beings or down on them as wild animals. They have never been able to treat them as friends, to consider them as people like themselves."

This sense of separateness has a long history. For 4,000 years, the Chinese rested secure in their superiority. The Chinese empire was unquestionably the greatest in the world, the "Central Kingdom," its boundaries coterminous with civilization. Outside it were only barbarians. The Chinese Emperor was the "Son of Heaven," mediator between heaven and earth; China had invented paper, gunpowder, and the compass; its poetry and art neared the sublime; its system of government by an elite of ethical bureaucrats had achieved perfect equipoise. Not even famines, floods, or conquest by alien nomads disturbed its serenity for long. In the early legends of the origin of the universe in China, there is an odd omission. There is no hint of any hero who led the Chinese to China from elsewhere. It was assumed that the Chinese originated in China.

The pride all this inspired among the Chinese is something beyond Western experience and comprehension. "Nationalism" is too paltry a word to describe it, for to the Chinese, China was a synthesis of people, territory, language, history, art, and philosophy, more like a religion than simply another nation state. In the twentieth century Chinese xenophobia became a potent force contributing to the Communists' victory, as many frustrated middle-class Chinese intellectuals and hungry peasants threw in their lot with Mao when they came to believe that only the Communists could expel the Japanese and make China strong again.

If nationalism has now gone out of style for many people in Europe and America, it has not for Chinese. At a banquet my wife, Barbara, and I attended in the immense East Room of the Great Hall of the People given by Pan American World Airlines to mark the beginning of its flights from New York to Peking, several Chinese officials were discussing the news they had just heard that John Lennon had been shot in New York. The menu that evening included sharks' fin soup with crab meat, roast goose with plum sauce, candied white fungus, and giant sliced prawns with chillies. Pan Am had added to the festivities by giving each guest a battery-operated quartz alarm clock, a trinket the Chinese at our table had never seen before. But they were concerned about Lennon. He was a famous singer, wasn't he, with some British musical group? a stern-faced cadre in a black Mao suit asked. Yes, said another, he had been honored by the Queen for his services to England. The shooting was a real tragedy, the second man added.

"Lennon certainly earned a lot of foreign exchange for his country." For the Chinese, that was John Lennon's epitaph; not the member of the Beatles, or the singer who pioneered a new musical idiom, or the pacifist, but the patriot.

History gave Chinese a unique sense of pride, and it also left them with an unusual style of dealing with foreigners. For several millennia foreigners who came to China were fitted into the tribute system—if they recognized China's superiority by bringing presents to the Emperor, they were allowed limited rights to live and trade in one of the ports farthest from Peking. In the seventeenth, eighteenth, and nineteenth centuries, as Europeans and then Americans began to buy Chinese tea and silk in exchange for silver and opium, they were added to the other barbarians, the Japanese, the Vietnamese, the traders from the petty states of the Malay Peninsula and the coasts of India. British and American merchants were confined to the "Thirteen Factories" outside the walls of Canton, a tiny area under a quarter of a mile long and two hundred yards wide. There, in the distant tropical south, they operated under irksome restrictions: they could not bring their wives with them, ride in sedan chairs, row on the river, or enter Canton city.

In 1793, peeved by these rules, an expansive British government sent an emissary, the Earl of Macartney, to the court of the Emperor Qian-long in Peking. His mission was to seek permission to open other ports for trade and an island depot where British goods could be stored and ships refitted. Macartney also brought magnificent gifts: 600 packages transported through the city walls by 90 wagons, 40 barrows, 200 horses, and 3,000 coolies. The Chinese instantly labeled these "tribute presents," confirming Britain's subservient position. The Emperor would not alter the traditional system. He issued an edict thanking King George III for his "respectful spirit of submission." But he pointed out, "The virtue and prestige of the Celestial Dynasty having spread far and wide, the kings of the myriad nations come by land and sea with all sorts of precious things. Consequently there is nothing we lack, as your principal envoy and others have themselves observed. We have never set much store on strange or ingenious objects, nor do we need any more of your country's manufactures."

In the end, the British broke down their confinement at Canton only with the Opium War of 1839–42, when British gunboats and soldiers forced a weak and reluctant Qing government to accept the import of opium from British India and the opening of a series of "treaty ports" to foreigners. There followed a century of humiliating Chinese decay and impotence. But in 1949 when a powerful Chinese government was finally reestablished once more, by the Communists, it moved to re-create some of the glory of the old empire, if in modern guise.

I was constantly struck by how much time and effort the Communist hierarchy devoted to receiving endless streams of foreign visitors in the Great Hall of the People, just across the street from the palace of the Ming and Qing emperors. It was a solemn quotidian ritual, the African colonels, the French bankers, the Japanese industrialists, the American congressmen, the heads of the Marxist splinter parties who came to pay court on the aging Chinese leaders in their new marble throne room. Once, when I accompanied the U.S. Defense Secretary, Harold Brown, on a courtesy call on Party Chairman Hua Guofeng, Deng was just emerging from another room next door where he had received the head of the lower house of the Japanese Diet. All these audiences were recorded on television and shown that night on the news. In no Western country would most of these visitors be newsworthy; certainly in no Western capital would senior officials devote so much time to greeting foreigners, however humble. But in China it was a signal to the Chinese people that their country was again the epicenter of the world, a strong nation that respectful foreigners came to pay homage to.

Since Confucius, Chinese have made a priority of entertaining visitors, making a good impression on them, and they have raised hostmanship into an art form. It is one of the most delightful aspects of Chinese society, and accounts in large measure for the vastly different perceptions Westerners have of China and the Soviet Union, even though their Communist systems have much in common.

I was often both flattered and amused by the efforts made on my behalf during my stay in China. Whenever I took a bus, invariably jammed, Chinese men and women both would insist on giving me their seats, just because I was a foreign guest. At first I tried to refuse, but that only made me more embarrassed because the Chinese passenger would get up from his or her seat and stay standing until I finally acquiesced and sat down. I remember going to a department store in Urumqi, the capital of Xinjiang, shortly before 7 P.M. as it was about to close for the day. I was with Wu, my government-assigned assistant, whom I called simply Lao Wu in the old Chinese informal style which the Communists have adopted. (*Lao* means old, and since he was forty-two, a year older than I, he became Lao Wu. Anyone younger than I, I addressed with the prefix *xiao,* "Little.") We needed to buy some of the string mesh bags Chinese use to carry their groceries in, for we had just purchased half a dozen succulent Hami melons, the sugary orange fruit that barbarians from Central Asia used to bring by camel caravan as presents to the Emperor. A sullen clerk behind the counter pointed to her watch.

"Too late, it's seven P.M., the store is closed," she said triumphantly.

But Lao Wu acted decisively, scoring the ultimate debating point in China. "But this is a foreign guest. He needs a shopping bag." The clerk looked at me, grunted with resignation, and then reached down and produced the bags we needed.

On another trip, in the northwest city of Lanzhou, it appeared Lao Wu and I would be stuck for several days longer than we wanted to because the once-a-day airplane flights to Peking were fully booked. "It's no big problem," my guide from the local foreign affairs office said with a self-confident smile. "I will use my connections to get you a seat." A prim, slender woman in her late twenties, she was as good as her word. A few hours later she reported success.

"I had to ask them to bump two Chinese passengers off the plane for a foreigner," she recounted. "The cadre in charge was reluctant to do it because he had already taken two other Chinese off for a foreign technician and his interpreter. But when I told him you are a journalist, he finally agreed. We can always do it for foreigners," the guide concluded.

Careful preparation and a dash of deception are other ingredients in the treatment for visiting foreigners. When I first took up residence in China in June 1979, I remember a trip to the Yiliu people's commune on the mile-high Yunnan plateau in the southwestern part of the country near the city of Kunming. It may be the only commune in China with its own parking lot, a big, paved empty space in front of the main administration building. Most of the peasants there still walk or ride in horse carts, so the parking lot is for visitors. At least that was my guess when I arrived for a tour in a snaking convoy of thirty cars and buses with the U.S. Secretary of Health, Education and Welfare, Joseph A. Califano. This was one of the obligatory stops on any visitor's itinerary of China, be he private tourist or foreign dignitary, an hour at a commune, a little look at how well agriculture has done since Liberation. Califano, an intelligent, energetic, and forceful man, a lawyer by training, asked if the commune was average for China. Yes, the local authorities assured him. Had other foreign visitors been here before? he pressed further, hinting the commune might be a showpiece. No, the officials responded, he was the first foreigner to be brought here.

But there were small telltale signs which suggested that the commune was not just average. The building where Califano was greeted and given a briefing on the commune's grain output had just been whitewashed—some of the paint had splashed on the dirt floor. In the back there were toilets thoughtfully differentiated by painted profiles of men and women, their large sharp-pointed noses and curly hair decidedly un-Chinese. Outside, I noticed, the dirt path leading toward a village of mud-brick houses, our next destination, had just been swept. The trace marks of the wicker brooms in the dust were still visible. At an outdoor public privy on our path, lime had been generously spread to dampen the usual rich, nauseous aroma. There were lines of peasant women in broad, flat bamboo hats weeding the knee-high fields of ripening green rice. Bent double at the waist, they were performing China's most ancient ritual. But on each narrow dike that led from the village to the fields, between the American visitors and the natives, there were young cadres in blue Mao tunics, just to avoid any untoward incident. It was easy to tell they weren't peasants themselves, for they bore the special insignia of those who have made it in Communist China, a fountain pen in their left-hand breast pocket.

Califano must have had his doubts about what he was shown, because that afternoon, driving back to Kunming, he suddenly asked his host, a deputy governor of Yunnan province, to stop as they passed through another village. Their long black Red Flag limousine screeched to a halt at the head of the long caravan of vehicles. To the consternation of the Chinese, Califano got out and tried to walk around the village. But there had been no official preparation here, and the peasants, caught by surprise, fled like chickens, scattering in all directions. So thorough was the panic that Califano couldn't find anyone to talk to.

When I recounted the episode later to a friend in Peking who worked for a government diplomatic agency, she snickered at my naïveté. Such precautions are typical of the lengths Chinese go to to entertain, please, beguile, and often manipulate foreigners, she said. A vivacious, winsome woman with large sparkling eyes and the standard short, bowl-cut hair, it was her job to escort state guests around Peking. One place she often took them was the big Chaoyang market in the northeast part of the city to show how well the Chinese are fed. When an important visitor was scheduled to arrive, the market would be given a "visiting task," she told me. Trucks would be sent to the market early that morning with extra supplies of live chickens and frozen fish, two delicacies often unavailable. The visitors were always impressed, she recalled. What they didn't know was that, though the Chinese customers could buy the goods on display, the fish would be counted against their monthly ration and most of the special fish were so large they were over people's quota of one pound a month. So all they could do was look.

Another key part of the treatment for visiting politicians, cultural luminaries, and assorted bigwigs is the airport reception by hundreds of clapping, singing schoolchildren, their cheeks rouged and their eyebrows blackened for the occasion, followed by a twelve-course epicurean banquet in the Great Hall of the People, complete with endless libations of fiery *maotai* liquor and toasts to friendship. The total effect of this hostmanship is like a powerful tranquilizer, enough to make otherwise rational and intelligent people suspend disbelief. I remember Mayor Ed Koch of New York, normally canny, self-assured, and unflappable, accepting a cigarette from the Party boss of Xian, the old capital in the west, and then lighting up. His aides were stunned. Koch never smokes and hates people to smoke in his presence.

"I didn't want to offend these people, they have been so nice to us," Koch said afterward. "It's the first cigarette I've smoked in twenty years, and I shall not take another for twenty more years."

Then there was Shirley MacLaine at the White House banquet for Deng Xiaoping in 1979. President Carter had invited her to sit at the head table with him and the diminutive Chinese leader since she had been one of the first Americans to visit China after Ping-Pong diplomacy began in 1971 and had both written a book—*You Can Get There From Here*—and made a movie extolling the benefits Mao's Cultural Revolution reforms had brought to a happy and prosperous China. At the White House dinner, Miss MacLaine enthusiastically recounted to Deng a meeting she had with a Chinese nuclear physicist who had been sent to a commune to grow tomatoes. The scientist had assured her he felt much happier and more productive on the farm than in his lab, Miss MacLaine said. "He lied," Deng cut her off. "That was what he had to say at the time." To her credit, Miss MacLaine told the story on herself on television the next day.

But there was also a less congenial, more sinister side to hostmanship as practiced by the Communists. Along with restoring the grandeur of imperial audiences for visitors, the Communists also reimposed the traditional hermetic restrictions on foreigners in China, both to buffer the outsiders from the less pleasant realities of Chinese life and to prevent any bourgeois contagion from infecting China. Just as in imperial times foreigners were confined to a small ghetto, so today virtually all foreigners in China must live in specially designated housing: diplomats and journalists in three-walled compounds of modern high-rise apartment buildings guarded by army sentries on the northeast edge of Peking, teachers in the isolated, rambling Friendship Hotel (originally built for Soviet advisers) to the northwest, and students in reserved quarters in the university dormitories.

Any Chinese who wanted to visit my office in the Peking Hotel had to register his or her name and work unit with the Public Security Ministry guards at the front desk; then the next day their office would receive a slip reporting their contact with a foreigner. I learned this when an earnest young Chinese journalist from Peking television daringly, but foolishly, it turned out, insisted on coming to see me in the hotel. Deng had said the officials should "emancipate their minds," and she took him seriously. But a few days later three policemen went to call on her Party secretary, who in turn summoned her to the meeting. "Why did you go to see Butterfield, what information did you give him?" they demanded. She was ordered to write a self-criticism and barred from seeing me again, she told me in one last rendezvous.

"We are supposed to be a socialist country, that means relying on the people," she said with disappointment. "But our government doesn't trust the people. What is there so secret that we can't talk with foreigners? This is no different from the Gang of Four." Several times later I ran into her at press conferences, but she cautiously turned her head so she wouldn't have to see me.

Another acquaintance, a college English teacher, reported that at a weekly political study session their Party leader had read out a new directive from the Peking city government prohibiting Chinese from meeting foreigners unless they first received clearance from their workplace. Afterward they were to make a full report of everything that was said. (Several other Chinese recounted being given the same instructions.) The regulation angered the teacher, and she insisted on inviting me to visit her apartment one Sunday afternoon on the school campus. I tried to decline, but she said I would be rude to refuse her hospitality. At her direction, we drove up to the front door of her building in *The Times*'s car, clearly marked by my foreigner's license plate, the usual 31 prefix denoting Peking but colored in red.

A plain, stocky woman whose passion in life was improving her already fluent English and going abroad to study, she lived with her retired parents. Her father, tall, stooped, and balding, a former government clerk, was clearly unsettled by my arrival. He understood the risks and saw little to gain from my visit. He called her into the bedroom and upbraided her. "You shouldn't have brought him here," he said, loud enough for me to hear through the thin walls.

I felt I should leave, but her mother, a round, kindly, former kindergarten teacher with short gray hair held firmly in place with bobby pins, blocked the door. "It's nothing, you must stay, besides I have already started cooking dinner," she said affably. I was caught in a dilemma. It would be an offense against Chinese manners to go, but a political offense to stay. Her mother sensed my unease. She took my arm gently and led me to a red plastic-covered armchair. "Just sit there till dinner is ready," she counseled.

Unfortunately, the next day the family received a visit from two neighbors, both Party members and administrators in the college. "We saw you had a foreign visitor, that was a mistake," they rebuked her. A few weeks later she took an English test for teachers in her school to decide who would win three coveted scholarships to spend a year studying in the United States. She got the highest mark, she claimed, but was turned down "for political reasons."

"For a Chinese to become friendly with a foreigner is like the old saying about a silk worm—you are just spinning a cocoon around yourself, ensnaring yourself in a web," she added. I felt guilty, as if I were radioactive and contaminated any Chinese I came in contact with. The government's restrictions were in hypocritical contrast to the large red illuminated sign in Chinese and English in the lobby of the Peking Hotel that I passed several times a day: "We have friends all over the world." Friendship to the government meant those carefully controlled tours of China for foreigners who came away full of sympathy for the People's Republic, or giving foreigners special privileges like access to the Friendship Store—the department and grocery store reserved for foreigners—where they could buy more goods than are available to ordinary Chinese. But friendship did not include intimacy with individual Chinese.

Many Chinese themselves resent the government's rules barring them from the hotels where foreigners stay and the Friendship Store. They see the regulations as discrimination by the regime against its own people. A doctor in Shanghai recalled the infamous sign that before 1949 blocked a small park by the city's waterfront: "No dogs or Chinese allowed." The Communists often dredged it up as an example of imperialist perfidy. But when the physician tried to visit me in the Jinjiang Hotel in Shanghai, the police guard at the gate wouldn't let him in without registering. "Nowadays dogs can go into the hotel, but Chinese still can't," he said with uncharacteristic animus.

The government is particularly sensitive about any romantic involvement between Chinese and foreigners, regarding it virtually as a form of national dishonor. When a precocious, outspoken high school student I knew began dating a European exchange student at Peking University, two agents from the Public Security Ministry paid a call on her parents, they told me later.

"What is the relationship between your daughter and this foreigner?" the police quizzed them. "Why has she been seeing him? You should educate her not to go out with foreigners, it is a shameful thing for China. Foreigners are always trying to ferret out our secrets and destroy the revolution. If your daughter loves her country, she will break off this relationship."

The student had met her European boy friend at a dance at the Nationalities Palace, a cavernous theater and office building where the government had opened an incongruous three-times-a-week discotheque in 1979 complete with flashing colored lights and Chinese beer and orange soda. The move was part of Mao's successors' gradual liberalization, "to satisfy the requests of our foreign friends," as one official said to me, for more to do on Saturday nights. The dances were supposed to be strictly segregated—foreigners only. But occasionally a few venturesome Chinese would sneak in, like the high school student, after dressing themselves up in tight-fitting trousers or putting on lipstick and eye shadow to try to confound the guards. What most Westerners didn't realize, she said, was that while the disco for foreigners occupied the first floor and the basement, there were also dances for Chinese on the second floor, no foreigners admitted.

For a Chinese woman to be caught sleeping with a foreign man is a serious offense. An acquaintance in the army related that a popular and attractive female singer in an air force music troupe had been arrested after spending the night with several Japanese diplomats and businessmen. He found out about the affair because the army mounted a confidential exhibit in Peking to display the tainted loot she had supposedly received for her promiscuity: a Japanese-made television set, a refrigerator, a tape recorder, and some clothes. The show hinted the police even had videotapes of some of the bedroom scenes.

Some love stories between Chinese and foreigners have a happier ending. Susan Wilf, a bright, outgoing graduate student from Harvard with curly brown hair and a voluptuous figure, managed to become the first American to marry a Chinese since the Cultural Revolution. She met her future spouse, a strikingly handsome accordion player in a Chinese band, Chen Daying, when a mutual friend arranged for her to tutor Chen in English. Government regulations required that they get permission to marry from their respective work units—for Susan, it was the Peking Second Foreign Languages Institute, where she was teaching. She wasn't sure what to expect. The couple had not even been able to buy an engagement ring until Susan pretended to the guard at the Friendship Store that Chen was already her husband. For ordinary Chinese are not allowed in the store, and it is the only place in Peking where precious stones are sold. But after a wait of six weeks, the minimum in a case of such magnitude, their union was approved by the State Council itself, China's cabinet, she was told.

At their wedding party, the couple opened the occasion by bowing four times to the one hundred guests, once for each of the directions of the compass, a Chinese custom. Then they startled the assemblage by kissing, for a full thirty seconds. In revolutionary China, kissing in public is still bourgeois.

A tiny pigtailed sixteen-year-old girl with rosy cheeks sitting in the rear of the room took it philosophically. "Each nationality has its own habits," she whispered to me. "It's all right for foreigners to kiss. Chinese might normally shake hands or something."

But the government also took steps to limit marriage between Chinese and foreigners as the number of foreign students, teachers, and tourists mushroomed in the late 1970s.* In 1980, Peking put out a decree prohibiting four categories of Chinese from marrying foreigners under any circumstances: all those in the armed forces, anyone in the political departments of the Party who handled personnel matters, those who worked with state secrets, and everyone in what was termed foreign affairs work, including diplomats, guides for the China Travel Service, and interpreters, like my assistant Lao Wu.

Chinese in this last group, who deal with foreigners on a daily basis, are selected for their jobs with extra prudence and kept under a number of special constraints. Over my twenty months in Peking, I gradually developed a genuine fondness for Lao Wu. Although he kept a discreet silence whenever I tried to discuss politics with him, I appreciated his conscientious work in the office. Without a complaint, he turned out reams of translations from the Chinese press and sparred on my behalf with the bureaucracy. But a friend whose father was a general cautioned me not to become too close to him.

"You know, every Saturday afternoon he and your driver have to make a full report about what you do and say during the week at their political study session in the Diplomatic Services Bureau," the general's son confided. He himself had a friend who was an interpreter for a European embassy, so he knew the drill. "They are told to draw a very clear line with you, they will never tell you anything, and it is part of their job to investigate you."

It was an unsettling sensation to know you lived with a spy, with yourself as the object of attention, and I sometimes tended to dismiss the notion as unthinkable. But one Friday afternoon when Lao Wu was out of the office running an errand, the Diplomatic Services Bureau rang for him on the phone. My other assistant, Jan Wong, answered. Jan is a Canadian-Chinese whose father runs a Chinese restaurant in Montreal and who had come to China to study at Peking University in the early 1970s. Because of Lao Wu's official role, I had hired Jan to help when I wanted to interview political dissidents or broaden my contacts among ordinary Chinese. At this, she was marvelous and soon became indispensable. Short, energetic, and engaging,

*The number of American students in China jumped from zero in 1978, before the normalization of Sino–U.S. relations, to 300 in 1981. In 1978, when China first opened its doors to regular tourism, the number of visitors reached 125,000, more than in all the previous years since 1949. In 1981, the number of tourists increased further to 218,000.

33

with a round, girlish face, Jan wore her hair in pigtails and dressed in plain, baggy proletarian blue like her former schoolmates. She had also learned to speak Chinese without a trace of a foreign accent. So she passed as a native. On that Friday afternoon when she took the call for Lao Wu, the woman at the Diplomatic Services Bureau assumed she was Chinese.

"Tell Wu he doesn't have to make his report tomorrow, the meeting is canceled," the caller said.

After the Chinese finally gave me an apartment and my family was able to move to Peking in September 1980, we had a similar problem with the woman the Diplomatic Services Bureau assigned to us as a maid, Wang *a-yi*, or "Auntie" Wang. Squat and expansive, with a full round face, she had the cherubic smile of a middle-aged Buddha. But she too reported on us each week, I was told, and she proved extraordinarily reticent about divulging even the most trivial personal information. When my wife asked her what her husband did, she replied, "He works." Several times when we asked her to stay late and baby-sit—you can't just call up a Chinese girl and ask her to watch your children for the evening—I was concerned that she would have difficulty getting home. She lived more than a half-hour bicycle ride from our apartment and the weather was very cold, so I offered to drive her home. But each time she refused. If she appeared in her neighborhood in *The Times*'s car, it would be reported and she might be accused of forming too close a relationship with us, we surmised. Another journalist, Tony Walker of the *Melbourne Age,* did manage to become friendly with his *a-yi.* Before her son got married, she extended an invitation to the Walkers, a great honor they thought. But a few days later she apologized with great embarrassment. The Diplomatic Services Bureau had found out about the invitation and ordered her to rescind it.

As a further precaution against foreigners, the general's son told me, there was a list of foreign diplomats who were regarded as intelligence agents. One copy was kept in the office at Peking University that handles foreign students, he added. That way the cadres who monitored the activities of the overseas students could check if they were in contact with the presumed spies. Among the names on the sheet he mentioned to me was that of a close friend, Roger Garside, a career diplomat in the British Foreign Office who has since written an informative book about contemporary Chinese politics, *Coming Alive, China After Mao.* I suspected his worst crime was that he spoke Chinese too well and had too many Chinese acquaintances. There was also a list giving the government's opinion about each foreign correspondent, a disaffected young journalist told me. Whenever I had an interview or took a trip, the officials involved were briefed on my rating. My name had an asterisk next to it, the journalist said. That meant I was considered *fan-hua,* "Anti-China," a particularly odorous label. He advised me not to be offended, it only meant the government was disturbed by my reporting. But it did warrant the Public Security Ministry giving me special attention.

Only occasionally was I aware of this vigilance. One fall afternoon when I carelessly arranged to meet a young unemployed high school graduate outside the Peking Hotel and got directly in *The Times*'s car from the hotel parking lot, I noticed a shiny black Mercedes 280 behind us—no underpowered Chinese-made cars for the police. My acquaintance was a tall, stocky young woman with a set of toothpaste-fresh white teeth. We were driving straight west on the Avenue of Eternal Tranquility, and the Mercedes stayed close behind, speeding up when I drove faster, slowing down when I tried a more leisurely pace. Finally, at the far western edge of the city, I suddenly cut across the middle lane and did a U-turn. The Mercedes, filled with four men, I noted, followed suit. We continued driving for an hour, till it grew dark, both of us increasingly nervous. Then, in hopes of shaking our pursuers, I turned into the side road next to the Friendship Store. It was filled with other foreign cars and a swarm of Chinese waiting for a bus. The police calculated we were going into the store and stopped a few yards back. In the protection of the darkness and the crowd, my friend jumped out and joined the straggling queue for the bus.

Of all the forms of control and discrimination involving foreigners, the one that most nettled Westerners was the government's double-price standard, one set for foreigners, another for Chinese. When I took a trip to Sichuan with Lao Wu, for example, my airplane ticket cost 200 yuan ($133), his only 85 yuan ($57). In the hotel in Chengdu, the provincial capital, I was charged 100 yuan ($67) a night for my room, food, and use of a car, Lao Wu only 40 ($27). The authorities presented both bills to me to pay, since I was Lao Wu's employer, so there was no attempt to hide the price differential.

This system was designed to extract badly needed foreign currency for China, so it could import more U.S. grain, West German coal-mining technology, and Japanese steel mills. Rich capitalists could afford to pay, this theory holds. But only in a country with China's heritage of superiority would the government be so blatant about overcharging, I felt, so contemptuous of standards of fair play. One evening I invited a scholarly editor to the Xinjiang Restaurant in Peking, which was famous for its spicy mutton shashlik and its fried bread, Chinese food with a Middle Eastern flavor. The editor knew the manager of the restaurant and volunteered to make the reservation to save me the trouble. After we finished, I went to the counter to pay the bill. The waitress looked confused and annoyed.

"If you pay, then we have to charge a different price," she announced. "We calculated the bill for a Chinese, because it was a Chinese who made the reservation." When I still insisted on paying, she carefully crossed out each price on the check and entered a new one, twice or more the original amount.

Sometimes this double-price policy turns into sheer greed. When a delegation from the American public television network, PBS, came to Peking to discuss filming a series of seven one-hour documentaries on China, the Chinese television authorities said it would cost them $1.5 million for local assistance. That was ten times what it would cost in other countries and what the Americans were prepared to pay, an outraged New York producer said afterward.

"But the Japanese have already paid four million dollars to make a documentary on the Yellow River," the Chinese countered.

From another foreign television crew that had shot a historical documentary in China, the PBS delegation heard how the costs mounted up. The crew was filming a scene involving a warrior. The Chinese first asked that the crew pay for the rent of the costume, which was reasonable. Then the Chinese demanded that the foreign company pay for the horse on which the warrior would sit; that was also fair. Next the Chinese asked for money for the actor who would sit on the horse; agreed, said the crew. After the scene was completed, the Chinese had another charge—the crew had to pay for the cancellation of the Chinese opera performance in which the actor was to have played that night.

When the Japanese filmed a movie about the Yangtze River, the PBS delegation heard, they needed a boat. The Chinese said they would have to rent it for a month, though they used it for only a few days. After the Japanese finished shooting, the Chinese presented another bill—they would also have to pay for all the passengers who didn't ride on the boat for the month it would be out of service.

But the most bizarre story of price discrimination was a simple one told by an American woman married to an American-Chinese who had come to Peking to teach. When they took a train trip to Loyang, in central China, she was charged double what her husband was for the ride, since he counted as an overseas Chinese. Then when they spent the night in a hotel, in the same double bed, her bill was triple that of her husband.

Despite China's self-assurance and xenophobia, there is a radical ambivalence about how China should deal with the West and its technological and economic superiority. Since China's ignominious defeat in the Opium War a century ago, this has been the pivotal issue for Chinese, how to make China "rich and strong" again, and the country's policy has swung back and forth like a pendulum. Some Chinese statesmen, like Mao, have preached self-reliance and shutting out the world, the nativist approach. Others, like Deng, who himself spent six years in France as a worker and student in the 1920s, have held that salvation lies in copying the secrets of Western science and opening China to expanded foreign trade. Deng's epochal trip to the United States in 1979 was designed to underscore the correctness of his plan, but it also helped stimulate an insatiable new appetite for the bounties of capitalism as Chinese television beamed back pictures of American suburban living, the split-level ranch-style home with two cars in the garage, and a color television set in every living room. When the Communists, partially as a result, then saw young Chinese letting their hair grow long and listening to Hong Kong rock music and putting up posters on Democracy Wall calling for freedom of speech, it made them nervous. A backlash set in. Deng muttered darkly about creeping "bourgeois liberalism" and the press tried to counteract the glamor of the West by painting it in unfavorable terms. American workers eat meat and draw high salaries, the *People's Daily* sermonized, but the United States is beset by inflation, crime, unemployment, racial conflict, and a collapsing family system.

I recall one especially venomous speech by Zhang Guangdou, a vice chairman of Qinghua University, China's equivalent of the Massachusetts Institute of Technology. People should not be misled by the material prosperity of capitalist countries but look to the nature of the system, asserted Zhang, a hydroelectric expert who had studied in the United States before World War Two and had recently returned from a two-month visit to America.

"Our revolutionary teachers have all said that capitalism must collapse and socialism must replace capitalism," Zhang declared. It is important to remember that America's wealth was based on a long history of exploitation, Zhang charged, of the Indians, of the blacks, of Chinese immigrant laborers, of the whole continent of Latin America, which the United States had converted into a colony. In recent years, "even second world countries, such as Japan, Germany, and England are victims of its bullying.

"The United States did not participate in the two world wars. You fight, and they come in near the end. They did not fight on their own territory, the battles were mainly fought in Europe and Asia. As a consequence they grabbed up many resources, many things, it is an imperialist country." After World War Two, Zhang continued, the United States "enlisted the service of many German scientists. So all of the scientists and technicians are foreigners."

In China, he said, "After our victory over Japan, the Americans came in. American soldiers pushed their way around, doing whatever they pleased, raping women. They did every bad thing possible. At the time our country was very poor and productivity was low. Everything bought on the streets was American, toilet paper, milk powder, etc." This explained why America is rich and China poor, Zhang argued. But young Chinese should also be aware of the troubles Americans face in their own daily lives.

"Americans are always figuring and figuring, worrying that there won't be enough money. My standard of living is low, but I am not anxious. If a son in America goes to his mother's home to eat, he must pay money. If the mother goes to the son's house to eat, she must also give money. I'm not joking in the least. I'll give you an example. A family invited me to eat dinner. Four of them invited me, and after eating, and in front of me, they took out a calculator and calculated who owed what."

But in a society already made cynical by the constant din of propaganda, the stridency of attacks like Zhang's are counterproductive, too exaggerated to be credible. Perhaps nothing illustrates the Communists' ambivalence toward the West better than the steady stream of children of the Party elite who have gone to the United States since the normalization of relations in 1979. One of Deng's sons, a physicist, is a graduate student at the University of Rochester; Deng's daughter lives in the Chinese Embassy in Washington, where her husband is a military attaché. A son of the Foreign Minister, Huang Hua, is an undergraduate at Harvard; a daughter of Liu Shaoqi, the late head of state, is enrolled at Boston University. From Chinese friends, I heard of over a dozen offspring of Politburo members and cabinet ministers now in the United States. There has been no comparable exodus from the elite of the Soviet Union. For the Chinese Communists, this represents a tangible investment, a belief that China can usefully learn from America and that Peking's relations with Washington will continue to improve. Otherwise these children could be a liability in a future internal Chinese power struggle.

2. "Where Are You, Comrade?"

你那几同志

IDENTITY

"If language is incorrect, then what is said does not concord with what was meant; and if what is said does not concord with what was meant, what is to be done cannot be effected."

Confucius, in the Analects

The new wing of the Peking Hotel is a handsome, seventeen-story concrete and glass edifice in the modern international mode. It could have been built in Chicago, Nairobi, or Istanbul. The front is graced with rows of recessed balconies climbing to flag poles on the flat roof, very different from the gentle curve of traditional Chinese tiled eaves. An elevated driveway leads visitors to a set of high glass doors that automatically glide open and closed each time a guest steps on a sensitized metal grille. Inside the entrance there is a marble-topped reservations desk, and in the rear of the vast high-ceilinged lobby, padded by yards of plush red carpeting, an electronic panel that controls twin banks of eight elevators flickers with red, yellow, and blue lights like a computer console. Off to one side is the main dining room, to the other a shopping arcade that offers, along with postcards and maps of the capital, Chinese elixirs for long life and flagging virility: powdered rhinoceros horn, deer's tail, and ginseng root. When I first arrived in June 1979 to set up *The New York Times* bureau, I took these merely as pleasant exotica. I was not prepared for what came next.

A balding, slightly stooped clerk in a loose-fitting brownish-gray tunic stood behind the reservations desk, which was identified by a sign in English that said, "Accommodation Center."

"Do you have a room?" I asked in my best Chinese.

After examining me for what seemed several minutes, he replied, "Where are you?" or *"Ni nar"* in Chinese.

Thinking I had heard wrong, I repeated my question. But he answered again, "Where are you?"

Finally, sensing my confusion, he amplified. "We only give rooms to units, not to individuals," he said, using the Chinese word *danwei*. *Danwei*, I knew, meant a person's workplace, their office, factory, school, or commune. "Where are you?" therefore meant "What is your unit?" But I had just arrived in China as a U.S. journalist; I didn't have a *danwei*.

"Everyone in China has a *danwei*," the clerk said definitively. "You must find your *danwei*, or we can't give you a room."

Thus began my first task in China, to find my *danwei*. The Information Department, which had granted me my visa, disclaimed responsibility. The China Travel Service said they couldn't help because I was a resident in China and not a tourist. The Diplomatic Services Bureau, which arranges housing for foreigners in Peking, turned down my request because they said they gave out only apartments, which they didn't have, and not hotel rooms. The American Embassy was reluctant to become involved because the press and the government in the United States are supposed to keep their distance from each other. Eventually, I did appeal to the American ambassador, Leonard Woodcock, who wrote to the Foreign Ministry suggesting they should take the awful responsibility and adopt me as part of their *danwei*.

This adventure was a useful lesson. *Danwei*, I quickly discovered, are the basic building blocks of Chinese society, almost a second citizenship for most Chinese. A Chinese is more likely to be asked his *danwei* than his name when he goes someplace new. Chinese telephone conversations usually begin "Where are you?" not "Who is this?" When I stopped for a night in the remote industrial city of Qiqihar in the far northeastern corner of China, the first question on the registration form of the local hotel asked for the guest's unit. Only the second line inquired about his name.

At the entrance to the Peking Hotel the Public Security Bureau stations two guards in plainclothes. One day soon after my arrival I stood outside the door to observe their ritual. They automatically let in all foreigners, Chinese they recognize as hotel employees, and Party officials who arrive in prestigious chauffeur-driven sedans. But any other Chinese they pull over and challenge, "Where are you, comrade?" On one occasion Martin King Whyte, a sociologist from the University of Michigan who was in Peking on an academic exchange program, invited a deputy mayor of the capital to lunch in the hotel. This official, Lei Jieqiong, was actually a distinguished seventy-four-year-old sociologist herself, a graduate of the University of California, who had only recently been appointed to the city post even though she was not a Party member. Since she did not arrive in the requisite limousine which transports most officials, the police guards didn't recognize her importance. "Where are you?" they snarled. When she answered that she was a deputy mayor of the city, they laughed and forced her to go to the security desk and show her work pass. Only then did they realize their mistake. The irony of the story, Miss Lei pointed out later, was that the Peking Hotel actually as a unit belongs to the Peking city government.

The reason for this stress on *danwei* is that a *danwei* to a Chinese is far more than just his workplace. A tall thirty-five-year-old woman who worked in the semisecret Fourth Ministry of Machine Building, which produces electronics for China's defense industry, explained how the system works. She lived in an apartment in a vast compound of five-story gray-brick buildings managed by her ministry. All her neighbors were also employed by the ministry. To go in or out of the one entrance, she had to walk past an army guard in uniform, and if she brought any visitors into the compound, they had to register in the sentry box. The woman's nine-year-old son went to school in another building inside the compound; she shopped for groceries in the compound store; when the family was sick there was a clinic in the compound. The ministry also issued her her ration cards for rice, cooking oil, cloth, and what the Chinese call "industrial goods," including radios, watches, sewing machines, or bicycles.

But the *danwei*'s authority over her went even deeper, as she related one summer afternoon when we drove by her compound. It would have been impossible for me to go in past the sentry, she apologized. When she wanted to get married a decade ago, she recalled, she had been required to apply to the Party secretary of her *danwei* for permission, a standard procedure. Her *danwei* then ran a security check with her boy friend's unit, and only after both *danwei* approved, could they wed. If she wanted to try to transfer to another job, her unit had to agree. When an elderly neighbor died recently, she added, the *danwei* had arranged for his funeral and cremation. To talk to me, a foreigner, she was supposed to receive permission from her *danwei* beforehand, and she was to report back on whatever we discussed.

Not every *danwei* in China is so well equipped that it can provide this full range of cradle-to-grave services. Some units don't have their own housing; only the largest have both their own schools and hospitals. But for the government the *danwei* structure means that society is organized as much as a security system as it is as a social or economic system. If the hallmark of the feudal system in medieval Europe and Japan was the peasant's inescapable bondage to the land, the essence of the Chinese system, I sometimes thought, was the individual's ties to his *danwei,* a kind of industrial feudalism.

There was no exact counterpart for the *danwei* in traditional China. Earlier dynasties did practice a mutual guarantee organization called the *bao-jia* system: families were organized in groups of tens and hundreds with each unit responsible for the acts of all the others. But the real antecedent probably lies simply in the Chinese penchant for bonding the individual to his group.

Chinese are more naturally comfortable with their group than by themselves. We say "everyone"; the Chinese equivalent is *da-jia,* "the great family." We select our own separate food from the menu, then eat from our own dishes. Chinese order their meals together and then eat from common plates, sharing the food. When Chinese drink alcohol at a meal, they never drink by themselves. They first lift their glass to a companion and offer a small toast, looking their dinner partner in the eye. To drink by oneself would be rude and selfish.

One Easter Sunday I found myself in Shanghai. I had been assigned to cover the China tour of a delegation from the U.S. Senate Foreign Relations Committee, and we were quartered in the Jinjiang Hotel, an elegant collection of dark-stone gothic buildings erected in the 1930s by some of the city's wealthiest Chinese and European residents. Somehow the Jinjiang has preserved that era—its rich mahogany floors and the brass fixtures on its doors are still polished every day. Richard Nixon stayed in the Jinjiang during his trip to China in 1972, and he signed the Shanghai Communiqué restoring ties between the United States and China after a hiatus of over two decades in a suite in the hotel. The hotel's roomboys, in crisp white uniforms, show an awareness of this tradition. Hence when I went to bed at 2 A.M. the night before, after filing a story to New York, I counted on a peaceful night's sleep.

But at 7 A.M. precisely I was awakened by a young roomboy carrying a large red thermos of hot tea which he proceeded to place on my bedside table. From years of habit, I don't wear pajamas when I sleep, and I can vaguely recall trying to gather the sheets around me.

"It's very early, would you mind leaving so I can sleep?" I ventured, probably with anger. "You might at least have knocked on the door."

But he was neither embarrassed nor daunted by my command.

"It's not important, please go ahead and sleep," he replied with a smile.

After he accomplished his errand, I was considering trying to go back to sleep when I heard his footsteps again. This time he had another thermos, for cold water. Five minutes later he was back for a third time, with a change of towels.

It was an experience that I was to have over and over again in China, as do other foreigners—roomboys who don't knock before entering and pay no heed to "Do Not Disturb" signs on doors. Chinese simply do not recognize privacy; indeed, there is no word for privacy in the 50,000 characters of the Chinese language. Life in China is so crowded and clamorous, privacy is normally impossible except by the hazard of circumstance.

Even in hospitals, patients often wait in the doctor's examining room while he is tending to another case. When I went to the Institute of Traditional Medicine to have a master in the art of Chinese massage see if he could repair the ravages of too much tennis in my shoulder, I shared the doctor's room and services with half a dozen patients. They nodded appreciatively as he discussed how my meridians had become inflamed and watched with interest as he pummeled and flexed my shoulder. David Eisenberg, a student from the Harvard Medical School who was the first American allowed to actually work in a Chinese hospital, said he had seen one case where the patient was dying of cancer and the other patients all sat there listening to the doctor's diagnosis.

Nor is there a word for intimacy in Chinese. In the summer of 1972, shortly after President Nixon's China trip, while I was stationed in Vietnam as a correspondent, *The Times* asked me to come back to New York to help act as guide and interpreter for the first group of reporters from the New China News Agency who wanted to tour the United States. For two weeks, in a rented car, we crossed Pennsylvania, West Virginia, Ohio, Michigan, Wisconsin, Illinois, New York, and Massachusetts, visiting a coal mine, a Ford automobile assembly plant, a dairy farm, and Niagara Falls. Some nights I had arranged for the Chinese journalists to stay with American families, but other evenings we ended up in roadside motels, like Holiday Inn. The dining rooms in these establishments all seemed to have been designed from a common plan: the atmosphere was subdued, the light was dim, some had artificial electric candles on the tables. It was suburban elegance. But one of the Chinese reporters, Ye Xiangzhi, a short, wiry man with a quick mind, was disturbed.

"Why do Americans like to eat in the dark?" he asked. "They can't even read the menu."

It was hard to answer him, for the Chinese have a value that is the flip side of privacy and intimacy—*renao,* for which there is no word in English or any European language. Literally it means "hot and noisy," suggesting the pleasure and excitement of a large group of friends and relatives who get together for a meal, with everyone talking and plenty of lights in the room. Anyone who has been to an ordinary restaurant in one of America's Chinatowns can get a hint of this, with the chopsticks clicking, the guests shouting out their orders, the waiters banging the dishes on the table without ceremony, and perhaps a game of Mah-jongg in a back room, the ivory tiles grating like the sound of surf withdrawing on a shale beach.

But the Chinese preference for the group does not mean any group; they are not indiscriminately gregarious. Walking down Peking's streets, as crowded as taking a subway in New York or Tokyo, it is almost impossible not to bump into someone, and at first when I did make contact I tried to preserve my American manners. "Excuse me, I'm sorry," I would say.

But Chinese friends laughed at my ignorance. I didn't even know the person, why should I apologize to him? I recalled an incident that happened when I first lived in Taiwan as a graduate student in 1961. I was coming back

43

on my bicycle from a language class and watched with horror as a pedicab, a three-wheeled bicycle-powered taxi, ran over an infant about a year old who had just learned to toddle. The child was covered with blood and screaming, but the pedicab driver kept on pedaling without slowing down and none of the many passersby in the street went to help. I tried to comfort the baby until its mother finally appeared. Later when I repeated the story to the Chinese family I was living with, they did not find it as outrageous as I did.

This is perhaps an extreme example, but I began to appreciate how differently Chinese order their mental universe than do Westerners. We tend to see people as individuals; we make some distinctions, of course, between those we know and those we don't. But basically we have one code of manners for all. Chinese, on the other hand, instinctively divide people into those with whom they already have a fixed relationship, a connection, what the Chinese call *guan-xi,* and those they don't. These connections operate like a series of invisible threads, tying Chinese to each other with far greater tensile strength than mere friendship in the West would do. *Guan-xi* have created a social magnetic field in which all Chinese move, keenly aware of those people with whom they have connections and those they don't. They explain why the Communist leadership, which was so grateful to Richard Nixon for helping make the breakthrough in Sino–American relations, could never understand Watergate and why Peking even sent a special plane to bring Nixon back to China for a visit after his disgrace. In a broader sense, *guan-xi* also help explain how a nation of one billion people coheres.

Take our friendship with the Wang family. Li, the husband, was an industrial engineer, a tall, reserved, aristocratic man with a high forehead and long swept-back hair. Xiao Miao, "Little Sprout," his wife, was a piano teacher with a quick wit and a pretty face that must once have been coquettish. We met at another Chinese friend's wedding. I gave the Wangs my card and they promised to get in touch. But I knew that only a tiny fraction of the Chinese I talked with once would dare to meet me again.

So I was surprised several months later, after my wife and children had moved to Peking, to hear Li's voice on the phone. Did I remember him? he asked. Yes, I said. Would I come to dinner at their apartment? Of course, I said instantly. To avoid arousing suspicion, we agreed to meet at the Telegraph Office, an easy landmark where both foreigners and Chinese went, and then drove with Li to his apartment inside the institute where his wife worked. There was a guard in the gatehouse, but to my relief he did not try to stop us, and we drove in past a tall white statue of Mao. The Great Helmsman was standing and staring expressionlessly into the distance, his long overcoat blown open by an unfelt breeze.

By the time we arrived it was dark. There were no streetlights, nor any lights at the front door or in the hallway; China is too poor to waste electricity in public places. Li picked up Ethan, our four-year-old, and began carrying him up the four flights to their apartment in the toal darkness. I could hear Ethan groan; he had been in China only a few weeks and was scared. I asked him to be quiet, we didn't want to alert the neighbors there were foreigners in the building and get the Wangs in trouble. Barbara carried Sarah, our one-year-old, and I took the baby stroller and the bag with Sarah's food. In the gloom of the stairs I could make out piles of cabbage left to dry for the winter—Chinese have no refrigerators—and bicycles chained to the railings.

When we reached the fourth floor, the door flew open and Yuanyuan, the Wangs' ten-year-old daughter, bounced out. "Uncle, Auntie," she chorused. "Welcome, welcome." Then she took Ethan by the hand, pulling him inside and simultaneously thrusting an enormous five-pound stuffed panda into his unprepared arms. It was the first of many gifts. Sensing his unease, she began tickling him in the ribs and taunting him to chase her through their tiny two-room home. Ethan still didn't speak more than a dozen words of Chinese, but he understood the challenge and was off with a whoop.

I looked at Yuanyuan with admiration. She was only ten, but already her instincts for playing the proper host were perfect. Her hair was cut in bangs, short on the sides, and her eyes were narrow slits, like a Japanese doll, her father said. She had on a new white blouse with a pair of well-tailored rust-colored corduroy slacks.

The Wangs' apartment was spartan by Western standards, but very much middle-class for a Chinese. Yuanyuan occupied one room about six feet long and six feet wide; the family used the other for eating, living, and sleeping. A double bed took up one corner, with four bright-green, orange, blue, and red quilts piled neatly on top of it. There was a small green plastic-covered sofa where we were directed to sit, and a folding card table the Wangs took out to eat on. On a small desk in another corner was a portrait of the late Prime Minister Zhou Enlai, almost everyone's popular hero, and on the wall a calendar supplied by Japan Air Lines with bathing beauties from all the countries the airline services. They had a squat-style toilet in a separate tiny cubicle, where they kept their supply of rice in a crockery pot, but no bathtub. The floors were bare concrete, with no rugs. The concrete walls could have used a coat of whitewash.

Dinner started with cold dishes, as good Chinese meals do: there were plates of chewy jellyfish and sliced cucumbers in a mustard sauce, tiny whole birds fried in a brown sauce which you ate bones and all, a cold noodle dish made from bean curd, preserved eggs with their distinctive brown and yellow color, sugared crab apples, and Chinese sausages. Yuanyuan kept piling Ethan's plate with the tiny birds and crab apples till I thought it would tip over. She would not accept Ethan's loud protestations.

Then came the hot dishes: first, dozens of spring rolls, vegetables and meat wrapped in crispy fried dough, then a spicy Sichuan-style pork with peanuts, a sweet and sour pork with honey, northern Chinese style, an omelette with tomatoes, and taro cooked in boiling sugar so that it had caramelized. Li's wife would appear for the presentation of each dish, then disappear back into their tiny kitchen, the size of a small closet, to prepare the next one. Her only equipment was a blackened metal wok, or Chinese deep-bottomed frying pan, which she heated over a coal-burning brazier. They also had a small sink with a single spigot for cold water. Both Miao and Li had taken the day off from work to shop and cook for us. I didn't realize it then, but to cook the spring rolls alone consumed their entire month's ration of one pound of peanut oil. When we finally were ready to leave, they piled us with large red apples, hard to find in the local market, and several bottles of special Chinese grape wine.

Barbara and I went home exhausted and ecstatic. Despite all the government's efforts to restrict contact between Chinese and foreigners, we had formed a friendship. The next week we invited the Wangs to our new apartment, on the eleventh floor of one of the high-rise buildings reserved for foreign diplomats and journalists. To us, it always seemed cramped, a mere six hundred square feet, with two tiny bedrooms, just big enough to squeeze in the beds, a modest combination living–dining room, a bathroom with shower, and a surprisingly large kitchen that occupied half the space of the overall apartment—the result of earlier complaints by Westerners that the Chinese made their kitchens too small. There were no closets. But after seeing the Wangs' dingy, poorly lit, and utilitarian quarters, we felt we were reveling in luxury. We had wall-to-wall carpeting and an American-made refrigerator, stove, and washing machine, all imported from Hong Kong.

Before Mao's death, it would have been impossible for a Chinese to enter our forbidden zone. But by 1980 the government had relaxed its rules enough that any Chinese with sufficient bravura could get in. All it required was that I pick the Wangs up in our car and drive them past the guard from the People's Liberation Army who stood outside our compound gate. Li covered his face with his hand as we passed the sentry, pretending to be rubbing his eyes. Then they had to accept the stares of the middle-aged women who operated the elevators in our building and reported to the Public Security Bureau on all visitors. For the Wangs, accepting our invitation was a risk. I often wondered about their motives; I sensed a mixture of curiosity, the thrill of the illicit, a practical eye for gain, and real friendship.

Miao had dressed for the occasion in a *qipao,* or *cheongsam,* the old Chinese dress with a high mandarin collar, side fastenings, a tight waist, and a slit up the side. She had kept it hidden when Red Guards searched their home during the Cultural Revolution. "I haven't worn it in years," she confided.

"It was too dangerous to dress up. To be beautiful or fashionable was bourgeois and could get you in trouble."

Miao had also uncovered a lacquer box with several exquisite jade hairpins and carved jade belt buckles which she presented to Barbara. It was an extravagant but delightful gift, for Barbara loves old Chinese jewelry and is a belt designer by profession. For me there was a Qing dynasty blue and white vase.

When we showed the Wangs around the apartment, Miao begged to peek in Barbara's clothes closet, a wardrobe we had also shipped up from Hong Kong. Miao giggled with embarrassment at several dresses with low-cut necklines, but she exclaimed with pleasure at a more chaste loose-fitting burgundy-red Calvin Klein dress with an ascot at the collar. She asked Barbara to try it on for her.

"You don't look like most foreigners," Miao observed after Barbara had disrobed. "They are so hideous, very big and fat, with huge noses. You are more petite." It was a high compliment.

Afterward Miao wanted to try the dress on herself but, with Chinese modesty, slipped it on over her dress. Luckily Barbara had a collection of magazines—*Harper's Bazaar, Vogue,* and fashion supplements from *The New York Times*—along with several sets of French pantyhose to give Miao and her daughter. But we clearly were getting in deeper than we had anticipated, for we soon began to sense that friendship to the Wangs, and to other Chinese, carries obligations that it doesn't to a Westerner. The next week we were back at the Wangs for dinner. This time Miao explained, with cautious circumlocutions at first, that cooking the spring rolls had consumed their entire month's ration of one pound of oil. Would we be willing to go to the Friendship Store, the large grocery and department store near our apartment, reserved in theory for foreigners only, and, at their expense, to buy them more? There is no limit on the amount of cooking oil foreigners can buy, she pointed out. When I assented she immediately produced a large plastic container like those we use to carry gasoline. It could hold ten pounds. We felt set up. Then she brought out another plastic bottle for me to buy four pounds of sesame oil. The Wangs' monthly ration was only two ounces. Li wondered if we might consider buying them a television set in the Friendship Store. A thirteen-inch Japanese-made black and white set cost only about $200 in the Friendship Store but $700 in a regular Chinese store. Moreover, a customer had to have the proper ration coupons and a letter from his unit saying that he was the person in the unit entitled to buy a television set that year. The wait could be a long one. Again we agreed, but we felt we were being subjected to a pressure that wouldn't have existed in the West. Barbara described it as claustrophobia. But I thought it was something more. Friendship in China offered assurances and an intimacy that we have abandoned in

America; it gave the Chinese psychic as well as material rewards that we have lost. We ourselves did feel close to the Wangs, but as Westerners the constant gift-giving and obligations left us uneasy.

Several weeks before we left China we had dinner with the Wangs in a restaurant. Ethan and Yuanyuan played hide and seek under the table; Li suggested we might let Yuanyuan come and live with us in the United States so she could learn English and go to better schools. It was a stunning proposal, that the Wangs would trust their only daughter's education to a foreigner.

"We feel you are really our friends now," Li explained, offering a toast of beer. "Our *guan-xi* are very close. We don't think of you as foreigners anymore."

From our friendships with the Wangs and other Chinese we came to realize that *guan-xi* provide the lubricant for Chinese to get through life. In a society which for millennia had no public law as we know it in the West to enforce impartial justice, people depended on their *guan-xi,* their personal relationships, particularly their contacts with those in power, to get things done. It was a form of social investment. Developing, cultivating, and expanding one's *guan-xi* became a common preoccupation. The advent of the Communists has not fundamentally changed that. As a result, the Chinese have turned the art of personal relations into a carefully calculated science. There are even people who live entirely on their *guan-xi*, or *guan-xi-hu,* as the Chinese term them, like a friend who returned to China in 1950 after studying political science in graduate school in the United States. This put him under immediate suspicion in the eyes of the Communists, though his motive in coming back had been patriotic, and he found himself without a job. But his English was excellent and he had read widely in Western books about China. Soon he discovered that many of the elderly Communist veterans, none of whom could read a foreign language, were curious as to what was being written about them abroad. It was the only place they could relive the glories of their past, because the Communists had banned all historical accounts about themselves in Chinese lest one faction get a better treatment than the others. Over a period of time my friend built up a circle of powerful acquaintances who asked him to come and read to them. In exchange he managed to get a comfortable apartment and access to special stores reserved for high-level officials by borrowing their identification cards. Eventually he parlayed his contacts into an exit visa for Hong Kong. There in turn he convinced some overseas Chinese businessmen that he knew Peking's leaders. The last time I saw him he was back in China, still with a Chinese passport but operating as a representative for a group of Hong Kong companies.

The importance Chinese attach to the distinction between people with whom they have *guan-xi* and those they don't is reflected in an idiosyncrasy of the Chinese language. There are a number of words that begin either with *nei,* meaning "inner," or *wai,* "external." A foreigner in Chinese is a *wai-guo-ren,* an "external country person." Any Chinese who isn't a native of Peking comes from *wai-di,* "an external region." An expert is *nei-hang,* someone who is "inside the profession," while a novice is a *wai-hang,* "outside the profession." Classified information in China, which can include even weather forecasts, is called *nei-bu,* "internal." Your father's parents are your grandparents, *zu-fu,* but your mother's parents are your "external" grandparents, or *wai-zu-fu.*

The family is the foundation of the Chinese social universe and the training ground for the proper application of *guan-xi.* In the past the function of the family was to raise filial sons who would become loyal subjects to the Emperor, a tradition the Communists have made their own use of. The father was a supreme autocrat, with power even to sell his children into slavery. Status in Chinese society was codified in the famous three bonds: the loyalty of subject to ruler, filial obedience of son to father, and fidelity of the wife to her husband (though not the other way around). Traditional Chinese homes had high walls around the outside, often topped with cut glass, emphasizing the family's distance from the rest of the community. But within the house the family lived and slept in the same rooms with much less sense of individual space than Westerners have.

"We grew up in a very complex world where you learned your proper place early," Mrs. Wang told me one evening as I drove her back home from our apartment. "I had two older brothers, an older sister, and two younger sisters, and we also had my grandfather and three aunts and uncles who lived next to us."

In Chinese, however, these relationships are much more carefully spelled out. An uncle is not just an uncle, but either a "father's older brother," a "father's younger brother," or a "mother's older brother," or "mother's younger brother." There is a separate term for each. Similarly, there are more than a dozen different terms for cousin to distinguish the exact form of relationship.

Foreigners have a difficult time appreciating the strength of the Chinese family, but I did get occasional glimpses of what it looks like from the Chinese side. When Deng Xiaoping, China's energetic, diminutive Deputy Party Chairman visited the United States in 1979, one of the stops he wanted to make was Houston. He was interested in the Johnson Space Center, the headquarters of the American space effort, and in talking with oil-drilling companies. But local boosters decided Deng should get a real Texas welcome and arranged a full-blown rodeo in the little town of Simonton, an hour's drive across the flat Texas range. Simonton consists of a liquor store, a post office, a general store, a pecan warehouse, and a huge enclosure for the dirt-floored indoor rodeo. In the parking lot outside a peeling sign proclaimed, "Simonton Rodeo Roundup, Where East Meets West." When Deng unexpectedly was whisked into an old-fashioned stagecoach and driven around the arena, I stationed myself behind two reporters from the New China News Agency. They were holding paper plates with slabs of barbecue and potato salad on their laps, uncertain how to attack the giant hunks of meat. Chinese are accustomed to eating their meat finely sliced into bite-size pieces—anything else is barbarian, reminiscent of the way the Mongols consumed their food.

At that moment, a tall slender blonde, with her honey-colored long hair combed so that it fell over one side of her face, sat down on the wooden plank next to one of the Chinese. She was dressed in skin-tight blue jeans and high leather boots; her face was made up for going on a movie set—and she had on more perfume than the Chinese had probably ever smelled before in their lives.

"Howdy, how y'all doing?" she inquired, giving the Chinese a broad wink. She introduced herself as Joan Shephard and said she had broken a Friday-night date to come out to help entertain the Chinese at the request of a White House advance man she knew vaguely.

After a moment's hesitation, the reporter asked shyly, "Are you a student?"

"No," she said.

"Then you live with your family?" he added, making an assumption natural for a Chinese that a young woman who wasn't married would live with her parents.

"No, I live by myself," she responded. The newsman's face fell. "Oh, I am so sorry," he said, as if in sympathy. He could only assume that her parents must be dead or that the American system had forced her to take a job far away from them. Her explanation that she had moved out of her parents' home because she wanted more freedom only left him perplexed.

A pert twenty-seven-year-old woman with a tiny turned-up nose who worked in Peking Radio related an encounter she once had in a department store in the city of Tianjin, China's third largest metropolis, which illustrated the depth of Chinese family feeling in a different way. She and her husband were shopping when suddenly a young man about twenty years old ordered them to give him 10 yuan, about $6.50. It was very crowded in the store, so the other customers couldn't see that he had taken a knife out from under his blue worker's jacket. My friend's husband was angry and didn't want to pay. Ten yuan was a quarter of his month's wages. But she was scared and handed over the money.

Then the robber apologized. "I am sorry to do this," he said softly, his head bowed in shame. "But I am unemployed and am too embarrassed to ask my parents for any more money."

Some foreigners who have visited China, particularly those who went during the Great Leap Forward in 1958 when Mao was experimenting with communal mess halls, have concluded that the Communists set out to destroy the family. Paradoxically, the opposite has happened. Xiao Yan, "Little Bird," a twenty-seven-year-old teacher, with the high cheekbones and broad face of a northern Chinese, explained how this occurred in her own case. Her father had been born a poor peasant and joined the Red Army as a teen-ager, rising to become a senior Communist officer. But he had died prematurely in 1960, and in the Cultural Revolution the family had been separated. Yan had been sent to work on a state farm on the frozen Soviet border in far northern Heilongjiang (Black Dragon River) province; her older sister had been ordered to move to a remote valley in Sichuan in the southwest when the defense factory where she worked was relocated there for security reasons; a younger sister was rusticated to a commune in Shandong, in east China, and her brother was sent to work in a factory in Shanxi province in the northwest. Their situation appeared hopeless, but eventually, Yan said, she won permission to move back to Peking after she was selected the best worker on her farm. Recently her younger sister has also moved back to the small apartment they share with their aged mother. Her older sister cannot move back to the capital, but she has sent her six-year-old daughter to Yan to enroll in school in Peking and get a city education. Yan also mails 10 yuan a month from the 43 yuan she earns to her brother since he makes only 23 yuan a month in his factory, "not enough to pay for his food," she told me. The family remained a magnet.

I wondered if Yan had any plans to get married. She had a lively mind, an infectious smile, and was pretty enough that a girl friend said, "Men would melt to look at her."

But Yan herself saw little chance of a wedding. "My first duty is to my mother and brother and sisters. Besides, I could never apply for and get more housing from the government. So there would be no place to live with a husband."

On one of the evenings we invited the Wang family to dinner at our apartment, Li arrived two hours late because he had to sing in a concert and we had already finished eating by the time he came. I explained to Li that since he was in an American's home he must now follow our customs. In Chinese, there is an expression, "When you cross the border, obey the local custom." In this case, I added, that meant he must be frank. If you want something, you must say yes. If you say no when you are offered something, we foreigners will take it as a refusal. I knew Chinese are trained to say no as a sign of good manners whenever they are offered food or a gift, no matter how much they want it. Li agreed he would comply.

So I asked him the question "Are you hungry?" By then it was after 8:30, and I was sure he had not had a chance to eat during his concert. But with a solemn look on his face he replied, "No, thank you, I am not hungry."

Guessing that he was still being Chinese, I went to the kitchen and brought out a platter of roast chicken with gravy and stuffing, some homemade bread Barbara had baked, and a dish of broiled tomatoes, onions, peppers, and carrots, all the vegetables then available in the market. I also put a large helping of crepes stuffed with an orange sauce on another plate. He devoured it all.

Li had been acting according to the traditional Confucian code which underlies Chinese character today much as *guan-xi* are the invisible threads that hold society together. It provides the public identity, the mask, the persona which enable Chinese to deal with the world with the least friction. In essence, Confucianism was the broad rules of conduct evolved for the relations of Chinese with each other. Confucius was a teacher and a gentleman, a very great if at times a pedantic gentleman, who with pious reverence had assembled all the details of etiquette practiced at the courts of the feudal lords of his day. (He was born in 551 B.C., a generation before the Buddha in India, and died in 479, a decade before the birth of Socrates in Greece.)

Fundamentally, Confucius wanted to establish the gentleman, or the princely man, as the ruler of the state. For Confucius, good was good and bad was bad, just as in a John Wayne movie. The princely man always knew where rectitude lay—in those rules of decorum, the *li,* which we translate variously as the rites or etiquette. Originally these abstruse rules may have grown out of a primitive animism in which the spirits of land, wind, and water played an active role in man's affairs. By Confucius' time this had congealed into a belief that improper conduct by man could throw the world of nature out of joint. A correct observance of the rites was a sign of perfect social order, and to abuse the rites must therefore indicate deeper decay. Confucius was particularly insistent that to neglect the outer form of the rites was to abuse the reality, the moral order, they represented.

To us the *li* may seem rather formalistic: where to stand in the presence of superiors, where to sit (a guest should face the door), how far to go in seeing off a visitor. A good Chinese host still walks his guest not only to the front door but out to his car and stands and waves till the visitor is out of sight. After I became accustomed to this elegant treatment, I have always felt somewhat cheated when leaving a Western friend's house to be shown just to the door and left standing there. The *li* dictated there should never be a touching of persons (a Chinese formerly shook his own hand, not yours, and Chinese officials still seem reluctant to grasp an extended hand). A slap on the back is more than indelicate, though American businessmen visiting Peking today insist on putting their arms around their Chinese hosts in picture-taking sessions. Nor should there be any immature enthusiasm. Western musicians, actors, and athletes visiting Peking are often puzzled by the lack of audience reaction to their performances. After a brilliant display of ice skating one November evening by the American star Peggy Fleming, the crowd of over 10,000 in the Capital Gymnasium offered a modest round of applause. Fleming, an Olympic champion, was genuinely hurt. She asked me afterward, "Why didn't the Chinese like me, what did I do wrong?" I had to try to explain that she got what amounted to a standing ovation for the Chinese. Confucius' ideal was to maintain composure at all times. Characteristically, his golden rule was phrased in the negative: "Don't do to others what you yourself would not like." The Western version—"Do unto others . . ."—might have seemed overly aggressive to him.

The influence of the rites, for doing things according to the correct form, created a fondness for ritual which has persisted under the Communists. At an important Party congress in 1977, foreign diplomats and newsmen were enchanted to watch the voting for the top leadership, which for the first time was shown on Chinese television. The officials marched up to the ballot box in the ornate Great Hall of the People in the exact order in which it was later announced they had been elected. First came Hua Guofeng, who at the time was Party Chairman, followed by Ye Jianying, the first deputy chairman, and then the other men who would win the post of deputy chairman, Deng Xiaoping, Chen Yun, Li Xiannian, and Wang Dongxing. It was as if at a bitterly contested Democratic or Republican convention the winning candidates for President and Vice President posed for their traditional victory celebration on the rostrum before any votes had been cast by the state delegates. When I asked a Chinese journalist why the Party leaders had acted this way, he insisted it was natural. Of course, he said, they would vote according to their rank in the hierarchy, and the new, forthcoming hierarchy was more important than the old, outgoing one.

The consummate ritual, I thought, was the series of toasts delivered at formal state banquets for visiting dignitaries. Most foreigners, delighted or dazed by the amount of food thrust on them at these twelve- or fifteen-course gastronomical extravaganzas, tended to miss the subtlety of the toasts, the host's well-turned knack of seeming to convey great warmth and friendship without ever revealing a personal feeling. To have been personal would have been to violate the *li*. The following is taken from my notes at a banquet given by a deputy mayor of Shanghai, Yan Youmin, for Senator Frank Church of the U.S. Senate Foreign Relations Committee, though it could have been delivered at many other such festivities.

"I am extremely glad to welcome you," Yan began, speaking through an interpreter. Senator Church did not know that the phrase Yan actually used was a stock expression, "I am ten parts happy," which showed up in virtually every toast I heard in China.

"You have come a long way from across the ocean and we are delighted you have chosen to honor us," Yan went on, another expression drawn from the standard phrase book. "Your journey has been hard."

How to end a party is often awkward for Westerners, but the *li* provide for that too. When the last course was served and consumed, Yan rose to speak again:

"Please forgive us, we didn't entertain you very well. Your stay in our city has been too short. Next time you must stay longer." (This is invariably taken by the visitors as an invitation to return to China, though it is just another of those stock polite expressions.)

"Tomorrow you have to set out early," Yan went on, speaking to Senator Church. "Everybody should go and get some rest now."

With these words, all the Chinese around the room rose and made for the door, knowing the banquet was concluded. It took the Americans a few minutes to realize what had happened.

To a Westerner, the Chinese penchant for ritual sometimes turns into a pattern of public make-believe. It is almost as if the Chinese live by the Stanislavski method, in which actors' words and actions imitate the correct outside gestures while downplaying their inner feelings. I think it is this quality which often makes frustrated foreigners feel the Chinese are inscrutable, and I remember an incident which drove me to the brink of apoplexy.

I was flying back with a group of Western and Japanese journalists after an exhilarating trip to Tibet. We were one of the first groups of reporters allowed into Tibet since 1949, and we were anxious to get back to file our stories. Since Lhasa, the small provincial town that serves as Tibet's capital, had only one telegraph line and a dubious phone connection to the outside world, we had agreed among ourselves not to send our material till we were back in Peking. Normally, at least one reporter would have tried to sneak his copy through, but perhaps because we were all delighted just to be in Tibet, no one broke the embargo.

On the last day we took off at 6 A.M. from Lhasa's airstrip, in a dry, brown valley at 10,000 feet, and headed over "the roof of the world" back to China proper in Sichuan. The four-hour flight is an endless succession of jagged granite peaks, covered with snow even in the middle of the summer, before touching down in the emerald-green paddy fields around Chengdu that simmered in the tropical sun like soup on a stove. Qi Mingzong, one of our escorts from the Information Department, explained that we would have an hour for lunch while our chartered plane, a Russian-built Ilyushin-18, a four-engine turboprop that belonged to the Chinese Air Force, was refueled and the crew had lunch. Mr. Qi, a slender man with a pinched face and an extraordinary, clipped upper-class British accent, was proud that the chief pilot had flown Chairman Hua to Lhasa when he visited Tibet the year before. We were scheduled to take off at 12:30 P.M. for Peking.

But just as we finished eating, Mr. Qi came over to our table. "I'm so sorry," he said with all the polish he could muster, "but there is a thunderstorm in Peking and we can't fly. We must wait."

Such delays are common in China—many planes and airports are not equipped with modern radar or instrument landing systems, and the Chinese are intelligently conservative about not flying when they risk danger.

But a few minutes later the public-address system crackled out an announcement that the regular afternoon plane for Peking, flight 622, was now boarding. It was a British-built Trident jet belonging to CAAC, or the Civil Aviation Administration of China (in Chinese the name is easier, simply People's Aviation). We looked at Mr. Qi, whose face grew tighter than usual. After watching it board and depart, we demanded an explanation.

"It will have to turn back, don't worry," Mr. Qi assured us. He suggested we sit down in the airport lounge and wait. With both the temperature and the humidity close to 100 degrees, we began to imagine arcane political reasons why the government would try to keep us out of Peking, or from filing our stories on Tibet. A coup perhaps had taken place.

Finally, three hours later, Mr. Qi emerged after another conference with the airport control tower and the air force to say that the weather in Peking had grown so bad that all flights into the capital for the day had been canceled.

"You will have to go into downtown Chengdu and stay in a hotel overnight, till the weather breaks," he insisted.

Only a vulgar foreigner would have questioned this story. Mr. Qi was obviously trying to preserve a correct appearance and the *li*. But we were vulgar foreigners.

When we got to the hotel, a run-down Soviet monstrosity of endless corridors that lacked both running water and electricity that afternoon, several of the newsmen phoned their wives in Peking. The weather there was beautiful, they said, the first day in a week it had not rained. Flight 622 from Chengdu had already landed on schedule. But a representative from the Information Department in the capital had called them a few minutes earlier to report that there was a terrible storm in Chengdu, so sadly our plane couldn't take off.

At dinner we tracked down Mr. Qi and confronted him again. There was no storm in Peking, we could say with assurance, and no storm here in Chengdu. Why were we being held hostage in a hot, miserable hotel in Chengdu?

But Mr. Qi was prepared. "Actually, I have checked and the storm was halfway between Peking and Chengdu, in Shijiazhuang," he said. That might have settled the affair, but on the drive into town I had seen that the local meteorological station was just down the street from the hotel, so we went there to check. There was no major storm that day anywhere in China.

It would have been easy to dismiss our hosts' explanations as just make-believe, and at the time I was angry enough to do so. But that would be missing an important distinction, I later came to realize. Mr. Qi was not being deliberately cynical, at least from his point of view. There was probably a real mechanical failure on the plane, or a problem with a crew member, and the Chinese felt it would have been embarrassing to tell us. Instead, they created the polite fiction about the storm, a happy pretense any Chinese would knowingly have accepted.

This same capacity for make-believe underlies the conventions of Chinese opera, where a headdress with long feathers signifies a general, flicking a whip indicates a man on horseback, and pacing about the stage means taking a journey. It is evident in a number of popular proverbs and historical incidents. In the third century B.C., a scheming prime minister of the Chin dynasty wished to determine who among his courtiers were really faithful to him. When a deer was presented in court, he pretended it was a horse. All those who insisted it was a deer were executed. In more modern times, the ambassadors from England and France considered it a triumph when in 1873, after fighting three wars with China, they were finally granted an audience with the Emperor. What they did not know at the time was that they had been taken into the palace reserved for tribute missions from smaller states. This preserved China's conceit that the Europeans were still loyal vassals.

This Chinese penchant for playacting stems from a different appreciation of appearance and reality. To the Chinese words are accorded a power of their own—they are power. As the American scholar of Chinese Buddhism, Holmes Welch, has pointed out, when a man died, his coffin would be decorated with the word "Longevity." It was not put there to celebrate the great age he had reached, since he may have died young, but to assert the immortality of the body. The Chinese language, in fact, is full of euphemisms to circumvent the ugly facts of life. When a poor family drowned an un-wanted girl child, since she could not bring in any income, they called it "bathing the infant." Two thousand years before modern communications and Marshall McLuhan, the Chinese had discovered the principle that the medium is the message.

The Chinese system of writing in ideograms may have contributed to the weight given words. Chinese characters have no innate phonetic value; but because they are often pictographic and the written language was held in almost religious esteem, each character has a life of its own, a magical po-tency. Confucius was deeply concerned with the problem of words—if the name, or the form, was correct, he asserted, things would follow their proper course. This Chinese belief in the power of language underlies the Communists' fondness for slogans. Walk into an office and you are likely to be greeted by large red letters on the wall proclaiming, "Serve the People," an apothegm of Mao. During the Cultural Revolution, friends said, they often felt it safest to begin conversations with a quotation from the Chairman like, "Good morning, Grasp Revolution." There is nothing new in this. In the Qing dynasty emperors instructed local officials to post villages with hortatory decrees for the edification of the peasantry. The Nationalists on Taiwan also cover walls with official sentiment; but in Taipei they are more likely to say, "Counterattack the mainland."

By make-believe we usually envision child's play. But there is nothing childish about the way Chinese can conjure reality out of illusion with the right words. When Chiang Kai-shek fled to Taiwan in 1949 after his ignominious defeat, he insisted that he was still the leader of "Free China" and that henceforth Taipei would be the capital of the Republic of China. Both Washington and the United Nations accepted this fiction for over two decades, keeping the Communists from what they felt was their rightful recognition. It is still a serious political crime in both China and Taiwan to suggest that Taiwan in any way is really separate from the mainland, whatever foreigners may think.

This same faith in the power of words has governed how Chinese name their children. In the past, girls were fitted with fanciful two-character given names like Jingxian, meaning "Quiet and Virtuous," or Yushuang, "Jade Frost." (In Chinese, the surname comes first, the given name after, so a woman whose family name was Li and who was called Yushuang, would be known as Li Yushuang.) These feminine names were to suggest the grace of birds, the delicacy of flowers, or the proper womanly attributes. Little boys were given names to develop their will or courage.

But after 1949 parents wanted to show their loyalty to the new Communist regime and they adopted a different nomenclature. One of the most common names, given to both boys and girls, was Hong, "Red." I had one friend whose name was Wang Xiaohong, "Wang Little Red," a common diminutive. Another was called Wang Yaohong, "Wang Who Wants to Be Red," and a third Wang Yonghong, "Wang Forever Red." Many parents picked the name Weidong, meaning "Protect Mao," *dong* being the last character in Mao's name. In the 1950s, in the era of good feelings between Peking and Moscow, some young Chinese ended up being called Xiaolin, "Little Stalin." A young high school teacher I met had been named Kangmei, "Resist America," because he was born during the Korean War.

With changes in political power, however, some names became bad magic. The daughter of a Chinese diplomat recalled that when she was in high school there were three sisters named Li. Their father was a former general in the Red Army, a genuine patriot, and so he called his first daughter Li Aiguo, "Li Who Loves Her Country," the second Li Aimin, "Li Who Loves the People," and the third, Li Aidang, "Li Who Loves the Party." But in the Cultural Revolution an earnest Red Guard noted that if you lined up the last syllables of each of their names, Guo, Min, and Dang, they came out, "Li Who Loves the Guomindang," the Nationalists. The father was clapped in prison.

During the Cultural Revolution, Red Guards also changed the name of the street that ran through the old foreign legation quarter to "Anti-Imperialism Street" and the narrow alley that leads to the Soviet Embassy to "Anti-Revisionism Street." Some radicals even proposed switching the colors of the city traffic lights because red was the symbol of revolution and ought to mean go, not stop.

In the last few years, as disillusionment with the Communists has spread, Chinese have stopped giving their children "revolutionary" names. A peasant woman I encountered had reverted to an old tradition and called her daughter, her first child, Zhaodi. The name means "Call in Younger Brothers," signifying her wish for a son. A young city couple named their daughter DoDo, not a Chinese name at all but the first two syllables from the musical scale made famous in China by Julie Andrews's song "Do, Re, Mi," in the movie *The Sound of Music.* She said that if she had another child she and her husband planned to call it ReRe, the next two syllables.

The Chinese belief in the importance of titles, of ensuring that the name fits the subject, may underlie one of the least attractive Communist practices, that of labeling people. Like the doctor I met on the train from Shanghai to Peking who had been stigmatized as a "Rightist" in 1957 and then attacked again in the Cultural Revolution because of his earlier label, millions of Chinese have had what the Communists call "caps" put on them. The term *dai-mao-zi,* to put a political hat on someone, is one of the cruelest in the current Chinese lexicon. The custom began on a large scale with the land reform campaign in the late 1940s as the Communists swept toward victory and won control in village after village. Detailed rules were drawn up for classifying everyone according to his economic, political, and social background. At the bottom of the scale the Communists eventually devised came the "five black elements": landlords, rich peasants, counterrevolutionaries, bad elements, and rightists. Officially Peking always describes these groups as a small minority, 5 percent of the population. But with a billion people in China, that would mean 50 million outcasts, about the same number of people that live in France or Great Britain.

Under a 1950 law, landlords were supposed to be able to shed their labels if they worked hard for five years and showed they had reformed. But as time passed, the classifications stuck and hardened into a permanent form of discrimination. Huang San, a short, intense man whose grandfather had been tarred with the label of rich peasant, related how serious a liability it could be. His grandfather had owned three acres of wheat fields in Hebei province near Peking, he said, along with a cart, a horse, and a small house. His grandfather had worked some of the land himself and rented out the remainder. After Liberation, his property had been divided up by what the Communists called the village's poor and middle peasants. Although Huang was not born until 1955, well after the family lost all its land, he found he too was labeled a rich peasant; whenever he filled in an official form, he had to give that degrading status as his *cheng-fen,* or "family origin." It meant that while he was one of the smartest students in his local primary school, he was not allowed to go beyond the fifth grade. His application to join the Communist Youth League branch in his village was rejected, and he was turned down later when he volunteered for the army, one of the few routes to upward mobility for rural youth. Huang's family was also excluded from their commune's cooperative medical insurance program. When his mother needed an operation for gallstones, they had to pay the full cost themselves, a charge of 45 yuan ($30), a year's income for Huang. Their neighbors with a better class origin had their medical care covered by a small monthly premium.

Moreover, Huang complained when I met him during a visit to some of his relatives in Peking, he, his father, and his older brother received less income for the same amount of work in the fields than the other peasants. As one of the bad classes, they were ordered to perform "duty labor," a kind of corvée duty, on the communal fields, and at the end of the year, when the village's harvest was added up and everyone's share was portioned out, half of their income was deducted for the "duty labor."

"What is left over is not enough to support our family," Huang charged. The family was constantly in debt to the production team (the lowest level of the commune) for which they worked, and his older brother, now thirty-three years old, had not been able to get married because of the family's status and low income. No peasant woman would want him.

In 1979 the Communists announced they had finally rescinded these class labels. But Huang said the officials in his village simply ignored Peking's order. "If they took away our labels, someone might look for a new exploiting class," Huang suggested. "That might lead to the Communist Party."

The road from the city of Lanzhou in northwest China to the Kushui, or "Bitterwater" commune, runs through endless small fields of sere brown earth, each carefully terraced upward toward the surrounding barren hills. Not a tree grows anywhere in sight. The land is as dry as desert, and it is hard to remember that millions of peasants make their existence in soil like this. Suddenly, as I was contemplating the peasants' hardihood, the Shanghai-model sedan I was driving in almost crashed into a man and his wife on the back of a bicycle. They were dressed in the faded and patched gray garb of farmers. The wife was holding a bundle of big green cabbages on her lap. Her husband obviously was not used to cars on his village road and he had wobbled out into the middle of the track without looking behind. Luckily, our driver pushed his brakes to the floor and our car swerved off onto the shoulder of the road. The two peasants toppled off their bike from fright, the cabbages spilling across the road.

When I retrieved my head from the windshield, I noticed the husband and wife were smiling and laughing as they picked themselves up. Our driver, hired from the Lanzhou Foreign Affairs Office, was also grinning, ear-to-ear. In the United States or Europe there would have been shouted imprecations, or worse. Death had been close. But this was another of those Chinese characteristics so baffling to foreigners—they laugh at adversity.

For "face" was involved here. If either party had gotten angry, face would have been forfeited, and the ancient *li* would have been violated. Face is an outgrowth of the extreme sensitivity Chinese have about personal dignity; it colors all personal relations. George Kates, in his charming, evocative portrait of life in Peking in the 1930s, *The Years That Were Fat,* suggests that it was so easy to wound this Chinese sense of dignity and so difficult for the wounds to heal that the condition might be called "spiritual hemophilia."

To salve relations between two Chinese, a middleman is often necessary. Not long after I returned to the United States, I invited a prominent Chinese editor to dinner at our home. He was studying at Harvard, spoke impeccable English, and seemed in every way Westernized. Professor John Fairbank and his wife, Wilma, also happened to be at the party. A few days later the editor called to thank me for the dinner and wondered if I would come to his place for a return meal. When I agreed, he inquired if I would call Professor Fairbank and ask him to come along also. As accustomed to the West as he was, he still needed a go-between to assure that he would not lose face if the famous professor declined his invitation.

This sensitivity has created a special reflex in the Chinese, an instinct to flee any situation where they might risk face. "Of the thirty-six ways of handling a situation, running away is the best," goes an old adage.

My Chinese assistant Lao Wu was a constant lesson to me in the importance of sensitivity; he was an expert at avoidance. On the first day we met, I tried to ease into our new relationship with what I thought were standard and innocuous Chinese questions. How many children do you have? I asked him.

After looking at me for a moment, he replied, "One or two." Here was a man who would never expose himself. The most I could learn was that he had previously worked at the Yugoslav Embassy as an English interpreter.

Gradually, over a period of time, I came to appreciate what in an earlier era would have been called his Confucian rectitude. He always arrived for work at 9 A.M. precisely, never a minute late. He never let slip an angry word, no matter how much I shouted at him. His sternest rebuff in a touchy situation would be a suggestion that my anger did not help get the job done. Lao Wu also endeavored to carry out all my requests: securing permission from the Information Department for a trip out of Peking, arranging interviews with a government official, reserving a table in a restaurant for lunch. But if I wanted him to plead my cause with a sticky bureaucrat, Lao Wu would seek shelter in his shell. These tests often came over my efforts to outwit the Peking Hotel. Among its rules that I felt were illogical was one that I could not let anyone else spend the night in either of the two rooms which I, or rather *The Times,* rented. One room was officially our office, where Lao Wu sat during the day, though because of another hotel rule about not moving furniture, the two beds remained. The second room I used for sleeping until I got an apartment in September 1980. On one occasion, our Tokyo correspondent, Henry Scott-Stokes, came through Peking on his way to North Korea and needed a hotel room. I asked Lao Wu to inform the hotel that another employee of *The Times* would be using the office overnight. With only a perfunctory check, Lao Wu said the answer was no, Scott-Stokes could not use a bed in the office. When I asked him to press harder, he looked at me and said, "You are making me feel like a sandwich."

Then I heard him mutter, *"Pa Ma-fan,"* an expression which literally means "to fear trouble" but which conveys centuries of wisdom about avoiding entanglements.

For all the pitfalls of face for the unsuspecting foreigner, there is one charming variation—a person must always express his abilities and even his name as being of less value than those of the person being addressed. Some of this formality has lapsed under the Communists, but much has survived. When a Chinese asked my name, they would preface it by saying, *"Nin gui xing?"* (What is your precious name?) In reply, I had to answer, "My humble name is . . ." The same formula is employed when asking a foreigner what country he comes from, though no Chinese seriously doubts that China is superior. If a Chinese compliments you on your appearance or your ability to speak Chinese, the *li* require that you must immediately decline the praise. "No, I speak very badly," which of course is nearer the truth. At dinner a Chinese host will invariably apologize after the tenth delicious dish has been served, "I am sorry, we had nothing to feed you tonight."

Sinologists love to dispute whether China today is more Chinese or more Communist. To me, it is like arguing about the number of angels that can dance on the head of a pin. The question is inherently unanswerable, since there are so many factors involved. But the longer I stayed in China the more

I was struck by the number of strong resonances to the past, if not exact similarities. It was not an accident that the Communists had made their Party headquarters in Zhongnanhai, a compound of lakes, palaces, and temples that was once part of the quarter in the old Imperial City reserved for the Emperors and their families. It was more than a coincidence that the Communist officials' claim to rule included their possession of the correct doctrine, Marxism, just as the mandarins in the past won their position by their superior knowledge of the Confucian classics. When I arrived in Peking, the first action Lao Wu counseled me in was to acquire a chop, or seal, with my name and position as *New York Times* bureau chief inscribed on it. Later, every time I wrote a letter, paid a bill, or sent in a request to the government, I affixed my chop to the document, tangible proof of my authority. It was a tradition carried on from the mandarins who served the dragon throne. In the Cultural Revolution, friends told me, Red Guards attacking an official they considered reactionary celebrated in triumph when they seized his seal of office. It was only then that they toppled him.

But most of all, I felt, the specific gravity of China's past came through in the patterns of personal relations in daily life, like *guan-xi* and the *li,* the importance of connections, names, and face. These shape the Chinese identity now much as they have for thousands of years. Even the trauma of the Communists' political campaigns have not shaken the Chinese people's unique consciousness of their own history and all that went with it. An American scholar, John Dolfin, who was married to a Chinese, once recounted an experience that befell him when he visited the village in northern China where his wife had been born. The hamlet lay in Henan province, just south of the Yellow River, the area where Chinese civilization began 3,000 years ago. It was unusual for the Communists to let a foreigner visit the village, Dolfin said, since it was far from the accepted tourist track and very poor. One afternoon, Dolfin, a tall, kindly man who speaks excellent Chinese, found himself in conversation with a group of elderly peasants who had gathered around his in-laws mud-walled house.

Had they ever seen a foreigner in their village before? he asked.

Yes, said several of the men, gnarled and browned from their years of labor in the fields. Was it a Russian? Dolfin suggested, thinking that a Soviet adviser might have happened through the area during the 1950s when relations between China and Russia were still good.

No, the peasants replied. Then could it have been a Japanese during Tokyo's long invasion of China from 1937 to 1945 in World War Two? The Japanese had come close, a talkative peasant said: "They reached a neighboring village and we buried all our valuables to hide from them. But we never actually saw a Japanese."

Perhaps it was a Western missionary in the late nineteenth or early twen-

tieth century? Dolfin then asked. No, again, said the peasants. One missionary had worked his way into the region in the 1930s, but the people had
driven him away after he spent one night there, assuming he was a spy.

Finally Dolfin had to give up.

"It was the Yuan dynasty," said another man with a white beard like a
patriarch, referring to the period from 1264 to 1368 when the Mongols
under Kublai Khan ruled China. "Some Mongol troops came through the
village."

3. The Giant Flight of Stairs

等級无边

RANK BUT NOT CLASS

"If a man becomes an official, even his chickens and dogs will ascend to heaven."

An old Chinese proverb

Under the shadow of the madder rose-stained west wall of the Forbidden City, the old sacred residence of China's emperors, is a large Chinese-style courtyard home with a sloping tiled roof. The house is invisible to passersby, hidden from the street by a gray-brick fence. But one afternoon a young Chinese graduate student acquaintance pointed out the location of the house as we drove by. It is the residence of a deputy chief of staff of the People's Liberation Army, she said, and contains the ultimate luxury in China—space. In a teeming city of four million people, where the average allotment of housing space is only a little over three square yards per person, the size of a dining-room table, and most families live squeezed in one- or two-room apartments, the general occupied a compound with two separate houses, a garden, and access to a small lake for swimming in the summer.

The general's family has four bedrooms, a living room with a piano and a large new Japanese-made color television set, and a commodious kitchen equipped with an American refrigerator. Unlike most Chinese houses today, which have plain concrete floors, the general's rooms are tastefully covered with polished wood. The general's family also has three modern bathrooms, each with flush toilets and bathtubs and regular running hot water, amenities Westerners take for granted but which the average Chinese can only dream about. Most Chinese still use public latrines and make do with cold water from a sink, if they have that. The house and its furnishings are all supplied by the army, free of charge, my friend confided. She knew one of the general's two children and so was a frequent guest in the residence.

Equally impressive, she said, was the general's retinue of servants, also supplied gratis by the military high command. There was an *a-yi,* or maid, to do the cooking, a driver for the general's army car, and an orderly who helped with the cleaning and errands. In addition, the general had two soldiers for bodyguards; they accompanied him whenever he left the house. All the help lived in a room attached to the smaller of the two buildings in the compound. The cook sometimes went out to buy food in a regular market, my friend added, but much of the time army trucks delivered special shipments of meat, rice, vegetables, and fruit from farms run by the military. In a society of constant food shortages, where grocery shopping consumes as much as two hours a day for most people (and seven days a week because there are few refrigerators), this service, too, was a "breathtaking" luxury, as my friend described it.

The general's main trouble was that despite the high front fence and the lack of any identifying name or number on his gate, some ordinary Chinese had discovered an important official was living there. In keeping with an old Chinese tradition, these people came to plead with the general for favors. "If you are poor, even if you live in the noisiest neighborhood, no one will ask about you," the general lamented, quoting a proverb. "But if you are rich, even if you live in the most remote mountains, people will seek you out."

In one case, my student friend related, a woman who had undergone an eye operation that left scars on her face repeatedly left letters on the general's doorstep asking for help in getting better medical treatment. She was in her late twenties and worried that her physical defect would prevent her from finding a husband.

"Please do something," she begged. "If you don't, I will commit suicide." The woman didn't address the general by name; in fact, she didn't know his name. She simply wrote, "To whoever lives here, I know you are someone important."

In another instance, a young man had deposited a package of liquor, cigarettes, and food in front of the house with a note asking for the general's daughter in marriage. A few days later the suitor dropped off a gift of 300 yuan ($200), half a year's salary for an average urban Chinese. He, too, wrote, "If you don't let me marry your daughter, I will kill myself."

The general, an aging veteran of the Communists' Long March in the 1930s, was disturbed. His two children are both young men. Clearly the letter writer was only surmising that whoever lived in such a house must be a senior official and therefore worth cultivating. The general turned all these letters and the money over to the police, but they couldn't catch the supplicants.

The story about the general's luxurious standard of living and the awe in which he was held by ordinary Chinese surprised me. For foreigners have long accepted as an article of faith that Mao Zedong had worked hard to create an egalitarian society—that was what the Communist revolution was about, putting an end to the excruciating injustices of the Nationalist era, the beggars, the opium addicts, the wealthy landlords, and the bloated warlords. Most Western visitors to China have reported that Mao succeeded. They have tended to see the uniformity of dress and the millions of Chinese pedaling their bicycles silently to work; they have been impressed by briefings from their China Travel Service guides on the low-cost housing and the inexpensive medical care, and they have believed the Maoist rhetoric about egalitarianism. But beneath this facade of the classless society, I gradually learned, some people are much more equal than others.

An American diplomat who traveled with Henry Kissinger on one of his first visits to China in the early 1970s recalled his own shock introduction to the subtle though significant differences between Chinese. It was the Foreign Service Officer's task to arrange the obligatory return banquet, the meal given by the visiting dignitary at the end of his journey to repay his Chinese hosts for their feast on his arrival. As it happened, China's Foreign Minister had entertained Kissinger in the Great Hall of the People, so under the adamantine rules of Chinese protocol, Kissinger would invite the Foreign Minister for the return banquet. When the diplomat came to the question of price with his Chinese counterpart, he suggested that 10 yuan a person might be a good figure. (Chinese arrange dinners by the cost per head, what they call the "standard," rather than by the price per dish.)

But the Chinese official looked troubled by the amount, in those days a handsome sum to pay for a meal in that country. That was much too low, the Chinese advised. The American should remember that the Foreign Minister himself would be coming. To which the American rejoined, with an attempt at humor, "I thought you had abolished class in China?"

"Yes," the Chinese said. "We have abolished class. But not rank."

A Chinese physicist I got to know, a specialist on lasers, put it another way. "All people in China may look alike, but they are not. The differences are narrow, but for that reason are keenly felt, and vitally important to us." He talked as we strolled around one of the unexcavated tombs of the Ming dynasty emperors in a broad valley north of Peking, just inside the Great Wall. It was one of the first warm days of spring, and the scientist, who had an unusual sartorial flair, took off his expensively tailored Mao jacket.

"You should imagine China as a giant flight of stairs," he continued. "There is a person on each step. Each person knows only what is on his step. No one sees the whole stairway from top to bottom. It is too vast."

The stairs begin with a labyrinthine system of grades and ranks, like a Chinese puzzle, into which each occupation has been divided by the Communists. First, there are twenty-four separate grades for the country's 20 million cadres. The Chinese term cadre, or *ganbu*, requires some explanation, for Chinese use it in two different though overlapping senses. Sometimes it refers to anyone with a position of leadership, from Deng Xiaoping on down to the heads of the village production teams. But Chinese also use it to cover all state functionaries, including a number of white-collar workers in the bureaucracy, like clerks and accountants, without any leadership role. A cadre may or may not be a member of the Communist Party. By Peking's count, there are 38 million Party members. At the bottom of the stairs on which the cadres are ranked are the ordinary clerks, grade twenty-four. Then come the section chiefs and department heads, grades fourteen to eighteen, bureau chiefs, grade thirteen, deputy ministers, grade eight, governors of the provinces, grades six and seven, and cabinet ministers, grades four and five. At the top of the pyramid only the late Chairman Mao, Premier Zhou Enlai, and Marshal Zhu De, the former head of the National People's Congress, were grade one, Chinese friends said. They were not sure, but they believed Deng Xiaoping and the former Party Chairman, Hua Guofeng, were only grade two or three. The reason, my friends insisted, was that the Communists, once in power in the 1950s, became very conservative and grades tended to become fixed. People were promoted very slowly, if at all.

Each rank has its corresponding salary: 40 yuan a month for grade twenty-four, rising to 190 yuan a month for grade thirteen, 280 yuan a month for grade eight, and then 400 yuan for grade one, ten times the lowest level. Office workers can tell a cadre's rank instantly by the type of chair he uses, a graying newspaper editor told me. Only cadres above grade thirteen are allowed a leather swivel chair, like those used by Western executives. Officials in the grades thirteen to sixteen range get a soft upholstered chair with springs and a velvet-covered seat. Grade seventeen cadres are entitled to a wooden chair with a cushion; those below that, only a plain wooden seat.

In determining an official's real authority, it is equally important to know the time and place a man joined the Communist movement, friends explained. Was it before or after the Long March, the epochal two-year trek across China in 1935 and 1936 that both saved and shaped the Communists? Did the cadre serve in Yanan, the Communists' wartime cave headquarters in the northwest, or did he work as an undercover agent in the Kuomintang, or "white" areas, a less prestigious assignment, at least in retrospect? Was he a member of the Red Army, or just a civilian party official? Such distinctions serve as pedigree and diploma to the Communists, like a family coat of arms, a place in the social register, or the name of the prep school one attended in some other societies.

The system of grades is virtually never mentioned in the official Chinese press, perhaps to help preserve the illusion of egalitarianism; but I gradually

67

came to learn about a range of other hierarchies too. In China's universities, professors are factored into twelve ranks, with salaries ranging from 56 yuan a month to 360 yuan, more than a six to one differential. Actors, stars of Chinese opera, and musicians have their own scale of grades one to sixteen. Artists and writers have been classified by the government along another index, and are paid, in addition to a regular monthly salary, a fee for their output calculated at so much per square foot of canvas or so much per 1,000 words of written text, depending on their ranking. I discovered at a cooking school in Chungqing, in Sichuan, where future experts in preparing the peppery cuisine of that province are trained, that Chinese chefs are graded from one to four, with master chef the highest encomium.

Technicians and engineers in factories have been placed on still another scale of eighteen grades, with a wage differential of ten to one; and factory workers are divided into eight grades, with wages ranging from about 34 yuan a month to 110 yuan. This spread of three to one is roughly equal to the wage differential in American and West European industry. The Communists' rationale for maintaining these differences is also similar to capitalist practice—to keep up motivation. Only Peking refers to the idea by the Marxist principle of "to each according to his work." This elaborate structure of ranks and wages has proven one of the most resilient of the Communists' accomplishments. Although it was originally established in the 1950s, it has remained largely unchanged, even in the face of repeated attacks on its inequalities during the Cultural Revolution. In fact, the laser scientist recalled his own experience in that tumultuous period when he was sent down to a May Seventh Cadre School for two years, supposedly to "be educated" by the local peasants. Here he helped plant rice and pulled carts loaded with hundreds of pounds of bricks. But he continued to draw his regular salary of 280 yuan a month—with one condition: he was ordered not to disclose how much he received to the peasants, for their total income per capita, for an entire year, at that time, the scientist said, was less than 40 yuan. Other city officials sent down to the countryside also continued to receive their normal pay, he added.

The physicist related another story to demonstrate how rigidly Chinese can adhere to the rank system. At an international conference on lasers in Peking, which he helped organize, the Chinese professors of grades one through four and the foreign scientists invited to attend sat in the first six rows of the conference hall. In front of each place was a white porcelain mug with scalding hot tea. One morning he arrived late for the symposium, because of some administrative details he had to clear up, and took a seat in a back row, assigned to professors of lesser standing. There he found the same white porcelain mug. But inside was only hot water, no tea leaves, to save money. Unless he had sat there, or one of the junior scientists had tried to grab a place in one of the front rows, no one would know the difference. The appearance of equality had been preserved.

This penchant for hierarchy is rooted in China's past, at least from the time when Confucius decreed that men who labor with their minds are destined to rule those who merely grovel with their hands. "The gentleman's part is like that of the wind; the smaller man's part is like that of the grass," Confucius said. "When the wind blows, he cannot chose but bend." In Confucian doctrine, each person's status was codified along the "Three Bonds," the loyalty of subject to ruler, filial obedience of son to father, and fidelity of wife to husband. Each of these was between superior and subordinate; none were between equals. The result was that each Chinese was enmeshed in a highly ordered system of kinship relations, with elder brothers, younger brothers, sisters, maternal aunts, paternal elder brothers' wives, all spelled out in a complex vocabulary which does not even exist in English or European languages. Each relationship also carried with it a corresponding set of rights and duties. Given this system within the family, Chinese were habituated to accept a similar pattern of authority and ranks in their government. It served to tell a man, or woman, where they stood automatically, providing a kind of security. If you fulfilled your prescribed role, you didn't need to worry about what others would do.

The Communists, of course, came to power dedicated to overthrowing China's past, the old love of hierarchy, cursed as feudalism, finding in it an explanation why the country that had invented gunpowder, the compass, and paper failed to keep pace with the West after the Industrial Revolution. While still guerrillas the Communists banned the old polite forms of address in Chinese for Mr., Mrs., and Miss: *xiansheng,* literally, "elder born," *taitai,* "great one," and *xiaojie,* "little miss." These smacked of feudalism, the Communists charged, and they replaced them with the simple Marxist term "comrade," *tongzhi.* They also adopted the old peasant convention of referring to other people, regardless of gender, simply as "Little Wang" or "Old Fung," depending on whether the person was younger or older than the speaker.

Yet somewhere along the way the Communists' Chinese heritage began to catch up with them. When I first arrived in Peking, I was very careful to avoid using the proper old-fashioned Chinese I had learned at Harvard and on Taiwan, and called people "comrade." But I noticed that almost no Chinese used it among themselves. Instead, I found, they often employed the same formal way of speaking that the Nationalists did, addressing people by their titles: Deputy Section Chief Wu, School President Mai, on up to Chairman Hua, never just Hua. I myself was addressed as Reporter Butterfield, or sometimes archaically as Mr. Butterfield.

As the Communists fell back into some of the old terminology of the mandarin class, they also worked out a system of perquisites to go with each rank, much like that established by the emperors for their retainers. Indeed, Chinese explained to me, you couldn't really measure a person's status by his salary alone, for many of the amenities of the good life, which in the West are acquired with money, in China can be gotten only through political position—better housing, cars, vacation trips, plane and train tickets.

"In China today it's not money but power that people want," said a tall, lean, crew-cut thirty-year-old son of an army general. "Money is very limited in what it can buy, you need connections and rank." On a hot July morning with the temperature in the nineties, he took me on a tour of some of the facilities which provide the politically annointed in China with what the Chinese call *te-quan*, "special privileges." These prerogatives had existed ever since 1949, he said, but with the breakdown in Party authority and public morality in the Cultural Revolution, they had become far more widespread and blatant. The constant political buffeting, the persecutions, and the economic dislocations of recent years had undermined people's devotion to the revolution and led to more self-seeking.

Our first stop was a few blocks east of the Forbidden City, Number 53 Dong Hua Men Street, a modern five-story concrete building with large plate-glass windows on the ground floor. Their curtains are perpetually drawn, so a passerby cannot peer inside. The only identifying clue to the structure was a small plaque, nailed to a post across a driveway, which described it modestly as the "Peking City Food Supply Place."

Yet it did not resemble any of Peking's ordinary markets, with their long patient queues of housewives and, occasionally, husbands, plastic airline-style bags in hand, waiting for the daily ration of whatever fresh vegetable or cut of meat happened to be available. Instead, there was a covey of vehicles drawn up outside, parked on a ramp leading to the entrance and cluttering the sidewalk, illegally. Among them were several Shanghai sedans, like a 1950s Packard, a few jeeps, a new imported Japanese panel van, a freezer truck, and a small three-wheeled truck that looked like an oversized motorcycle. Several chauffeurs squatted idly under the shade of a locust tree. Stacked in the back of the three-wheeler were a dozen chickens, two sides of pork, a crate full of large yellow croaker fish, each big enough to feed a Chinese banquet table of twelve, and packages of frozen giant prawns from the Bohai Gulf. My Chinese acquaintance was stunned by the abundance of meat, the proportions of the fish, the biggest he had ever seen, he said, and the number of prawns, an item that ordinary Chinese cannot buy except at the New Year's holiday.

The store, he explained, is for China's highest ranking officials only—members of the Communist Party Central Committee, the heads of the eleven large military regions into which command of the army is divided, and a few nationally prominent non-Communists who had collaborated with Peking. A number of aged Party veterans had also been given the "special purchase cards" required for admission. In addition, the store provided daily supplies to the capital's top restaurants and hotels patronized by China's leaders and foreigners.

A few blocks farther east, on the ground floor of a dark-brown, granite-faced apartment building, was a shop identified only by its address, Number 83, Chao Yang Men Street. The store's windows had been shuttered up with red-painted boards. Just inside the door sat a fat, middle-aged woman atten-dant with short hair trimmed in the shape of a bowl. When I tried to walk in, she demanded, "Have you got a card?" When in turn I asked, "What is this place?" she responded, "You're in the wrong place." I tried the question again, but got the same answer. Inside, a large screen shielded the contents from view. Only a large portrait of Chairman Mao was visible.

According to my companion, it was a special bookstore for high cadres only. Occasionally, he said, he borrowed his father's "special purchase card," which allowed him to go inside. Unlike the regular bookshops, which are always jammed with customers clamoring for attention from rude salesclerks, the officials' bookstore had banks of easy chairs for the cadres to sit in while they decided on their selection. Most of the volumes for sale were marked *Nei-bu*, "for internal distribution only," or classified. They included transla-tions of popular foreign novels which the Party authorities deemed unfit for ordinary Chinese to read, like *Love Story.* There were also Western political tracts, including former President Nixon's memoirs, *RN,* and his earlier book, *My Six Crises,* which are not available to the public. But the most important service of the special bookstore, my friend explained, was simply that it had books. Chinese have long loved to read, given the value tradition-ally placed on the written word and education. But because of the vast size of China's population and the country's scant forest cover, denuded centuries ago by peasants who needed wood for fuel, there is a terrible shortage of paper. It had been aggravated during the Cultural Revolution by the deluge of propaganda materials, notably the hundreds of millions of copies of the little red plastic-covered edition of Mao's quotations venerated by the Red Guards as their bible. Hence most books today are issued in small editions of perhaps 10,000 to 20,000 copies, hardly enough for a country of a billion people. Popular works, like English-language textbooks or a Chinese-English dictionary, are sold out in a few hours. Not so in the special book-store, which keeps adequate reserves. The most eagerly sought-after book, my friend confided, was a recent photo-offset edition of a sixteenth-century copy of the *Golden Lotus,* China's classic of pornography. It has been banned in ordinary bookshops since the Communists' victory in 1949.

Continuing our drive, opposite the northern wall of the Forbidden City, across from the old moat, my guide pointed to an unmarked edifice built in imitation of a Chinese temple. The roof was set with mustard-yellow tiles, and the front was decorated with a series of red-painted columns and three tall red doors. Two army sentries stood stiffly beside a driveway lined with pine trees that led to the rear of the building. It is the Three Gates Theater, my friend said, where high cadres can see current American, European, and Japanese hit movies not otherwise shown in China. From 1966 to 1972, under the cultural despotism of Jiang Qing, no movies at all were produced in China, and only ten were filmed in the next four years up to Mao's death and the overthrow of the radicals. Even today the offerings of the Chinese film industry tend to be hackneyed and bombastic, avoiding sex or politically sensitive plots. So watching foreign movies has become something of a passion for those lucky enough to have the proper political credentials.

Two blocks away, also facing the northern wall of the Forbidden City, is a two-story gray-brick house with a sloping tile roof partially hidden behind a ten-foot-high wall. From the outside the building is unpretentious, but my friend identified it as the home of Deng Xiaoping, the vice chairman of the Party, who is China's most powerful leader. Rumor has it that the gray steel gates to the house are equipped with an electronic device to let Deng's car in without stopping, a common gadget in America, though still rare in China. But Deng now spends most of his time in a more spacious villa in the Western Hills outside Peking, a quiet wooded neighborhood off limits to foreigners and ordinary Chinese. In imperial times the area where he lives, known as Jade Spring Mountain, was reserved for the Emperor's pleasure during the summer months.

My friend was especially proud to be able to show me Deng's in-town residence, because only a few high ranking Chinese know where their country's leaders live. The locations are a state secret. He found it difficult to believe that Americans not only know where their President lives but can visit the White House as tourists. This Chinese penchant for secrecy stems partly from the Communists' mania for security, born of their guerrilla days, but it also follows an old imperial tradition under which dignitaries sought to maintain their exalted status by aloofness from the public. The greater their distance from the people, the higher their prestige. In his later years, Mao almost never appeared in public, with the exception of the monster rallies of hundreds of thousands of Red Guards during the Cultural Revolution, and even then he stood atop the tower of the Gate of Heavenly Peace, with no personal contact with the worshipful masses below. Mao's successors also tend to appear only on ceremonial occasions, like China's National Day on October 1 or at Party congresses. Members of the Politburo, the inner sanctum of power, do not hold press conferences for Chinese journalists or work crowds at airports or kiss babies.

Other officials below the highest rung on the ladder also are assigned cloistered and special housing according to their rank, I learned. One new development in the western part of Peking, across the street from the State Guesthouse, where former President Nixon stayed in 1972, has been sardonically dubbed *Fu-pi-lou,* roughly translatable as the "Capitalist Restoration Building," since many of its residents are officials who were purged as capitalist roaders during the Cultural Revolution but have since been rehabilitated. It is actually two separate sets of buildings divided by a black-topped driveway. On one side is a series of three-story red-brick residences with ample balconies, large picture windows, and grassy yards planted with small pine trees, a rarity in a city so sere and dusty that grass does not seem to grow. The apartments on this side are reserved for cadres of grade eight and above, like the Minister of Education, Zhang Nanxiang. But after the many stories I had heard about how luxurious the *Fu-pi-lou* was from Chinese, I was surprised that the apartments were comparable only to a lower-middle-class housing project in an American city.

On the other side of the driveway is a group of more modest six-story gray-concrete apartment buildings. Among the residents are the son of Fang Yi, a Politburo member who is head of the State Science and Technology Commission, a daughter of Ulanhu, another Politburo member, several prominent movie stars, and the artist Huang Zhou, popular in China for his ink wash paintings of donkeys. But even here the quarters are spacious by Chinese standards. One senior scholar I met who lived there had three bedrooms, a living room, a kitchen, a toilet with a bathtub, and even a telephone, still a novelty for the average Chinese, for they cost 1,900 yuan ($1,267) to install, over three years wages for an urban Chinese, and the telephone company can take years to act unless a person has the right political connections.

I did manage to visit the home of one senior Chinese, Madame Sun Yat-sen, the widow of the leader of the 1911 revolution that overthrew the Manchu Qing dynasty and herself a deputy head of the National People's Congress, the nominal legislature. Madame Sun, who was born Soong Chingling and was an elder sister of Madame Chiang Kai-shek, was in frail health at the time and died in May 1981, a few months after I left China, of leukemia. Her position in Peking was largely symbolic, representing the tradition of her husband and other non-Communist patriotic Chinese, and she had little real power. But her regal life-style resembled that of an American millionaire. She lived in an extraordinary house built by a Manchu prince in the late nineteenth century where the last Emperor of the Qing dynasty, Henry Pu Yi, was born. It is located on a quiet street on the north side of the Back Lake, one of the man-made imperial lakes which stretch out behind the Forbidden City. Today the house is hidden by a fifteen-foot-high gray-brick wall.

When I drove up at 6:20 P.M. precisely, as called for in the letter of invitation sent by Madame Sun's personal secretary, three sentries of the People's Liberation Army, in green fatigues, emerged and checked my name against a master list. Then they swung open a high red iron gate topped by a ceremonial Chinese tile arch. I had wangled the invitation because for years *The New York Times* had been sending Madame Sun free copies of the Sunday paper, at her request.

The broad driveway led through several acres of parklike grounds set with pines and willows, a large pond, and several gardens. The house itself appeared only after the visitor navigates a sweeping curve. The roof was sloped and finished in tile, Chinese-style. But the proportions were Western, three stories high, and the floors were covered with thick carpets spread from wall to wall.

Madame Sun was waiting in an anteroom, a tiny woman of ninety-two, with a round, cherub face, her long hair, still black, pulled back in a bun. She was dressed in a simple though elegant blue silk jacket with high mandarin collar and Chinese cloth fastenings. A woman aide and one of her foster daughters supported Madame Sun when we went into dinner.

The dining room suggested a Chinese re-creation of a European château, a long rectangular room, decorated with portraits of Mao and Hua at one end, and a huge piece of Mao's calligraphy, a gift to Madame Sun, hung on the other. The table was set with antique Chinese blue and white porcelain, and silver knives and forks, along with chopsticks. Servants in white livery produced a meal, part Chinese, part Western, unobtainable in any Peking restaurant, that reflected Madame Sun's own mixed upbringing. Although she was born in Shanghai, to a wealthy business family, she was educated in Macon, Georgia, and spoke English with an American accent.

The meal began with a Chinese hot and sour soup, strips of pork and bean curd in a broth laced with pepper and vinegar. Then came a Shanghai roast duck, rich with tender meat, and served cold. There followed a cold chicken dish, a grilled white fish, Western-style, a curried beef, stewed cucumber in brown sauce, and what Madame Sun announced as "the house specialty," macaroni with cheese, American-style. Dessert was cold almond-paste soup, a Chinese delicacy made from real almonds in the old-fashioned way, by crushing them between two stones, she said. "In the restaurants they don't use real almonds anymore," she insisted. Here again was a true luxury well beyond the means of normal Chinese.

After dinner, Madame Sun's personal doctor appeared at the door, made a signal to her secretary, who gave a sign to her woman assistant seated next to her. "It is time for you to rest," the aide declared.

As she was led upstairs for the night, I was taken on a tour of the rest of the house, which included her private movie theater. It was another long room with high ceilings, large glass windows facing the gardens, and ten rows of stuffed easy chairs covered with brown and gray slip covers. The room was equipped with two projectors and a screen that stretched full across it. When she was in good health, Madame Sun was famous for her screenings of the latest American films, often double features, and sometimes, I was told, triple features. The shows could last till the middle of the night, and it was considered rude to leave before they were over. Under the protocol of privileges for the elite, only members of the Politburo were supposed to be able to show movies at home, but Madame Sun was granted an exception because of her advanced age, Chinese said.

In the gravel driveway of Madame Sun's house stood another of the perquisites that go with being a member of the elite, a long black Hong Qi, or Red Flag limousine. There are no private cars in China; all automobiles are assigned by the state, usually with a chauffeur. Technically the vehicles belong to the government office, school, or factory which allocates them, rather than to the official, and the *People's Daily* periodically admonished against personal use of cars, meaning cadres should not let their wives take them for shopping or sending the children to school. Yet pick any day to visit one of Peking's major department stores or first-class restaurants and you will see fleets of these cars, disgorging families, lined up outside.

"I used to worry about my wife using the office car," a graying engineer in Shanghai told me, "since the car belongs to the people. But then we talked about it, and she pointed out that we are the people, too. I couldn't argue with her," and he laughed. Many people seem to share in this joke.

In a country where most people must still rely on bicycles for transportation, the Red Flag is a special wonder, a hand-tooled luxury car designed in the 1950s, with the interior modeled after the Mercedes and the rear end copied from the Cadillac. The inside sparkles with polished wood; there are jump seats for extra passengers, like the stretch version of the Cadillac; a lace antimacassar is spread over the rear upholstery, and brown curtains shield passengers in the back from public scrutiny. Only two hundred Red Flags are produced a year, at a truck factory in Changchun, in the northeast, so they are alloted only to the highest officials.

When traffic policemen spot a Red Flag on the road, they will often push other cars, trucks, or bicyclists aside. And Red Flags are excluded by special right from having to brake to a sudden stop if confronted with an unexpected pedestrian or bicyclist, constant hazards in Peking. I discovered this when a friend who worked in the computer center of the Academy of Sciences reported that a man in his office who had recently learned how to ride a bike made an abrupt turn without signaling. A Red Flag behind him smashed into the man, braking only slightly. He lay in a coma for a week, then died. Ordinarily, the family of a victim in an accident would receive a substantial settlement under the system of strict accountability in Chinese law. But his family got nothing, the office mate said. For Red Flags, they learned, are exempted from these regulations for fear that if they brake to a sudden stop they might injure a high cadre riding in the back seat. Ironically, this Red Flag had been loaded with foreigners, businessmen who can now rent the prestige cars to help China earn foreign exchange.

Driving a Red Flag, I saw on other occasions, gives its passengers a license to go almost anywhere. One fall afternoon when I was playing tennis with an Australian diplomat on the bumpy, leaf-strewn courts of the International Club—supposedly reserved for foreigners only—I watched as the familiar long black shape of a Red Flag pulled up and an elderly, white-haired man in an air force uniform disembarked. One aide carried two new American-made graphite tennis rackets, worth over $200 apiece; another aide brought out a thermos and cups for tea. When I quizzed the aides about the identity of their boss, they shook their heads and replied, "I'm not too clear." But a Chinese attendant who looks after the courts told me later that the mystery player was a general in the air force.

When I repeated the incident to my friend whose father was a general and who had given me the tour of the special facilities for the elite, he nodded in recognition.

"The real power in China is in the military," he said, with more than a touch of pride. Indeed, as he explained it, the military in China is a state within the state. His own father, who held a rank equivalent to lieutenant general, got a salary of 400 yuan ($267) a month, higher than any civilian except Mao. But the figure was meaningless, because his father, like the deputy chief of staff who lived under the shadow of the Forbidden City, also got a free house, car, and food from the army. In addition, his father had access to a store in the Western suburbs of Peking that sells cheap consumer goods made by the nation's huge network of defense industries, like the post exchange, or PX, system in the United States. That was how he and some of his friends had bought motorcycles, an item not available in regular stores.

Privilege in the military is not only for high-ranking officers; ordinary soldiers in China's 4.5 million-man armed forces are also better off than their civilian counterparts. While only 3.8 percent of China's population as a whole are members of the Communist Party, 35 percent of the military have been accepted into the Party, an important route to the better life in China. When soldiers are demobilized, they are often given important leadership posts in factories or communes, despite their lack of training, because of their presumed political loyalty. Families of soldiers in the villages have tradition-ally been given an extra share of the harvest at the end of the year. During the Cultural Revolution, Mao called in the army to take over many universities and factories riven by factional battles. The military units were supposed to go back to their barracks in the early 1970s, but some found their new quarters so comfortable that they have stayed on despite repeated orders from the State Council. The Ministry of Education reported while I was in Peking that the army still occupied 20 million square yards of school land, more than the government could build in several years. In Peking, when students and faculty at People's University organized a protest march in 1979 over the continued occupation of two thirds of their campus by the Second Artillery, a missile command, the leaders of the demonstration were expelled from school. The students had no classrooms or cafeteria because of the soldiers' presence.

But the most surprising feature of army life to me, in a Communist state, was the amplitude of servants allotted to officers. Every officer, from company commander up, is assigned an orderly, my friend said. His father's orderly did everything from shining shoes and sweeping the floor in their house to setting out his father's toothbrush and putting toothpaste on it. One former army general, Wang Meng, now head of the Sports Commission, took his orderly on a trip to Mexico with him. Later I learned that all civilian officials of grade eight and above, from Deputy Minister up, receive allowances of 50 yuan ($33) a month to hire maids. Many of these servants in Peking come from Anhui, a province in central China that is one of the poorest in the country, a kind of Chinese Appalachia, other friends related. They had come to the capital in search of a better life and managed to stay on, without the necessary legal identification papers, because of their employment.

And yet, for all this consciousness of rank, all the privileges and prerogatives, the Communists have made efforts to reduce the gap between the top and the bottom. The distinctive feature of the Chinese system has not been to eliminate all the differences but to try to mute them. People in high positions are entitled to their rewards, but they should not flaunt them.

This strange sweet and sour, elitist–egalitarian ambivalence comes out in the way Chinese handle their chauffeurs. On the one hand, officials shouldn't labor with their hands, and therefore don't drive. But on the other hand, chauffeurs are a living reminder they are not practicing socialist equality. So when cadres go out for dinner they have worked out an ingenious compromise to resolve this dilemma. The first time I invited some Chinese to a banquet, a group of journalists from the New China News Agency, I thought I had made all the necessary arrangements. I had called the restaurant and negotiated the price per head, the number of guests, and the date. But then the man on duty at the restaurant caught me off guard.

"What is the standard for the chauffeurs?" he asked.

It took me a minute to realize that I had to buy dinner for the newsmen's drivers as well. For of course they would come in chauffeured cars, their drivers would wait, and would expect to be fed.

But I did not have to pay as much for the chauffeurs' meals, the clerk in the restaurant assured me. I had agreed to pay 20 yuan apiece for the journalists. Five yuan would be more than sufficient for the drivers, and would include beer and cigarettes, he said.

The most obvious way in which the Chinese have sought to minimize or blur the distinctions between people is by the uniformity of dress. Proletarian blue and peasant black, like the baggy pants and formless jackets, are a defense against charges of trying to be better than one's neighbors, of being too interested in fashion and therefore bourgeois. The degree of shabbiness and shapelessness varies with the political season.

"When a major campaign develops, like the Cultural Revolution, we bring out all our oldest, most tattered clothes," an English teacher related. "My family still keeps our patched pants and jackets, like peasants' clothes, in the bottom of a trunk, just in case."

But with China's more relaxed mood since Mao's death and the downfall of the radicals in 1976, style consciousness has made a comeback. Most Chinese feel they can now judge a cadre's rank by the cut of his tunic—the higher his status, the finer the fabric, the better the fit, and the neater the crease in his trousers. Cadres still have their own tailor shops. In Peking it's the Hung Bin, near the old foreign legation quarter. In Shanghai it's the Paramount, on Nanking Road, the main shopping street. When I stopped in there, drawn by a tuxedo displayed in the window, an elderly white-haired salesman assured me all their products were hand-stitched. "We make suits for the senior cadres," he went on. "They appreciate our workmanship."

In an effort to reduce inequality in the army, Peking abolished formal ranks in 1965. To foreigners the results are impressive. Members of China's armed forces wear no epaulets, no insignia of rank. But the difference may be more cosmetic than real. It does not mean that privates can give orders to generals, or that their pay is the same. Enlisted men still know who their officers are and salute them. The head of a company, instead of being called a captain, is merely identified as company commander. Everyone wears baggy green fatigues. But officers' jackets have four pockets, enlisted men's only two.

The government has also taken a number of deliberate steps to try to equalize social and economic differences. To ensure that in a country of one billion people with limited resources everyone gets a minimal supply of food and consumer goods, the Communists have strictly rationed key items like rice, cooking oil, and cloth. Housing may be scarce, and often shabby by Western standards, but the government has held rents to the very low level of three or four yuan a month, affordable by all. Salaries are low—the average urban worker earns 64 yuan ($42) a month—but there are no income taxes and over one quarter of the gross national product has gone to investment. Much of this is in industry, but Peking has also devoted it to expanding education and health care, which benefit the public. Each occupation has its scale of ranks and corresponding salaries, but they are virtually identical all across China. To try to make up for the higher cost and scarcity of goods in remote areas, like Xinjiang and Tibet, or the higher cost of living in the most expensive cities, like Peking and Shanghai, the government employs an eleven grade cost-of-living index. On this scale, a small town in Anhui, where meat and vegetables are cheap, is pegged at four, the provincial capital of Hefei at five, Peking six, and Shanghai eight. Tibet is at the top, eleven. All state employees are given minor adjustments in their salaries to reflect whether they live in a cheap or expensive area. Nobody, I learned, has to suffer by being classed as being in a one, two, or three region, which would cut their incomes. The lowest is a four.

One of the best examples of how Peking has attempted to mute differences is in its policy toward athletes. For a long time I found it difficult to learn about how China trains its sports stars. I knew there was a system of state support for sports, based on that in the Soviet Union, organized under the State Physical Culture and Sports Commission, a cabinet-level agency with a large headquarters in Peking. It is public knowledge that China is dotted with what are called spare-time sports schools, after-school gyms, and swimming pools where promising youngsters are sent; and it is an open secret that members of the national teams draw government salaries. But even my best Chinese friends, including one who worked in the Sports Commission and lived near the special dormitories for members of the national teams on Sports Street, refused to discuss the system.

"It's supposed to be a secret that Chinese athletes are professionals," he said, and indicated he would rather express his disillusionment about Marxism than discuss the nurture of athletes. This clandestine atmosphere suggested a massive, richly endowed program, like that in Russia or East Germany, where athletes are pampered and have the chance to become millionaires.

But when an acquaintance whose daughter was a fast-rising young swimmer finally broke this code of silence, her revelations seemed tame. Her daughter had begun swimming when she was five years old, the woman said, after being discovered by a coach from their neighborhood spare-time sports school. She used to work out four or five hours a day in the school's pool. Then at eleven she was picked for the Peking city team, and to help her train full-time, her mother enrolled her in what is called a "training camp." The daughter attended regular classes only in the morning, with a reduced academic load, mathematics, Chinese language, and politics, the three R's for Chinese. "Then she has all afternoon and evening to practice, swimming laps, jogging, doing flexibility exercises, and lifting weights," her mother said. Her daughter now comes home only on Sunday afternoons.

Thanks to this regimen, her daughter has won a national championship meet in her event, freestyle, and has been awarded the honor of being named a first-grade athlete, one short of the top, master of sports. The lowest is third-grade athlete.

But the rewards for such achievement are slight by American or Soviet standards. In fact, the mother is worried about her daughter's future, for Chinese athletes don't draw any salary until they are seventeen years old. Then they get only the wage of a beginning factory worker, about 40 yuan a month. Promotion comes slowly, as it does for other Chinese, and even China's world champion Ping-Pong player, Zhuang Zedong, who won favor with Jiang Qing and was named head of the Sports Commission, earned only 80 yuan a month. For a period before the Cultural Revolution any Chinese star who placed in the top three in an international meet received a bonus of 100 yuan, but that has been scrapped as too bourgeois. Moreover, the mother pointed out, her daughter will have nothing to fall back on when she finishes high school, for she has sacrificed her education and won't be able to go to college. She might be sent to work in a factory or, if she is lucky, be named a coach.

Still, her mother admitted, there are rewards that set her daughter apart. She gets a food "supplement" of 60 yuan a month, more than an average worker's salary, which is paid to the training camp for more nourishing meals. She gets all her uniforms free; she will get a bonus of six yuan a month if she becomes a master of sports, and there is frequent travel around China, a privilege few Chinese enjoy in a country where transportation is inadequate and buying tickets takes official approval. Besides, her mother observed, "athletes have more fun." In China, then, even the smallest difference looms large, magnified by the very ordinariness of most people's lives.

The same system of small gradations, minor to an outsider, but of real significance to a Chinese, applies to other occupations. Peking's supporters often note that China has not allowed its favored writers, movie stars, or nuclear physicists, those who have contributed to the glory of the state, to become millionaires, as the Soviet Union has. Many of them do, however, live very comfortably, practicing discreet rather than conspicuous consumption. Perhaps the wealthiest writer is Ba Jin, a left-wing novelist whose semiautobiographical trilogy, *Family,* made him China's most popular writer before 1949. Today he still lives in a large Western-style house he purchased in the 1950s, secluded behind a wrought-iron gate and a long driveway. He doesn't draw a state salary, he said in an interview, he doesn't need to.

During the Cultural Revolution, Red Guard pamphlets estimated his fortune, derived from his royalties, at 200,000 yuan ($133,000). Like other cultural figures, he was attacked by the Red Guards and his property confiscated, but he has since been rehabilitated and his house returned.

There are many ways those with the proper rank and credentials can beat the asperities of life without being too conspicuous about it. If they are ill, there are special hospitals. In the capital, it's the Peking Hospital, a modern tree-shaded complex around the corner from the Xinqiao Hotel, where Prime Minister Zhou Enlai was treated for cancer till his death in 1976. A Chinese scientist who visited a high-ranking relative there was amazed at all the latest American, West European, and Japanese medical technology he found, including a large computer that was not in operation, apparently because no one knew how to run it. He contrasted the equipment with that in his neighborhood clinic, which did not have a working X-ray machine. In Kunming, in Yunnan, a doctor told me, he worked in a special wing of a hospital reserved for high-level cadres who got the small supplies of foreign drugs when they were available. During the Cultural Revolution the doctor came under attack for being a Christian and was forced to clean the lavatories. But when one of these ranking patients arrived, the doctor was called back for consultation.

Cadres get the same ration coupons as ordinary Chinese. But officials get extra allowances for entertainment and, friends related, often spend up to twenty days a month engaged in meetings where they will be well fed, largely at state expense.

Some special consumer goods are available only to the favored. Panda brand filter cigarettes, which are made with imported tobacco, cannot be purchased in any store. But a number of leaders smoke them, and once during a press conference given by Deng, in the Great Hall of the People, I found a blue packet of Pandas, decorated with its namesake, on a desk in front of my chair, along with a pad of paper and pencil.

The Peking Hotel is strictly off limits to Chinese, and gray-uniformed security guards rigorously question anyone they don't recognize as working there. But I was charmed one fall afternoon to watch a Red Flag pull up to the entrance and observe an orderly in military uniform jump out to help the passenger in the back seat open the door. Slowly a portly white-haired gentleman in his seventies emerged, accompanied by his wife. Without a word from the guards, they trundled in, took the elevator to the mezzanine floor, and went to the hotel barbershop. I discovered later that cabinet ministers, generals, and their sons and daughters are regular patrons of the men's and women's hairdressers, theoretically reserved for foreigners. The daughter of one senior general, now an army officer herself, said she had been coming there to get her hair cut since she was a girl.

Similarly, only ranking cadres, army officers, and others with special status can buy tickets for China's limited number of daily airplane flights or purchase "soft seat," first-class accommodations on the nation's railroad network. ("Soft-seat" means literally that, plushy stuffed chairs, windows shaded by lace curtains, no extra passengers pushing in the aisles. "Hard-seat," or second-class, means flat wooden or wicker-framed seats, and usually more passengers than seats.)

Passengers going "soft-seat" or "soft-berth" usually board their train through a special entrance, set off to the side of the main railroad station for discretion. In the old lakeside city of Hangzhou, China's capital during the Sung dynasty, the first-class waiting room is in a small building hidden behind a closed iron gate and up a gravel drive. It is furnished with easy chairs and carpeted with soft rugs. From there passengers enter the far end of the platform, undisturbed by the crush of people pushing through in the main station, which has only hard wooden benches to sit on. I came to be familiar with many of these first-class waiting rooms, because they are also where foreigners are taken.

China does not have private dachas, the country retreats available to the privileged in the Soviet Union as a reward for service to the state. But cadres on trips have access to well-appointed "guesthouses," zhao-dai-suo. In Hefei, the capital of Anhui, I accidentally got a glimpse of the style to which China's most senior leaders are accustomed. I was traveling with Governor Harry Hughes of Maryland, who had come to sign a sister-state agreement with Anhui, and was housed in a villa built for a visit by Mao in 1958. The villa lay in a sprawling compound of guesthouses set on a hilly park overlooking a lake. Mao's residence was a modernistic brick and glass structure, with something of early Frank Lloyd Wright in its lines, though it was trimmed in a dubious shade of pea-soup green, perhaps to match the surrounding pine trees. Next door was a small power station to ensure electricity for important visitors, presumably a reflection on the city's wavering supply. The power station included a building where an attendant lived, and on a hot June evening he was sitting on a chair on the roof. The door to his own room was thrown open, revealing a bed under a tangle of wires.

The entrance to Mao's bungalow was gained by a fifty-foot-long corridor carpeted in red. The entire suite of eight rooms was finished with dark wood paneling, a rarity in China, where wood is in short supply, and it had a somber, Victorian feeling. The master bedroom contained a full-length double mirror, a voluminous wardrobe, and a dark rosewood four-poster double bed hung with a mosquito net. The windows were covered with light-brown patterned-silk curtains. Off to one side was a small sitting room with a sunken leather sofa built into three of its walls. Two other bedrooms also came equipped with four-posters and their own private sitting rooms. The combination living–dining room was furnished with three heavy sofas, large porcelain vases, and a color television set.

The most luxurious feature, however, by Chinese standards, was the enormous bathroom. The bathtub was formed in the shape of an L, five feet to the side, with a short set of steps leading up to it. The stairs were topped with steel handrails, to assist the elderly or infirm bather. The bathroom contained a choice of a Western flush toilet, a Chinese-style seatless squat toilet, and a urinal. It was also furnished with a reclining leather couch beside the tub, so a guest could be given a rubdown after his bath. The villa was staffed by twenty attendants.

The Communists have also set aside a number of villas and hotels for the faithful at China's favorite resorts like Beidaihe, the old summer colony for European businessmen, diplomats, and missionaries on the Yellow Sea coast east of Peking, Huang Shan, or Yellow Mountain in Anhui, and West Lake in Hangzhou. At Qingdao, another resort and port on the Yellow Sea which also produces China's most famous beer, Robert Piccus, an American businessman, recalled his difficulty in penetrating the secrecy which surrounds the occupants of the seaside villas. Before coming to Qingdao, Piccus had arranged to meet a Danish executive whose company was negotiating a deal to improve the harbor. Piccus was put up in the regular city hotel, but the Dane was quartered in a special guest house and Piccus couldn't find him. Finally the Dane managed to call Piccus to explain.

"I can't tell you where I am, since the people in charge of the guesthouse say they don't know the name of the building or our address," the Dane said, suppressing a laugh. "I also can't tell you how to call me, since they say they don't know the phone number here."

Although the elite have veiled many of their privileges behind this kind of secrecy, ordinary Chinese are still aware they are not equal and often bitter about it. Mao's impassioned pleas for revolutionary egalitarianism made a deep impression on both urban and rural Chinese, though the Great Helmsman may not have been an exemplar of his idealistic doctine.

At Fudan University in Shanghai, one of the three most prestigious colleges in China, a group of journalism majors conducted a daring public opinion poll in which they asked other students what they thought China's most serious problem was. The pollsters went to the school library, locked its doors, and passed out their questionnaires. Of the several hundred students who responded, 60 percent listed *te-quan,* special privileges, an American exchange student at Fudan said.

From time to time a member of the leadership does get into political trouble because of overstepping the fine line between legitimate enjoyment of the spoils of office and arrogance. Chen Muhua, the tall, formidable woman who is an alternate member of the Politburo and a deputy premier, came under attack after a trip to Rumania. She was about to fly back to Peking when a group of Chinese students studying in Rumania who were sick arranged through the Chinese ambassador in Bucharest to return with her on her special plane. The ambassador thought it would help the students and save the government some money. But when he informed Chen at the airport, she was piqued. According to an account published in a Communist magazine in Hong Kong, she declared:

"Since you have arranged to have so many students board the plane, I will let them return home first. I will not leave for the time being." The ambassador was forced to reverse his plan and take the students off the plane.

Not long afterward the *People's Daily* observed that such abuses have helped undermine the prestige of the Party. "Why is it that in the early days of the present regime we could discard the dirt of the old society without delay and establish a new spirit?" the paper asked. "One of the main reasons is that the spirit was sound then and the Communist Party enjoyed high prestige among the masses."

But now, the paper added, Party members and cadres "are demanding special privileges not only for themselves but also for their children. They let them enter the Party, get them back from the villages to the cities, put them into schools, and get permits for them to go abroad. They treat their children as their private property. . . . Such behavior in cadres can seriously damage the Party among the masses." The paper blamed this decline in idealism and rise in selfishness on the Gang of Four, a euphemism, most Chinese knew, for the whole Cultural Revolution decade.

Indeed, the abuses that have aroused the most resentment are those involving the children of high cadres. The most notorious case of nepotism—or "the shade of the Emperor's favor" in Chinese—is that of the family of Ye Jianying, the pudgy, balding eighty-four-year-old vice chairman of the Party, marshal of the People's Liberation Army and head of the National People's Congress. Ye is so frail that in his rare public appearances he often has to be propped up by a bevy of nurses. But Chinese friends reported that on his eightieth birthday he had staged a party for himself that cost 300,000 yuan ($200,000), and whether or not the story was true, it received wide credence. To honor him, his children had approached a number of China's most famous artists and hinted that papa, an avid art collector, would appreciate a gift for the occasion, one of the painters told me.

Ye's eldest son, a man in his forties, is married to the daughter of a senior navy officer in Canton in the south, my friends related. But Ye's son had lost interest in her and, while she lived with her father, he courted other women in Peking. The roommate of a Chinese woman I knew who worked for Peking television was dating the son. She was slender, attractive, a stylish dresser who got her clothes from relatives in Hong Kong and had learned all the latest Western dance steps. The son usually appeared in a Red Flag to collect her and carried a wad of 10-yuan bills, the largest denomination in which China's currency is minted, that was as thick as you could hold in your hand, the woman boasted. Ye's son actually held a senior command post in the air force, she added, though it was not public knowledge, and with this job was able to travel abroad frequently, a much-coveted privilege. Another son had been appointed deputy mayor of Canton, a job which gave him the chance for frequent trips to Hong Kong.

One of Ye's daughters, Ye Xiangzhen, had been a leader of a virulent Red Guard faction during the Cultural Revolution. She had personally taken part in harassing Peng Zhen, then the mayor of Peking, now rehabilitated and restored to the Politburo. But Ye's prestige had protected her from retribution. In school she had first studied art, lost interest in that, then somehow gone to medical school, the kind of switch ordinary Chinese could not make. Recently she has formed a movie company of her own, an improbable achievement in a country where all film studios are owned by the state; but an American businessman reported talking with her about distributing one of her films in the United States. She is married to China's most famous pianist, Liu Shikun, a tall, gaunt, crew-cut man. But their relationship turned sour and Liu often showed up at the bar in the Peking Hotel with other fashionably dressed young women, I noticed during the year I lived there.

Ye's younger brother, I also learned, who was a businessman in their hometown in Guangdong province before 1949, is now manager of the large Xinqiao Hotel in Peking where I often ate dinner. But the most talked-about member of the clan is one of Ye's grandsons. In 1980 the Peking police caught him when they set a trap for a group of Chinese smuggling gold out of the country in exchange for Japanese tape recorders and digital watches. The grandson arrived at the supposed site for the smuggling operation in one of his family's Red Flags and proved to be the ringleader of the gang. But once the embarrassed Public Security Bureau realized his identity, he was set free, several Chinese related.

Another member of the capital's fast set is Yolanda Sui, one of the two foster daughters of Madame Sun Yat-sen. The first time I encountered her was in the dining room of the Peking Hotel. She was dressed in a short, hip-hugging wool skirt, high brown-leather boots, and a bright-orange blouse. Yolanda was in her mid-twenties, slender, and very tall for a Chinese, about five feet eight. She had on heavy eye shadow and lipstick; not pretty, but haughty, striking, and sexy. She looked like a movie star from Taiwan or Hong Kong.

Later a mutual acquaintance introduced us and I asked what she did. "I'm in movies," she replied, saying she had just returned from shooting a film with an army movie production studio on location in Hunan. I noticed her often after that, on her way to the beauty parlor in the hotel or driving in her Red Flag to the evening movies at the International Club, reserved for foreigners. When I was at Madame Sun's house for dinner, I asked her about Yolanda's background. Madame Sun explained that she had adopted Yolanda after her father, who was one of her bodyguards, had become paralyzed from drinking too much.

On the night the head of the Party Propaganda Department bestowed China's version of the Academy Awards for the best movie of the year and the most popular actor and actress, I spotted Yolanda sitting at a table with Li Rentang, the man who had just won the best actor trophy. The ceremony was held in a ballroom of the Peking Hotel and was televised around China. Yolanda was outfitted in a red silk blouse and a long, embroidered red-print skirt, a dazzle of color and style in a forest of baggy blue. She was also smoking a cigarette, something very few young Chinese women do in public. When a Canadian television crew also noticed her, she pulled a compact out of her handbag and checked to see if her nose was shiny. Inside her bag, I saw, was a packet of Marlboros; foreign cigarettes are not available in regular Chinese stores. A middle-aged Chinese woman who works in the movie industry and witnessed the scene commented later, "She will be a movie star until Madame Sun dies. Then it's all over." Shortly before Madame Sun did die in 1981, Yolanda married a dashingly handsome movie actor. I often wondered what her final fate was.

Not all children of high cadres slip into such a free-wheeling life-style. The leading dissident in Peking's short-lived democracy movement in 1978 and 1979 was Wei Jingsheng, whose father was a senior economic official and Party veteran. Several other Chinese I met whose parents were ranking Party or army officials accepted the benefits of their parents' positions, though tried to be more discreet about it. Little Liu, a tiny, twenty-eight-year-old woman with a small, up-turned nose and a Doris Day smile, admitted that she had managed to get out of the village where she had been sent after high school because her father was a provincial leader. Both her father and mother had been born into poor peasant families, she said. As a teen-ager her father had run away to join the Red Army guerrillas, and in retaliation the Nationalists had executed his parents. That gave her an outstanding class background, an asset that was useful in getting transferred out of the village and gaining admission to Peking University at the end of the Cultural Revolution. After graduation her father had secured a plum job for her in the Central Broadcasting Station in Peking, where she screened Western movies. Half of her colleagues there were sons or daughters of cadres, she said. But Little Liu dressed in plain blues and grays and didn't brag about her father's rank.

Her admission to college, making use of her father's position, was not unusual. The New China News Agency once admitted in a candid report that

39 percent of the freshman class at Peking University were offspring of cadres or army men. Since cadres and soldiers make up only about 2 percent of the total population, that suggests that an official parentage is a clear advantage in education, much as being from a well-to-do upper-middle-class family in the United States is.

But Little Liu turned down an offer from some of her father's friends in Peking to help her join the Communist Party. "I don't believe in turning black into white, and white into black, the kind of things you have to do to curry favor and get ahead in the Party," she explained. "When I told my father my decision, he was very upset, but in his heart he knows too that the Party is not like it was before Liberation or in the 1950s. It has changed."

Her refusal to join the Party despite its promise of added privileges and a better life raises a question about how successful the Communists have been in passing on their real power, their political positions, to their children.

"This worries them a lot, they talk about it with their families," said a thoughtful, taciturn economist who was trained in America. "The best the old man can do is to arrange a good education and job for his kids before he dies." This was largely true, I found. With a few exceptions, like the sons of Marshal Ye, children of Politburo members have not risen to important Party or army posts. Instead, most of the elite's offspring have sought, or been guided into, careers elsewhere, as scientists, like Deng's son who is studying physics in the United States, or movie stars, guides for the China Travel Service, or doctors. Perhaps these are safer from the vicissitudes of the constantly shifting political line and the frequent purges in Peking. Perhaps the younger generation, spoiled by growing up comfortably, lack their parents' ambition, as happened in imperial times to the spoiled sons of the court mandarins. Unlike Europe, China has never had a hereditary aristocracy that managed to survive over a period of generations.

When the patriarch does die, my economist acquaintance explained, there is a gentle process of diminution. After a Central Committee member whom he knew passed away, his wife and children were asked to move out of their spacious, sun-lit old Chinese courtyard-style home. They were given a grace period of six months, however, and furnished with a handsome apartment. Then when the mother died, the children were requested to move again, to somewhat smaller quarters, all arranged by the Party. They were stepping down the stairs.

"This illustrates something about the Communists," the economist said. "They can be brutal. But they can also do things in the old humane Chinese way."

China's apologists have argued over the years that Peking has created a model revolutionary society, one that has gone a long way toward eliminating inequality. In the Communists' cave headquarters in Yanan in the 1930s and 1940s and in the early days after Liberation in the 1950s there was some truth to this. But the endless political campaigns of the past three decades combined with the shortages of food, consumer goods, housing, and jobs have weakened the Communists' revolutionary fiber. The cadres have become protective of their positions and their families and hungry for the better material life.

In purely monetary terms, it is true, the Communists still maintain the appearance of their old egalitarianism. All salaries are limited. But money by itself is not a good measure; the real differences are the hidden privileges, prerogatives, and perquisites that go with political status: the better housing, the chauffeur-driven cars, the special food stores, and the ability to travel. It seemed to me that the Chinese obsession with rank is at least as blatant as the snobbery of New York debutante society. The life-style of high cadres, with their lavish guesthouses, home movie theaters, and imported tobacco is as far beyond the grasp of the peasant in his rice paddy as the doings of a successful Hollywood rock-music impresario or a wealthy Wall Street lawyer billing $200,000 a year are from the life of a West Virginia coal miner or a black dropout in Harlem.

Attention to rank in China does not end even with death. At the Babaoshan Cemetery in Peking, where many of China's Communist leaders are buried, there are several different funeral halls for mourners and a number of separate vaults where the ashes are kept. By law everyone in the cities now must be cremated, to save land for productive agriculture, and the fee of 20 yuan is automatically paid for all state employees by their workplaces. But vaults are numbered, and the number one room is for the highest cadres only, the number two room for the next rung on the ladder, and so on, a Chinese whose mother was cremated there told me. The result is often fights over which vault a person's remains will rest in.

In the past the ashes could stay forever. But with China's population squeeze, there is now a time limit of five years for ordinary Chinese. After that, their families must come and move their remains elsewhere. High cadres' ashes may still stay indefinitely.

4. The Back Door

走 后 门

GETTING ALONG

"Our minds are on the left, but our pockets are on the right."
A current Chinese saying

I had never had a crank phone call in China before, but one Saturday
morning shortly before I was scheduled to leave Peking, I received a call that
I was certain was either a friend playing a practical joke or a daft Chinese.
The caller identified himself as an employee of the restaurant in the Peking
Exhibition Hall, a huge Stalinesque confection built during the halcyon days
of Chinese–Russian relations in the 1950s. The caller asked if I was the
American correspondent Bao Defu. That was the Chinese name a teacher
had given me years before in Taiwan—it was as close as one could get in
Chinese to the English pronunciation of Butterfield while retaining the sound
and meaning of a real Chinese name.

Why hadn't I come last night to eat the dinner I had ordered and the
restaurant had prepared? he demanded.

I was mystified. I had never been to the restaurant, and I certainly had not
ordered a meal there. Perhaps he had the wrong name, I suggested.

But the caller was insistent. "You came here two days ago with your name
card and ordered a banquet for forty guests. You must pay." His voice was
edged with anger.

It is common practice in China's better restaurants to order ahead of time,
and for foreigners, it is almost mandatory. That way, you will be seated in
a special reserved room at the back, or upstairs, and charged double, triple,
or quadruple the price. The cost of a meal is fixed by the "standard," the
amount you set per head, not by the price per dish, as in Western restaurants.
If a guest fails to appear, and the number of people is fewer than you ordered,
the host must pay anyway. I was familiar with all these rules. How much was

the price for each of the forty guests I supposedly had ordered for? I asked the caller. Forty yuan each, he said, about $27, a mere total of $1,080 for dinner.

That convinced me he must be a crank and I slammed down the phone.

But the next day the phone rang again. This time it was the Dong Lai Shun restaurant, an eatery popular for its Mongolian hot pot, strips of thinly sliced lamb which diners cook for themselves in a Chinese chafing dish. The caller had the same question for me: why had I failed to show up and pay for a dinner I had ordered for the previous evening? After all, he said, encouraging me to confess, "your own secretary came here to place the order."

My secretary? I said. I don't have a secretary. Was it a woman? Yes, he assented, a woman with your name card. That offered a new view—someone was impersonating me. Was this woman Chinese or foreign? I inquired. Chinese, was the answer.

Over the next two weeks, the calls kept coming, almost every day. The Peking Vegetarian restaurant claimed I had ordered a banquet for sixty people and twelve chauffeurs at 60 yuan a head for the guests and five yuan for the drivers. That was a mere $2,440. A large department store phoned to say that four hundred pounds of wool thread I had ordered was now ready to be picked up. The odd thing was, no one ever appeared to eat those lavish meals or pick up the material that had been ordered.

Finally, one morning, I received a call from the police. An officer of the Public Security Bureau began with the usual routine—was I the American correspondent named Bao? When I replied yes, he said he wanted to check some details about the complaint I had lodged the day before at a local police station in the northern part of Peking. I had stopped in to report that a man named Chen from the Central Philharmonic Orchestra had swindled me in a business transaction, the officer continued. I was tempted to interrupt and protest the story was fraudulent. But here was a glimpse at how real Chinese life might work. I was fascinated and let him go on. This fellow Chen had supposedly asked me to buy him a bicycle, liquor, and cigarettes in the Friendship Store, using my foreign currency. After I bought the goods for him, Chen absconded without paying, and now I wanted the police to catch him, or so the officer said.

This added a new twist. Now the imposter was brazen enough even to walk into a police station using her false identity. I thought it would be easy to persuade the policeman that it wasn't me. Was the person who went to your station yesterday Chinese? I asked. Yes, he said.

"I am not Chinese," I said, springing my trap.

"But you are speaking Chinese," the policeman responded.

I had underestimated the situation again. There was only one more thing

I could think of to do. I offered to go to the police station to show them that I was not Chinese.

"But how will we know you are not Chinese?" the officer asked. I was flattered that anyone would be so impressed by my ability to speak Chinese, but was rapidly losing patience.

Eventually, I persuaded the policeman to let me come down to the Foreign Affairs Section of the Public Security Bureau that afternoon to give my evidence. This agency for dealing with foreigners is housed in a lovely old Chinese-style courtyard building, set behind a circular moon gate, that must once have belonged to a wealthy capitalist. The office has bright-red wooden pillars and a sloping roof covered with green and blue tiles. Five policemen were waiting for me, including a tall handsome man with long gray hair, a Chinese Cary Grant, a woman stenographer who kept laughing at my story, and a lean, crew-cut man whose sober face never betrayed any expression. He was the only Chinese I met during my time in China who still wore a Mao button. "I like Chairman Mao," he said when I asked why he kept what had become an anachronism, something like an American wearing a Nixon campaign button. He asked if I would please supply a list of all my Chinese friends to help the police track down the culprit. I politely declined. That seemed too obvious a subterfuge.

Soon after, the police did catch the impersonator. The *Peking Evening News*, China's closest thing to a spicy Western tabloid, disclosed that she was Cui Xinfeng, a twenty-three-year-old worker in a Peking phonograph-needle factory. Cui had also claimed to be a Hong Kong businesswoman called Su Lina, whose calling card she showed when she arrived in restaurants and shops. That was how I had originally met her. One night when I was filing a story at the high-vaulted Peking Telegraph office, I had encountered a woman standing at the counter arguing with the clerk over the address on her cable. She wanted to send it to the Kowloon Trading Company of Hong Kong, but she had no other address for the firm and the clerk would not accept the message.

I noticed that she was dressed like an ordinary Peking resident, with a wool scarf over her head and a short, bulky black coat. She also suffered from acne. But her accent sounded Cantonese, the dialect of south China that is spoken in Hong Kong, as thick in its way as a Georgia drawl in America. Finally, after she stepped aside, the clerk began reading my cable, and she asked me who I was. I gave her one of my name cards, a common practice among foreign correspondents in Peking, like a fisherman putting out a line, hoping for a new Chinese acquaintance and possible source. She volunteered that she worked for the Kowloon Company and lived in the Overseas Chinese Hotel in Peking. Only later did it occur to me that both her accent and her identity might be false.

I was intrigued and at first baffled by the incident. Only once had Cui actually gotten any material benefit by her impersonation—the manager of the Mongolian hot-pot restaurant was so impressed by the size of her banquet order that he invited her to stay for a sumptuous lunch, free of charge. But Chinese friends instinctively understood and helped explain her bizarre behavior. In China, they said, the bureaucracy is so clumsy and rigid that there are constant shortages of food, housing, and consumer goods. Communist Party cadres avoid the problem because of their privileges: the special food shops, the bookstores, the hospitals, and resorts. But "the masses," ordinary people, must be more inventive. To survive, they have created a nationwide system of informal exchange; more than a black market, it is a second, or countereconomy, that exists in tandem with the regular state-planned economy and helps it function. Chinese call it "taking the back door," *zou-hou-men.*

The ultimate back-door ploy was to impersonate a Party official or foreigner, someone who had regular access to luxuries most Chinese could only dream about. I heard of a number of other cases of imposters. In Shanghai, the local paper, the *Wenhuibao,* reported in tantalizing detail the exploits of a Chinese pauper turned prince, a peasant who masqueraded as the son of a deputy chief of staff of the army. The trickster, Zhang Longqian, a twenty-five-year-old farmer of no distinction, began his adventures during a visit to Shanghai when he wanted to see a performance of Shakespeare's *Much Ado About Nothing* but found, as often in China, that all the tickets were reserved for distribution to special *danwei.* So Zhang rang up the theater, using the name of a department head of the city Communist Party committee, and said in an authoritative manner that a friend of his, a deputy chief of staff of the army, had a son who wanted to watch the play. The theater director who took the call was flattered, and soon Zhang not only had a ticket, he was also introduced to a pretty young actress whose affections were easily won by the son of such a prominent official. One deceit led to another, and Zhang found himself with gifts of new clothes, a watch, a house to live in, and a car, loaned by the Communist boss of Fudan University. Zhang's fairy-tale life ended only when a member of the street committee where he was living developed scruples about a demand Zhang had made to have his new girl friend promoted to a more prestigious theater company. The transfer required permission from the street committee, and the local cadre didn't approve of such back-door deals done on the request of high officials. He launched an investigation, and Zhang's real identity was uncovered.

The woman who impersonated me was less successful; she never showed up to collect. Perhaps she was a trifle zany, perhaps for her it was just acting out a fantasy, the psychic thrill of using a foreigner's name to order what she could never get on her own. Sometimes madness is a more accurate mirror of reality.

Most examples of the back door are more mundane, simple everyday arrangements by which individuals as well as factories, communes, and offices cope with the centrally planned economy, using their ingenuity to coax, wheedle, or procure items and services that are normally unavailable or may require months of waiting. It may be extra food for a wedding, a coveted job assignment, or a ticket on an airplane—plane travel is normally reserved for officials.

I recall one afternoon, when I was trying to finish a story for *The Times,* a Peking journalist I knew called to invite me to the movies. When I asked her what the name of the film was, Ling said she didn't know. All she could tell me was that a friend of hers, who had given her the tickets, promised it was an American movie. It would also be a *neibu,* literally "an internal," or restricted, show not intended for the public. In Peking, where screenings of foreign movies are rare and tickets to such events are a highly sought-after commodity, it hadn't occurred to her to find out the title.

The theater itself was a small private screening room inside a hulking brick office building. There was no sign outside advertising the showing. I noticed that in contrast to the usual concrete floor and hardwood folding seats in Peking's commercial theaters, it had a plush blue carpet and stuffed armchairs covered with gray cloth. We had agreed to arrive separately because of the regulations against Chinese having contact with foreigners, but Ling contrived to sit next to me just before the lights went out. It was a bold gesture on her part; she delighted in challenging the authorities, savoring the thrill of the illicit. She whispered that she had recognized several other members of the audience: in front of us was the wife of a deputy foreign minister, herself an official in the ministry, while behind us sat the son of a member of the Politburo. When the projector began to roll, the movie turned out to be *Patton.* I was bemused by the choice of the film, but Ling and the other members of the audience enjoyed Patton's unconcealed patriotism and the scene at the end when he snubs a group of Russian generals as American and Soviet troops meet to celebrate their victory over the Germans.

Afterward I asked Ling, a brusque, determined, middle-aged woman who had recently treated herself to a permanent in a beauty shop, how she had gotten the tickets. "Through the back door," she replied. A man she knew who worked for Peking Television desperately wanted to find a new apartment since he lived a fifty-minute bicycle ride away from work, and Ling had introduced him to one of her relatives who was an official in the city housing office. In return, from time to time he gave her tickets to private movies. Another evening, she recalled with a chuckle, the film was *The Red Nuptials,* a French soft-porn movie. Later she discovered that it had been borrowed from a French diplomat by a so-called foreign expert, a foreigner who taught French under contract to the Chinese government. The movie had then been enthusiastically traded from *danwei* to *danwei;* it finally ended up being shown at the Peking Exhibition Hall to a large audience, including senior officials, most of whom were caught unaware and were embarrassed.

Ling's tickets to these movies were classic back-door deals. As Chinese friends described the workings of the back door, these exchanges usually do not involve money. That would be considered bribery and therefore illegal. Instead they are based on the traditional use of *guan-xi,* the cultivation of contacts and connections among friends, relatives, and colleagues. The longer I stayed in Peking, the more I sensed that almost anything that got done went through the back door. A nurse in Peking recalled that during the Cultural Revolution, when teen-agers were shipped off to resettle in the countryside, she wanted her son to have a special skill that might help him avoid being rusticated. So she asked a neighbor, a famous pianist, to give him lessons. There are no private music schools or lessons, but the neighbor, out of long-standing friendship, consented. Later, when the pianist's mother fell ill, the nurse arranged for her admission to a good hospital. The piano lessons also did their trick—the nurse's son was kept in Peking and not sent to the countryside.

"No money changed hands, for that would have been condescending in China today," the nurse said. "It was just friendship. Even the Communists can't replace friendship with class struggle."

But I was puzzled why the pianist's mother couldn't get into the hospital on her own. The Communists have greatly expanded medical care in China since 1949 and made much of it free; it was one of their greatest accomplishments. The nurse shook her head at my naïveté. Yes, that was true, she admitted. But the hospitals were still terribly overcrowded—in part because medical care was so cheap—and doctors had to see an average of ten to fifteen patients an hour, like an assembly line. Western drugs were also in short supply because they were given low priority in the state plan.

"Patients in my hospital have to line up three times," said a balding, gregarious physician who had been trained by American missionaries. "First they have to queue at the registration desk, then at the doctor's office, and finally at the pharmacy counter for their prescriptions. You can spend the whole morning just waiting.

"Many doctors are so busy they just make a casual examination of the patient and then scribble something out. It's not good medicine and the patients know it.

"So many of the patients use the back door," the doctor added. "If you know a doctor, you don't have to line up for him but just walk right into his room. He will give you better attention.

"Patients who have an even closer relationship with a doctor will go see him at home, after hours. That's where the best care is.

"Of course, in exchange, the patients must give presents to the doctors. At the New Year's holiday, they will bring around good cuts of meat, or a fish, or some fruit.

"That's why we say being a doctor in China is a 'fat job,' " he continued. "There is a joke that doctors, drivers, and shop clerks are the 'three treasures,' because they have more access to things that can be traded through the back door." He himself admitted that it was easier for him to get clothes made at one of the good tailor shops on Wangfujing Street, which often turn down customers, because the tailors knew him. And it was simple for him to get a table in the popular Mongolian hot-pot restaurant, where other diners had to buy tickets a day or more in advance, because the manager was his patient.

Drivers of trucks, buses, and cars are valued, I learned, because there are virtually no privately owned motor vehicles, and drivers therefore have an unusual ability to move around the country. Once in a noisy restaurant that stays open late and is frequented by drivers, I met a swarthy man in his late twenties who said he drove a truck for a farm machinery factory in Shandong province, east of Peking. After we exchanged a few toasts of beer and cheap white grain alcohol that stung my throat, he began recalling his adventures. It seemed that his factory often had slack periods, when there weren't enough raw materials or there was a shortage of electricity. When these occurred, he would take off in his truck to haul coal from another province. The scheme worked well, with him splitting the profits with the factory Party secretary, until one evening he fell asleep at the wheel and crashed into another vehicle, wrecking his truck.

"It was too bad," the driver said wistfully, pouring both of us some more beer. "On Sundays I used to be able to use the truck to take my girl friend and some of our other friends on picnics."

On another occasion, I went with a student acquaintance to a small, crowded eatery that served peppery Sichuan-style cooking. The tables were full, but we finally found two empty stools and squeezed down. The previous customers' dishes and chopsticks still lay scattered on the table, along with small piles of chicken bones picked clean of their meat. My friend often patronized the restaurant and recommended its "home style" bean curd, cooked with fried red chili peppers and another form of pulverized pepper powder.

But when the waitress arrived, she said she was sorry the bean curd was sold out. My friend then casually took out a pack of China brand cigarettes, one of the more expensive varieties, and placed it on a corner of the table. If I hadn't been watching closely, I might not have seen that she scooped up the cigarettes along with some of the used dishes. My friend, a bright, outgoing fellow who liked to practice his English on me, smiled at the transaction. She was an old classmate of his from junior high school, and she saved bean curd, a Chinese favorite, for her friends, he explained. A few minutes later she came back from the kitchen with a steaming bowl heaped full of chunks of the soft brownish delicacy.

In China's rigid system of state job assignments, where an impersonal government agency determines a person's career, getting a favored job or a transfer requires even more artifice and use of the back door. The same college student had an older sister who had been sent to Tibet as part of Mao's utopian program to resettle city high school graduates in the country-side. She had been there ten years already; she was thirty years old, and, from her family's point of view, was in critical danger both of becoming an old maid, since almost all Chinese women get married before they are twenty-nine, and being stuck forever on the remote, backward, 10,000-foot-high plateau of Tibet, which most Chinese abominate. Something had to be done fast.

"So my parents looked around very carefully," the student told me. "They knew that few men would marry a thirty-year-old woman. But my father located a very ambitious junior clerk, only twenty-seven, who worked in his office. Then they sounded him out through an intermediary. If he would agree to marry my sister, he could use his Peking household registration certificate to apply to bring my sister back to the city. In return, my father found him a much better job, with a promotion to be a cadre, in one of the hot, new, state import and export corporations that do a lot of business with foreigners. My father had an old comrade-in-arms from Red Army days in the trade corporation. It was all a matter of connections."

The arrival of large numbers of foreign businessmen, after Mao's succes-sors moved to expand foreign trade as part of their modernization program, provided new opportunities for the back door. A Texan in the oil equipment business recalled that during a banquet hosted by the Ministry of Metallurgy his Chinese dinner partner became very expansive.

"You Americans just don't know how to do business," the Chinese official said. "Look at all the new Mercedes we are driving in our ministry. Where do you suppose they come from?" Then he laughed and waved his hands. "From our good friends in West Germany."

Another time, said the Texan, a short, stocky man who spent much of his time traveling in China, he had been in the final stages of negotiations with the Machinery Import–Export Corporation for the sale of some American oil-drilling parts.

"There is just one more thing we will need," one of the officials told him. "The deal will cost you two percent of the value of the sale. If you agree, the money should be deposited in a bank account in Switzerland whose number I will give you."

96

The Texan was stunned. It was the kind of pitch he expected in Indonesia or the Philippines, not in socialist China. As they talked further, the American added, the Chinese insisted that the money was not for his personal use, but for his corporation. Normally, as a state agency, they had to turn over all the foreign exchange they earned to the government. But this way they would have a special discretionary fund for their own use, outside the state plan, to buy equipment not allocated to them in the budget process. Still, it was illegal.

What astounded me was not such tales of misdoings—every country has its corruption—but that factories and communes in China routinely had to depend on the counter economy just as individuals did. A letter to the *People's Daily* from a county in Jiangxi province in central China disclosed that communes in the area had to buy 60 to 70 percent of their chemical fertilizer through the back door since the amount of fertilizer allocated to them by the central plan fell far short of what they had to have for their crops. The communes actually signed private contracts with the fertilizer factories, the letter writer charged, paying the plants with their produce: pork, peanuts, soybeans, melon seeds, or timber. To conclude such deals, he added, the commune officials also had to treat the factory cadres and their drivers to banquets and ply them with liquor and cigarettes.

Chinese factories have a whole category of employees just to help them cope when they can't get what they need from the plan. They are called *cai gou yuan,* literally, "purchasing agents" or "buyers," though the way Chinese described their functions they might better have been termed "fixers." Another article in the *People's Daily* estimated that every day 50,000 to 60,000 buyers arrive in Peking and Shanghai on urgent errands for their factories.

I got to know one of these agents, a husky, full-faced, energetic man in his mid-thirties who by sheer artfulness and use of *guan-xi* had worked his way up from being an orphan son of poor peasants to travel abroad as a private agent for a senior government official. At the outset his good class background, "poor peasant," had enabled him to wangle a job in an electronics factory in Peking and escape his village origins. From there his acumen quickly got him a job as the factory's buyer. Then, by chance, when he was sent to work on a so-called May Seventh School in the countryside where cadres were supposed to be purified by farm labor, he met a deputy mayor of the capital. The official sensed something special in him and assigned him as fixer to a new high-powered agency Peking set up to handle foreign trade in the city.

By the time I encountered him he was operating out of his own room in the Peking Hotel, one of the very few Chinese permitted to live there. He proved endlessly useful to his business associates. If a foreign businessman needed a room in the hotel and it was full—it always was—he could arrange it. If you needed a seat on the CAAC flight to Tokyo or Canton—they were always booked too—he could take care of that. If the hotel itself needed customs clearance for a new shipment of imported Japanese television sets, he knew how to handle it, no matter that the ultimate recipient of the TV sets might be a cadre outside the hotel who used the hotel's involvement in the tourist trade as a cover for a private back-door transaction.

One day when I went to his room he had on a new gold Seiko quartz watch. It was a present given him during a month's trip to Hong Kong and Tokyo which was paid for by grateful foreign firms.

The phone rang. It was a friend advising him that the manager of the hotel was in the hospital. He picked out a Japanese calculator from his desk and prepared to pay a solicitous visit to the sick man.

Later his contacts paid off further. He was able to arrange a trip to the United States, a feat in itself, requiring clearance from the Public Security Ministry and the Foreign Ministry. When he came back, he was wearing a Western-style blue pinstripe suit. He had also had business cards printed up identifying him as president of a newly formed import–export company in New York that would trade with China. Before I left China, an American businessman who worked closely with him said they had gone together one day to the office of a cabinet minister. The official had briefed them on the latest shift in economic policy, which industries were being cut back in a new retrenchment, and which factories would get special subsidies. It was classic inside information. The purpose of the leak, the American surmised, was that the fixer was acting as an agent, buying Chinese commodities for the official which they then sold overseas.

Even policemen participated in the back door, I discovered. During the fall of 1980, I noticed that more and more Chinese were gaining access to the Friendship Store. To use the store, you had to pay in special script issued only to foreigners in exchange for dollars, marks, or yen. And to get into the marble entranceway, you had to pass several guards in gray Mao tunics from the Public Security Bureau. They lounged around the door, letting anyone with a foreign face pass but questioning Chinese.

One morning, as I was sitting in our car outside waiting for Barbara to finish some shopping, I saw an unusually pretty girl, with red cheeks and hair worn loose to her shoulders, in a black wool coat, pacing up and down in front of the store. She looked anxious. After a few minutes one of the younger guards came out to talk to her, and I wondered if she would be in trouble for loitering. But they smiled at each other, he took her hand, and then he led her into the store. The other guards looked on benevolently as they went in, boy friend and girl friend apparently.

When Barbara came out, she said she had seen a Chinese family of father, mother, and two children on a wild buying spree. First they had bought three suitcases in the store, then they began stuffing them as fast as they could, as if time might run out on them or the back-door connection they used to gain entrance might be detected. Barbara was standing at the woolen-goods counter when they came by and ordered a half-dozen scarves, five cashmere sweaters, a dozen pairs of socks, and ten pairs of gloves. The items they bought, she observed, were all of a much better quality than what was available in regular Chinese stores.

Another time I came across a Chinese friend in the store. I was curious how he had gotten in.

"It was simple," he replied. "What you need is a letter of introduction from your *danwei* saying that you are going on an official mission abroad or that the *danwei* needs certain goods for an official purpose." It was a stratagem cadres sometimes used to buy things for themselves.

What he had done, he confessed, was to forge a letter. Then he persuaded a friend who had access to the *danwei*'s seal to chop the letter for him, making it look correct. A friend who worked in the People's Bank had arranged to get some of the foreign script for him. Properly prepared, he bought three television sets in the Friendship Store, one for each of them.

Before 1949 the Chinese had long practiced a form of petty corruption that foreigners call "squeeze," demanding a little extra money or a cut of any deal before it is consummated. The Communists claimed with pride they had eradicated such malfeasance. But the very nature of the Chinese Communist economy and its inefficiencies—the shortages, the endless waits in line, the shoddy quality of goods—reproduced "squeeze" in a new guise, the back door. In 1957, when the population of China stood at 600 million, the *People's Daily* reported, there were about one million stores in China, grocery shops, bicycle repair shops, laundries, barbers, cobblers. But by 1981 the population had swollen to one billion, an increase of 400 million, almost equal to the total of the United States and Western Europe combined, yet the number of stores had shrunk to only 190,000. The rest had fallen victim to the Communists' distaste for private enterprise and zeal for unified central control. In Peking alone the number of restaurants plummeted from 10,200 in 1949 to 679 in 1981. Mao had proclaimed, "Serve the People," a slogan emblazoned on the walls of thousands of offices and stores. But less than 10 percent of the Chinese work force are employed in the service industry compared to 48 percent in the United States and 42 percent in France and Japan. For Peking had decided to copy the Soviet model of industrialization and put emphasis on the expansion of heavy industry, like steel, rather than on agriculture, consumer goods, and housing. This produced glamorous annual statistics of growth in the gross national product and added to the leaders' sense that China was becoming a modern industrial power. But it did not keep up with the needs of a swiftly growing population. It was a costly mistake in priorities avoided by other nations in the region, including Japan, South Korea, and Taiwan.

To cope with the resulting shortages, the Communists have devised a rationing system so Byzantine in its complexity that many Chinese themselves are at a loss to understand it. In Peking people have to carry as many as seven or eight different types of coupons and ration booklets, explained Fuli, a soft-spoken woman factory worker with a weathered face and prominent teeth. First, she said, is your grain ration book, in a red plastic cover; new pages for it are issued each month by your local government grain store, if you are a legal resident of the neighborhood and have a valid household registration. The Communists have added to the intricacy of the rationing system by an egalitarian attempt to tie a person's food allotment to the energy they expend in their work. Fuli herself, as a worker in a musical instrument factory, got thirty-five catties a month (a catty is 1.1 pounds, or half a kilogram). Her father, a cadre, got thirty-one catties, since his work is less physically taxing; her younger brother, a construction worker, got forty catties. Infants get six catties a month, she said, with the maximum of sixty catties for men tending blast furnaces in steel plants. In Peking, she added, people get 50 percent of their grain ration in wheat flour (northern Chinese prefer noodles and steamed bread to rice), 20 percent in rice, and 30 percent in coupons good for buying bowls of rice or noodles in restaurants. The first time I went out to eat with Chinese I was surprised when the waiter asked them for their grain coupons before accepting their orders. As a foreigner, I was exempt. If a Chinese cadre is sent on a business trip, there are special national grain tickets which he has to use on trains or in restaurants outside his hometown.

In effect, the system means that any time you go out and get hungry, you have to have your grain coupons with you as well as cash. When Judy McCahill, the wife of an American diplomat, was on the operating table in the Capital Hospital in Peking, about to have a baby, one of the doctors suddenly announced he was hungry.

"Should we get some doughnuts?" a nurse suggested.

"I don't have any grain coupons," the doctor said.

"That's all right," another nurse cut in. "There are some in a drawer in the office."

Next come a series of separate coupons: for cooking oil (a catty a month in Peking, but as little as two ounces a month in Yunnan), for cotton cloth (sixteen feet seven inches a year, in Peking), for coal, and for cooking gas. Since 1979 meat has not been rationed in Peking, but in some other provinces the allowance is as little as a pound or two a month.

In addition, each neighborhood state grocery shop issues another type of ration booklet. It includes monthly allotments of soap, sugar, bean curd, corn starch, some types of fish, and several Chinese delicacies like sesame paste and vermicelli noodles made from green beans.

Finally, Fuli explained, her factory gave each worker four industrial coupons each January good for purchasing manufactured products. Two or three of these coupons could buy enough wool to knit a sweater; half a coupon was necessary for some brands of tea. Ten industrial coupons, two and a half years' worth, were required to make the most important purchase of all, a bicycle, as indispensable to a Chinese as a car to twentieth-century Americans. But that was not all. To buy a bike you also had to have a special bike purchase coupon. In her factory, Fuli said, out of every one hundred workers, only two were given these treasured certificates each year.

"The chance to buy a bike is so important to us," she said, "that when a new worker is assigned to the factory, the first thing they do is go to the quartermaster to put their name on the bike list. Some of my friends who already have bikes of their own register their names on the list again when they have a baby. That way, by the time their kids are in their teens and old enough to need a bike, they will be able to get one.

"If you lose your coupons, it is a real disaster," Fuli continued, contorting her face into a grimace. Once a friend of hers had all the family's coupons in an envelope and his wife threw them out by accident. The government wouldn't replace some of them till the next year; but in Chinese fashion, their friends and colleagues chipped in and shared some of their own coupons. It was the kind of generosity I was to witness several times.

An astonishing example of the rationing system is that to buy a light bulb a Chinese has to turn in his old one. Each bulb bears a serial number—those used in factories are different from those intended for home use, and those sold in Peking are marked with a different sequence from those in other places. That way, you can't cheat and bring in a light bulb from anyplace but your home. If your bulb is stolen, you have to get a letter from the police before you can replace it.

In a developing country like China with a population of one billion, some rationing may be essential to prevent inequalities, Chinese I knew conceded. But Fuli saw another purpose to the government's program. "It's really a way to control you," Fuli remarked. "If you don't have the proper residence certificate, you can't get your ration cards, and, without them, you can't live."

With Mao's death and the ascension of Deng Xiaoping, Peking recognized that its stress on heavy industry had been a strategic mistake. The *People's Daily* reported that heavy industry had actually grown ninety-fold between 1949 and 1980, while light industry, which turns out consumer goods like shoes, textiles, bicycles, radios, and television sets, increased only nineteen-fold. Deng and his practical-minded colleagues understood better than Mao that centuries of living with scarcity had bred a strong strain of materialism in Chinese, a craving only intensified by the shortages of recent years. When Chinese friends came over to our apartment, they often began by walking around and asking how much the television set, the refrigerator, or the furniture had cost. In elevators, when I was able to overhear conversations, much of the talk was about where a person had bought something or what he had paid for it. In 1972, when one of the first groups of Chinese journalists came to the United States and I was asked to help escort them around the country, they confounded a vice president of the Ford Motor Company by asking him what his salary was in front of other employees. To a Chinese, it was as normal as asking an American his name or where he went to school.

To satisfy the pent-up desire for a better standard of living, Deng gave Chinese their first wage raises in twenty years; he restored bonuses, which had been banned as capitalistic, and he openly encouraged a new consumerism by ordering factories to expand their production of goods like television sets and allowing advertising on television and street billboards. The results were immediately apparent. I remember on a chilly January afternoon, under a dull gray sky, I came across a crowd of twenty people jammed around the entrance to an old, unmarked brick building on East Single Arch Street, not far from the Peking Hotel. The fading-red wooden door was closed, but the group stood there patiently, stamping their feet against the cold and chatting with an air of excitement. Eventually, the door opened and a man came out clutching his prize, a carton containing a new twelve-inch Sony black and white television set made in Japan. He and his wife, who had waited outside, strapped it to the back of their bicycle and walked off with care.

I was curious at what was happening. A middle-aged woman standing in line, her shape lost in a heavy blue overcoat, explained. They had drawn lots in their offices, she said, and the lucky winners got coupons to buy the TV sets. They let only one customer at a time into the store to prevent a crush, she added, and no one was permitted to take the sets out of their cardboard cartons to examine them before buying. They cost 600 yuan ($400), over ten months' salary for an average urban Chinese. Americans would have been outraged by the price; the government was exacting more than a 100 percent sales tax on the sets. But the woman didn't mind. She said she hadn't had any luxury goods to buy for many years, so she had accumulated a substantial savings account, and she and her husband's brothers had pooled their money for the purchase.

"We're happy to buy them, whatever the price," the woman said after I told her I was a foreign correspondent. "Tell them to send us more."

But I wondered whether the government, having unleashed this new consumerism, would be able to satisfy it. To appreciate what daily life really meant, despite the regime's new policy, Chinese friends suggested I should go grocery shopping, for that was where the continued shortages and rude service hit hardest. So on a cold, crisp December morning I went with our friends the Wangs, Li and Miao, to the Chong Wen Men market, a cavernous building shaped like an airplane hangar, with a rounded roof and skylights to let in shafts of sunshine. It is considered one of the biggest and best-supplied markets in Peking, and on the day we went was jammed with several thousand people. Unlike Western supermarkets, where the shoppers pick out their own food and then pay at the check-out counter, the Chinese customers had to line up separately for each item: vegetables, fruit, pork, chicken, fish, bean curd, and canned goods. Inefficient as it might be, that was the rule, and there was no changing it.

We joined the line for live chickens, the way Chinese prefer to buy their fowl. There were twenty-seven people in front of us, I counted, and it took almost half an hour to get to the clerk who was pulling the birds out of their metal cages. Because of lines like this, the Wangs calculated, it took them two hours a day to shop for food, about average among Chinese I knew. And since refrigerators have made their appearance only in the homes of top officials, grocery shopping means a seven-day-a-week chore for Chinese. One way to cut down on the time, Miao said, was pooling. She and her friends often went shopping in teams   onc woman bought the chickens, another the vegetables, and so forth.

Most of the salesclerks, or "service personnel," as they are known in Chinese, were young men and women in their late teens or early twenties dressed in long white or blue smocks over their blue trousers. They wore high rubber boots since they were constantly washing down the brown marble floor with buckets of water to keep it clean. The walls of the market were covered with large red characters urging them to "raise higher the level of service" or "work hard to serve the people." But it didn't do for a customer to get too picky. At the chicken counter, a short, elderly man with a heavily wrinkled face upbraided a woman clerk with long pigtails for waiting on another shopper who had pushed his way into the line. The queue jumper had on a well-tailored black-wool overcoat and a Mao cap; "a cadre," Miao remarked under her breath.

When the older man's turn finally came, he complained that the chicken the clerk handed him was a cock rather than a hen. "Too tough and lean, give me a fatter one," he said.

The clerk responded by walking to the other end of the counter where there was another line of people waiting to have the chickens they had already bought killed and their feathers plucked. The customer tried to entice her back with several calls, but she ignored him. Finally he left in defeat, empty-handed.

Salespeople, Li explained, are among the lowest paid in China, and get few of the benefits of factory workers like free medical care and large pensions. In a state that equates heavy industry with socialism and commerce with capitalism, salesclerks are generally looked down on and their only revenge is to give customers a hard time. Once when the Wangs and I went to a restaurant to eat, the waitress forgot to bring half our order. I tried to get her attention by waving, and then by shouting, but the Wangs looked at me as if I were a madman.

"We try to be as polite and nice as possible to get them to wait on us," Li said. "They are used to shouting at the customers, not the customers shouting at them."

When we moved on to the market's fish counter, where there were forty people waiting in line, there was only one variety for sale, a small, thin, silver-skinned fish with a sharp snout. They were frozen and imported from North Korea. The Wangs had never seen them before and didn't know the name. Two clerks were taking clumps of the icy fish off a steel dolly, throwing them on the floor, then beating them with long-handled wooden mallets to separate them before selling. During the 1950s and early 1960s, before the Cultural Revolution, Li commented, it was easy to buy fish; but now it had become increasingly difficult, and the most popular variety in Peking, the yellow croaker, had disappeared entirely, unless you had a friend with access to the special food shop for high cadres. I noted in the *People's Daily* that China's total catch of fish had remained stagnant since the 1950s, while the population had soared, and that the intake of freshwater fish had dropped from 600,000 tons a year two decades ago to 300,000 tons now, because of overfishing, reclamation of land for planting grain, and pollution.

On our way out of the market, we passed a green metal stand with a sign: "Please Raise Your Precious Ideas." It was supposed to hold a "comment book" for customers. But someone had taken the book away. Next to it was a blue-painted wooden stand labeled "Public Scales," a thoughtful device so shoppers could weigh their purchases and ensure they had not been cheated. But the scale was missing too. The absent book and scale were an ironic reminder of the gap between Mao's call to "serve the people" and the everyday neglect of consumers.

As we walked a few blocks down the street, we came across several peasants in from the countryside squatting on the sidewalk and offering some of their produce for sale. There were live chickens trussed up in the small, black-plastic airline-style bags that many Chinese like to carry, piles of dried watermelon seeds, and candied crab apples on skewers. Knots of people had gathered around two of the hawkers; we pushed closer to look. A middle-aged man in a heavy, faded blue overcoat was holding out mimeographed papers. I couldn't see what they were, but Li laughed. They were crib sheets for the college entrance exam in math. A younger man with a mustache and hair down to his collar—a small sign of rebellion—had a stack of women's shoes. The Wangs explained that he had probably bought up all the popular styles and sizes when they came on sale in one of the few government shoe stores. Now he was reselling them at a markup of 20 percent. All these forms of private enterprise had been prohibited during the decade from 1966 to Mao's death and the overthrow of the radicals in 1976 as a "tail of capitalism." But Deng had decreed that China still needed some free markets to supplement the state-planned economy. The trouble was, the government never clearly defined how much private commerce was permitted, so selling chickens or reselling shoes was always risky and remained part of the quasi-legal back-door system.

The practice of "taking the back door" had begun on a small scale in the 1950s, the Wangs and other Chinese said. But with the breakdown of governmental authority in the Cultural Revolution and a stagnant economy, the back door had really blossomed in the 1970s into a major nationwide phenomenon. It had become so widespread, the Wangs told me, that it had spawned its own jokes. Peking residents liked to tell the story of the old woman who waited in line all day at the market to buy a fish. After hours of queueing in vain, she spotted several well-dressed customers walk past with large fresh fish in their straw baskets.

"Comrade, where did you get the fish?" she inquired.

"Through the back door," was their reply.

But when the woman went around behind the market to look, all she found was a locked gate.

"There is a back door," another elderly bystander told her, sensing her plight. "But it is closed to you and me."

The Wangs, however, like other Chinese, did not find anything amusing about their difficulty in buying food. For to Chinese, food is an obsession. When Chinese greet each other, they don't say, "Hello, how are you?" but "Have you eaten or not?" When Chinese measure population, they don't count heads, as Westerners do, but *kou,* or "mouths." The word for population is *ren-kou,* "people mouths." When Chinese want to express appreciation, I found, they don't give flowers; that would be too ephemeral and is reserved for funerals. Instead they bring fruit, something to eat. To entertain, Chinese don't host cocktail parties, they put on lavish banquets, sometimes costing several months' salary. Then as soon as the eating is over, the guests depart. The food is the thing, not the talk.

I remember a spectacular nine-course luncheon in an unpretentious little restaurant in the Nine Dragons Slope district of Chongqing, the city in Sichuan that was Chiang Kai-shek's wartime capital. Cooking in Sichuan is a serious business, dating back two thousand years to the legendary Three

Kingdoms period, and the head chef in the restaurant, Zhang Kaichi, was one of only eight men in the city of six million people to earn the title of master chef. In the kitchen, a dark smoky chamber warmed by a bank of six open coal stoves, Zhang explained that the essence of Sichuan cuisine is *ma-la-tang,* or numbing, spicy, and scalding hot. The numbing taste derives from tiny Sichuan peppercorns, which actually left my lips insensate. His own favorite dish, Zhang said, was an explosively hot concoction with the misleading name of "meat slices cooked in water." I had never seen it on the menu of the burgeoning number of Sichuan restaurants in the United States; when it arrived, I understood why. It was a formidable sight; an almost inch-thick reddish-brown sauce laced with ground fried chilies and crushed pepper-corns was still bubbling on its surface, hiding strips of pork and vegetables beneath. Although long an aficionado of Sichuan cooking, I hesitated before digging my chopsticks into the dish. The meat, prepared with egg whites, was tender, but the spice was ferocious. Sensing my plight, a waitress immediately proferred a hot towel to wipe my forehead.

Other dishes that followed included a salty duck smoked with camphor and tea, a Sichuan specialty, a chicken with peanut granules, spiced with garlic, ginger, and pickles, a peppery bean-curd treat, and a clear—and blessedly mild—fish-ball soup. Then came a delicate velvet chicken, Sichuan-style, chicken breasts pounded to a gossamer texture and served with fresh mush-rooms, bamboo shoots, and spinach, with just a hint of chili. The meal was completed with another Sichuan favorite, "fish fragrance meat shreds." The name, Zhang explained, does not mean fish is used in the cooking, but simply that it is prepared in the same fashion as any sensible Sichuanese would serve a fish—with a blend of ginger, onions, garlic, vinegar, and chilies.

The Chinese preoccupation with food grows out of the country's condi-tion. For three millennia, though China's chefs had unlocked the secrets of sauce and spice, millions of Chinese have not been sure where their next meal was coming from. The Communists ended the tragic famines of the past, an important accomplishment, and have doubled grain output since 1949. But I was surprised how meager the diet of many Chinese remains. The *People's Daily* reported that Chinese eat only fourteen pounds of meat a year, thirteen pounds of fruit, twelve pounds of fish. Chinese consumption of sugar is only one tenth the world average. Consequently most of the protein and calories Chinese get—and they get an average of only 2,000 to 2,100 calories a day, far below the U.S. figure of 3,200—come from rice, wheat, corn, or other grains. This takes its toll on energy levels.

In the industrial city of Shenyang, in the northeast, I met a crew-cut twenty-seven-year-old student who used the English name of John. Tall, self-confident, and outspoken, he had worked for five years in a factory before being admitted to college and, under the Chinese system, continued to receive his full salary of 40 yuan ($26) a month while in school. That was lucky, he calculated, because he spent almost the entire amount to supplement the university cafeteria diet so he would have enough stamina to study.

"Some of my friends, if they jog in the morning, the way the university president tells us to, get drowsy and doze off in class," John said. They had to live on the regular government subsidy for college students of only 19 yuan ($12.60) a month. Their daily diet, as John described it, was a breakfast of steamed bread and salted vegetables; a dish of vegetables and some fatty pork for lunch—which by itself cost 50 fen (Chinese cents), a total of 15 yuan a month—and more steamed bread with some cold vegetables for dinner. On Sundays the school cafeteria served only two meals, at 10 A.M. and 3 P.M. "Sundays, we often end up hungry," John said.

Although at first I was inclined to dismiss his account as too bleak to be true, I found that students at other colleges across China ate roughly the same way. At Yunnan University, in the southwest, an American woman teaching there, Elizabeth Booz, told me her students got meat only three times a week, and it was usually just fat. Even so, their government allowances tended to run out before the end of the month, so some of the students would pool their resources. The girls, being smaller, tended to eat less rice than the boys, Mrs. Booz said, and so again they would share their grain ration coupons with their male classmates. At Peking University, some American exchange students studying there said they felt their own energy slipping when they ate only in the university dining room for more than a few days at a time.

"Because of the constant shortage of food, your mind isn't on your work a lot of the time," a reserved, courteous, but intense archaeologist said. "People are always thinking and scheming how to get some food for their next meal. It is one of the greatest causes of inefficiency in China.

"The cadres are not aware of the problem because they don't have to go through it," he went on. "They have maids to do their shopping, or special purchase cards to get into the shops for cadres only, and they have more opportunities for back-door trade-offs.

"But it affects people's working habits. In my office, you are supposed to be at work at eight A.M. But many people are not there till eight fifteen or eight thirty. What they are doing is shopping.

"Then at ten, when we get our fifteen-minute morning break, some people take off for half an hour, forty minutes, or even longer in search of food. When lunchtime comes, people break at eleven thirty instead of twelve to make sure they get the daily dish in the cafeteria with meat in it. If they are late, the meat will be all gone."

This propensity of Chinese to bolt their offices at 11:30 sometimes baffles and frustrates foreigners, who put it down, mistakenly, to laziness. Not long after I arrived in China, John Rich, a former NBC television correspondent who now represents RCA in Asia, checked into the Peking Hotel with a team of RCA specialists to present a seminar to the Chinese on satellite communications. They had flown to China at their own expense, and they were enthused that they were offering the Chinese their first chance at some highly advanced technical information. But on the first day, with the Americans in the midst of their talks, their Chinese host suddenly asked them to stop. It was 11:30, he said, all the Chinese scientists present had to leave for lunch. The Americans were stunned; couldn't lunch wait a few minutes? No, said the Chinese official. And the Chinese walked out.

If getting enough to eat remains an obsession for Chinese, other routines of daily life which Westerners take for granted—buying furniture, taking a bath, finding a house—require all the connections, luck, and artifice that Chinese can muster. When Jan Wong, my Canadian-Chinese assistant, and her husband, Norman Shulman, wanted to buy furniture for their apartment, they quickly discovered that to purchase three of the most essential items, a double bed, a folding dinner table, and a dresser-cabinet, you had to have a special ration coupon issued only to newly married couples. To prevent cheating, you also had to present your marriage certificate, which the furniture shop stamped on the back. Even so, it took a six-month wait to get a bed, the *People's Daily* once disclosed.

There was a terrible shortage of wood. In a scathing article, the *Workers' Daily* reported that in 1957, when the population was only 600 million, four million cubic meters of timber were allotted for carpentry in the state plan and 40 million articles of furniture were produced. But because of lack of concern with the consumer, in 1979, with close to a billion people, only two million cubic meters of timber were designated for carpentry and only 20 million pieces of furniture were turned out, half the production of two decades earlier. And 50 percent of that lumber went to government offices, the paper added.

When Norman, an American from New York who had lived in China since 1965 and worked as a computer technician for the Academy of Sciences, investigated the state shops that sold new furniture, he learned that you had to line up by 6 A.M. on a day when the stores expected a shipment of new goods. Otherwise, within a few hours, everything would be sold out and the shops would close up for the day, leaving only a blackboard outside with the date of the next arrival. One back-door alternative was to hire a group of unemployed young men who had set themselves up in business and for a fee would take your place in line, starting as early as 3 A.M.

Given these difficulties, what most Chinese did, I learned, was to become amateur carpenters. Soon after arriving in China I visited the apartment of a man whose father was a general in the People's Liberation Army. From upstairs came a constant sound of hammering, shaking the room and making conversation difficult.

"They are building the Four Modernizations," my friend said sarcastically, referring to the government's program to develop farming, industry, science, and national defense. "They start at seven A.M. and then after work they go at it again, making their own furniture."

His wife, a slender woman with long hair and a finely shaped up-turned nose, laughed at his complaint. She pointed to the small two-seat sofa I was sitting on. She called it a *shafa,* one of the few foreign words to make its way into Chinese, by nature an exclusive, xenophobic tongue that rejects imports. They had built the sofa themselves, she said, from metal springs they had bought in a store and pieces of wood scavenged from a nearby apartment under construction. Since lumber and other building materials are in such short supply, pilfering had become a major business, other Chinese said. I noticed that at night, though cars in China are forbidden to drive with their headlights on, evidently to save energy, and many streets and buildings are not lit, construction sites usually basked in floodlit splendor as a precaution.

In the building where Jan and Norman lived when she first began working for me, Jan had to share a shower with the other women. They got hot water three times a week in the summer, twice a week in the winter, for one hour at a time. It was from 5 to 6 P.M., the hour before people got out of work, so they took their baths on office time, just as many Chinese did their grocery shopping. The odd bath times of different *danwei* were a frequent topic of conversation among Chinese, I noticed. At the Second Foreign Languages Institute, located in farmland east of Peking, the students and faculty got their showers two afternoons a week, from noon all the way to 6 P.M. But the two afternoons were Wednesday and Thursday. The reason, a teacher explained, was that the workers who ran the bathhouse wanted to work only two consecutive days and took the rest of the week off. "There has been criticism from the students and teachers, but there is nothing we can do about it," my friend said.

The short hours for bathing were presumably also designed by the government as an economy measure to conserve scarce fuel. But Chinese I knew regarded the situation as a serious inconvenience because most were fastidious about keeping themselves clean. This led to still another set of stratagems. Jan used to take baths in our office in the Peking Hotel, which had hot water twenty-four hours a day, a royal privilege. Lao Wu didn't have hot water or a bathtub in his apartment either. Sometimes, he said, on his way home from work he would stop at the headquarters of his *danwei,* where they had showers for their employees. Other times he would bathe in *The Times*'s office.

Equally inconvenient and uncomfortable was the government's strict policy of not turning on the heat in buildings until November 15, no matter what the weather. My first year in Peking, winter arrived early. By the first few days of November the lakes in the North Ocean Park behind the Forbidden City were frozen, a bitter, dry wind blew down across the Gobi Desert from Siberia, and the temperature fell to 10 degrees fahrenheit (−10 degrees centigrade). But Chinese who lived in apartments or worked in offices with central heating still had to wait till the magic date of November 15. The only remedy was to pile on layers of undergarments, sometimes as many as four or five—long, knitted woolen pants called *maoku*, silk-padded long underwear, sweaters and more sweaters, till people moved with the grace of penguins. Americans who balked at turning down their thermostats to 65 degrees or even 68 degrees because of the oil shortage could hardly imagine what it is like to live in a house that is close to freezing inside. At the Second Foreign Languages Institute, some of the classrooms had no heat all winter. To make matters worse, a teacher told me, his room had many empty windowpanes, the result of fighting during the Cultural Revolution over ten years before. Students had to stamp their feet during class and wear gloves in order not to get frostbite.

One afternoon when I was walking around an old section of Peking, down a series of narrow alleys fronted with anonymous gray-brick walls, I was intrigued by a series of small handwritten signs affixed to a lamppost. Several were written on bright, eye-catching red and yellow paper, the others merely on sheets torn from a school notebook. They all involved one subject— housing. "Wanted to exchange," one of these notices read, "a two-room apartment at 125 Andingmen Street, of 11.8 square meters, for a home nearer to Qianmen or the Number 7 trolley bus route." The author, whose name was Huang, went on to explain in cursive but plaintive form that he needed to be closer to his job and that he had been looking for a new place for two years.

Unlike the United States or Europe, where there are classified ads in the newspapers or real estate agents to help you find housing, in China most people have only one choice—to apply to a government housing office. Only 10 percent of the housing in China's cities is still privately owned; the rest is allocated either by city housing departments or by some of the larger factories, offices, and schools that have their own buildings.

"When you register for a new apartment," said a translator who worked in the Academy of Social Sciences, a government think-tank, "the first thing they do is measure your current housing. If you have more than three square meters per person, forget it. They won't consider you. You will have to find something on your own, through the back door or by putting up a sign and hoping." She herself had been married for three years, but still lived with her husband's parents and his brother in their old Chinese-style courtyard house, a low, one-story structure with a tile roof. It had three small rooms, one of which she and her husband had built themselves so they could have a room of their own. It was just large enough for their bed and a tall wooden cabinet. They shared a kitchen and toilet with neighbors in a surrounding compound that had once belonged to a wealthy merchant.

She and her husband were victims of the acute housing shortage that has hit China's cities. The Communists have pointed proudly to their record of keeping the cost of housing low and affordable to all. Most Chinese I knew paid only two or three dollars a month in rent, a fabulous bargain compared to the $1,000 a month it can cost for an apartment in New York or Tokyo and the $500,000 it takes to buy a fashionable house in Los Angeles. But the other side of the coin has been that the average allotment of housing space per person in China's cities is only 3.6 square yards, about the size of a large dining-room table. That is less than half the average amount in the Soviet Union, which itself has long had a serious housing problem. I noted once that the New China News Agency reported that 35 percent of all urban families in China had a "housing problem" and "5 to 6 percent of them do not have proper housing at all." A forty-five-year-old schoolteacher I met slept on the desk in his classroom because he did not have an apartment. His housing had been confiscated in the Cultural Revolution when he was declared a capitalist roader, and the government had not found him new quarters since.

The major cause of the shortage has been that the government, following Stalin's lead, treated housing as an item of consumption and therefore saw it as having less legitimate claim on the country's scarce resources than construction for factories or office buildings. This was another of those strategic errors which Mao's successors belatedly recognized and tried to correct, with a burst of new housing projects in the late 1970s. In 1979 alone the government put up 118 million square yards of housing, one sixth of the total built nationwide since 1949. But even this figure is less impressive than it sounds. In the United States in the same year, 267 million square yards of housing were built, for a population that is only one quarter of China's and was already far better housed.

Even after people finally are assigned a new apartment, their troubles aren't necessarily over. Jan and Norman were told by the Academy of Sciences that they would soon be given a new apartment in a series of luxury buildings being put up for high-level officials of the academy, senior scientists, and overseas Chinese researchers who had volunteered to come back to the motherland. They waited expectantly for word to move, but a year elapsed before they were allowed to occupy their new quarters. Part of the delay, they discovered later, was that the construction workers objected that the interior of the apartments was too bourgeois—they had terrazzo floors, wallpaper, and a frosted-glass partition between the living room and the dining area, all unheard of in Peking. So the workers had gone on strike.

When they actually did move in, Jan and Norman found other reminders of the shoddy workmanship that often gives Chinese buildings a predilapidated look. Plaster was falling from the ceiling, the bathtub was cracked in two places, the closet door was too big to close, and a pile of lime lay frozen on the kitchen floor.

The lime got hacked away when fellow workers in Norman's *danwei,* including his unit's Party secretary, volunteered to come over to help. But Jan then discovered that the telephone company would not install a phone and the local government grain shop would not sell them rice or wheat.

"We were baffled at first," said Jan. But later they learned that their trouble was just part of another back-door practice. "Some friends told us that the telephone company was negotiating with the Academy of Sciences to try to get a share of the new apartments for itself before it would put in any phones. It was extortion."

Still, she considered herself lucky. The *People's Daily* reported that in some new buildings there was no running water or electricity because the city water and electric power agencies had demanded a number of the apartments for themselves from the *danwei* that put them up. Jan's aunt, a ranking intellectual in Tianjin, China's third largest city, was assigned an apartment in a special new project for high-level officials. The post office used a similar ploy. It would not recognize the existence of her building, so every day her aunt had to go back across the city to her old apartment to fetch her mail.

5. Eating Bitterness

吃 苦

LIHUA

"Everyone is given a difficult sutra to read."

A Chinese proverb

She was only six years old when it happened.

Until then, Lihua ("Strength for China") had lived in a spacious apartment in Peking with her three older brothers, a younger sister, her father, who was a scientist, and her mother, a nurse. They thought of themselves with pride as what the Chinese call intellectuals, the carriers of the great tradition. Her mother used to tell the children about her own grandfather, who had passed one of the imperial exams under the Qing dynasty before the turn of the century and had held a sinecure job in the court in Peking.

But they had a neighbor who was jealous of them. He was a worker and a Communist Party member, in Chinese terms a good class status. But he drank and smoked a lot, his wife was unemployed, and he had a hard time supporting their five children. In 1966, at the start of the Cultural Revolution, the neighbor moved quickly to organize a radical faction in their apartment building in support of Mao. His new position enabled him to examine Lihua's father's confidential dossier in the Party's files; in it he found her father had once been briefly a member of the Kuomintang before 1949 when he was a student. That was enough to convict him. A rally was held, Lihua's father was judged a "hidden counterrevolutionary," and he was stripped of his teaching post.

"Red Guards came to search our house, they confiscated everything," she recalled. "They took my father's books, my mother's jewelry, her college photo albums, our furniture. Then they built a bonfire in the yard outside and burned everything.

"That was the end of my childhood," Lihua said.

Afterward, the Public Security Bureau ordered her entire family to move to a village in a remote part of Hunan province, eight hundred miles south of Peking. It was punishment for her father's supposed past sins. Lihua's ancestors had come from the village, Gold Mountain, but neither her mother nor father had ever lived there, and no one in the family knew how to farm. Six teen-age Red Guards accompanied the family on the three-day train trip to make sure they got there.

"When we arrived, the local cadres took away the few things we had left, our clothes and our bedding. They left us only what we had on our backs." The family was put in the village schoolhouse, a small one-room building with holes in the walls where the windows should have been and a roof that leaked. There was no furniture. Lihua had to learn to sleep on the mud floor. The school had already been closed by the Cultural Revolution. The teacher had been arrested as a reactionary.

"The peasants and the cadres made my parents parade through the streets every day for several weeks," she related. "They hung a placard around my father's neck, they made him kneel down to confess his crimes, and they beat both my father and mother with iron bars.

"A person is made of flesh. If you beat them long enough, they will die." Within a month her mother was dead and her father was left deaf and unable to use his right arm.

"My mouth is very stupid because I didn't go to school, but these are a few of the facts."

Lihua recounted this story the first time we met in September 1979 on the steps of the Peking Municipal Party Committee Headquarters, a functional gray-concrete building. I had gone there when I heard there were a number of petitioners from the countryside standing outside the Party office trying to present their grievances to the city authorities. It was one of those periods when China's leaders temporarily relaxed their control. Some young factory workers and students took advantage of the slack to put up wall posters or print unofficial journals criticizing the regime, what we foreign correspondents came to call the "democracy movement." Thousands of other people materialized from the countryside asking to have their own personal cases reexamined. The Chinese referred to them as *shang-fang*, meaning they were "entreating a higher level for help." Lihua was one of these.

I didn't notice her at first. I was interviewing an eighteen-year-old man, dressed in a faded, soiled pair of loose blue trousers, who said he had been sold by his father for a pig after the family had been forced out of Peking during the Cultural Revolution. Lihua had come over and stood quietly by my side, waiting for me to finish asking the other man questions. She didn't look like a petitioner. She was wearing a neat tomato-red cotton jacket, with a blue- and white-striped shirt underneath. Her long hair, worn in braids to her waist, was carefully combed; her skin was creamy, unlike most peasants, who have been burned brown by years in the sun; and her teeth were straight and white. Above all, it was the easy smile on her broad face—she didn't look angry. She talked in a calm, dispassionate voice, almost as if all this had happened to someone else, but her story soon gathered a crowd.

After her mother died and her father became an invalid, she had to find a way to earn a living, for the cadres in charge of the village retroactively labeled her family "landlords" and at first wouldn't let her brothers take part in working in the collective fields or have their own small private plot for raising vegetables. The one thing she found she could do as a six-year-old was to go out to the mountains around the village to collect firewood to sell to a brick kiln nearby.

"I would walk thirty li [ten miles] up to the hills at sunrise every day, then back that evening. Sometimes I had to carry a hundred pounds, almost twice my weight. But I was inexperienced and often cut myself with the ax," she said. When I looked down at her hands, there were long scars on the backs of both hands and a gash down the middle finger of her left hand from the tip of the nail to the first joint. "We didn't have enough money to pay for a doctor to stitch it," she explained. The village, as part of a commune, had a cooperative medical program, but families of landlords were not eligible to join.

"In that first year, our clothes soon became like tattered pieces of paper. I had to teach myself how to sew for the family by taking apart our old clothes and then putting them back together.

"I was born into the new society," she went on, using a Chinese expression for the years after the Communists' victory in 1949. "I grew up under the Red flag and at first I didn't understand how such things could happen. But gradually I came to realize that I represent many thousands of people. It is just like in the old feudal society before Liberation. We Chinese must still chi-ku, 'eat bitterness.' Nothing has really changed.

"As humans, we should have rights, the right to a job, to get an education, but the cadres often treat us like dogs and pigs," she said, still speaking in her level, matter-of-fact tone, addressing both me and the crowd around her.

I broke off our talk here. It was as much as I could listen to that morning, and I was getting nervous about the size of the crowd, now over a hundred people. It was noontime, and a number of Party officials were coming out of their offices. A cadre in his fifties, gray-haired and dressed in a well-tailored Mao tunic, walked down the steps and into a chauffeur-driven black Mercedes that was waiting. He did not stop to talk to any of the petitioners. I was with Jan Wong, my assistant, who dressed and looked like a Peking college student, a useful disguise. Jan wrote out *The Times*'s office phone number, and Lihua agreed to meet us again.

I felt depressed by Lihua's story, but euphoric about meeting her. Confined to Peking, it was rare for me to encounter someone from the countryside. Most Chinese I knew were city people, and the Information Department had rebuffed all my requests to live even for a few days in a village. Yet four fifths of China's one billion people were peasants, and perhaps 200 million of them still lived in isolated areas in conditions that the government itself described as verging on poverty. By chance, Lihua's village was in one of the most remote and poorest regions, the Jinggangshan, a legendary belt of forested mountains on the border of Hunan and Jiangxi provinces. Mao had taken advantage of its isolation and backwardness to set up his first guerrilla base there in 1928. At our next meeting, I asked Lihua if she would describe life in Gold Mountain. I didn't have to put another question to her—she was a born raconteur, like one of the traditional storytellers who recited picaresque sagas of adventure and misfortune at rural fairs.

Evidently little had changed since Mao's Red Army days in the Jinggang-shan in the 1930s, she indicated. From her village it was still a half day's walk to the nearest road. There was no electricity—most villages now do have electric power, the government claims—and no running water. The peasants used ponds and irrigation ditches to wash their clothes. Gold Mountain had seven hundred inhabitants, in one hundred families, larger than the average village because the government had formed it by consolidating four separate hamlets scattered across a mountain during the Great Leap Forward in 1958. Officially it was designated as a production team, the lowest of the three tiers that make up a commune, but in size it was more like a brigade, the middle level.

"Our village used to be in an area the people called the land of rice and fish," Lihua said. "The land was fertile, rainfall was plentiful, rice grew in the paddies, and the peasants had to work only half the year to survive."

But the Great Leap Forward in 1958, when Mao ordered the formation of the communes, altered all that, she asserted. Mao had calculated that China could be transformed almost overnight from a poor agricultural country to a modern industrial power if the peasants labored hard enough in the fields and began enough small-scale rural factories. In Gold Mountain, the cadres tried to produce Mao's miracle. Some officials in Peking believed there was coal in the area, so the peasants were told to dig tunnels in all their fields. The rice and sweet potato crops were left to rot in the rush, though no coal was found. Some other ministry determined that the peasants could increase their supply of fertilizer by cutting down all the trees around the village, and spreading the ashes on the fields. That left them without fuel for cooking and heating their homes.

When Lihua's family arrived in the village a few years later, it had still not recovered. They found themselves constantly short of food. "We had to

borrow or beg a few ounces of rice or sweet potatoes from the other peasants," she remembered. "My brothers didn't know how to cook, so I had to
learn that also. I would put the rice in a pot, with too much water for it, to
make a thin gruel, then add in whatever vegetables we could scavenge,
maybe some cabbage, turnips, scallions, wild herbs, or mushrooms from the
mountains. The peasants say, 'There are poor people, but no poor mountains.' You couldn't cut down the mountains."

Her hunts in the mountains were not always successful. "I was still very
young, and I didn't know what I could pick and eat. One day I was poisoned
by something I had gathered. My face turned purple, I vomited, and was
delirious. An old woman saved me with some herbal medicine she had.

"Sometimes we were so short of food we had to eat the husks of the rice
too. I would make them into pancakes. But they were so hard, I couldn't
swallow them unless I was very hungry. I would carry one up to the mountains and eat it when I was cutting firewood.

"For years we couldn't get cooking oil," she said, meaning vegetable oils
like peanut or rapeseed oil that the Chinese use for frying their food. "There
was so little oil our cooking pot got rusty."

Lihua blamed this diet for her current health problems. Her hair was
falling out in clumps when she brushed it, she said; her eyes hurt when she
read, and she often felt weak or dizzy. I noticed that at lunch she ate only
two or three mouthfuls of rice and some chicken soup. She had no appetite
for more, she insisted. Over the next few months, as we met several dozen
times, I never saw her eat a normal meal.

Lihua's family faced other shortages too. They couldn't buy soap or
matches. Each peasant family was supposed to get a pack of 1,000 matches
a year, but the cadres in Gold Mountain took that ration away from Lihua's
brothers and sisters, as they had been labeled landlords. "We had to take a
bundle of loose straw to a neighbor's house to borrow fire," she recalled.
"They took pity on us." Soap simply wasn't available.

The peasants in Gold Mountain ate meat only five or six times a year, on
the traditional festival days like the lunar New Year, she said. Before 1949
the peasants never had much meat either, but the problem had been compounded by the Communists' limits on the number of chickens and pigs each
family could raise. Mao had been afraid that a family that grew more than
a few animals would turn into capitalists. So each household in Gold Mountain, Lihua related, had been restricted to raising one pig and two chickens.
They had to be sold to the state, at the state's low, fixed price.

"If you slaughtered them yourself, the cadres would ask for a piece," she
said. "Once at New Year's, they asked us for a whole pig. If they were being
polite, the cadres would say, 'Such and such a cadre is coming down for a
visit from a higher level for a visit and we need some money for his food.

It is your duty to give it.' Sometimes they would just get people to write a slip to the production team to borrow money from the collective account. Then they took the money for themselves. It was up to you to repay it." Lihua claimed her family had lost about $600 this way, counting chickens, pigs, and cash.

"We called the head of the prodution team the local emperor. He was master of all. They weren't any different from the landlords in the old society."

The man who was head of the production team when she first arrived in Gold Mountain was a veteran of the Red Army who had gained local prestige by fighting in the Korean war with China's troops. He had now retired and his son had taken over the post. Although China's official policy is that the heads of production teams are to be elected, Lihua said she had never heard of any vote in her village. As far as she knew, the cadres were all appointed by some higher authority.

The team leaders were faced with the problem of trying to make Gold Mountain's production figures look better. The average distribution to able-bodied male peasants at the end of the year in the village, when the harvest of all the crops was added up and state taxes were deducted, came out to 550 pounds of unhusked rice or its equivalent in sweet potatoes, Lihua recalled. That works out to about 380 pounds of edible rice. When she said that, Jan Wong, who was helping me interpret, was shocked. Jan calculated that she, herself, consumed 350 pounds of rice a year in Peking, but that was in addition to the generous amounts of meat, fish, and vegetables she ate every day. Published Chinese government figures suggest that 330 pounds of rice a year is semistarvation rations. Moreover, Lihua added, unlike better-off teams, Gold Mountain had no cash to divide at year's end because the village had no sideline occupations, like growing oranges or silkworms, and no local factories.

One year the cadres decided they could raise production by introducing a new high-yield variety of rice with short stalks they had heard about. But it required extra amounts of fertilizer, which they didn't have, and, as the peasants soon discovered, it was susceptible to insects. To try to overcome the pest problem, the cadres bought new chemical sprays; the pesticides soon killed most of the fish in the village ponds. In the end the crop failed, and the peasants had to go for a year without rice, begging from a nearby village. Even the stalks left in the fields weren't as good for fuel as the old long-stemmed strain.

But the team leader reported an increase in output anyway, Lihua charged, and consequently had to deliver a larger amount to the state. "To cover up what had happened, he ordered us to put what good grain we had on the tops of the rice sacks, to put stalks at the bottom, and rocks in the middle.

"This was our education from the Cultural Revolution.

"Before, the peasants were very *lao shi*," a Chinese virtue that translates as "honest and upright." "Afterward they became evil. People began to steal from each other's private plots. You had to watch out your neighbors didn't take your chickens or pig. People's philosophy became *guo yi tian, suan yi tian* [get through the day and forget it]. Everyone was very pessimistic."

Lihua herself was growing up in these years. At the early summer and fall harvests (they grew two crops a year), she made her way to a state farm fifteen miles away where they paid 50 cents for every bag of 110 pounds of husked rice she brought in. They also gave her eight pounds of rice to eat.

"That was my best chance of the year. I would work day and night till I couldn't bend from the waist. Then I would lie down and crawl to harvest the rice. In the war the soldiers used to sleep while they marched. I used to sleep while I worked, I was so tired."

Some of the other workers on the state farm were young people who had been sent to resettle in the countryside from their homes in Shanghai. They were part of the 18 million urban Chinese school graduates rusticated on Mao's order after the start of the Cultural Revolution. "When they first arrived, their heads were full of beautiful ideas about the villages," Lihua remembered. "They believed what they had heard, that the land was rich, that the peasants were revolutionary." But once they found how hard life was, they changed. Many of the city youth couldn't work hard enough to support themselves and had to depend on money sent by their parents. Some of the men took to carrying knives and going around in gangs.

"When they showed up in Gold Mountain, it was just like a scene in a movie about bandits. The people all scattered and ran indoors. The chickens flew in the air."

One afternoon when she was thirteen, Lihua recalled, she set out for a small rural market with eggs from their chicken to sell. Her family didn't eat the eggs themselves, they were too valuable. She was walking through a sugar cane field, the maturing cane over her head, and had just crossed a small stream when she saw a man in his early twenties in front of her. He was wearing a watch and glasses, and his clothes were clean, not like a peasant. He asked her to sit down and talk with him.

"I was afraid, my heart was beating fast," Lihua told me. Then he produced a knife from under his shirt. He ordered her to take off her clothes.

"I don't know why I thought of it, but I said, 'You take off your clothes first.'"

The man agreed and, in a bout of modesty, turned his back before loosening his pants. He also put the knife down on the ground.

"When he did, I rushed forward and grabbed it and began stabbing him. Blood spurted all over the place. He fell to the ground, and I kept stabbing

119

him until I thought he was dead. Then I fainted, I can't remember exactly."

When she awoke, it was dark, and she washed herself off in the stream. On her way home she came across the graveyard where her mother was buried. "I dug at her grave with my hands. I wanted to crawl inside." Then she passed out again. The next morning an old man on his way to the mountains to gather wood found her and notified one of her brothers, who came to get her.

"He thought I was overtired. I didn't tell him what had happened." After the incident, she went on, she didn't feel like living anymore. "But I had responsibilities. My little sister was four years younger than me, my father was weak. I decided I would never get married and just devote my life to taking care of them. Men are a bad thing."

There never was an investigation, she said. At the time, with the large number of discontent rusticated students in their area, violence was not uncommon and there had been a number of violent fights and murders in the village.

It was at this period in her life, in her early teens, that Lihua began to listen to the stories of other peasant women about spirits, demons, and ghosts. "I wondered how life could be so cruel. Sometimes at night, when I had gone out to wash our clothes after my day's work was done and hadn't had anything to eat, I would look up at the moon and wish some fairy would come down and save me. I began to burn incense, and I thought that I must have been a criminal in an earlier life. When I walked down the road, I imagined that every plant, every tree, was cursing me for my previous life."

There had been a Buddhist temple with a priest in the village before Red Guards destroyed it in the Cultural Revolution, she said. "Some of the peasants said that was the reason the era was so poor." But many of the villagers continued to practice their old rites at home. On the first and fifteenth day of each month they burned incense and put a bowl of rice in front of a picture of the kitchen god, which they kept on an altar. "You were supposed to put meat or fruit in front of the god, but they were too poor," she said.

Lihua's description was the first authentic account I had heard of continued folk religion in the countryside. In theory China's constitution guarantees freedom of religion; but in practice the Communists have tended to see religion as a rival claim to Marxism and have imposed tight restrictions on most religious rituals and beliefs. I was curious, therefore, if other traditional ideas that the Communists had derided as superstition and tried to eradicate had survived. Yes, she said.

"There was a witch in our village. The authorities couldn't do anything about her because she was protected by the *lao bai xing,*" literally, the "old hundred names," the Chinese word for common people. "She and the witches in some other villages were really mad, so they weren't treated as commune members by the cadres. They didn't work in the fields. But the people gave them food for their services, like curing illnesses. For example, they will place a bowl of clear water on the altar table in the former temple. That night, the person who was sick would drink it, believing that in the meantime the gods have added some medicine to it."

The peasants in Gold Mountain also practiced a Chinese form of voodoo, she said. "If someone you hate is very sick and you want them to die, to speed up the process you must find out the exact date of their birth. Then you learn some chants for that date, make a wooden doll, and stick it with seven pins. Finally, you burn it at night. The person is guaranteed to die by morning."

Somehow during all these years Lihua managed to educate herself. Her only formal schooling was part of a year in first grade before the family was forced out of Peking. "But I wanted so much to learn," she explained. "My language teacher was a dictionary. Everyone I met was a teacher to me, I could ask them questions. I got a copy of the *Three Character Classic,*" the Confucian moral primer and grammar that generations of Chinese schoolboys had to master. It contained short homilies that rhymed in Chinese and could easily be memorized: "At men's beginning their nature is fundamentally good, by nature they are similar but in practice they grow apart." This appealed to Lihua. "Even though the government said it was decadent, I thought it had a lot to teach," she said.

One of her older brothers also tried to continue his education. He had managed to save an English and a Russian dictionary when the family was exiled and he took them with him to the fields during the day. When the peasants took a break from their labor, he would go to a corner of the field to study.

"The peasants didn't understand foreign languages and didn't know what he was doing," Lihua told me later. "They accused him of maintaining illicit relations with foreign countries and being an American spy." She laughed at the memory, her large almond eyes wrinkling up and almost disappearing in the folds of her heavy eyelids. But it wasn't funny at the time. "The peasants took him to a struggle session. They beat him and took away all his notes. But they couldn't find anyone else who could read them to tell them what the notes said." After that, her brother gave up studying.

By now we were meeting once every two or three weeks. I would write her a letter setting the time, and Lihua's short, solid figure would appear at the magazine kiosk across the street from the Peking Hotel. Chinese are always punctual; it is a mark of respect and character to be on time. But Lihua was inevitably late, the only Chinese I knew who was less punctual than I. I finally realized why. She lived on the outskirts of Peking and it took her over an hour's ride on the city's crowded bus system, with three transfers, to get into the center of town. Each ride was an adventure because she didn't have any money, and when the conductor asked for her fare, Lihua would plead that she was in Peking as a petitioner. Lihua also did not have a watch. When I discovered this, the next time I went to Hong Kong on vacation to visit my family, I bought her an inexpensive Japanese wristwatch.

Each time we met we would go for lunch in a different restaurant, hoping to avoid suspicion. Lihua would start talking, and if we managed to get a table in a quiet corner, I would scribble notes as fast as I could, holding my notebook in my lap against the waiters' prying eyes. Some days I had to wait till I got back to my office to type up my recollections. Lihua didn't mind my writing about her; in fact, she said she had kept a diary herself but her father had found it and burned it. He was worried about further retribution. But Lihua seemed to have an endless supply of grit and courage; she was already taking a giant risk by coming to Peking as a petitioner; and she wanted her story to be told. "I want people outside China to know what the Cultural Revolution was like and what the Chinese have been through," she said during one lunch.

I was curious how she had managed to get back from her village to Peking. Her father had made the first effort, she said, in 1969, three years after they had been sent out of the city. He had written to his old institute in Peking appealing for reconsideration. But the school sent his letter back to the village and the cadres had him dragged through the streets and beaten again. He himself never sought redress after that.

"People like him have ink in their stomachs," Lihua remarked. "They are learned, but have no courage."

In 1976, after Mao died and Jiang Qing, his widow, was arrested, Lihua wrote an appeal. But she discovered that the institute had by then been converted into a factory, not an ususual fate for schools during the Cultural Revolution. The officials in charge of the factory didn't recall her father's case, but they were considerate enough to dispatch two men to the village to investigate her charges. Several months later she got the reply. Her father had indeed been wronged. He would be rehabilitated. But he was now so old and weak—he was fifty-eight years old, two years short of normal retirement—that he should retire. There would be a small pension, but no financial compensation for all the years lost. Nor would the factory consider letting the family back into Peking. They had too many members for that. Government policy was to keep the size of the cities down. Therefore the officials would not give Lihua what she most wanted, a change in her *hu-kou*, the household registration certificate that is a key form of identification in China. It specified whether a person lived in the countryside or a city, and which city. A peasant could not get a job or an apartment in the cities without an urban *hu-kou,* nor could he buy grain, oil, or cloth in the cities, since these depended on city ration cards. For Lihua, a Peking household registration certificate was to become the magic talisman, "like a fortune-teller's card in the old society," she remarked. "It held your fate in its hands."

By the summer of 1979 Lihua had turned twenty and was impatient. She had heard about the petitioners coming to Peking and she decided to try herself. Her oldest brother, now thirty-three, had managed to move back to the capital because he had been sent down to the countryside separately, in a different campaign, just before the beginning of the Cultural Revolution. He was working for a construction company and lived in a tiny dormitory room. She could stay with him there temporarily. But this risked a neighbor turning her in to the police. So she developed the first of a series of stratagems, creating good, new *guan-xi.* She discovered that the neighbors needed clothes—the ready-made clothes in the stores fit poorly and Peking's few tailor shops were always busy. Lihua knew how to sew. It was a natural way to ingratiate herself.

"These days you have to do things to buy a person's humanity," Lihua commented.

Then she began making the rounds of all the government offices she thought might help: her father's old school (which had now been converted back to its original teaching function), the Public Security Bureau, the State Council, or cabinet, the High Court, and the Peking city Party Committee, where we met. I asked if she wasn't afraid of being picked up as a troublemaker and put in jail, as I knew some petitioners were.

"No," she replied. "I have no future anyway."

At her father's former institute, an official assigned to deal with petitioners invited her in to talk. They spent two hours each morning for several weeks discussing the case and drinking tea, but an investigation the official promised into her plight never took place. "To the Communists we are just like noodles in the hands of a noodle-maker, something to shape as you like," she said afterward.

One day during her rounds she met another woman petitioner. The woman had a neighbor who had a relative who knew someone in the police. "It was very roundabout, but I began going to the police officer's house. I found they needed clothes for their children, so I began to sew for them, too. They would give me the material, since I couldn't buy any myself."

There was one problem with all this sewing, however. Lihua did not have her own sewing machine. By this time Jan and I felt as caught up in her tale as she was, so we went out and bought her a Chinese copy of an early Singer.

Four months after her initial meeting with the policeman, he also felt sorry enough for her to invite her to write out her story so he might submit it for official consideration.

"I had to be very careful not to complain in explaining how my mother had been killed," she told me a few days later. "I couldn't blame the police. But who do I say is responsible? Even though nobody had done anything, I had to say I was grateful to the Party for its help." She was smiling her girlish smile again. I thought she showed a tenaciousness and sense of strategy beyond her twenty years. She was a gentle diplomat; her only resource was the sympathy she could evoke. "I hate them, but I never let it show," she once explained.

By now it was winter in Peking, and one day I dropped in to see her in the room, thirty feet square, she shared with her brother, his wife, and her younger sister and father, whom she had recently brought up from Gold Mountain. She had sent for her sister so she could get an education, but Lihua had had to use all her negotiating skills to get her into a school because of that missing household registration. Lihua also attended the parent–teacher meetings, since her father remained an invalid. Their room faced north, the undesirable vantage in Peking, letting in the cold and the wind but little light. The room was heated only by a small coal-burning stove, though to save money they didn't use it during the day and my breath showed in little puffs. It might have been forty degrees in the room. Lihua had freshly whitewashed the walls, and even the bare concrete floor she kept spotless—not a speck of dust in a city where most people seemed resigned to the daily damage visited by the dust storms from the Gobi Desert.

Their only furniture was two wide wooden planks planted on sawhorses and covered with cotton pallets the entire family used as its bed. A short wire strung along the wall near the stove was hung with newly washed laundry. On the window sill were twenty bottles of medicine and traditional Chinese tonics, testimony to Lihua's chronic ailments.

After a day's sewing, Lihua got out a low stool, spread a newspaper over the spotless sheet, and used the bed for a desk on which to study. She was trying to learn English.

Finally, the next July, a year after she had come to Peking, she received a notice from the police reporting her family could get its household registration transferred to the capital. But there was a catch. The permission would expire in three weeks and within that time she had to show they had permanent housing in Peking. That was the law: without a city household registration, you couldn't get an apartment; but without an apartment, you couldn't get a household registration.

"I am frantic," Lihua told me the next day. "China is too hopeless." She was wearing her summer costume, a white cotton blouse and yellow flowered skirt she had made herself. (After Mao's death, such departures from orthodox blue were allowable.) In the winter she had one set of clothes she wore every day, in the summer another one. That was all she could afford.

She had gone to the construction company where her brother worked and asked them to write a letter saying she and her father were entitled to live in the company's housing. She promised to move out as soon as she found her own quarters. But the company refused. They were afraid she would stay, like many people in Peking. Eventually, I learned, she got a letter from her father's former school saying they would find housing for him within two months. It was a fib, but with that note she got the construction company to write to the police certifying her residence in their dormitory.

Lihua felt triumphant, but the saga was not over. The cadres in Gold Mountain wouldn't let her two remaining brothers leave. The family still owed the production team $300, they claimed. In Lihua's view, it was a debtor's trap. Because the family had long ago been labeled as landlords, half of all the work points they earned for their daily labor in the fields were deducted as "duty points." As a result, they got only half as much grain at the year-end distribution as other peasants and had to borrow money to live on. Her brothers also had to spend time cultivating land assigned to the team cadres as so-called duty labor. She deduced that the cadres didn't want to lose this form of free serf labor.

"They treated my family as criminals," she complained. In 1979, Peking had announced that the stigma of the landlord class label would be removed, but she claimed it had not been in their village. That left the cadres free to do what they liked with her family. One time she had mailed a packet of shirts and pants she had made for her brothers to Gold Mountain, but they never received the clothes. When Lihua visited the village later, she said the team leader was wearing some of her handiwork.

The situation now appeared hopeless; the three-week deadline was approaching and her brothers were still down in the village. They had to arrive in Peking before the end of July or the permit for them to live in the city would expire. Lihua made one last appeal to her father's old school. They agreed to send an official on the three-day train trip to Gold Mountain to talk with the cadres there. Finally, the team leader consented; he would reschedule the debt. The family could repay from Peking. The two missing brothers appeared a day before the deadline.

I saw Lihua a few more times after that. She was busy studying. She had spotted an advertisement for a new school set up by the city for unemployed young people. It would train them to be primary school teachers. Admission required a high school education, but Lihua spun her usual story and the head of the school agreed to let her take a test to see if she had taught herself as well as a regular school would have. She passed.

After my wife moved to Peking and we had our own apartment, Lihua came over for lunch one day. It meant walking past the two middle-aged women who operated the elevator in our building. But that was easy for her.

When the elevator women stared at her on the way up to the eleventh floor, trying to fix her description for their report to the Public Security Bureau, she smiled back and asked the polite Chinese question, "Have you eaten or not?"

She had brought a pair of tiny cotton shoes she had sewn for our baby, Sarah, and a piece of lace she had made for Barbara.

I noticed she was not wearing the watch I had given her. Now that her brothers had come, she explained with embarrassment, she was worried that they would be jealous about such an expensive item, so she had hidden it. "I don't want to cause a contradiction in my family. We have managed so far to stay together despite our problems. I don't want to spoil that."

In her modest way, she had the virtues Chinese have always prized: devotion to her family, carefully controlled emotions, a willingness to work hard, and a passion for knowledge. At the same time, she also had that ability to use people and situations, *guan-xi,* to her own advantage. In others it might have seemed manipulation; in Lihua it grew out of desperation and added to her attraction. To me she was the quintessential Chinese, proof that the Confucian character had not been wiped out.

There was another Chinese trait too—her righteous anger. Confucius taught moderation and never losing one's temper, but China did not have the moral of turning the other cheek. The last time we met I asked Lihua if, now that her family was safely in Peking, her unhappiness with the Communists had abated. No, she replied.

"People say that now that I've got my household registration, I should be happy. But I won't be happy till I die. I've never lived a good day in my life. My mother was beaten to death, my father was left senseless, and I still have to beg for everything.

"That is what the Cultural Revolution did. It is unfixable. My scars will never heal."

PART

2

PASSAGES

—

6. Sex Without Joy

爱情与婚姻

LOVE AND MARRIAGE

"To die over an unhappy love affair is absolutely worthless. You should plunge yourself into the hot struggle for production and gradually your wounds will be healed."
Advice from the editors of China Youth News *to a lovelorn young man jilted by his girl friend*

Lili was an exceptionally pretty teen-ager, with smooth white skin, shiny black hair, and delicately carved features. Her father was a senior general in the People's Liberation Army, and she had always led a comfortable life. She went to a special school for children of high cadres, her family had a spacious house, and there was a maid to help with the chores. Until the Cultural Revolution in 1967. Then her father was arrested on trumped-up charges of being a capitalist roader. He was taken to a struggle session where he was shouted at, insulted, and spit on, and then dragged off to prison where he was tortured to death. Lili's mother, the daughter of a former landlord and a woman unaccustomed to hardship, went mad and died. Because her father had been branded a traitor, the family's house was confiscated and Lili was expelled from high school. At the age of seventeen Lili was left alone to fend for herself and her younger sister, who was twelve.

A mutual friend who recounted Lili's adventures said that her only recourse was to become a beggar, for her only other resources, her clothes, a silk bedspread, her cello, were soon sold off for food. Her younger sister fell ill, probably from eating nothing but boiled cabbage leavings from the market in the city of Hangzhou, where they lived. Lili was desperate.

That was when the envelopes began to arrive every month with 50 yuan ($33) inside and no return address. It was more than an average month's wage at the time. At first Lili could not believe it and put the money aside.

"But," she said, "when no one came around knocking at the door, I decided to use the money for my sister." The money continued to come until two years later when Lili made it into the army. Because of her good looks and her musical talent, she was put into a military song and dance troupe that traveled around the country entertaining high-level officers.

It was only then, during a visit to Peking, that she discovered who her mysterious benefactor was. He was an old friend of her father's, a general himself, named Cao, who had found out where Lili was and sent the money. Naturally Lili felt an enormous debt to him and went to see him whenever her ensemble performed in Peking.

There was one slight problem. Cao had a son who was also an army officer, stationed in Sichuan, in the southwest, and Cao very much wanted Lili to marry him. Cao brought the subject up many times, but Lili had never met the son and she always put Cao off good-naturedly, pleading that she was too young to get married. In fact, Lili did not like the old-fashioned idea of an arranged marriage, which the Communists had formally declared illegal with their progressive family law of 1950, one of their first pieces of legislation after Liberation. But Cao persisted. He got his son transferred up from Sichuan to Peking so Lili could meet him—that only increased the trouble. She didn't like him at all. He was "empty-headed and interested in nothing but his own pleasure," she found.

Then old Cao fell ill and Lili got a leave of absence to rush to Peking to be with him in the hospital. On his deathbed he pleaded with her to marry his son and let him die a happy man. Lili was distraught. She not only felt a great sense of obligation to Cao, but she was an orphan and had no relatives who could act as go-betweens in the traditional Chinese way to argue her case. Finally she spoke with the son, striking a deal. They would agree in front of Cao to be married, so he could die happily, but she would not marry him.

But as soon as Cao was dead, the son "rushed all around Peking," Lili related, telling his relatives and friends that they were engaged. Lili ignored him, but he increased the pressure. He tried to kill himself, citing his loss of face when Lili reneged on her pledge. Cao's widow then went to the Party secretary of Lili's army *danwei*, charging her with improper conduct. She had agreed to the marriage, now she was backing out. Lili's Party leader called her in for investigation and "advised" her—it was tantamount to an order in the army—to marry the son since she had already committed herself.

The son proposed what looked like a happy solution. "I'm losing too much face with things as they are," he said. Why not just go with him to the local civil affairs office and register their marriage—the official process for getting married in China today—and then they could forget it. She believed him and went to register. But that night he broke into the house where she was staying and, in her view, raped her, since she was unwilling. "I left a nice scar bite on his shoulder as evidence," she recalled.

The friend who told me about Lili's quiet tragedy did not do so to titillate me. She meant only to offer a personal insight into one of the most secretive aspects of life in China, sexual mores. Peking publishes a cornucopia of data on everything from the production of pigs and wristwatches to hydroelectric power. Since Mao's death it has sanctioned the press to write about crime and investigate corruption in the Party. It has even disclosed an official figure for the percentage of the national budget devoted to defense. But sex has usually been treated as if it didn't exist. Indeed, for more than a decade after the start of the Cultural Revolution, love was denounced as a sensual, unnecessary, and decadent bourgeois conceit and banished from public discussion. The Communists themselves came to power as Marxist revolutionaries dedicated to reordering what they decried as the backwardness and injustices of China's feudal society. But their revolution stopped at the bedroom door. Instead, in a state which has "put politics in command," in Mao's phrase, sex and love have become entangled with politics too. Much as the government impinges on the individual through controls over jobs and housing, by restricting travel, and by grouping people into *danwei,* so, too, Peking has helped shape the sex lives of millions of Chinese. Romance, marriage, the number of children a couple can have, divorce, even intercourse, are all subject in one way or another to Communist Party dictates. The result is a mixture our grandparents would be more familiar with than we are. On the surface China seems remarkably chaste and moralistic, Victorian, to borrow a Western term; but behind this apparent primness often lie frustrations and problems of sexual repression.

It is the outer modesty which charms and intrigues foreign visitors. Women eschew makeup, and even after the downfall of the radicals, the majority still dress in formless Mao jackets and baggy trousers that discourage a young man's fancy. Shirts on men and women should always be buttoned up to the top. When I first took up residence in Peking and was still infected with the macho Western custom of leaving my top shirt button undone, a roomboy in the Peking Hotel where I was staying kept reminding me to close it. He thought I had simply forgotten and would be embarrassed when I discovered my omission. In the summertime, a woman with her blouse open, even one button, is considered lewd, and in some cities, Chinese say, her affectation will be taken as a sign she is a prostitute.

In the winter, women are always expected to wear jackets in public. My assistant Jan Wong recalled that, when she was a student at Peking University, her Chinese roommate would always pause to put on her jacket before going to answer a knock at the door, even if she was already wearing a sweater.

But when Chinese women are alone among themselves, without men around, they are not shy about their bodies the way Western women often are. Jan remembers the first time she went to a public bathhouse—many Chinese must use them because of the lack of modern plumbing—and found small groups of naked women happily scrubbing each other's backs with soap and towels. Men do the same thing; in fact, part of the pleasure of going to the bathhouses is to go with a friend or two. There is no implication of homosexuality in this.

In high school and college boys and girls still sit separately, as they did in schools in the United States until a generation or two ago. Female students blush and giggle if asked whether they have a boy friend; few would admit it. Indeed, Chinese themselves usually use the circumlocution "Do you have a friend?" without any romatic overtone, to spare a person embarrassment. During a visit to an English-language class at Yunnan University in Kunming, I tried to coax an admission that the students sometimes thought about members of the opposite sex. "We'd rather study," they chorused in response.

Art Buchwald, the columnist, who was along on the trip, tried to press the question further. "But what do you dream about?" he asked. They only giggled.

It is not unusual to find people in their mid-twenties who have never been on dates, much less have steady boy friends or girl friends. In Shanghai once I quizzed my guide from China Travel Service, a pert twenty-seven-year-old woman with jaunty short pigtails named Yang Guidi, on what she wanted in a husband. "I haven't thought about that," she replied, covering her mouth with her hand in an old Chinese gesture of shyness. "I'm conservative. I have never been out with a boy. I don't like to watch television or dance. Some young people get so excited by such things they forget to study or work. I prefer to read at home, to improve myself, before I go to bed. Then I get up every morning at six thirty and go for a jog." On Sundays, insisted Miss Yang, who is a Party member, she stays home with her father and mother.

For a man to kiss a woman, many Chinese feel, is tantamount to a proposal of marriage, or should swiftly lead to it. A foreign woman who is married to a Chinese and has lived in China for many years recalled an episode when her twenty-eight-year-old daughter came to her in outrage. The daughter was deeply in love with a young Chinese man and was scheduled to marry him the next week. But then her fiancé tried to kiss her. "It's disgusting," the daughter complained. She argued vehemently that she wanted to call off the wedding until her mother explained the facts of life to her. "The average twenty-year-old Chinese woman knows as much about sex as our grandmothers did a hundred years ago," the woman later told me.

According to the Chinese press, kissing is not only in questionable moral taste, it is also downright unhealthy. The *Workers' Daily,* a paper published for factory workers, warned in one memorable article that kissing helps transmit the hepatitis B virus, which is found in 6 to 10 percent of all people, even those in good health. "That's a terrible figure," the paper cautioned. "You could say that these people are dangerous people who could at any moment contaminate their loved ones," since the virus is contained in saliva and works its way from there to the bloodstream. "So one can see that kissing is really dangerous behavior. Adults and children, we must all rid ourselves of this kissing habit," the paper concluded.

Jokes with sexual innuendos are not told in public. Once during a banquet for a delegation of foreign journalists hosted by the deputy governor of Fujian, the province opposite Taiwan, a Yugoslav correspondent was commenting on what China might want from the United States. America is already exporting its technological revolution, the Yugoslav said, raising his glass of *maotai,* the fiery clear liquor. "And now the Americans are trying to export their sexual revolution too." At this, the official interpreter, a pleasant middle-aged man with an excellent command of English, suddenly turned silent and looked at me.

"I think, if you don't mind," he said in English, "it's better not to translate that."

Foreigners, coming from our own overly sex-conscious societies, often applaud this innocence and the downplaying of the erotic in China as a healthy sign—the absence of sex on television, the clothes that aren't designed to reveal every curve of the body. Some visitors have even hypothesized that the Chinese have somehow conquered their libidos by making sex invisible or thinking the good thoughts of Chairman Mao. An earnest Harvard undergraduate who spent the summer working on a commune in China confided afterward that the experience had provided him an unexpected benefit. "Back in Cambridge, I'm always obsessed with sex, I'm always thinking about making it with some girl," he told me. But on the commune, where the women dressed without a thought to sexual attraction and conversation did not turn to boy friends and girl friends, "I just stopped thinking about sex. It wasn't in the air."

No doubt most Chinese are more straitlaced than Westerners today, less sexually flamboyant and promiscuous. We were too, a generation or two back. But the Chinese are not made of plastic either, and the notion that they have learned to surmount their sexual appetites without any consequences is another of those home-grown perceptions which foreigners have projected on China.

To some extent, China's prudish attitude toward sex is an inheritance from the Confucian past. The notion of romantic love was never a respectable one in China. The very term for love between men and women, *lian ai,* is a modern linguistic creation designed to meet the need for an equivalent to the Western expression. In classical Chinese the two components of *lian ai* appeared separately, each meaning love or affection, but in connection with the concept of loyalty between emperor and subject or father and son. Western-style dating, dancing, and necking, any public display of affection, were regarded as licentious by the Chinese. Chinese women could not, as Americans and Europeans do, justify intercourse by invoking a claim to be in love. Since ancient times, relations between men and women had a more serious purpose, marriage. And marriage meant a careful arrangement between two families, to ensure their prosperity and provide for progeny. It was too important a business to be left to the young people themselves. Love came second to parental wishes and was not a reason for acting impetuously. Often the first sight the bride and groom had of each other was when she was brought to her new in-laws' house for the wedding in a covered sedan chair. All this worked in a society where the individual had his center of gravity more in his social relations than in himself and was willing to give first place to the feelings of others.

At the same time, however, Chinese were not burdened by the Western notion that sex itself was sinful. There was no Chinese counterpart to the Christian dogma of immaculate conception and the virgin birth, or the biblical injunction that got Jimmy Carter into trouble in his first campaign: "But I say to you that everyone who looks at a woman lustfully has already committed adultery in his heart." Sex was simply a natural urge, like eating, sleeping, or moving the bowels, to which, said Mencius, the great early expounder of Confucianism, expression should be given in the right time and place. Chinese did not need to feel guilty when making love, as long as they did it with the proper party.

This traditional Chinese view of love and sex is reflected in the country's literature. Chinese novels did not turn on romance, the great theme of Western writing, since romantic love did not play such an instrumental role in Chinese life and thought. But pornography was a highly developed genre, and though Confucian literati might not admit it, few had qualms about viewing the most graphic pictures in private with their spouses or teahouse girls. One of the greatest Chinese novels, *The Golden Lotus,* widely printed before 1949, recounts in salacious detail the roisterous doings of a rich, wastrel merchant named Hsi-men Ching, his relations with his wives and concubines, and his affairs with his neighbors' wives, maids, and prostitutes. The novel, by an unknown sixteenth-century author, was condemned by outraged Western missionaries, but to the Chinese it had artistic appeal. It was the earliest Chinese book about the personal lives of believable, middle-class characters and the first to deal with women as individual personalities. Western writers of erotica did not match it in candor till very recent years.

In the first tryst between Hsi-men Ching and Golden Lotus, one of the heroines of the story who later becomes his concubine, the author sets the scene thus:

> In the days when Golden Lotus had performed the act of darkness with Chan [an earlier lover], that miserable old man had never been able to offer any substantial contribution to the proceedings, and not once had she been satisfied. Then she married Wu Ta. You may imagine the prowess which might be expected from Master Tom Thumb. It could hardly be described as heroic. Now she met Hsi-men Ching, whose capacity in such matters was unlimited and whose skill was exceptionally refined and cunning.
>
> Soon they had drunk as much as they desired, and a fit of passion swept over them. Hsi-men Ching's desire could no longer be restrained; he disclosed the treasure which sprang from his loins, and made the woman touch it with her delicate fingers. Upstanding it was, and flushed with pride, the black hair strong and bristling. A mighty warrior in very truth.
>
> Then Golden Lotus took off her clothes. Hsi-men Ching fondled the fragrant blossom. No down concealed it. It had all the fragrance and tenderness of fresh-made pastry, the softness and the appearance of a new-made pie. It was a thing so exquisite all the world would have desired it.*

In the traditional Chinese view, both prostitution and concubinage were part of nature, not subject to moral denunciation. Much the same casual attitude still prevails in Taiwan today. Once, when I lived in Taipei, I reported to the local police substation for our annual neighborhood security registration, a kind of census. At the head of a line of people stood two women—one, grown into comfortable middle age, with a plump figure and nondescript clothes; the other, ten years her junior, still slender and well made up. When queried by a policeman, they both gave their surname as Huang and listed the same address and apartment number.

"But you can't both be Mrs. Huang," the policeman objected. From the middle of the queue came a voice of explanation. "One's the wife, the other is the concubine." The crowd chuckled at the information, but the two women did not appear embarrassed and the police officer dutifully recorded their names, though taking a concubine is theoretically illegal in Taiwan.

From this traditional approach to sex, the Communists have adopted the first half—that the needs of society should take preference over an individual's pursuit of love—but they have reversed the second half—that sex itself is not sinful. Instead, as part of their effort to control society, the Communists have substituted something new, a rigid puritanism that does lead to guilt and repression. Peking's view comes through in the current vocabulary. There is no widely accepted polite expression in China today for "making love,"

*The Golden Lotus, translated by Clement Egerton (London: Routledge and Kegan Paul, 1939), Vol. I, p. 67.

though the term exists in Taiwan and Hong Kong, probably adopted from the West. When intercourse is mentioned in the Communist press, it always turns out to be lewd, deviant, described by phrases like "improper relations between men and women" or "relations between men and women done in a messy way." Even the vernacular term, "having relations," now has a sordid ring to Chinese.*

"You shouldn't talk about such things," Yang Wanhua, one of my closest friends, chided me when I asked for her reaction to the word. "It is a very dirty thing."

Slim and short, with a pixie turned-up nose, freckles, high, prominent cheekbones, and a forward, direct manner for a Chinese, Hua, as I called her, looked much younger than her age of forty. Her hair was cut very short, in boyish fashion, and her face was unlined. She kept herself in good physical condition by jogging three miles every morning at 5:30 on a track near the Physical Culture and Sports Commission where she worked. She was a reporter for the sports agency's English-language magazine, *Sports of China.* Hua was also, I came to learn, a Party member and cadre who had enjoyed a brief meteoric promotion during the Cultural Revolution when the radicals who took over the Sports Commission needed a token woman to show they were adhering to Mao's ideas.

Hua had been born to a family of schoolteachers in a small town near Canton. Soon after the Communists came to power and then the Korean War broke out in 1950, she dropped out of primary school. "It was the time of the revolutionary high tide," she explained. "I was very young and innocent and believed everything the Party said. I was an activist, so I joined the revolution at the age of twelve." Translated, it meant she went to work as a clerk in a Canton Party office. At night she continued to study on her own and practiced swimming with the local city team where she was a champion backstroker. She still moves gracefully, with the gait of an athlete, her legs springing rather than walking.

By the time Hua was nineteen, she had already been selected as a Party member, a very early age for the honor. She also had a boy friend. "He was the captain of the city soccer team," Hua told me with a hint of pride not long after we first met while we were both looking at rugs in the Friendship Store. She was acting as guide and interpreter for a group of visiting Australian sports coaches.

For a year, Hua and her boy friend used to go for walks in one of Canton's parks. Parks are one of the few places where young Chinese couples can find

*There is, however, a substantial lexicon of vulgar slang terms men use to describe sexual activity. "Give her a blast" is a street term meaning to screw. One ingenious Chinese ideogram is composed of two characters—one for the word enter, the other for flesh. It, too, means to fuck someone.

privacy, since there are almost no automobiles and unmarried people can't get their own housing. "It was very serious, almost like getting married, we were very much in love," Hua recalled. "We kissed a lot, but we never did more than that, there was no way." Her boy friend lived in a dormitory run by the Sports Commission where Chinese athletes stay with all their expenses paid. "Every day he had practice, and when he wasn't practicing, he had games to play," Hua continued. "So mostly I just went to watch him practice or play. On the night before a game, they wouldn't let the players out of the training camp."

But then something went wrong. "He came from a very bad class background," Hua related. "His father had been an officer in the Kuomintang, his older brother had been labeled a rightist in 1957. It didn't matter to me, but it did to him. He worried that I was too good for him, since I was a Party member and an activist. Later, when we broke up, he said it was because he didn't want me to have trouble because of him. He was the only person I ever loved."

Not long afterward, Hua's boss, a ranking city official, decided to send her to Peking to college, though she had only five years of formal education. Most of the other students were children of ranking cadres, diplomats, or army officers from Peking and on Sundays would go home, leaving her with only a few other male students on campus.

"Sundays were the worst days," Hua said. "The boys tried to flirt with me, and even though I used to lock my door, some of them would manage to get in." Her rebuffs angered her would-be suitors, who accused her of being unfriendly, a serious charge against a rising young Party member who should always be convivial and outgoing, a paragon of Communist rectitude.

"One boy in particular chased after me," Hua went on. "He told me he loved me and threatened to commit suicide if I didn't marry him. We had just had a student who killed himself by jumping in the furnace, so it worried me."

One day the Party secretary of her class, a man who could play an important role in her later life by what he wrote in her personal dossier, and a man she recollects as a good person, asked her for a talk. He counseled her to accept the boys more, and if the one student wanted to marry her, she should consent. The young man was already an officer in the People's Liberation Army, it would be a fine match. As happened to Lili, Hua was at the mercy of her Party leader, even in her most private life.

"I was afraid of getting in trouble. When that boy kept after me, finally I said yes, but on one condition. We had to have separate beds and he had to leave me alone. We were not to sleep together. I had been taught that sex was very dirty. It was all we ever heard in study classes and read in the papers."

This prudishness was also to be the seed of years of unhappiness. Hua unfolded her story gradually over a period of months, as we got to know each other better, each time stripping away another of the protective shells she had constructed to shield her psyche. I wondered if she wasn't taking a great risk, meeting me, a foreign journalist, and offering such a personal tale. But she usually took the initiative herself, calling me to arrange a meeting somewhere circumspect, on a street corner or in a bookshop. "I never tell any of my friends, or anyone in my office, about my life. It would be too dangerous. Even if they didn't report me, the next time there is a campaign, they would be forced to speak out," she said. "With a job like mine and a husband who is an army officer, I am supposed to be very happy." So ironically she found she could confide to a foreigner what she dared not say to another Chinese.

There was another reason for her friendship with me. She had once been a determined activist, throwing all of her considerable energy into working for the Party. But her sudden promotion in the Cultural Revolution and then demotion after it, all because of factional quarrels, had soured her on the Party. Now she found a new, illicit pleasure in defying the system—meeting with a foreigner, practicing her English, sometimes even affecting Western dress with a pair of tight-fitting slacks she had made at home from material a relative had sent her from Hong Kong. It was in this way she eventually came to the heart of her story.

It was an unhappy marriage from the start, Hua insisted. She and her husband soon had a baby girl, but she tried to resist him whenever he wanted to make love.

"We would get into terrible arguments about it. He was away most of the time, the army separated us, but when he came home, about once a month, he would look at me and I could tell what he wanted. How I hated it. He would take off his pants, and it made me so angry, sick, and tired. He kept trying to touch me, to caress my breast, but I wouldn't let him touch me, not even my hand. I was disgusted."

In the end, though, Hua said, her husband was stronger than she was and would overpower her. "It was always very painful. I didn't get wet, so he had a hard time getting inside me. It hurt me, and it hurt him too."

Eventually she developed a better defense mechanism. "Later, when he came after me and began to play with me, I felt like I was having a heart attack. My chest grew tight and I couldn't breathe. I would cry out. He would get afraid and leave me alone." Sometimes after they had intercourse, Hua recalled, she would rush to the toilet down the hallway to throw up.

"I went to the doctor many times for a check-up," Hua told me one day during a walk through the Forbidden City. "I was worried about my heart. He examined me very carefully. He did an electrocardiogram test, and made me run on one of those machines. But, of course, I was an athlete and still jog for an hour every morning, so there wasn't anything wrong with my heart."

I asked if she had told the doctor what brought on her symptoms. "No, I never told the doctor what caused it. That would be too terrible." Hua said she had never heard of Freud, but the Viennese psychiatrist would have recognized her symptoms, so much like those of nineteenth-century hysterical women he saw.

When I asked if she had ever experienced an orgasm, Hua's face furrowed into a frown. Just to make sure, I used a slang expression common in Taiwan and Hong Kong, and one some Chinese on the mainland I have talked to do know, *gao-chao,* literally, "high tide." "What is that?" she asked in reply. She had never had any such sensation. Intercourse, as she knew it, consumed three or four minutes and ended when her husband withdrew. The only position they had tried, she said, was for her to lie flat on her back and her husband to climb on top of her.

Had she ever tried oral sex then? I asked. "What is that, kissing?" she responded.

She was incredulous when I tried, with considerable embarrassment, to explain that in the United States and Europe fellatio and cunnilingus had become an accepted part of sexual conduct between men and women. "How could people do that, it's disgusting." When informed of the plot of the movie *Deep Throat,* she commented, "People in China would not watch such dirty things."

Despite our conversations, Hua did not feel she had missed anything sexually. "I am very strong. I never had such desires. I never think about doing such kinds of things. We are not like you people in the West, you kiss a girl and then you are changeable as the wind." Still, Hua liked to describe herself as a romantic. She said she had enjoyed watching the film *The Way We Were,* with Robert Redford and Barbra Streisand, which she had seen at an unofficial showing in a small theater, courtesy of a friend who had given her a coveted ticket. Hua could even sing the theme song from the movie, though in a hoarse, infelicitous voice. Once in a rare admission, she said, "Sometimes when I wake up at night, I dream about meeting a man who will really love me and make me happy. But I think that will never happen to me."

Hua was skeptical about the suggestion that she might be frigid and that the cause was psychological. She had not heard of the term. When told that in the United States some doctors and social scientists, like Alfred Kinsey and the team of Masters and Johnson, had spent years studying human sexual response and that books on the subject usually could be found on the bestseller list, she laughed. "What a waste of time for a doctor."

By this time I had grown increasingly nervous about the frequency of our contact—we saw each other about once a week—and over Hua's habit of phoning me in the Peking Hotel. Sooner or later, I suggested, the Public Security Bureau would get curious. It might be safer if we didn't see each other for a few weeks, I ventured. But Hua remained insistent on keeping up our meetings. "China is a socialist state, a people's state, we should have the right to pick our own friends," she contended. Then one evening she called to say she had been asked to accompany an official delegation to Shenyang, in the northeast, to examine some new sports facilities and would be gone for a week or two. She was surprised by the order to go, it was out of her usual line of work, but there was no hint of suspicion or foreboding in her voice.

A month later, when I hadn't heard from her, I became worried. I decided to risk calling her office from a pay phone. The man who answered wouldn't say where she was and demanded to know, "Where are you?" or what my *danwei* was. I hung up, thoroughly alarmed. I decided to ask Jan Wong to call Hua's office and pretend to be a relative visiting from Canton. This time the man in her office said, "She's away on business." How long would Hua be gone? Jan inquired. "A very long time," he replied. When would Hua return? Jan pressed him. "I don't know," he said with finality. Jan agreed it sounded very bad.

But it was not until a few months later when I met another person who worked in the Sports Commission that I found out what had happened. Hua had been arrested and sent to a labor reform camp for talking to me about her sex life. I had written an article about sex in China for the Sunday *New York Times Magazine* and, without mentioning any names, referred to some unhappy marriages in the Sports Commission. Unfortunately, the article had been reprinted in a classified bulletin that was circulated to members of the Party Central Committee. Evidently some official had taken offense at the revelation of such intimacies to a foreigner and ordered the police to investigate. Eventually, Hua was tracked down. Talking about sex in China, it turned out, was a crime. I was appalled, both at this realization and by my culpability in Hua's fate. Later another Chinese friend who had read a secret Central Committee document on Hua's case said I should not blame myself completely—there were other factors. But I never found out what they were.

China has not put out any statistics on the incidence of frigidity among women, or what percentage reach orgasm, so any conclusions on the subject must be fragmentary. But the more Chinese I talked with, the more it seemed that Hua was not unusual: that many Chinese women do not enjoy sex, or feel they shouldn't, that a number of Chinese men do not know how to satisfy their partners, and that there is widespread ignorance about sexual performance and fulfillment in China.

Susan Wilf, a Harvard graduate student who taught English in Peking and married a Chinese, recalled her amusement at the reaction of a fellow Chinese teacher when he heard her tape of the Donna Summer song "Love to Love Ya." The teacher, a happily married forty-year-old man with two children, whom Susan recalled as being very smart and a Party member, was puzzled at the recording. In it, the "Queen of Disco" moans, sighs, and pants as she sings, suggesting a woman reaching climax. But the teacher asked Susan, "What is she doing? Having a baby?"

Soon after my arrival in Peking, I witnessed an incident which suggested how people felt they had to mask their sexual feelings. I had gone to the large drugstore on Wangfujing Street to buy some medicine. As I was standing at the counter, a matronly looking woman in her early forties came in and asked a salesgirl for a packet of birth-control pills. These are dispensed free to all Chinese, either by pharmacies or a person's local street committee, as part of the government's ambitious program to cut the population growth rate to zero by the year 2000. So the transaction should have been perfectly natural.

But when the salesgirl, a young woman in her early twenties, with braids to her waist and wearing a white sanitary smock, noticed the customer's age, she raised an eyebrow.

"For you?" she inquired of the woman, whose salt and pepper hair was cropped in a severe, short bowl cut and firmly anchored with bobby pins.

"Oh no, for my daughter," the customer replied.

It seemed an obvious subterfuge. For given the woman's own age, her daughter was probably not old enough to get married in China. Legally, women in the cities must wait till they are at least twenty-five years old, men till they are twenty-seven or twenty-eight, depending on the location. This provision for delayed marriage is another part of Peking's birth-control plan to cut down on the number of offspring by requiring people to put off wedlock until they have fewer childbearing years left. Delayed marriage is even enshrined in China's 1978 constitution, like other rights and duties of individuals. So it seemed likely that the customer in the drugstore was too embarrassed to admit that she and her husband still made love.

"Most Chinese women I know treat sex as a duty to be performed and complain when their husbands want too much," the American woman who is married to a Chinese related. "After forty, they feel they have completed their duty and can stop it altogether." Her own husband, who is fifty years old, gets ribbed when he goes to pick up his monthly allotment of condoms because people think that by that age "neither he nor I should be interested anymore."

Another woman I got to know, a schoolteacher named Li Mei, did have a serious complaint against her husband. When we were walking in the park behind the Temple of the Sleeping Buddha, in the Fragrant Hills area to the west of Peking, she recounted why she wanted a divorce. Her words came in a rush, blunt for a Chinese, and seemed out of character for a plain-looking thirty-six-year-old woman who had been raised by a grandmother so strict that when she was six years old she was not allowed to play in a neighbor's house because they had a little boy. "Grandmother thought it was bad for a girl to do that. She was very feudal, a real Qing dynasty lady.

"I never refused my husband's demands to do it," Li Mei explained of her own troubles. "I had never been to bed with a man before we were married, so I didn't know anything about it. But he had a disease. He came too quickly, as soon as he penetrated me.

"Then he would fall asleep immediately. After the first year of marriage I developed insomnia. My husband would lie there and snore. At first I would just lie awake and think. But then I began to weep. I have cried a lot. For twelve years."

Both Hua and Li Mei said they had never had any sex education in school, or advice from friends. The closest Hua came to such instruction was a birth-control lecture given in her office, but she had not listened carefully. "It was too dirty." Their experience in this is typical—counseling in sex therapy, either in schoolroom courses or private consultation with doctors, simply does not exist, according to every Chinese I queried.

Much of this ignorance about sex and official puritanism prevail in the Soviet Union, too. For love and sex are usually equated with being cheap and bourgeois, with promiscuity; they are unrevolutionary, not worthy of brave hearts that should be beating with thoughts of building a new socialist nation. It is not so much that the Chinese Communists borrowed their sexual mores from the Russians, along with their ideology and Party apparatus, but that revolutionaries traditionally see themselves as dedicated, ascetic souls, and sex as a libertine sideshow that detracts from the more important tasks of economic development and preserving Party discipline. When the Chinese press, in a rare sensual moment, does offer advice on sexual matters, it is usually to urge that people sublimate their improper passions into more constructive work or study for the benefit of the nation, like the following exchange between a high school student and the paper *China Youth News:*

> *Comrade Editor:*
>   *I've already fallen in love with a girl student. But I don't have the courage to break off relations. What shall I do?*
>
>   *Tao Jie*

The response was written by a man who identified himself as a high school teacher.

"You have fallen in love with each other and it is not easy to break up," the teacher wrote. "But you have to make a decision. High school is a time of high aspiration. If you fall in love now, you will lose precious time. Your generation will play a vital role in modernizing China. You should concentrate on training yourself to be useful to the motherland. Love at your age is too soon. Besides, it will lead to a neglect of your studies. It takes will power to give up bad habits and will power to control emotions. You can keep your friendship with the girl, but avoid intimacy. See more of your classmates."

Peking's view that proper thinking can overcome biological imperatives was also reflected in another delicate colloquy between a youthful letter writer and the *China Youth News* on the subject of masturbation. The paper translated it as "hand lewdness."

> *Comrade Editor:*
> *I have a problem which I am embarrassed to talk about, that is, masturbation. For over a year now I've wanted to change but I can't. I feel my strength draining from me, and want to see a doctor, but I'm afraid of being laughed at. What should I do?*
>
> *Xiao Li, Henan province*

The answer was provided by a professor at the Peking Medical College:

> *After reading your letter, I feel it necessary to talk a bit about some facts of biology and hygiene.*
> *At first, many young people are simply curious and use masturbation to satisfy their sexual needs. But gradually it becomes a bad habit. While young people are developing, if they lack correct understanding of sex or are influenced by pornographic reading materials, they will masturbate. Done once in a while, it will have no harmful effect on one's health. But if it is done regularly, it will stimulate sex nerves to a certain degree which will produce fatigue, dizziness, listlessness, bad memory, and other phenomena which will hamper work and study. In more serious cases, it will lead to nervous breakdowns. After marriage, many disorders and premature ejaculation are very much related to masturbation.*
> *Second, what should you do about masturbating? I can tell you with confidence that this problem can be completely overcome and that it will not leave any aftereffects. You must put your main energy into study and work, and arrange your extra time to take part in cultural and sports activities in order to have a regulated life.*
> *Before sleeping at night, go jogging, wash your feet in warm water, and try to fall asleep immediately upon getting into bed. In the morning when you wake up, don't lie around. When sleeping, be careful not to sleep on your*

stomach, and don't use covers that are too heavy. Don't wear underpants that are too tight, and maintain cleanliness of the penis.

Will masturbation affect sex life after marriage? If your health is normal it generally won't be a problem. If your health is poor and you commit masturbation, then there may be some adverse effects.

Some people say that one drop of sperm is equal to many drops of blood, but there is no basis for this. Sperm is mainly made of protein, and the more you lose, the more you can produce. However, it causes wear and tear on the body. Therefore, young people already married should restrict themselves somewhat in terms of sex.

A pocket-sized pamphlet written by two other professors entitled *Sexual Knowledge,* the only sex manual I ever saw in China, took an even stricter view of the need to limit the frequency of intercourse. "Newlyweds will have very, very frequent sex right after marriage: that is, once every three to seven days," the professors postulated. As passions cool, they went on, married couples can expect a more normal routine of "once every week or two." But the guidebook, which was sold out within hours after it went on sale in the New China Bookstore near the Peking Hotel, suggested that individuals should make their own choices based on how they feel the morning after they have intercourse.

"When the frequency is balanced, they will not feel tired the day after. In fact, quite the opposite, their whole bodies are light and loose and relaxed and their temperaments are happy."

A sure sign of overindulgence, the professors caution, is if the sexual partners "feel tired, heavy-headed, if their legs are tingly and ticklish, if their heart beats rapidly, and they're short of breath or lose their appetite."

The good professors' view that sexual activity causes bodily deterioration and therefore should be conducted with moderation might spring straight out of a nineteenth-century tract inveighing against the evils of fornication. But they do not deal with a major conundrum for all Chinese young people. What are they supposed to do if by law women in the cities cannot legally marry till they are twenty-five and men twenty-seven or twenty-eight, for premarital sex is also taboo, if not actually illegal, and the penalties for being caught are often harsh. When Jan Wong was at Peking University, one of her friends, a very bright and attractive young man, passed the tough exams for entrance to a graduate school of engineering. But only a few weeks after the semester started, the school authorities received a letter signed by three women all claiming that he had "tricked" them into sleeping with him on the promise of marriage. Such a scoundrel, they charged, should not be allowed to have a chance at graduate school, a very prestigious opportunity since there are only about 8,000 places for all of

China's one billion people. The school agreed, and he was kicked out, a serious blow to his career.

When A. M. Rosenthal, the Executive Editor of *The New York Times,* visited China in 1981, he was taken to a reformatory for teen-agers in Shanghai. In the girls' wing he walked into a room where a dozen youths were fixing boxes. Rosenthal asked one of the girls why she was there. She stood up immediately, looked him straight in the eye, and said with pain, "My name is Ma Xiulan. I am eighteen years old. I am here because I had affairs with boys." In another room where a group of girls were working on sewing machines, Rosenthal repeated the question and got the same answer. Later the principal explained that most of the girls were in the reformatory for having affairs with boys—not prostitution, but the crime of sex without sanction.

If masturbation can be dangerous to your health and making love must await marriage, homosexuality is truly *terra incognita* in China. I have never seen a reference to it in the Chinese press—it is too deviant even to mention. Classical Chinese literature contains a number of examples of homosexual lovers, but most Chinese today seem to have only a vague idea of what this means. A twenty-eight-year-old man who had special access to American newspapers and magazines and had read about Gay Liberation once asked me how two men could possibly mate. He was genuinely puzzled. When John Roderick, the veteran correspondent of the Associated Press, arrived in Peking to open his agency's bureau in early 1979, his government-assigned interpreter startled him with a seemingly irrelevant question soon after they met. "Do you know what we do with homosexuals here in China?" he asked. No, replied Roderick, he didn't know. "We shoot them," the interpreter said.

On the other hand, it is also true that Chinese, like other Asians, accept certain forms of behavior as natural that Westerners have tended to see in homosexual terms, like men walking down the street holding hands, or helping each other scrub down in public bathhouses. When I was studying Chinese in Taiwan, it took me some time to get accustomed to a Chinese male student friend taking me by the arm when we went downtown. I was also surprised later when another acquaintance put his hand on my thigh as we drove in a taxi and kept it there for much of the ride. It was only a gesture of companionship. Foreign tourists in China often misunderstand when they see two People's Liberation Army soldiers in uniform locked hand in hand.

Nevertheless there do seem to be a few, a tiny handful, of homosexuals in China, tucked away deep in the closet, and they face a real threat of social ostracism and political reprisal. A middle-aged Chinese intellectual told me of an instance of which he knew. In a Peking factory there was an older worker who was a homosexual and who knew that one of the younger workers had not confessed he had a close relative who was a former landlord. The older man used this knowledge to blackmail the junior man into engaging in sex with him. Finally the younger worker calculated that the political charge against him was the lesser of two evils and reported the affair. Both men were heavily criticized in meetings in the factory.

A friend of Jan's told her about a distant relative who has been a lesbian for years. She and her partner, both nurses, have been together since the 1940s. They sleep together on the same bed and make no secret of their relationship. All the neighbors know, but have not interfered, partly because the two women haven't caused any trouble, and partly because the neighbors feel the women's only problem is that they haven't found a man to straighten them out. Both men and women normally come under enormous pressure from relatives to get married, so there are few "old maids" in China.

The two nurses did get in trouble during the Cultural Revolution, however. They had adopted a young girl, a relative of one of them. The daughter hated them for the unusual situation in which she was raised. After the Cultural Revolution began the girl became a Red Guard and one day led her faction to the women's home and exposed them. She also pointed out where they had buried their savings under the floor. Jan's friend speculated that establishing such a lesbian union today would be impossible. "You couldn't apply for housing, like other newlyweds," she explained, laughing with a mixture of shock and amusement. Even straight couples often have to wait for several years for an apartment, given China's housing shortage.

Still, the strict puritanical morality prescribed by Peking is beginning to give way, eroded by the troubles of the Cultural Revolution just as education, factory production, and Communist Party discipline have been undermined. When Mao encouraged gangs of youthful Red Guards to traverse the country, going from city to city to batter Party cadres, they often ended up sleeping together, regardless of sex, in railroad trains, crowded barracks, or whatever shelter they could find. The old barriers against intimacy began to tumble. When Mao also shipped millions of city school graduates off to the countryside, supposedly to toughen their revolutionary fiber, they again found themselves thrown together, away from parental authority. The commune authorities often housed them together for convenience, and the young city men and women discovered the best solace against the rigors of village life lay in companionships they could not have formed at home.

As a result, I found, while many young men may still want their wives to be virgins, fewer are. A radar technician in the air force whom I met in a small restaurant when I sat down at a table where he was dining confessed later that he himself was still a virgin. "But I'm almost the only one of my friends who is," he explained. It was hard to tell whether he was boasting or complaining.

"My father is a high-ranking cadre," he said, "and I'm afraid to have relations with a woman. If I did, and I didn't like her and didn't want to marry her, she might charge me with rape," the same problem which got the student expelled from Peking University. Most women, he seemed convinced, were interested in him only because of his family's standing.

A tall, good-looking lathe operator in a Peking machinery factory said that premarital sex was definitely on the increase among his friends in the past few years. "It started in the Cultural Revolution when there was no law," he observed. "But the real problem is, the government says we can't get married till we are twenty-eight. How can anyone wait that long to have relations?" He also blamed China's housing shortage. "Even when I got to be twenty-eight and my girl friend was twenty-five, we still couldn't get our own apartment. We had to wait three more years for it. Both of us were afraid that if we waited till we finally had our own housing to make love, we would be too old." So he and his girl friend, a fellow factory worker, started sleeping together in his parents' apartment. There is a term for this arrangement, he said, a pun, *zhu-li.* It means "assistant," but also "live-in." Among his friends, he said, almost everyone now has been a "live-in" before they get married. "My parents understood, I just didn't tell my *danwei,*" the worker related. He was then thirty-three years old and happily married, with a two-year-old daughter.

Another indication of the changing morality is that despite all the official pressure, some Chinese women now do get pregnant before marriage, even teen-agers. David Eisenberg, a graduate of the Harvard Medical School who spent a year working in the Institute for Traditional Chinese Medicine in Peking, said that when a European doctor there had the rare chance to observe the institute's gynecology ward, he saw twelve pregnant and unmarried women come in for abortions during a two-week period. They ranged in age from seventeen to twenty-four, Dr. Eisenberg said. One, who was twenty-two, had come in for the second time. She was with her boy friend and was weeping.

In the countryside, where the government's hand sits more lightly, premarital sex may be easier than in the cities even though rural life is supposed to be more conservative. Maggie Mosher, an American-Chinese woman who spent a year with her sociologist husband conducting interviews in her ancestral village in Guangdong province, near Hong Kong, calculated that 70 percent of the young women she talked to had been pregnant before getting married. This was not true of women above thirty, she said, so it seemed to be a new development. That so many young people ignored the regime's official policy suggested how deeply cynicism has spread.

Maggie remembered an incident when a neighbor of hers, already six months pregnant, was collected by her new in-laws and driven to their house on the back of a bike (bicycles have replaced sedan chairs in the contemporary wedding party). "It was a wonderful sight, sitting on the bike with her belly sticking out."

In the cities, women in the past few years have started to complain about men pinching their bottoms or slipping hands inside their clothes while riding on the tightly packed buses. On a December afternoon, after I boarded the number 1 bus near the old Democracy Wall on Changan Boulevard, I noticed a comely woman in her late twenties berating a man squeezed next to her. He had his hand pressed firmly between her legs, though she was still well protected by layers of winter cotton-paded pants.

"If you touch me again, I'll hit you," she warned loud enough for most of us passengers to hear. People stared. A minute later, making good her threat, she cracked him in the chest with her elbow. She was still muttering when she pushed her way to the door and got off at the Square of the Gate of Heavenly Peace.

The women's dormitory at the Foreign Languages Institute has occasionally been troubled by flashers. An American student related an incident that happened to her as she was reading one evening in her room. A man in his early twenties she had seen hanging around campus, dressed in a Western-style jacket belted at the waist, walked in and took down his pants. She had to scream to get him to leave. The woman suspected he was a factory worker rather than a student, but he managed to get into the dorm more than once.

The same things happen in New York and Tokyo; but that's the point. Chinese are like other people. They get hungry, sleepy, and feel the tug of sexual desire. The Communists in the end have not been able to legislate sexuality. Paradoxically, it's easier for Chinese to break the rules when they are in a crowd. At home, or in their unit, they would be subject to the usual pressures and likely to be detected. Perhaps that's why young men in China's cities have become increasingly brazen in trying to pick up girls on the street, something unheard of until the past few years.

Xiaopei, a translator at Peking Radio with large almond eyes and a button nose, said it happened a number of times to her as she was riding her bicycle downtown. "The surprising thing was, they were rather cultured types, well-dressed, not like those punks you see with mustaches and foreign-style sunglasses," she recalled.

"One day when I was riding along, I heard a voice behind me call, 'Miss, let's go to the movies. I have lots of tickets.'

"I suppose he meant to impress me, that he was the son of a high cadre with all those tickets, so I told him to get lost. I said I was already old and married. But he laughed. 'You look only like a sixth grader.'

"Eventually we were approaching the Peking Hotel and I told him I had to go in on business," also an an impressive remark for a Chinese, indicating that she must hold an important post necessitating contact with foreigners. "But not to be outdone, he retorted, 'What's so great about that? I often go in there to eat.' " But when she pedaled into the hotel parking lot, he couldn't follow her and had to ride off.

To the Chinese this increase in attempted pickups is one of the clearest indications of the general breakdown in authority and morality that accompanied the Cultural Revolution. For most Chinese have always felt awkward just striking up friendships in the office or during chance encounters on a train or in a restaurant. They are much more comfortable waiting to be introduced by a friend or relative, in the traditional style. Connections, *guan-xi,* in China are not formed haphazardly and on individual whim, as in the West, but are built up guardedly over a long period. It is the opposite of the American craze for singles bars. A Chinese depends on his group and uses a go-between to deal with strangers.

Our friend Miao, Mrs. Wang, sometimes acted as a matchmaker, she told me one evening at dinner. She usually became involved because she knew either the young man or woman and their families asked her to help locate a suitable partner. Her first step, she explained, was to study details of any prospective candidate's class background, his or her family's income, the education record of each, job, and physical appearance. Cadres looked for other cadres, she said, intellectuals were picky about wanting to marry only intellectuals, and workers preferred other workers.

The other main principle she noticed was that "boys want a girl who is good-looking, while girls want a boy with a good job and money."

In the past few years, she added, young women had become almost obsessed with money in deciding on a potential husband. "It's a bad thing, but they are all doing it," Miao commented. In her view, it was again a result of the Cultural Revolution, for with the Communists' denunciation of love as vulgar, cheap, and bourgeois, ironically what took its place was the very unrevolutionary notion that a woman should make a good match in material terms.

In fact, she related, there is a popular saying that a bridegroom in the cities must be able to supply "the ten musts for marriage." Number one is one set of furniture. Two is both of the husband's parents out of the way or a separate apartment. Three stands for the "three things that go around," a wristwatch, sewing machine, and bicycle. Four is "four seasons all wearing fine material," or to have good clothes. Five is "the five extremities in good shape," or be in good health and handsome. Six is "the six relations not concerned," or no poor relatives to take care of. Seven, a 70-yuan-a-month salary, well above average. Eight, "eight ways flexible," someone who is smooth and slick in social relations. Nine, a pun on avoiding liquor, which rhymes with the word for nine in Chinese. Ten, "ten parts," or completely obedient to one's wife.

The Communists actually outlawed the old practice of bride price in their progressive family law of 1950. But the New China News Agency admitted that during 1980 newlyweds in Peking spent an average of 1,554 yuan ($1,036) on purchases connected with their marriage, the great bulk of it by the groom and his family. The figure represents more than a year's salary for both bride and groom.

Miao said that after she located someone whom she thought would make a good partner for her own young man or woman, normally through another go-between, she fixed a day for the couple to meet. Her preference was for a neutral location away from both sets of parents. That way, if either party didn't like the prospective mate, there would be no need to go through with the marriage and no loss of face. Miao always consulted an old family book of Chinese astrology in picking the day for the first meeting.

It was on a propitious Sunday afternoon in September that I followed Miao and one of her young men to the Sun Yat-sen Park at the side of the Forbidden City. The park, set with potted plants tended by gardeners, had stone paths for walking and rows of cypress trees and gnarled pines. It is also dotted with old pavilions dating from the time when it was part of the Imperial City. The young woman Miao had chosen showed up dressed in a neatly pressed white blouse and gray slacks, her hair in two long braids. While Miao and her counterpart chatted for fifteen minutes, sitting on a wooden bench, the new couple eyed each other gingerly, exchanging a few sentences. Later, the young man expressed his general satisfaction, though he felt the girl's neck was too short and her skin too dark. The first criterion of beauty, and sex appeal, to most Chinese men, is white skin, a heritage perhaps of feudal days when proper upper-class ladies stayed indoors and protected their delicate bodies from the sun, unlike peasant girls. For her part in the affair, Miao was rewarded with presents of cloth, some extra grain coupons, and a second-hand bicycle.

One time, Miao confessed, she had great trouble finding a suitable match —it was for a thirty-one-year-old woman who hadn't gotten married because she had been sent to work as a teacher in a village several hours' bus ride from Peking. The woman was a university graduate and, as an intellectual, in Chinese terms, was not interested in any man on the local commune. "She also wasn't exactly good-looking," Miao added with a wink. Few Chinese men want to marry a woman over thirty, the year is a kind of magic cut-off date, the difference between being eligible and being a spinster. But Miao finally, after interviewing twenty-four candidates, found a scientist in his fifties who had been trained in the United States and then attacked as a rightist because of his American education. His political label had prevented him from finding a wife before.

Not all couples go through formal matchmakers. Miao and Li had met while they were both in the army. He was a dashing actor in a theater troupe, and she spotted him when he came to her company to perform. She knew a friend of his in the troupe and boldly asked for an introduction after the show. "It was she who chased after me," Li recalled. "She kept asking me to the movies or to go for walks in the park." She even took the initiative in kissing him, he claimed, over Miao's mock protest. He still remembered the place—it was in her barracks. Her roommates had all arranged to go out and leave them alone for a few hours, the only way for them to get privacy. But it had taken him four years to make up his mind, a decision he reached only when he was about to be sent off to labor in the countryside late in the Cultural Revolution. Their wedding was simple; they registered at the local civil affairs office, then he hosted a small dinner party with beer and *maotai* in his quarters. His commanding officer came and made a speech urging them to contribute to the Cultural Revolution. Then they had to bow from the waist three times to a statue of Chairman Mao. There was no honeymoon. Like many Chinese, they had neither the money to afford one nor were they given any time off by their *danwei*.

The most startling of all the changes in sexual mores that have come with the breakdown in the Communists' authority after the Cultural Revolution has been a small revival of prostitution. It is a very sensitive subject to Peking, for in the early 1950s, when the Communists were at the zenith of their zeal and power, they moved forcefully to eradicate the world's oldest profession, condemning it as a scourge of the old feudal society. The brothels were closed and the whores rehabilitated, an accomplishment of which they often boasted.

While reporting on China from Hong Kong, I heard rumors that street-walkers had reappeared in some cities. A construction worker from Canton, who escaped to Hong Kong, claimed he had paid two yuan ($1.33) to procure a woman he met on a busy street near the Pearl River in the downtown part of the city. Such women, he said, were called "roadside chickens," after the name of a Cantonese dish, and were easy to spot if you knew the signals. Some left the top two buttons on their shirts undone; some kept a handkerchief sticking halfway out of a pocket; others combed their hair so it covered one eye in an alluring fashion.

Still, I was skeptical about such stories. So many visiting foreigners for years had said China had abolished prostitution, it was an accepted fact. Hence I was not prepared for what I found at the Peace Cafe in Peking. It was a ten-minute walk from the Peking Hotel, past the sycamore trees on

Wangfujing Street, the darkened headquarters of the *People's Daily* and the bustling Peking Number One Department Store, or "One Hundred Goods Big Building" in Chinese. Turning right at the Four Unities Hair Salon, now decorated with photos of Western models, you enter Goldfish Alley, one of the thousands of narrow streets, or *hutongs,* which make up the heart of old Peking. The darkened alley was jammed with bicyclists, all clanging their tinny horns in the shadows—Chinese bikes don't have lights. On the outside the Peace Cafe was a nondescript gray-brick edifice with two small carved-stone lions guarding the Chinese-style red doors. A drunk had vomited neatly in the doorway. Inside, a heavy cloud of cigarette smoke hung in the glare of the bare fluorescent lights, mixed with the smell of stale beer. The cafe was made up of two rooms, each jammed with customers seated on folding chairs at tables covered with dirty plastic cloths. By the door was a small fishpond with several orange carp floating lazily in it. Despite its lack of decor, for six months during 1979, before the police cracked down, it became a hangout for Peking's trendy young set, the scene—in American terms a cross between the old neighborhood drugstore and a seedy Eighth Avenue bar in New York. Some of the patrons—factory workers, soldiers, unemployed high school graduates waiting for their job assignments, children of high-ranking cadres—went only to drink beer or indulge in the Peace Cafe's special, a chocolate sundae complete with whipped cream and nuts. They were there to see and be seen. Others went to make assignations.

One of the first nights I went, a group of four soldiers in uniform were sitting near the entrance transfixed by the blare of a large, shiny, new Japanese cassette tape recorder with twin speakers. It was playing the beat of a pop recording star from Hong Kong, and on the table in front of them they had strewn a collection of other cassettes, emblazoned with pictures of crooning female vocalists from Taiwan and Hong Kong. The tapes were a boast of the connections which had enabled them to purchase such forbidden material, and a challenge to the authorities.

At another table a woman in her twenties, dressed in a bright-blue sweater, with a metal chain around her neck and blue pants that had been cut several inches closer to her hips than normal, jumped up and embraced a man who had just strutted in. She had brightened her mouth with lipstick, and her hair had been curled by one of those machines used in Chinese beauty parlors that look like a relic from the set of a Frankenstein movie, all wires and tubes designed to electrocute rather than coif the hair. The effect was disastrous. But it was evidently the effort and daring that went into it, rather than the aesthetic result, that counted. When the man and woman sat down, he thrust his hand into her lap and began rubbing between her legs.

Later, outside, as I was walking home, I was approached by a short, wiry, crew-cut young Chinese who had also just left the Peace Cafe. He was dressed in the green garb of the People's Liberation Army, minus the red tags on his collar, which are worn to denote a soldier on active service. Many soldiers after they are demobilized continue to wear their old uniforms, but strip the red tags off. It saves money on clothes and carries extra prestige.

"I'm in the army, but I take my tags off so no one will know," the man explained, as if by way of introduction. "My name is Wang Wei," "Benefit the People" Wang. He spit the words out staccato, like the sound of a machine gun. "My father is a general. I've got a lot of foreign friends," and he mentioned the Dutch ambassador.

"I can fix you up with a young girl, if you want," he went on, with hardly a pause or a connecting link. "She's fourteen, very cute. You can take her home. But you'd better show up if I get her. The other day I got one for a foreign friend and then he didn't come. She was very mad."

I wasn't sure if he could really be what he sounded, a pimp, or whether this was just braggadocio. To find out, I arranged to go back the next evening with Orville Schell, the writer, and an old Harvard classmate, who was visiting Peking.

But Wang Wei was there, sitting in the back of the Peace Cafe with three women. They looked to be in their twenties, not fourteen, but he assured us they were, in fact, *yeh ji,* "wild pheasants," the Peking slang for a strumpet. Did we want to take them out? One was a square, solidly built woman of twenty-three clad in a faded gray jacket and baggy pants. Her figure and clothes matched her daytime job as a steelworker in Peking's Capital Iron and Steel Plant. But she had put on lipstick and cut her hair in the China-doll style, with long bangs over her eyes. To a foreigner that might not make much of a difference in her overall appearance. But in China, nuance can be everything. She was also smoking a cigarette, another tip-off. Almost no young women smoke in public in China.

"How about it?" Wang Wei asked us. After some shuffling, Orville and I decided that if we wanted to see how the operation worked, and if we were going to talk with the women themselves, we should go outside with them. Wang Wei followed. From somewhere he had acquired a trench coat and an old battered felt hat, the kind worn in China in the 1930s during the Nationalist period. We stood in a dark corner of the alley, under a stone wall, where the dim streetlights did not reach. The sharp stench of urine from a public toilet nearby carried to us. The whole scene conjured up a Chinese gangster film, the kind the Communists like to make about the bad old days before Liberation.

When we asked how much, Wang Wei suggested 200 or 300 yuan, or $133 to $200. We laughed. The price for Chinese is $2.78 I replied, repeating what other Chinese had told me. Fifty-three dollars then, he retorted.

Eventually we agreed on $20 for the two of us. The price for foreigners is always higher—in restaurants, museums, even for underground journals or prostitutes.

Wang Wei turned over a share to one of the women, named Wu Yao, who had been selected to go with us. We only wanted to talk, we told her. She looked puzzled but, having been paid, wanted to get whatever it was over with quickly.

"I have to get home," she advised, placing her hands on her broad hips and staring at us. She, too, had put on lipstick and blackened her eyebrows, but there was little alluring about her, except her availability. "My parents try to keep tight control over me. They want me back home by nine o'clock every night," she told us in a hard voice. Then how did she manage to go to the Peace Cafe? "I fool them. I tell them I am going over to a friend's house."

She was a nurse, she continued, and earned 22 yuan ($15) a month, less than half what Peking officially calls an average salary. She began making love when she was seventeen, in high school, she said. "It's pretty common now in school." Where could people go to do it, we asked, given the absence of privacy? "It's not so hard. You can use someone's house when their parents or brothers and sisters are at work."

She had been to bed with a large number of men, including overseas Chinese, Pakistanis, and Africans. She didn't think it was too risky. "You can get an abortion if you need it. Take the back door. Pay the doctor some money, there's no problem."

A group of men walked by where we were still standing. One called to her. It was her brother, she said. Her parents were looking for her. She had to go.

A few months later, after a number of foreign correspondents had written about the Peace Cafe, Wu was arrested. She and the pimps "corrupted the reputation of China and detracted from the fame of our country," the *People's Daily* charged.

If the Cultural Revolution had unintentionally contributed to a breakdown in sexual mores, the Communists had very deliberately set about politicizing marriage. Since 1949 any couple that wants to get married must first receive clearance from the Party secretary of their *danwei*. Only then can they legally register their marriage. For many people, those with "clean" class backgrounds, this is routine. But for Communist Party members and army officers, who carry extra responsibility, a more thorough investigation is made of their intended mate's political record. The higher the rank, the more careful the scrutiny, Chinese say.

And some couples with political blemishes are denied permission, evidently to preserve public security. Yang Fuguo, a clerk in a hospital in Canton, was turned down when he applied to marry a petite, pretty nurse.

"They didn't have to tell me the reason, only the verdict—no," said Yang, a short, direct man in his late thirties with wiry hair and crooked teeth.

"I never found out why, but eventually we began to piece things together, from hints. Apparently someone had branded her a spy risk during the Cultural Revolution because she had a sister in the United States and other relatives in Hong Kong. This was put in her dossier. Of course, we never saw the dossier, that was impossible. And they wouldn't confirm it."

Yang kept on seeing the nurse, however, and was ordered not to talk to her anymore. When he still refused to give her up, he was transferred to a remote state farm in the mountains. Only six years later, after the downfall of Lin Biao, the former Defense Minister, when the political leadership in the hospital changed, were they allowed to marry.

The Communists' strict regulation of marriage and their puritanical sexual code have not deterred China's leaders from enjoying active sex lives themselves. High political position, if not an aphrodisiac, has proved a definite advantage in romantic conquests, much as it does in securing such privileges as better housing, chauffeured cars, and good jobs for one's children. Mao married four times. His first marriage was arranged by his father when he was only thirteen to a local peasant girl and was never consummated. His second wife, Yang Kaihui, was the daughter of a favorite professor. What began as an intellectual affair, however, led to her pregnancy and then a swift wedding. Today the official interpretation of Mao holds that Yang was the Chairman's favorite, but he had left her before she was picked up by the Kuomintang and beheaded.

By this time, in fact, Mao was already living with a Communist woman partisan, He Zizhen, who accompanied him on the Long March despite being wounded badly enough to require being carried on a stretcher. In the caves of Yanan, the Communists' wartime headquarters in the northwest, this relationship, too, deteriorated. Mao's fancy was caught by a comely, aggressive young actress from Shanghai who ventured to Yanan and made herself conspicuous by sitting in the front row at one of his lectures. He Zizhen was packed off to the Soviet Union for medical care—on her return to China she was confined to a mental hospital from about 1939 until recently—and Mao married the actress, who took the name of Jiang Qing.

"Sex is engaging in the first rounds, but what sustains interest in the long run is power," Jiang Qing later told her American biographer, Roxanne Witke. The Great Helmsman put it somewhat differently: "Political power grows out of the barrel of a gun," he said in his most widely quoted aphorism.

Before the Cultural Revolution, China's Party leaders used to hold dances to which attractive and politically reliable young women were invited. A middle-aged woman cadre who worked for a film studio recalled she often had been escorted to these dances on Saturday nights in the Peking Hotel in the early 1960s, when she was a college student in the capital, by a deputy mayor. On several other occasions she was invited to a special guesthouse behind the Forbidden City, where a number of senior officials lived, for dances given by Foreign Minister Chen Yi, a veteran military officer. Twice she found herself included in parties for Mao and Premier Zhou and ended up dancing with them. "Zhou was very light on his feet," she recalled. "Mao just asked me questions like, 'Where do you work, what is your parents' background?' I was too nervous to really talk to them." From the outset of the Cultural Revolution in 1966, of course, dancing was proscribed as a decadent bourgeois diversion, and even today, despite a certain revival, it can lead to political trouble for those who dare take the floor.

Even in Mao's later years he seems to have sustained a fondness for the opposite sex and surrounded himself with young women, like the Brooklyn-born Nancy Tang, his English interpreter, and Wang Hairong, the daughter of a distant relative, whose job was to put his Delphic utterances into more comprehensible Chinese. Peking gossip holds that Mao also had a final mistress, a very pretty woman named Zhang Yufeng, whom he appointed his personal secretary. To pacify her husband, Mao awarded him a handsome post as deputy chief in a Central Committee office. But Jiang Qing hated her, the story goes, and, when Mao died in September 1976, had her arrested. A month later, with Jiang Qing's own downfall, Zhang was ordered to write a confession detailing her knowledge of the Gang of Four's conspiracies, which was then used in compiling the official dossier against them.

The story did not end there, however. Hua Guofeng, then the newly appointed Party Chairman, is said to have feared Zhang because of all she knew about Mao's last years (the basis of Hua's claim to legitimacy was that Mao personally selected him as his successor). So Hua, too, had her locked up in a house outside Peking until she eventually committed suicide by slashing her wrists with glass from a bathroom window.

Several Chinese acquaintances regaled me with accounts of the adventures of Lin Like, the son of the late Defense Minister Lin Biao who reportedly died in an airplane crash after trying to assassinate Mao. The younger Lin, a ranking air force officer, had looked at nearly 10,000 photographs of young women in search of the most beautiful wife in China, they said. The wives of two senior Party officials also cruised Wangfujing, Peking's Fifth Avenue, looking for candidates. Eventually, using the pretext of a hunt for actresses and dancers, ten semifinalists were selected, my friends said they had read in a Central Committee document on Lin. Lin then picked three—one a Chinese, one a member of the Bai minority, and the third a member of the Miao minority in southwest China. (China, too, has its myths that ethnic minorities somehow are sexier or enjoy more sexual prowess.) But Lin died in the plane crash with his father before he finally got married.

On a more mundane level, there is evidence that local party officials and army officers have more than occasionally utilized their ranks for sexual favors. Once on a train from Hangzhou to Shanghai I was seated behind three elderly navy officers who looked to be in their sixties. Each was accompanied by an aide. Only, unlike in the United States, the aides were all women, in their early twenties, and pretty. The car was hot from the steam radiators, and the three women had taken off their blue uniform jackets. Underneath, each had on a matching outfit, with a round-collared blouse, sweater, and socks, one in blue, one in pink, and the other in yellow. Few ordinary Chinese could indulge such tastes.

The most flagrant abuses, however, cropped up in Mao's idealistic program to resettle young school graduates from the cities in the countryside. Rusticated in villages far from home, these young women had no relatives to protect them and were at the mercy of the local officials for food, work points, and housing. The *China Youth News* once printed a letter accusing the head of a state farm in Heilongjiang province, a certain Yan Ziyang, of raping or "behaving indecently" toward eight of the eleven rusticated women stationed there. The letter was signed "Families of the Victims." In response, an investigation was carried out and the paper published the findings in the form of a letter to the families:

"The facts in your letter are basically true. Yan raped two female, educated youths [the term for people resettled in the countryside], and had indecent behavior toward five others. This is very bad."

Yan was dismissed from the Party and arrested, though the paper never reported what further punishment he suffered.

A number of Chinese I knew told similar tales of advances by superiors, sometimes ending in rape, but the most poignant story came from an accountant. He had a girl friend who was a nurse in an army hospital in Chanjiang, a port in southern China near Hainan island. She was very idealistic, always kind and sympathetic to her patients, and they adored her, the accountant recalled.

During the Cultural Revolution, the political commissar of the local garrison took a fancy to her and began coming around to her apartment, first asking, then demanding, that she sleep with him. She was unusually pretty and delicate and had little defense. She told her boy friend that the officer had threatened her with a pistol to coerce her. But the accountant suspected the intimidation was more political—a suggestion that she might be sent to a labor camp.

So she gave in—not once, but many times over a period of several months. And she was not the only victim on the base. The officer also raped twenty other women, the accountant charged. Several years later, when the Cultural Revolution was over, he persuaded her to press a complaint against the officer.

"It was a daring and foolhardy thing to do," the accountant recalled. They took the case to a military tribunal in Canton, but after a cursory hearing, the court dismissed her charges, for the officer argued that he was a veteran guerrilla fighter; she was from a bad class background with relatives overseas. How could he have raped her? It was she who had seduced him, he asserted.

"He turned the dead cat toward her," the accountant commented, a Chinese phrase equivalent to turning the tables on someone.

Now the officer really had her at his mercy. First she was put on half pay. Later all her income was stopped. Next he ordered her transferred to a remote state farm in the mountains where she was made a cattle herder. Unable to endure the hardships, she finally ran away, back to her family home in Canton. Her sister, who was also a friend of mine, was shocked by her appearance, emaciated, with large welts from insect bites that had not been treated, because she was denied medicine.

Unfortunately, her mother was not sympathetic. "Mother said she was a fool for trying to get justice," her sister related. "Mother's view was, you have to live with the system." Because she had absconded, she did not have a valid household registration certificate for Canton and therefore no ration cards for food and no hope of getting a job.

Finally, driven by her family's rejection, she committed suicide. By Chinese practice, that sealed her guilt. At the state farm, when her sister went to claim her belongings, she found her dormitory window had been painted black and her name on the local records was marked with a black cross.

In the aftermath, her mother was officially accused of driving her to suicide, for their neighbors in Canton had overheard a family quarrel the day before her death.

China does not release nationwide figures on crime, so it is difficult to judge the incidence of rape. But during a visit to the main Shanghai municipal prison, a somber compound of concrete buildings stained dark gray by the years, the political commissar told me that rape was the second most common crime for which his prisoners had been convicted, trailing only robbery. Indeed, in the prison infirmary, of the three inmates I talked to, one had been convicted for rape, another for robbery, and a third for being a Kuomintang spy.

The impression that rape is a widespread problem is confirmed by other pieces of evidence. Many of the posters I have seen outside courthouses around China, detailing the misdeeds of recently convicted criminals, are for rape. Then there was the story of Lihua, the young petitioner I saw many times in Peking, who killed a youth after he tried to rape her in the countryside. Lihua also told me about the case of a sixteen-year-old high school student in her dorm. The girl had trouble with her homework, Lihua said, but her father and mother, illiterate construction workers, were of little help. Hence, she often went across the hall to a thirty-year-old Communist party member and technician for assistance. Their relationship was so close she even called him "Uncle." One day, however, when her mother came home she noticed the girl was distraught. When her mother asked why, she cried but would not explain. So her mother took out a large kitchen chopper, like an American butcher's knife, and threatened her. "Uncle" had raped her, the girl confessed. He was arrested by the Public Security Bureau.

American psychiatrists now generally believe that rape is less a sexual crime, less an overwhelming need for sexual gratification, than an act brought on by "uncontrolled hostility, a sense of inadequacy or a quest for power," as Dr. Carol C. Nadelson, a specialist on rape, put it.* Whether this finding applies equally in China remains a matter of speculation, for no Chinese I talked with ever heard of a study of rape. Indeed, they were not aware of any counseling for rape victims either. Rape remains off limits, a subject too sensitive for discussion.

Yet the evidence for an interconnection in China between the urge for power and rape, and between politics and sex, is there. The most spectacular case that occurred during my stay in Peking was that of the Xiong twins, a pair of twenty-seven-year-old brothers in the lakeside city of Hangzhou whose father was an army general. The brothers, Xiong Beiping and Xiong Zhiping, developed a bad reputation from an early age. In school they refused to study, often were truant, and beat up their seventy-year-old principal when he tried to discipline them, according to later accounts in the Chinese press. After they were admitted to the army, they would not take part in physical training. Returned to civilian life and given jobs in a factory, they failed to show up for work. They lived in a large house, walled off from the street, with their own garden, a "pleasure nest," the China Youth News later called it. From here they sallied forth to a nearby park to lure young women with blandishments like tickets to concerts, the chance to watch television (a novelty in China), or the promise of love and marriage. Over a period of four years, from 1974 to 1978, they and a gang of their friends, nicknamed "Rotten Eggplant," "Big Head," and "the Nun," raped 106 women. On occasion they also held kangaroo court in their house, forcing women they had brought in to kneel on the floor and be tried. Their neighbors and the police were aware of the twins' activities but did nothing.

One day the twins' younger sister invited a classmate to spend the night at their house. Beiping entered the room where the girl was sleeping and

*Dr. Carol C. Nadelson, "Rapist and Victim," The New England Journal of Medicine, Vol. 297, No. 14, Oct. 6, 1977, p. 784.

raped her at knifepoint. The twins' mother heard the girl's cries but pretended nothing had happened. "Don't tell anyone," she advised the girl the next morning. "If you do, no one will believe you."

The explanation for this extraordinary episode was that the twins' father held what the Chinese press referred to without elaboration as "a leading post." In fact, diplomats concluded after consulting their files, he was a major general and a former commander of the local military district. When the twins were eventually arrested and brought to trial as part of a general crackdown on juvenile crime, one brother was sentenced to death and executed immediately—with the shooting shown on national television; the other, because he showed some repentance in court, was given a two-year stay of execution to test his behavior. What the press did not say, however, was that the brothers' father had himself been purged in 1971, as a follower of Lin Biao, several years before their crimes began. That suggested just how great the power of senior army commanders was, some Chinese acquaintances said—enough to intimidate the police and the civilian authorities even from jail.

For all China's strict official puritanism, adultery is hardly unknown, though less widespread than in Europe or the United States. Jan Wong related with amusement her discovery of a triangle of a husband, wife, and her lover, all of whom worked in the Foreign Languages Press, China's large publisher of foreign-language books and magazines such as *Peking Review* and *China Reconstructs.* The wife, whom Jan called Ping, was a slim and attractive thirty-two-year-old with a penchant for well-cut jackets and blouses that gave more than the usual hint of her figure. She met her boy friend, Jan learned, after she returned from a sojourn at a May Seventh Cadre School in the countryside at the end of the Cultural Revolution when her husband was still sequestered in the village. Chen, the lover, is a good-looking, dark, strong man, a photographer a few years younger than Ping. He is married to a factory worker and has a son, as do Ping and her husband, Song. But even after Song discovered their affair, he did not take any action. Indeed, the three often ate in the Foreign Languages Press dining room and went to the movies together.

The reason, Jan finally learned, is that Chen is only half Chinese and therefore has access to the Friendship Store, normally open only to foreigners. Chen used this privilege to buy goods Song never could: better meat and vegetables, high-grade Chinese cigarettes, electrical appliances. Then the three of them shared the bounty.

In the countryside also there is considerable sexual promiscuity, friends who have lived there assured me. A Harvard-educated professor who worked for a year in a village in Shanxi province, in the northwest, during the Socialist Education Campaign in 1964, just before the Cultural Revolution, remembered the chagrin of the Communist Party cadres on his work team when they tried to get the local peasants to meetings in the evenings.

"The peasants were too busy with their mistresses," he told me. "They called it hiding in small rooms." Some of the women were single, some married. It usually occurred among the men who earned a better than average income and could treat the women to gifts, the professor explained. One shepherd, a job considered taxing and therefore well paid, actually had ten mistresses.

But legally the government views adultery, like premarital sex, as a crime, disruptive of social order. A hotel roomboy I knew in Peking, who was married, was sentenced to three years in prison for sleeping with a waitress who also worked in the hotel.

My unlucky friend Hua told me about a well-respected Party member and middle-ranking cadre in the Sports Commission who on the surface seemed a happily married man with two children. But then one day he was discovered having an affair with another woman in their *danwei* who was also married. In the United States, their infidelity might have been passed over by their colleagues; their spouses perhaps would have filed for divorce. But sex in China is not a private matter between individuals. Under the Communists it has become a highly politicized act which the regime regards as part of its legitimate area of control. To get a divorce, the lovers had to apply to the *danwei* for permission. It was refused. The cadre, mortified by being found out and unable to resolve the situation legally, tried to save his family further embarrassment. He walked to the railroad line that runs behind the Sports Commission headquarters and waited till a train approached. Then he lay down on the tracks and let himself be run over.

Yet his final act failed. In keeping with regulations, the Sports Commission drew up a detailed document on their indiscretion and circulated it around the *danwei*. His lover was ordered before a public rally and criticized for several hours. For good measure, her husband was forced to attend.

7. Holding Up Half the Sky

WOMEN

"If a woman marries a chicken, she should act like a chicken; if she marries a dog, she should act like a dog."

Old Chinese proverb

The Peking First Infectious Diseases Hospital is a forbidding complex of gray-brick buildings set incongruously inside what remains of the ancient Altar of the Earth Park. In Ming and Qing times, this was where the Emperor came at the summer solstice to offer sacrifices to the earth, rising an hour before sunup from the Hall of Abstinence to present the meat of a yellow bull, a cup of wine, a bolt of silk, and then prostrate himself nine times. Neither the hospital—which now largely houses victims of tuberculosis and hepatitis—nor the Altar of the Earth are on the usual tourist itinerary, and I might never have visited the area except that my wife, Barbara, developed a serious bout of what was diagnosed as bacillary dysentery. It was so serious, with a temperature of 104° and constant vomiting and diarrhea, that the doctor at the Capital Hospital, where foreigners are normally treated, ordered me to take her immediately to the Infectious Diseases Hospital so she could be quarantined.

When we tried to drive into the hospital, I saw what quarantine meant. The high green-painted steel front gate was bolted shut, and after we finally were able to summon a guard to admit us, we found the door to the second-floor ward where Barbara was to be ensconced was padlocked both on the inside and outside. Eventually, after pounding on the door for several minutes, a petite nurse, her face hidden by a surgical mask, materialized to usher us shyly into a large private room with its own toilet and the usual concrete floor. Our anxiety did not subside when one of the nurse's first acts was to bring Barbara a large dusty apple to eat. From a decade in Asia, we at least knew that the first remedy for stomach ailments is a rigorously bland diet, excluding fruit. Our trepidations increased further when the nurse reappeared with an apparatus to feed Barbara intravenously. The old bottle on top had an open mouth, with a black rubber stopper hanging beside it and a piece of worn, frayed cotton bandage to bind it closed. Next she brought in another bottle, filled with an unidentified solution, which she poured into the one that would trickle into Barbara's veins. Barbara said she felt too weak to argue about American notions of sterility. Outside we could see a number of the other patients, clad in striped blue and white pajamas and brown robes, convulsively clearing their throats and then spitting in the courtyard below. We looked at each other, thinking that many of them had TB.

Finally the doctor arrived, Wang Chaoqi, a plump, jolly, benign woman of forty-five. Calm and self-confident, with straight black hair cut short, proletarian style, at the nape of her neck, she brought Barbara back to health over the next week despite our initial doubts about the quality of the medical care. To Barbara's further surprise, she discovered that the entire hospital staff of over two hundred doctors and nurses was women. During Barbara's week there, she never encountered a male physician. Even the hospital director, who came solicitously to call on her foreign patient, was a woman.

I was intrigued by this plentitude of women. Like other foreigners who have traveled in China, I had been introduced to a number of Chinese women who had achieved prominence—the director of a submarine shipyard in the industrial city of Wuhan, a lawyer who was head of the China Democratic League, one of the tiny non-Communist parties permitted to survive. Most of them were really examples of Chinese tokenism, women who held figurehead positions. But Dr. Wang and the staff at the Infectious Diseases Hospital had achieved genuine responsibility. When I asked Dr. Wang if she had ever felt any discrimination as a woman, she smiled, showing two rows of perfect white teeth.

"No, why should I?" she replied. She said she had graduated from the Peking Medical College, the best in the city, which before 1949 had been the Peking Union Medical College, built early in the century by the Rockefeller Foundation. She was married to a doctor, and they drew equal salaries, she said.

"I have read that some American women's groups are disappointed when they come to China and Chinese women they meet tell them everything is good," she added with another smile. "Don't you think I am telling the truth?"

Dr. Wang and the staff at the Infectious Diseases Hospital were not a showpiece; they were too far off the beaten track. But they were the best example I encountered of the great leap forward in human dignity that Chinese women have made since 1949. In the past, women's subservience to men was summed up in the injunction in the *Classic for Girls:* "If the wife does not serve her husband, the rules of propriety will be broken." Every Chinese grew up knowing the ancient adages, "An ignorant woman is virtuous" and "A woman should be a virtuous wife and a good mother." Chinese baby girls were more likely than boys to suffer infanticide in poor families. A daughter was referred to as an "outsider" because she would eventually be given away in marriage and no longer bring any economic benefit to her family, "like spilled water," the proverb decreed. After the wedding the new bride fell under the tyranny of her husband's mother. In a wealthy family, she might have to suffer the indignity of a second wife or concubine being brought into the household, especially if she was childless. Her husband could repudiate her; but if he died, she could not easily remarry.

Women were expected to stay secluded inside the home and never venture out. Before 1949 the very word for wife was *neiren,* "inside person." As the classic *The Book of Rites* put it, "A man does not talk about affairs inside" the household, "a woman does not talk about affairs outside" the home. The Chinese ideogram for peace and harmony is a woman under a roof: 安. In this scheme, a woman's labor was absorbed within the home and brought in no income. Women were largely illiterate and could not inherit property.

This traditional inferiority was given philosophical legitimacy in an elaborate cosmological explanation which held that the world is divided into two interacting elements: yin, the attribute of all things female, which was dark, weak, and passive, and yang, the male characteristic, bright, strong, and active.

Until well into the twentieth century women's subordination was reinforced by the crippling practice of foot-binding. From the age of about five to fifteen, a young girl's feet were tightly wrapped, with the arch broken and the toes curled under, to produce the "lily foot." Men's interest in these small sensitive objects made them genuinely erogenous but a terrible pain for women. Even today it is not unusual in Peking to see elderly women with short, stumpy feet hobbling across the roads, trying to dodge the rivers of bicycles coming toward them. In all this, women were supposed to be tolerant. "Obey heaven and follow fate," counseled another saying.

When the Communists came to make their revolution, women represented easily the largest disinherited group in China—in Mao's phrase, they "held up half the sky"—and the Communists moved quickly to tap this latent force with favorable policies. Their main line of attack was to break down the barriers to women working, for Marxists have argued since Engels that the key to women's subservience is their exclusion from the marketplace. Articulate Chinese women I talked with quoted Lenin's comment that to assure woman's "complete emancipation and make her the equal of man . . . it is necessary for women to participate in common productive labor."

On paper, Chinese women today have made far more gains in this way than their American sisters. While American women are still struggling to get the Equal Rights Amendment into the Constitution, China's constitution, in Article 53, proclaims, "Women enjoy equal rights with men in all spheres of political, economic, cultural, social, and family life. Men and women enjoy equal pay for equal work." Elsewhere, the Chinese constitution guarantees everyone's right to work. In practice this means women must work; they no longer have the choice between career or family. A liberal 1950 family law, the first law passed by the Communists, provided for freedom of choice in marriage, abolished concubinage, and gave women the right to own property, use their own names, and sue for divorce. In recent years the Communists have also legalized abortion and made it free on demand. Women in the cities get a minimum of fifty-six days paid maternity leave, six months if they sign the pledge to have only one child. The government has set up a network of child-care centers. Many Chinese women now go to college, and one third of all scientists and engineers are women.

Yet despite these achievements, China is still a man's world; Chinese women may be liberated but they are still not equal. On every plane ride I took on the Chinese airlines, CAAC, almost all the passengers were men; only the stewardesses were female. In the small provincial city of Foshan, outside Canton, in the south, I stopped to eat lunch in a nondescript three-story concrete restaurant. There were hundreds of male patrons busy gobbling down bowls of fried noodles, dishes of pork and mustard greens, and tureens of soup—young factory workers in their undershirts and old peasants in their traditional black pajamas. But I didn't see a single woman except for the waitresses. When I remarked on the absence of female customers, my guide, a cheerful, rosy-cheeked woman in her late twenties, responded, "the men don't have housework to do." Jan Wong reported that when she traveled "soft-berth" class on the trains, she often drew suspicious looks, for none of the other passengers, all men, could figure out how a woman, and such a young one at that, got access to this privileged status. Most of the men, she learned, were on business trips, or "missions," as the Chinese termed them.

In the countryside, I noticed, women now work in the fields, giving them new economic independence, especially important for young wives who can begin to prove themselves to their mothers-in-law before they give birth to a son. In the past that was the critical test—providing a male heir to continue the family line. But today women are usually assigned the most backbreaking labor, transplanting rice or picking beans while many of their menfolk are off driving tractors or acting as cadres. Steven Butler, an American sociologist who lived on a commune in Hebei province, in north China, calculated that women actually did 80 percent of all the fieldwork. And while in theory pay is supposed to be equal, I found on visits to over a dozen communes that men normally were awarded about ten work points per day while women got only seven or eight for much the same labor. (Work points are the system of remuneration for peasants. Each person is given a certain number for his day's work, and at the end of the year, after the harvest is in, the total number of work points is added up and the peasants are paid according to their share of the overall output.) Cadres at the communes I toured explained that the discrepancy in awarding work points was the result of the natural physiological difference between the sexes—men are stronger and should be paid more for doing harder work. Similarly, in industry, women tend to be shunted into light industry like textiles, electronics, and neighborhood cooperative handicraft factories making embroidery, lacquerware, paper boxes, toys, and silk flowers. These are the most repetitive jobs, which draw the lowest pay and other benefits.

In education, a nationwide survey by the Ministry of Education found that girls make up 50 percent of all the pupils in primary schools. But by high school the number has shrunk to 40 percent of the total student body and by college only 30 percent. At Peking University, according to the New China News Agency, the entering class in 1980 had only 23 percent women. Kang Keqing, the septuagenarian president of the All-China Women's Federation, the largely toothless official government women's organization, complained in a meeting once that women account for 80 percent of the illiterates in China today. Females, she added, in an unusual burst of candor, also make up 60 to 70 percent of the young people in the cities who have not yet been assigned jobs after finishing school. And, she charged, "pass grades for recruiting workers in factories and enrolling students are arbitrarily raised for women." It was the only time I heard a Chinese leader admit to continuing inequality.

One reason for these statistics is that, contrary to Marxist expectations, mass access to the job market has not proved a panacea because the old assumptions of male superiority and female subservience endure. I was surprised one evening when our friend Miao commented on the natural difference between our son and her daughter.

"Boys are more inclined to rough sports, they are more naughty, and they will do better in science and math," she said over dinner. "Girls are better-behaved, more partial to music and dance, and they are better in school in languages. It is their nature."

These stereotypes remain even stronger in the countryside, where the level of education is lower. Lihua, my petitioner friend, recalled that in her village girls were not sent to school at all, for their parents still regard them as "outsiders" in whom such an investment is really being made for another family, she explained. At marriage, they will move away. Girl babies in her village are called "a thousand ounces of gold"; but a boy child is called "ten thousand ounces of gold."

A confidential study on the status of women and marriage prepared by a team of investigators for the Women's Federation in 1980 discovered the persistence of other old customs which the Communists claimed to have eliminated. (I was given a copy of the document by a woman student at Peking University.) In one commune in Shanxi, there were 146 girls under the age of five who were betrothed, accounting for 43 percent of their age group, the investigators found. Among those five to ten years old, 81 percent were engaged. In a county in Fujian, on the southeast coast, the investigators said that, because of the continued selling of child brides, parental interference in their daughters' marriages, and ill treatment of new brides there were four suicides by poisoning, four cases of nervous breakdown, and two attempted murders, all within the first five months of 1980. In the Tungfang commune of the county, three women and one young man left home to join Buddhist nunneries and a monastery because of marriage problems. The report described these troubles as a "feudal remnant."

The report also uncovered a new problem, one caused by modernization —"the abandonment of wives is on the rise," it said. This occurred largely among men who were promoted to be cadres and were then transferred to urban areas or among young men who got into college. The investigators cited the case of a teacher at Guizhou University, in the southwest, Zhang Guangxi. He had originally married a peasant woman in his native village, but after he was appointed a professor in the university he divorced her to marry an elementary school teacher. Later, however, he fell in love with a student in his school. To complicate matters, his second wife was pregnant and Zhang pushed her into getting abortions, twice. In the meantime, without bothering to get a second divorce, he went to register his marriage to the student at the local civil affairs office. The pair were convicted of bigamy.

The investigators also turned up evidence of battered wives. "The major reasons for maltreatment of wives are male chauvinism and a desire to force the wife into divorce," the authors of the report stated. Of the 2,128 letters the Women's Federation received in 1979 about marriage problems, evidently from women who had no other outlet for their grievances, 436 of them, 20 percent, concerned physical abuse. The report related the gruesome example of a former peasant turned soldier, Qiu Haichi, in Henan province, in central China. Qiu was engaged to a local peasant woman before entering the army, and even after he suffered severe burns, which covered much of his face, his fiancée went through with the wedding. But after Qiu's scars healed, the report found, he had an affair with another woman and pressed his wife for a divorce. She refused. Their quarrels then worsened, and "on January 3, 1980, he attacked her with a knife, slicing off both her arms and digging out her eyes. After this, he trampled her eyeballs underfoot. Neighbors heard and rushed to save her, but she was on her last breath," the report concluded.

Within the Communist Party itself, despite its lip service to equality, Chinese women have fared no better, and perhaps not as well, as American women in gaining access to political power. Women now make up 4.7 million of the 20 million Chinese cadres, 24 percent of the total, it is true. But there is only one woman among the twenty-four regular members of the ruling Politburo, which makes the key decisions, and she is the widow of Zhou Enlai, Deng Yingchao. Although Madame Deng herself is regarded with saintly affection, she was selected for the post only after her husband's death as part of respect for his legacy. There are no women among the eleven members of the Party Secretariat, the powerful organization that runs the Party on a daily basis. And while several American women have been elected governors of their states, none of the first Party secretaries and governors of China's twenty-nine provincial level units are women. One woman, Chen Muhua, a tall, robust, former engineering student, has become one of the two alternate members of the Politburo. She is also the only woman among the dozen deputy prime ministers who administer the government apparatus. But Chinese friends cautioned against looking to her as a future national leader. They noted that her areas of responsibility—family planning, day-care centers, and China's economic aid program to Third World nations—are not the portfolios given to members of the inner circle. They also said her career had been blunted by charges of corruption and arrogance, including an incident, as mentioned earlier, when she refused to give a ride on her special plane to a group of sick Chinese athletes when she was returning from a trip to Rumania. Instead, she brought back a load of West German furniture for herself.

Virtually all the other women who have risen to prominence in Communist China have done so by marrying well—Jiang Qing, Mao's widow, Soong Qing Ling, the widow of Sun Yat-sen, who was a deputy chairman of the National People's Congress until her death in 1981, and Miss Kang, the head of the Women's Federation. Her late husband was Zhu De, the leader of the Red Army and a revered military hero. The Women's Federation, despite some activities like the confidential study of women's status, devotes much of its energy to urging women to support the current Party line. I was amused at the opening ceremony of the fourth, and most recent, national women's congress in 1978 when the welcoming speech was delivered by a man, Wang Dongxing, the former head of Mao's bodyguards who has since been purged. In her own address, Miss Kang declared that "the major task for the new period" set by the Party "was also the task for Chinese women." That is, she said, "To steadfastly continue the revolution under the dictatorship of the proletariat, deepen the three great revolutionary movements of class struggle, the struggle for production and scientific experiment, and transform China into a great and powerful socialist country with modern agriculture, industry, national defense, and science and technology by the end of the century." Stern rhetoric, but not what American feminists would applaud. In China, class struggle comes before the battle between the sexes.

Perhaps because of the tradition of women shunning involvement outside the home, the wives of Chinese leaders do not play a regular ceremonial role accompanying their husbands on trips abroad or appearing with them on podiums as do the spouses of American presidents and astronauts. In fact, while Hua Guofeng was Party Chairman and Prime Minister, the Chinese press never even disclosed the name of his wife. But, Chinese friends advised, senior officials ensured good jobs for their wives in keeping with another tradition, family solidarity. Hua's wife, they said, had been a political commissar in the Light Industry Bureau before his selection as Party Chairman, when she was given a plum post inside Zhongnanhai, the Communist headquarters. Deng's wife, Cho Lin, a short, round-faced woman who did travel with her husband on his epochal trip to the United States in 1979, is said to be head of the General Office of the Party Military Affairs Commission. That innocuous-sounding title would put her in charge of communications between the Party and the army, a critical post from which she can help Deng exert authority over the armed forces.

"Wives may not play an important role in public," the daughter of an army general said. "But as we say, a lot of decisions are made by whispering in the ear on the pillow, especially when the family may benefit in some way."

If wives of the leaders share their husbands' rise to fame, they also share their ignominy. Wang Guangmei, the sophisticated, articulate, attractive wife of the former head of state, Liu Shaoqi, was dragged before mass rallies and imprisoned for a decade after her husband was denounced as China's leading capitalist roader in the Cultural Revolution. Now that Liu has been posthumously rehabilitated—he died in 1969 in prison—she has been released from jail and given a new job. The most famous downfall, of course, was that of Jiang Qing, who was arrested less than a month after Mao died in 1976. But to me an equally telling example of how wives are tied to their husbands involved Cao Yiou. She was the widow of Kang Sheng, a Politburo member who was a close supporter of Mao and for many years the dreaded head of China's secret police. Cao was a deputy to the National People's Congress. But when Kang was posthumously criticized for his role in the Cultural Revolution and then expelled from the Party in 1980, four years after his death, she suddenly lost her legislative seat. Cao herself was not attacked.

In the countryside also women's entry into the job market has not translated into greater political power. Whenever I visited a commune I made it
a practice to ask how many of the local cadres were women. The answer at
the Bitter Water commune in Gansu, in the northwest, was typical. Of the
thirty-three cadres in the commune and its composite brigades and production teams, only two were women. One of these was Deng Meisheng, the
deputy commune chairman. Tall and lithe, with short straight hair, a strong
flat nose, and broad cheekbones, she bore a striking resemblance to an
American Indian. During an interview with commune officials in a peasant's
mud-walled house, she sat on a low stool in a corner. I noticed she was not
dressed like a peasant—under her regulation blue-cotton cadre's tunic she
had on a tan cardigan sweater and a pale-blue flower-printed blouse with a
high round collar. When I asked what her duties were, the commune chairman replied for her. She was in charge of work with women, youth, family
planning, public health, education, and culture, the chairman said. In other
words, everything excluding actual farm production and its financing, the
critical sectors for the peasants. In the communes I was taken to, the women
cadres I encountered almost always were responsible for what the Chinese
call "women's work," meaning family planning and encouraging women to
work in the fields, not the consciousness-raising activity Western feminists
think of by the same term.

There are several reasons why women's increased work in the fields has
not had the effect the Communists, and some American women's groups,
expected. For one thing, in a traditional Chinese way, the payment of work
points at the end of the year is handed over to the family head, usually a man,
not to an individual, since the income is regarded as the earnings of the whole
family. Because women still move to their husband's family at marriage, they
aren't able to build up the network of *guan-xi* necessary to be selected for
leadership posts. And equally important, women are still expected to do the
household chores, which gives them less time than men for cadre duties.

It is this wearisome double burden, of trying to juggle the conflicting
demands of a job and a family, which seems to press hardest on Chinese
women today, both in the cities and villages. Unlike American women, many
of whom feel torn about embarking on a career, Chinese women have no
choice—by law, they must work. When we went to the Wangs' house for
dinner, Miao had to shop and do the cooking. Li was the polite host, keeping
us company, pouring us beer, and filling our bowls with the latest dish of hot
food, which Li would bring from their tiny kitchen with its cold-water sink
and coal brazier for cooking. Only at the end of the meal, after she had
finished all the cooking, did she come in and sit down to eat herself. Giving
a dinner party is particularly hard for a Chinese wife, Barbara pointed out,
because none of the food can be cooked ahead of time and must be served

immediately after each dish is individually fried. Like most other Chinese, the Wangs did not have a refrigerator and Miao had to shop seven days a week.

When we were together with the Wangs, they seemed a happy couple. But once when I was driving Li home alone in the car he complained that his wife was too involved in her work and too tired and moody at the end of the day. Miao, on the other hand, confessed in private that she felt like the character in a popular new novel, *At Middle Age,* about a hardworking, middle-aged eye surgeon who finds herself exhausted after a day's work in the hospital, which may include performing several operations. Gradually, she realizes, she is neglecting her husband and children.

American women who have children and also work can sympathize with Miao's plight. But even the most energetic Western woman would find it difficult to cope with life in China, for many of the labor-saving devices she takes for granted simply don't exist there. There are no vacuum cleaners to do the cleaning. Nor has Chinese industry yet produced dishwashers, clothes washers, or dryers. Chinese workmen are so unfamiliar with these appliances that when my colleague Michael Parks of *The Los Angeles Times* moved into his apartment, he discovered the technician assigned to help him had connected his American-made clothes washer to the sink to bring water into it. But he had not attached the hose in the back of the machine to drain the water out. When Parks suggested politely the washer might not work that way, the worker assured him that was how he always installed them for diplomats. Some Chinese who can afford it take their clothes to a neighborhood laundry; others do them in buckets at home, often using cold water. But whatever that ingredient is, advertised in American television commercials, that gets clothes "whiter than white," Chinese soap doesn't have it; it leaves them gray.

China has not yet developed a tampon either. During their menstrual period, Chinese women make do with a roll of coarse grayish toilet paper which they form into pads; then, if they have enough money, they buy some cotton to wad around the paper pad. All this fits into a belt that is made of reddish rubber on one side and flowered cotton on the other. Peasant women use rags which they must wash over and over, since it is impossible to buy paper or cotton in the countryside, friends told me. Before the influx of tourists in the late 1970s, a customs official confiscated a box of tampons from an American woman who had planned a lengthy stay in Peking. He didn't believe her explanation of what they were for and evidently thought they were a new smuggling technique. The proper Chinese word for menstruation is *yue-jing,* "monthly passing." But the colloquial term is *dao-mei,* "rotten luck," reflecting Chinese attitudes toward the problem.

The double burden of worker and wife is especially difficult for mothers with infants. Although China has sired more babies than any nation on earth, there are no disposable diapers yet, only the old cloth variety which must be washed by hand and hung to dry in people's small apartments. Nor has Chinese industry manufactured any canned baby food or even maternity clothes for pregnant women.

China is still a developing country, of course, and it would be wrong to expect it to reach the same level of creature comforts as the United States, Japan, or Western Europe. But given the Communists' proclaimed devotion to equality for women, I was surprised that there are still far from enough nursery schools and kindergartens. Mao once told André Malraux, the French writer, that "to liberate women is not to manufacture sewing machines." In his cryptic way, the Chairman was suggesting that the real path to emancipating women from household drudgery lay in providing collective social services like day-care centers and communal dining facilities. But despite the fanfare with which Chinese display their nurseries to foreign visitors, Miss Chen, the Deputy Prime Minister, admitted in 1980 that only 28 percent of China's babies and young children are in nurseries and a slightly smaller number in kindergartens. The majority of mothers, even though they work, still have to fend for themselves. By comparison, 53 percent of Americans' three-, four-, and five-year-olds were in some kind of day-care center, nursery school, or kindergarten in 1980.

The most common solution for Chinese families, said Lao Wu, my Chinese assistant, was to call for grandmother to come and live with the family until the child reached school age. He had brought his own mother from their native town in Fujian, as far south of Peking as Miami is from New York, and a four-day journey by train. Some parents whose apartments were too small to accommodate a visiting relative farmed their children out to grandparents in the countryside, as did a woman I knew in the Foreign Ministry. But her four-year-old daughter, after a year in the village, refused to call her mother. Those who could afford it, high cadres, some army officers, and well-paid technicians, hired maids.

All this work, managing a family as well as a job, takes its toll on Chinese women. "Women have a harder life than men," observed an astute woman professor at Peking University who was married herself. "Have you noticed," she asked me, "how women in China age faster than men? By their early thirties they look like they are forty, heavier around the middle, the jowls, and with lines showing in their faces. Our husbands stay slimmer and younger-looking." She, at thirty-five, had become very conscious of her diet and was fighting a battle with her waistline and hips. To me, her husband did look ten years younger.

The imperative for women to work in China, ironically, has created a strong countercurrent of anti-women's liberation feeling among some educated Chinese women, much the same segment of well-educated, affluent women who in America have been the most active feminists and for whom a career is the panacea. Where the Americans are rebelling against having to be housewives, the Chinese are unhappy about having to be breadwinners. Having a career, once it becomes a necessity, can be transformed from a means to self-fulfillment and independence into drudgery.

The professor at Peking University complained that what she really wanted to do was to stay home and raise her son and daughter, who currently live in a government kindergarten from Monday morning till the parents pick them up after work on Saturday. Their only real chance to be with the children is on Sundays.

"If I had my choice," she said, "I would devote my time to tutoring my son, to make sure he gets into the best school." Surprisingly, she was less concerned about her daughter's education. "It is our boy who must make a career," the professor explained, reflecting the persistence of the traditional attitude.

But it is the difficulty women often have in getting a divorce which more than anything else illustrates the ambivalent position Chinese women have reached—freed from some of the old fetters, yet not fully equal. In theory, divorce in China should be easy. The Communist family law, specifically amended in 1980 to make it more progressive, provides that "in cases of complete alienation of mutual affection, and when mediation has failed, divorce should be granted." The language is clear and simple. But a number of Chinese women I met complained more bitterly about their trouble in getting a divorce than about anything else.

Take the case of Guiying, a slight, cheerful worker in a battery factory with tiny eyes and short pigtails. She recalled that she and her husband, another worker, had been married only a few months when they began quarreling about the money she spent on clothes and he consumed on cigarettes and alcohol. Soon, she said, he had turned violent and she moved back into her old cubicle in the factory dormitory. Three years after they separated, she felt sanguine about applying for a divorce, particularly since her husband had found a new girl friend and agreed to apply, too. But when she went to her factory Party committee, in accordance with proper procedure, they told her it would take time to investigate. Six months later, she asked what had happened. Her application had been handed over to the security section, she was told. Finally, a full year later, she was notified—the request was turned down.

"The Party secretary said it would be better if we got together again," Guiying told me during a meal in a small restaurant near the Peking Hotel. "He wouldn't say why we had been refused, but I think personally it is a matter of face. The authorities are very feudal. They want it to look as if everyone is happily married. Divorce to them is still immoral."

Guiying then quoted another proverb: "A good horse won't accept two saddles; a good wife doesn't marry twice."

I wondered why she didn't apply to the court directly.

"If your *danwei* doesn't agree, there's no hope," she explained. "The court will always come back and ask your *danwei* before looking into the case. Marriage is for life."

Just how sternly many Chinese still feel about divorce I discovered when I had the rare chance to attend a divorce trial in Shanghai. It might have been a tale out of an old Chinese novel. The wife, Wei Jingfeng, who was the plaintiff, charged that her "contradictions," or troubles with her husband, began because he was too filial to his mother. A dour, round-faced, thirty-five-year-old worker in a meteorological instruments factory, she testified that her husband had insisted they live with his mother and grandparents. Then when she gave birth to her first child, her in-laws were unhappy. It was a girl, not a boy.

"They had very feudal ideas," Wei recalled in the makeshift courtroom, the headquarters of her neighborhood committee. The building was an old Chinese-style structure with a sloping tile roof; inside, the only adornments on the high yellow walls were color portraits of Mao and Hua.

"After I was discharged from the hospital, when I entered our house, my mother-in-law followed an old custom," Wei continued. "She took a young boy in her arms, meaning she wanted a grandson next time.

"I was very unhappy when I saw this. My husband's grandmother is over eighty. She told me, 'You had flowers, now the next time bear fruit.'"

Later, Wei said, she and her mother-in-law quarreled over the number of eggs she ate; her husband's family thought she was wasting money. Things reached a crisis when Wei had an abortion without consulting the family rather than risk giving birth to another girl. Finally, she moved out with her daughter to a small apartment of her own, she related, but it was an impossible situation because her husband kept all their ration cards.

As she recounted her story, the couple's now five-year-old daughter wandered around the packed room, seemingly oblivious to the family tragedy. But when her mother concluded her testimony, she suddenly came up to her mother's side and put her straw sun hat, with a red ribbon, on her mother's head. Then she climbed on her mother's lap.

The estranged husband, Hong Songdao, thirty-nine, a tall, slim and solemn man who worked as a cadre in a machine exporting agency, told the story differently. He claimed that, when his wife came back from the hospital, one of his nephews happened to be visiting and his mother had picked the boy up to look at the new baby. In his view, the trouble was that his wife had shown no respect for his mother; she had smashed much of his family's furniture in fits of anger, and she had ripped his clothes one day when she encountered him on the street. She had also gone to his office "over 140 times" to complain about his behavior, causing him serious embarrassment.

"Because of her shrewish temperament, we're incompatible," Hong testified. "But because of my daughter, I felt contradictions in my heart and don't want to be divorced."

My Chinese guide, a cherubic woman with graying hair from the Chinese People's Association for Friendship with Foreign Countries, looked at me knowledgeably. Most men oppose divorce, she whispered, and most divorce cases are now instituted by women, one mark of their progress. In the past, men could discard their wives, while women had virtually no right to seek divorce. But my guide hinted she already knew what the court would decide. It was composed of a male judge and two so-called lay assessors, one each from the husband's and wife's *danweis*.

"Our duty is to educate people, not to attack them," the judge began. "You should both be more patient. Our country needs stability and unity and families need stability and unity." It was a Confucian plea for social harmony. Then, the judge counseled the wife, she should withdraw her petition for divorce. It would be economically wasteful, he implied. Two apartments and two sets of ration tickets for one couple were more than a crowded city could afford.

To the judge's opinion, the lay assessors added the weight of community pressure, always strong in China. "I think it's not a case where divorce is necessary," a middle-aged male worker from the husband's office interjected. "It is only a problem of some lingering feudal ideas by the mother-in-law."

He turned to the wife. "You should tell your mother-in-law that today in our society there are women airplane pilots, like men, so girls are not less valuable than boys. Both you and your husband should carry out more ideological work to reeducate her." Here again was a Confucian idea, that people are inherently maleable, that had made its way into Chinese Communist practice.

A woman worker from the wife's factory, with a broad, full face and blue tunic, also chastised the plaintiff. "You should know it is not a happy result to get divorced," she said to Wei. "You must consider your daughter's happiness as well as your own. My suggestion is, the wife should show more respect for the old generation. Otherwise, in the future, how would you feel if your child did not respect you?"

This was not exactly sisterly solidarity, and it was more pressure than the wife could bear. She assented to a reconciliation. It was their sixth, she said as she left the courtroom.

Still, the Chinese press often reported that divorce was on the increase, as in other countries undergoing modernization. Some articles applauded the trend as a sign of liberation for women; others railed that this was degeneration into capitalist licentiousness. The confidential investigation prepared for the Women's Federation on the status of marriage charged, "Under the influence of bourgeois attitudes toward matters of love and marriage, ethics are sliding. Some young women think that women's liberation means sexual freedom.

"Some young people think of marrying as a sort of game, marry carelessly and divorce lightly. They choose a partner only on the basis of family background, how good their job is, or how good-looking they are. As a result, they don't get along and fight right up to divorce."

The report found that in the city of Wuhan, in central China, in one recent year there were 110 cases of divorce, five of them within six months of marriage, 60 percent within three years. In Peking, the investigators said, there was even a case where a couple went to register their marriage in the morning, in the afternoon when they went to buy furniture, began to argue, and by late in the day were back at the local government office to try to get their marriage annulled.

One woman I met had succeeded in getting divorced, Limei, a plain-looking schoolteacher who felt sexually unfulfilled with her husband. The divorce had actually been her husband's idea, she insisted, but she now regarded it as a disaster.

"My friends and people at school treat me like a strange animal," she lamented. "At school they talk about me behind my back, and in person my friends pretend they don't know I'm divorced. It's as if there was something evil about it."

She had become depressed. She would call me one day on the phone in high spirits just to say hello; then the next day she would upbraid me morosely for not inviting her over to our house more often. I came to dread her calls, not knowing how to respond and feeling guilty when I took refuge in saying I was too busy working to talk.

The situation was awkward for her, because she and her ex-husband taught in the same school and they were constantly bumping into each other. Neither had yet been able to get a transfer, or to get separate housing, though he had finally moved out and slept in his classroom.

I learned just how correct Limei's complaint about gossip was from another teacher in her school who didn't realize we were friends. One day the other teacher recounted the story of her divorce as if it were the school scandal. "She dresses fashionably, she likes to sing and dance," he said of Limei, "and she got divorced." It was as close as Chinese come in polite conversation to saying that someone is loose and fooled around.

And yet, for all Limei's troubles, when I once asked her if she felt women in China had achieved equality, she looked at me as if I had said something foolish. "Certainly," she answered. "A lot of work has been done for women since Liberation." Her response was typical. Most Chinese women simply did not seem concerned with the issues that agitate American feminists: equal pay, promotions, exclusion from political power, sexism in the office.

Jan Wong came to the office angry one day. She said a notice had just been put up on the bulletin board of the *danwei* where she then lived, the Foreign Languages Press. It announced the summer schedule for use of the communal shower room. Women would get three hours per week, men nine. She had scrawled a sarcastic comment using a thick red-felt pen: "What kind of male-female equality is this?" The next morning someone had retorted, "This is a scientific arrangement." Another person wrote, "This is equality." Jan could not induce any mutters of protest from other women in the building, though, as she pointed out, they were equal in number to the men.

At first I was baffled by this lack of feminine consciousness. But the woman professor at Peking University who wanted to stay home to tutor her son helped put it in perspective. At her college, she said, if a husband and wife were both teaching in the same department and they came up for a raise at the same time, the husband would get the money first. She knew, because that was what had happened to her and her husband.

"You may say that's unequal. It is. But that is not important. It doesn't matter who gets the raise as long as one of us does."

For, she went on to explain, "in China we still operate on the family system. Everything still goes to the family. What is important to me is to see that my children get properly cared for and get ahead." She did not see women as a separate category.

Another woman, a slender, graceful Chinese-American architect who was born in China, summarized the crux of the issue. "Part of the story is that Chinese women have made real progress," she said. "But you must also remember China's level of economic development. Chinese women can't afford to be interested in feminist issues. They focus on the things that are important to them—getting a decent apartment with a toilet of its own, buying groceries, figuring out who will take care of the children while they work. They don't yet identify with their jobs or careers. Fulfillment for them comes at home with the family."

But it was an incident that happened during Deng Xiaoping's tour of the United States in 1979 which helped me realize Chinese men and women have not yet gone through the arguments feminists in the West advance. Among the large contingent of Chinese correspondents covering the trip was Deng Qin, a short, wiry, nervous, and very aggressive television camera woman, no relative of the Party leader. At the welcoming reception at the White House, she burst through the other reporters and a cordon of Secret Service guards to get close to Deng and President Carter. Later, at a formal state dinner in the White House, she again shoved past a line drawn by the Secret Service. But the third time she did it, one of the agents, a tall, heavyset, muscular man with a mustache and dressed in a brown three-piece suit, cuffed her hard on the shoulder and pushed her back behind the rope set up for the press.

Miss Deng was incensed. She complained, in tears, to her leader, an official of the Central Television Station, and he in turn demanded a formal apology from the U.S. government.

"It would have been okay if it had happened to a man, but she was a woman," the Chinese official said sternly to an American diplomat. "It shows a lack of manners." There was a scare that the episode might mar Deng's visit.

When told about her grievance, the Secret Service agent responded, "They may think that way in China, but in the United States now men and women get equal treatment. My job is to protect the President."

Later on in the trip, Miss Deng began to relax. Coached by an American interpreter, she sang a song to the Secret Service man, "Getting to Know You." He leaned down and kissed her on the forehead.

8. No Road Out

没 出 路

YOUTH

"Youth must be put to the test."
Mao Zedong to André Malraux, 1965, at the outset of the
Cultural Revolution
"Don't read too much. Too much study can kill people."
Mao to his niece, Wang Hairong, 1965

Lao San was tall and slim, with smoothly combed back hair and handsome, even features. Like many children of Party cadres, he was self-assured and gregarious—his friends said debonair. He never appeared in rumpled blues, like other Chinese; his pants were always well tailored and neatly pressed. The last night I saw Lao San (the name means "Number Three," as in third-born son), he was wearing a Western-style dark-gray dacron and wool suit, an expensive and daring affectation in proletarian Peking. Lao San, who was in his late twenties, was a reporter for the English-language magazine *China Reconstructs,* and that evening had been assigned to cover a press conference at the Peking Hotel given by the World Wildlife Fund to announce its plans to help save China's giant pandas. There wasn't anything unusual in his behavior. He sat next to Sir Peter Scott, the chairman of the Wildlife Fund, taking notes. After the press conference, an office car took him home to the one-room apartment he shared with his slender, pretty wife and eighteen-month-old son.

Two plainclothes detectives from the Public Security Bureau were waiting outside in the mild spring air to arrest him. Later that evening other policemen searched his home and found five stolen tape recorders and a typewriter, only a fraction of the loot he had purloined over the past few years from his office. For Lao San, it turned out, had been the leader of a juvenile gang since his high school days over a decade before.

I was intrigued by his story, which was pieced together by my assistant Jan Wong. He had first been caught stealing as a teen-ager when he lived across the street from the Foreign Languages Press, which housed *China Reconstructs* and where his father was an official. But because of his father's position, his peccadillos were covered up. He was able first to join the Communist Party and then to be "recommended by the masses" for admission to college as one of what were called the worker-peasant-soldier students. At the time, during the Cultural Revolution, Mao had abolished the regular college entrance exams—he felt they discriminated against peasants and workers—and replaced the tests with a system of admission by recommendation according to a candidate's political background. In college, Lao San was again charged with theft, but he made a public self-criticism and his father's friends managed to get his wrongdoing expunged from his dossier, a difficult trick.

After graduation, when he was assigned to *China Reconstructs,* things began to be missing from the office. First there was one comrade's copies of *National Geographic,* a treasured item since at the time foreign magazines were contraband. Next it was a typewriter; then an English dictionary (they were unavailable in stores). The office owned a collective bicycle, ostensibly for the proofreaders to use when they had to travel to the printing factory; but most of them were lethargic, middle-aged women who preferred knitting and grocery shopping. When Lao San discovered no one used it, he asked if he could keep it for riding to work. Shortly after he was given the key, he reported the chain had been stolen. The office had no choice but to give him money to replace it. A few days later he announced the tires had been snatched.

Still, Lao San hadn't been caught in the act, and government policy was to try to "reform" errant Party members like him, not arrest them. Besides, he proved useful. The Foreign Languages Press often screened "internal" movies in its auditorium. The neighborhood kids inevitably learned about the showings, though they weren't advertised, and would storm the doors if they weren't let in. Officials at the press discovered that Lao San was the only person who could control them, friends recalled. He would go to the front gate and say, "Humph, don't you recognize me?"

They were immediately respectful. "Oh, it's you, Lao San."

Lao San's downfall came when he broke into the apartment of a fellow employee whose boy friend had just been to Japan and brought her back an expensive sterco tape recorder. After stuffing the recorder in his satchel, he arrived at the office late to find a meeting in progress in the hallway. Everyone noticed the large bag on his shoulder. During the morning break, still cool, he laid the satchel on a radiator and played Ping-Pong with a friend on the office table. But the victim happened to go home and found a window smashed and her apartment in disorder. The cadres immediately suspected

Lao San and, while he was engrossed in his game, peeked in his bag. They hesitated to arrest him on the spot, afraid he might have accomplices.

Shortly after he was detained, I asked Jan to interview his wife. She had permed hair and a reputation as a fashion plate. On the day of the last robbery, she had created a sensation in the collective cafeteria when she appeared in a fake leopard-skin coat.

"I am a person who cares a lot about face," she told Jan. "When all this happened, I felt extremely depressed." Jan noticed there were dirty clothes soaking in the sink, dirty dishes on the small stove, and garbage in the pan on the floor.

"It was society that made him do it," his wife complained. His father had been an important cadre in the Foreign Languages Press, had led delegations abroad—a mark of authority—and his mother was also a Party member, his wife related. But in the Cultural Revolution his parents were attacked and sent to prison. "The big character posters against his parents were even pasted up outside their front door. He began to get disillusioned." She sighed. "Some people say that the old cadres suffered during the Cultural Revolution, but in fact an entire generation was destroyed, the young people."

His wife also lashed out at all the campaigns of the past three decades and all the changes in political line.

"One day our big brother, the Soviet Union, becomes our revisionist enemy. Then, overnight, our staunch and loyal ally, Albania, is wrong and always has been wrong. Next it is our lips and teeth neighbor, Vietnam, who attacks us. What are we supposed to believe?

"In the 1950s morality was taught in class. It was the new Communist morality, but there was a definite sense of right and wrong. Now right and wrong is simply a matter of the current line; it depends on who is in power. So people care only about themselves and getting ahead. Everyone does it."

Whether one agreed with all his wife's claims or not, Lao San did seem to me a casualty of the Cultural Revolution, one of those young people under thirty whom the Chinese now call "the lost generation." Mao had always looked on youth as the bearers of the new society. It was young people who had fueled the May Fourth movement of 1919 which rekindled Chinese nationalism and led to the founding of the Chinese Communist Party in 1921. Mao himself was only twenty-eight years old when he took part in the Party's first session. But the Cultural Revolution had turned China's younger generation into a social and economic problem. The problem is particularly serious because 65 percent of China's population is under thirty, or 650 million people. There are over 200 million teen-agers, almost as many as the entire population of the United States.

Generalizing about Chinese youth is as impossible as generalizing about young people in America. In sophistication and life-style, the brilliant son of Foreign Minister Huang Hua, who won a scholarship to Harvard and lives in a dormitory with friends who smoke pot, is a world apart from a young factory worker in Peking, not to mention the youthful peasant in tropical Sichuan who may have had five years of primary school before he took his place behind a water buffalo tilling the fields the way his ancestors did.

But the predominant mood of all these young people when I was in Peking —from 1979 to 1981—was cynicism, apathy, and indifference. The first political joke I heard in China came from a crew-cut twenty-seven-year-old graduate student at People's University in Peking, a school that trains cadres.

"Do you know about the son who asked his father what communism is like?" he asked me.

" 'Well, son,' the father explained. 'Communism is like the horizon. The more you approach it, the farther it recedes.' "

My first winter in Peking, the *People's Daily* reported with outrage that a group of youths had stood and jeered when three soldiers attempted to rescue a young boy who fell through a lake in Peking while skating. "Run, soldiers, you want to join the Party," the crowd was said to have shouted, alluding to the Party's reputation for trying to recruit activists who are always the first to volunteer.

In the southern port city of Xiamen, I watched with fascination from my hotel-room window as a small teen-age boy across the street let the air out of the tires of an olive-drab People's Liberation Army truck. Each time, before bending down to his task, he looked around carefully to see if anyone was watching. Ironically, on the wall behind him was a red-painted poster extolling China's young people to copy the heroic deeds of a model soldier named Lei Feng, who has long been held up an an exemplar of Communist rectitude. Earlier that day, I had heard children in a local school reciting a ditty about Lei Feng, who had died in 1962, the victim of a prosaic automobile accident:

> "In the winter Lei Feng repairs cars regardless of the cold.
> Lei Feng walks a thousand miles and does 10,000 good things.
> Working for the Party and the people, his heart is red
> and never changes."

But such Communist pieties about him had spent their force, as witnessed by the boy deflating the tires of the army truck. The cynicism of young people was the flip side of the earnest idealism of the early years of the People's Republic, the Boy Scout enthusiasm which showed in all the pictures of innocent, rosy-cheeked city youngsters going off to be resettled in the countryside "in accordance with Chairman Mao's great call," as the Chinese press liked to say. Some of this may always have been a sham. But for a foreigner conditioned by years of reading official propaganda and listening to glowing accounts from tourists, it came as a shock to meet some of these rusticated youth.

Lu Hong could have been a model for a propaganda poster—she had a beautiful, round, open face with high cheekbones, a vivacious smile, and those perpetually pink cheeks. Her shiny black hair was cut short on the sides and back and fell over her eyes in thick bangs. She was thirty years old, born in the same year as the People's Republic.

"I was very young when the Cultural Revolution began," she told me over a meal of *guo-tieh,* fried dumplings stuffed with cabbage and pork. "My schoolmates and I were among the first in Peking to become Red Guards, we believed deeply in Chairman Mao. I could recite the entire book of the Chairman's quotations backward and forward, we spent hours just shouting the slogans at our teachers."

Hong remembered in particular a winter day, with the temperature below freezing, when she and her faction of Red Guards put on their red armbands and made three of the teachers from their high school kneel on the ground outside without their coats or gloves. "We had gone to their houses to conduct an investigation, to search them, and we found some English-language books. They were probably only textbooks, but to us it was proof they were worshiping foreign things and were slaves to the foreigners. We held a bonfire and burned everything we had found."

After that, she recalled, the leader of her group, a tall, charismatic eighteen-year-old boy, the son of an army general, whose nickname was "Old Dog," ordered them to beat the teachers. He produced some wooden boards, and the students starting hitting the teachers on their bodies. "We kept on till one of the teachers starting coughing blood," Hong said. "Then Old Dog told us to stop. We felt very proud of ourselves. It seemed very revolutionary."

Two years later, Hong went on, she was one of the first to volunteer when Mao proclaimed, "It is very necessary for educated young people to go to the countryside to be reeducated by the poor and lower-middle peasants."

"They put me on a train to the northeast. There were two thousand four hundred other high school students in the cars. We were traveling for four days and didn't know what our destination was until they let us off at a state farm near the Soviet border. At the time, I was full of patriotism and wanted to protect the motherland.

"Then they put us in a dormitory made of mud, with mud walls and mud floors," she continued. "Sixty people slept in one room on two *kangs,* made of mud, straw, and manure." (A *kang* is a raised platform heated by flues running underneath which northern Chinese use for sitting on during the day and sleeping on at night to keep warm.) "At night, if you came in late, all you could see were sixty heads sticking out of the covers, down a narrow aisle."

The only way for her to bathe, Hong said, was in a small enamel basin. In the entire eight years she spent on the farm, she never got to take a bath or shower.

But the worst problem was boredom. The nearest town was a three-hour walk. That was where she had to go to see a movie. But in the first five years on the farm, she saw only three movies, all of which she had seen before in Peking. There were no books or magazines for sale, and many of her friends had not brought any with them.

"After getting up at five A.M. to work in the fields, you were too tired to read at night anyway, so some of the young people forgot how to read and write."

Still, Hong was lucky. Her father was a cadre and eventually arranged through the back door to get her transferred back to Peking.

"I spent eight years fanning the flames of revolution; it was like losing a big chunk out of your life. Now I would like to contribute to the motherland, but what do I have? I never finished high school. It's like my friends say, the Chinese people don't live, they just exist."

Hong was one of 17 million city youngsters sent down to the villages, nearly one in every ten urban residents. There were over one million from Shanghai, 620,000 from Peking, the greatest forced movement of population in history. Mao's purpose was threefold: to narrow the gap between the cities and the villages, to revive the young generation's flagging revolutionary spirit, and to relieve some of the excess population pressure on the urban areas. But these high-minded goals were lost on the young people themselves. What they found were the hardships, the boredom, and the frustration of rural life, and it sapped their revolutionary zeal.

Song Mingchao, a wiry, emphatic man who smoked constantly, said he had been revolted at first when he had to carry night soil—human excrement saved from the common privies around the village—and spread it on the fields by hand. Song was a southerner, from Canton, who was sent to Hainan Island, then still a remote backward area covered with jungle and inhabited by ethnic minorities.

But far worse, he said, was that he could never earn enough to support himself. The local male peasants, accustomed to the hard labor, drew ten work points a day, the women eight; but he never could get more than six or seven. "So we were always hungry. We scrounged in the fields, looking for sweet potatoes, roots, wild herbs, whatever we could find.

"Chairman Mao said we were supposed to learn from the peasants, but the peasants didn't want anything to do with us. We couldn't understand their dialect. And they said we were lazy; they blamed us for consuming their food without earning our share.

"The boys had another problem," Song added. "We couldn't find girl friends because the peasants wanted to marry someone who was a good worker and could earn lots of money. Once three of my friends shaved their heads. The cadres were angry and asked why. 'We might as well become monks,' they answered."

Eventually, Song decided, "There is no future for me in China." He and some friends forged travel documents and made their way to Canton. There he lived for six months illegally. He had no household registration and no ration coupons, so he joined an underground gang of other young people like himself. Some of the boys became pickpockets, hanging around the markets and movie theaters; a few of the girls acted as prostitutes. Whenever he had a chance, he practiced swimming in a park. After two attempts, he escaped to Hong Kong, swimming three hours across a bay where other refugees often drowned or were bitten by sharks. In 1980 the number of illegal refugees who managed to make it to Hong Kong reached as many as five hundred a night.

It was in the British colony where I talked with Song. He still read the Communist press, and he noted that after Mao's death the government largely abandoned the rustication program. Only five million of the seventeen million youth sent down to the villages were still there; the others had found their way back legally or illegally to add to the pressures on the cities. Song also liked to recite from Chairman Mao. He wondered if I knew what Mao had said in a talk at the caves in Yanan in 1939:

"How should we judge if a youth is revolutionary? There can be only one criterion, namely whether or not he is willing to integrate himself with the broad masses of the workers and peasants and does so in practice."

By that test, Song said, the revolution had failed.

It sometimes seemed as if young people had now deliberately inverted Mao's values, creating their own counterculture. Instead of calling each other "comrade," in good Communist fashion, I noticed, they addressed people as *shi-fu,* or "master," a traditional term for skilled craftsmen or experts. At the Peace Cafe, the restaurant and bar on Goldfish Alley where I encountered prostitutes, one of the customers was a tall, swaggering twenty-year-old who dressed in what looked like a zoot suit—a Western suit jacket with broad lapels, high padded shoulders, and gray bell-bottom pants, or "trumpet trousers," in the Chinese vernacular. He had teased up his hair and greased it into a pompadour, like a Chinese John Travolta.

When we met, he grabbed my hand in a gesture of bravado, identifying himself as Liu Guanghua, or "Liu Glory to China." (When he was later arrested for procuring, the *People's Daily* delicately changed his name to Liu Xiaohua, Liu Little Flower.)

"Do I look like a Chinese?" he asked proudly. "Not many Chinese can dress this way; but I do." When I told him he looked like a Hong Kong Chinese, he beamed.

"When I was a boy, I was very bad," he went on, his conversation and manners a parody of all the Maoist virtues. "You know what I liked to do? Fight. Every day I would have fistfights. Not just one on one, but gang fights, twenty at a time. I was the best." He gestured with his thumbs up to show he was tops. He also pointed to his nose. It looked like it had been broken half a dozen times.

"I studied Russian in school, but I never learned any. I could write only one letter, R. I didn't learn many Chinese characters either. I was a really bad student."

Liu had to go, some business with women, he said. I was curious to learn more about him and asked for his address. He hesitated. At first I thought he was nervous about having a foreigner visit his house. But then another friend of his explained, "He really doesn't write well." When he scribbled down the address, his calligraphy was almost as bad, I thought, as my own misshapen Chinese handwriting.

The younger generation's reversal of Maoist values also showed in their music. Chinese young people, unlike Russian youth, have not shown much interest in American rock music or jazz, perhaps because the sounds are too foreign and harsh. But while I was in Peking, people in their teens and twenties were swept by a craze for soft, wistful love songs from Taiwan and Hong Kong, many of them set to the music of Hawaiian guitars and electric organs. To Western ears, they sound old-fashioned, like a Chinese version of the Andrews Sisters from the 1940s. But to Chinese, who for years have been able to hear only the drumbeating ditties cranked out by the People's Liberation Army band like "The Night Soil Collectors Are Coming Down the Mountain," the new songs had a strong emotional appeal. The music made its way quickly around the cities as Chinese who began traveling abroad in the late 1970s or overseas Chinese coming back to visit relatives brought in cassette tapes. I found one of the most valued presents I could give young Chinese friends was a handful of Hong Kong cassettes; every time I returned from a trip to the British colony the roomboys in the Peking Hotel would stop by to see which new tapes I had brought.

An eminent Chinese journalist told me with a wry grin that the official Chinese Music Association had gotten itself into a dilemma over a contest it sponsored in the spring of 1980 to pick the fifteen most popular songs. It was the first such competition since 1949, and the association received over a million letters. The trouble was, the writers voted overwhelmingly for Teresa Teng, a glamorous, svelte chanteuse from Taiwan who had never been to the mainland, and Li Guyi, a petite, controversial soprano who imitated the beat of the Taiwan hits. Li had divorced her husband—on the grounds that he was sterile—to marry the son of the commander of the navy, shocking the Communist hierarchy. While the Music Association tried to figure out what to do about the results of its contest, the press fulminated against "bourgeois, decadent" songs. A paper in Tianjin declared that Teng's songs "are either too bitter or sentimental and should be resolutely resisted because they can only impair our physical and mental health and corrupt our revolutionary will." Finally the Music Association decided to manufacture its own list of the fifteen winners, all what the government called "militant" songs, including "Good-bye Mother," about a soldier going off to fight in the 1979 border war with Vietnam, and "Our Lives Are Full of Sunshine," about the Four Modernizations.

But people were not so easily hoodwinked. Several weeks after the official results were announced, the League of Left-Wing Writers held a large party to mark the fiftieth anniversary of its founding in Shanghai, well before Liberation. Li Guyi was one of the singers. After she performed, the audience gave her a standing ovation, unusual in China, but when she did not come back for an encore and was followed by an army chorus, half the people at the party walked out, the journalist later said. The event was being shown on live television, and a microphone picked up shouts of, "If Li Guyi isn't going to sing anymore, let's go home." The situation was doubly embarrassing because one of the participants was the deputy head of the Party Propaganda Department, Zhou Yang, who for years has been the Communists' cultural czar.

Just as the sudden availability of cassette recorders helped spread the rage for Hong Kong music, they also fueled a new passion for dancing. Before the Cultural Revolution some Party leaders had held sedate dances in the Peking Hotel on Saturday nights; but from 1966 to 1979 dancing was banned as a corrupt capitalist pastime. As a result, Barbara and I were not prepared for what happened the second night we went to our friends the Wangs for dinner. After the meal was finished, they folded up the table, stowed it in a corner, and turned on their new Japanese recorder, a present from a relative in Hong Kong. The first song was by Donna Summer. Miao and Li began clapping for Barbara and me to demonstrate the disco for them. Neither of us is a good dancer, but there was no choice, and soon we found ourselves on their tiny living-room floor switching partners not only with the Wangs but with several neighbors and relatives who had been alerted to the arrival of the hip foreigners. Somehow the Wangs had taught themselves a stiff facsimile of disco, and they had not forgotten the fox-trot, waltz, and tango they had learned before the Cultural Revolution.

"Life in China is dull, so dull," Mrs. Wang exclaimed. "It's why young people get in trouble." It was a comment I heard repeated often.

Another evening a young friend in his twenties, Yining, who worked for Peking Television, called to say he had tickets to a dance in the Great Hall of the People. I was incredulous. I was accustomed to thinking of the Great Hall as the holy sepulcher, the mother church of Chinese communism. In my mind its polished marble steps and hushed grand meeting rooms, always guarded by soldiers at attention with bayonet-tipped rifles, recalled the late Zhou Enlai feting Richard Nixon. But in 1980, in keeping with the government's new stress on profits to spur economic development, the Party began renting out some of the rooms in the Great Hall on a commercial basis. The dance that evening began early, at 6:30, in a huge room on the third floor with giant pillars and a green marble floor. Two bands played a medley of approved tunes, including several Western songs that have become part of the Chinese repertoire: "Red River Valley," "Auld Lang Syne," and "Do Re Mi" from the movie *The Sound of Music*. The lights had been left on bright; intimacy was impossible; but that didn't bother the dancers—they had come to dance, not hold hands or embrace in a dark corner. There were men dancing with men, women with women, even a mother essaying a new step with her small daughter. Several times an announcer warned over the loudspeaker, "It is forbidden to do rock and roll," but a number of young couples ground away anyway, behind a high lacquer screen. The illicit dancers were wearing sunglasses with the price tag and made in Hong Kong sticker still on them, a kind of magic talisman assuring their modernity. One of the women swung to the beat with her long waist-length hair loosed from its usual braids. She was tall for a Chinese, and had on a fur coat, tight red sweater, and hip-hugging bell-bottom slacks.

"The daughter of a high cadre," Yining said, pointing to her. "Only cadres' kids are well fed on milk and meat, and it shows."

At 9:30 the announcer abruptly declared the party over and the guests immediately streamed out, docile and obedient, without a pause. Americans would have hung around, hoping for another dance, I said to my host as we walked down the majestic steps looking toward the Gate of Heavenly Peace.

"We may be compliant on the surface," he replied. "We are conditioned to accepting authority. It is just like in *1984* by George Orwell," he said, adding that he had recently read the book. "It is an exact description of the Cultural Revolution; I loved it. But something else happened in the Cultural Revolution which Orwell didn't foresee—many people became disillusioned. Mao sent us out as Red Guards to topple the capitalist roaders. 'To rebel is justified,' he told us and we believed him. We pulled down the power holders. But then Mao said stop, and he called in the army to get rid of us and packed many of us off to the countryside. All he really wanted was for us to get rid of his enemies in the Party. We felt manipulated and betrayed." It was a widely shared sentiment among young Chinese I met.

He himself had spent three years on a commune planting rice before his father, a county official, had used a back-door connection to have him "recommended" by the peasants for admission to university under one of Mao's reforms. "It wasn't the peasants who picked me, it was the commune Party secretary," my acquaintance recalled. "You were supposed to be selected on the basis of your political background. Actually, my father was born into a poor peasant family, ran away to join the Red Army as a boy, and his parents were executed by the Kuomintang, so I did have a clean class record. But that wasn't what Mao intended."

After he graduated, his father again used his influence to have him assigned to the television station, a prestigious and easy job. But even this presumably fortunate young man was now disgruntled. For all Chinese who had entered college when the "recommendation" system was in effect, from 1970 to 1976, were stigmatized as "worker-peasant-soldier students." They hadn't had to pass the old exams to get into college—many had only a few years of primary school education before being selected—and while they were in university the classrooms were in chaos. Yining said he had never had to take a test during his college career. Mao's successors had taken their revenge on the worker-peasant-soldier students by excluding them from several national wage raises after 1976 and putting them in a separate category outside the regular salary grades. Yining was paid only 43 yuan a month ($28.67), less than the average factory worker's income of 58 yuan ($38.67).

"We're not all stupid, it isn't our fault we didn't learn anything in those days," Yining lamented.

In some ways the worker-peasant-soldier students are the most tangible result of the Cultural Revolution. Almost a million of them are spread throughout the country—in research laboratories under the Academy of Sciences and in far off Tibet, where some volunteered to go. But Yining sees little future for them.

"Now people discriminate against us everywhere, they look down on us as the afterbirth of the Cultural Revolution. We just missed getting thrown out with the Gang of Four."

For all the difficulties of the worker-peasant-soldier students, they were not as bad off as another even larger group of young people who began to surface after I arrived in China. The Chinese called them dai-ye, "waiting for work"; it was a euphemism for unemployed. One of the Communists' great accomplishments in the 1950s was that in a poor, overcrowded country they had given everyone a job—indeed, most Chinese had come to look on their jobs as having a lifetime guarantee. The system was administered by labor agencies which coordinated among factories, schools, and neighborhoods; students finishing school didn't have to go out to look for a job, they were assigned one. But in 1979 the government suddenly discovered it had a major unemployment problem. The trouble had actually been building for several years because of the effect of the great baby boom in the 1950s and 1960s, after the return of peace and stability; but it had been obscured by Mao's down-to-the-countryside program, which siphoned off excess city youth to the villages. With Mao's death, his successors recognized that the policy had become unpopular and unworkable and millions of discontented people flooded back to their homes, some legally and some without permission. The seriousness of the situation was brought home to the Communist hierarchy at New Year's in 1979 when youths returning to Shanghai to spend the holiday with their families extended their stay to demonstrate against their continued rustication. Westerners in the city reported that tens of thousands of these young people had looted shops, blockaded the railway station, tying up trains, and marched on the city Party headquarters along the waterfront. To compound the employment problem, there are an estimated four million Chinese coming on the job market in the cities each year after finishing school. Government officials indicated there were anywhere from 10 to 20 million young people in the cities "waiting for work." That does not sound like a large figure in a country of one billion, but what it meant in human terms was revealed in a New China News Agency story claiming that 70.4 percent of all urban young people now had jobs. Looked at in reverse, that also showed that 29.6 percent did not—almost as high unemployment as black youth suffered in America.

Because the government could not create new jobs fast enough in state-run factories, the coveted sector of the economy, Mao's successors reversed the Great Helmsman's contempt for small private and cooperative enterprises as a "tail of capitalism" and encouraged youngsters to work in them. Some of these proved a minor success—I visited a small hotel with 110 beds started by a group of unemployed young people in an underground bomb shelter in the capital, and a three-table restaurant in a family home. But this kind of enterprise didn't resolve the problem.

On a crisp November day I encountered a twenty-one-year-old woman, Kang Keli, who had been given one of these new and often makeshift jobs as an attendant in a small bicycle parking lot near the Forbidden City. It was the best weather of the year in Peking; the persimmons had ripened into bright-orange spheres on the gray branches of the trees inside the emperors' old residence; the high sky was an azure blue and free of pollution for a day. Keli said she had graduated from high school two years before but only in the past month had been assigned her first work, guarding the bikes. Her pay was only 24 yuan ($16), less than half the average for a factory worker, and she got none of the usual benefits in China—a bonus, free medical care, housing, or a pension.

"It's better than sitting at home doing nothing," said Keli, who had short braids and large round eyes. Her younger sister had just graduated from high school the previous July and also still hadn't been assigned work. A younger brother would finish school next spring.

"For us young people, there is no road out," she said, using a phrase I heard often. "There is no future." Keli smiled when she said it, as Chinese do when confronted with an unkind fate, but her words conveyed a finality. In the 1950s, when the Communists' triumph was still fresh, a surge of optimism had swept China—there was hope that the country could finally be transformed from its backwardness and poverty. But now the mood was pessimistic again. It was partly an indictment of the Communists, of their wasted opportunity, and partly a reflection of the intractability of poverty in a country with a quarter of the world's population.

Not long before I had come across a lanky teen-ager with horn-rimmed glasses hawking copies of a four-page newspaper called *The Torch,* a daily bulletin put out to publicize the results of the then ongoing national games, a Chinese olympics. He was carrying the papers in a bag around his neck, but unlike newspaper boys elsewhere wasn't shouting the headlines to attract customers.

"I don't want to cheat people," he explained. "It's bad enough if they buy it on their own because there's nothing in it, but I'm not going to encourage them."

He said his neighborhood committee had given him the job a few days ago, but it would end when the games were over. Then he would just have to wait for another assignment. Suddenly he shoved the papers in his hand into the bag and began to run. "Bottle caps," he whispered, teen-age slang for the police, because of the round red national emblem they wear on their hats.

"Isn't it legal for you to sell papers?" I half shouted at him, assuming that his neighborhood committee must have cleared the job with the police.

"Not in this place," he shouted back ambiguously before he was out of sight.

I never discovered whether he was violating the law; but I did learn during my stay in Peking that juvenile delinquency and crime among young people had become a serious problem in China. Here was another of those shibboleths. The Chinese had long boasted that they had virtually eliminated crime. Yet a radio station in Changchun, an industrial center in the northeast, reported an incident that sounded like a scene from the movie *Blackboard Jungle.* At the city's Number 9 High School, the broadcast charged, two "gangster students," miffed that one of their classmates had been chastised by a teacher, broke into the teacher's room and "violently attacked him with sticks and stones.

"When the teacher ran to the teachers' office on the second floor," the radio went on, one of the students "caught him from behind and shot him with a zip gun, shooting a nail in his back."

The *Southern Daily* in Canton once reported that a twenty-one-year-old rural youth went on a thirteen-day joyride across Guangdong province in which he stole two bicycles, two cars, and four trucks and hit and killed two cyclists. The young man, Wang Yonghe, began his adventure when he was caught stealing peanut oil that belonged to his production team. Looking for a means to escape, he spied a truck belonging to a local cigarette factory. The door was not locked, so he loaded the bike he was riding in the back and took off. But because he had learned how to drive only on a tractor, the paper said, "the truck ran like a mad horse. In less than two hundred meters, he hit and damaged a cart, a bamboo fence, and a bike repair shop." Eventually, after a chase through the Canton airport and a swim across the Pearl River in Canton to avoid his pursuers, Wang was captured when he tried to steal some clothes from a theatrical troupe performing in a park. The *Southern Daily* noted with dissatisfaction that Wang's father was Party secretary of his production brigade and should have disciplined him more as a boy.

People like Wang and the students who shot the teacher were what the Chinese had come to call *liu-mang,* an old term that originally meant vagabond but had been appropriated to connote hoodlums. A number of Chinese I knew showed the same anxiety about meeting *liu-mang* on the street as New Yorkers do about being mugged on the subway. One evening when I invited a Chinese teacher to a play in a workers' club away from the center of the city, she was visibly upset when she arrived at the theater. She had come by herself on her bicycle to avoid arousing suspicion. Halfway through the performance, she whispered that she wanted to leave early before the crowd got out. I couldn't figure out what was bothering her, but the next day she called to explain.

"That is a very bad section of town," she said. "You shouldn't have asked me there. The streets are very dark and there are lots of *liu-mang.* You never know what could happen."

How can you tell a *liu-mang?* I asked. "They have long hair and mustaches, and they smoke a lot on the street," she answered. "Sometimes they drink too much in the restaurants and then they throw up on the floor. It's terrible. It never happened before the Cultural Revolution." She almost sounded like an outraged American parent describing hippies in the late 1960s.

Like other journalists and diplomats in Peking, I wondered whether juvenile crime had really grown or whether with the greater openness of the Chinese press and the freer contact between Chinese and foreigners after

1976 we had just become more aware of what had been going on all along. Both explanations probably had a measure of truth. But Chinese officials insisted the increase was dramatic. The president of the Supreme People's Court, Jiang Hua, said in a speech that juvenile delinquency was ten times higher in 1980 than in the early 1960s. A professor of law at Peking University, Shen Zhongling, stated in an interview that young people now commit 60 percent of all crimes in China. That is about the same proportion as in the United States, where people under twenty-five accounted for 57 percent of all arrests in 1980, according to the FBI. A leftist magazine in Hong Kong, *Tunghsiang,* reported that one district of Shanghai registered 1,042 thefts and burglaries in 1978, 87 percent of them committed by young people. In compliance with a new national policy, the district subsequently set up a reform school to "reeducate" juvenile offenders. In its first year it took in 104 students.

The growing alienation of young people baffled the older generation of Chinese. Many times I heard Party cadres wonder why young people were not more grateful for what the Communists had done for China. But they had forgotten that the majority of people were born after 1949 and didn't remember what the bad old days were like. The most noticeable improvements in the conditions of life took place in the 1950s—the more equitable and secure supply of food, the new security of employment, the increased availability of education and medical care. These were impressive changes, but young people now took them for granted. There had not been similar gains in the 1960s or 1970s and the major event in the lives of everyone under thirty was the Cultural Revolution.

Perplexed by young people's attitudes, the government was tempted to see the handiwork of the devil—in their case, capitalism, just as rightists in America often blame rising crime rates and drug addiction on the Communists.

"A few young people are deluded by the temporary prosperity of the capitalist countries," the *People's Daily* fulminated in an editorial. "They see the prosperity and technological advances of the capitalist nations and the backwardness of the socialist states and conclude that capitalism is better than socialism. This leads them astray. But this is completely wrong. Only socialism can save China."

A conscientious, hardworking high school teacher offered a more subtle but similar interpretation of what troubled young people. "What is happening is that the government now says it wants to learn from the West. By that it means Western science and technology and the rule of law.

"But when young people see it is fashionable to copy the West, what they imitate is all the superficial things, sunglasses, long hair, bell-bottom pants, dating in high school."

We were on a picnic at the tombs of the Ming emperors, northwest of Peking, with the teacher's husband, a scientist, and the couple's sixteen-year-old daughter. As we sat on the grass under a cluster of pine trees facing a three-arched gate, the sound of a woman singing drifted across the broad, grassy valley from a loudspeaker at another of the tombs a mile away. It was Li Guyi, the pop star.

"I hate to say it, but students today are not as good as those before the Cultural Revolution," the teacher continued. She had on a mannish pants suit made from a check material and spoke with a quiet intensity and sense of uprightness I noticed in many Chinese.

"There are a few good students, of course, but most don't have the habit of hard study. When they were young all they read were the thoughts of Chairman Mao. Worse, they don't believe anything you tell them. They argue with you about everything. After all the changes in the Party's line, they have seen through things." She used the same phrase, *kan to le,* that young people used themselves.

Her own teen-age daughter, Lingling, in some ways bore out her lament. The first time I met Lingling, when we were both reading a poster on Peking's now defunct Democracy Wall, she confided her cynicism.

"I am afraid China is going to end up just like the Soviet Union, with a powerful army, lots of factories, and no freedom," she said in her soft, girlish voice. "I don't like to go to the zoo, all those animals locked up in cages. It reminds me of how we Chinese are trapped."

That sounded precocious coming from a sixteen-year-old, I suggested.

"I'm almost seventeen," she said at first, defensively. Then she added, "I had to learn early. I was only three years old when the Cultural Revolution hit us. My father and mother were both criticized and taken away—they said she was a Kuomintang agent. By the time she came home, all her hair had turned white."

Lingling had a willowy figure and a perfect oval face, but she was mortified that she suffered from acne and so wore a *koujiao,* a white cotton surgical mask that many Chinese use against the cold and dust of Peking's winter. On the first day we met, she had on an ordinary blue worker's jacket, but she had left the top two buttons undone in a gesture of daring. Under it she wore a tight-fitting turquoise T-shirt, with a matching turquoise scarf around her neck. Her pants were made of blue denim, cut tight at the hips, a Chinese version of blue jeans. To complete her outfit, she had on open sandals with two-inch heels, very high for China, and black patterned stockings which showed through her shoes. Her father had bought them in Shanghai, China's center of fashion. When I commented that she was unusually well dressed for China, she smiled with pleasure.

"Most people just like those fatty pants, they're so ugly, but they are afraid of being stared at."

Lingling had tried wearing her tight pants to school, but her homeroom teacher stood in the door with a ruler and measured to see if the students' trousers were either too tight at the hips or too wide at the cuff. Another time, she recalled, she was taking her noon nap in school when she heard an announcement over the loudspeaker.

"It was a new government directive. Students must no longer wear foreign sunglasses, boys can't have long hair, girls can't get their hair permed or wear makeup, and no more listening to love songs from Hong Kong.

"So I will be careful about what I wear in school, but I'll do what I like at home. Life in China is a big play. We are all actors." Then she paused for a moment. "But I don't like to think about this too often. One has to have some illusions to live."

For all Lingling's cynicism, however, she was actually a bright, diligent youngster who was determined to get high grades and pass the college entrance exams, which had been restored in 1977. In this she was like many other young Chinese—their disillusionment was real, but presented with an opportunity to get ahead, they were still capable of hard work. The trick for Peking lay in providing them more hope to advance within the restricted, conservative confines of Chinese society. Once when Lingling opened her school notebook, I saw that inside the front cover she had written out her daily schedule. It began with getting up at 5:30 every day for half an hour of exercise, then fifteen minutes for breakfast, and an hour of study before classes started. Every subsequent quarter of an hour during the day was accounted for, till lights out at 10 P.M.

Lingling's mother had used her connections to get her into one of the better high schools and, because their apartment was over an hour's bus ride from the school, had also gotten permission for both mother and daughter to sleep in the teachers' room at night so Lingling wouldn't waste valuable study time commuting. In the evenings her mother tutored her in Chinese, her mother's own subject, and had other teachers give her extra help in math. Lingling's father lived by himself at home during the week, cooking his own meals.

"I don't mind," he said when we were on the picnic. "We just hope Lingling will be able to pass the exams and someday be able to go abroad to study." This dream of getting into college and ultimately going overseas to study was the last great motivation for young people and kept many of them from falling into the apathy that had overtaken the country's bureaucrats, factory workers, and less-talented youngsters.

Even during the Cultural Revolution when the universities were shuttered, the traditional Chinese passion for study did not slacken. At the University of Science and Technology in Hefei, in central China, a tall, gangly physicist in his early thirties named Chen Ping recalled how he had been assigned to work as an electrician in a small railroad station in a remote part of the country after his school was closed in 1968.

"I didn't have much work to do," he remembered, fingering his wispy mustache. "Maybe two or two and a half hours a day. There weren't many trains. They were stopped by all the factional fighting."

But during a trip to the local provincial capital, he found a 1947 edition of the Encyclopedia Britannica gathering dust on the shelves of the railroad office. It had been bequeathed to the railway by an old employee, but no one knew what the books were. Chen asked to buy them.

"At first they said no, but then they said I could borrow the books."

So with the help of his girl friend, a conductor on a train that passed through his lonely station, he began to read. She brought him one volume at a time, until he finished all twenty-eight. He might have gotten into political trouble, given the radical temper of the time, but his fellow workers were tolerant.

"They said, 'Why don't you tell us a story each day from what you read?' "

After the Cultural Revolution, Chen returned to his university as a teacher. He had mastered English. And he married his railroad conductor.

This reverence for education, which dated to Confucius, made Mao's reforms of the school system one of the most contentious issues in China. Like some progressive American educators in the 1960s, Mao felt the schools had become too elitist, that they discriminated against children from less-advantaged families like those of peasants and workers. That was why he had abolished the college entrance exams and simplified the curriculum in the schools. To lessen the traditional authority of the teachers, which Mao also believed was elitist, he had encouraged student attacks on teachers. And to make education more practical, he called for combining study with work in the fields and factories.

But since his death, most Chinese agree Mao's experiments only ended up lowering standards. The New China News Agency stated in one sensational report that China now has 140 million illiterates, 120 million of them under forty-five. In another article, the *People's Daily* revealed that while 95 percent of Chinese children do start out attending primary school, as the government has long claimed, "in reality only 60 percent finish their five years of primary school and only 30 percent can be said to have reached the five-year primary school standard." The problem lies with the poor quality of rural schools, the severe shortage of government funds for them, and the continued belief among many peasants that it is more useful for their children to work in the fields than go to school. As a result, the Chinese school system, like many American schools, is turning out functional illiterates.

Education is also an emotional subject in China because along with membership in the Communist Party and promotion to the officer corps in the armed forces, it is one of the three main avenues for moving up in society. Competition for survival starts early. The Communists have rapidly expanded the number of schools—there are 210 million Chinese in school today. But 12 percent of those who finish primary school are unable to go on to junior high, and there is no room in high school for 50 percent of the students who complete junior high. At the top of this pyramid, only 3 percent of the college-age population in China, about a million students, can get into university. In the United States, by comparison, 35 percent of the population between eighteen and twenty-one are in college; 23 percent of young people in the Soviet Union go to college, and even in the Philippines, which has a total of 40 million people, there are 1.27 million college students, more than in all of China. The *Guangming Daily* groused that China ranked 113 out of a list of 141 countries in the world in percentage of its young people who get a post-secondary education.

This figure startled me, given the value Chinese place on schooling. The major reason is money. Peking has not released exact data for its expenditure on education, but some rough calculations can be made. The 1980 national budget for education, plus health, culture, and science, of which over half went to scientific research, was 14.8 billion yuan ($9.87 billion), or about $10 per person. The real total would be somewhat higher, since Peking requires the villages to finance their own schools out of local revenue. But another article in the *Guangming Daily* disclosed that in the late 1970s, after the downfall of the Gang of Four, the government invested only 1.12 percent of China's gross national product in education. That would put China about 110th on the United Nations list of spending for education, after such countries as Somalia, 2.7 percent, Guatemala, 1.7 percent, and Bangladesh, 1.2 percent. The United States invests 6.4 percent of its GNP in education, the Soviet Union, 7.6 percent. Chinese friends traced Peking's miserly appropriations to Mao's contempt for expertise and the Communists' failure to understand the role of technology in the modern world. Mao had derided intellectuals as "the stinking ninth category," after landlords, capitalists, and assorted other bad elements. The Chairman's view became national policy. "For quite some time," the *People's Daily* said in a revealing 1980 article, "some people considered education as an item of consumption that had no connection with production. When they thought of expanding production, they considered building factories, buying machines, constructing irrigation works. They seldom considered, or simply did not consider, the question of training people."

For the lucky few who do get into college, the rewards are immense. Unlike those young people who finish only junior or senior high school and may have to wait a year or two before being assigned to work in a neighbor-hood cooperative or at best a factory, they are assured some of the most prestigious jobs in China: as scientists, engineers, interpreters for the China Travel Service. "It is a lifetime meal ticket," said an affable professor at Fudan University in Shanghai who had been trained in the United States. "You have to realize that under our system, almost no one flunks out once they get into college. Professors just don't fail students. It would go against the idea of a guaranteed lifetime position once they make it into college."

The key to success, since Mao's death, is passing the national university entrance exams, twelve and a half hours of tests in six subjects spread over three days. In 1980, of the 3.3 million students who qualified through a preliminary screening process to sit for the tests, only 285,000 were admitted to college. Most were high school seniors, seventeen, eighteen, or nineteen years old, though there were a few people in their mid- or late twenties whose schooling had been disrupted by the Cultural Revolution or who had flunked earlier exams. Americans are familiar with the ordeal of taking the college boards—the competition, the preparation, the anxiety; but the Chi-nese exams involve even more tension. The very word for test in Chinese, *kao-shi*, resonates with a hallowed significance, evoking memories of the old imperial exam system where thousands of scholar-candidates steeped in years of study of the Confucian classics were locked in cubicles for several days at a time. Those who succeeded became the Emperor's mandarins. Exams to Chinese are almost a religious ritual, admitting priests to a cult, a kind of theocracy.

For the current college exams, the teachers who have been picked to prepare the questions are kept incommunicado in a secret mountain resort for two months before the test date in July. They are not allowed to make phone calls, write letters, or send telegrams, to prevent cheating. Parents become as involved as their children in preparing for the exams. A teen-age acquaintance told me that for a month before he took the exams, his father and mother wouldn't let him have any friends over to his house, though they did excuse him from his household chores. For an entire year in advance, he said, he studied six hours a day in addition to his regular homework, studying texts of earlier exams. After he passed, his parents threw a large dinner party that cost several months of their salaries. His homeroom teacher wrote an inscription in an album he bought for the occasion: "Now you will be a success for life."

The pressure to succeed is intense. Each summer the Chinese press reports several cases of suicide among students who fail. Many students who do not succeed are unwilling to accept their defeat and try again the next year. The Ministry of Education once arranged for me to visit the Number 35 High School in Peking which was being used as a test site and talk with a group of fourteen students who had just finished their three days of tests. When I asked what they would do if they didn't pass, all fourteen said they would study on their own for a year and take the exam again.

Another young woman, a lathe operator in a Peking factory who had not been able to finish high school because of the Cultural Revolution, recounted her attempts to take the exams on her own. She had already tried twice. Why, I asked, was she not satisfied with being a worker in a socialist state?

"In the early years of the People's Republic, many people were very happy to be workers," she replied, arching her thick black eyebrows. "The pay was good, welfare was guaranteed, and it gave you a Red status," meaning you were politically safe. "But now people want to be intellectuals. There's a lot of prestige being a scientist. It may be a workers' state, but workers have a poor position. There is no equality between us and the cadres."

One of the consequences of the return to a conventional exam system has been the open creation of the kind of elite that Mao abhorred. Just as in America, children from families with a higher standard of living and better educational backgrounds now have an advantage in getting into college. The New China News Agency conceded that of the entering class of 2,000 students at Peking University in 1979, 39 percent came from families of cadres and soldiers, though these two groups make up only 2.2 percent of the overall population. Another 11 percent of the freshmen were offspring of intellectuals, who constitute perhaps 2.5 percent of the population. Friends who taught at Peking University, however, cautioned that the situation was not really that different while Mao's reforms were in effect—the only change was that his successors were more candid about the figures.

The government also returned to the pre-1966 system of "key schools" in which it could concentrate its scarce resources on the individuals with the greatest intellectual potential to provide the economy with talent in the speediest, most efficient fashion. At one of these favored institutions, the Fuzhou Number 1 High School on the southeast coast, the principal, Zhang Junshi, said 37 percent of his senior class had gotten into college the previous summer. Before the Cultural Revolution, when he was beaten by some of his students and packed off to work in a factory, the school had achieved the stunning record of placing 90 percent of its graduates in college, Zhang recalled. A tall, erect, courteous man with a high forehead, Zhang took obvious pride in his work. As a key school, the Fuzhou high school got an extra subsidy from the city government for each student, and admission was by exam only, as for college.

Walking through the high-ceilinged, whitewashed corridors of the school, I was struck by how different it was from an American high school. Chinese complain about how unruly their teen-agers have become, but the students in Fuzhou seemed serious, disciplined, dedicated, like my teen-age friend Lingling. These youngsters knew they had a chance to succeed within the system and reap its rewards. So no one ran in the hallways, there was no talking in class, the students stood when the teacher entered, they folded their hands behind their backs and recited in unison when the teacher read a lesson. Rote memory is still the main instructional technique just as it has been for over 2,000 years—Mao's strictures to the contrary. There were no frills—no audio-visual aids, no student cars in the parking lot, and no drugs. It was the kind of school in which my grandfather, who started out as a teacher in a one-room village schoolhouse in upstate New York at the turn of the century, might have felt comfortable.

The Chinese school system is designed to inculcate technical skills rather than teach students to think or develop their capacity for creativity, the goals of an American liberal arts education. The curriculum in the Fuzhou school, like those elsewhere in China, is largely determined in Peking. Electives are few. There are no music or fine arts appreciation courses, no homemaking, and no economics, sociology, or psychology—all regarded as too frivolous or too politically sensitive. Classes in Chinese history are carefully circumscribed. Even students majoring in history in the universities study events only up to 1949, the founding of the People's Republic. There is only one authorized textbook on the history of the Chinese Communist Party from its founding in 1921 to 1949, and none for the period since then, for with the incessant political purges and shifts in the Party line, the Communists have had difficulty deciding what the correct version of history is. Was Mao good or bad? In what degree? Why was Liu Shaoqi, the head of state until the Cultural Revolution, denounced as a capitalist roader and jailed only to be posthumously rehabilitated? Examined too carefully, these questions might threaten to unravel the whole fabric of the state. Students in high school and college are given compulsory political education, and politics is one of the six subjects tested on the college entrance exams.* But the courses stay away from sensitive issues like the roles of Mao and Liu and students say the content of the politics courses consists of dull memorization of the current Party line. On the 1980 politics test, the major essay question, worth twenty of a possible one hundred points on the whole exam, was "Why do we have to strengthen the leadership of the Communist Party in order to realize the Four Modernizations?" Under fill-in-the-blanks, students were asked, "What is the root cause of the inevitable crisis of capitalism?" The correct answer, the lathe operator in the Peking factory told me, was private property. She had no difficulty with the politics test because all the questions and answers

---

*The others are Chinese language, math, and a foreign language, mandatory for all candidates. Those concentrating in science must also take tests in physics and chemistry; those in the humanities and social sciences, tests in history and geography.

were provided in a review outline which she had purchased several months beforehand at the night school she was attending.

As another measure to try to assure conformity, the Ministry of Education admits it takes a student's political attitude into consideration along with his test scores in deciding who gains admission to college.

"What this means is that you have to join the China Youth League if you want to go to college," said Lingling. The Youth League, modeled on the Soviet Komsomol, is the training organization for Party members. "I didn't want to join, but my teacher and mother insisted. They said that if you apply for college and two students have the same grades, the one who is a Youth League member will get preference.

"So my mother wrote my application for me. I didn't know what to put down. She made up a wonderful essay, that the Youth League is important for China's future and only with the Communist Party can China achieve the Four Modernizations.

"Then when the day came we were to be sworn in, luckily I was sick. I don't know if I could have taken the oath with a straight face."

Only 20 to 30 percent of the students in her class belong to the Youth League, Lingling calculated, a sharp drop-off from the early years of the People's Republic when membership was usually over 50 percent. The league members' main activity is to stay at school on Saturday afternoons—most Chinese go to school regularly for half a day on Saturday mornings—and either do extra political study or voluntary labor, like planting trees or digging in the school garden.

"When it's time for the league members to perform labor, the rest of the students laugh at us and say, 'Bye, we're going home,' " Lingling concluded.

This cynicism makes today's Chinese young people hard to predict. The Communist Party was founded on idealism and willingness to sacrifice. It was the Communists' belief in their cause which enabled the older generation to accept privation and tight political controls during the revolution and up to the 1960s. But in the Cultural Revolution something snapped. The Communists lost popular confidence, a critical ingredient to ruling such a vast country as China, like the mandate of heaven, the traditional principle that gave legitimacy to China's emperors. Today, if China is to meet its goal of becoming a modern industrial power, it needs productive factory workers and creative scientists, not semieducated malcontents and frustrated cynics. I was surprised how disillusionment has spread even to the best universities, where the students have the most to gain from the system. At Fudan University in Shanghai, a group of journalism students decided to take a poll to find out what their colleagues believed in, a graduate student there told me. One afternoon they went to the library, locked the doors, and daringly passed out questionnaires. Only a third of those who responded said they believed in Marxism; nearly a quarter said fate; a few replied Christianity, and 25 percent said "nothing at all." In a similar unofficial sounding at the Peking University library, a friend told me, 95 percent of the students said they doubted China could achieve the government's modernization program.

But it was a compulsory freshman class on Marxism at Peking University that really brought home to me how deep this alienation is. A nervous young woman teacher, standing on a raised platform at the front of the room, had just explained what she called the five basic principles of socialism. Then she scanned a roll of her students and called on one to repeat the cardinal points. The student was absent.

The professor read out another name, and again there was no response. This time an embarrassed giggle went around the large, sunny room, perhaps because an American was present.

Finally, with the sixth name, the professor found a student who was actually there. "Well?" she asked.

"I don't know," the student replied.

The teacher's inability to evoke an answer about a subject so sacred to the Communists and the absence of so many students from a required class summed up for me a conundrum Peking's leaders now face: China has become an authoritarian country with an authority crisis.

9.　Growing Up *Guai*

THE CHINESE PASSAGES

"We wax happily, but wane with ineptitude. The last part of life we tend to abandon, even to despair, whereas for the Chinese it is a summit, for the very reason that it has been built by human wisdom alone upon a notoriously fragile and transitory base."
　　　　　　　　　　George Kates, The Years That Were Fat

In a large sunny room with a bare concrete floor, ten one-year-olds were squeezed next to each other on a tiny wooden bench, their backs against a wall. For minutes they sat motionless. None cried, pushed, or shoved.

Then a middle-aged woman attendant, with short salt and pepper hair, took a windup toy chicken out of its carton, turned the key, and let the metallic yellow bird strut across the floor past the infants' feet. Again, none of them moved or tried to grab the toy, as my two children would. They simply followed it with their eyes.

Finally, one boy, dressed in a red jacket and green padded trousers, with hair that stuck up straight in tufts, couldn't resist. He toddled over and pounced on the chicken. The attendant, clad in a full-length white nurse's smock, gently picked him up and deposited him back on the bench with the others.

The episode took place during a visit I made to the four-story gray-brick nursery school and kindergarten run by the Peking Printing and Dyeing Factory for 270 children of its workers. But it was similar to scenes I saw acted out in other nursery schools in a dozen Chinese cities. Like many American visitors to China, I was constantly struck by the almost universal good behavior of Chinese children, what some Westerners interpret as passivity. They are quiet, obedient, quick to follow their teachers' instructions, and they seldom exhibit the boisterous aggressiveness or selfishness of

American children. Nor do they cry, whine, throw tantrums, or suck their thumbs, some of the typical signs of anxiety and tension to which Western kids are prone.

In the Printing and Dyeing Factory's nursery, the attendants had already begun to toilet-train the one-year-olds. In a corner of the room there was a pile of white enamel spittoons. "As soon as the infants wake from their naps, we put them on the potties," Li Jianzhi, the head of the school said. "They stay there till they defecate. When they want to urinate, they have learned to go by themselves."

I was incredulous. Our daughter Sarah was one herself and nowhere near ready for such discipline, I felt. But just then a fourteen-month-old girl wearing a green apron with the factory's name stenciled on the front wandered off the communal bench and picked up a spittoon. Then she sat down and accomplished her mission. Her pants had a slit in the rear, as all Chinese children's do, to make the task easier.

Afterward she returned to the bench where several of the attendants had begun to feed the kids their lunch, rice porridge mixed with scrambled eggs. Each woman, perched on a low stool in front of the bench, held three metal cups and spoons, one for each of the children they were charged with helping eat. I watched with growing amazement as the attendants managed to give first one of the kids a spoonful and then moved on to another. None complained or grabbed for more, out of turn. They were learning to share and take their place in a group.

An American woman resident of Peking who enrolled her five-year-old son in the local Chinese kindergarten that accepts foreign children was crestfallen to be told that her child was the only member of his class who misbehaved.

"The teacher said that when they had visitors, my son refused to stop playing with a toy and return to his seat like the others," she recalled. "The teacher was disturbed that my son lay down on the floor and had a fit. She couldn't understand it."

How Chinese induce their children to be so well-behaved, in an age of rampant permissiveness and disobedience in the West, was one of the mysteries about China that fascinated me. One key, I found, was that Chinese parents strive to create a special sense of closeness with their offspring—Americans might call it smothering. At the same time, in order to build in discipline and self-control, Chinese fathers and mothers carefully restrain any restless moves toward what we would see as independent activity and self-expression.

At birth, many Chinese mothers still swaddle their babies, binding their legs and arms in blankets or cloth so they can't move. Laura Chandler, a ginger-haired American teaching in the provincial town of Hefei, discovered that when she had a baby daughter in the local hospital the nurses tied its hands to its sides with strings. They were afraid otherwise the baby would wake itself. A Chinese from Shandong said the peasants in her native village still practiced an old custom of putting their newborn babies inside a sack which they tied up to the infants' necks. Rather than using diapers, they then filled the sack with sand, which acts like cat litter. When Chinese parents take their infants out for a walk, they usually hold them in their arms or tie them to their backs rather than push them in a stroller or pram, out in front. Hence where Western infants get their own independent view of the world around them, Chinese children tend to see it through their parents' prism.

Chinese children sleep in the same room and often on the same bed with their parents till they are at least three or four years old. Chinese friends were invariably surprised to find that Sarah slept in her own room and managed to get through the night without waking.

"How can she go to sleep by herself?" our friend Mrs. Wang inquired. "When Yuanyuan was small, she always slept in our bed. She would wake up five or six times a night, to urinate or be fed. I had to be there." In part, this custom may grow out of the small, cramped apartments that Chinese must accept because of the housing shortage; but it also produces an intimacy American children don't get.

The Wangs were also aghast when they came to supper and found that we let Sarah play on the floor by herself. She was just learning to walk and was determined to crawl and toddle while Barbara cooked.

"You shouldn't let your baby play on the floor," Miao reproved us. She picked Sarah up and held her on her lap. "She could get cold or dirty." Again, this was partly testimony to the economic conditions of Chinese homes—the lack of adequate heating and bare concrete floors, which are hard to keep clean from all the dust in Peking.

But I could see Barbara bristle at someone else telling her how to raise her child. When she finished cooking, it was already eight o'clock, and she put Sarah to bed before serving the meal. The baby's room, however, was only ten feet from the dinner table, and she could hear the conversation. She stood in her crib and voiced her displeasure at being excluded. Miao looked uncomfortable. After taking a few bites of roast chicken, she rushed into Sarah's room to comfort her, despite Barbara's protests that crying wouldn't hurt her and she wouldn't go to sleep if someone kept picking her up.

"When my child cried, I cried even harder," Miao explained. "I had to go to her."

Later that night, after I had driven the Wangs home, Barbara observed that neither of them ever reprimanded or punished Yuanyuan, even when she and Ethan, our four-year-old, charged around the living room yelling and throwing pillows. This, too, is part of the closeness between Chinese parents and children. Chinese cherish harmony, one of the central Confucian virtues, and I noticed that Chinese are reluctant to use harsh words or physical punishment.

"It is no use to beat children, they don't understand," Lao Wu, my Chinese assistant, said once when we discussed Chinese child-rearing practices. "If my boy misbehaves, I try to persuade him to stop. For example, if there is a thermos of hot water on the table and he tries to climb up and get it so he could burn himself or break it, I move it away. If he still goes for it, I tell him a neighbor's boy would not do that." He was almost serene in his confidence, born of Chinese belief in the power of education, that his son of course would do what he was taught.

I was skeptical of such comments at first, but as we stayed in China I realized that no country has greater love for children. The word for "good" in Chinese is a pictograph of a woman next to a child (好). It was also apparent that after Ethan and Sarah joined me in Peking, the reaction I got in the dining room of the Peking Hotel changed dramatically—the waiters and waitresses I had jousted with for a year to get service suddenly began coming over to our table immediately. Everyone wanted to talk with Ethan and pinch Sarah's cheeks. *"Nemma bai, nemma pang,"* they exclaimed (So white, so fat), almost an insult in English but the ultimate compliment to a Chinese, signs of a healthy, well-fed baby.

On the day the family first flew up from Hong Kong to Peking, Ethan insisted on exploring the CAAC plane by himself. Soon he had locked himself inside the lavatory in the rear of the Russian-built Ilyushin jetliner. I didn't realize what had happened until I saw all the Chinese passengers turned in their seats staring aft. A muffled cry of "Daddy Fox," Ethan's appellation for me, was coming from the toilet. He had turned the heavy latch and it couldn't be released from the outside. But a young engineer with a pitted face who had been sitting across the aisle feeding Ethan a steady diet of candy and apples leapt from his seat faster than I could and rushed to the rescue. First he whipped out a penknife and tried to pry the lock open. When that didn't work, he slammed himself against the door like a detective in the movies. Soon several stewardesses and even the pilot arrived, all to no avail. But after thirty minutes of coaxing, Ethan finally got the inner knob to turn, and as the sign on the outside swung from "Occupied" to "Vacant," he emerged. The engineer grabbed him in his arms like his own son.

Some Western Sinologists have observed that Chinese tend to indulge or spoil their children (the word for "spoil" is *ni-ai,* literally, "drown with love"). It is true that they often save the best food, like meat or milk, for their children, when they must subsist on a tight budget. It is also true that while Chinese adults today stick to somber proletarian blue and unisex baggy Mao tunics, they dress their children in brilliant oranges, reds, and pinks, as if they reserved all their pent-up interest in fashion and individuality for their off-spring. The most beautiful piece of clothing we found made in China today —in contrast to the lovely embroidered robes and dresses sewn before 1949 and sold in antique shops to foreigners—was a pink satin cloak with hood for Sarah.

But Chinese parents don't glorify their offspring the way child-centered middle-class Americans do. The quality they prize in their children is *guai,* a word that means "well-behaved," but which also coveys the sense of submissive, quiet, and placid. I can recall dozens of times, both in Taiwan and on the mainland, when a child made too much noise or got out of line, their parents would cluck at them, *"Guai, guai, guai,"* using the term like "shush," or "shame," "behave yourself." Ethan, by contrast, was *tiao-pi,* "naughty." Once when Barbara was sick, we sent our *a-yi,* or "maid," to pick him up from the kindergarten he attended, run by the wife of a Filipino journalist. The *a-yi* arrived home livid. Ethan had slapped and kicked at her all the way home, she said. He was crying. When I asked him what happened, he said she had tried to hold him by the hand. To an American child it was confining; to a Chinese it was natural and necessary.

Chinese parents don't ask what they can do for their children—as American fathers and mothers do—but what their children can do for them. This is a carry-over of the old virtue of filial piety, which lay at the heart of Chinese personal relations. A professional couple we got to know, the Hu's, have a girl eight years old and a boy twelve. The children never called their parents by their first names, as some American kids do, only by their titles of mother and father. Each is assigned his or her chores: the daughter goes to fetch the milk every morning from the neighborhood collection point (there is no home delivery); the son washes the supper dishes without a whimper. The two children rise at 6 A.M., get dressed quietly, and go out jogging, then come back and heat the milk and slice some bread for their Western-style breakfast, all without waking their parents. The son and daughter share a tiny room, and at night they sit face to face at two small desks doing their homework under a single lamp. I never saw them fight or quarrel. The absence of sibling rivalry, given the predatory instincts Ethan and Sarah sometimes showed for each other, was remarkable. One day the son came home late for dinner; he claimed he had stayed late at school to study. When Mr. Hu, a pleasant, polite man with neatly combed short hair, later found out he had actually been out turning cartwheels with some friends, he made his son kneel for an hour for telling a fib.

Before 1949, the anthropologist Francis Hsu has observed, China "was a country where children came last."* Parents had a completely free hand with

---

*Francis L. K. Hsu, *Americans and Chinese* (New York: Doubleday & Co., 1970), pp. 76–77.

their progeny. Infanticide was not a common practice, Hsu wrote, but in times of poverty parents who did kill their children were seldom punished by law or publicly censured. Children may not fall into such a benighted position today—the Communists have banned infanticide. But I was intrigued that, unlike in the United States, there is no public debate over abortion, though under the government's stringent birth-control campaign some commune clinics I visited handle more abortions in a year than live births. Traditionally there was no specialty of pediatrics in China, and even now I could not find any books in bookstores on how to make Chinese better parents. There is no Chinese equivalent of Dr. Spock, or Piaget, and no widely published studies of how children learn or behave.

Instead, in the past at least, Chinese were raised on the classic *The Twenty-four Examples of Filial Piety,* from which three- and four-year-olds were told stories like that of the boy who allowed mosquitoes "to feed without restraint upon his blood until they were satisfied" in order to prevent them from biting his parents. The most impressive of all was the tale entitled "On Account of His Mother He Buried His Child":

> A poor man by the name of Kuo and his wife were confronted with a serious problem. His aged mother was sick in bed. She needed both medicine and nourishment which Kuo could ill afford. After consultation between themselves, Kuo and his wife decided that the only way out was to get rid of their three-year-old and only son. Kuo and his wife said to each other, "We have only one mother, but we can always get another child." Thereupon the two went out to the field to dig a pit to bury their child alive. But shortly after they started to dig, they struck gold. It transpired that the gods were moved by the spirit of their filial piety and this was their reward.*

Such stories are now condemned as a relic of the feudal past, but Chinese children still learn early to see the world in terms of a network of others. By design or not, it is in the government-run day-care centers where this social training and discipline are the most intense, as if the Communists had transmuted filial piety into acceptance of the authority of the state. Some working mothers bring their infants to nurseries as early as fifty-six days, the end of their paid maternity leave. At the Peking Printing and Dyeing Factory, children under one are placed in a "feeding station," a large poorly heated room dominated by a single collective crib. Ten infants, spaced at intervals of two feet, were lying immobile on their backs on a plastic sheet the day of my visit. They were so bundled in their three or four layers of padded winter clothing they could not roll over. Three mothers were feeding their own babies in an anteroom from large bottles.

"The mothers can come to feed their children twice a day, during their

*As translated in Hsu, *Americans and Chinese,* p. 78.

work breaks," explained Miss Li, the head of the school. "Otherwise, we have nurses to take care of the babies." There were no toys in the crib, and no mobiles strung over it, no indications that the attendants were concerned about stimulating their sensory perception or intellectual development. "If they cry, we comfort them," added Miss Li, a benign woman with a radiant smile and a green sweater under her blue jacket. She felt that infants under one year old are largely passive and helpless and likely to learn little.

Children in the nursery school and kindergarten are divided into age groups—the one-, two-, three-, four-, and five-year-olds each had separate rooms—but as they grow older every activity is still highly organized and, I noticed, initiated by adults. In the room for three-year-olds, the teacher was playing a small pump organ and teaching the class a new song. As I entered, the entire group of twenty-four children chorused, "Good morning, Uncle," as if there had been a cue. They were seated at three low tables; none was pushing or poking the other. The teacher, a robust woman in her early twenties, commanded, "Sing," and they divided into girls and boys. The girls chanted first:

Little brother, where are your little hands?

My hands are here.
They can grasp guns, they can fire, pow, pow, pow.
Little sister, where are your little hands?

My hands are here. They can do physical labor.
When the kerchiefs are dirty, they can wash them.
Little brother, where are your feet?

My feet are here, they can play football.
Little sister, where are your feet?

My feet are here, they can dance.

In earlier years the song would have been a paean to Chairman Mao. The Great Helmsman is out of fashion, but the moral tone was still strong, if sexist by current Western standards. The girls all had red- or blue-velvet bows in their hair, held in place by a plastic strap that ran behind their ears.

It was a charming and impressive performance, far beyond anything Ethan could sing or memorize. He could never get beyond the first line of "Mary Had a Little Lamb" or "Silent Night." He didn't have the power of concentration or ability to follow the teacher's instructions that these Chinese children did. But there were no books on display in the classroom, and during my day's visit to the school I didn't see any attempt by the teachers to encourage individual play or improvisation. The songs and dances were all collective behavior, requiring only a memorized response. They bred conformity and role-playing.

Next door, in the class for four-year-olds, the teacher had drawn a handsome ocean liner on the blackboard, green for the ship, blue for the waves, red for fish in the ocean, and a pennant flying from the ship's mast. All the students had dutifully copied the outline, some with more skill than others, but all with little deviation. Again, Ethan would have been put to shame; the art work he did was primitive free-form finger painting. But unlike American teachers, the instructor had not festooned the walls with the students' handiwork. "We don't glorify the work of individual students," the teacher explained. The only decoration was somber color portraits of Mao and Hua and a copy of the week's schedule for the class. Each activity was listed in advance.

As a left-hander, I was curious if there were any left-handed pupils in the school. Chinese for centuries have forcibly converted their heathen southpaws; calligraphy written with the left hand is infelicitous, they say.

"We have only one left-handed student in the whole school, a girl," Miss Li responded. "She is very stubborn. We have gotten her to use her right hand to write, but it will take more time to make her use her right hand to eat."

Some Chinese parents, however, do worry that the tough regimen of nursery schools like this tends to make their children too placid and uncreative. A professor at Peking Normal University was concerned that his two-year-old son just sits quietly and doesn't speak when he comes home. Sometimes he doesn't move or make a noise for an hour at a time. "We worry whether the treatment in the nursery is destroying his intelligence," the professor said. Because the professor and his wife both work and because their jobs are over an hour's bus ride from their apartment, they board their son in the nursery. They drop him off on Monday mornings before going to work and don't see him again till they pick him up on Saturday afternoon. About a third of the children in Peking's nurseries and kindergartens are boarders like this.

Chinese parents and teachers also recognize that children who are raised at home tend to be less disciplined and more individualistic than those sent off early to nursery school. (Despite the impression given visiting foreigners, only about a quarter of Chinese youngsters are in nurseries or kindergartens, a much lower figure than in the United States.)

Niannian is a four-year-old daughter of parents who are technicians in a factory. Living with them are their old servant, from before Liberation, and the families of two relatives who lost their own homes in the Cultural Revolution. So Niannian has grown up at the small center of attention of an adult world peopled by assorted uncles, aunts, and a nanny. She was used to eating her meals with the family and took part in the grown-ups' conversation until her mother shushed her. She hadn't learned the skills of cooperation necessary to life in kindergarten—and Chinese society as a whole. When her parents finally did start her in their factory nursery, she cried and wouldn't let her mother leave her. Even when she came home for dinner she was so miserable she wouldn't eat for the first few weeks.

Once during a visit to their home, Niannian wanted to go to a nearby park where she liked to ride on the slide. There was a long line of patient children behind the ladder, standing quietly, without visible parental supervision. They climbed up and slid down without a sound, sometimes even without a smile. Niannian did not want to stand in line. She started to climb the most direct way—up the front of the chute, to the chagrin of her mother. And when her mother pulled her off, she hollered, as an American child would.

As Chinese grow up, they also trace a different set of passages from Westerners, making the transition to young adulthood more slowly and with less disruption, for they are still circumscribed, and sustained, by their network of mutual dependence, their *guan-xi,* and therefore feel less compulsion to assert their own independent development. In traditional China there was no recognized period of adolescence; even today there is no term for it in the language. The cult of youth has never existed in China. As the psychiatrist Robert Lifton has observed, "One's importance lay, not in the youth he was, but in the man he would become, and mainly in relationship to his family and his society. A Chinese youth became a man not by casting off his father's influence and control, but rather by adapting himself to them, by becoming like him."* Youthful rebelliousness was countered by stories from the *Twenty-four Examples of Filial Piety.* Today this sense of loyalty to one's parents and other superiors remains strong, despite the outburst of youthful rebellion encouraged by Mao in the Cultural Revolution and the growth of cynicism about Communist society. Martha Ritter, an actress from New York who taught English for a year at Peking Normal University, recalled that her students were deeply puzzled when she assigned them to read *The Catcher in the Rye,* J. D. Salinger's classic account of American teen-age restlessness.

"Why if Holden Caulfield is sent to the best school, if his parents are well-off, and his teacher is a good person, why does he hate all of them?" one of her pupils asked. "Why do young Americans like this book, why is it considered great literature?" others inquired.

"They have no sense of adolescent rebellion," Ritter concluded. "They are not burning with rage to find themselves, to distance themselves from the institutions they grew up with."

No matter how old, Chinese must still defer to their parents, at least on

*Robert Jay Lifton, *Thought Reform and the Psychology of Totalism* (New York: W. W. Norton and Co., 1961), p. 363.

the surface. A nineteen-year-old college student, a lively, inquisitive boy with a fondness for reading American novels, told me he took his parents to the movies every weekend, something American teen-agers would be mortified to do. Lihua, my twenty-year-old petitioner friend who had been sent to the countryside, devoted much of her time to caring for her invalid father and her sister and brothers. Jan Wong noticed that, among her friends and roommates when she was an undergraduate at Peking University, most matured later than Westerners because of the prolonged child-parent relationship.

"A twenty-one-year-old here is probably equivalent to a fourteen-year-old in America in terms of independence from his or her parents, economically, philosophically, and psychologically," Jan said. "I was astounded by the number of times my Chinese friends asked me if I was homesick—they always were. My roommate, who lived in Peking, went home every weekend." When she attended McGill University in Montreal, her own hometown, Jan recalled, "I went home only when I had to.

"Twenty-one-year-olds here tend to still be giggly, unthoughtful about their future, and childlike in behavior. They take delight in pranks that would amuse a junior high school student in America, like throwing water on each other when they are sent to a village for labor stints, hiding things from one another, or popping out from behind doors to scare someone."

But the political and social breakdown of the Cultural Revolution has produced something of a chasm between generations in China. The parents of Lingling, the precocious sixteen-year-old high school student, summoned me urgently to their apartment shortly before I left China. Lingling wasn't there, and her mother was agitated. She had found a diary Lingling had been secretly keeping and discovered her daughter was involved with a foreign student at Peking University. She was also concerned that Lingling was no longer maintaining her spartan study routine.

"We don't understand her anymore," her mother said, talking rapidly. "She has been affected by all the things young people are thinking and copying from the West. Her school is near where Democracy Wall was, and last year she read all those posters. Now she has those ideas."

"Maybe we are too old now," added her father, who had been sitting in a corner silently. "There is a generation gap emerging in China."

They wondered if I, as a Westerner, could persuade Lingling to concentrate on her studies. Later, when I next saw her, she had just been ice skating with her foreign boy friend. She had on a new purple knit sweater and matching scarf and had cut her hair very short, in pixie fashion, like an early Audrey Hepburn. There was a dash of red lipstick on her mouth. She looked very pretty. It was the kind of daring display of fashion some Chinese women had begun to try out in private after Mao's death, though, as Lingling had told me, she couldn't do it in school because it wasn't officially sanctioned.

"My parents don't understand me," Lingling protested. "Since I am an only child, I am spoiled. My parents do everything for me. To put it nicely, they love me very much. To put it more candidly, they insist I spend all my time with them. They don't like me going out of the house without them. If we go to the movies and there is a boy sitting in the same row, they make me sit between them.

"I like to be free. But the more innocent and stupid I act, the better they like it. So I don't show them I am sophisticated and can think for myself."

A thoughtful Chinese editor, with two teen-age daughters of his own, related that they had occasionally laughed at him as old-fashioned. "They say I am a person of the 1930s. There is a growing generation gap in China. But I think it is a political problem rather than a biological or cultural phenomenon as in the West. It is a result of the frustrations of the Cultural Revolution, not a permanent trend." He believed the traditional Chinese family was still intact.

There may be the makings of a generation gap in China, but as Chinese young people move into their twenties, they do not yet go through the trauma or triumph of an identity crisis, as Americans and other Westerners do. They don't have that luxury, for they are hemmed in by a society that offers them little choice or mobility, the prerequisites for the full-blown, do-your-own-thing individualistic life-style that Americans now take for granted. Indeed, there is no word in Chinese for either identity crisis or life-style. Instead, Chinese tend to follow a carefully prescribed pattern with little deviation or exploration of alternatives. By law, Chinese men must wait until they are at least twenty-two years old to get married, twenty-seven in the cities; women must be a minimum of twenty, twenty-five in the urban areas. Then when they reach the legal age, all Chinese seem to rush to get married in the next year or two.

Lan, a twenty-six-year-old scientist with an impish smile, lives in a dormitory with three roommates. She had started living in the dorm two years ago when she was twenty-four and her roommates were the same age. At twenty-five the other three all got married; within the next year they all had children. Now she has a second set of twenty-five-year-old roommates, and all of them have boy friends and plan to have weddings soon.

Lan is worried. There are no eligible men in the institute where she does research, and she has found it hard to meet anyone with the same high education level she has. As an intellectual, she wouldn't consider marrying a factory worker or peasant. And the pressure for her to get married is intense.

"There is a telephone operator in our institute who is thirty-five and not married," Lan told me one day as we drove to the Summer Palace in the northwestern suburbs of the city. "She lives in a tiny room with her switchboard and a bed. Everyone gossips about her and ridicules her because of her condition.

"You can be the dumbest person in the institute, do no work, and no one will laugh at you," she went on. "But if you aren't married by thirty, they will laugh."

David Eisenberg, the Harvard Medical School graduate who worked in the Institute of Traditional Chinese Medicine, related that Chinese physicians frequently encountered a complaint from women in their late twenties. When they came in for treatment, the women said they were suffering from stomach pains or other common ailments. But after the doctors examined them, they found nothing wrong. Then the patients admitted their real problem; the symptoms were only an excuse. They had been married for a year and hadn't yet gotten pregnant. They felt they had to produce on schedule.

To make this social straitjacket tighter, young Chinese are dependent on their parents for many of the necessities of life. Housing is so scarce that newly married couples must often live with their parents until well into their thirties. In her best seller, *Passages,* Gail Sheehy classifies people like these in America as white ethnics and comments that "having missed out on the experimental round trips that help middle-class youth to pull up roots," they maintain dependent ties to their families.* Sheehy adds, disparagingly, that the white ethnics often have no vision of themselves. When they marry, it is mainly to comply with what they believe they should do. The white ethnic "may do his time on earth making a living, rather than committed to a lifework." But Chinese have little choice. They often have to count on their parents to use their connections to secure them a job, and, once assigned employment, there is scant opportunity to change it. Women are not confronted with the dilemma of whether to pick career or motherhood—they must work. There is no equivalent in China to the old American admonition "Go west, young man." The only time Chinese are likely to move to another city is when their *danweis* order them to go, often against their wills, having to leave their wives, husbands, or children behind. The kind of mobility Americans are accustomed to is totally alien to Chinese. I remember in 1972, on my tour of the United States with a group of Chinese newsmen, they were mystified by the sight of cars on the New Jersey Turnpike pulling house trailers behind them. What are these strange contraptions? they asked. I saw looks of disbelief when I explained that some Americans actually moved their homes with them.

*Gail Sheehy, *Passages* (New York: E. P. Dutton, 1976), p. 256.

But where Americans might chafe at this lack of choice, it can also provide Chinese with a psychological security that rootless Americans lack. Chinese are so accustomed to having everything decided for them—to having their jobs, their housing, sometimes their marriage partners picked out by someone else—that they are baffled when confronted by the uncertainties of life in the United States. When two of the first Chinese scholars to study in America arrived at Boston in 1980, they expected officials from Harvard to meet them at the airport, as visiting foreigners always are met in China. But no one was there. Then when they managed to collect their baggage and take a taxi to Cambridge, they had no idea where to go. The driver deposited them at the Faculty Club, where they could spend the night. When a university administrator told them they would have to find their own apartment and arrange their own class schedule, they felt insulted.

In middle age, this same constricted mobility again dictates a different voyage for Chinese—not having been able to dream as grandiosely when they were young, they have fewer illusions to abandon as their physical powers begin to falter. In the United States, Gail Sheehy found that "the transition into middle life is as critical as adolescence and in some ways more harrowing."* As Americans realize they will not become president of the bank and time is running out, they can be tormented into depression, sexual promiscuity, power chasing, alcoholism, and violent swings of mood.

But Chinese in their middle years are less likely to press down on the career accelerator and more likely to try to build themselves a safe niche in their old *danwei,* immunizing themselves from the dangers of political campaigns. They have already crossed the critical divide. If they didn't show political activism when they were in their late teens and join the Youth League, they have been labeled passive and can't recover later and join the Party, the major path to success. Otherwise promotion is almost solely on the basis of seniority—the year a person began working in his *danwei*—and it is dangerous to appear too ambitious.

"People resent anyone who is better than they are," a soft-spoken forty-year-old clerk in the Academy of Sciences said. "It is part of our heritage from Mao. They instinctively feel everyone should be equal." Because her father had been labeled a rightist in 1957, she had not been able to go to college; but her parents, who had been educated at schools run by American missionaries before 1949, taught her English at home. "I am only a typist, the lowest grade, but my English is much better than anyone else's in the office, so I volunteered to do some translations we needed. But the other

*Sheehy, *Passages.* p. 360.

people in the office said I put on airs, they said I should be satisfied with what I am. They are always gossiping about me."

Finally she considered asking for a transfer, but that would mean going to the personnel section of her institute, which is run by an old Party cadre who formerly served as a political commissar in the army. "Then they would make an investigation, they would go to my dossier, and the old issue of my father being a rightist would come up again." So she dropped the idea as too dangerous.

Middle-aged Chinese are also trapped in a much slower pattern of career promotion than Westerners. In Communist China, people in their forties and fifties are often still on the lower and middle levels of the ladder of success where their counterparts in the West would already be in top executive positions. Senior posts in China today—in the Party, the army, factory management, science, medicine, and the arts—are all reserved for elderly veterans who have reached at least their sixties and more often their seventies or even eighties, the men who joined the Party long before 1949.

"Among my friends," observed a newspaper editor in his mid-fifties, "the great frustration is that they are still lowly paid and don't have important posts." He himself earns only 75 yuan ($50) a month, not as much as many factory workers, and has not been promoted in over twenty years, though he is intelligent, dedicated, and respected by his colleagues. The problem is that his superior at his paper joined the Party in Yanan in the late 1930s and, while approaching seventy, has no intention of retiring.

"This is a problem for all Chinese who went to university or started their careers in the 1950s," the editor added. "They are at the height of their mental and physical powers, but they have to accept being in a low or mediocre position."

Even those few middle-aged Chinese who are successful are cautious about pressing ahead too far or too fast. A diminutive actress with a sensitive face and tiny hands that she waves as she talks said she prefers staying home with her husband and two children to appearing on television.

"There is a saying in Chinese—'A person fears fame the way a pig is afraid of becoming fat.' "

A one-time teacher who was imprisoned in the Cultural Revolution, she worried that her former colleagues would become jealous of her current good fortune. "No one can tell what will happen when Deng Xiaoping dies, there could be another campaign," she said. "Now my motto is, I don't want fame or money, only to avoid making mistakes." She still lives in the same apartment building where she has for years, and every day passes the people who were responsible for her earlier incarceration.

"Before when I walked past them, I wouldn't say hello, nor would they.

Now sometimes we greet each other. But I haven't forgiven them, and I wonder how they feel."

The greatest contrast to the West comes with old age. To Americans, it means the lonely end of life, the loss of vitality, lowered income, insecurity, and perhaps a small retirement home in Sun City or a bed in a nursing home, far away from family. But as Chinese approach old age, they become more content. It is the summit of existence, honored as a minor form of immortality. To be called *lao,* "old," is a compliment to a Chinese of either sex. Traditionally, as a person's physical powers waned, he was thought to gain in wisdom. Confucius told his disciples: "At fifteen, I set my heart on learning. At thirty, I was firmly established. At forty, I had no more doubts. At fifty, I knew the will of heaven. At sixty, I was ready to listen to it. At seventy, I could follow my heart's desire without transgressing what was right."

The elderly were also compensated by an increase in respect in their family. This was where the web of mutual dependence really paid dividends. A Chinese retained the parent–child relationship as his fundamental social tie as he went through life, adding other relations to it, not moving from one family to another as Americans do, like a snake shedding skins. Social security for a Chinese was just that. I knew of a forty-five-year-old cadre with two children of his own who wanted to exchange his old, cramped, Chinese courtyard-style home for a modern apartment, with a toilet and kitchen, closer to his office. His *danwei* was willing to arrange the switch. But his mother, a crotchety, senile eighty-year-old, refused to move. She was used to her neighborhood, though she seldom went out anymore, and got around their home only by supporting herself from table to chair. The son felt obligated to honor her wish.

Far from undermining this chivalry of age, the Communists have reinforced it. China must be one of the few countries in the world where children are actually bound by law to take care of their parents. Article Fifteen of China's family law stipulates that "children have the duty to support and assist their parents. When children fail to perform the duty of supporting their parents," the law continues, their parents "have the right to demand that their children pay for their support." Article Twenty-two makes it mandatory for grandchildren to assist their grandparents, if their parents are deceased. The *People's Daily* once reported that three peasants in Shandong, two sons and a daughter-in-law, were sentenced to up to seven years in jail for neglecting their eighty-year-old parents.

The Communists have also instituted a munificent welfare plan that ensures financial security for the elderly. In the cities, men can retire at sixty, after twenty years of service, women at fifty if they worked in a factory, or fifty-five if they spent their career in an office. They then draw a pension of 75 percent of their preretirement wages, up to 90 percent if they were model workers or veteran Communists who joined the Party before 1949. By a quirk of history, older people who started working in the 1950s are usually paid much higher salaries than those who joined the labor force in more recent years. (For the Communists awarded bigger starting pay to people in the 1950s than they do today, and in addition in the 1960s and most of the 1970s there was a national wage freeze.) Moreover, some retired men can find second jobs, particularly if they are technicians or skilled workers. The result is a strong incentive to keep the old three-generation Chinese family still living under one roof. For in an urban household with a retiree and four working members (father, mother, son, and daughter-in-law), the retired person's income often accounts for half of the total. This is the conclusion of Deborah Davis-Friedman, a sociologist at Yale who is working on a book on the care of the elderly in China.

Unlike young people, who are angry and frustrated, the elderly in China are genuinely grateful for what the Communists have done for them. Pick any morning, if you rise at five-thirty or six o'clock, and go to the Altar of the Sun Park near our apartment. There will be two hundred to three hundred elderly men and women gliding through the movements of China's ancient form of calisthenics, tai ji, performing as if in slow motion. Now and then they pause to chat with a neighbor or acquaintance.

"We are very thankful to Chairman Mao and the Communist Party," a white-bearded patriarch with a deeply furrowed forehead told me one morning when I went to watch their ritual. "The young people today don't understand, but we remember how hard life was before Liberation. In those days, old people could starve to death." His own father, a day laborer, had died of malnutrition and disease at the age of thirty-two, he recalled.

There are other economic imperatives holding the extended family together. When a factory or office worker does retire, under a unique system the Communists have devised, they have the right to turn over their job to a son or daughter. Given the current employment problem, this is a significant benefit. At the giant Lanzhou Petrochemical works, a sprawling oil refinery and complex of chemical plants, with 36,000 workers, a factory official said that of the six hundred workers who retire a year virtually all are replaced by their own children.

An acquaintance who worked as an accountant for the People's Bank said he planned on taking advantage of a new government offer to retire early —for him at age fifty-eight—so his son could take over his job. His son had finished high school two years before but still hadn't been assigned a job by the local labor office, and the accountant was concerned he might become a delinquent, like other unemployed young Chinese. When combined with Peking's program of delayed marriage and single-child families, the system of inherited jobs almost guarantees that if parents follow the rules, their offspring will be employed by the time they reach maturity.

Elderly people have another advantage. They are often the only members of the family who have been assigned housing—the authorities don't consider a desire by young people to set up their own separate household adequate reason for granting a new apartment. The cost of housing and food is relatively cheap; but prized new consumer goods like television sets, wristwatches, and bicycles, by which Chinese measure the improvement in their living standard, are much more expensive and require the combined savings of several family members. Grandparents are also useful for looking after small children when day-care centers are far away or unavailable.

In the countryside, the financial motives for keeping families together are even more powerful. Only a few of the richest communes have established pension plans, so the elderly must depend on their grown children for support, as they always have. But the aged can still play an important economic role themselves. Most housing in the villages is privately owned, and to build a new house takes years of joint savings. Public child-care facilities are rare. Those peasants over fifty are allowed to stop working on the collective labor teams, but this frees elderly men and women to devote full time to private sideline occupations like their small family plots, raising pigs and chickens, or growing fruit trees. For many peasants, this sideline work may account for over 30 percent of their total family income, and almost all their cash, as opposed to their payments in grain or oil which they get from their work in the collective fields. As a consequence, having older people in a family can be an economic asset, not a liability.

The Communist Party leadership itself is a tribute to the Chinese veneration for age. The average age of the Standing Committee of the Politburo, the inner sanctum of power, is seventy-two. Perhaps the two most powerful figures in China are Deng Xiaoping, who was born in 1904, and Chen Yun, who was born in 1900. Chen spends much of his time in the hospital, friends said. There is no legal requirement for senior Party or army officials to retire; they have lifetime tenure, like justices of the U.S. Supreme Court. At the last national congress of China's leading writers, artists, musicians, and actors in 1979, two of the delegates died during the conference. The average age of the nine men selected as the new heads of the various cultural associations was seventy-three.

At a session of the National People's Congress in September 1980, Ye Jianying, the stooped, fragile eighty-three-year-old chairman, was chosen to give the closing report. The meeting took place in the main auditorium of the Great Hall of the People, a giant amphitheater with seats for 10,000 people on three levels, a red star in the ceiling surrounded by four circles of lights, and a rostrum flanked by huge portraits of Mao and Hua and rows of red flags. Some of the delegates hobbled in on crutches or had to be helped to their seats by nurses. When the time came for Ye to begin, he was so weak a woman radio announcer actually read most of his speech for him. But at the end of the talk, Ye took over himself. He said the delegates should congratulate several aging deputy prime ministers who had agreed to retire at the congress, thus "raising the efficiency of the leading apparatus of the state. . . . They have, through this deed of theirs, set a shining example.

"I hereby propose that we all rise and give a standing ovation as a sincere tribute to them," Ye added. As he spoke, a group of a dozen women nurses in white coats and male attendants rushed onto the stage to help Ye and several other aged leaders to their feet. When he had finished, four of the nurses escorted Ye off the stage.

But China's cult of longevity may eventually be affected by the very success of the Communists' policies. With life expectancy up from thirty-two years in 1949 to sixty-four years now, there are many more elderly people surviving. And if the Communists follow through on their stringent one-child-per-family program, that will mean that each young person may be forced to help support as many as four aged parents and parents-in-law. A number of Chinese worry privately that this will prove an excessive burden unless the state moves in with an even larger and more costly social security plan, something the government can't afford. "It is a social problem waiting to happen," said the newspaper editor whose own career is blocked by an elderly boss.

10.   Report in the Evening

BING

"From the Red East rises the sun,
There appears a Mao Zedong."
                    From "The East Is Red," China's revolutionary anthem
                    during the Cultural Revolution

It was a large room, with hundreds of people sitting on wooden chairs and
standing in the aisles, she remembers. Her mother had been ushered to a
prominent seat in the front row, to watch. Her father, a veteran general of
the People's Liberation Army, a wounded hero in the wars against the
Nationalists and the Americans in Korea, was placed on the rostrum. Then
several armed guards with red armbands forced him to kneel, made him bow
his head, and thrust his arms up behind him and tied his hands. It was what
the Red Guards called the jet position, from the victim's resemblance to a
plane with swept-back wings. The time was 1967, early in the Cultural
Revolution, and her father had the misfortune to be in an army faction that
had come under attack by Lin Biao, the Minister of Defense and Mao's chief
ally. He was accused of being a capitalist roader and traitor, and the army
command had organized the meeting as a mass criticism session. With everything in readiness, Xiao Bing, "Little Soldier," his thirteen-year-old daughter, was marched onto the stage to testify against him. Given the ancient code
of filial piety, for a Chinese to denounce her father was the ultimate symbolic
act, a rejection of the old system of parental authority and an acceptance of
the new Communist regime as its replacement.

"It sounds incredible now, you can't understand it unless you were
brought up in the system," Bing told me after I had met her by chance at
a restaurant in Peking. Following the Chinese practice, I had sat down at a
table where there was an empty chair.

"I was very young and naïve at the time," Bing explained about her attack on her father. "I thought I was a child of the Revolution, not of my parents." She saw herself, as millions of young Chinese did in the 1950s and 1960s, as belonging to Mao and to communism and to China.

"That was the way my parents had brought me up—to be very disciplined. My father himself had betrayed his own brother in 1958 during the Anti-Rightist movement because he had said something in private about China being too reliant on the Soviet Union. To my father, that was the meaning of loyalty and honesty, to be devoted to the Party. My parents felt revolutionaries shouldn't show personal affection.

"I remember one day when I was nine, I was feeling very lonely. My parents both worked late. I wanted to do something to show them that I missed them. So after I came back from school, I made the bed and fixed some tea. When my father came home, he laughed at me. It was not a mean laugh, but it hurt. After that, I was determined to be a good revolutionary myself and not show my feelings either."

Bing learned her lesson in self-discipline well. When her father came under criticism, she was the first to denounce him. "I said I wouldn't be sacrificed for a capitalist roader." Thousands of other Chinese youngsters were caught in the same situation.

At the mass meeting to attack her father, a panel of military interrogators asked Bing to report any of her father's crimes she could recall. "I said he sometimes ate meat at home, something a reactionary like him shouldn't be allowed to do." To an outsider, this might seem a trivial charge, irrelevant to the heinous crime of counterrevolution. But in the arbitrary and hothouse atmosphere of the Cultural Revolution, it was the kind of evidence that zealous radical prosecutors took seriously. They encouraged her to go on.

"I also remembered that during a conversation at home with us he had told a story of how during the civil war with the Nationalists he had once temporarily lost contact with his company. I said there might be something suspicious in that." Pressed for more, she related that her father had urged her to drink milk to make her tall and healthy. "That was a bourgeois idea, I told them." Bing did not know how much her testimony counted—only later had she realized the verdict was predetermined—but her father ended up spending almost ten years years in an army detention center.

Bing has since grown into a lithe, twenty-eight-year-old woman with short, wiry hair and tiny, narrow eyes, triangular at the corners, the kind foreigners think of when they say Chinese have slanted eyes. She was not pretty in a conventional way, but she had a verve and directness and an engaging way with words that helped her charm friends. Whenever we met she first put on what she termed her "costume" to avoid recognition. On the outside she wore a full-length olive-drab army overcoat—unlike Chinese military coats, it had a hood and there was something about its color that looked familiar though wrong for China. "A souvenir," she said, crinkling up her eyes into even narrower slits, "from the U.S. Army in Korea. My father brought it home." Through other relatives in the Party who had made official trips abroad, she had acquired a pair of high brown-leather boots, tight green corduroy slacks, and a green ski parka, all foreign-made. It was enough of a disguise to deceive the guards at the Peking Hotel, who let her pass as an overseas Chinese.

One day, several weeks after we first met, she tried to explain more fully how she could have denounced her father.

"In those days, Mao was really like a god in my mind," she went on. During the Cultural Revolution, there had been a ritual everyone had to follow. Every household had a white plaster bust of Mao, and each day all the family members had to bow before it twice. "The saying was, 'In the morning ask for instructions; in the evening report back what you have done.'" It was an imitation of an old imperial practice, Bing noted.

"Suddenly one morning when I bowed to the statue, he looked like he was smiling at me. I got very angry with him. But then I was horrified at my reaction."

At the time, Bing added, the cadres were preaching the idea that people's lives were determined by a sudden flash, like a photographer's flash, which would leave an imprint on your mind. Whatever the flash was, it would decide whether you were a revolutionary or a reactionary.

"I was scared I was a reactionary, and they had told us we must report immediately any reactionary thoughts. I was afraid they would take me before a criticism session like my father and throw me into prison. I was only thirteen, and there was no one for me to turn to.

"Those were times when we kept personal feelings to ourselves. For months and years, I didn't have a real conversation with friends." She was living in a school dormitory. It was near her parents' apartment and she passed her mother every day on the street, but she couldn't talk with her. It was too awkward. She feared her mother was angry with her for her betrayal of her father; she was embarrassed, and she was also afraid to be seen with the wife of a known counterrevolutionary.

Despite her rigorous training in controlling her emotions, Bing admitted there were times she did get homesick. "Once I went home on a weekend —my mother was away, but my younger sister was there. She was only ten. She said, 'Big sister, we really miss you.' I broke down and cried." Bing lacked the support systems Westerners take for granted. She was cut off emotionally and politically from her parents. She didn't dare talk with friends. There were no guidance counselors at school or psychiatrists to turn to.

"For many weeks I was close to a nervous breakdown," she continued her story. "Each morning when we woke up, we heard the loudspeakers playing 'The East Is Red' and it set my mind going. I asked Chairman Mao to forgive me. I prayed to him. I kept reading as many of his books as I could, to keep the terrible thought of what I had seen out of my head.

"I got a Peking city map, with the bus routes on it, and I would recite, the Number Seven bus goes here, the Number Eight bus goes there. At night I would leave the radio on. I couldn't sleep unless I was distracted.

"I thought about jumping off a tall building. But if you commit suicide, they would automatically take it as proof you were a reactionary."

Finally, she said, she couldn't stand the pressure anymore. She wrote on a piece of paper what had happened and turned it in to the authorities. "They actually were very kind to me, because I was so young," Bing said. "They didn't handle me," she went on, using a Chinese term meaning to be punished. "They just assigned another girl to watch me twenty-four hours a day."

But Bing's troubles weren't over. Even though she had publicly denounced her father, under the Communists' bloodline theory of guilt, in which several generations are implicated in the sins of one member of the family, she was also labeled a reactionary by the officials at her school. They would not let her join the Communist Youth League; they expelled her from the city Ping-Pong team, where she was a rising star, and they banned her from meetings where Party documents were read out.

"Finally one day when they taunted me as a reactionary, I couldn't stand it any longer," Bing recalled. "I ran out of the building. I didn't know where I was going. I was in a daze."

She ended up at the Peking Railroad Station, a vast Stalinesque structure with marble floors. She sat there all afternoon and evening until eleven o'clock when the militia went through the station rounding up everyone without a proper residence certificate.

"I didn't have mine with me," Bing said. "They thought I was a prostitute and took me next door to a police station. They put me in a cell with a dozen other people—thieves, beggars, a crazy old man in rags who kept shouting to himself. It was horrible, like gong to hell and finding yourself alive. I refused to sit down on a bench with the others, they were so dirty, so I stood all night near the door."

The next morning at 5 A.M. a guard came to interrogate her. By chance she remembered that a friend of hers on the Ping-Pong team had a relative who worked in the police station and asked to see him. "Luckily I recalled a lot about the girl—that she had just been to Albania, that she had come back with a pair of sunglasses. Those were big things in those days." Finally he said she could leave.

But the episode meant the end of her formal education at the seventh grade; she was expelled from school and assigned to work in a factory. In 1976, when Mao died, Bing related, the Party leader of her factory called the workers together to watch a memorial service on television. "The Party secretary expected us to cry and show grief for Mao. There was a lot of pressure. I couldn't get a tear out. But my clothes were soaked with sweat."

Only later, after the Gang of Four were arrested, did she learn that some of her friends hadn't been able to cry either. "They just faced the wall, so no one could see."

It was a few months after Mao's death and the arrest of the radicals that her father finally was released from prison and rehabilitated. He did not blame Bing for what had happened it turned out, and the family was reconciled. "He understood, he knew I had been very young and that I didn't do it for myself but for the revolution. But still, it was very stupid of me to do it, it is not something I will ever forget."

There was a ceremony in the Great Hall of the People to honor her father, she told me, but she refused to go. "It was too late." Her father had been dishonored, attacked, imprisoned for a decade; she had been forced to stop school and was isolated emotionally and politically. Her faith in the Communist system had been shattered.

Still, she found irony in the situation. "For those of us who survived," she said, "the Cultural Revolution was a good thing. We learned a lot. I could never put another god in my heart like Mao." As it was for millions of other Chinese, the Cultural Revolution had been a watershed for Bing. She was no longer a revolutionary.

Bing was nervous about our meeting—she lived in dread of being spied on and criticized. "You learn to live with fear from the time you are born in China, it is the condition of our lives," she said. "At every door there is a policeman, every pair of eyes is watching you." We were eating lunch in the Russian Restaurant, a vestige of the days of better relations between Peking and Moscow, where you could still get a bowl of borscht and chicken fried with butter à la Kiev. The restaurant is next to the Peking zoo, but outside our window on a bitter January day, with patches of ice on the ground, stood an army sentry, his coat bulging with layers of padded undergarments. Was he protecting the restaurant or the zoo, I wondered? Neither, Bing said. Behind the restaurant is a theater, and theaters are considered important political institutions. She had telephoned to arrange the time for our rendezvous that day—we had already agreed on a place to meet at our last encounter—so she didn't have to identify herself or the location over the phone. With all the dangers a Chinese faced making friends with a foreigner,

I wondered why Bing was so willing to talk to me. I sensed it stemmed from the terrible isolation she had felt since childhood. Paradoxically, since she couldn't trust her family, friends, or colleagues, she felt safe telling her innermost thoughts only to a foreigner.

When she was twenty-two years old, Bing went on with the story of her life, she had attracted the eye of the son of another general, Guoqiang, "Strengthen the Nation." Her friends reckoned he was a prime catch. He was handsome, with smooth white skin and a flashing smile; he was a brilliant student in university, and his father was a deputy chief of staff of the army, an excellent family to marry into, a critical consideration to Chinese. He also liked Ping-Pong and was impressed by how well Bing played in a game he chanced to see.

"I didn't think he would like me, because I thought of myself as an ugly duckling, but I was very flattered. It was a low time in my life. My father was still in prison, and I didn't have much of a future."

Guoqiang began writing her letters, to court her, and she eventually agreed to go to the movies with him. She was startled when he kissed her at the end of their first date, unusually fast for a Chinese. It turned out he was very interested in sex, though Bing used a circumlocution in talking about making love.

"He put a lot of pressure on me to do it," she said. "I felt an obligation to him, he had been kind to me when I was in a precarious position and he helped me in my effort to study English on my own, since I wasn't allowed to go to school." One day he invited her over to his parents' house, a spacious home given his father by the army. It had its own garden, two servants, and separate rooms for each of the family's four grown children, one of whom had two infants of his own. There was even a guest room, where Bing was to spend the night. Late that evening, after Guoqiang thought his parents had gone to sleep, he called her to his room. He had asked a friend to secretly change the lock on his door, so his parents couldn't get in.

But after Bing entered and undressed, his mother became suspicious and knocked at the door. When she found it was bolted, she was even more upset and kept pounding until Guoqiang finally had to open up.

"There was some laundry drying on a line in the room," Bing recalled. "I hid behind it, feeling ashamed. His mother pretended she didn't see me, to save face. It was terrible. After that, I never enjoyed doing it. I just closed my eyes. I could go without it."

The experience of Bing and Guoqiang seemed typical of the shifting sexuality of the younger generation of Chinese. They were moving toward a freer standard of sexual behavior in the aftermath of the Cultural Revolution, though they still had to keep it secret, and they had not rid themselves entirely of the government's officially encouraged inhibitions.

A few months later Bing discovered she was pregnant. They were not married, and it presented a dangerous situation. "Any hint to my *danwei* that I was pregnant would ruin my reputation," Bing said. "The Party thinks women are supposed to be virgins till they are married, and it would go straight into my dossier. It is the worst thing that can happen to a woman." Fortunately, Guoqiang had an old high school classmate who was a nurse in a maternity hospital.

"When we went to her house to see her, we didn't have to say anything. She knew. She just said, 'How many months pregnant?' That was all. Then she made the arrangements with her hospital through the back door. She put me down as married, so there would be no questions and no report to my *danwei*.

"Guoqiang was supposed to come with me, but on that day he started making excuses. He said he had to go to work. I felt embarrassed. I was supposed to be married and my husband didn't even show up at the hospital. At first the doctors figured I was just being selfish and having an abortion without telling my husband. They asked if I had his permission."

Bing was put in a room with a dozen other women. When they called her name, she walked across the hall to the operating room. "They used a hose and pump to suck the fetus out," she recalled. "Afterward they pieced it together, the little bits they had, to make sure some of it wasn't left inside to cause bleeding." Then they told her to go back to the ward and rest for half an hour before going home.

There are usually taxis at the hospital, one of the rare places in Peking where Chinese can get cabs—they are normally reserved for foreigners, and are too expensive for Chinese anyway. But that day there weren't any taxis. Bing had to take a bus back to her parents' home, a crowded, jostling half-hour ride. The nurse had come to the hospital door with her.

"I am sorry I have to stay and work," she said to Bing.

"The look in her eyes said she knew how lonely I was.

"The next afternoon Guoqiang came over. He wanted to make love. I said, I can't, I've just had an abortion, I'm in pain. But he complained, 'I've ridden my bike all the way over from school.'"

Six months later, Bing was pregnant again; they were still not married. This time Bing was certain the hospital would criticize her, so she decided to claim that she was married and already had one baby and didn't want a second, in keeping with the Party's effort to limit families to one child. But the woman physician who came to examine her before the abortion saw right through her. The doctor had brought along three medical-school students for a class.

"She started talking to the students," Bing said. " 'Look at her abdomen, you see it is still tight. Notice her breasts, they don't sag. She's lying. Come on miss, confess.' "

This time, after the abortion was performed—without anesthetic as before —Bing fainted from the pain. She had to sit down on the steps leading downstairs not to pass out again when she left the hospital. By chance the doctor came by and saw her.

" 'I hate men,' " the doctor exclaimed. Actually, Bing said, the doctor was even younger than she was, but was very serious. " 'Men cause so much suffering. I see it all, and they never know what they do. I will never get married,' " she told Bing.

Bing had pedaled her bicycle to the hospital and rode it home.

With free contraceptives available under the government's birth-control program, why didn't she take some precautions against getting pregnant? I inquired. "It's just so humiliating to go in there and ask," Bing replied. Chinese prophylactics, she explained, come in three sizes. "You have to say, large, medium, or small. Guoqiang refused to go, he said it was my job."

Bing's parents never chastised her for her denunciation of her father, they understood it. But her parents were disappointed with her cynicism about the Communists. Despite his mistreatment, her father remained steadfast in his belief in the Party.

"He is an old-fashioned cadre, selfless and dedicated," she said. "Even my mother says his thinking is back in Yanan in the 1940s. After dinner he will still get up to sweep the floor and wash the dishes, though we have a servant and an army orderly to do that for us. Everyone else uses his office car for personal errands, but my father never lets me take it. He doesn't bring mother to official banquets to enjoy the food, even when other generals now routinely take their wives." Her father, she said, had grown up in poverty —his own father was a peddler, his mother was an opium addict. He had managed to attend a primary school only because of the indulgence of a local merchant family who sponsored a free school for the indigent. Ironically, one of his teachers was a radical and took him to join the Red Army guerrillas in the early 1930s.

"He doesn't like young people today," Bing said. Once, at a family meal, they were discussing a student protest demonstration in Hunan over Party interference in an experimental campus election. "My father was furious. 'These young people, all they do is make trouble, don't you join them,' " she quoted him as warning her.

"I said, 'What trouble? Student action is a good thing for democracy.'

"He only got madder. 'You should listen to me. My membership in the Party is fifty years, your mother has forty years. Between us, we have ninety years. You must believe what we tell you.'

"I couldn't stand it," Bing added. "I said, 'Look at the Soviet Union. It has an even longer history, and see where it has gotten.' There is a generation gap growing in China. My experience has made me a cynic. I believe nothing, like my friends. Recently I heard a joke people were telling about the Soviet Union, but I thought you could apply it to China as well. 'Adam and Eve were Russians. They were naked and had only an apple to eat between them, but they thought they were in paradise.' My parents are like them, they don't see," Bing said.

Bing's parents were also unhappy with her decision not to have children. She had finally married Guoqiang, her boy friend, when she was twenty-six. His father had pulled strings to get her admitted to a university, and her gratitude to him had increased. "But I made it an absolute with him that we would never have children," she said. "It is a growing trend among intellectuals. Our interests are changing," she explained. "If you have a child, it ties you down. You don't have the money to spend on new things like tape recorders, you don't have the time or the energy to continue your studies." Her reasoning was symptomatic of the new materialism in China, but her calculations were also much the same as those of young people in the West who are delaying marriage and deciding against having babies. There is a rise of concern with the self, with seeking one's own fulfillment, and less commitment to society or the state. Not long before, Bing said, one of her friends had a baby boy. The parents nicknamed him, in English, "Mistake." But Bing was aware of the hurt her position caused her parents, who thought along more traditional lines despite their Communist Party membership. Mencius, the great early expounder of Confucian doctrine, had said, "There are three unfilial acts, and of these, lack of progeny is the greatest."

Most of all, her parents were shocked to learn that she had recently had an affair with another man. He had been her first sweetheart when they were teen-agers during the Cultural Revolution, but then he got involved in a factional fight, was accused of being a counterrevolutionary, and had fled to Hong Kong. "I hated him for leaving the motherland, I thought he was a traitor," Bing told me, "but I loved him too." That was seven years ago. Now suddenly he had come back, on a business trip, with a Hong Kong passport, and he had looked her up. "It was as if the seven years never existed. I found I was still in love with him."

To make matters worse, she was having problems with her husband, troubles an American woman approaching thirty might recognize. "I discovered we were very different people," Bing said. "I began to realize I want to grow, to expand, to continue my studies and go to the United States, if I can. All he cares about is doing well in his job and that I be presentable to his friends." Guoqiang had gotten a coveted position with CAAC, the

Chinese airlines, thanks to his father's connections. "At night I have to get in bed first to warm it up, our room is so cold. Then after we do it, he just falls asleep." Their tastes varied also. Guoqiang liked to go to *gung-fu* movies starring Bruce Lee, which he could see in special "internal" film shows. Bing liked books about women. An American teacher at her college lent her a copy of the feminist novel *The Woman's Room.* She asked Guoqiang to read it; he refused. When he went on an official trip to Western Europe, she felt "liberated." "My schoolwork was better, my teacher gave me higher grades, even my roommate in the school dorm where I lived during the week noticed I was more relaxed."

Then the foreign professor also gave her a copy of Gail Sheehy's book *Passages.* "It was a revelation. I was really going through a crisis, and it showed me there are turning points in your life. I fit right in to what Sheehy called 'Catch 30.'" There was a restless new vitality inside Bing, a side of her that had been suppressed, and she felt a need to reappraise and reconstruct her life. Reading the book didn't make her problems go away, she said, but it helped her understand what was happening.

Bing was sitting on the couch in my apartment. It was late afternoon, the day before New Year's, and as we talked, the leaden winter sky grew dark. I didn't want to move to turn on a light and break her train of thought. Outside construction workers putting up another apartment building were shooting off fireworks, green and red rockets that burst in the air, casting flashes on the walls in the room. It should have been a time for celebration.

Bing, I realized, had come full cycle in a single generation, like China since 1949. She had been Chairman Mao's good little revolutionary as a girl, dedicated to the cause; then she was disillusioned by her experience in the Cultural Revolution; now as she approached thirty she had become, in Chinese terms, a postrevolutionary woman. Like women in the West, she was launched on a voyage of self-discovery, questioning the roles she was supposed to play. And for her, each step in this process had been a lonely one.

Picking up the thread of her story, Bing recalled that soon after her old boy friend came back to Peking he asked her to spend a week night with him in his hotel.

"I didn't really want to do that with him, but he said he had gone those seven years without caring for another woman, without ever touching another woman. I felt sorry for him."

But when they got in bed, she discovered he was an expert at making love and knew far more than she did. "I couldn't do the things he wanted me to, they were awful. I was surprised and upset. I also felt guilty about what I was doing to my husband. I couldn't sleep. I left very early in the morning and went home, but I was crying, so Guoqiang knew something was wrong. I told him what I had done."

That changed everything, Bing said. "He could never trust me after that. He isn't a bad man. He didn't deserve what happened. But I didn't love him anymore."

Her husband's first reaction, she said, was that he had failed. He had never failed before in his life, and he was afraid people would laugh at him. It was a severe loss of face. Then he threatened to go to the police to have her lover arrested for adultery, a punishable crime in China. He also accused her of a lack of gratitude, of not repaying all the *guan-xi,* the connections, his family had arranged for her when she was in political difficulty.

Bing had entreated her lover to leave Peking to avoid any trouble with the police and assumed he had gone. But a month later she got a call from him saying he was departing the next morning and couldn't forget her. She was touched and decided to risk a last visit to say good-bye, an inviolable Chinese custom.

But when she knocked on his hotel-room door, she found him in bed with one of her girl friends. She was surprised, embarrassed, and wounded, but he did not seem flustered. He asked her to go down to the dining room and wait to have breakfast with the two of them.

After this encounter, she was in a quandary. She couldn't bring herself to tell Guoqiang; he would only ridicule her. But every night he was keeping her awake till four or five o'clock, pressing to know if she really loved him. All she wanted was to go to sleep and blot it out. He demanded an answer. If she said no, she didn't love him, he would ask for a divorce. That would go into her dossier and probably scrap any chance she had to get a passport to study abroad. Guoqiang had already told her parents about the affair, as a form of revenge, and her father had counseled her, "A divorced woman is ruined. Everyone has arrows at your back, ready to shoot."

I wondered if many Chinese women go through such crises, as American women now do. Yes, Bing replied, two of her girl friends were having similar trouble with their husbands.

"There are turning points in our lives, too. The difference is, we have much less room to maneuver. We know what is expected of us more clearly than Americans do, the rules are much more strict. And we know we can't break the rules so easily. So usually we just drag along. We never resolve our crises."

When I left China, Bing and her husband were still quarreling. There were no marriage counselors for her to see, no psychiatrists to help her, no lawyers she could hire to defend her. She reminded me of a heroine in some tragic nineteenth-century novel, a woman trapped by the conventions of her time, unable to gain understanding or support. She had become deeply pessimistic. From a dinner conversation at her parents-in-laws' house, she had heard that Chen Yun, one of the Party's most respected elder statesman, had prophesied that China would soon suffer from one of three disasters: the economy would collapse, the army would stage a coup, or there would be a popular rebellion.

"We should lead our lives with the lights turned out," she told me the day I departed, "so we don't have to see too clearly where we are going."

PART
3

SYSTEMS

II.   A Pig Under the Roof

PEASANTS

"You may rob the Three Armies of their commander in chief, but you cannot deprive the humblest peasant of his opinion."
Confucius, the Analects

When William Hinton first visited Long Bow village in 1948, it was just starting to emerge from centuries of medieval poverty and ignorance. In the past, if the harvest was good, the peasants had to give much of their crop to rapacious landlords to repay debts. If the harvest was bad, some peasants had to sell their children to survive; others starved. Babies died screaming from tetanus after untutored midwives used rusty scissors to snip their umbilical cords. Hinton, an American writer and farmer, recorded this misery and then the impact of the arrival of the Communists in Long Bow in the classic account of revolution in a Chinese village, *Fanshen** (*Fanshen* literally means to "turn over," or in Communist usage, to undergo a revolution). When Hinton left later in 1948, the Communists had just carried out a traumatic land-reform campaign which killed or dispossessed the landlords and enfranchised the poor.

In 1980, Hinton, a tall, jovial man of sixty-three, with a craggy face and thatch of snow-white hair, returned to Long Bow to work on a sequel to his original book and help the village with mechanizing its agriculture. It was like a journey to a different world, he told me later.

Where the mule-cart track used to run, linking Long Bow to other hamlets in Shanxi province in central western China, there is an asphalt highway now. And beyond, where there were only small fields of corn and millet, there is a main north–south railroad line now, a locomotive repair shop, a cement

---

*William Hinton, *Fanshen. A Documentary of Revolution in a Chinese Village* (New York: Random House, 1966).

mill, and a saw-blade works with 5,000 employees. Another 30,000 workers are constructing a new east–west railroad that will run through the Taihang Mountains, which had long isolated the region.

Long Bow itself really isn't a village anymore. It's an industrial suburb of the new city of Changzhi, which has a population of 300,000 people. When Hinton stayed in Long Bow in 1948, Changzhi was only a small, walled town where Long Bow's peasants went to market several times a week.

Some of these changes have come to other areas of China's countryside under three decades of Communist rule. But what really distinguishes Long Bow, Hinton said with avuncular affection, pushing back a lock of white hair, is its new success in mechanizing corn production. With his guidance, the village took a risky experiment. It laid off fifty peasants and formed a team of twelve young people who opened up one hundred acres, which they farmed entirely with mechanized means, from plowing and spreading manure to spraying with herbicides, planting, picking, and drying. Although elsewhere in China mechanization has proved more costly than traditional hand cultivation and local officials were skeptical, Long Bow proved them wrong.

"We doubled the yield, cut the costs in half, and raised the earnings of the peasants to the level of factory workers," Hinton said with a boyish grin. As he talked, he paced around my hotel room with a loping stride, as if he were measuring off another field to plant. In his enthusiasm and sympathy for the villagers, I sensed something of the old left-wing ideals of the 1930s in Hinton, a folksy man whose easygoing manner masks his keen intellect. Output on the mechanized fields in Long Bow, he said, averaged 112 bushels of corn per acre, far above China's norm, and well beyond the 89 bushels an acre he had been getting on his farm in Pennsylvania.

As a result, Hinton found when he returned to Long Bow the following spring, "there was corn hanging all over the village—from trees, all sorts of platforms and boards. They never had such a harvest. It's one of the few places in China where they have really done this complete mechanization." There were other bonuses too. The fifty people who had been displaced by the new machinery were put to work in the local factories.

"It's hard to believe, but they even said the corn tasted sweeter, too," Hinton related. "It could be, because for the first time they had a complete fertilizer." In the past the peasants had used only night soil, excrement from the public latrines and pig sties. Now they added potash, phosphorus, and nitrogen from small local factories they ran themselves. The new fertilizer also helped account for the high yield.

"It's not sweet corn like we have in the States. They just raise what we call field corn and feed it to the cattle." The Chinese plant this kind of corn because it is much higher-yielding than sweet corn, he explained, and they must worry about getting the maximum possible return. For Long Bow, like many other rural areas in China, has lost some of its land to the new factories. And with peace and prosperity, its population has soared. So where in 1948 there were a thousand peasants farming a thousand acres, an acre per person, today there are 2,400 people living on only about 600 acres, a quarter of an acre per capita, about the national average.

To further increase their income, Long Bow's peasants now plant much of their acreage in vegetables, which they sell to the new industrial city nearby. In 1948, Hinton recalled, the only vegetables the peasants ate were wild herbs they picked in the mountains. Their diet in those days was corn cakes for breakfast, more corn cakes for lunch, and noodles made from wheat for dinner, if they were lucky. Today almost every family raises a pig and eats meat on occasion, unheard of before the Communists' arrival. But it is still not a mainstay of their cuisine, as Hinton discovered from the local cook assigned to feed him during his most recent visit. The cook did not know how to prepare meat dishes.

One key to Long Bow's success, Hinton felt, has been the brigade leader, Wang Jinhung, a brilliant thirty-nine-year-old man born to a poor peasant family. In the 1950s he was sent off as an apprentice with a construction gang working for Russian engineers. "He always carried a ruler, measured things, and kept a notebook," Hinton said. Consequently, as he served variously as a welder, crane operator, electrician, mechanic, and building designer, he kept picking up new skills. After the Sino–Soviet split in the early 1960s, Wang was sent back to Long Bow as an electrician and eventually made brigade head.

The other vital ingredient in Long Bow's success was Hinton himself. Because of his book and long-standing sympathy for China, Peking classified Hinton as a "friend" and allowed him to make several return trips to the village over the years, an unusual privilege for a foreigner. He helped Wang design a grain dryer, using local coal for fuel, and a center pivot irrigation system. Then, drawing on his good connections with China's leaders, he took Wang to the provincial capital of Taiyuan and "borrowed a lot of machinery we found sitting around with a half inch of dust on it in the local agricultural machinery institute." No one else was bothering to use it.

This year, Hinton said, Long Bow will double the acreage farmed mechanically and lay off more peasants, who will be absorbed in the brigade's factories, further stimulating the village's growth.

I was fascinated with Hinton's account. He was virtually the only Westerner allowed to observe intimately the development of a Chinese village from before 1949 to the present. Three quarters of the country's population, 800 million people, still live in the countryside, an almost unimaginably large number; yet for most foreigners and even many Chinese it remains an unknown continent. After my arrival in Peking, I made repeated applications to the Information Department to let me live and work in a village so I could more accurately report on the peasants. I even received an invitation from a Chinese-American who was doing sociological research for a year with her husband in her home village in Guangdong province, near Hong Kong. They had built their own house, where I could stay, and had purchased a car, to drive me back and forth to the village, so I would not be a burden to the local authorities. But this request, like all the others, was turned down as "inconvenient." It was as if there was something secret about the peasants that the government wanted to hide.

I did manage to visit a dozen communes for the usual two- or three-hour inspections foreigners get, with briefings by the local officials and quick stops at peasants' homes. But each time, the communes I toured turned out to be well above average in their economic development. According to the State Statistical Bureau, the average per capita income for peasants from work in their collective fields was the equivalent of $57 in 1980. But of the twelve communes I visited, the lowest per capita income was $87. Several had earnings of over $200 a year, and one outside Shanghai claimed $540, almost ten times the national average. To Westerners, accustomed to measuring their salaries in the tens of thousands of dollars, these figures may all appear small; but they have real significance to Chinese. They also meant that I was seeing only the most prosperous segment of rural China. Less than one quarter of China's production teams—the team is the lowest level of rural organization, under the brigade and the commune—have an average per capita income of over $67 like those I was shown. Half of the teams make between $33 and $67. Another 27 percent get less than $33. At the bottom, in Jingyuan county in Ningxia province, in the arid northwest, the Communist Party theoretical journal *Red Flag* reported, the peasants receive a mere $10 a year. That is far below the level Peking itself has defined as the minimum for subsistence, an income of $27 a year.

More important to the peasants themselves than these monetary figures is the amount of grain they receive for their work, for on most production teams the peasants actually get the bulk of their income directly in kind at the end of the year when the harvest is added up and divided among the laborers. They get cash only to the extent that their team is prosperous enough to have surplus grain to sell to the state or has small industries like brick kilns or fruit orchards. Hence the monetary figure that Peking uses to measure peasant income, and gives out to foreigners, is somewhat misleading. It is based on an artificial conversion from farm production. If the subsistence level is calculated in grain, Peking reckons that peasants must get at least 330 pounds of wheat or rice a year. That works out to 1,500 calories a day, 100 calories less than the critical limit of 1,600 used by the U.N. Food and Agricultural Organization to measure malnourishment. But the Communist-controlled periodical *Cheng Ming* in Hong Kong reported in 1979 that 200 million peasants, almost as many people as live in the United States, receive less than that 330 pounds ration a year. "That is to say," the magazine stated, "they are living in a state of semistarvation."

These figures suggest that there is not one vast uniform countryside, rural China, but a wildly variant patchwork pattern of emerging prosperity and continued poverty. China has its equivalents to the Imperial Valley of California, rich farming communities, like Long Bow, but also its Appalachias. In their excellent 1978 study, *Village and Family in Contemporary China,* William L. Parish and Martin King Whyte estimate that in Guangdong province, in south China, the richest fifth of the peasants receive about 36 percent of the total per capita income, and the poorest fifth, 9 percent.* These figures indicate less inequality than rural India, Honduras, or the Philippines, but more than Taiwan, South Korea, or Egypt. Living on a commune does not automatically guarantee equality.

The more affluent villages tend to be where the natural conditions favor them—where the land is flat and fertile, in river valleys where water is adequate, and in rings around the cities, which provide a lucrative market for the nearby peasants and in turn send back bounteous quantities of night soil to fertilize their fields. The latter factor contributed to Long Bow's growth. The poorer areas lie in the remote mountains and in the drought-prone north China plain and northwest. Several of the poorest pockets are still the old areas that in the 1930s furnished bases for the fledgling Red Guerrillas because of their backwardness, like Yanan and the Jinggangshan Mountains where Lihua lived.

It is difficult for Americans and Europeans, who are accustomed to relatively stable rainfall, to appreciate how capricious and destructive the weather in China can be. On my tour of the United States with Chinese journalists in 1972, they told me that the single most striking sight to them was hundreds of acres of corn growing near Ottawa, Illinois, on a farm owned by a heavyset, gregarious man named Adrian Pike. As we stood examining the ripening green stalks, higher than the heads of the Chinese, one of the reporters turned to Pike with a mystified expression.

"How do you irrigate your fields?" he asked. Pike replied good-naturedly that he just depended on rainfall. I could see the look of incredulity on the Chinese faces. Irrigation ditches for rice, wheat, corn, and cotton are the lifeblood of the Chinese peasantry.

*William L. Parish and Martin King Whyte, *Village and Family in Contemporary China* (Chicago: University of Chicago Press, 1978), p. 376, fn. 1.

Since I was not allowed to visit any of the less prosperous parts of the Chinese countryside, I had to depend on others for descriptions of them. A scholarly, bespectacled economist who was sent to labor in a cadre school for several years in the mid-1970s in southern Henan province, in the valley of the Huai River, said there had been a devastating flood while he was there in 1975. Not a word about it appeared in the Chinese press, but he later read in a confidential report that 360,000 people had died. Historically, the economist said, the region has always been one of China's poorest: "It was either drought or flood every year, as long as the peasants could remember. Everyone builds their houses of mud, so that if they get swept away, the loss will be less."

In Gold Mountain, the village in the mountains of Hunan in central southern China where my petitioner friend Lihua was sent in the Cultural Revolution, the nearest road is still a half day's walk away and the peasants still don't send their daughters to school. Until recently, she told me, the peasants had never seen a tractor. The first time the team leader brought in a small hand-operated tractor, not much bigger or more powerful than a lawn mower, the peasants were very excited. They called it the "iron ox." But after running it for an hour, they became anxious and then frustrated when it inexplicably stopped. "Some of the peasants got angry and began beating it with sticks," Lihua said. The next day a mechanic arrived from the commune center. The tractor had run out of gas.

In a few provinces, Chinese told me, some communes are so poor that in the slack season they give their peasants what amounts to a license to go off to beg in the cities. In Ningxia, the province with the county that had an average income of only $23 a year, a doctor who worked there said he regularly had beggars come to his house. "They were mostly women and children," the doctor said. "Their communes give them a slip of paper which says they are entitled to go out begging. That way they won't be picked up by the police. There simply is not enough food for them at home; some places I knew of were reduced to three ounces of grain a day. The teams give it all to the men, who need their energy to work in the fields."

Once the physician went on a medical inspection of a poor commune inhabited by the Moslem Hui minority in Ningxia. "The people stayed hidden inside their homes. At first I thought it was because they were afraid of us. But when I went inside, I saw they were filthy dirty and so poor they didn't have any clothes on."

Stories like these helped me realize that the government's sensitivity about letting foreigners visit the countryside was because it represented both the triumph and the tragedy of the Chinese revolution. Unlike the Bolsheviks in Russia, who won a quick victory in the cities, the Chinese Communists had to battle their way to power through years of organizing discontented peasants into a guerrilla army. After Liberation, Mao recognized his debt to the countryside, in theory at least, by proclaiming that agriculture was the "foundation" of China's economic development. But for every success the Communists have achieved since 1949 in the villages, there have also been stupid blunders in policy, surprising discrimination in favor of the cities over the countryside, and terrible neglect. Some regions have made enormous progress. But others, contrary to the impression of many foreigners, are no better off than they were in 1949 or have even slipped backward in comparison to the cities and more advanced rural areas. For them, Mao's revolution has not delivered.

The most obvious success is that in the past three decades, thanks to improved rural organization, increased irrigation, better seeds, and more use of chemical fertilizer, the Communists have managed to double China's grain output. But since the population has nearly doubled at the same time, the per capita consumption of grain has remained at roughly the same low level. Nicholas Lardy, a professor of economics at Yale, has calculated that at the end of the 1970s per capita farm output was actually no better than it was in the early 1930s, before World War Two.*

The Communists also brought new security and vastly improved public health care to the villages. They introduced large-scale immunization programs, persuaded the peasants to remove refuse from around their houses, and pushed campaigns in the 1950s to eliminate the "Four Pests," rats, flies, mosquitoes, and grain-eating sparrows. Before 1949, with wars, banditry, famine, and pestilence, the average peasant lived to be only twenty to twenty-five years old. By the mid-1970s the average life expectancy had risen to sixty-four, according to a careful study by two American specialists.** Hence China has gained over 1.5 years of life expectancy for each calendar year since Liberation. This is a far better record than the other large developing nations, including India and Brazil, and is matched only by a few smaller countries like Taiwan and Sri Lanka.

Infant mortality is another useful index of improved living conditions. Prior to 1949, there were about 200 deaths at birth for every 1,000 children. By 1955, the number had declined to 74 per 1,000, and by the mid 1970s to 35 or 40 per 1,000, a dramatic change.

But the same discipline and organizational genius that produced these advances could also prove destructive when the orders from Peking were poorly conceived. The worst example of what the Communists call "com-

*Nicholas Lardy, "Food Consumption in the People's Republic of China," 1980, an unpublished paper. In using these figures and those that follow, I am deeply endebted to Professor Lardy, who is writing a book on Chinese agriculture.
**Judith Banister and Samuel H. Preston, "Mortality in China," *Population and Development Review*, Vol. 7, No. 1 (March 1981), p. 107.

mandism" was the Great Leap Forward in 1958 when Mao sought to transform China overnight into a purer form of communism, pushed the consolidation of the communes, set up communal mess halls and backyard iron blast furnaces, confiscated all private property, and guaranteed food, clothing, and even haircuts to all. "I have witnessed the tremendous energy of the masses," Mao said after a rural inspection tour in September of that year. "On this foundation it is possible to accomplish any task whatsoever." The real extent of the disaster that followed has long been hidden from the outside world. But data released by Peking in 1980 indicate that about 16.5 million more people than normal died in the three years of food shortages caused by the Great Leap, probably from malnutrition and its effects.*

In the aftermath, Mao also had to retreat from the full-blown commune structure established in 1958. The commune became more an administrative apparatus of local government in the countryside than a way of life, as Mao intended. Instead, the real functioning farm unit became the production team, which was natural for the peasants, since most teams were based on the old pre-1949 villages. It is the team to which the peasants report for work and which keeps track of the peasants' work points. Today there are five million production teams in China, with an average of thirty to forty families, or about 150 to 200 people, farming anywhere from 15 to 100 acres. A brigade normally has about 450 households, or 2,000 people. There are 50,000 communes, with an average of 16,000 members, though the actual size varies greatly depending on local geography. For most peasants, the commune is a dim and distant organization. They normally visit the commune center, located in the old market towns, only if they need more medical attention than the barefoot doctor attached to their team can provide, or if their children are lucky enough to go to the commune high school, or perhaps to visit the barber or the carpenter. Over the years Mao tried repeatedly to increase the powers of the communes, arguing that they are a more advanced form of communism than the team. But he failed, and since his death Deng Xiaoping has pushed in the opposite direction, contending that even the teams are sometimes too large for efficiency and allowing some teams to subdivide into groups of families for farm work.

Given the Communists' success as guerrillas in the countryside and their accomplishments in the 1950s in agriculture, I was surprised by the number of stories Chinese told about the cadres' mismanagement. An American married to a Chinese woman from Henan on the north China plain recalled what happened in his wife's native village after an order came down from Chairman Hua Guofeng in Peking to level all the hilly land in the area during the winter slack season. The commune Party secretary had picked one person

*Ansley J. Coale, "Population Trends, Population Policy, and Population Studies in China," *Population and Development Review,* Vol. 7, No. 1 (March 1981), p. 89.

from each family to join work gangs to get the job done. At first they had worked carefully, removing the valuable topsoil, putting it in an adjacent field, then leveling the hilly ground and replacing the topsoil. But as spring approached, it became obvious they wouldn't finish the task on time so the cadres ordered everyone to speed up. The good topsoil was simply plowed under.

"That meant no good crops for four years," a local peasant told the American with bitterness. Then he paused and looked at the American. "Tell me," the peasant asked, "in the United States, how does the government organize agriculture?" He was incredulous when told that farming in America is up to the farmers.

The combined effect of such mismanagement over many years and a prolonged drought had produced a serious food shortage, and the peasants were hungry and hostile toward the cadres. When the American and his wife visited the village in 1976, they were surprised to be given an armed escort from the provincial capital of Zhengzhou. Two policemen with AK-47 assault rifles rode in a jeep in front of them. Asked why the guards were necessary, a local cadre explained that a few weeks earlier, at the junction of the main road and the path to the village, *tu-fei*, "bandits," had held up some peasants. "But the bandits are not as bad as a few years ago," the official added reassuringly.

The American discovered that the best-fed people in the village, the men who did the hardest labor and earned the most work points, ate a diet that consisted of only about two pounds of wheat flour a day. Once or twice a week they also got some pickled vegetables and perhaps an egg; once a month they might get a small piece of fatty pork. While he and his wife stayed in the village, the police brought in special food in a jeep for them every morning. As a gesture of courtesy, the American's in-laws held a banquet for the local cadres. Again, the police delivered extra rations. The meal was held in the family compound, with high mud walls around the house.

"The peasants were so curious and hungry, they climbed to the top and sat there watching, craning their necks for what must have been a marvel for them," the American recalled. "We had three kinds of dishes with fatty pork. I couldn't eat it, but the cadres slurped it down like a banana split."

The final and crowning course was a fish. The Yellow River was only two miles away, and many of the nearby fields had fishponds in them, but when the American later asked the peasants about the last time they had eaten fish, they shook their heads and said they couldn't remember. "Only the cadres are allowed to catch fish," one elderly man with a wispy goatee told him.

A professor of engineering from Peking who was dispatched with colleagues from his institute to work on a so-called May Seventh School for cadres in the early 1970s in another part of Henan remembered a deep chasm between the peasants and the officials. Although he and his fellow teachers and administrators were supposedly in the countryside to be "reeducated" by the peasants, the newcomers kept to themselves. "The peasants lived in their mud huts, we built ourselves brick dorms with concrete floors. We had meat and cooking oil, they had none.

"When we went out to work in the fields, if we didn't leave someone behind to guard the place, the peasant children would sneak in and steal things. One time I left my mud boots on the windowsill to dry, and when I came back they were gone."

At harvest time, he recalled, marauding bands of local women and children would steal the school's crops. Finally when the school was ordered closed down and the professor returned to Peking, the peasants invaded the compound and carried everything away—the bricks, the boards, even the light fixtures. "There was a platoon of soldiers left to guard the compound, but they were helpless to stop it without shooting everyone."

Paradoxically, another of the reasons for the Communists' failure to bring about more equality in the countryside was Mao's very demand for egalitarianism. In the periods when the Chairman and his radical supporters held sway—like the Great Leap Forward, the Cultural Revolution, and parts of the early and mid-1970s—they sought to abolish the last traces of individual enterprise in the villages, the peasants' private plots and the free markets where the peasants could sell their extra grain or pigs and chickens they raised themselves. Mao condemned them as a vestige of capitalism and feared they would increase differences in income among the peasants. But since Mao's death it is now clear that when the private plots and rural markets were closed, farm production declined and peasant income everywhere dropped. Equality and economic efficiency don't always mix.

Equally ironic was the effect of Mao's insistence on self-reliance, that each province should produce all its own grain and not depend on others for supplies of wheat or rice. This was an outgrowth of the Chairman's guerrilla experience in the 1930s, but with the deepening Sino–Soviet conflict in the 1960s, he saw it as part of a strategy to render China less vulnerable to Russian attack. In a speech to the Politburo in March 1966, he warned that it was "dangerous" for individual provinces to rely on the government to ship them grain to meet their basic needs. The trouble was, some regions were better suited to grazing cattle or growing commercial crops like cotton and sugar cane and had long been grain-deficit areas. But to enforce Mao's policy of regional self-sufficiency, Peking began procuring less grain and reduced its shipments to grain-poor areas. Hence by 1977, Professor Lardy estimates, the government was transferring less grain than it had twenty years before even though overall output had nearly doubled. As an example of what happened, Professor Lardy points to Hunan, a rice-rich province in

Buddhist pilgrims pray at sunrise on Mount E-mei in Sichuan, one of five mountains traditionally considered sacred by Chinese. Religion was proscribed during the Cultural Revolution but has made a comeback since Mao Zedong's successors adopted a more tolerant attitude. *(Photo © 1981 Liu Heung Shing/Contact Press Images)*

Young dissidents sell transcripts of the trial of Wei Jingsheng at Peking's Democracy Wall shortly before the police arrested them. The leader of the group was sentenced to a labor reform camp. *(Photo © 1981 Liu Heung Shing/Contact Press Images)*

Getting a permanent in one of China's revived beauty parlors. *(Photo © 1981 Liu Heung Shing/Contact Press Images)*

Three young *liu-mang*, or toughs, sport the latest fashion — sunglasses. *(Photo © 1981 Liu Heung Shing/Contact Press Images)*

Courtship Chinese-style. In crowded Peking, privacy is where you can find it. *(Photo © 1981 Liu Heung Shing/Contact Press Images)*

Peasants load a truck with cabbages at harvest time near Peking. Many farm products are spoiled by poor handling, since the peasants, like factory workers, are rewarded for quantity, not quality. *(Photo © 1981 Liu Heung Shing/Contact Press Images)*

Commune members divide their potato harvest in Gansu. An accountant, squatting on the left, has an abacus and an official seal to certify each peasant's share. *(Photo by Fox Butterfield)*

Skating and taking a stroll on the frozen moat outside the wall of the Forbidden City. *(Photo © 1981 Liu Heung Shing / Contact Press Images)*

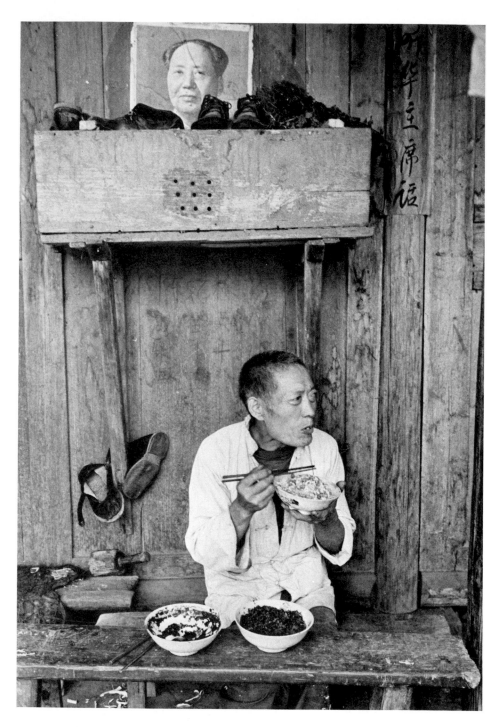

A cobbler in Sichuan eats his lunch. In the past few years the Communists have encouraged a limited revival of individual enterprise to soak up the unemployed and create more consumer goods and services. *(Photo © 1981 Liu Heung Shing/Contact Press Images)*

One-year-olds in the nursery school of a Peking factory drink their morning apple juice. None moved or jostled the others. *(Photo by Fox Butterfield)*

School children in Tibet recite in unison after their teacher, with their hands dutifully clasped behind their backs, in the old pedagogical fashion. *(Photo by Fox Butterfield)*

A Chinese guard from the Bureau for the Preservation of Cultural Relics keeps Tibetans out of the Jokhang, the seventh-century temple in Lhasa that is the holiest shrine of Tibetan Buddhism. He is in charge, not the monks. *(Photo by Fox Butterfield)*

A Tibetan waits outside the Jokhang. The temple was closed during the Cultural Revolution and now is open only three mornings a week to Tibetans, though they come from all over Chinese Central Asia to worship at it. *(Photo by Fox Butterfield)*

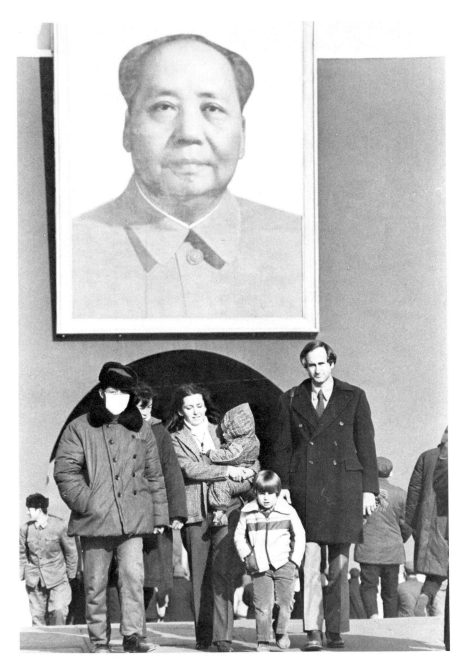

Sarah, Ethan, Barbara, and the author in front of the Gate of Heavenly Peace. The man on the left is wearing a surgical mask against Peking's cold and dust. *(Photo © 1981 Liu Heung Shing / Contact Press Images)*

Confession in the Roman Catholic cathedral in Peking. Since the Cultural
Revolution, Chinese have become hungry for something spiritual, Chinese
Christian leaders say. *(Photo © 1981 Liu Heung Shing / Contact Press Images)*

Tibetan women at a pastoral commune 14,500 feet above sea level, on the great Tibetan plateau. *(Photo by Fox Butterfield)*

A young porter carries a 130-pound load of cement up Huang Shan, or Yellow Mountain, in Anhui province. *(Photo by Fox Butterfield)*

Roller skating in Shanghai, one of the few pleasures for young people in China's largest city. *(Photo © 1981 Liu Heung Shing/Contact Press Images)*

At China's Academy Awards night. On the right is Yolanda Sui, the foster daughter of the late Madame Sun Yat-sen, a member of the pampered elite and an aspiring movie actress. On the left is the woman voted best actress. *(Photo by Francis Deron, Agence France Press)*

Wang Keping, the dissident sculptor, in his tiny studio apartment. The carving is Chairman Mao as Buddha, with one eye closed and the other slyly open to see who is praying to him, Wang says. *(Photo © 1981 Liu Heung Shing/Contact Press Images)*

A propaganda poster painter enjoys his *xiu-xi*, or siesta, a right enshrined in China's constitution. *(Photo © 1981 Liu Heung Shing / Contact Press Images)*

Left: Youthful peasants working on a treadmill to irrigate rice paddies, just as their ancestors did. *(Photo by Fox Butterfield)*

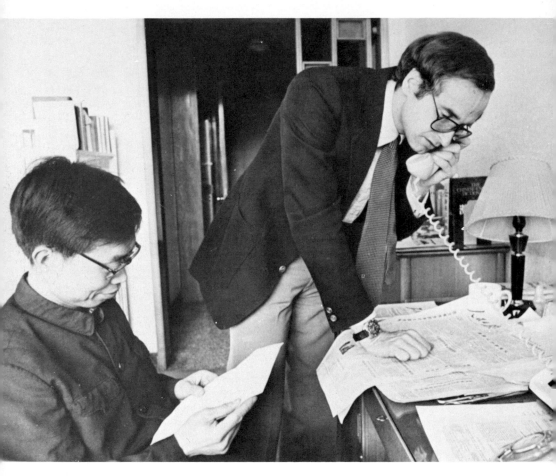

The author and Lao Wu, my government-assigned assistant, in *The New York Times*'s office in the Peking Hotel. *(Photo by Liu Heung Shing / The New York Times)*

central south China, which by the late 1970s was able to distribute two thirds more grain per capita to its peasants than arid, grassy Ningxia. Under Mao's policy of enforced grain planting, Ningxia's pasturelands turned into a dust bowl and the province as a whole averaged only 334 pounds of grain per person, scarcely above the subsistence level of 330 pounds.

To compound the problem, Mao became obsessed with grain production as the key measure of farm success, like the Russian fixation on steel output as an indicator of industrial might. "Take grain as the key link," Mao proclaimed, and all the provinces and teams, even those that had previously grown large amounts of other food crops that are important sources of protein in the Chinese diet, like soybeans and edible oils (peanuts and rapeseed), had to fall in line. As a consequence, Professor Lardy has found, the output of these valuable food sources declined in per capita terms as much as 30 to 50 percent from their high point in 1956, before the Great Leap Forward, to the late 1970s. This, too, added to the peasants' hunger.

But what is far more startling than these persistent differences between one rural area and another and the Communists' mistakes in farm policy is that the Communists, despite their rhetoric of putting the countryside first, have not done more to close the gap between the cities and the villages. From earliest times there have always been two Chinas, one urban, one rural. Ensconced in Peking, with its broad avenues, sophisticated bureaucrats, and crowded department stores, I tended to forget how the vast majority of Chinese lived. But I remember once stopping at a village in Fujian province, on the southeast coast, at planting time in the spring. The weather was already hot and humid, with banks of heavy white clouds hugging the low green mountains inland from the rice paddies along the shore. The noonday sun shimmered off the flooded fields like a mirror, the newly transplanted rice sprouts an emerald green. Young peasants, their backs hunched under swaying bamboo shoulder poles with buckets at each end, were walking along the narrow mud dikes between the paddies, ferrying loads of night soil. Then they waded barefoot into the unplanted fields, sinking ankle deep in the mud, and upturned their buckets of slop. The pungent, choking smell of excrement hung in the air for yards around, the most basic reality of village life. Part of the manure came from the local privy, a piece of granite with a circular cutout suspended over a small pond. The rest came from the village's pigs. The importance of the pig in rural life is reflected in the Chinese ideograph for home—it shows a pig under a roof. Out in the fields, other peasants, bent double at the waist, were moving backward step by step as they transplanted the rice seedlings, an operation that multiplied millions of times is the greatest expenditure of human energy in the world.

Four teen-age girls, their loose-fitting black pants rolled to their knees, were working on a long wooden treadmill to pump water into another field. When I approached and tried to talk with them, they smiled and giggled, but none spoke Mandarin, or "the common language," as it is now called, only the local Fujian dialect. It was a sign they had not gone far in school, since all education is now supposed to be in the unified language. During a full day's drive the length of Fujian, I saw only a handful of tractors, most of which were being used as trucks to pull loads of bricks, rice, or trussed pigs. Plowing was still the work of men hitched to lumbering water buffaloes. The pace of life was slower than in the cities, the work harder.

It is hard for Americans, accustomed to mechanized farming, to realize how primitive and backbreaking Chinese agriculture still is. But in a 1978 speech, Deng Xiaoping gave a neat vest-pocket guide. The average annual output of grain per farm worker in China is about 2,200 pounds, he said. In the United States, it is over 110,000 pounds, a disparity of "several dozen times," Deng noted.

In Anhui, in central China, another of the poorer provinces, I recall climbing Huang Shan, or Yellow Mountain, whose oddly shaped peaks, pines, and clouds traditionally make it one of the wonders of nature to Chinese. A pilgrimage to Huang Shan has been a goal of Chinese since the great eighth-century poet Li Bo celebrated its phantasmagoric beauties. To accommodate the thousands of Chinese and foreign tourists who now flock to its summit, the government is enlarging several mountaintop hotels and restaurants. But since there is no road, all the cement, timber, and prefabricated sections must be carried up the mountain on foot. On the thousands of steep stone steps cut into the mountain over the centuries by laborers, I passed convoys of porters. Most were teen-agers and young men and women in their twenties from villages hidden by mist in the valley below.

At one level spot, where I stopped to catch my breath, a girl of fifteen, less than five feet tall, vaulted past me. Her two long, thick black braids bobbed as she climbed with an eighty-pound basket of rice strapped to her back. The load must have been more than equal her weight. Beads of perspiration stood out on her forehead, and her blue plaid shirt was soaked through. She had begun her trek at 5 A.M., to avoid the noonday heat, she said.

In the past Chinese peasants faced the harsh reality that their labor was worth less than land; good muscles were more plentiful than good earth. The Communists have preserved this tradition in their own way, friends who had worked in the countryside said. In figuring the cost of farm production, commune accountants do not include human labor.

In the 1930s, surveys made at the time suggest, the ratio of urban to rural income was about two to one. But from reports of friends and data I was able to piece together, the gap today looms much larger. Exact comparisons are difficult because of the way the government furnishes data. In 1980 the average city worker, not counting dependents, earned the equivalent of $508. The average per capita income for peasants, including men, women, and children, was $57 from their collective labor and another $20 from sideline occupations like growing vegetables in their private plots, raising pigs, or weaving straw baskets, for a total of $77. Both of these figures must then be deflated, the urban one to allow for the number of dependents, the rural one because economists believe the government's use of grain prices in calculating peasants' income overstates the real value they receive.* When these deductions are made, urban per capita income was about $276 in 1980, peasant per capita earnings around $58. That would be a differential of nearly five to one in favor of the cities.

But the real difference between city and countryside goes beyond income figures. The peasants' livelihood is still at the mercy of the weather. With drought or flood, the team's harvest goes down and so does a peasant's income. City workers have fixed wages and guaranteed lifetime jobs. In 1981 international relief officials were invited for the first time by Peking to inspect the ravages of drought in Hebei, in north China, and a flood of the Yangtze River in Hubei, in central China. They estimated that up to 130 million people were facing food shortages in a total of nine provinces and reported widespread cases of rickets and anemia among children.

In the cities, the state provides free education, medical care, old-age pensions, and low-cost housing. By government count, its subsidies for these services total $351 a year for every urban resident, more than doubling city income. In the countryside the Communists have established a widespread network of schools and clinics; but unlike the cities, the local teams and brigades have been left largely to pay for them out of their own slender earnings. This happened because of a critical decision by Peking in the 1950s to concentrate its investment resources on building up industry and the cities to support it, despite the Communists' claim to give preference to agriculture.

Lihua recalled that in Gold Mountain the peasants had to pay tuition charges that amounted to the equivalent of $4 a year—calculated in work points—to send their children to the small one-room primary school. The rickety building, once a landlord's residence, had holes for windows, its roof leaked, and it had no desks or even stools, so the students had to squat on the mud floor or bring their own seats. The teacher was a young woman peasant from a neighboring village who had managed to get as far as junior

*Most peasants receive the bulk of their distributions from their teams in grain and oil, not in cash. But Peking, in converting their income to a cash figure for statistical purposes, uses grain prices, which have gone up several times in recent years. That of course does not change the amount of grain the peasants really receive. Professor Lardy suggests true peasant income from collective labor in 1980 should be about $38.

high school. There were no books, only some materials she prepared herself and sold to the students for the equivalent of another $2. These expenses might seem small, but the total cost for a year's education amounted to a quarter of a villager's annual income, and the high price kept attendance down. The only high school was in the commune center, a four-hour walk, and parents who wanted to send their children had to pay additional charges for room and board. Lihua's team had a rudimentary clinic staffed by a barefoot doctor, or paramedic, with a cooperative health insurance plan that cost another $2.67 a year. But Lihua's own family was excluded from the benefits of the insurance scheme since they were labeled landlords. They had to pay full cost if they used the clinic. The village had no pension plan, like city factories, and all housing was built at the peasants' expense.

Badly funded village schools like those in Gold Mountain are no match for government-supported city schools in getting their pupils into college. The *People's Daily* once conceded that there is only one person with a college-level education for every ten communes, or about one out of every 160,000 peasants and rural cadres.

The daughter of a county Party secretary who had been able to go to college and get a job in Peking told me that the brightest student in her primary school had been the son of a peasant. "He was fantastically intelligent," she said. "I was already in third grade. He had not been able to go to first or second grade because his parents were very poor and they held him out of school to help with work at home. But he jumped right into our class and learned to read and write. He always got the highest marks." His career ended in fifth grade, the final year of primary school. His parents could not afford to pay his school fees anymore.

There are other ways also in which the countryside is discriminated against. Under China's election law, the rural areas get only one eighth the representation of the cities in the National People's Congress. The Congress is largely a rubber stamp, but the peasants have a more difficult time joining the Communist Party too, the real locus of power. Once, to make the comparison, I noted that in a lacquerware factory in the southern city of Fuzhou, with 836 employees, there were ninety-three Party members, a ratio of more than one out of ten. But at the Huluzhen brigade outside the city, only fifteen of the 634 adult peasants belonged to the Party, less than one out of forty. Professor Lardy has calculated that from 1956 to 1978, while the consumption of grain per capita for China as a whole dropped slightly, it declined 5.9 percent in the countryside but rose 15.8 percent in the cities.* This was the result of a deliberate government decision to favor the urban areas.

The government's tilt in favor of the cities is obvious to Chinese. In the

*Lardy, "Food Consumption in the People's Republic of China," p. 19.

1950s, before Peking imposed tight restrictions on migration from the countryside through the household registration system, millions of peasants
flooded into the cities. The great divide in China today, friends explained,
is between those who have an "agricultural status" household registration
and those with a "non-agricultural status" registration. Peasants, with a farm
registration, depend on the erratic work-point earnings from their fields. But
cadres at the commune level, the lowest group to be given the coveted
non-farm registration, are paid a fixed salary regardless of the harvest. For
many peasants the greatest success in life is to get a member of their family
elevated to non-farm status, a kind of insurance policy. In turn, the government has devised countertactics to try to prevent this. Under the Communists' complex system of labels, people inherit their class backgrounds from
their fathers—landlord, capitalist, poor peasant—but they get their household registrations from their mothers. For more men than women are assigned jobs as commune cadres, picking up non-farm registration, and when
they die, their children revert to being peasants.

Another way to escape from the countryside is to go to work for a high-
ranking cadre in the city as a maid. Bing, the daughter of the general who
denounced her father during the Cultural Revolution, said her family had
recruited an eighteen-year-old peasant girl from the village where her father
had been born many years before. She was a shy, stocky youth who had never
seen a bus or heard of airplanes and railroad trains until she came to Peking.
Her father had died not long after she arrived in the capital, but she was
consoled by a letter he wrote: "I feel very content, at least I managed to get
one of my children a city household registration."

Most Western Sinologists have given Peking credit for not following
Stalin's model of exploiting the peasants to spur China's economic growth.
They have been impressed that the Communists set the grain tax on the
peasants at a low, fixed level in the 1950s and as production has risen, the
proportion paid in taxes has fallen, now perhaps an average of 3 to 8 percent
of a team's annual income. The government also taxes the villages by requiring the peasants to sell additional amounts of their grain at a price set by the
state. To benefit the peasants, this price has been raised several times in the
past few years.

But as Peking has become more candid after Mao's death by publishing
more economic data and letting a few foreign specialists do field research on
communes, a different picture of the government's relations with the peasants has emerged. It suggests that Peking, like Moscow, has systematically
squeezed the countryside, albeit in hidden fashion, to support industrialization.

Despite the recent increases in the state purchase price for grain, Professor

Lardy estimates that Chinese peasants are actually being paid the lowest amount of any villagers in Asia relative to the cost of the industrial products they must buy back from the cities, like tractors, chemical fertilizer, and electricity. The state charges $2,000 for a tiny 12-horsepower tractor, the size of a lawnmower, and $12,000 for a medium-sized 75-horsepower tractor, ensuring the factories that produce them a tidy profit. This difference between what the peasants get for their crops and what they must pay for manufactured goods amounts to a substantial indirect levy on the countryside. The reason the government has been reluctant to raise farm prices to a more realistic level is that it would hurt urban residents who have had to live with fixed wages for years and who the Communists evidently fear are more volatile and a greater threat to the regime. In the three decades of Communist rule, the cost of rice to urban consumers has never gone up. Most Chinese I knew in the cities treated stable rice prices as a matter of faith, a sacred obligation of the government. But to keep food prices down for these privileged city residents, the government has been forced to pay a subsidy of roughly $4.67 billion a year, a whopping 7 percent of total state revenue in the 1981 budget. The subsidy goes to the peasants, but even with it most peasants feel they are getting too little. As an indication of the real value of their grain, if they sell it in one of the rural free markets, they can still get 70 percent more than what the government pays.

To make the problem worse for the peasants, as China has begun to mechanize its farming, they must use more and more of the costly industrial inputs. In Hebei province, near Peking, an American scholar who was permitted to live on a commune there, Steven Butler, found that the ratio of peasants' costs to their gross income jumped from 25 to 30 percent in the early 1970s to 50 percent by 1980. "The cities are ripping off the countryside," Butler remarked. Farming costs have become so high, he estimated, that the peasants may actually get a negative return on their collectively planted grain crop. The key to their survival is in private sideline production where they can plant other crops or do other jobs with a good return on capital.

At the same time, the level of government investment in agriculture is actually much smaller than Western economists had believed. Farm investment comes from two sources—local profits the government allows the teams and brigades to retain for reinvestment and national appropriations. Recently published figures show that the total profits the government let the teams keep amounted to $4.2 billion in 1978, the latest year for which figures are available. That is only the same amount as in 1956, though the number of peasants climbed from 450 million to 800 million in those years. Put another way, it means that the teams can save only about $5 apiece for each peasant, the cost of a hoe, hardly enough to modernize agriculture. As for national appropriations, Peking has masked its actual amount of investment in agriculture in conflicting data, but Lardy estimates that it may have come to less than $3.3 billion in 1978. Added together with local investment, that would give a total investment in farming of only $7.3 billion. Since the real overall value of farm output in 1978 was $71.3 billion, that gives a rate of investment of only 10 percent. By comparison, in 1978 Peking reinvested the staggering total of 36.8 percent of its gross national product. That means that the great bulk of funds went to industry, a particularly lopsided figure remembering that 800 million Chinese, 80 percent of the population, are peasants.

Mao's successors have taken some measures to try to redress these imbalances. At a critical meeting in December 1978, the Third Plenum of the Eleventh Central Committee, where Deng Xiaoping asserted his predominance, the Party committed itself to a liberal new program to speed agricultural development. It promised to raise the purchase prices the peasants are paid for their crops, it sanctified the controversial private plots and free markets, and it offered the peasants much greater control over what crops they plant. In 1980 Peking took an even more controversial step by letting peasants in some of the poorer production teams farm their own land, abolishing the system of collective work points, and allowing the peasants to keep whatever they produced above a fixed quota. In many areas the initial results have been good. On the commune in Hebei where Steven Butler did research, he found the peasants there in the midst of what he described as an historic change. "They are no longer worried every day about where their next meal is going to come from," he said. The average grain ration has gone up from 330 pounds a year in the 1950s, the minimal subsistence level, to 550 pounds in 1980 with another 90 to 100 pounds from the peasants' private plots. Instead of raising only corn and sweet potatoes, as they did in the past, which the peasants regard as coarse, inferior food, they now plant wheat, a tastier product.

For the first time, Butler went on, "the peasants are beginning to think of buying things with their earnings—new houses, clothes, wristwatches, bicycles. Many of them have savings accounts in their local collective banks. It's the good life."

Most of the production teams he visited on the commune had purchased their own black-and-white television sets, which they set up on metal stands outdoors for everyone to watch. "It makes a huge difference in people's lives, having something to do in the evening, and they love it," Butler observed. "Some of the richer families were thinking of buying their own sets, but no one wants to be the first because they will be inundated with neighbors coming to watch." One prosperous team resolved the dilemma with a collective decision. They waited till every family in the team had enough money;

then they all went out and bought television sets simultaneously. In Butler's view, the people in his commune are ready for what economists call the take-off stage of sustained economic development which farmers in Japan, Taiwan, and South Korea have already moved into.

But despite the new prosperity of Butler's commune, some Western economists feel that Peking is still not going far enough to stimulate agriculture. The government has not followed through on two other pledges made at the December 1978 Party meeting: to reduce the costs of manufactured products sold to the villages by up to 15 percent and increase state investment in farming from the current 10 percent of national income to 18 percent. Nor are there any signs that Peking is prepared to bite the bullet and make urban consumers pay a realistic price for grain, which would provide a real incentive to the peasants. But unless the government does shift more resources into agriculture, farm output may continue to grow only at the slow pace of the 2 to 2.5 percent a year it has averaged over the last three decades and food will remain a serious problem for China. As an indication of the country's troubles, grain imports climbed upward throughout the late 1970s and in 1980 reached an all-time record of 13.7 million tons. Almost all the imported grain was funneled into the cities.

If Mao shortchanged the countryside, the peasants also outlasted the Chairman. The villages remain more traditional, more tied to their ancient customs and rhythms, and more centered around the family than the cities. This gives the peasants a certain autonomy, a kind of insulation from government dictates.

The very form of rural organization today is itself a compromise between what the Communists tried to impose from above, the commune, and the old system of villages, clans, and neighborhoods. Mao and the radicals long wanted to make the large commune what they called the basic accounting unit—the group that works together and shares its income. But in the Great Leap Forward this proved unworkable, and the Communists instead accepted the production team, which was based on the old small village, or a clan or a neighborhood of a larger village, as the basic unit. This meant that the team cadres were natives of the villages where they worked, and not only natives, but brothers, uncles, or cousins of the peasants. Having kinsmen in charge made collective farming acceptable to the Chinese peasant and reinforced his interest in the team's welfare. But it also gave the peasant leverage over local officials that city people don't have.

A trim, serious-minded woman in her late twenties with short pigtails who was sent to live in a village in Sichuan for six years recalled how the peasants took advantage of their natural connections with the team leaders. The legal minimum age for marriage for men was twenty-three and twenty-one for

women, but every year several girls as young as sixteen or seventeen succeeded in getting married despite the restriction.

"They had to have a letter of introduction from the team leader to the
brigade office before they could register their marriage," the woman said,
"but everyone was related and the cadres didn't object." It was another
example of the use of *guan-xi,* or "connections." Being related to the team
leader or accountant also made it easier to get extra work points if someone
was sick or to get your name on the list for the one bicycle team members
were allowed to purchase every two years. In the city, such decisions are in
the hands of the Party secretary of your office, factory, or school, the woman
pointed out. City living requires more ingenuity to arrange things.

There was also less political pressure in the village, she remembered. Most
of the families belonged to a single clan, and the team leader was always a
member of that clan. The current team head, a hardworking, respected
forty-nine-year-old man, was anxious to quit the post. He complained that he
got no extra remuneration for the hours he spent on team chores and that
his duties kept him from cultivating his private plot. Like team cadres
throughout China, he was paid work points rather than a fixed state salary
and had to work in the fields with the peasants. The team had political
meetings only about twice a year—the peasants were too tired if meetings
were called at night, after a hard day's work, and if they were held during
the daytime, the peasants demanded work points to compensate them for
time lost.

"Most times when the cadres did read out a document from Peking, the
peasants didn't understand it anyway, unless it was directly about farm
work," the woman said. She said that when Mao died, everyone was ordered
to observe three minutes of silence. At the time, she had been assigned to
brigade headquarters to make announcements over the loudspeaker system
because as a native of Peking she had a proper accent.

"The militia were told to keep watch to make sure everyone obeyed the
order for silence for the Chairman. But there was one old man who was
selling tree ear fungus [a Chinese delicacy, like mushrooms] and he just kept
right on selling. He didn't stand and close his eyes as required. When the
militiaman demanded to know why he was behaving so badly, he asked,
'Who is Mao?' " She was stunned by this display of rural ignorance.

But it is in their marriage practices that the peasants remain most traditional and the old role of the family continues to predominate. When the
Communists introduced their family law in 1950, they envisioned abolishing
the old arranged marriage decided on by the parents for economic reasons
and intended to replace it with free choice between young partners. But the
confidential study prepared for the Women's Federation in 1980 on the
condition of women in the countryside found that 75 percent of rural mar-

riages are still arranged. For most peasants spend their entire time living and working in their own village, which is now also their team, and "opportunities to meet people from an outside village are small," the document reported. In villages with only one clan, there are still taboos about marrying a person with the same surname, and "there is an old-fashioned notion that for young people to bring up the matter of marriage independently is not correct. They must rely on an introduction." The study notes there has been one area of progress—in the past, many of these arranged marriages were blind, the couples never even met before their wedding. Now they may have one chance to eye each other in a village teahouse or the home of the prospective groom in the company of the matchmaker, with both partners having the right of refusal.

A young refugee in Hong Kong recalled how one of his cousins in Guangdong, Wang Guoying, had gotten married. When Wang was twenty-five years old, his parents hired a matchmaker who found a suitable bride for him in a nearby team. She was tall and strong, a good worker, so she would be as asset in earning work points, and her family was classified as poor peasants, a good class background, the two most important criteria to them. In an old peasant term, "the doors and the windows matched."

There was only one hitch. Her family wanted a high bride price for her, 1,000 yuan ($667), with a third in cash and the rest in food, clothes, and jewelry. That amounted to nearly two years' income for Wang's whole family. There was some bargaining, the amount was reduced slightly, and after the Wangs borrowed heavily from their local credit cooperative and pooled savings from relatives, the money was raised.

Such marriages by purchase, as the Communists call them, were prohibited by the family law, but friends told me they remain universal in the villages. Parish and Whyte conclude in their book about the countryside that expenditures by a bridegroom's family have actually increased on the average from about half a year's family income before Liberation to over a full year's earnings today.* One reason may be that since peasant women now work more in the fields than before 1949, their economic value has increased.

The refugee in Hong Kong related that their brigade Party secretary once called a meeting of the local cadres to read out a new directive from Peking inveighing against the feudal practice of buying brides. The refugee himself at the time was serving as a brigade financial officer, and so took part in the session.

"We laughed at the Party secretary," he remembered. "Everyone knew his own wife had cost his family 600 yuan [$400]. So some of us jeered at him, 'You should have gotten her free.'"

*Parish and Whyte, *Village and Family in Contemporary China,* pp. 188–89.

The Communists have largely succeeded in abolishing concubinage, another objective of the family law, but not entirely, as they have claimed. The report prepared for the Women's Federation found cases of women being sold as concubines in nineteen different provinces, ranging in age from fourteen to fifty. In a detailed investigation in several counties in Anhui province, the researchers discovered 22,339 women who had been sold there. Curiously, 83 percent of them were from Sichuan, long reportedly a center of the trade because of its rural poverty. The report did not give details on how these women had been purchased, but it said, "Some of the women had been raped at some point and then sold to the rapist as his wife. Some had been sold many times."

Lihua related that in Gold Mountain some of her poorer neighbors still sold their children. There was a former wounded veteran of the Red Army who had eight children but whose wife had died and who had become lazy and unable to support his large family. Because of their impoverished condition, he couldn't purchase a bride for his oldest son, who was twenty-six. The father took care of that by arranging to have him "adopted" for a price by an elderly widow who had no son of her own to look after her in her advanced age. Then he sold his fourteen-year-old daughter to a family in a village ten miles away for 1,000 yuan ($667) and a fat pig. They wanted to ensure finding a wife for their son, who had a badly pockmarked face and a reputation as a lazy worker.

"The father was an uneducated man and really didn't care about his children's happiness," Lihua said. "When he had spent all the money from the fourteen-year-old, he went around the village asking who would like to buy his eleven-year-old daughter. No one did. She was too young and not very pretty." But eventually in another village he found a former landlord's family who had a son that was already thirty-two years old but couldn't find a wife because of his class label and age. The family agreed to purchase the young girl for 200 yuan ($133). "They put her to work in the kitchen," Lihua said. "When she reached eighteen, they would have a wedding ceremony."

Finally the father sold another son, who was only nine years old. He found an old couple who didn't have any children and wanted a son. The price was 50 yuan ($33). "When he left home, his father didn't give him anything, not even a set of extra clothes."

The Communists have also largely eliminated the Buddhist and Taoist priests and nuns, the geomancers and shamans, who lived in the countryside and said prayers at village festivals or chanted incantations at funerals. But as Lihua had told me about her life in Gold Mountain, the peasants continue to practice some of their folk religion underground. On a trip back to her village after I met her, she had consulted a blind fortune-teller who appeared in Gold Mountain. A hunched and grizzled man in his late fifties, he lived as an itinerant, wandering from village to village, stopping in the homes of whatever peasants would give him food and shelter. He had quickly earned a reputation for clairvoyance in Gold Mountain. A family who had not had a male heir for several generations and had just had a newborn male child brought their son to him to ask about his future. The fortune-teller told them the boy had a black spot behind his ear, a mark even his mother hadn't noticed. That meant his fate would be good, the fortune-teller prophesied. The parents were delighted. They gave the blind man eight yuan ($5), over a month's income for them.

In the cities, the Communists have made cremation mandatory because of the severe shortage of land and have succeeded in getting urban residents to simplify the elaborate, costly funerals which Chinese practiced for centuries, giving substance to the cult of the ancestors, China's native religion. In the countryside the government has also attempted to introduce cremation to save farmland; but here the Party's writ sits more lightly and the peasants have resisted these changes. In many villages, friends told me, the peasants still begin saving to buy coffins for themselves after they pass sixty, the number of years considered a normal life cycle.

A professor of English from Peking who was sent to labor in a village in Jiangxi, in central China, was assigned to live with a family in a small one-room mud hut. The floor was also mud and the roof leaked when it rained, but the grandmother in the family had already purchased a handsome camphor-wood coffin for 60 yuan ($40). She kept it stored in the family's single room, in readiness. When she died, her body was laid out for three days in front of a Buddhist altar that the family had kept hidden from the cadres during the Cultural Revolution. Little clay bowls were placed around her body, each labeled with the names of her favorite food. At night her sons and grandsons took turns "guarding the spirit," or standing in front of the body. Then for one night she was placed in the coffin, which was propped up on a sawhorse, and in keeping with local superstition her eldest son had to sleep under it.

If a person in the village died before reaching sixty, the professor said, the peasants called him a "short-life devil" and believed he had committed some misdeeds in this life or a previous one. His body was not honored inside the house. One peasant who was run over by a truck was left where he fell.

The village lay in a narrow valley topped by hills covered with fir trees, and the grandmother was buried on one of the hillsides. An elderly villager who was familiar with the ancient wisdom of *feng-shui,* the spirits of "the wind and the water," or geomancy, selected a favorable site for her grave. Several dozen peasants took part in the funeral procession, the close relatives dressed in white robes and white caps with strips of white paper over their shoes—white is the color of death. For seven days after her death, her close relatives were forbidden to eat meat, and her sons and daughters were not allowed to bathe or wash their hair for forty-nine days.

In early April, by our calendar, comes one of the most important traditional Chinese festivals, Qing Ming, when people are supposed to visit their family graves to "sweep" or clean them of weeds. The Communists do not give the peasants a holiday for Qing Ming, since it is regarded as a superstitious custom that interferes with work.

But I remember driving through the Fujian countryside on the day of Qing Ming and looking with astonishment as we passed hillside after hillside strewn with red, green, blue, and yellow paper flowers. They had been placed there to mark the low brick tombstones. Outside Quanzhou, which when Marco Polo visited China in the thirteenth century was one of the world's great ports, then known as Zaytun, a knot of a dozen peasants was tending a graveyard with hoes. One middle-aged woman, in loose black pants, was bent over a circular grave. She had just placed an offering of cooked rice in front of it and was kneeling in a posture of prayer, oblivious to the noisy traffic of trucks and buses on the road, a symbol of the hardy resistance the peasants had displayed to those parts of Mao's revolution which they didn't care for and the persistence of rural rhythms and traditions.

12.   The Iron Rice Bowl

铁 饭 碗

INDUSTRY

"An Immortal said: 'In playing chess, there is no infallible way of winning, but there is an infallible way of not losing.' He was asked what this infallible way could be, and replied: 'It is not to play chess.' "
Feng Yulan, A History of Chinese Philosophy

Not long after I took up residence in Peking in June 1979, I got out an old pre-World War Two guidebook to the city and tried to retrace the site of the capital's ancient walls. Except for a short stretch around the Forbidden City and Zhongnanhai, where the country's leaders work, these magnificent barriers—forty feet high and sixty-two feet thick at the base—were torn down by the Communists in the 1950s as an obstruction to traffic and a sinful waste of space. Instead, I found, as I walked on an east–west line from the old Qian Men, or Front Gate, which still survives, the government had recently replaced the walls with a two-mile-long series of ten-story buff-colored apartment buildings. The concrete apartments, more than forty blocks in all, were a sparkling contrast to the shabbiness of most Chinese buildings, with their dingy exteriors badly in need of paint and cracked windows. The new buildings had large glass windows and small balconies, with space for shops on the ground floor. In a city where the average urban resident has only about three square yards of living space, this new project looked like a splendid attempt by the government to resolve one of its worst problems.

But as I walked farther, I began to sense something amiss. There were no children playing outside, no curtains in the windows, no laundry hanging out to dry, no sound of laughter or shouting reverberating from within. The apartments, in fact, were virtually empty.

"They are beautiful buildings," a taxi driver said to me over his shoulder a few days later as we drove along the avenue where the apartments stood, as mute as the tombs of the Ming emperors in the hills northwest of the city. "But whoever built them should be shot." Then he spit out the window in the universal gesture of contempt.

They had been completed over a year before, I learned from a dour, middle-aged man who worked in a photography shop nearby, but most people to whom they had been offered as new housing had refused to accept them. He himself had been assigned an apartment on the sixth floor of one of the buildings and had managed to stall for several months before his *danwei* ordered him to move in. The trouble with the buildings, he explained, was that they lacked adequate pressure to lift water above the third floor, there were no gas mains for the stoves, no elevators, and the heating system didn't work. He had to pump his water by hand with a makeshift device and he dreaded the coming of winter. The buildings were all supposed to be heated by hot water from a thermal power plant, but it was so far away that by the time the water arrived it was only 41 degrees fahrenheit and the radiators gave off no heat. The reason for the mess, he confided, was that there had been no coordination between the different government construction, engineering, and architectural agencies involved.

"Whoever arrived at the job first just set to work," he said, his tone a whisper so that other people in the shop couldn't hear. "That way, one group of workmen came to lay the foundations and put up the structures and walls before the water company came to install the pipes. No one cared about the results, because no one had overall responsibility."

He had clipped out an article from the *People's Daily* which chastised the construction industry for "anarchy." But, he added, the paper did not say anyone had been punished for wasting millions of yuan.

The apartment project symbolized for me both the achievements and blunders of Chinese industry. Before 1949 China's modern industrial sector was microscopic: a smattering of textile mills in Shanghai, a fledgling iron and steel industry in what was then called Manchuria, developed by the Japanese, and a skeletal railroad network linking only the major cities. But since the First Five-Year Plan in 1953, China's industrial production has grown at an average annual pace of 10 percent, one of the highest anywhere. China is now the world's leading producer of cotton textiles and tungsten; the second largest manufacturer of radios; the third biggest miner of coal; it ranks fifth in output of steel and tenth in oil. China manufactures its own computers, electron microscopes, nuclear missiles, and jet fighters.

These are impressive accomplishments, and during the four years I covered China from Hong Kong I regularly reported Peking's year-end claims of production increases in steel, oil, and chemical fertilizer as a measure of progress. But it wasn't until I lived in China that I realized these conventional indices of economic growth masked colossal waste, monumental miscalculations, an inefficient economic system, and bureaucratic bungling that China could ill afford. The rapid expansion of China's gross national product also obscured the lack of any real increase in living standards. Indeed, since the mid-1950s, the average amount of housing space has decreased, and until a sharp redirection of economic policy by Mao's successors starting in 1979, there was no significant improvement in the supply of consumer goods or food. Real wages in the cities fell from 1965 to the end of the decade of the 1970s. Chinese industry was much like the gigantic white-elephant apartment project in Peking—on the surface, the government had scored success, but somehow it didn't connect with people's livelihood.

A graying government economist, Lao Hu, offered an explanation of what went wrong. Tall and thin, erect and dignified, if a bit rigid in his bearing, he was courteous and formal in the manner of an old-fashioned upper-class Chinese. He spoke in quiet measured tones, always intense, thoughtful, and serious. He seldom smiled, but he retained an enthusiasm for his subject. One critical problem, as Lao Hu outlined it, was that in the early 1950s China had adopted the Stalinist model of intensive industrialization. Despite Peking's subsequent split with Moscow, the Russian system became Chinese orthodoxy.

"It was like shooting one's self in the foot," Lao Hu said. The Soviet model called for high forced savings, financed by keeping wages low, the cost of manufactured products expensive, and factory earnings high. There was no personal income tax, but the government siphoned off all the factories' profits to reinvest in the development of more industry, especially heavy industry like steel. These new heavy industrial plants produced glamorous annual gains in the gross national product which China's leaders could report with pride. But they also brought waste, imbalances, and inefficiency, he charged, because there was no attempt to measure the state's return on the capital it invested. Profit was considered a dirty capitalist word, and factory directors who worried about red ink were accused of "putting profits in command."

"It was a great blind rush to build as many factories as possible," Lao Hu went on. In the three decades of Communist rule, China constructed a grand total of 355,000 factories, with an investment equivalent to $213 billion, a staggering sum for a poor country like China. To achieve this the government reinvested an average of 30 percent of the country's gross national product each year, with the figure rising as high as 36.5 percent in 1978, leaving proportionately little for consumption. By comparison, total private investment in the United States in 1980 was 6.6 percent of America's GNP.

But in Peking's rush, it ignored the profitability of its new investments and their efficiency declined precipitously. In 1957 every $67 of assets (factories and their machinery) generated $23 in profits and taxes for the state. By 1976, the figure had fallen to $13.*

An American businessman with the Xerox Corporation, one of dozens to take up residence in the Peking Hotel in the late 1970s, recalled inspecting a number of factories managed by the Fourth Ministry of Machine Building, which produces electronic equipment for the armed forces. The ministry was interested in manufacturing an improved copying machine, and Xerox engineers were impressed by the quality of the research and workmanship they saw in the factories. But the Americans also found that the Chinese plants were greatly overequipped with machines, overstaffed, and were operating at only about 20 percent of capacity.

"One factory we visited was turning out only one hundred to two hundred copiers a year," the businessman related. "One of our own factories at home turns out that many in a single day."

On the day of his visit, the American noticed that many of the workers were idle, sitting in groups smoking, talking, or playing cards. The only ones working were constructing a new wing for the factory.

"I was amazed," the businessman added. "Here was this big factory with most of its workers and machines idle and they are expanding. What was the investment for? Finally I had an inspiration. They were just constructing a new plant because the workers didn't have anything else to do and the factory director had to use his allotted funds for the year or lose them. I asked the director if this was true, and he agreed with embarrassment it was."

A middle-aged factory worker with broad shoulders and a prominent scar on his right hand told me about another worker in his plant who had recently retired at the mandatory age of sixty. The factory gave a farewell party for him, but in the middle of drinking beer and eating small sweet cakes he began to cry. "Why are you crying, now your life will be easy?" his colleagues quizzed him.

"Yes," he replied. "But I have been a worker in this factory for twenty years, since they first started construction on it, and I have never done a day's work in the plant." The others knew what he meant. The factory was still under construction and had never opened because there was such competition for building materials that the plant could not get the supplies it needed. He had simply reported for work each day and then idled his time attending political study sessions, playing cards, or chatting with his friends.

His story was not unusual. Almost every Chinese I met had a favorite tale about a factory that was never finished or couldn't be used once it was built because some official had been too ambitious. In Urumqi, the capital of

*People's Daily, March 2, 1981, p. 5.

Xinjiang, the vast westernmost province of China that is as big as all of Western Europe or Alaska, my local guide joked about an oil refinery the government had constructed there at a cost equivalent to $140 million. The complex had been finished for over a year, but it was not in use. Xinjiang is the site of some of China's most promising new oil fields, but their output is shipped by railroad to another even larger refinery in Lanzhou, to the east, which would have to be shut down if the Urumqi plant was put on line.

This goof was small, however, compared to the blunders in building a $500 million addition to the steelworks at Wuhan, in central China, the country's second largest iron and steel complex, and the projected $13.3 billion Baoshan iron and steel mill near Shanghai designed to be the largest industrial undertaking since the founding of the People's Republic. When the Wuhan addition, which included five separate rolling, casting, and sheet mills built by Japanese and West German firms, was completed in 1978, it was supposed to manufacture three million tons of high-grade steel a year. But the Chinese builders had forgotten about electricity. When the plant was turned on, it drew more electric power than the entire surrounding province of Hubei could produce. Its operations had to be limited to one or two days a week.

The even larger Baoshan complex was to be the centerpiece of Peking's Four Modernizations program—the ambitious plan to modernize the country's agriculture, industry, science, and defense by the year 2000—a mammoth plant to turn out 6.7 million tons of steel a year with the most advanced technology imported from Japan, West Germany, and the United States. It was the kind of project that China's leaders once liked to show off as an example of how massive amounts of manpower and revolutionary spirit could produce an economic miracle. The Communists regarded it with such importance that for its ground-breaking ceremony a planeload of Politburo members had flown down to Shanghai to officiate. But when I visited the site, an hour's drive from Shanghai on the muddy banks of the broad Yangtze River, few workers were in sight and hardly a hammer blow could be heard. The girder skeletons destined to house two blast furnaces, a hot and a cold rolling mill, a tubing mill, cokers, converters, repair shops, and a power plant stood in various stages of noncompletion. The only activity was at a large wharf, still under construction. Although no official announcement had been made at the time of my trip, the project had been suspended. It was a victim of Peking's sharp retrenchment in 1980 and 1981 when the government finally began to recognize the effects of its overbuilding. The national budget for 1981 was slashed 13.4 percent, twice the size of President Reagan's precedent-making cuts in U.S. government spending the same year.

At Baoshan, a deputy director of the construction team admitted there had been a series of miscalculations. The Japanese blast furnaces proved too sophisticated for the low-grade ore China produces, so Peking had to buy higher-grade ore from Australia, which was too expensive. Then the location chosen for the steel mill was on swampy ground; it required 300,000 tons of steel supporting piles, some of which sank out of sight. The shallow Yangtze River estuary could not accommodate the 100,000-ton carriers bringing the ore from Australia, so the Chinese had to build a new port and storage facilities 130 miles to the south and transship the ore on smaller vessels. All of these unexpected expenses meant huge cost overruns. An official of the Ministry of Metallurgy admitted publicly that the real price for Baoshan might run to the equivalent of $27 billion, twice the original estimate, and an astronomical 40 percent of China's national budget for 1981 of $65 billion.

Lao Hu, the economist, suggested a historical reason for Peking's fascination with steel production as an index of national strength. "Many Chinese have long believed we were beaten by the imperialists starting in the nineteenth century because of our lack of steel," he said in a talk in his spacious apartment, a mark of his rank. "Mao himself put forward the slogan, 'Take steel as the key link.' But they turned this into a fixation with heavy industry." Over the last thirty years, he said, more than 50 percent of all government investment in construction has gone to heavy industry, with only 5 percent for the consumer-goods-producing light industry and 8 percent to agriculture. At the same time, he added, China's leaders had badly neglected other critical sectors—energy, transportation, and housing. "Last year we lost twenty-five percent of our potential industrial production because many factories didn't have enough electric power and had to accept brownouts." In 1980 the output of oil, coal, and natural gas actually decreased 2 percent because of the government's failure to put sufficient funds in new energy development and in 1981 fell further.

Paradoxically, part of the explanation for this incredible waste and inefficiency is central planning, the Soviet system of managing the economy by annual quotas rather than by profits and market forces. My friend Lao Hu saw it as another contagion China had picked up from the Soviets. In theory, he explained, central planning is very scientific: the state sets the target for each factory every year, then it delivers the necessary raw materials and workers, and the plant manager need only ensure that he meets his annual production quota.

"It is a command economy, like running an army, and it has strong appeal to men like Mao who came to power as generals," Lao Hu said. "The tragedy was that it did work remarkably well in the First Five-Year Plan," from 1953 to 1957, when the country was just recovering from decades of civil war and the Communists were full of energy and idealism. "But that was a one-time phenomenon," Lao Hu continued. The flaw, he said, is that the plan measures success by whether a factory turns out the correct number of radios or tractors according to a pre-set target, not by whether the products are actually sold or how much profit the factory earns.

As an example of what happens when the fetish for building factories is combined with central planning, Lao Hu suggested I look at the automotive industry. China has 130 car and truck plants, the largest number in the world. Indeed, twenty-eight of the twenty-nine provinces and independent municipalities into which China is divided each have at least one such factory —Tibet is the exception. But their total output is only 220,000 vehicles a year, putting China about twentieth in the world.

The biggest automobile factory in Peking manufactures jeeps, and I decided to ask for a tour of the plant. When I first called early in the month of December, a factory official apologized. They were sorry they would have to turn down my request. The plant had met its quota for the year in September, he explained, and it had been closed since then. The workers still reported each day, but only to maintain and repair the machinery. Perhaps I would like to apply again in January when the factory received its target for the next year and reopened.

I was intrigued. In January I renewed my request and this time was met by the head of the director's office, Wen Zhenxiang, a former army political commissar with a high forehead and longish hair that he combed straight back, much like Mao had. Wen was attired in a green cap, blue jacket with a gold pen in the left breast pocket, like cadres everywhere in China, and green army pants. The sickly sweet smell of a distillery a few blocks away hung over the sprawling brick factory.

Piles of parts waiting to be assembled lay scattered seemingly at random on the concrete floor: oil pans, radiator grills, headlights, drive shafts, crates of nuts and bolts. Two workers in their twenties were feeding metal panels for the jeeps' bodies into a 1,000-ton press, extracting their hands a split second before the machine crashed down, stamping the steel like a cookie cutter shaping dough. The workers, like those I observed elsewhere in Chinese factories, wore no protective goggles and had no device to shield their hands from the devouring press. The factory had only been a repair garage until 1958 and had been built up largely through the efforts of its own staff, Wen said. Over the years they had designed their own simple automated assembly line and automatic painting and drying shop in a model application of the dictum of self-reliance. Their jeep, though, remained unchanged, a copy of a Russian original, a boxy, no frills, four-door vehicle with a high running board, olive-drab paint, and an unsophisticated four-cylinder engine like those found in American cars in the late 1940s. The plant's production quota in 1980 was 15,000 jeeps, Wen said, or less than two for each of the factory's 9,700 workers. Could it produce more? I asked. Yes, he replied, it had a capacity of 30,000 vehicles a year. Then wouldn't it be more profitable to manufacture more instead of closing down for several months at the end of the year after they met their quota? I persisted. Wen chuckled at my question.

"We cannot produce at will, we must follow the task assigned us by the State Planning Commission. That is the path of socialism."

The planning commission also relieves the factory manager of responsibility for selling the jeeps—it issues certificates to the Machinery Equipment Agencies of each province and they in turn distribute the right to buy the vehicles to individual offices, factories, or communes. The customers must come to Peking themselves to collect their jeeps and are responsible for getting them home. Foreign customers might balk at that condition, except that for the Chinese cadres designated to make the pickups it means an all-expense-paid trip to Peking, a special treat.

The jeeps are not cheap. The selling price is equivalent to $9,333, high by American, Japanese, and European standards considering the quality of the vehicle. But the price, too, is fixed by the State Planning Commission, not the factory. Wen estimated the cost of production at $6,467, for a handsome profit of 44 percent per jeep. American automobile manufacturers mark up the price of their cars an average of only 15 percent; even the Cadillac never exceeded 25 percent. But when I congratulated Wen on the size of the margin, he again laughed at my ignorance. As a state-owned enterprise, the factory must turn over 95 percent of its profits to the government and retains only 5 percent. So neither the manager nor the workers have a vested interest in cutting costs or raising profits.

Under the rules of central planning, the director of the jeep factory lacked other types of authority which Western managers would take for granted. He cannot hire or fire a single worker, he can't raise an employee's salary, he can't purchase new machinery, and he can't redesign the model of the jeep. All these powers lie with the several layers of the bureaucracy above him to which he must report. The manager's lack of power added to the inefficiency.

An enterprising reporter from the *People's Daily* once interviewed the manager of the Heavy Machinery Plant in Shenyang, a major industrial center in the northeast, on the frustrations of his job. To build a new dormitory for some of the factory's 10,000 workers, he complained, he had to get permission from eleven separate government agencies and twenty-four official chops, or seals. In one three-month period, the manager was required to read 518 government documents and attend forty-eight meetings at offices outside the plant. First the national ministry in charge of the factory, the First Ministry of Machine Building, would hold a meeting, then the provincial agency would copy it, and next the city department involved would hold its own conference on the same topic. Each supervisory agency also bombarded the factory with inspection teams—quality inspection teams, financial rules inspection teams, production safety inspection teams, and family-planning inspection teams. On one day, when a reporter from the *People's Daily* was there, seven different inspection groups arrived at once and the factory's three reception rooms proved insufficient.

"Each team insisted its work was very important and demanded the leading comrade of the factory meet with it," the journalist wrote. "They wanted the director to mobilize the masses of workers in his plant to 'fight a people's war of annihilation' on their particular topic," a Maoist term borrowed from the Party's guerrilla days meaning an all-out effort. The problem, the director said, using a Chinese metaphor, was that he had "too many grandmothers."

John Bing, for many years the representative in Peking of Pullman Kellogg, a Texas-based company which constructed half a dozen large chemical fertilizer plants in China, once found himself in a discussion of American management practices with the director of one of the factories he had helped build. The Chinese official wanted to know how American managers raised productivity.

"I told him, we just concentrate on finding out what is wrong and then fix it," said Bing, a tall, slightly stooped sandy-haired man who had such affection for China that he gave up his retirement to come back to live and work in a small hotel-room office in Peking with his wife.

The Chinese cadre looked bemused. "I couldn't do that," he told Bing. "I have to spend ninety percent of my time dealing with personnel and political problems that have nothing to do with production."

By coincidence, I met an engineer and accountant from the American Motors Corporation, the makers of the U.S. Jeep, who were in Peking to negotiate a joint venture enterprise with the capital jeep factory. Under the proposed deal, A.M.C. would supply its technology to upgrade the Chinese jeep, whose antiquated engine gets poor gasoline mileage and can't meet most international standards for emission control. The talks dragged on inconclusively for over two years, but they gave the Americans an unusual opportunity to inspect the Chinese factory. The men were surprised, they told me, by how overbuilt and underutilized it was. It should actually be producing 45,000 jeeps a year, triple its current output, they estimated.

"They have more equipment than they can use for years," the engineer commented. "In the machine shop, where maybe they need five lathes, they have twenty-five. They have all these forges and presses, too, which they may use only once or twice a month to make some small part they don't need in quantity. It's very uneconomical." In the United States, he said, a company would farm out such work to specialized subcontractors. The best way for the joint venture to make money, he joked, would be to sell off its excess machines to companies in the United States, where there is a market for used equipment.

There were two reasons the jeep factory felt it needed so much machinery, the accountant surmised after talks with Chinese cadres. One was the old Chinese Communist stress on self-sufficiency, dating to the Party's guerrilla days when each army band had to be self-contained. That was also why almost every province has its own car and truck assembly plants, regardless of the size of its population and road network. But there was a practical reason too. The jeep factory had found that if it didn't make all its own parts, like wire for its sparkplugs, and depended on deliveries from other factories under the state plan, the necessary materials tended not to arrive on time. The plan was constantly fouled up. So each ministry, each province, and each factory jealously guards its own turf, and they sometimes act more like warring nations than components of the same economy.

In a county in Shanxi province, in the west, the *People's Daily* related, such a conflict developed between a coal mine and an electric generating plant located next door to each other. "They are separated by only a wall, and all the coal produced in the mine is supposed to be consumed by the plant," the paper said. "According to the original design, only a conveyor belt is needed to move the coal from the mine to the generating plant. But the present situation is different." Because the mine comes under the Ministry of Coal and the plant under the Ministry of Electric Power, they refused to cooperate with each other. So the coal was first transported by truck to a railroad line four miles to the east. Then it was loaded on freight cars and shipped back to the power plant.

In Urumqi, the ramshackle capital of Xinjiang, built on an oasis between the perennially snow-capped Mountains of Heaven and the Dzungarian Desert, I came across an American sales manager for a company that makes giant trenchers to lay oil pipelines. His firm, Barber-Greene, had sold five of the $150,000 machines to China's Ministry of Petroleum the year before, plus $100,000 in spare parts. Two of the trenchers had been assigned to Xinjiang to help construct a new pipeline there. The American had flown out to Urumqi, a four-hour plane ride from Peking, to see how his equipment was performing. To his consternation, he could find only one of the two trenchers sent to Xinjiang.

Where was the other? he asked. It's not working, a cadre from the provincial office of the Ministry of Petroleum replied.

Why not, what went wrong? the American inquired.

"Oh, nothing's wrong with it. But we had to take it apart to get spare parts for the one that is working," the Chinese explained.

The American's perplexity deepened. "But why didn't you order up some of the $100,000 in spare parts you bought?" he asked.

"We don't know where they are," the Chinese answered. "And even if we did, we couldn't get them. They are in another province."

Such lack of concern with efficiency, by the standards of Western management, is not unusual. Although Mao's successors have condemned the leftists' attacks on "putting profits in command" and have called for more attention to the bottom line, 23 percent of China's state-owned factories operated at a loss in 1980, according to the State Statistical Bureau. Even though industrial production increased 8.4 percent that year, total profits from the country's factories dropped 1.3 percent, the bureau also reported. Since without an individual income tax the major source of the government's revenue is factory profits, this is a critical problem.

Lao Hu charged that devotion to central planning created a number of other practices antithetical to good cost accounting. "We have always tended to keep a lot of inventory and not turn it over very quickly," he said, "since no one is responsible for whether goods sell." Factories just produce to meet their quota; no one ever takes a market survey, he added.

A friend who was employed in a state corporation that handles electrical machinery estimated it had the equivalent of $400 million in stock in warehouses around China. But the government budget for 1981 to buy electrical machinery was only $200 million. So it would take two full years of purchases just to sell off their inventory, without any further production, he said. An official of the State Economic Commission, which oversees the economy, told delegates to the National People's Congress in 1980 that the total value of goods in warehouses in China is equal to a full year's income for all Chinese wage earners.

Poor quality, another trouble that has plagued Chinese industry, is also traceable to the plan, Lao Hu argued, for a factory's performance is measured only by the number of goods it produces, not their quality. A youthful Chinese who works in a Peking factory that makes components for computers told me the rejection rate for parts in his plant was over 50 percent. The New China News Agency once disclosed that a tractor factory in Canton had manufactured more than 7,000 tractors since it started in 1966, but not one of them met the specified quality standards. An article in the *People's Daily* lambasted a county farm-machinery plant in Jilin province, in the northeast, one of the rural small-scale industries which China's leaders have counted on to help mechanize the countryside. It turned out only fifty small hand-operated tractors a year, with a bad reputation for being too expensive and often breaking down. Nevertheless, the county Party secretary, to ensure the factory made a profit, forced the communes in the area to buy them. Some of the comrades in one commune rebelled and challenged the factory. They offered to buy as many tractors as the plant could drive to them. The plant picked out ten tractors; only three arrived.

During the four years I covered China from Hong Kong and dutifully reported Peking's annual year-end economic claims for *The New York Times,* I sometimes wondered how accurate the figures were which the government released. Western economists I talked with, from universities, the U.S. State Department, and the CIA, were reassuring. Almost all of them agreed that the Chinese data was reliable, though for the period from the Great Leap Forward in 1958 to the late 1970s it was often only fragmentary and expressed in percentages. Peking might assert, for instance, that the output of railway cars had met the yearly target. But that didn't say what the actual production was, or whether it had increased over the previous year. The Chinese didn't deliberately lie, the foreign specialists felt—they just issued their statistics selectively.

But a member of the State Statistical Bureau, the high-level agency responsible for gathering and collating data from every factory and commune across the country, essential to the centrally planned economy, presented a very different picture. During the Cultural Revolution, he said, the staff of the bureau in Peking had come under severe attack from the radicals because most of them were highly trained intellectuals. Many of the statisticians were packed off to labor in the countryside, and the number of employees in the office had been reduced from two hundred to a mere fourteen, to assemble data on hundreds of millions of people. Only in 1980, he related, had the State Statistical Bureau regained its pre-Cultural Revolution size, and their first task was to work out a new standard form for factories to report their production figures. Each factory had to turn in its statistics within three days after the end of every month.

How accurate had these reports been? I asked him. "After the chaos of the Cultural Revolution, we suspect a lot of factories just reported their planned targets as their output," he replied, "but we had no way to check on them." His bureau was only now establishing its own independent audit mechanism. The figures for agriculture were probably even more misleading, he added. Here again was an example of incalculable harm done to the country by the Cultural Revolution.

The worst problem had been created by the Communists' belief that the fastest way to spur an increase in grain production was to urge communes to concentrate on raising their yield per acre. This created a national mania for per unit yield, and at every commune I visited the cadres were always ready with a briefing on their own per unit output. But this also gave the cadres an easy way to doctor their achievements, for by reporting less land than they actually had, they could inflate the harvest per acre. So many teams and communes routinely did this, an official of the Ministry of State Farms and Land Reclamation told me, that Peking's estimates of the total amount of arable land in China had become unreliable. Using locally supplied figures, the government reckoned China had 250 million acres of cultivable land. But American satellite photographs given to the Chinese showed 350 million acres, a 40 percent discrepancy. This outright deceit was part of the breakdown in morality that followed years of political campaigns.

The most controversial figures Peking put out were for its population. Like a fat man sensitive about his weight, the Chinese estimates often seemed too low to foreign specialists. But China's leaders themselves were sometimes surprisingly candid about their own ignorance. In 1972, Li Xiannian, then the country's chief economic planner, was asked by a Japanese visitor about the size of China's population. The State Planning Commission uses a figure of less than 750 million people, Li responded; officials responsible for food go by the number of 800 million, and the Ministry of Commerce prefers 830 million. China is conducting a full-scale census in 1982, with the help of United Nations–provided computers, to clarify the mystery.

One morning when I was reading our daily intake of nearly a dozen Chinese newspapers with my assistant Lao Wu, he let out a loud cry of *"ai-ya,"* roughly, "my god." The story was about a team of peasants who had been working on their commune's fields in the suburbs of Peking. It was wintertime, and the peasants had built a fire to warm themselves. But when one farmer threw some of the burning brushwood into a nearby river, the stream caught fire and rapidly consumed a bridge and high-tension power lines. An investigation revealed the surface of the river was coated with oil discharged by five factories upstream.

The incident was one of a series of cases the Chinese press began to expose in 1980 as the Communists belatedly recognized that their industrial growth over the last thirty years had brought serious pollution. The government has not made public any studies of how foul the air and water have become, and in a country where political power is monopolized by the Communist Party there has been no popular movement to stop offending factories and cars. But to live in Peking in the winter is to be aware of the problem. For days at a time after Barbara and I moved into our new eleventh-floor apartment in one of the areas reserved for foreign diplomats and journalists, when we looked out the window in the morning all that was visible was a thick gray haze. It was like the effect of a white-out on skiers during a blinding snowstorm. The city below us disappeared.

A delegation from the U.S. Environmental Protection Agency that visited China confirmed our worst fears. One of the Americans had brought along a small instrument known as a "personal air quality monitor" which measures the number of particles in the air per million. The safe level is considered no higher than twenty-five or thirty, he told groups of Chinese. The highest level ever recorded in Washington was fifty.

But when he turned on the machine inside a classroom in Peking, it reached 120. In Wuhan, the heavy industrial center on the Yangtze River, the meter rose to 400, its highest point. Then the machine sputtered and broke.

For many years the Communists had insisted that pollution could occur only in capitalist countries where corrupt industrialists "make their enormous profits by rampantly discharging harmful substances into the environment at will and in complete disregard for the fate of the people," as the *People's Daily* once charged. As recently as 1972, a Chinese delegate to a United Nations environmental conference in Stockholm denounced the United States and other industrialized nations for causing the world's environmental troubles and demanded "compensation" for undeveloped countries, presumably including China. But Mao's more pragmatic successors have shown a greater ecological awareness and in 1980 enacted the first environmental protection law in China. How far China can or should now move to check pollution, however, poses a difficult dilemma for Peking. For the government owns the factories, and as Li Hongyuan, an official in charge of pollution control in Heilongjiang province, in the northeast, put it, "There is often a severe contradiction between production and protecting the environment."

A short, energetic man with an endless supply of facts and figures and an engaging passion for his job, Li took me to visit the Song Hua River, which flows through Harbin, the capital of Heilongjiang. The river has become contaminated, Li said, and virtually all the fish are gone from it. Fishermen who ate large quantities of aquatic products in recent years now show high amounts of mercury in their bodies. Some peasants who live downstream from factories that discharged chromium into the river have complained of vomiting, diarrhea, and stomach pains. Li's office has fined several of these factories and persuaded some of them to start cleaning up, but it may be too late to repair the long-term damage to the river.

Until the early part of this century, the land in Heilongjiang was virtually unsettled, a vast fertile prairie rimmed by lushly forested mountains. For China, overpopulated for centuries, it was a last frontier. But now the plains are peopled with peasants in mud-walled houses like the rest of the country, and the forests have been endangered by widespread felling of trees and by fires. Some Chinese scientists believe the destruction of the forests may account for a 50 percent drop in the province's rainfall since the early 1950s. As a result, in the past decade alone the average flow of water though the Song Hua River, which irrigates much of Heilongjiang, has fallen by half. In Harbin, an industrialized city of over two million people originally laid out by the Russians, the river now occupies only about half of its old course.

"There is a medium linking the lord of the earth with the lord of heaven —that is vegetation, which evaporates moisture into the air and produces rainfall," said Chen Zhong, an official of the Ministry of State Farms and Land Reclamation. "But the lord of heaven is a merchant. He doesn't give if he isn't paid."

The offshore oil rig in the South China Sea, near Hainan Island, was on a high-priority project—it was running delicate tests with an air-pressure gun lowered down a well hole to try to confirm earlier seismic data about the presence of rich petroleum deposits in the area. So when an American engineer from a major U.S. oil company went aboard the rig he was astounded to find that the Chinese crewmen stopped drilling as lunchtime approached, turned off all their machinery, and then vanished for long midday naps, what the Chinese call *xiu-xi.*

It costs $50,000 a day to operate the platform, the American pointed out to the captain of the vessel. It is also technically dangerous to stop the drill —the equipment is more likely to get stuck. That's why foreign rig crews work twelve-hour shifts around the clock without resting. "You just can't interrupt the drilling," the American argued. But the captain was unpersuaded.

For since 1949 *xiu-xi* has become one of the most important and satisfying rituals of Chinese life. Few Chinese would consider doing anything else but sleep during their siesta, which lasts a full two hours in the winter, up to three hours in summer. Lunch is eaten on office time before 12 P.M.; shopping is accomplished during "tea" breaks in the morning and afternoon, which may last from fifteen minutes to a couple of hours. Workmen at a construction site outside our apartment building napped on heaps of gravel; I often drove past peasants dozing in the backs of donkey carts as they clattered down the street; office workers I knew slumbered on couches in their offices. At the *People's Daily* some offices come equipped with their own beds. When Jan Wong worked at the Foreign Languages Press, many of her fellow employees kept bedrolls on a shelf. At noontime they cleared all the books and papers off their desks, spread their blankets atop them, and nodded off.

So partial are Chinese to *xiu-xi* that nothing—even airplane travel—is allowed to interfere. On a CAAC flight from Canton to the old lakeside city of Hangzhou, about the distance from New York to Chicago, we put down at noon at a military airfield near the small provincial city of Nanchang. The stewardess explained it was time for lunch, and all the passengers trouped into an air force mess hall where we were fed steaming dishes of fried pork and peppers and bowls of hot soup. But after the meal we were still left waiting for another hour. The sky was a bright, cloudless blue, there was no problem with weather, and I passed the time watching several antiquated silver MIG-17's practice takeoffs and landings. When the crew finally reappeared, I quizzed the stewardess about the delay.

"The pilot had to have his *xiu-xi,*" she answered.

Xiu-xi grows out of the ancient and natural rhythms of peasant life, rising early with the sun to labor hard in the fields, then taking a break during the heat of midday. But the Communists have enthusiastically embraced it as an accomplishment of socialism in an industrial society. It is even enshrined in China's constitution, Article 49: "The working people have the right to *xiu-xi.*"

The siesta is only one of a number of comforts Communist rule has brought to urban Chinese as Peking has created an elaborate all-encompassing welfare state. There is free medical care, free public education, and heavily subsidized low-cost housing. Even the lowest paid factory workers get monthly coupons good for haircuts and trips to the public baths; most offices give out free movie tickets, and women get a small extra allowance to purchase paper for sanitary napkins.

But the centerpiece of the system is guaranteed lifetime employment, what the Chinese call the "iron rice bowl." In China, unless you commit a serious crime like robbery or murder, it is virtually impossible to be fired. At the huge Lanzhou Petrochemical complex in the west, the biggest of its kind in China, with 36,000 workers, a plant official told me they had never dismissed a single employee. And every worker has the right to pass on his post to one of his children, creating a system of inherited jobs.

"From my point of view, it is not good to fire workers, that would cause them troubles in their livelihood," remarked the cadre, Zhang Lianchang, a thin man with a pinched face who is the deputy head of the director's office. "That is not the socialist way. Before Liberation, workers were at the mercy of capitalists and could be laid off anytime, like you do in the United States. Lifetime employment is one of the great achievements of the revolution," he went on, sounding more like a Western union leader than an executive.

Such claims are not the hyperbole of propaganda. In 1981, when the government moved to close over 1,000 inefficient factories to cut its budget deficit, Chinese friends reported that the workers in these plants were still being paid. A tall, muscular young man with a pitted face whom I met during a stroll in the North Ocean Park said the tractor factory where he had worked for four years had been ordered to stop production. He was still drawing his regular salary. His biggest concern, he said, was what to do with his free time.

Socialism has brought other unique benefits to urban Chinese in their work life. Many people now take for granted that their *danwei* will supply them with what in the West would be considered personal property. Not long after arriving in Peking, I hired a driver for *The Times*'s office car, a necessity in

China to help with chores like paying bills, which is still done in person and not by mail. At the suggestion of Lao Wu, we asked the Diplomatic Services Bureau for an older man—they are much more reliable than youngsters these days, Lao Wu contended. The driver assigned to me turned out to be an affable, burly former peasant in his late forties, with a square jaw and a dry sense of humor. His surname was Shi, meaning stone, and because he was older than I, I addressed him as Lao Shi, a phrase that rhymes with the word for honest and upright, a description that fit him neatly.

But his good humor broke down on the first rainy morning. What was wrong? I inquired through Lao Wu, using a middleman in the Chinese fashion. The driver was unhappy, Lao Wu answered, because I had not bought an umbrella and thermos for the office car.

But he has an umbrella, I said, pointing to the black object standing dripping in a corner of the room. Yes, Lao Wu counseled patiently, but that is his own umbrella. After he arrives at the office, he should not be expected to have to use it.

This is part of the system of *bao-xiao,* or "putting it on the office expense account." Bing, the woman who denounced her father during the Cultural Revolution, told me that whenever she went to the airport to see off or greet a colleague she got a free meal at the airport restaurant. "You just tell the waiter you are on an official mission, and he marks it on the bill," she explained. "Then when you go back to your *danwei,* you can collect from them."

In Chinese eyes, these state-provided comforts help compensate for the continued low standard of living, the lack of individual choice in important decisions like education and jobs, and the frustrations of daily life, the standing in line to buy groceries and the overcrowded buses.

"If you are not overly ambitious and don't have any political troubles, life in China is pleasant, like living on a slow-moving conveyor belt," commented a balding professor at one of Peking's universities. "Everything is provided for you, you don't have to worry, and there is little pressure to make you hurry."

Not long before, his daughter, a woman in her mid-twenties, had managed to arrange a visit to Hong Kong on the pretext of seeing an uncle. The professor was afraid she might stay on in the British colony, as thousands of Chinese do each year, attracted by the bright lights, the job opportunities, and the much higher standard of living. But after two months she returned.

"It was too hectic, people have to work so hard," she told her father.

But some Chinese worry that the custom of *xiu-xi,* the iron rice bowl, and the welfare state mentality have eroded the old work ethic that made Chinese famous, the ability to *chi-ku,* or "eat bitterness." (The word "coolie" in English comes from a variant of this, *ku-li,* "bitter strength.")

"People in the cities don't work as hard as they used to," complained a talented surgeon who was trained before 1949. In his hospital, he said, many of the patients just come in to get medical excuses from work. They don't have to pay for the hospital visit, and simply by making a trip to the clinic they get a half day off from work. Some of them try to feign illness by tinkering with the thermometer or squeezing the blood-pressure apparatus.

"It's easy to tell that so many people are faking," the doctor continued. "On a day that is an official holiday, they suddenly vanish."

Our *a-yi,* whose surname was Wang, was a skilled practioner of life lived at the slow-motion pace of *tai-ji,* Chinese shadow boxing. Plump and middle-aged, with her hair worn short in the proletarian bowl-cut style, Wang *a-yi* had not gone past primary school, but she had a native shrewdness we soon learned to appreciate. When Barbara first asked her to iron some of our clothes, she requested that the ironing board be lowered and that we let her do the ironing sitting down. Barbara was incredulous—she had never seen anyone iron from a chair.

But Wang *a-yi* explained blithely, "Ironing is too hard to do standing up."

Then she pointed out she would need a special large cloth to spread on the floor; otherwise, with the board so low, the ironing would drag on the ground and get dirty. Of course, sitting down, she could not exert as much pressure on the iron, and in a full afternoon's work, accompanied by frequent sighs, she managed to iron three shirts, Barbara reckoned.

Since factory workers can't be fired, malingering on the job has become endemic in industry, and several foreign businessmen who had concluded deals with Chinese enterprises recounted their troubles with lazy employees. The owner of a large textile firm in Hong Kong I knew had decided to take advantage of Peking's new policy, starting in 1979, of allowing foreign companies to establish joint-venture factories in China to help China earn foreign currency and upgrade its technology. He had calculated in advance that the productivity of Chinese workers would probably be only one half of what it is among their cousins who labor across the border in Hong Kong, but with the lower wages in China, he was confident he could still earn a profit. To his chagrin, he said, he discovered that labor efficiency in the new plant in China was only one quarter of that in his factories in Hong Kong.*

In Shanghai, a Japanese businessman said, his company had furnished sophisticated new machinery to manufacture black-and-white television sets to a Chinese factory. The equipment enabled the plant to greatly speed up its production, but the Chinese workers rebelled. They claimed that since

*Hu Qiaomu, a senior adviser to Deng Xiaoping and head of the Academy of Social Sciences, once disclosed in a public report that labor productivity in Chinese factories did not increase between 1958 and 1978. That, Hu admitted, was a catastrophic problem that had undermined China's economic growth.

they were producing more, the machines made them work harder. Therefore, either they should be paid more or the machines should be slowed down. In the end, the Japanese agreed to change the machinery.

This is not to say that all Chinese are lazy. Lihua, the petitioner sent to the countryside, and my other Chinese friends were all conscientious and, with an objective to strive for, indefatigable. Chinese officials whom I watched accompany delegations of foreign dignitaries around the country inevitably exhausted their guests with their energy. But hard workers and those with initiative have become the exception, at least in the cities.

The system actually makes it hard to work hard. For students trying to study at Peking University, the library closes down for lunch from 11:30 A.M. to 2 P.M. It is open again from 2 P.M. to 5 P.M., but closed from 5 P.M. to 7:30 P.M. for dinner. In the evenings only the reading room is open and students cannot check out books because the staff has all gone home. The library is also closed on Thursday and Saturday afternoons so the students and staff can attend political study sessions. Lights in the school's dormitories are turned off at 11 P.M., and if students want to study late, they have to go outside and sit under the dim streetlamps. At Fudan University in Shanghai the administration became concerned that this practice was interfering with the students' sleep and turned off the streetlights too.

Goldbricking has been compounded by Peking's ideological difficulty in devising a wage system with built-in incentives. Mao held that the masses would work hardest out of revolutionary élan, not for material gain, and he abolished piece-rate wages, merit raises, and bonuses, the kinds of income that reward performance. It is no doubt true that in the 1950s and early 1960s, when many Chinese still ardently believed in communism, railroad workers and longshoremen were flattered to win a crimson banner identifying them as labor heroes. But in the two decades from the end of the 1950s to the late 1970s wages remained frozen across the country. Prices were also kept under careful check, but many Chinese felt a sense of genuine frustration and stagnation after years without a raise.

In the summer of 1975, the government had to dispatch 100,000 regular army troops to occupy eighteen factories in Hangzhou after a series of strikes at least partly connected with wage demands. Mao's more practical successors have pronounced his policy mistaken, the fallacy of "everyone eating from the same pot," and they have reinstituted the socialist principle of "to each according to his work," or, less grandly, material incentives. Peking's key reform has been to order factory managers to start paying bonuses again. In theory, to be effective, they should go to the best workers. But in more than twenty plants I visited they were given out to almost all the workers, with only small variations in amount, and tended to become part of the workers' regular pay package. For the Maoist ethic of egalitarianism still runs deep, and both cadres and workers seem ill at ease with a system that encourages differences. The result is that most workers still feel little motivation to excel.

"You get the same pay whether you work hard or not," observed Fuli, a worker in a musical instrument factory.

All the seven members of her workshop earn the same bonus, six yuan ($4) a month, she said, though the amount is supposedly based on a complex calculation that includes a worker's output, quality of labor, safety record, and attitude in political study sessions. "If you report for work regularly, you will get your bonus, and there is an upper limit on how much you can get for it," she added.

The tendency toward egalitarianism is reinforced by the public way in which the workers are paid. On pay day, once a month, Fuli related, one employee from her workshop goes to the factory office to collect the batch of envelopes containing their wages. Each person's name and salary is written on a slip glued to the envelope, so everyone knows what everyone else earns. But even without this overt tip-off, Fuli said, it is easy to tell what anyone makes. For over the years, pay raises have been granted almost entirely on seniority. "All you have to do is to look at a person's face to tell how much he earns," she advised.

In the late 1970s, after Mao's death, his pragmatic successors became increasingly aware of the inadequacy and waste of the Communists' fixation with heavy industry and rigid state planning. Starting in 1979, Deng Xiaoping introduced a two-pronged economic shake-up that was the most ambitious revision of Chinese industrial organization since the 1950s. The first part called for readjusting Peking's priorities: the government ordered curbs on investment in heavy industry and directed that more funds be channeled into the previously neglected sectors like energy, transportation, housing, consumer goods, and agriculture. This readjustment also meant lowering the rate of forced savings for reinvestment and funneling more of the country's national income to consumers in the form of higher wages. The second part of Deng's plan was intended to break out of the straitjacket of central planning by borrowing ideas of flexible market socialism from the innovative countries of Eastern Europe, Hungary, and Yugoslavia. Six thousand factories were given permission to experiment with a limited form of autonomy under which they could keep up to 20 percent of the profits they earned above their state quota. Managers in these factories were given new authority to reinvest their extra earnings as they chose, either in new plant and machinery or in higher wages for their employees. These managers were even given the unheard-of right to fix some prices—the most sacred power of all for central planners—alter their production quotas, and perhaps hire and fire a few workers. The experimental factories were also to be forced to take responsibility for selling their products; no longer would the state buy whatever they manufactured, regardless of the quality. In a final phase of the experiment, the factories would no longer automatically receive their accustomed annual operating funds from the People's Bank. Instead, they would have to apply to the bank and borrow the necessary funds in the form of loans, repayable with interest. The key word was profitability.

But in early 1981, amid considerable confusion, Peking suspended further implementation of the second half of its program, the structural reforms. The government had become nervous that the factories granted the new self-management rights often used them to raise their prices, contributing to inflation, or to build new plants, adding to the state's budget deficit of $11 billion. To the fiscally conservative Communists, both inflation and deficit financing are anathema. To counteract these problems, Peking ordered central planning and controls tightened again.

There was also another reason for Peking's suspension of its reforms, I heard from Chinese friends—resistance by factory managers and other bureaucrats who were unhappy with changing habits built up over the past thirty years. Both factory managers and workers alike were uncomfortable with the idea of firing a lazy or incompetent worker—it would break their iron rice bowl and might lead to retribution in the next political campaign. Then there was the problem of making a profit—it smacked of capitalism, and it was also much harder than simply fulfilling a quota. It required managers to curb expenses, monitor the quality of their products, make sure their goods sold, and raise labor productivity. Under the old system, too many people were doing nicely out of doing very little.

Peking has continued to try to readjust its economic priorities, cutting back the national budget and lowering the level of investment in heavy industry. But the Communists' failure to push through on Deng's badly needed structural reforms raises serious doubts about how successful the regime will be in achieving its Four Modernizations program. The Four Modernizations has always been something of a hollow slogan, like "a chicken in every pot," without a clearly defined goal beyond Peking's oft-repeated phrase of making China into a "powerful modern socialist state by the year 2000." Perhaps the clearest definition of what it really will mean was given by Deng himself in an important speech to high-level officials in 1980. The target of the Four Modernizations, he said, is that by the end of the century China's per capita gross national product reach $1,000. "This represents a *xiao-kang* society," Deng added, using a classical Chinese term implying a peaceful era with a simple though sufficient standard of living. Deng's plan must have struck his audience as modest. In 1958 Mao had boasted that China would overtake Great Britain in industrial production and technology within fifteen years. When Deng spoke he knew that the per capita GNP of Hong Kong was already over $2,000 a year and that of Singapore, $3,000. That would leave China far short of its Asian neighbors and mean that it would probably not be a really powerful modern state, not a great power in military terms, certainly. Yet Deng's target is still ambitious. China's per capita GNP today is about $470 (he put it at only a little over $200 in another of those statistical inconsistencies). Can China achieve this?

Most foreign businessmen I talked with who had visited Chinese factories or spent months helping build new mines, ports, and plants were skeptical. To them it was critical that the Communists overhaul their management system.

"Chinese industry will continue to grow, it can't help but expand with all the reinvestment they pour into it," remarked an American engineer who has helped construct multimillion-dollar projects in several parts of China. "But it will be slow, and uneven, and wasteful," the engineer added.

He recalled an incident when his firm had just completed building a large chemical fertilizer factory. Everything looked wonderful. There was a big celebration for the opening, and the Chinese lined up a row of trucks to pick up the first production of fertilizer.

But the next day the plant manager summoned the American to his office. How could he shut the machinery down immediately? he inquired. The American was puzzled. The plant was running smoothly.

"Yes," the manager replied, "but we have run out of trucks. They belong to the local counties and communes and there is no way to tell when they will return to pick up more fertilizer."

The American was horrified. It would take several hours to shut off the equipment, then a week to restart production.

13. Follow the Leader

服 从 领 导

THE ORGANIZATION

"Bureaucratism is an ulcer of countries which uphold proletarian dictatorship."
Red Flag
"Veteran revolutionaries only end up as monsters and ghosts."
Deng Xiaoping

Well before I arrived in China, I harbored a secret ambition—as a fanatic skier, I wanted to be the first foreigner to ski in China. I had seen photographs in one of Peking's glossy color magazines of Chinese skiers descending the piste, smiles pasted to their rosy faces; and shortly before I took up residence in Peking I was encouraged by an article released by the New China News Agency reporting that the China Travel Service had decided to allow foreigners to ski in China as part of its plan to expand the country's tourist industry. So my first December in Peking, I applied to the Information Department for permission to go to Heilongjiang (Black Dragon River), the province in the far northeast described in the articles about China's ski slopes. After a month's delay, the Information Department replied that I was mistaken. There was no skiing in China.

Thinking there might have been a misunderstanding, I reapplied, this time enclosing the pictures and copy of the news story. Four weeks later, they answered again—yes, there is skiing in China, but it is in an area closed to foreigners.

I was ready to accept defeat, but a few days later I spotted an American lawyer who represented U.S. business firms in China sauntering through the lobby of the Peking Hotel with skis on his shoulders. He and his wife had just been skiing for a week in Heilongjiang, they said, and while there had encountered a team of journalists from the American magazine *Ski*.

Armed with this fresh evidence, I approached the Information Department for the third time. After several more weeks passed, they finally conceded that yes, there is a place foreigners can ski, but they were very sorry it was now too late in the season—it was early March—and the snow had all melted. They would be happy to let me go to Heilongjiang to write about other subjects, but without my skis.

I decided to test their story. When I arrived in Harbin, the capital of Heilongjiang, it was 5 degrees below zero fahrenheit and my guide from the local Foreign Affairs Department said there was plenty of snow at the ski slope, a four-hour drive from the city. "You should have brought your skis," he suggested.

I had run into the Chinese bureaucracy. There was no way, I realized, I would get a straight answer from the Information Department about why they wouldn't let me go skiing. The Chinese invented bureaucracy over 2,000 years ago, and their capacity for it is endless. Avoiding responsibility has been raised to a national art form. The great early historian, Si-ma Qian, who lived from 145 to 90 B.C., had warned, "Do not take the lead in planning affairs, or you may be held responsible." In one of the red pavilions of the Forbidden City, where the Ming and Qing emperors kept their imperial seals, hangs a large inscription in gold letters on a blue background—Wu-wei, "Do nothing," or action through inaction. It is the old motto of the Taoist mystics; the key to merging with nature is not to strive. By this they did not mean complete inaction, rather, do only what is natural. "Do nothing, and nothing will not be done," the sage Lao Zi counseled. The favorite figure of the Taoists is water, which, though the softest of all things, wears away the hardest. The pavilion with its message was one of my favorite places to wander to get away from the hurly-burly of my office in the Peking Hotel. It seemed to explain the knack Chinese officials had for spontaneous inactivity.

In January 1979, shortly before Deng Xiaoping made his historic journey to the United States, *Time* magazine arranged an exclusive interview with him. It was a journalistic coup; Deng's picture would be on *Time*'s cover the day he arrived in Washington, and Hedley Donovan, *Time*'s editor in chief, flew in from New York along with Marsh Clark, the magazine's Hong Kong bureau chief. They were staying at the Peking Hotel, a five-minute drive from the Great Hall of the People where the meeting was to take place at 9 A.M. At 8:45 that morning the two men met an official from the Information Department who was to accompany them to the interview and went to the desk in the lobby that assigns taxis. But there weren't any cabs; Peking's taxi drivers were staging a go-slow strike to demand higher wages. Clark, anxious about being late, an unpardonable offense in China, especially when meeting the country's paramount leader, asked the official if they could use his Foreign Ministry car, which was parked out front, with the chauffeur sitting idly in the front seat.

No, the official replied tartly, that was impossible. Clark and Donovan were not guests of the state, therefore they couldn't drive in a government car. He was adamant.

Nine o'clock came and still no taxis appeared, Clark told me later. He was desperate. But the Information Department cadre wouldn't change his mind. Only at five minutes past nine did a cab finally arrive and they rushed down the Avenue of Eternal Tranquility. Deng was standing at the top of the marble steps of the Great Hall to greet them, a smile on his deeply furrowed face. Certainly he understood what it is like to deal with the 20 million cadres and 38 million members of the Communist Party who make up the heart of the bureaucracy.

Bureaucracy was so prevalent, I found, such a factor in people's daily lives, grinding them down with frustration, that it had spawned its own lexicon. In the past the Chinese had a special set of words to ease the pain of life. They all related to fate, to the vagaries of nature. When I lived on Taiwan, if something went wrong, friends would say, *"Suan-le-ba"* (Forget it), or *"Mei-yu fa-zi"* (There is nothing you can do about it). When the Communists came to power, they sought to overcome this passive, defeatist thinking; Mao's promise was that China had stood up. I noticed that in Peking people had stopped using the old phrases about fate. Instead they had been transmuted into a new vocabulary, the kinds of answers bureaucrats give when asked a question: "I must study the problem," "I will consider it," "I will get in touch with the responsible comrades," or the two most common replies, *"Bu fang-bian"* (It is not convenient), and *"Bu qing-chu,"* (I'm not too clear about it). They all meant the same thing; nothing would be done.

"The real problem in China is not the special privileges of the elite which everyone complains about," an outspoken scientist told me. "It's incompetence in the bureaucracy."

To prove his point, the scientist tipped me off to a big news story—a Chinese oil rig had collapsed in the Bohai Gulf off the coast of north China, and all seventy-two people aboard it had drowned. The tragedy had taken place eight months before, but not a word about it had appeared in the Chinese press, for the Minister of Petroleum, Song Zhenming, was a close personal friend and political follower of one of China's top officials, Kang Shien, a deputy prime minister. Song had served under Kang since Kang had been head of the Daqing oil field, the wonder child of Chinese industry, and each time Kang was promoted, he had brought Song, his subordinate, up with him. In Chinese terms, they had close *guan-xi,* connections, the cement of Chinese politics. Kang had helped stall off an investigation because it could reflect on him too. The scientist was furious about the cover-up, he said, offering me a crockery jar of yogurt in his living room, and he felt exposure would be good for China.

Indeed, a few weeks after I published an article about the disaster in *The New York Times*, the *People's Daily* followed up with its own detailed report. At 3:30 A.M. on November 25, 1979, the paper charged, a rig China had purchased from Japan for $25 million had capsized while it was being towed to a new drilling site. The skipper of the ship that was towing the rig did nothing to rescue the men in the water and did not transmit a distress signal. It took twelve hours, in fact, before the Ministry of Petroleum notified China's coast guard of the accident.

Song, the oil minister, said in his official report to the State Council, or cabinet, that the incident had been caused by unforeseen and exceptionally strong winds that reached gale force 11. Records of meteorological stations along the coast revealed they had correctly predicted a storm for that day, though the real winds were not nearly of such magnitude. According to the *People's Daily*, the oil-drilling platform had been bought from Japan seven years before, but no one had bothered to translate the operating and safety manuals for it. Top officials of the oil ministry had made a series of trips to Tokyo, presumably to ensure they knew how to work the rig, but they had not trained the workers aboard it, who had "a low education and technical standard," the paper asserted.

The month the accident occurred, the ministry was pushing to fulfill its annual quota for discovering new oil reserves. To meet its target, 20 million more tons of reserves had to be found in the shallow Bohai Gulf region by the end of the year. So on November 24, the day before the disaster, the director of the Ocean Petroleum Exploration Bureau, under the ministry, ordered the rig moved to a new site. Information on the impending storm was handed to him, but he simply ignored it, the paper said. He also over-ruled three protests from the rig's captain. The crew should apply the Party's old spirit of not being afraid of hardship or death, the official advised. Even so, the accident might have been averted if proper procedures had been followed. But the crew did not know they were supposed to pump the ballast water out of the rig to reduce its draft and make it more seaworthy before moving it. In the end, when the storm did blow up, the high waves just washed over and into the rig's cabin, making it turn turtle.

It was almost a textbook case of the troubles that plague China's bureau-cracy, which is responsible for running both the government and industry: lack of technical competence, arrogant officials who ignore advice from subordinates, factionalism, worship of state quotas, and the old guerrilla mentality that holds that sheer willpower can overcome any obstacle. There was even a scurrilous epilogue. When Song was promoted to be oil minister in Peking, he had brought with him his chauffeur of twenty years. His driver had the habit of cruising the streets at night in the minister's large Red Flag limousine looking for women to pick up. One woman later reported to the police that he had molested her in the back seat, a serious offense in puritanical China. But Song had interceded and gotten the charge dropped. A few months later the driver picked up another woman, near the Peking railway station, drove her to the suburbs, then raped and murdered her. This time he was tracked down and executed. Song was sacked for his role in the rig disaster, and Kang, his benefactor, was given a humiliating "big demerit."

Many Chinese now blame these bureaucratic troubles on their feudal past, the old love of hierarchy, obedience to authority, the lack of a scientific attitude, and the clannishness of factions in the imperial court. The Communists made a strategic error after 1949, an editor at the *People's Daily* confided to me.

"We thought the fundamental problem in China was capitalism," he said. "Actually, China was not yet industrialized and didn't have a large bourgeois class. The real problem was feudalism." This was a shorthand way of saying China was burdened by its past and not a "blank sheet of paper," as Mao had opined, on which anything could be written.

On one of my first trips to China, as a tourist, before the normalization of relations between the United States and China, I had an encounter that helped me realize just how ingrained the Chinese desire for authority is. At the railroad station across the border from Hong Kong, my guide from the China Travel Service greeted our group with the announcement that he had selected a leader from among our delegation. The group leader would be responsible for rounding us up each morning and evening, make sure we were on time for meals and bus rides, and pass on any complaints or suggestions we had to the Chinese. But in a case of mistaken identity, the Chinese had picked an eighteen-year-old American high school student who had come to China with his mother under protest. He didn't like China, and said so. His name was the same as that of his father, a U.S. diplomat, and the Chinese had calculated that a senior foreign service officer would be a suitable group leader. But no matter how many times the teen-ager tried to resign or we appealed for a change, the travel service guide declined.

"He is your leader, how can you change him?" the guide declared. "You must learn to follow the leader. That is what we Chinese do."

Behind this seemingly inexplicable incident, to us as Westerners, I discovered, was the instinctive Chinese penchant for authority. More than 2,000 years of imperial tradition have created in the collective unconscious the desire for a supreme, quasi-mystical leader. The collapse of the Qing dynasty and the abolition of the position of emperor in 1911 left a vacuum which Mao later shrewdly manipulated, building a personality cult for himself that verged on turning him into a deity.

The popular image of Mao in the West is that he was the great leveler, the crusader against bureaucracy and privilege. Wasn't it Mao who summoned the millions of Red Guards to humble Party cadres who had grown soft and fat with their years in power? An articulate, thoughtful historian who was trained in schools run by American missionaries before 1949 scoffed at this perception of the Chairman. Mao may have sensed that the Communists were slipping back into the old hierarchal and feudal ways of the imperial mandarins. But paradoxically Mao himself was no different. He lived in luxurious villas with servants, isolated from the common people, and he always demanded his own way. When he found he was outvoted in the Party Central Committee, he ignored the Party's normal procedures and went outside the Party to the Red Guards, to his wife, Jiang Qing, and then to the army. "There was nothing democratic about him," the professor contended. In fact, by his imperious ways, he unconsciously encouraged the old Chinese taste for separation between the leader and the masses. The Cultural Revolution for Mao was to overthrow his enemies in the Party, not authority itself, the professor added. When youthful rebels in Shanghai threatened to get out of control in early 1967 by establishing the so-called Shanghai Commune, modeled on the Paris Commune of a century before, Mao backtracked. Having heard that the rebels wanted to get rid of all "heads," Mao declared, "This is extreme anarchism, it is most reactionary. In reality there will always still be heads." Eventually in many factories and schools he called in the army to suppress Red Guard activity.

The professor saw irony in the Red Guards' almost mystical veneration of Mao and their ascription of "supernatural powers" and "magic" to the small red plastic-covered book of his quotations. "When we were supposedly attacking feudalism, bureaucracy, and all the bad old things, the Red Guards were out in the streets yelling *wan-sui* to Mao," literally, "10,000 years," or "eternal life." "That was what the mandarins and the people used to say for the Emperor," the professor related, pausing to shake his head in disbelief. "Even I myself was out in the streets shouting *wan-sui.* It was ridiculous."

The urge to be ruled by a strong leader remained in the countryside too. A wiry, thirty-two-year-old graduate student who had been sent to work in a village for nine years related the reaction of the peasant family where he was quartered in 1976 when Mao died. "That night they talked a lot, almost till dawn, they were very upset," he remembered. " 'The Emperor is dead, there is no one to replace him,' they kept saying. 'What will China do without an Emperor?' They really believed it, China must have an Emperor," the graduate student said.

Deng Xiaoping has proclaimed that Mao's deification of himself was a mistake and that there will be no more personality cults. There are no icons to Deng, no pictures of him in people's homes, no plaster busts of him in stores, as there were for Mao. But traces of the old Mao cult and the affinity the Chinese had for it remain strong. During a visit to a hilly tea-growing commune in Anhui, in central China, I noticed a red-painted sign prominently displayed over the entrance to the mill where the tea leaves are dried: "The great leader Chairman Mao came here on September 16, 1958." Another plaque announced, "It was here Chairman Mao gave his great instruction, 'Plant more tea bushes on the sides of mountains.'" Even his most banal utterances still conveyed apocalyptic force to some Chinese. After I inspected the mill, the commune Party secretary escorted me to a freshly painted yellow and white stucco meeting hall for a briefing on the commune's production figures. Above the doorway was an inscription: "The hall where Chairman Mao came to view the tea."

In the early part of the twentieth century, modern-minded young Chinese had tried to cast off filial piety as being outdated and an obstacle to China's progress. But the attitudes it inspired persisted—loyalty, respect for authority, self-discipline. These were ready-made for communism, and in the early 1950s, at least, as the psychiatrist Robert Lifton has put it, the Chinese became filial Communists.* The Cultural Revolution eventually undermined some of this discipline and replaced it with cynicism. Even so, I detected, the Chinese still have a far greater respect for the old virtues of loyalty and authority than Americans do.

The Communist revolution in China is often described as the triumph of the countryside over the cities. This usually refers to Mao's brilliant strategy of organizing peasant guerrillas in the villages and then using them to conquer the Nationalist-dominated urban areas. But I found the manner of the Communists' victory had a more far-reaching significance—it literally meant that when the Communists entered the cities in 1949 and found themselves governing the country, they took their peasant soldiers and installed them as Party secretaries and security chiefs in every office, factory, school, and hospital.

Fang Guanghua, a quiet, intense, twenty-six-year-old lathe operator with smooth skin, high cheekbones, and strong white teeth, explained what this meant in personal terms. For a year he had been going to night school six evenings a week, after finishing his shift in a truck factory, to brush up on his physics, chemistry, and math. He had been assigned to the plant after spending several years in the countryside and he desperately wanted to

*Robert Jay Lifton, *Thought Reform and the Psychology of Totalism* (New York: W. W. Norton and Co., 1961), p. 386.

further his education. It was the only way for him to get ahead and avoid a dreary life of working in a factory with little chance for promotion. His ambition was like that of Lingling, the bright sixteen-year-old high school student. He had actually passed the university entrance exam the year before, but his factory wouldn't let him go to college. Now he hoped to pass another test that would qualify him for China's new and highly popular television university. It was organized for workers like him, giving them screened lectures in the mornings, then live tutors in the afternoon. After a two-year program, he would get a degree and perhaps a better job as a technician or engineer. There was only one catch. He had to get approval to register for the exam from the Party secretary of the factory, a man named Ke. The Party secretary was the real boss of the plant; there was a professional factory manager, but he was a weak second. As everywhere in China, the Party forms a parallel system—to the government, to industry, to the universities, even to the army—and it is Party representatives placed within these organizations who exercise the real power. They in turn are responsible to the Party officials in the hierarchy above them, assuring strict central control.

Ke turned Fang down flatly. "Study is useless," he said. "Nothing you can learn will help the factory," and he refused Fang permission. Fang then tried asking the four other members of the factory Party committee. Each said no. Their opposition to his attempts to improve himself seemed at odds with the government's modernization program, and I was puzzled. But Fang understood, he told me, during a rendezvous in Jan Wong's apartment. Jan had originally met him when I sent her to cover a demonstration in front of Party headquarters at Zhongnanhai by disgruntled students and workers who were not being allowed to continue their schooling. Since Jan was ethnically Chinese and dressed in plain blue, like a native, she had been able to join the protestors and make friends with Fang.

Ke, Fang explained, was from a poor peasant family and had marched into the capital with the Red Army. By hard work and loyalty, he had made his way up the Party ladder to become boss of the factory, which had been a small shop to make rickshaws before Liberation. Ke had never attended school, Fang related, so at public meetings, when he was supposed to read out government documents, he had to call on a younger cadre to do it for him. Ke still retained some of the rough peasant ways of his boyhood. Once at a factory-wide gathering to issue handbooks on labor safety, he warned the employees not to use them as *hou-men-piao*, "back-door tickets," a euphemism for toilet paper. "The women workers thought he was very crude," Fang said.

The other members of the factory committee were former rickshaw pullers, part of the poorest urban class before 1949, and they couldn't read or write either. They had been with the factory since it was converted from making rickshaws to trucks and were very proud of their homemade accomplishments.

"They have a deep-seated distrust of intellectuals and get angry when they see me reading around the factory," Fang said. "But they are staunch Party members. They never question the Party's orders." During the campaign to criticize Deng in 1976, the second time he was purged, they energetically attacked him. After Deng was rehabilitated in 1977, they swung 180 degrees "without the slightest difficulty," Fang said.

Ke had never had any technical training, but he was a fanatic about keeping the factory clean. Recently he had shut down the plant for three days because it was due for inspection by the ministry which had jurisdiction over it. "We polished the same windows over and over to get it in perfect shape," Fang recalled. The reason Ke was so concerned about appearance is that he knew the higher-level cadres didn't know anything about production either and that neatness is what most impressed them, Fang added.

When Ke first became factory boss, he had still kept his wife, a peasant, in their home village. He had taken lumber from the plant and gotten some workers and one of the factory's trucks to help build himself a new home in the countryside. That offended Fang, but he was even angrier when Ke arranged through a back-door connection to get his wife's household registration moved to Peking. He then got her a job in the factory, and moved her and his children into a room in the plant, though the factory had no dormitories to offer its workers. Ke was finally forced to move them out only when one of his children had caused a serious accident by pulling a switch in the boiler room when a worker was inside a machine that feeds coal to the furnace.

Ke ate in the factory canteen with the workers in good proletarian style, Fang continued, but he had a weakness for presents. Anyone who wanted a promotion had to send him little gifts of eggs, chickens, or fruit. At the last Chinese New Year's, or Spring Festival as the Communists call it, eighty of the plant's four hundred workers had gone to his house with presents. Ke's petty corruption, his self-serving behavior, was another indication of how the Communists' early reputation for honesty and idealism had broken down after three decades in power.

Most studies of how China is run focus on a few top leaders like Mao, Zhou, and Deng, on their personalities, their foibles, their policy disputes. But as I traveled around the country, I was repeatedly impressed by the importance of the simple rural background of the bulk of the members of the Party and the bureaucracy, like Ke. He was not unusual in his peasant upbringing and lack of education. A study by the *Guangming Daily* revealed that only 22 percent of the Party secretaries and managers of China's factories have what it termed "technical knowledge." Hebei province, in north China, conceded in a radio broadcast that of its 700,000 cadres, only 227,000 had graduated from junior or senior high school. Then there was the Surgeon General of the People's Liberation Army, whom I met at a reception. He turned out not to be a trained physician but a former medic on the Long March in the 1930s. The Party secretaries of several university departments I visited were one-time political commissars in the army, not teachers.

When Mayor Ed Koch of New York came to Peking to establish a sister-city relationship with the Chinese capital, I had the unusual chance to sit at banquets next to three of Peking's deputy mayors. They all were born into peasant families in the same county in Shandong province, east of Peking, they told me in hesitant snatches of conversation; they had joined the Red Army as teen-agers, and they had marched victoriously into Peking in 1949. Now they were in charge of housing, finance, and industry for the city, though none had specialized training. They were all protégés of the mayor of Peking, a friend later explained, who came from their home region and had been their army commander.

Men like these had been revolutionaries in their youth, rebelling against the corrupt Kuomintang, but in power they have reverted to the inward-looking, conservative values of their rural homes: respectful of authority, suspicious of change, interested in their family's comfort, skeptical of the importance of technology, the intellect, and things Western, and, above all, xenophobic. For most, their only real training had come in the army, where they learned discipline and the thoughts of Chairman Mao. It is not surprising that, like other peasant revolutionaries in Chinese history who overthrew earlier dynasties, they re-created something of the old imperial state, with its pomp and privileges, once they rose to power. They were not prepared to run a modern state, and China suffered.

With their country accents and rough manners—even Deng keeps a spittoon by his feet during meetings with foreign heads of state and sometimes punctuates his sentences with an expectoration—these cadres are viewed by the more sophisticated natives of Peking and Shanghai as urban Americans would view hillbillies from Kentucky or Tennessee. Our friends the Wangs liked to tell jokes about the typical cadre.

"In a village the county authorities had announced they were going to form the militia and issue rifles," Li began one of his favorites stories. "It was a big event in a place where nothing ever happens and the peasants got very excited. But then days and weeks passed, and the county authorities were having trouble reaching a decision.

"Finally, after two years, a jeep came down to the village. An important-looking cadre got out and declared there would be a big meeting about forming the militia.

"At the meeting, he got up and began speaking slowly, 'I- am-the-county-

Party-secretary,' and with those words the audience burst into thunderous applause. It was a great honor to be visited by such a high cadre.

"But then the speaker added, 'That is, I was sent by the county Party secretary.' " Li told the story employing the thick dialect of Hunan province, where Mao and many other cadres came from.

" 'We have decided, about the guns, that one gun for each person,' and again there was a chorus of applause, 'is absolutely impossible.'

" 'We have reached the conclusion that one gun for every two people,' and there was still clapping, 'is not right.'

" 'So I want to announce the final decision of the county Party committee is, one gun for every three people,' which set off more applause. 'But they are wooden guns,' the cadre concluded."

A university diploma, of course, is not necessarily a qualification for leadership in any society. But it is striking how few of China's top leaders have any higher education. Of the twenty-six members of the Politburo, only one, Fang Yi, who oversees science, went to college, and his official biography does not say where or for how many years. Of the twelve men who make up the Secretariat of the Central Committee, which runs the Party apparatus, and the eighteen deputy prime ministers, who administer the government, only five have a college education. This means there is an enormous cultural gap between China's political leaders and the country's highly trained doctors, scientists, and professors, many of whom were educated at schools run by Western missionaries or in colleges in the United States, Europe, and Japan.

"We have very little common language," said an introspective, soft-spoken physicist in his fifties. "The cadres believe what Mao told his niece, Wang Hairong—'The more you learn, the more stupid you become.' They still see intellectuals as what Mao called us, 'the stinking ninth.' " (The ninth in a list of "bad elements" blackballed by the Communists.)

Not long before, he had applied for permission to do advanced research in the United States. The director of his institute, a scientist himself, had approved. But his application also had to go to the cadres in the institute's personnel department and security section, both former peasants and army political commissars. They vetoed it. The physicist says they had long distrusted him because he had spent two years studying in America and had come back in 1950 after the outbreak of the Korean War. He returned out of patriotism, he told me, but in the Cultural Revolution he was accused of being an American spy and arrested. He was later cleared of the charge; yet it remained in his dossier.

His older brother had also gone to the United States as a student before 1949 but had decided the political risks of returning to China were too great and had stayed on in America, where he had become a distinguished scientist.

The previous summer the Chinese Academy of Sciences had invited him to return to give a series of lectures, and he was accorded a hero's welcome. My acquaintance saw irony in this, but, instead of expressing bitterness, used it to make a significant point. China had been forced to pay a high price for the Communists' ignorance, incompetence, and distrust of intellectuals; several generations of talent were wasted, he charged.

"The reason China has not developed a powerful technocracy like the Soviet Union, with world-famous scientists and advanced military weapons, is because the Communists distrusted the intellectuals so much," he said. "They came from peasant families, they fought for years in the mountains. It was all they knew. After 1950 these men might have developed some expertise, but then Mao launched one political campaign after another. There was no time for education. Besides, Mao proclaimed it was better to be Red than to be expert," more important to be correct politically than to be educated and professional.

Chinese certainly are intelligent enough to produce great scientists, he added. "Look at Yang Chen-ning in the United States," one of three Chinese-Americans to win the Nobel Prize. China had succeeded in a few scientific fields where the government had felt urgency and concentrated its resources, my friend said, notably physics, with the production of nuclear weapons and ballistic missiles. In medicine Chinese doctors had also made pioneering advances in a few areas—burn care and limb transplants (in part because of the high rate of industrial accidents in China).

"But a lot of us were wasted," he went on. "Mao ordered us to be self-reliant, so instead of doing experiments, we spent our time making our own microscopes." For four years during the Cultural Revolution he had labored on a farm planting corn. After he returned to his institute, he found the supply of scientific journals from the outside world had been terminated as politically dangerous. For almost a decade he had worked on one project, he said, only to discover that another Chinese physicist had already done the same experiment in a separate research facility. "We weren't allowed to telephone or write each other for security reasons."

After Mao's death, Deng and his associates sought to correct some of these abuses. In a sharp departure from Maoist orthodoxy, Deng announced that henceforth intellectuals should be considered part of the working class, not members of the bourgeoisie, as they had been, because "science and technology are part of the productive forces." Deng lashed out at ideologues who still haggled over preserving Mao's sayings—"They sit on the pot, but they can't manage to shit," he exclaimed in a party meeting. In 1981 the Academy of Sciences officially elected a sixty-six-year-old chemist who had been trained in England and the United States, Lu Jiaxi, as its president, a move designed to show that scientists now are gaining more authority over their own work.

What was not said publicly, my friend pointed out, was that a veteran Communist and member of the Central Committee, Li Chang, remained as Party secretary of the academy, the key position, and also served as one of its three executive chairmen. The *People's Daily* disclosed in a survey of twenty-three institutes under the Academy of Sciences that only 25 percent of the officials in these organizations were really scientists. The rest were Party administrators and watchdogs. "A large number of college graduates who according to the original plans were to be assigned to scientific and technical work were instead appointed as buyers, sales workers, custodians, typists, cooks, etc.," the paper said in another article. "Some specializing in rocketry were assigned as doorkeepers. Remote-control specialists were turned into butchers. Mathematicians became bakers." At a national congress of the academy in 1981, Hu Yaobang, the new Party chairman, chastised the Party, charging that many comrades still did not trust intellectuals. The cadres feel "they are not docile, they think too much, and have too many views" of their own.

The predominance in the Party of older men from humble rural backgrounds makes it difficult to categorize the Chinese Communists with neat Western political labels like left or right. How to deal with this problem, how succinctly to identify the different Politburo factions for the readers of *The New York Times* was a never-ending conundrum for me. Mao and his cohorts, we journalists liked to write, were leftists, and, accepting Chinese terminology, Deng was a rightist. But this obscured as much as it clarified.

A young chemical engineer I met on a muggy summer afternoon when he was sending a telegram at the marble-floored cable office and I was filing a story to New York helped shake my tendency to oversimplify Chinese politics. After a brief, guarded talk at the cable office, he asked if he could meet me later at my hotel room. He had an uncle who was a senior official and often came to the hotel for a haircut, a carefully restricted privilege, and the engineer said it would be no problem for him to get past the hotel guards with his relative. A few days later he appeared, dressed in a loose, short-sleeved white shirt worn over gray pants and plastic sandals, standard summer garb for urban Chinese men.

Was I a leftist or a rightist? he wanted to know.

I said that in American political terms I considered myself a liberal, probably left of center.

"That's too bad," he said, obviously disappointed. "In China, we intellectuals don't like leftists. They are too conservative."

To a Westerner, where the political left has been associated with progressive and the right with conservative, the engineer's sentiment was a contradiction. But he went on to elucidate.

"In the Cultural Revolution, Mao and the Gang of Four called themselves leftists. They opposed individualism, freedom of speech, democracy; they preferred collective behavior and control and a closed door to the outside world." Now Deng Xiaoping is following a rightist policy, he continued, more moderate, more practical, with material incentives, more freedom of expression, and more open to trade and cultural contacts with the West.

The average cadre, like his uncle, he said, was nervous about Deng's experimental program. He had spent his entire career in the Party learning the Maoist catechism. "My uncle thinks that giving scientists like me the right to run our own institutes or travel abroad is an invitation to anarchy and the spread of capitalism," he said. We agreed that conservative might be a better word to describe these cadres, in the sense of resisting change, rather than as leftists, to avoid misunderstanding by foreigners.

Getting up from his chair to pace around the room, he wondered if I was aware of the central fact of Chinese politics—the importance of *guan-xi,* which are the real basis of all factions, not ideology. His uncle was from Sichuan, he said, the province where Deng was born, and had served in the army in Sichuan in the early 1950s when Deng was the senior army political commissar and Party secretary there before being promoted to Peking. That made his uncle part of the Sichuan *bang,* or Sichuan gang, currently the strongest faction in Peking. Another key member of the Sichuan group was Hu Yaobang, whom Deng installed as Party chairman in 1981. Hu had first met Deng in 1941 when, as a twenty-six-year-old army political commissar, he was assigned to work under Deng in the 18th Red Army group operating in the arid Taihang Mountains in the northwestern part of the country. The two men became practically inseparable. They served together in the army for eight years. They marched south into Sichuan in 1949 and helped set up the first Communist administration there. They were transferred simultaneously to Peking in 1952, and then, when Deng was purged in the Cultural Revolution as a capitalist roader, Hu was toppled along with him, labeled by the Red Guards as a member of Deng's "club." The pattern was repeated in 1976 when Deng was disgraced for the second time. It was probably not a coincidence, the engineer observed, that the two men share a striking physical resemblance—both are barely five feet tall.

Another leader with a Sichuan connection is the new Prime Minister, Zhao Ziyang. Deng had sent Zhao to Sichuan in 1975 as first Party secretary at a time when the vast province, with 100 million people, China's largest, was suffering from serious political infighting and an acute food shortage. Zhao's performance in transforming the province's bankrupt economy and then introducing some of Deng's pet economic reforms quickly won him Deng's favor.

As an example of how the factional system worked, the engineer said that recently his uncle had been having trouble in the ministry where he worked.

The minister belonged to a different clique—he had served in another army group during the civil war—and wanted to get rid of his uncle. His uncle had known Hu Yaobang since they both worked in Sichuan almost thirty years before, and though they didn't share the same political philosophy, his uncle had appealed to Hu to intercede on his behalf. After several months, Hu arranged a face-saving compromise: his uncle was transferred to another ministry but with a higher rank as deputy minister.

After a few months in China, I had made several Chinese friends and had become aware there was often a gap between the happy posture they assumed in public and the cynicism they expressed privately. But they were students, workers, and teachers, not Party members, and I was curious how cadres viewed communism after three decades of political campaigns, factional wrangles, and economic ups and downs.

That was when I met Mulan, a slight, frank woman whose pretty round face and large bright eyes concealed her forty-five years. I was walking down the Avenue of Eternal Tranquility on the eve of China's national day, October 1; in celebration, the government had strung clusters of lights in front of all the large offices lining the street, illuminating it like an amusement park. The broad sidewalks were jammed with hundreds of thousands of people, more I thought than live in some member states of the United Nations. Unexpectedly, I felt a tap on my arm and turned to see a woman smiling at me.

"How do you like our national day?" she asked, a careful, neutral gambit. Then she introduced herself and said she was an office worker who was trying to improve her English.

It wasn't until we had met several more times that I had the courage to ask if she was a Communist Party member. Mulan laughed. "It's no secret. Communist Party members are humans too. They are not monsters." Then she turned the question on me.

"Do you work for the CIA? I read that many American journalists are really CIA agents." I wasn't sure she believed my denial. But over a period of weeks she gradually unfolded the history of how she had come to join the Party and what she now felt about it.

"When I was young I was an activist—I always volunteered for everything, staying late in school to help clean the dormitory, speaking up at political study sessions, helping the slower students with their homework. That is the first thing they look for in selecting Party members.

"My family background was good too," she said. "My father was a poor tailor. That was the other thing they demanded in candidates." She was formally admitted to the Party when she was twenty, as a college student.

"Those were happier days, in the 1950s. I believed everything the Party said. I wanted to work to build up my country. We were very patriotic. It was the same as being a Communist. I remember being angry when I saw some foreign tourists aiming their cameras at people pulling carts. It was a shameful thing for China."

Mulan still was very disciplined in her personal life. She rose at 5:30 A.M. each day to jog, then went back to clean the tiny closet-size apartment she shared with her son and husband, and was in her office by 7:30. She was often still there till 9 or 10 P.M. taking care of extra work, I discovered when I called her on the phone.

During the Cultural Revolution, when the army was sent in to take over the ministry where she worked and restore order, she was selected to be one of the five leaders of the ministry, though she was only in her early thirties. That meant, she conceded, that she had been a radical and had been promoted like a "helicopter," in the Chinese expression, jumped over much more senior people. In 1970, when the cadres from her ministry were all sent to labor in the countryside, she remained one of the leaders.

"It was hard being a leader," she told me one day during a walk around the old Summer Palace just west of Peking. "You were supposed to set an example and to serve others. I had to be up at five A.M. when we were in the village, to get everyone out to the fields, then I had to pull carts all day loaded with bricks and bags of grain." One morning she was so sleepy she caught her hand in a threshing machine and severed the tendons in several of her fingers. At night, she said, when everyone else could rest, she had to go to meetings, often till midnight. "We examined people's cases, to determine if they were capitalist roaders or counterrevolutionaries, and we had to listen to people's grievances." Mulan had a four-year-old son—because of her schedule, she had to keep him in a nursery during the week and saw him only on Sundays.

"But I was happy. I believed I was helping my country," she recalled.

There were, however, the beginnings of doubt. "Something terrible happened. Some of the cadres put people accused of being counterrevolutionaries in bags and then slowly beat them to death. Every day I had to work side by side with these cadres and the families of the people who were tortured."

She also got into trouble when she turned down a man's petition to join the Party. "He had no qualifications, but he was very angry and later accused me behind my back of having an affair with another of the leaders. My husband was very upset."

After Mao's death and Deng's ascension, political power in her ministry shifted. Mulan found herself in the wrong faction, isolated, humbled, almost a pariah, though by then she had lost much of her interest in politics.

"The real power is at the top, too far away, what does it matter what we discuss in our meetings?" she said. "I used to put forward suggestions, but they were never acted on, so I've stopped being an activist." Instead, she related, she started finding excuses to skip political meetings or leave early. "I would say my job was very busy. If I couldn't leave, I just sat there and read the newspapers."

Mulan also detected a different spirit in the Party from what she knew in the 1950s—too many people were in it to get back-door privileges for their families. Her office handled large blocks of tickets for movies and plays, and every day dozens of people she barely knew called to ask her for some. "I finally had to put the phone on someone else's desk," she said. "In the old days, we talked about the Party with almost a mystical reverence, we referred to it just as the 'organization.' If you were a Party member, you spoke about leading 'the organization life.' But now the old spirit of sacrifice for the nation is gone."

Mulan hid her feelings. "I live a secret life now. No one knows. There is no room in our Communist society for human feelings. They think we should be made of wood. I can't discuss it with anyone in my *danwei,* that would be too dangerous." Only with a foreigner, who had no connection with the Party, would she share her inner turmoil. What she really wanted to do, she said, was to resign from the Party, but no one did that and she was afraid to go first. It would arouse intense suspicion.

One spring day, after a lengthy meeting she had to attend, Mulan was visibly depressed. Her usual smile had vanished, but she wanted to go for a walk. The Central Committee had just issued a major new set of guidelines for tightening Party discipline; all Communists would have to write confessions of their innermost thoughts; then they would have to undergo a screening by a review panel. If they passed, they would be issued Party cards, something the Chinese Communists had not done in many years. The purpose was to weed out those members whom Deng described in a confidential speech as "below standard." There had been only two million Party members in 1949 when the Communists came to power; now the Party had burgeoned to 38 million members, half of them recruited since the start of the Cultural Revolution in 1966. Deng wanted to retire some of the oldest members, now senile, and get rid of younger ones who had joined through their connections to the radicals. The program wasn't necessarily aimed at Mulan, but she was scared. We decided it was best not to see each other again.

From Mulan and other Chinese, I learned that the attitude of many people toward joining the Party had undergone a profound transformation since the 1950s. Instead of a calling, like the priesthood, it had come to be seen as the quickest, surest way to a better life.

"The first thing when you meet someone and they say they are a Party member, you wonder why," my friend Bing remarked. "What did they have to do to become a member? Sell their souls? Who did they have to turn in?" Among her girl friends, she said, "No one would want to marry a Party member now. They would worry about what kind of man he was."

It was only later that I learned her own husband was a Communist. She was candid about his reasons for joining. "If you are a Party member, there are lots of rewards. You get promoted faster, you are assigned more interesting and sensitive work in your job, and you have a better chance of being sent abroad." He had gotten a cushy job at CAAC, which enabled him to travel overseas, a rare privilege.

There are strategies for getting into the Party, she added. The easiest way for her husband to join was while he was in university, for the Party reserves a quota for new members in each college class. If you haven't been picked before you graduate, it is much harder later—offices have smaller quotas. For peasants the best hope is by joining the army first; the military has the largest of all quotas.

But for ambitious peasant youths who want to join there is also intense psychological pressure. For if a soldier doesn't get into the Party before his first tour of duty is up—three years in the army, four years in the air force, five years in the navy—he may be demobilized and will have lost his chance. Those who fail are sometimes resentful. Bing's father, a general, had told her that at a mustering-out banquet for a group of peasant soldiers, one disgruntled man who had not been accepted into the Party had stolen a hand grenade and hidden it under his bulky uniform jacket. He was sitting at a table with his regimental commander; when the officer rose to propose a farewell toast, the soldier pulled the pin, killing himself and a dozen others.

Admission to the Party is still not easy, Bing added. Her husband had to spend a year on probation, writing confessions nearly every day during that period to report everything he thought and did. "He had to put on a big show of being hardworking and making lots of sacrifices," she recalled. He also had to *pai-ma-pi,* "pat the horse's rump," or curry favor with his Party secretary.

A scholar in the Academy of Social Sciences, though not a Communist himself, deplored this new opportunism in the Party.

"The Party was built on the principle of selflessness," he said in a talk in his cramped fifth-floor walk-up apartment. "That was what enabled the Communists to beat the Kuomintang and to launch our industrialization in the 1950s. It was something all Chinese could be proud of."

The Party was still able to attract talented, capable people, but they no longer were willing to make the personal sacrifices, he said. His younger sister had recently been accepted for membership, but she had refused an assignment to Tibet after finishing college. In the old days no one would dare do that.

"In China, moral leadership has always been considered the basis of good government," he continued, pouring me a cup of steaming tea. "It is like Confucius said—'If a ruler himself is upright, all will go well without orders. But if he himself is not upright, even though he gives orders, they will not be obeyed.'"

This was what had happened in China after the Cultural Revolution—there had been a breakdown in moral authority. In the 1950s and early 1960s, one of the unique features of Chinese communism was Mao's mass line—he mobilized hundreds of millions of people for projects ranging from killing flies and sparrows to building giant dams with shovels and wheelbarrows. Voluntarily or not, everyone took part in weekly, sometimes daily, political study sessions, reading, memorizing, and reciting the latest editorial from the *People's Daily* or quotations from Chairman Mao. In those days, no one could afford to be labeled passive. Prudence dictated even opponents of the regime remain politically conscious. "If you didn't, your leader would make you wear tight shoes," the scholar from the Academy of Social Sciences related —he could make your life uncomfortable.

But by the late 1970s the malaise in the Party—the years of factional quarrels, the persecutions, the quest for special privileges, the twists and turns in the political line—had made popular participation increasingly formal, empty, and ritualistic. The masses retreated into indifference as their best defense.

On one of my early trips to China, in August 1977 to accompany Secretary of State Cyrus R. Vance, I happened to arrive in Canton from Hong Kong on the day the Eleventh Congress of the Chinese Communist Party ended. Rumors had circulated in Hong Kong that a high-level Party gathering was under way because the provincial Party leaders had vanished from public view for several weeks; but Peking had made no official announcement about the Congress, not even acknowledging its existence. Yet that afternoon in Canton, a drab, crowded city of old buildings with peeling paint built along the muddy Pearl River, people were putting up red flags, colored lanterns, and large banners proclaiming, "Warmly welcome the victorious outcome of the Eleventh Party Congress." This was an important news story for me, and I asked my China Travel Service guide what the results of the congress were, who had been elected to the Politburo, and what decisions had been reached.

"I don't know anything about a Party congress," he said, looking me straight in the face. "There has been no announcement. You can listen to the news on the radio tonight."

Then how did the people know there was a congress and why were they so certain it was victorious? I persisted.

Without a flicker of emotion, he pointed to another red sign. It read,

"Long live the great, glorious and always correct Chinese Communist Party."
"That is how we know it was a success."

At my guide's suggestion, we decided to go to a downtown park that evening where a dance troupe was to perform to celebrate the Party meeting. At precisely 8 P.M., as the national news program began over loudspeakers strung through the park, thousands of firecrackers exploded and the band accompanying the dancers clanged their cymbals. It was impossible to hear a word of the news. Thousands of people were jammed into the park, but few of them seemed intent on hearing the tidings from Peking.

Peking's leaders are acutely aware of this growing disenchantment with their rule. Few Communist regimes have been as blunt about recognizing their own faults. The *People's Daily* in 1980 called it "a crisis of faith" in Marxism. The paper, which is distributed nationally with a circulation of 5.3 million, blamed it on distortions of Marxism by the Gang of Four and the appearance of "some new situations and new questions" for which Marxism does not yet have an answer. Among these, the paper said, is the problem of why capitalism has not yet collapsed, as Marx had predicted, and why most socialist countries are poorer than capitalist ones. These were questions most Chinese I knew were already asking among themselves.

The Party's theoretical journal, *Red Flag,* confessed in another 1980 article, "The Party's prestige is not high—this is a fact." Echoing Lord Acton's dictum that power tends to corrupt, *Red Flag* suggested there may be a "basic difference between a ruling party and an underground or nonruling party. What is the danger to a party after it has assumed power? The danger is that it will degenerate if it works carelessly. After it has assumed power, the party cannot order the masses and must not become the rulers and the ruling class of the old society." It is theoretically possible for a Communist party to degenerate into a fascist party, the journal added. "This is a very serious problem."

The Party seemed to hope that such candor would help recoup its declining prestige. In 1980 and 1981 the Communists also took several steps to try to return to their earlier, more democratic and popular ways. Peking called for an end to the system of lifetime tenure which allowed senile patriarchs to keep their posts in the Party, the government, or the army no matter how infirm or incompetent they became. It instituted limited local elections for people's congresses, the first since 1949. It promulgated China's first criminal code since Liberation to create a more equitable system of justice. And it installed a new team of leaders, including Hu as Party Chairman and Zhao Ziyang as Prime Minister. They succeeded the hapless Hua Guofeng, whose major claim to legitimacy was that a dying Mao had told him, "With you in charge, I'm at ease."

I met Zhao when I went to Sichuan in early 1980 to report on the industrial and agricultural reforms he had introduced there, giving factories more autonomy and peasants a greater say over what they planted. At the time he was only the Party boss of the province, though there were already rumors in Peking that Deng wanted to name him Prime Minister. Before making the trip, I had requested an interview with him, but ranking Chinese officials tend to avoid resident foreign journalists like the plague and I didn't expect to see him.

To my surprise, Zhao not only assented to the interview, he came over to my hotel himself and arrived without the usual retinue of aides. In person the sixty-three-year-old Zhao is unprepossessing. He has a medium build, receding gray hair—which he started to dye after his promotion to Peking—soft brown eyes, and a quiet voice. But part of his appeal is his low-key approach, his modesty, his avoidance of the grand visions and neat ideological solutions that got China into trouble in the past. Explaining his interest in experimenting with market forces and new forms of socialism borrowed from Hungary and Yugoslavia, he said, "In China, we have a saying—'When you cross the river, you grope for the stones.' But you must cross the river. You can't just jump over it. Sometimes things don't work and you have to start again."

But despite the Party's efforts, its reforms haven't rekindled the lost enthusiasm of its earlier years. An American graduate student at Peking University, whose Chinese roommate was a cautious, correct Party member and the daughter of a high cadre, recounted what happened after a campus meeting to distribute copies of the Party's new guidelines for discipline. It was an important document, but when her roommate came back to the dorm she unstapled it and used the pages to cover her books against Peking's dust. Paper is scarce and expensive in China, she explained; she didn't want to waste it.

An investigative team from the Propaganda Department of the Central Committee found that at the South China Teachers College in Hunan one third of the students didn't show up for a compulsory course on Marxism. Others sat in the classroom reading novels, writing letters, or doing their homework for other classes, according to an article in the *Guangming Daily*. The students complained that there wasn't much point in studying Marxism because the line always changed depending on who was in power. To add to the problem, most of the professors teaching the course on Marxism are of low quality, the paper reported. The better ones were purged in past campaigns and now most teachers are scared to deal with the subject.

Even among the country's leaders there is a ferment, an uncertainty, about what Marxism means for China. "We are having trouble defining what our system is," an official in Yunnan province, in the southwest, told an American diplomat visiting there. "We are trying a number of experiments. Those that work, we will call socialism. Those that don't, we will call capitalism."

Deng Xiaoping himself has defined Marxism simply as the principle of "seeking truth from facts." As a corollary to that, he has added, "Practice is the sole criterion of truth." Some older cadres I met abhorred this as reducing socialism to mere pragmatism.

Perhaps to help compensate for the reduced appeal of Marxism, Deng has dusted off the old nationalistic slogan of the reform-minded mandarins of the late nineteenth century who wanted to modernize China to catch up with the West. Their goal was to make China *fu-qiang,* or "rich and strong." In a 1980 meeting with a Rumanian delegation, Deng said concisely, "The purpose of socialism is to make the country rich and strong." At bottom, that is what most Chinese I knew really wanted out of communism.

The most volatile and sensitive issue for the Party has been what to do with the legacy of its Great Helmsman, Mao. For over two decades Mao was a demigod; his cult was China's secular religion. But many urban Chinese had long wearied of his incessant calls for class struggle and despised him for the chaos of the Cultural Revolution. At the large New China bookstore on Wangfujing Street, one of Peking's busiest shopping centers, the central counter opposite the glass front doorway is reserved for Mao's writings. But I noticed on several visits to the store that there were no clerks behind the counter and no customers anywhere around it. Instead, they were lined up to buy traditional Chinese novels or books on studying English and physics, two of the most popular subjects today since they are looked on as a way to get a better job or possibly earn a trip abroad.

A middle-aged college teacher told me that one morning, when she was disappointed with her students' performance on a test, she upbraided them by quoting a well-known essay of Mao's on the need for diligence. It involved a Canadian doctor, Norman Bethune, who had come to China in 1938 and had died serving the Red Army in its guerrilla bases. "We must all learn the spirit of absolute selflessness from Dr. Norman Bethune," Mao had written. But her students snickered.

"After class several of them came up to me," she recalled. " 'Teacher, you are really something, quoting Chairman Mao,' and they laughed."

In the middle of the vast Square of the Gate of Heavenly Peace, bigger than half a dozen football fields, sits Mao's last resting place. The mausoleum is a chunk of white marble, a neoclassical temple transplanted to China, looking more like the Lincoln Memorial in Washington than a traditional Chinese edifice. Only the roof, double-tiered and painted orange, in imitation of the imperial mustard-yellow tiles of the Forbidden City across the square, has a Chinese touch. In defiance of the laws of geomancy, the mausoleum faces north, a bad omen to some Chinese. Four members of the People's

Liberation Army, in long dark-green winter padded coats and fur caps with red stars, guarded the entrance the December day I paid my respects. Mao lies in an inner chamber with a floor of polished black marble, his body encased in a crystal sarcophagus. Only his head and upper chest are visible; the rest is draped with a Chinese Communist Party flag, red with a yellow hammer and sickle. Rumors after he died hinted the government had trouble preserving his body and had to call on the Vietnamese for help—they had earlier enshrined Ho Chi Minh. Mao's face looks very old and tired, the skin drawn and wrinkled, like a man who had an unhappy ending.

In Chinese fashion, visitors are admitted only in groups, not as individuals. You must come with your *danwei*. I was curious to check some facts about the construction of the memorial hall and asked a guard.

"I am a soldier," he replied. "I don't know."

Then I queried several other attendants in civilian dress; they also professed ignorance. They pointed me to a young, pigtailed woman at the entrance with padded shoes and a blue scarf over her head against the cold. She was the official greeter, they said. How long did it take to build the hall and when did it open? I asked, details I had read in the Chinese press several years before but had forgotten.

"I don't know," she said, too, turning away.

Unlike guides elsewhere, she had no briefing to give, and there were no signs or exhibits inside to recount Mao's exploits. The subject was too nettlesome. So the Chairman had become just another dead ancestor whose role was best left ambiguous.

Not long after I left China, the Central Committee issued a lengthy and carefully worded analysis of Mao's life. The document took over a year to prepare. Deng wanted to undercut once and for all those cadres who still harkened to Mao's calls for revolution. But he couldn't let the criticism go too far—if Mao had been wrong for so many years, wasn't the Communist Party itself in error? So the analysis was a compromise. "Comrade Mao Zedong was a great Marxist and a great proletarian revolutionary," it said; it was Mao who led the revolution to triumph in 1949. "It is true that he made gross mistakes during the Cultural Revolution"—he had become increasingly arbitrary, undemocratic, even irrational. "But if we judge his activities as a whole, his contributions to the Chinese revolution far outweigh his mistakes. His merits are primary and his errors secondary."

Yet I wondered how the older cadres, those who had served with Mao felt, whether they were saddened by his sharply reduced stature and this verdict. By lucky chance, on the night before I left China, a friend arranged for me to have dinner with a member of Mao's family. My friend specified we could meet only if I agreed not to divulge the man's identity—he lived a precarious existence—and I assented.

He turned out to be a dignified, reserved middle-aged man with a high forehead and swept-back hair reminiscent of Mao. Whenever he mentioned Mao, it was always as "the Chairman." He wanted to talk with me, he said, because he felt there was misunderstanding about Mao. Mao was not a conservative, he insisted, he was always open-minded. He loved to read books—when he went on tours of the provinces, the one thing he took with him were cartons of books, and his bed was always half covered with unread volumes.

"Let me give you an example," the relative said. "Even in his seventies he became interested in the United States, read about it, and this resulted in the invitation to Nixon to visit China.

"Many cadres now seek privileges for themselves, but the Chairman was always democratic. He lived very simply. Sometimes people did things for him which he didn't know about. Once when he went on a trip, they built a swimming pool in his garden. The Chairman loved to swim, but he was very mad.

"He told his children, 'Don't depend on me, don't depend on others, depend on yourselves.' He told us that when he died, he would leave all his money and possessions to the Party and the state.

"I remember once I went off to do labor on a commune," the relative continued, offering me some peanuts with his chopsticks. "When I came back I was very dirty with long hair and a beard. I was embarrassed about joining the family for dinner, but the Chairman said, 'Good, you look very good.' "

It was true, he added, that Mao and Jiang Qing, the Chairman's fourth wife, really had not gotten along, as the government claimed after Mao died and Miss Jiang was arrested as the ringleader of the Gang of Four. Their troubles started in Yanan in the 1940s, he asserted, and after the Communists' victory in 1949, they had not lived together in Peking as husband and wife.

"Mao didn't see her for long periods of time. At first it was his working schedule. He would work at night and sleep all day. They would have only one meal together a week, Saturday evening dinner. For him it was breakfast.

"Later they separated. When he was in Peking, she would go to the provinces. When he went on a tour, she would come back to the capital. Mao couldn't stand her, all her nagging and her ambitions. In his last years, sometimes he gave orders not to let her in the house. The guards kept her out."

When dinner was finished, Mao's relative wanted to ask me a question. Why, he pondered, was China so backward compared to Japan? One hundred years ago they had been at the same level. "Is it because socialism is not as good as capitalism?" he asked.

It was an awkward situation. I felt embarrassed to evaluate China's adoption of communism in front of a member of Mao's family. But then he answered for me.

"In theory, socialism is excellent," he said. "It provides for economic as well as political democracy. But in practice it has shown weaknesses. We let the state and the bureaucracy grow too strong and prevented the development of individual initiative. China needs to find some way to combine the two systems."

Would the Chairman feel that way? I asked.

"The Chairman was always prepared to learn," he answered.

14. A World Turned Upside Down

上 下 顛 倒

HONG AND WEIDONG

"Victorious, you are a king;
But vanquished, a bandit."
A Chinese adage

He was home on leave from the army. It was a hot August day, and
Weidong ("Protect Mao") and another soldier from his regiment had been
out drinking. They had consumed two bottles of *bai-jiu,* a potent Chinese
version of white lightning with a burning, heavy taste of alcohol, when his
companion suggested they look up a very pretty girl he knew named Hong
("Red").

She had a soft oval face, creamy white skin, liquid eyes, and long shiny
black hair. Hong was bound to be at home, the friend said, because that
was where she had been every day for the past five years since she had
pretended to be sick in 1967 and had refused to "volunteer" to be resettled in the countryside like most of her high school classmates. Her teacher
had come to her house repeatedly to urge her to go as her patriotic duty.
Still she declined. She had also turned down an assignment from her neighborhood committee to work in the local collective laundry. It meant washing clothes by hand, often in cold water, even in the middle of Peking's
long winters.

Hong was too proud and too angry to go along with the government's
orders. Her father and mother were both professors, intellectuals by Chinese
reckoning. They had come from prosperous merchant families, had gone to
schools run by foreign missionaries before 1949, and spoke excellent English. Several of her parents' brothers and sisters had gone to college in the
United States and Britain and stayed abroad after the Communists' victory.
So when the Cultural Revolution broke out, her father was a prime target

—a bourgeois intellectual with "overseas relations," as the radicals put it. Just having a relative outside China was cause for suspicion by the Communists. Radicals in his college accused him of being a counterrevolutionary and put him in what was euphemistically called a "study class" for two years. It wasn't a prison, but he had to spend all his time reading Mao's works, writing confessions about his supposed dealings with foreign agents, and could come home only one day a month.

Hence when Weidong and his friend arrived at Hong's apartment in their army uniforms, red in the face and smelling of liquor, she pushed them out. She had no use for the Communist Party or the People's Liberation Army —especially, she thought, for a soldier who probably came from a family of high cadres, for Weidong was very tall for a Chinese, well over six feet, and only officials could afford to feed their children the milk and meat to help them grow that big.

But Weidong had been taken by her good looks and her coquettish pout when she rebuffed them. He was equally determined and headstrong. His father, in fact, was a former poor peasant who had joined the Red Army in its guerrilla days in Yanan in the 1930s and had risen to become a senior officer in the navy after its creation in 1949. Weidong was a star on the army's basketball team—tall, lean, rawboned, with large hands, an athlete's grace, and clean, handsome features. His voice was deep and resonant, with an air of authority. When he talked, everyone in the room listened. There was also something roguish about him, a boisterousness and bravado, and taken all together, he reminded me of a young Chinese John Wayne. Later I learned "the Duke" was his favorite movie star.

That evening, after it was dark, Weidong returned to Hong's apartment building, climbed over the brick fence around it, and snuck in a back window.

"Why wouldn't you let me in before?" he demanded to know.

Hong was startled. But an elderly woman neighbor, who was a member of the building's public security committee, had chanced to see Weidong slinking into the apartment. She had immediately summoned the police and they arrived within minutes.

"Who are you?" they began by questioning the tall soldier. When he revealed his identity, they called his father to check. Satisfied about his background, the police let Weidong go.

The next day he came back to Hong's to apologize. But she wasn't there. The police had taken her away, her mother said curtly. They gave no reason. For several more days, as long as his leave lasted, Weidong visited Hong's home to see if she had been released. She hadn't.

A month later, when he got another furlough, he came back again. By then, he learned, she had been officially arrested.* The accusation against her was that as the daughter of an intellectual with suspect "overseas relations" she had tried to seduce a soldier and the son of a general. In revolutionary China, where Mao ordained "take class struggle as the key link" and "put politics in command," the old notions of class had been reversed.

Weidong was contrite. He felt guilty about what he had done to Hong and tried to use his father's connections to get her released. He even went to a Peking court and confessed he was to blame. But it was a few months after Lin Biao, the Defense Minister and Mao's designated heir, had tried to assassinate the Chairman, and the police were jittery. Hong ended up spending a year in jail. When the Public Security Bureau finally let her out, she told me later, they warned her she had not been cleared of the charge against her. There just wasn't enough proof. The incident would remain in her dossier.

By now Weidong felt a deep attachment to her. She still had no job and he asked his father to help arrange employment for her. But his parents were suspicious of Hong's family and opposed to his seeing her again.

"They said I would become 'unreliable' in the Party's eyes if I had any relationship with her," Weidong said. "Since I was a boy I had dreamed of going to a military academy and becoming an officer like my father. I had good expectations of being promoted."** But when he continued to see Hong, his commanding officer told him his military career was finished and he was demobilized. The army officer in charge of assigning jobs to veterans made him a mechanic. It was a shocking loss of face for someone with the background and energy and talent of Weidong.

His only consolation was that the girl with the beautiful face had started to like him too. They took a trip hiking in the mountains west of Peking, just the two of them, and they fell in love. Unlike many young Chinese, who look on marriage as a way to enrich themselves, get a better job, or marry into a well-connected family, Hong and Weidong said theirs was a relationship based on real feeling. When he reached twenty-eight and she twenty-five, the legal minimum, they got married. For China, it was an uncommon match, the general's son and the professor's daughter.

I first met them at a party at a diplomat's house. It was Christmas, 1978, and the government had only recently begun its experiment in liberalizing the rules on freedom of expression and contact between Chinese and foreign-

---

*Chinese law makes a distinction between simple detention and formal arrest. In theory, the police can arrest a person only after they have filed charges against him and obtained a warrant from the prosecutor's office.

**In the Chinese armed forces, officers are selected from among the enlisted men rather than enrolled directly in officers schools from civilian life.

ers. Peking's Democracy Wall was jammed every day with avid readers. Hong had been invited to the reception by some foreign students she knew. But she was pessimistic about how long the era of greater openness would last.

"This is a very unusual opportunity," she confided to me at the end of the evening. "It is unlikely we will have the chance to meet again." She did give me her phone number, however, in a gesture of daring. I was in Peking for only a ten-day trip to mark the normalization of relations between the United States and China, and it wasn't until six months later that the government let *The New York Times* open its bureau and I returned to live full-time in the Chinese capital. One of the first things I did was to try calling Hong. The woman who answered asked me who I was. This presented a dilemma—I didn't want to get her in trouble by mentioning my name or *The Times*—so I said I was an American student from New York and hoped she would get the connection. Hong was not home, the woman then reported. After three more futile phone calls, I was ready to give up. But one day, as I walked out of the hotel at lunchtime, Hong and Weidong were standing on the sidewalk. They had guessed it was me, braved a call to the U.S. Embassy to ask where I was staying, and decided to wait outside the hotel, hoping to catch me.

Hong explained why she had not answered the phone. "The telephone is not in our apartment, but in the room of the people in the public security committee. They report to the police whenever there is a suspicious phone call, especially from a foreigner like you. The police came right over to ask me who you were. I was scared." Only officials have telephones of their own, she said, and all public phones are in shops, offices, or apartments of people who work for the police. It is one of the most basic mechanisms of government control.

Hong and Weidong were in a quandary, they told me. Her mother had arranged a trip to the United States for her where she would visit her mother's sister who lived in New York. The aunt hoped Hong would stay on and go to college in the United States. Mao's pragmatic successors, to increase the number of Chinese able to get a higher education, had instituted a new policy that permitted anyone with relatives overseas and the financial means to support themselves to go abroad to college. It was another turnabout. The Communists were once again recognizing the importance of education, and intellectuals were regaining some of their lost prestige. Suddenly millions of young Chinese dreamed of going to college and studying overseas. It was a marvelous opportunity for Hong.

But she was reluctant to go. Her mother, she admitted, had an ulterior motive. "She doesn't like Weidong—in fact, she hates him," Hong said. Her parents, like Weidong's, had been against their marriage. They didn't like cadres and particularly the children of high cadres, Hong added. Her mother was scheming to break them up.

Later, when I met her mother, a slender, well-preserved middle-aged woman with a brittle manner, I understood. "In 1966, in the Cultural Revolution, the Red Guards in our school came to our apartment and searched it for a whole day," her mother recounted. "They took all our furniture, my jewelry, all our books and records, many of which had been gotten from abroad. They left us with only one set of clothes. They made us carry our books and records down to the courtyard by the armloads. Then they held a bonfire on our campus. It lasted for three days.

"But it was very unfair. Later we learned that many of the most valuable books and records had been taken to warehouses around Peking. There the children of high cadres bought them back for fifteen cents a pound, not per record or book, but per pound.

"Before the Cultural Revolution, we Chinese lived under a great illusion. We believed the Communists could save China and make it prosperous and strong again. People were very idealistic and hardworking. Now people have seen through this, and they have suffered a terrible loss of faith. This is the key to understanding China today. The cadres have become concerned only with their own privileges, the factory workers are lazy, and the young people have lost ten years of schooling and don't have jobs. People have become selfish."

Her mother became more bitter as she spoke. "The great problem today is that there is no public morality. The old Confucian morality was destroyed, now the Communist morality is gone, too."

Although she detested Weidong because of his father's military rank, I found they had more in common than she realized. The Cultural Revolution had made Weidong cynical, too. With his dream of being an army officer shattered by his love for Hong and his role in life reduced to working as a mechanic, Weidong saw little future for himself or other Chinese of his generation.

"Young people now have no sense of purpose, we only *hun-xia-chu,*" he said, using a popular expression meaning to muddle through from day to day. "If you give them a job, they will do it, but they won't put any energy into it." His only pleasure in life, apart from Hong, was going to watch American Western movies. Thanks to his father, he still had access to "internal" film shows.

I remarked that many young Americans are also lost and alienated. A surfeit of affluence—of growing up with everything the world has to offer, cars, television sets, comfortable houses—has left American young people without a sense of purpose, with nothing behind them to propel them forward.

"For Chinese, it is the opposite," Weidong commented. "We have something in front of us blocking our way. We can't get around it, the Party." The only hope he could see for China, he said one evening, was war with the Soviet Union. "Then all of China will be destroyed and we can start over."

It was an extraordinary statement for someone whose father was a veteran Communist general. How did his father feel? I asked.

"He is a very dedicated Party man, but he has lapsed into silence," Weidong replied. "When I go home, we don't talk anymore. My father has nothing to say. It is too dangerous for him to say what he thinks about what is happening." Deng Xiaoping had once declared in a confidential talk that China's generals could be divided into three groups, Weidong went on. One third supported Deng's modernization program, with its departures from Maoist orthodoxy, one third didn't care, and one third opposed it. His father was among the conservative third who preferred the old Maoist ways. He expected Deng would put pressure on him to retire, though he was only in his late sixties, still middle-aged in Chinese terms.

His father had bestowed one incalculable privilege on Weidong. Not long before, his father had moved into a large new house built especially for high-ranking generals and had left his comfortable old apartment to Weidong. It had two large bedrooms, a living room, and a toilet and kitchen of its own, far more space and amenities than the three square yards allotted to the average urban resident. On their own, Hong and Weidong would have had to apply to the city housing authority and might have had to wait three to five years for a tiny one-room apartment. On one wall was a black-bordered portrait of Zhou Enlai, modern China's one unblemished popular hero, a Communist with the moderation and subtlety and manners of a Confucian mandarin. On a bookcase was a white plaster bust of the Venus de Milo, covered with clear plastic to ward off the Peking dust. Weidong was an amateur artist, and idealized portraits he had painted of Hong and his father hung from other walls. A Chinese copy of Richard Nixon's book *My Six Crises* lay open on their double bed. Weidong had bought it in the special bookstore for high cadres with his father's identification card. Cartons filled with other books—*The Great Gatsby,* short stories of Mark Twain, traditional Chinese novels—were stacked in corners of the room. Given the political difficulties and shortage of books in China, they had assembled a sizable library.

Weidong was a natural leader. If he had not aroused the regime's suspicions, he might have gone far in the system. Whenever I dropped into their apartment in the evening, there were always three or four of his friends there —young men like him, about thirty, other sons of generals with whom he had grown up and gone to school. They enjoyed listening to him talk. One cold winter night, one of the visitors was a short, crew-cut, boyish-looking cadre in a green army jacket. Weidong introduced him without hesitation as head of the China Youth League branch at one of Peking's main colleges where he was responsible for recruiting new Party members and ensuring good classroom discipline. Was he as cynical as Weidong? I asked. Surely he believed in the Party and Marxism?

Weidong snorted. "He is a Party member, yes. But if he tells you he believes any of that stuff, I'll punch him in the face," and Weidong leapt off the bed where he was sitting and pretended to smack his friend, slamming his right fist into his left palm.

The young cadre laughed, too. "I'll tell you how I came to join the Party. I was in the army, and when it came time to be demobilized, my job assignment officer told me, 'If you join the Party, it will be a lot easier to get a good job. Right now we have some Party members who can't get decent jobs, so if you aren't in the Party, it will be even worse.'"

Does the Party still get good recruits? I asked. "Yes, some, but they join for the wrong reasons. We say they enter the organization but not its ideology. They want the material benefits." Many other people who should be in the Party, to strengthen it, don't want to join. "The hardest thing is, you have to curry favor with your Party secretary all the time. They always say, 'Please express your own opinion, the Party is very democratic.' But if you do, you are in trouble."

Another winter evening, there was a sharp knock on the door and Weidong ushered in a heavyset young man with a pockmarked face clad in a gray greatcoat with a tan scarf thrown around his neck. He was clutching a round bundle wrapped in copies of the *People's Daily.* Weidong introduced him by his nickname, Big China. Inside the package was a Ming dynasty landscape scroll; Big China was selling it on commission for a person he identified only as "the old man." He would not say more because by law all artistic works and antiques must be sold through a state agency so the government can reap the profit. Big China was a closet capitalist.

Weidong ordered the girl friend of another of his visitors to unroll the painting for him while he inspected it from a distance. "Put on your gloves, don't leave fingerprints," he commanded. It proved to be almost five yards long, a delicate depiction of mountains, rivers, and pavilions painted in pastel shades of green and brown. Weidong examined the style, the painter's signature, and several red seals stamped on it and then pronounced it was a sixteenth-century original.

How much? he asked Big China. Five thousand yuan ($3,333) was the answer. "Please give me some face," Weidong countered, the signal for bargaining. Finally they settled on 4,000 yuan ($2,667).

I was incredulous that Weidong could even consider buying it. His salary was only 48 yuan ($32) a month. "It's a great price," Weidong remarked.

"In a state shop, they would sell it to you foreigners for at least 30,000 yuan [$20,000]. But it's not for me, but for my father."

His father had been collecting Chinese art since 1949, when his Red Army division moved into the cities and he confiscated the holdings of several wealthy families. The art was better off in his father's possession, Weidong reasoned, because during the Cultural Revolution no Red Guards had dared to invade his home and destroy the paintings.

"The real power in China is the army, not the Party," Weidong added with a touch of pride. It was a comment I heard from other Chinese.

But in China even generals draw a limited salary, I interjected. The highest income I knew of was 400 yuan ($267) a month. That is true, Weidong agreed, but I was overlooking the host of other perquisites his father received: free housing, a car, driver, servant, orderly, food from military farms. Almost his entire salary went into the bank. "In China today, it's power, not money, that people want." Money by itself can not buy these other privileges.

Weidong's drifting, his marking time, came to an abrupt end a few months later when Hong became pregnant. The first I knew about it was when I stopped by to see them and Hong was holding a tiny tiger-striped kitten on her lap.

"Weidong gave it to me, so I could learn to take care of a baby," she ventured with a smile. In its way, it was still another of his boyish, daring gestures. Keeping cats and dogs is illegal in China's cities. They consume scarce food and the government believes they contribute to filth and disease.

"Having a cat is safer than a dog," Weidong said. "They stay inside where foreigners don't see them. Dogs go outside. What the government can't stand is if foreigners see their regulations aren't being obeyed."

But Weidong had become more serious: he was thinking about his career for the first time since his involvement with Hong had ruined his chance of becoming an army officer. Now he had a family to provide for. With his father's help, he had gotten a post as the lowest level cadre in a foreign trade corporation.

"All he thinks about now is business," Hong said. "He gets up early to go to work and is gone all day long. There isn't time to go to the movies so much anymore."

To her disgust, he was also thinking about joining the Party. "If I was in the Party, I could get promoted faster, get a little extra income, our family would be better off," Weidong said, running his hand over his brush-cut hair. "It's not that I don't care about China, I do, just as much as when I was young and an activist. But now I know what the Party really is." It would not be easy for him to get into the Party, but the atmosphere was more relaxed than in the early 1970s when his trouble with Hong occurred, and he hoped his father's rank and his many friends in the Party would help.

Hong disagreed with his plan. "I am an intellectual. I have always been apolitical. There is no way I can believe in the Party or Marxism. Politics is just the same as it has been since Confucius, a matter of manipulating people." With her stomach swelling, she was wearing one of her husband's large old army jackets—there are no ready-made maternity clothes in China.

Hong had gone out looking for books on child care but couldn't find any in the government bookshops. Pediatrics has only recently become a recognized branch of medicine in China, and most families always depended on folk wisdom passed on from generation to generation. But Hong had borrowed a volume from her father's college library that turned out to have been written by an American physician. Was the author any good? she asked me. It was Dr. Spock.

After their baby was born, I dropped by to see the new family, bringing a case of American disposable paper diapers, an invention they had never seen. Weidong had hired an *a-yi* for 20 yuan ($13) a month to help take care of the baby and wash the endless train of cloth diapers in their sink.

Hong, who had taken to wearing a hint of bright-red lipstick and darkening her eyebrows, in keeping with the gradual liberalization of the period, was enjoying being a mother. Before the baby was born, they had signed a pledge to have only one child. It was part of the government's stringent new campaign to reduce China's birth rate to zero by the year 2000. "There was a lot of pressure on us to sign from the neighborhood committee and our workplaces," Hong said. "They kept coming around to talk about it. We really couldn't refuse." Weidong was disappointed when their only baby turned out to be a girl; like most Chinese, he wanted a boy. But in exchange for their promise, Hong was granted six months of paid maternity leave from the ministry where she had finally gotten a job. She was employed as a translator. During the Cultural Revolution, when she stayed at home and had nothing to do, her parents taught her English so she would at least have some skill.

Now Hong wished she didn't have to go back to work. "If it was permitted, I'd just stay here after my leave is up and be a mother." It was a sentiment I heard from many Chinese women who face the opposite dilemma from American females. They don't confront a choice between career or family— they must work, by law.

Hong had also cut her long hair and gotten it permed, as many Chinese women began to do after the arrest of Jiang Qing. Mao's widow had demanded proletarian purity in hair styles as in everything else—only pigtails or the short, chopped, bowl cut were allowed. "I liked it long myself, but Weidong wanted me to get it curled, he said it looked more modern," Hong explained. On the bottom shelf of their bookcase, I noticed, was a set of plastic hair curlers, the ultimate bourgeois artifact, a sign of the changing times in China.

With a new career at stake, Weidong became more circumspect about our meeting. When I invited them over to our apartment for dinner, he took the precaution of first calling a friend who worked in the Public Security Bureau to see if I was on the list of foreigners being watched by the police. "We are very close, I can ask him anything," Weidong said. I had been on the list for a time, it transpired, but now I was off it. Weidong didn't offer any explanation, but I was safe.

We arranged the date for the meal over the phone. When I called his new office, another man answered and for a moment I hesitated. He began with the usual question, "Where are you?"

"I am an old friend of Weidong's from out of town," I responded, trying to hide the tremor in my voice.

I could hear him shout across the office, "There's a friend of yours from Shandong on the phone." I was both relieved and flattered. I had been mistaken for a Chinese. But Weidong laughed at me later. A Shandong accent is one of the worst in China, he said.

That evening, when Hong and Weidong came over, he played guns with Ethan, hiding in back of the sofa and popping out from behind a wall. "When you grow up, you should become a soldier," Weidong counseled him with nostaligia for his own lost dream.

Weidong had been under growing pressure from the city housing office to vacate the apartment his father had left him, he told me. "The other people in the building have been complaining. They say we have such a huge home for only the three of us when they have families of five or six living in a single room. They say it is only because I am the son of a high cadre that I can live like this. But I'm not going to move out. They can do what they want, they will have to throw me out." It sounded like his old bravado, but he was serious.

Eventually, the city government had given him a ten-day deadline. If he wasn't out, they would evict him. On the crucial day, Weidong stayed home from work. He had invited a group of a dozen friends over, "the biggest, meanest, toughest boys I could find."

At the appointed hour, a truck from the local housing office appeared with a cadre. But the official wasn't prepared for a fight and left. It was another lesson for me. In a totalitarian society, the Chinese Communists often relied on persuasion in dealing with their citizens. Mao had believed it was the most democratic and effective technique. But after the popular loss of faith in the Party in the Cultural Revolution, many people were no longer willing to cooperate; it often left the government paralyzed and impotent, an authoritarian country with an authority crisis.

"The people say we children of high cadres stink, with all our privileges," Weidong said. "But we don't have anywhere else to move to. I can't just put my family out in the cold." He, too, had become a survivor, battling the system and finally making it work for him.

PART
4

PERSUASIONS

—

15. Soldiers in the Grass

THE CONTROL APPARATUS

"The dictatorship of the proletariat is ravenous, more fearsome than the dictatorship of the bourgeoisie. In a bourgeois society, one can run when one violates the law, but when society is so tightly organized, where can one run to? There is no place to vent one's grief and no place to submit an appeal. . . . In our society, there is indeed the phenomenon that men are not treated as men."

> Zhou Yang, Deputy Director of the
> Party Propaganda Department, 1966

Using the telephone in China, I learned on my first day in residence, requires a special technique—not in dialing the number, but in eliciting a response from the person you are trying to reach. I had just arrived in Peking and was calling the personnel office of the Diplomatic Services Bureau to inquire about hiring a Chinese assistant for *The New York Times*. The conversation went like this:

"Hello, is this the personnel office?"

"I'm not too clear," said a diffident voice.

"Is there anyone there who knows if this is the personnel office?" I tried again.

"They've just gone out," the voice answered. "What do you want?"

"I'm the new correspondent of *The New York Times* and want to hire an assistant. Who do I contact?"

"I'm not too clear," the voice said, retreating once more.

"Can I make an appointment to come over and talk to someone in your office about an assistant?" I said, trying a new tack.

"Please give me your phone number."

"Will someone call me back later?" I asked, my hopes by this time fading.

"I'm not too clear." With that, the voice hung up.

It was my first taste of the Chinese national mania for security and secrecy. Rule number one in making a telephone call, I learned, is never give out any information—it could be a state secret and get you in trouble. To the Communists, who fought their way to power as clandestine guerrillas, this originally had a useful purpose. But the lengths to which people go to avoid identifying themselves or divulging facts on the phone often reach comical proportions. When one Chinese calls another, the person answering the telephone always begins by saying *"wei,"* an all-purpose, neutral response. Even if you are calling an office, like the Information Department of the Foreign Ministry, the official government spokesman, the clerk who picks up the phone never answers by saying "This is the Information Department." It is up to the caller to guess whether he has dialed correctly.

But to add to the confusion, most times the person who initiated the call is also unwilling to identify himself. Instead of saying "This is Lao Wang calling" or "This is the Academy of Social Sciences," the caller will only say *"wei"* also. So neither party can be sure whom they are talking to until one finally relents and takes the daring step of giving out their organization or name. This sparring can consume several minutes. An exasperated American businessman told me that one slow afternoon he decided to play a game. He dialed numbers at random and said only *"wei,"* counting how many times the person answering would chime in with a *"wei"* of his own till he eventually gave up. The highest number of *"wei's"* he reached was thirty-four.

The same rule of discretion applies to important buildings. There is no sign in front of Zhongnanhai, the tall red-walled compound next to the Forbidden City where the top Party and government leaders work. There is no plaque to identify the drab yellow-brick building in the western suburbs of Peking that houses the Central Party School. In Shanghai, I noticed, there is not even a sign outside the imposing gothic Jinjiang Hotel, now largely reserved for foreign tourists. If you don't know what the building is already, it's none of your business.

Throughout China most offices, factories, schools, and even apartment buildings have walls around them and guards at the gates. Outside the new, whitewashed, walled compound of the *People's Daily,* two sentries of the People's Liberation Army stand guard with rifles. Everyone going both in and out must show a special work pass from the paper. There are uniformed guards now in the lobby of *The New York Times,* a result of recurrent bomb threats during the political turbulence of the late 1960s. But in China the reason for security is different. When I asked a tall, gaunt editor of the *People's Daily* why they needed so much protection, he replied, "Because it is one of the most secret places in China. Much of the information we handle is secret."

The Peking Hotel does not have a wall, but it does have its own company of army sentries who live in barracks near the hotel. Sometimes on Sunday mornings they woke me at 6 A.M. by practicing goose-step marching or the Chinese version of judo on the narrow street behind the hotel where my room faced. The shouts of fifty or sixty men yelling *"sha"* (kill) and stamping their feet in unison aren't conducive to sleep. When Jan Wong moved into her own new apartment building, her Chinese friends were delighted that it didn't have a fence or gatekeeper. That meant they could visit her without having to register and disclose their identity. Hoping this would be permanent, Jan asked the building manager if there were plans to erect a wall.

"Don't worry," he replied, misunderstanding her intention. "As soon as the two other high-rises in the compound are done we'll get on to building the wall and put in a gatekeeper. It will be very safe."

This passion for security sometimes reaches the point of being a danger itself, as I discovered when I often went out around midnight to file stories for my paper at the cable office, after the New China News Agency had finally released its daily bulletin. Late at night the employees in the Peking Hotel not only locked the fire exits and gradually shut off all the eight elevators, they also for a period began barricading the only internal stairway. I never found out why, but it was done with great care. The doors to the stairs were tied with rope and then tables and chairs piled in front of them. It was a good precaution against unauthorized entry, if someone managed to slip past the army sentries on the street and the Public Security Bureau guards at the door. But what about fires? Several times when I went to the movies or drama performances and decided to leave early, I found that all the doors had been padlocked, from the outside. Once when I protested to a guard, he reassured me that it was to keep people without tickets from crashing the show.

A professor at one of Peking's universities laughed when I recounted my complaints to him about these precautions. He invited me for a half-mile walk down the Avenue of Eternal Tranquility to the western wall of the old Forbidden City. There, running for several hundred yards, was a three-story building that looked like part of the palace, with the same madder-rose walls and mustard-yellow tiled roof. But my companion urged me to look closer. The windows on the west side of the building, which faced across the street to the Party and government headquarters in the Zhongnanhai compound, were only painted to look like windows; the whole edifice in fact was a facade. In 1973, the professor related, when the new seventeen-story wing of the Peking Hotel was completed, the Public Security Bureau discovered to its horror that a guest, looking west, could peer down across the Forbidden City and into the secret recesses of Zhongnanhai—if he had very strong binoculars. Wang Dongxing, then head of Mao's Praetorian Guard, a special army division known only by its numerical designation as the 8341 unit, devised the idea of putting up the fake palace building as a security screen. "It was outrageous," the professor lamented, "squandering millions of yuan on that hoax when satellites can look right down and take photos from the sky. It shows how well-informed some of our leaders are."

But such precautions are only the outer signs of an all-encompassing control apparatus, as intricate as the microscopic patterns etched on a silicon chip. Foreigners who visit China, including some experienced in traveling elsewhere in the Communist world, often come away saying proudly that they were able to walk wherever they wanted, poking down old lanes, looking into people's houses, without being followed. China really isn't a police state after all, they conclude. But an American who has lived in Peking since before 1949 scoffed at their naïveté. The control system operates the other way around, he explained, from the inside out, for the government has organized society as a security system as much as it is a social or economic system. It is built on three overlapping and mutually reinforcing components: the *danwei,* or workplace, the street committee, and the "small group" where political study sessions are held. "The Communists have created such a thorough organization, it is like radar, it picks you up wherever you go," the veteran American resident observed.

During a visit to the smog-bound industrial city of Wuhan on the Yangtze River, I looked up an American scholar who was doing research there at the Central China Normal Institute. To my surprise there was no gatehouse or guard at the school entrance—security is often more lax outside Peking—so I just drove in my taxi through the campus to the brick building on a hill where the American, Michael Gassiter, was living.

A few minutes after my arrival, the phone rang. I could hear a loud woman's voice ask, "Do you have a foreigner visiting you?" She did not identify herself, but when Gassiter answered in the affirmative, she probed further. "Is he an American reporter? We need to know."

It was Mrs. Zhou, said Gassiter, a specialist on China's 1911 Revolution. He recognized her voice. She was the cadre in the college security section assigned to watch him. I had not been overtly followed, but her intelligence was excellent. Everyone in the school, everyone who belonged to that *danwei,* was required to report to the security section when a stranger appeared on campus, and someone had glimpsed me arriving.

Gassiter was already accustomed to the constant monitoring of his daily activity. "If I go downtown to go shopping, the next day Mrs. Zhou will say to me, 'I suppose you went into town. I suppose you went to the department store. I suppose you bought two shirts.' "

Every Chinese, as discussed earlier, belongs to a *danwei* through his office, factory, school, or commune. Although technically a person's place of work, the *danwei* also often provides the housing where a Chinese lives, the school where his children get an education, clinics for when he gets sick, and ration cards for his rice, cooking oil, and soap. Before a Chinese can get married, he must get permission from the Party secretary of his *danwei;* if a couple want to get divorced, their *danwei* must first approve.

In a sealed envelope in the personnel section of each *danwei* is a confidential dossier for every employee. It contains not only the normal elements of biography—a person's education and work record—but also any political charges made against him by informers in the past and the Party's evaluation of the individual as an activist, for example, or a suspected counterrevolutionary. In addition, in keeping with the Communists' "bloodline" theory, the file lists the person's class background for three generations, whether his grandfather and father were landlords and capitalists or poor peasants and workers.

"Your dossier is strictly secret, only the cadres know what is in it," said a taciturn electrician in his early thirties. "You yourself can never find out." During the Cultural Revolution, though he himself was a Red Guard, he was labeled a Kuomintang agent and spent two years in jail. "Someone in another Red Guard faction must have made the charge against me, but I could never find out who or what it was," he said.

Before anyone can be transferred from one city to another, or from one job to another, he added, you must have a letter from your *danwei* confirming that your dossier has already been forwarded to your new unit. Your *danwei* also controls your right to travel. Before a Chinese can make a trip from his city or village that will take more than a day, he must get approval from the Party secretary of his *danwei,* like a soldier in a Western country getting a pass. He must come up with a concrete reason for needing leave, like a sick parent, because the only regular vacation time in China is six national holidays a year. To enforce this restriction, there are policemen at checkpoints on the main roads leading into Peking and other large cities who stop anyone they don't recognize. If a traveler wants to get a hotel room, he must first present a letter from his *danwei.* This is recorded and his name sent to the local police station.

It is difficult for foreigners to appreciate how much control this system gives the authorities over Chinese, but an American woman graduate student at Peking University related an incident that brought the totality of it home to her. It was soon after she arrived from her own college in the Midwest and she was shocked by the primitive living conditions on campus—running water only two hours a day, greasy, inedible food. So she had written a vivid description of her life to her husband, who was still back in the United States.

A few hours after she mailed the letter, the proctor in charge of foreign students at the school knocked on her door.

"May I talk with you?" he inquired politely. "Are you having any difficulty in China?" He then proceeded to quote her letter verbatim.

Not long after, another American student she knew received a letter from his girl friend in the United States. The letter was in good condition, except that the last page was in Danish. The proctor had made a mistake. "After that I knew what a *danwei* meant," the American woman said. "It's like a womb, you can never escape from it."

Chinese friends told me the Public Security Bureau maintains its own agents in the post office to open mail. China's original 1954 constitution guaranteed "privacy of correspondence," but this provision was dropped in the 1975 and 1978 revisions of the constitution. All letters I received mailed from inside China had been torn at the corners, opening a tiny slit through which an experienced operative could slip out the contents by first rolling it up with a round instrument like a pen, my acquaintances added.

Another part of the *danwei* organization in the universities is the "class monitor," a Party member whose job is to ensure political rectitude and discipline. When Jan Wong was at Peking University in the mid-1970s, the monitor assigned to her class in the history department was a former peasant in his late twenties, Pan Qingde (Qingde means "Celebration of Virtue"). With a square face, even white teeth, crew cut, and clean features, he reminded Jan of the movie stars typed to play the young hero in Chinese films. Pan stayed with her class for its entire three years on campus, sitting in on their courses and living in the dorm with the students, though he had his own private room. Some of her classmates liked to practice their English with Jan, but, she learned later, Pan had warned them, "I'm not against studying English, but the main thing we should do at school is engage in class struggle." At the time, Jan admitted, she had looked up to Pan as the Party leader in the class and entrusted him with confidences about her romance with Norman Shulman, an American who had lived in Peking since 1965. What she didn't know was that Pan suspected her of being a "secret agent" because she was an overseas Chinese and often spoke out frankly in political meetings. He had her Chinese roommate report every time Norman visited her and passed along the information to Norman's *danwei,* trying to stop their affair. When Jan and Norman decided to get married, Jan gave the invitations to their wedding party to Pan to hand out to her classmates. She felt wounded when not a single one of them showed up. It wasn't until four years later that one of her friends told her Pan had not distributed the cards.

If the *danwei* exercises control over Chinese in their workplaces, the street committee provides the government with a mechanism to watch them at home. In the five-story concrete building where my friends Hong and Wei-dong lived, the representative to the local street committee was a rotund, graying, illiterate woman in her fifties named Ma whose husband had been a poor waiter in a restaurant before 1949. Mrs. Ma was not a Party member, but she was energetic, shrewd, and had carefully cultivated good relations with the police by offering them a cup of tea or a cigarette whenever they happened to stop by the building. In time, at the annual meeting of all the adults in the building, Mrs. Ma was put forward by the neighborhood office, the lowest level of government, as the official candidate for street committee member. The ballot was not secret, and everyone knew whom they were supposed to vote for, Weidong related. Mrs. Ma won all the votes.

In action, Mrs. Ma was a cross between a building superintendent, police informant, social worker, and union-hall hiring boss. The powers of the street committee are not codified in law, for they are considered representatives of the "masses" rather than the police, but that only gives them more authority, Weidong said.

"Their most terrifying power is that they can search your house whenever they want," Weidong related. "The police are supposed to have a warrant, but the street committee cadres can come in when they please." Usually three or four members of the street committee, middle-aged women like Mrs. Ma, would just barge in without knocking after midnight when Hong and Wei-dong were asleep. "Their excuse is that they are here to inspect our *hu-kou,*" the household registration certificate. The street committee was checking for any people living in Peking illegally from the countryside, relatives of the family, perhaps, or rusticated youth who had snuck back into the capital. "I give them our certificates, but then they always look around the apartment and examine anything they are interested in.

"If we have friends over, even for dinner, Mrs. Ma may walk in and ask who they are," Hong interjected. "It is very humiliating. If you don't cooper-ate, she can call the police and they will come over and ask the same ques-tions." Once when Hong and Weidong quarreled late at night, Mrs. Ma stopped by the next day to chastise them for not resolving their domestic problems. "There is no way to be alone, she even watches what time we go to bed," Hong complained. "We are like caged animals."

Mrs. Ma also keeps a strict eye on the residents' neatness and sometimes reprimanded Hong for not washing the dishes or sweeping the floors. Often during the winter, when dusk falls early, Mrs. Ma and the other street committee cadres would hide in the unlighted entryways to the buildings to watch for strangers, Weidong cautioned me. He had seen her carrying a club. For me, it gave each of my nocturnal visits to their house an added and unwelcome sense of adventure. One evening, when walking through a dark field toward their apartment, I was accosted by two young men in ordinary blue workers' clothes. They demanded to know what my *danwei* was and what I was doing in the area. I offered the fiction that I was a foreign teacher on my way to visit the home of one of my students. Weidong explained that they were members of the local urban militia, another link in the security network.

The street committee cadres are not paid a regular salary, but they can count on small gifts of meat, vegetables, and rice from residents who want to keep on their good side. More important, their posts put them in position to help their families and friends, for it is the street committee that passes on recommendations about job assignments to the city labor department for unemployed young people in the neighborhood. It is also the street committee that advises the municipal housing office about which families need new quarters.

"Just look around and see whose children come back first from the countryside and get good jobs, and you'll know who the street committee people are," Weidong said.

In recent years the street committee has gained a further and extraordinary power—the right to decide which couples in the neighborhood may have children. This prerogative is part of the government's tough new birth-control campaign that aims to reduce China's rate of population increase to zero by the year 2000 by encouraging families to limit themselves to one child. Under the drive, each province and city has been awarded quotas for the number of babies they are allowed to sire per year, and the street committee then determines which families may use the quotas.

"We give first preference to couples without children," said Mrs. Tian, another energetic middle-aged woman street committee member I got to know. She took pride in her job and pointed out that she had helped establish a small cooperative for unemployed youngsters in her building making soles for shoes. She also made sure that elderly people in the building without children to support them got their small monthly welfare subsidies. But she took a firm attitude toward birth control.

"If a family already has one child, we ask them to wait at least four years before having another, or better, not to have a second baby. If a couple already has two children or more, we tell them not to have any more."

For those who agree to have only one baby there is a package of rewards: a monthly bonus of five yuan ($3.30) for each parent until the child reaches fourteen (or about 8 percent extra pay for an average urban worker), preference for their child in school enrollment, and, theoretically, the right to housing space normally allotted to a family of four.

Mrs. Tian was frank about how her street committee administered the program. "We assign a person to keep track of each woman's menstrual cycle. If someone misses her period and isn't scheduled to have a baby, we

326

tell her to have an abortion. There isn't room for liberalism on such an issue."

The reason for this stringent program, the most ambitious family-limitation plan in history, is the dismal arithmetic of China's population figures. In A.D. 2, when China's first census was taken, there were 59.6 million people in the country; in 1840, 412 million, and in 1949, 540 million. In other words, it took about 4,000 years of recorded history for China to reach its first 500 million people. But in the past three decades, under Communist rule, the population has almost doubled to one billion, all in a country only slightly larger than the United States. In the early 1950s a respected economist, Ma Yinchu, warned that the country's population was expanding too fast and would interfere with China's economic growth. For his temerity in challenging the Marxist belief that more people mean more production, Ma was attacked and purged from his job as president of Peking University. (Only in 1979, at the age of ninety-eight, was he rehabilitated and named honorary chancellor of the school again.) With so many births since 1949, Peking calculates there are 20 million people a year reaching the marriageable age and that, even if everyone accepts the one-child family, the population will still climb to 1.2 billion by the turn of the century. After that, the government would like to see the total decline to 700 million before it gradually eases its restrictions.

Chinese government figures show that the I.U.D., or intrauterine device, is the most widely used method of birth control, accounting for 50 percent of all contraceptive practice. Sterilization is the next most common form, accounting for 30 percent, with female sterilizations outnumbering male sterilizations by ten to one nationwide, though the procedure for men is simpler to perform. China has also developed its own range of oral contraceptive pills, including a highly publicized experimental male pill made from a component of cotton seed oil, gossypol. The male pill was developed after an investigation of perplexing symptoms, including infertility and cardiac irregularities, which beset peasants in a cotton-growing area of Henan province, in north China.

Peking has not released national figures on the number of abortions a year, but in many communes I visited they outnumbered live births. Since Peking first instituted its serious birth-control campaign in the early 1970s, the rate of population increase has already fallen dramatically, especially in the cities. From its high point of 2.34 percent a year in 1971, the growth rate dropped to 1.2 percent in 1980. But that still fell short of the government's target of less than 1 percent a year. The real question remains whether the peasants, who make up 80 percent of the country, will accept having only one child when they know from experience that under China's economic system larger families tend to earn greater incomes. On a visit to the Xihong production brigade near Shanghai, I saw one technique the government is using to try to break this resistance. Pasted on a wall of the brigade's clinic was a large pink chart that displayed precisely how each local cadre was complying with the campaign. Of the brigade's twenty-nine officials (twenty-seven of them men), ten men had had vasectomies. Fourteen other cadres or their wives were using I.U.D.s or pills. Of the remaining five, three were too young to get married under China's policy of delayed wedlock, one had no children, and the other, a refractory type, had three children and wasn't taking any precautions. Aren't the cadres embarrassed by this public accounting of their private sexual decisions? I quizzed the brigade head. "Not at all," he replied with a diplomatic smile.

This constant exposure to public scrutiny and peer pressure makes life in China like living in an army barracks. I was reminded of this on my overnight train ride from Shanghai to Peking with Ding, the stocky drill sergeant conductor who tried her best to keep me comfortable and segregated from the Chinese passengers. The train was due to arrive in Peking at 6:10 A.M., much too early for my taste, but at 4:35 A.M. Comrade Ding used her passkey to open the door to my compartment and sound reveille.

"Time to get up," she said cheerfully, flipping on the light in the darkened room. "Wash your face." It was a clear command, but when I looked at my watch and saw the time, with still an hour and a half to go before we reached our destination, my decadent bourgeois body wanted to go back to sleep and I turned off the light.

Ten minutes later, when I failed to appear, Ding returned, opening the door again without a knock and switching on the light. "You'd better hurry, go to the toilet," she barked.

Why now? I implored her, rubbing my eyes. It isn't even 5 A.M. and we have well over an hour to go. "We will be locking the toilet at five thirty when we get close to Peking," she replied, closing off my line of retreat. "Here are your clothes"—and she reached up and took my shirt, pants, and sweater off the top bunk where I had put them.

This time I obeyed and stumbled down the corridor to the toilet. But it was locked. Comrade Ding rushed after me to open it.

"We keep it locked so the people in the next car won't use it," she explained. The adjoining coach was "hard berth," for the masses, jammed with triple-decker hard wooden bunk beds lining an open, smoke-filled corridor. I was traveling "soft berth," in a private compartment for four people with lace curtains and thick mattresses, the section reserved for cadres and foreigners.

By the time I had shaved and returned to my more opulent quarters, the loudspeakers started, to the stirring tune of "The East Is Red."

"Good morning," said a bright, soothing woman's voice from the black

328

round box just above my head. "Today is Tuesday. We will now commence our broadcast. Our train will soon come to its final stop, our service personnel are already starting to clean up the train for hygienic purposes. Everyone should go to the toilet, brush your teeth, and fold your blankets."

The radio announcer was like a combination of a disc jockey and catechist. Soon she began reading the morning's news and political lessons, quoting an editorial from the *People's Daily* on the need to work hard to increase grain production. "We must always remember that Chairman Mao taught us to 'take grain as the key link,'" she intoned. Generally I like listening to the news; it is my profession. But this was too early and I searched for a button to turn off the voice. There wasn't any. After the news, the announcer then recited the day's train schedule from Peking, for the benefit of connecting passengers. I stopped counting after the twentieth train. She also had useful advice on which way to walk when disembarking from the train and what the bus routes of the capital were.

Amid all her statistics, there was one she didn't rattle off that morning that kept popping into my head. A New China News Agency article I read when I first began working in Hong Kong in 1975 reported that there were 106 million loudspeakers in the Chinese countryside. They formed a network that gave the government direct access to 70 percent of all the homes of peasants. The article didn't say how many loudspeakers there are in the cities, but certainly a few million more would be a modest number. And judging from the peasants' homes I have sat in when the day's broadcast was beamed over the air, few of them had knobs that allow the listener the privilege of extinguishing the sound. China is a captive audience of hundreds of millions of people.

It has become commonplace among Sinologists to say that the Communists have combined the techniques of modern totalitarianism, like the loudspeaker network, with the traditional Chinese tendency toward conformity. Explanations repeated too often have a way of losing their force, which in this case would be too bad, because this one is still a cogent insight into how Peking's control apparatus works. There is no exact equivalent in Chinese for the word "conformity," for it is only a person doing what is expected, showing understanding of human relations and the *li,* the old laws of ritual and etiquette. Unlike the West, where we have glorified the individual, in China conformity enjoyed social approval. My friend Bing, the woman who as a teen-ager denounced her father, offered a series of Chinese aphorisms on the subject: " 'A tall tree will be crushed by the wind; a rock that sticks out on the riverbank will be washed by the current.' . . . That is what we were brought up on," she added, "not to show our talents. Instead you should be 'worn smooth like a cobblestone.' People are supposed to learn to have 'eight

329

faces polished like jade,' " meaning to be all things to all people. "Your expression should be unreadable."

It is this quiescent quality, this tendency toward compromise and conformity, which sometimes leads foreigners to think the Chinese are inscrutable. I remember on my tour of the United States with the group of Chinese journalists in 1972 a sweltering August afternoon when we stopped for gas on an interstate highway. While our car was parked at the gas pump, the three Chinese reporters announced they would go to the nearby Howard Johnson's restaurant and buy us ice-cream cones. Fifteen minutes later, when they hadn't returned, I went inside to find out what had happened. They were locked in a mutually uncomprehending discussion with the soda-fountain waitress. They had asked for ice-cream cones, but she had pointed to the board behind her listing all the available flavors. Which kind do you want? she asked. They couldn't bring themselves to express personal preferences. "Any flavor will do, just make them all the same," one of the newsmen finally said.

The great issue in Chinese philosophy has not been what is truth, or the difference between good and evil, but how the ruler should govern wisely and ensure that the people live harmoniously, accepting compromise and conformity. For Confucius the answer lay in education—he believed that everyone could be reformed through proper ethical schooling. "The cultivation of the person depends on rectifying the mind," he taught his disciples.

The Communists shrewdly exploited this tradition to try to transform the thinking of the nation and create a new socialist man. Their weapon was political study, which became another of their control mechanisms. Borrowing also from Lenin's ideas about small, tightly organized Party cells, the Communists in their cave headquarters in Yanan in the early 1940s worked out a technique to indoctrinate the thousands of disparate new adherents that were flocking to their cause: young nationalistic students, older intellectuals, poor illiterate peasants, and former warlord and Kuomintang troops. Everyone was divided into small groups, ten was a good number, and then spent several months undergoing intensive "thought reform," as the Communists called it. First came a period of study of assigned Party documents, then mutual criticism of their past attitudes and activities, and finally a time for submission and rebirth where each individual had to write and rewrite his personal confession until it was accepted by the Party. This process resembled a religious conversion, like our own revival meetings, but with added elements of physical isolation, psychotherapy, manipulation of a person's guilt, and often real terror. In the early 1950s, when the Communists had the whole country to govern, they applied this system to millions of other Chinese in special large "revolutionary" colleges they established.

By the time I arrived in China in the late 1970s, however, after the cataclysms of the Great Leap Forward and the Cultural Revolution, political study had become much less intensive, more formal, and often only a hollow ritual. As the psychiatrist Robert Lifton observed in his 1961 book on thought reform, it was subject to a law of diminishing conversions.* "Repeated attempts to reform the same man are more likely to increase his hostility . . . than to purge him of his 'incorrect' thoughts." The balance between genuine enthusiasm and coercion gradually shifted to the latter, Lifton concluded.

At Bing's college in Peking, the students now have only two hours of political study a week, which are held on Saturday afternoons in their *xiao-xu,* or "small groups," a permanent subdivision of their class. "In theory that is what we do," Bing told me on a warm Saturday noontime when we met for lunch, "but actually many of the students don't go at all anymore or are put to work cleaning up the dorm. If they have to go, some of my friends knit sweaters to kill the time." Only when there is an important new Central Committee document to be read out do people take a real interest, Bing added, since it is likely to contain major political or economic news that won't show up in the newspapers until much later, if at all.

At the end of each semester all the students must still write out a "summing up," a personal report card on their behavior. "In the past you had to be frank and describe your inner thoughts. They said everybody has three levels of consciousness. The first is the one you thought about yourself, your everyday feelings. The second level is the things you tell only your closest friends. The third is feelings you hide even from yourself, your unconscious. This is what you were supposed to report. It was very scary in those days.

"You were also supposed to be very hard on yourself, to tell about your failures," Bing continued. "It was a matter of loyalty to Chairman Mao and it was voluntary and sincere. But nowadays people just lie or emphasize their achievements.

"Last semester, for example, I wrote, 'I have been working very hard to study the thoughts of Chairman Mao.' That was not true, of course. Then I said, 'I took part in political study sessions very actively.' That was also not true. Finally I wrote, 'I studied very hard for my classes.' That was true.

"You have to read these out loud in front of your small group. The other students must comment on them, guided by the teacher, who is a Party member. In the past the others would be very critical of you, but no more. People are afraid that if they speak out, in the next campaign you will find something to use against them. That is our lesson from the Cultural Revolution."

*Robert Jay Lifton, *Thought Reform and the Psychology of Totalism* (New York: W. W. Norton and Co., 1961), p. 412.

If a student makes an error, he still has to write out a self-criticism, but this is used more for punishment now than as part of an effort to convert the sinner, as it was in the past. "One time when I lost my plastic college identification badge, I had to write a confession saying how inconsiderate it was because someone who was not a student could sneak onto campus," Bing said. With that, she picked up a copy of a book I had lent her, *The White Album* by Joan Didion, and announced, "I'm off to make revolution." I doubted she was headed for her Saturday afternoon political study session.

But the process still retains some of its rigor for Party members. Guo was a senior at Peking University who had been a factory worker before passing the college entrance exam and had a wife at home who was also a worker. At school he met and fell in love with a woman in his class who, like him, was a Party member. Unfortunately for Guo, one weekend his wife found a note from his girl friend that he had carelessly left in his pocket. She was furious and reported them to the college authorities. Their Party branch called a meeting where they both had to make self-criticisms, orally and in writing, and promise never to see each other again. An acquaintance at Peking University who told me about the affair said that if they hadn't confessed, they would have been expelled from school and their careers ruined.

Of all the examples of how the Communists control their people, the one that impressed and horrified me the most—perhaps because for much of my time in China I had to live apart from my family—was the casual, routine way Peking assigns husbands and wives to work in different parts of the country. The left-wing magazine *Cheng Ming* in Hong Kong once estimated that there are eight million people in China who have been forced to live separated from their spouses because of their jobs, two million of them cadres and six million ordinary workers and office employees. There is no official rationale for it, except that it is the way the labor offices have decided to assign people, for the convenience of the state.

Shen is a tall, thin, bespectacled man in his mid-forties with thinning hair and an anxious expression in the corners of his eyes. When I first met him, I thought he was a bachelor. He lived by himself in the dormitory of his scientific institute, with only a narrow bed and a trunk in which he kept his few possessions. Most days he also ate all his meals in the institute's mess hall. It took time for Shen to confide that he actually was married. Many years ago, in the late 1950s, he and his wife were students together at Qinghua University in Peking; they fell in love, and at graduation were wed. They had a total of one month living together. Then the state labor bureau assigned him to a post in the capital and her to a job in Shanghai. There was no appeal. He got to see her about three weeks a year, usually at Chinese New Year's, when they combined the three-day national holiday with the special two-week leave they were entitled to for working apart.

Even when his wife gave birth to a baby girl nine years ago, the government would not relent. They belonged to separate *danwei,* and neither unit would let them go, because of bureaucratic jealousy, Shen felt. His wife's troubles were compounded in 1975 when she criticized Jiang Qing in front of some office mates who informed on her. For that she was exiled to a village in the countryside outside Shanghai. In 1979 she was rehabilitated but still is confined to the village where she works as a peasant planting rice and raising her daughter.

Sometimes in the evenings Shen played with the children of neighbors outside his dorm, holding the babies on his lap or kicking a ball with young boys. "My prime is passing by," he said one such summer night, "and I'm still separated. My daughter knows me only as the man who visits once a year and brings presents. How many years does one have to live?"

In addition to couples like Shen and his wife, who were separated by their job assignments after graduation from college, there is also a large group of people from the countryside who were split up when the husbands became cadres and were promoted to work in the cities. Because of the government's tight restrictions on urban growth, they have not been allowed to bring their wives with them.

Sometimes, when I wandered down Wangfujing Street in Peking, or looked around outside the railroad station, or noticed the telephone poles near the Peking University campus, I saw small handwritten signs. At the top each had two horizontal arrows pointing in opposite directions. They are appeals to exchange jobs and housing from husbands and wives living in different cities.

"My family lives in Peking, but I work in a state-owned factory in Tianjin," one notice stuck on a telephone pole near the Peking Hotel read. "I have received permission from the leadership in my factory to transfer to Peking. Comrades wishing to return to Tianjin and work in a liquor factory should please contact me," and it gave the man's name and his plant's phone number.

The government's tardiness in resolving these problems of separated families struck me as more than mere bureaucratic rigidity. There was a certain callousness, much like the Party's attitude toward anything touching on sex, as if people could live for the revolution without love. When I reported on China from Hong Kong, I employed for a period a pretty young British-Chinese woman as my assistant, Lynn Kirkpatrick. She and her husband, Andrew, had studied for two years at Fudan University in Shanghai. Although they were married, the school forbade them to live together and assigned them to different crowded dormitories. When a British businessman in Shanghai allowed them to spend the night together at his home a few times, he was reprimanded by the local public security office.

The Public Security Ministry, which administers this vast control apparatus —the police, the security agents in each *danwei,* the street committees—is not as well known in the outside world as its Russian counterpart, the K.G.B. But many Chinese I knew referred to it as the *Ke Ge Bo,* Chinese for the initials K.G.B. The Public Security Ministry oversees both the regular blue-uniformed traffic policemen who work on city streets and plainclothes agents. Friends told me the ministry is divided into thirteen bureaus, with one especially delegated to monitor the activities of foreigners in China. While I was in Peking, this was the sixth bureau, but the ministry frequently switches the numerical designations for added security. The ministry also has its own armed troops, like companies and battalions of the People's Libera-tion Army, who guard some key Party organizations and prisons. But none of my Chinese acquaintances could estimate the total number of employees in the Public Security Ministry. The ministry's headquarters are located in a vast compound facing the Gate of Heavenly Peace and bordered by the Museum of Revolutionary History. Part of the ministry, including the court-room where Jiang Qing and other members of the Gang of Four were tried in December 1980, occupies the old grounds of the pre-1949 British Lega-tion. More than any other part of the regime, the Public Security Ministry is secretive about its operations, and a request I made to visit their offices was turned down. But Western diplomats in Peking say that from what little they know, the Chinese police don't make as much use of sophisticated electronic bugging devices as the Russians do. It may be because they don't have the advanced technology, or perhaps it's because the Chinese already have their own elaborate and dependable human intelligence-gathering network. In any case, the American Embassy in Peking has not found bugs planted in its walls or high-energy sensing devices aimed at it as has the U.S. mission in Moscow.

The factional quarrels of the Cultural Revolution took their toll in the Public Security Ministry as they did elsewhere. One head of the ministry, Li Zhen, disappeared in 1972 after reportedly being assassinated in the base-ment of his office. The real story of his demise is such a carefully held secret that even his wife and daughter have never been informed what happened to him after he left home in his chauffeur-driven Red Flag limousine that day, Chinese friends told me. Li was quietly succeeded by Hua Guofeng, though Hua's appointment to the post was not made public till three years later in 1975. In retrospect, it may well have been Hua's stewardship of the police post which helped him gain Mao's favor and be catapulted to the jobs of Prime Minister and Party Chairman in 1976 after Zhou Enlai and Mao died.

But Hua's connection with the ministry also meant that he ran the prisons where many of Mao's opponents, now China's leaders, were incarcerated.

The Public Security Ministry does not handle China's intelligence activities overseas—for that, there is an even more clandestine organization. On a crisp, sunny autumn afternoon, when Bing and I were driving to the Fragrant Hills, west of Peking, she called my attention to an unmarked drab gray concrete building just beyond the old Summer Palace. It was the Institute of International Relations, she said with a meaningful glance. The innocuous name meant nothing to me, I confessed. Bing looked triumphant.

"Top secret," she said with a grin. "It belongs to the Central Investigation Department.

"It's so secret that most Chinese don't even know about it," Bing explained. "It's like your CIA. They are in charge of spying on foreign countries. They send people abroad under cover as diplomats, cultural attachés, trade delegates, or journalists. The institute is where they train their recruits."

The Central Investigation Department is so important, she added, that it comes directly under the Party Central Committee, not the government. "If they want you, they can get you transferred from any *danwei,*" Bing said with awe, the ultimate sign of bureaucratic clout in China. The husband of one of her friends at college worked for the Central Investigation Department in the Chinese Embassy in Paris and her friend consequently was the envy of all her classmates. "They think he must send her lots of good things, like French clothes, television sets, cassettes."

Given the immense power of the police in China, I was surprised that many Chinese had a casual, almost contemptuous attitude toward the uniformed policemen on duty on Peking's streets. Although the government has made efforts to instruct Chinese in traffic safety—creating reserved lanes for bicyclists, putting up billboards with rules for cars and pedestrians —traffic in China's cities is routinely chaotic. Pedestrians cross the street against red lights without even looking at the signals; cyclists cut into the fast automobile lanes without warning; cars operate by the rule of the horn —whoever honks loudest or drives fastest has the right of way. Several times I had to slam on my brakes in astonishment to avoid hitting people who were walking backward across busy streets because of an icy or dusty wind. This makes the Chinese very different from the self-disciplined Japanese. In Tokyo no one even steps off the curb until the light has turned green. "The Chinese have a rough edge, like animals in a jungle," a Japanese diplomat I had known in both Taiwan and Peking observed. "Just think what would have happened if it had been Japan that went Communist in 1949 instead of China."

Once on a cold winter afternoon, driving back to the Peking Hotel, I noticed a young policeman on his elevated traffic box hail a woman cyclist who was trying to cross the intersection. He was shouting at her for some apparent violation, but she wouldn't stop. So the policeman dismounted from his stand, grabbed her bike by the luggage rack on the back, and threw her off balance to the pavement. The woman was incensed. She jumped up, whacked the policeman on his shoulder, punched him in the chest, and then for good measure yanked off his stiff blue-cotton cap and hurled it across the street. In turn he took her by the arm and marched her over to a white-painted police sentry stand at the corner. She was a poor woman, in her late thirties, with tired eyes and rough skin. I noticed she was wearing a worn corduroy jacket, baggy blue-cotton pants, and thin cotton gloves, which had been crudely mended. Her cotton shoes were old and much too thin for that time of year. Several more police soon arrived and confiscated her bicycle, ordering her to report to a nearby police station to be questioned.

"But how can I get there if you have locked up my bike?" she protested. By this time a crowd of several hundred bystanders had gathered. There are few movies and plays to go to in Peking, and tickets are hard to come by anyway, so a crowd will gather to watch almost anything, especially a fight with a policeman. A teen-age boy stepped up to the woman, ignoring the police, and said, "Here, ride my bike to the station." His gesture was another sign of the breakdown in the Communists' prestige in the wake of the Cultural Revolution.

Yet despite such occasional acts of bravado, the ubiquity and intensity of the control apparatus have generated tremendous psychological pressures on the Chinese, creating mental strains that few Westerners can imagine. "People live under constant tension," remarked a dignified, taciturn engineer. "You always have to worry about someone you know betraying you," he explained, someone in your *danwei,* your street committee, or your political study group.

This pressure has been compounded by the years of political campaigns, the constant shifts in the official line, and the widespread political persecution, the engineer added. To try to minimize the dangers, he said, he follows one major precaution—he never talks about anything personal with people in his *danwei.* "For the next time a campaign comes up, the Party will order criticism meetings in your *danwei* and people will be compelled to say anything they know about you, whether they like you or not. So I make my friends with people outside my office."

The engineer and his wife both complained about suffering from what they called *shen-jing shuai-ro,* literally, "weakness of the nerves," or medically, neurasthenia, what Westerners identify as nervous tension, depression, and anxiety. Over time, I found, many of my Chinese friends talked about having *shen-jing shuai-ro.* Hua, the woman journalist who was arrested for talking with me about her sex life, said she suffered from constant headaches and insomnia. Often she slept only two or three hours a night, she said, and felt endlessly fatigued. When we went out to eat together, she said she had no appetite and only picked at her food. Miao, Mrs. Wang, also had headaches and couldn't sleep, and according to her husband, Li, was often irritable and listless. When he and I were alone, he diagnosed her problem as *shen-jing shuai-ro.* Some other Chinese I knew had nervous tics. Lao Wu, my conscientious assistant, had a habit of jiggling his foot. Whenever I put a difficult question to him or asked him to make a phone call to a government office that embarrassed him, the arc of his swing increased radically. Some Americans, of course, have nervous tics also, but it was the number of Chinese I encountered with habits like Lao Wu's which shocked me.

David Eisenberg, the young American doctor from the Harvard Medical School who was doing research at the Institute of Traditional Chinese Medicine in Peking, said that often when Chinese learned he was a physician they immediately began telling him about their cases of nervous tension. During a vacation trip to the old lakeside city of Hangzhou, south of Shanghai, Dr. Eisenberg related, he stopped to buy some cookies in a small shop.

"When the man behind the counter and I got to talking and he discovered I was a doctor, he said he had suffered from neurasthenia for a year. 'I've been to a traditional Chinese medicine doctor and to a Western-style doctor, but I can't sleep at night and I feel tired, nervous, and irritable all the time. Please give me some medicine.' "

In response, Dr. Eisenberg, a soft-spoken twenty-seven-year-old with curly blond hair and a neatly trimmed beard, asked the clerk if he had any problems in his personal life. It turned out he had been sent to Hangzhou over a year ago, far from his home. "I haven't seen my family in over a year, I can't ever see my girl friend again, and I hate my job," he told Dr. Eisenberg. "I wanted to study English, but when the Cultural Revolution came, I had to quit school. What future is there in selling cookies?"

Dr. Eisenberg himself was cautious in drawing conclusions from such random encounters, but he was very struck later when he spent a month observing how patients were treated in the acupuncture clinic of the traditional medicine hospital, the first American permitted actually to work in the hospital. Over a quarter of the one hundred patients he saw also complained about nervous tension.

"The patients themselves believed their problem had a purely physical origin," Dr. Eisenberg recounted. In part, he felt, this was because traditionally it was much more socially acceptable for Chinese to have physical rather than emotional sickness. Chinese have long felt a stigma in admitting to mental illness in the family.* But the Chinese doctors also encouraged this interpretation because they don't accept Freud's theory of the unconscious and therefore don't look into a patient's emotional background.

The government has added to the confusion by its own skittishness on the whole issue of mental health in China. Several Chinese doctors I talked with said the Communists officially insist that mental disorders have no biological basis and therefore are the result of social or ideological troubles—which the regime presumably should have resolved. In 1957, at a time when relations between Peking and Moscow were still close and China was under strong Soviet intellectual influence, the government abolished psychology as a field of study, branding it a "bogus bourgeois science." Most of China's small number of Western-trained psychologists were arrested and packed off to labor camps, a psychologist who earned his Ph.D. at Columbia University before 1949 told me. Psychiatrists were excepted, but most of China's medical schools stopped offering courses in the subject.

In his work at the acupuncture clinic, however, Dr. Eisenberg decided to try an experiment. While the Chinese doctors prescribed a course of treatment with needles for the headaches, insomnia, and fatigue, he inquired whether the patients had any emotional problems that might have triggered their symptoms.

"One young man said no, he didn't have any personal problems, but a few days ago his fiancée was stabbed to death by two guys," Dr. Eisenberg recalled. Among the other patients, some were depressed by their failure on the college entrance exam or by conflicts with the cadres in their *danwei* from whom they couldn't escape. Another man was catatonic. He couldn't speak or move and seemed numb. When Dr. Eisenberg asked a companion who had brought him into the clinic about his history, it turned out he had just been released after spending nine years in solitary confinement in prison.

In particular Dr. Eisenberg remembered an obese forty-five-year-old woman who came into the hospital sweating and breathing heavily. Her pants

*For instance, Chinese are still very reluctant to discuss the problem of mental retardation. In schools and nurseries I visited, whenever I asked how the teachers dealt with mentally retarded students, school officials denied there were any. The reason, I discovered, was that children with mental difficulties are usually kept at home and cared for by their families in the traditional style. The Communists have set up some special schools for the blind and a few factories where other handicapped people work, but I never found any facilities for the mentally retarded. A famous composer Jan Wong knew had a sixteen-year-old son, a tallish, bulky youth who talks in a thick low voice that is largely incomprehensible. When he was six, his parents sent him to first grade, not realizing his trouble. But he failed all his courses and the teachers refused to allow him to stay in school. Now he lives at home, where he can wash himself and do simple housework. When he was younger he loved to play with the children in the neighborhood, but now they laugh at him and he hides in his room when visitors come to the apartment.

were too short and her long gray woolen underwear hung down two inches below her cuffs. She complained that she was hysterical.

"Look at my mouth, it's crooked," she groaned. Only then did the Chinese physician in attendance and Dr. Eisenberg notice a strange overbite, her mouth twisting slightly to the right. When the woman talked or smoked, it went away, but when she was silent, there it was, like a comedian's grimace.

"I've had nervous tension for the past fifteen years, it started with the Gang of Four," the woman insisted. "Can't you give me some needles?"

While the Chinese doctor stuck needles in her, Dr. Eisenberg probed her personal life. She had not worked since 1965, after the birth of her fourth child, she said, since she was so busy at home taking care of her progeny. Her lack of employment was unusual for a Chinese woman. Then in 1966 her husband was packed off to the countryside to be a welder, separating him from the family, and had returned only a few months before. In the city, he couldn't find work.

"My two oldest children are big troublemakers," the woman went on. "Neither one has a job yet. I'd hoped they would get into university, but they just fight and get into mischief," she lamented. But when Dr. Eisenberg asked her if she saw any connection between these difficulties and her illness, she responded, "I don't see any relationship."

Until recently, China's psychiatric hospitals have been shrouded in almost as much secrecy as its nuclear test sites. There is no evidence that the Chinese systematically used their mental institutions as the Russians have done for dealing with troublesome political dissidents, but there have been reports of individual cases where the government did lock up political prisoners in mental clinics. During the Cultural Revolution, Red Guards found by accident a group of followers of Hu Feng—a prominent Marxist literary critic who had long been an outspoken opponent of Party intellectual policy—in a mental ward where they had been confined for several years. During my stay in Peking I saw a movie entitled *Dark Willows and Bright Flowers* about the conflict between youthful radicals and veteran cadres in the countryside. The heroine, who sides with the veteran cadres, is put into a mental hospital by a scheming leftist and tied to her bed. The villain's action did not produce any reaction from the audience, which suggested they were familiar with the practice.

But the main problem with China's mental hospitals, Chinese told me, was simply that there aren't enough of them. A balding engineer in Shanghai from a family that was affluent and middle-class before Liberation said that his brother had become chronically depressed and unable to work after he was sent to teach in a mountain village in 1958. His brother couldn't adjust to the rigors of rural life and had moved back to stay with his aged mother in the city, illegally. His symptoms grew progressively worse, but the large

Shanghai Psychiatric Hospital would not accept him for treatment. They were already overcrowded, and his condition was not considered severe enough. The hospital only took schizophrenics. He was a victim of depression, neurotic rather than psychotic. Eventually, the engineer said, he had arranged through a doctor he knew who treated members of the Politburo to get his brother into the hospital, using the back door.

Since Mao's death the regime has been more relaxed in its attitude toward the mental health question and has allowed a number of foreign delegations to visit the Shanghai hospital and another modern clinic in Peking. I toured the Shanghai hospital with Joseph A. Califano, then the U.S. Secretary of Health, Education and Welfare. It proved to be a pleasant rectangular compound of three-story concrete and brick buildings set around a garden in a suburb of the city. American doctors in the group thought its facilities and treatment compared favorably with large public hospitals in the United States. They were also interested that the Chinese staff used many of the same powerful new tranquilizers and other psychotropic drugs developed in the West in the past few decades. But they did note a major difference from American hospitals. The director, Dr. Xia Zhenyi, a slight, graying man trained in the United States, confirmed that 85 percent of the 1,000 inmates and 500 outpatients the hospital treats each day were schizophrenics, the most severe form of mental illness.

Talking as we scurried along the high-ceilinged corridors, Dr. Xia insisted China simply did not have the widespread problem of depression and other neuroses that exist in the West. "The incidence of mental disease in China is much lower than in America," he asserted. In China, he said, it occurs in only about seven people per thousand. But in the United States about 15 percent of the population suffer from some form of diagnosable mental disorder, according to the National Institute of Mental Health.

Shortly before I left China I met a woman psychologist in her late fifties who had been allowed to resume teaching her specialty again in 1978 after a twenty-year hiatus. Her books had all been burned years before, but her own spirit was still youthful, almost feisty, and she was deeply interested in the implications of psychology for China.

Did she agree with Dr. Xia that Chinese don't suffer from depression or had she noticed that many Chinese complained about nervous tension? I asked. Her dark eyes stared at me intently for a moment and I wondered if I had trespassed onto forbidden territory. But then she broke into a passionate discussion.

"After what we have gone through in the past thirty years, the whole country is depressed," she said, her eyes flashing. "Depression and anxiety are our psychological scars. I worry about this every day.

"But that is why we must find more positive things to say about our country and the Party. Otherwise we won't be able to cure ourselves and we will go around depressed. Try to be more cheery."

My friend Bing also saw depression and paranoia as the price China had to pay for the exigencies of the control system. "I talk about it sometimes with my very close friends," she said. "But you can talk only by stationing a guard at your mouth. You have to know exactly who you are talking to and the limits of what you can say to them."

China's condition, Bing suggested, was like a proverb that grew out of an incident in the late fourth century, a time of imperial disintegration in China, similar to the Dark Ages in Europe. A rebel named Fu Jian had gathered an army—said by Chinese historians to number a million men—to overthrow the state of Jin. The government commander had only 8,000 troops. But the usurper's soldiers mistook the moving grass and trees for advancing government forces and fled in terror. From the episode the Chinese have extracted a four-character phrase which has come to be a parable for paranoia and the fear of being surrounded by hostile spying eyes: *Cao-mu jie-bing*, or "In the grass, the trees, everything seems a soldier."

"That is the way it is for us," Bing said, "always soldiers in the grass."

16. *Lao Gai*

THE CHINESE GULAG

*"The Struggle . . . is a peculiarly Chinese invention, combining intimi-
dation, humiliation, and sheer exhaustion. Briefly described, it is an
intellectual gang-beating of one man by many, sometimes even thousands, in which the victim has no defense, even the truth."*
                                        Bao Ruo-wang, Prisoner of Mao

It began innocently enough. I was traveling in a delegation with the U.S.
Secretary of Defense, Harold Brown, the first senior American military
official to visit China since 1949, and our hosts from the Information Department wanted to be sure that when Brown left China via Shanghai, those of
us who were resident correspondents in Peking would be able to get home.
They were very solicitous and attentive to detail. For several days before the
scheduled end of the trip, Lin Qingyun, an Information Department cadre
of whom I was fond, asked how I planned on returning to Peking. A pleasant,
boyish-looking man with a dark-brown complexion, Lin said he would buy
a ticket for me, a great help in China where planes and trains are often
booked weeks in advance. I said I intended to take the train, but I politely
declined Lin's offer because I wanted discreetly to look up some Chinese
friends in Shanghai and didn't know how long it would take to find them and
arrange meetings. Then after we arrived in Shanghai and I had a chance to
contact my friends, I went and bought my own train ticket for two days after
the group was to leave.

But in the afternoon, a few hours after my purchase, as I was sitting at the
large wooden desk in my hotel room rushing to finish a story for *The Times*
on the significance of Brown's trip for Sino–U. S. relations, two officials from
the Shanghai city government knocked on the door. They said they wanted

to collect payment for the train ticket they had bought for me according to my request to Lin.

It was then I made a fatal mistake; I took a stand on principle. Perhaps because I was in a hurry to write my story and it was close to dinnertime, I reacted like a foreigner and refused to pay. I pointed out that I had not asked anyone to purchase the ticket for me. They replied courteously that I knew very well I had requested them to buy it, but if I didn't want the ticket, I could just pay the cancellation fee, six yuan ($4). I still refused. I felt I shouldn't have to pay for something I didn't order.

Later that evening, just as I returned to my room after dinner, an officer from the People's Liberation Army Foreign Affairs Department, Tang Yin-chu, who had accompanied the delegation, walked in. A square-jawed, crew-cut man with ramrod posture, Tang was visibly agitated.

"Why did you refuse to pay?" he demanded, his face flushed. I explained again that I had never asked for the ticket.

"But you did," he went on, calling my erstwhile friend Lin to the room to confront me. "You must recognize your error," they shouted at me in unison. My error? With that phrase I finally realized the seriousness of the situation. I was beginning to feel like the victim of a Chinese struggle session, a meeting where the target is surrounded by a group of his friends and colleagues and criticized, insulted, and screamed at, even slapped and spit on, till he is hopelessly confused and terrorized and confesses to whatever the charge against him. In real struggle sessions I had heard about, the process lasted anywhere from two or three hours to several days or even weeks. My plight was obviously not so severe, but it had many of the same elements.

Lin was transformed from the kindly man I knew. His face was red with anger, even with his dark skin, and he had assumed a mask of moral superiority.

"You are denying the facts," he lectured me. "I have proof. I have notes of our conversations and of all your phone calls. You cannot deny the facts." At least I had learned that my phone had been tapped.

"Mr. Lin, this seems to be a misunderstanding," I responded, trying to keep my temper and find a compromise.

"There are no misunderstandings in China, you are wrong," Lin replied, this time screaming. There was clearly no possibility of my proving my innocence. But I still hadn't learned there was no escape except total contrition.

"Mr. Lin, sometimes in the United States and China we do things differently," I tried a different tack. "In America people have to buy their own tickets, the government doesn't buy them for us."

"The problem is, you don't respect China," Lin returned to the attack.

"Secretary Brown has just completed a very important visit to China. It was to improve relations between our two countries. You don't want your mistake to harm those relations?" he asked. It was true the visit had been significant. Brown had disclosed that the Carter administration was prepared to sell China some nonlethal American military hardware. Lin was trying to manipulate my feelings of guilt, a common technique in struggle sessions.

Tang, who had taken off his green uniform jacket, joined the assault. "You are a bad element," he hissed, using a phrase usually reserved for reactionaries. "Of the forty correspondents on the trip, you are the only one who has given us trouble." Here was another of the standard techniques, isolating the victim.

Then Lin dredged up the past, the Chinese inquisitor's ultimate weapon. "You have had a bad attitude ever since you came to China. You caused trouble for the Information Department on your first visit to Peking."

I knew exactly what Lin was referring to, an incident that happened during a trip in August 1977, but Lin wasn't even in China then, he was stationed in the Chinese Embassy in Mexico. So he must have read about it in my dossier. In China, nothing is thrown away—not old bits of rag, twisted pieces of metal, scraps of paper, and especially not information. The earlier episode had occurred when I wanted to send a story to New York but discovered that the press card the Information Department had prepared for me listed the wrong filing address. The mistake had been inadvertently made by the State Department in Washington which passed on the wrong information to the Chinese. Instead of the telex number for *The Times* in New York, the State Department had provided my own incoming cable address in Hong Kong. When I pointed out the error to the Information Department officer accompanying me, he flew into a rage.

"China does not make mistakes," he pronounced categorically. "You are an imperialist trying to impose your will on the Chinese people." He was not mollified when an American diplomat admitted it was the State Department's fault and we discovered similar errors had been made on the press cards of the reporters for *The Washington Post, The Los Angeles Times,* and *Newsweek.*

By the time Lin recalled this past transgression from my dossier, I realized my cause was lost. "Mr. Lin, I will happily pay for the ticket, it is a small matter," I said, trying to sound conciliatory. But this wasn't enough; the guilty must confess fully. The Chinese are very formalistic. Even though the government has decided a person is guilty, he must confess to make it clear that justice has been done.

"I will not accept your money," Lin said, contempt showing on his face. "You must apologize and pay it to our hosts in Shanghai, whom you have offended."

By this time the discussion had dragged on for several hours, and it was after midnight. The two Shanghai officials who had originally come to see me that afternoon were asleep in rooms on a different floor of the hotel, billeted there for the duration of Brown's visit. I wasn't sure which they themselves preferred—sleep or a middle-of-the-night apology. But we marched together downstairs to their room, woke the two men, and after they pulled on their clothes, I handed over the money and apologized.

"You should draw conclusions from your behavior and improve your attitude," Lin chastised me as I started back for my room, exhausted, angry, and frightened.

It was only a minor encounter, I realized later, I suffered no harm, but it gave me a better appreciation for the accounts some Chinese acquaintances told of what it had been like to undergo a real struggle session. And millions of Chinese had been put through these pulverizing, humiliating, and terrifying experiences over the past three decades to purify them for the revolution. There were many targets: former landlords and capitalists, of course, but also professors, journalists, and lawyers, labeled as rightists, Christian ministers, even workers, peasants, and students who joined the wrong political faction.

A short, round-faced thirty-five-year-old former Red Guard with wavy hair and a high-pitched voice, Lo, recalled the two years he spent undergoing interrogation, much of it in struggle sessions. The questioning took place in a specially built prison run by the Public Security Ministry in a remote mountainous area in Jiangxi province, in central China. Lo was confined to a tiny mud hut by himself, with one guard stationed inside his cell and another just outside the door. Even at night a light was kept burning to monitor his activity. Lo was forbidden to talk with the guards, or with any of the other prisoners in the camp; hence for the entire two years, he said, the only words he heard were those of his inquisitors and other inmates when they shouted at him in struggle sessions.

Lo was accused of being a member of an ultra-radical group that seized control of the Foreign Ministry during the height of the Cultural Revolution. He didn't deny he had participated in the takeover, one of the most sensational Red Guard actions, but he claimed his group had followed direct orders from Jiang Qing. In 1972, when he was detained, she was still Mao's wife and at the height of her power. But Lin Biao, the Defense Minister and Mao's putative heir, had just died in a plane crash after trying to assassinate the Chairman, and the Public Security Ministry wanted Lo to admit that it was really Lin who gave the command to occupy the Foreign Ministry. The police were compiling a document for the Central Committee to use to discredit Lin.

Throughout his two years in the prison, the interrogators were always the same four men—two from the Public Security Ministry and two from the security section of the Foreign Ministry. They had accompanied him by train from Peking after his arrest.

"They would start every day at eight A.M., to twelve P.M., then from two P.M. to five P.M. and again in the evenings from eight P.M. to ten P.M.," Lo recalled. "They would never interrogate me when their stomachs were empty," he added with a laugh. He told me his story over a glass of beer in a small restaurant in Canton where we had met during a stopover I made in that southern city. Lo spoke dispassionately about his experience. The Chinese are a sober, unemotive people, and, like most Chinese I knew, he had a way of understating the horror of his misadventures.

"It was not fair questioning," Lo recalled. "They wanted to squeeze things out of me which just didn't happen. They wanted me to write a confession according to their version of events. It didn't do any good to deny it. Whenever I refused, they put me into a struggle session with other prisoners.

"Sometimes they held the struggle sessions in a pigsty," Lo went on. The guards would shove him down among the grunting animals. "They forced me to kneel on the dirt floor, with all the shit, and they held my head down so my nose practically was in the stuff. You weren't allowed to look up. Reactionaries aren't supposed to be proud. The police interrogators would say, 'Who ordered you to take over the Foreign Ministry?' When I said Jiang Qing, they would have everyone jump up and shout at me, 'You are slandering Chairman Mao.' Some of the other prisoners had to hit me and spit on me. If they didn't do it, the guards would criticize them for their bad attitude and they would be struggled with also.

"Actually, I was fortunate. They never beat me too badly. To get you to confess, the Communists prefer to use psychological pressure." But Lo recalled when he had taken part in a struggle session where the inmates beat a former leftist cadre from the Overseas Chinese Affairs Commission who refused to confess. "We pounded and kicked him so hard he spit blood. A few days later he died," Lo remembered.

While Lo was in the prison, he also related, three prisoners committed suicide. "They couldn't stand the pressure and humiliation. One slashed his wrists with some glass, another slit his throat, the third one hanged himself. They always announced it over the loudspeaker. The camp commander said, 'They died for fear their crimes would be discovered.'" Lo was anxious to know whether his father and mother had been affected by his arrest. But he never received any mail from home. Only after he was released did he learn that all his father's and mother's letters had been returned by the prison authorities.

As the inquisition wore on, the police promised Lo that if he admitted he had acted on Lin Biao's orders, they would release him immediately. But he declined. Finally they wrote out a confession for him.

"We had to rehearse it. First I had to memorize the whole thing, so there would be no mistakes when I spoke in front of the struggle session. They would tell me, 'This sentence you must say very sadly. This paragraph you must say with real emotion.' In some places they wrote 'pause' for the other prisoners to talk. In other places they wrote 'slogans' so people could shout at me. Once I couldn't remember what came next. The guards said I was trying to cover up; actually I just forgot. Eventually they gave me the paper so I could read it.

"The first time I was put in a struggle session, after fifteen minutes I felt numb, I was so scared. But eventually I got used to it. When they didn't beat me very hard, it was just like a pig going to market. Since my head was bowed and I couldn't see anybody, all there was was a lot of noise and shouting."

Finally one day the guards told him he would be released. "I never knew why. They told me, 'You are an enemy of the people, but your attitude is good.' "

Almost every Chinese I got to know during my twenty months in Peking had a tale of political persecution, many far worse than Lo's. From their stories it seemed as if a whole generation of Chinese (and 650 million of China's one billion people have been born since 1949) had known nothing but arbitrary accusations, violent swings in the political line, unjustified arrests, torture, and imprisonment. Few Chinese I knew felt free from the fear of physical or psychological abuse and a pervasive sense of injustice. There was Lihua, the girl who at the age of six was driven out of Peking and had to watch as her mother was beaten to death, and Bing, the thirteen-year-old who felt compelled to denounce her father, and Hong, who was thrown into jail because the drunken son of a general took a fancy to her. During a banquet in the provincial city of Hefei for Governor Harry Hughes of Maryland, I was seated next to a petite woman reporter from the New China News Agency, Zhang Wei. Her tiny frame, her short hair, an unlined face, and a perpetual girlish smile made her look much younger than her fifty years. Conversation with Chinese officials you haven't met before at formal dinners is often strained, so to try to find a safe beginning, I asked what her husband did.

"My husband is dead, he was a victim of the Gang of Four," she replied without elaboration, the smile never leaving the corners of her mouth. It was a simple statement of fact, a commonplace for China, shocking only to a foreigner.

At lunch one day in the Peking Hotel, an American businesswoman who was involved in bringing Chinese musical and theatrical groups to the United States invited me to join her and a woman pianist from the Peking Philharmonic Orchestra. The Chinese musician had a narrow, sad face and was silent

347

for long periods of time. Before the Cultural Revolution, she explained, her husband was a leading violinist with the orchestra.

"But one day he made a mistake," she said in a flat voice. "During the Cultural Revolution the streets were a sea of red, all the shops were covered with red banners and their windows were filled with Mao's books. My husband was shopping with a friend. He remarked it was impossible to tell which store was a restaurant and which a barber shop." His friend then informed on him, and the police arrested him.

"When I tried to see him and find out what had happened, the police said, 'It is not good to ask,' " the pianist continued, putting down her chopsticks. "Later they came to see me. 'Your husband is a counterrevolutionary. You should divorce him. If you don't draw a clear line between yourselves, it will look like you support him in his crimes.' I had no choice. Usually it is very difficult to get a divorce, but my *danwei* approved immediately." Her husband ended up spending ten years in prison. After his release, he did not want to remarry her.

Across the room from us, eating at another table, I noticed, was China's leading pianist, Liu Shikun, a tall, gaunt man with brush-cut hair and black horn-rimmed spectacles. Liu had free access to the Peking Hotel because he had married a daughter of Ye Jianying, the octogenarian chairman of the National People's Congress. During the Cultural Revolution (from 1966 to 1969) Liu had originally been a leader of a virulently radical faction of Red Guards who paraded the leaders of the Peking city Party committee through the streets with placards around their necks. But later he became embroiled in a factional dispute with another leftist group, and they deliberately broke his hands. Playing Chopin, Mozart, and Beethoven on the piano, after all, was a bourgeois art. Then, for reasons never made clear, Liu was also thrown into prison for nine years. The only way he could practice his fingering exercises was on a bamboo shoulder pole, a fellow musician told me. Since the overthrow of the radicals in 1976, Liu has resumed his musical career.

There are statistics on the scale of persecution in China during the Cultural Revolution—since the arrest of the Gang of Four, the *People's Daily* has been a cornucopia of information. But the figures are contradictory, and fragmentary, and one could hardly expect the police and all the Red Guard groups to keep accurate records of how many people they arrested, tortured, or killed. So the numbers are only suggestive. The *People's Daily* once calculated that 100 million people were affected by the Cultural Revolution, one out of every nine Chinese at the time. Agence France Press, whose correspondents in Peking were among the best-informed and hardest-working I knew, reported in 1979 that a reliable Chinese source had told the agency that 400,000 people died as a result of the Cultural Revolution in the late 1960s.

During a tour of Fujian province, along the southeast coast, the Deputy Governor, Wen Fusan, told a group of us foreign newsmen that in the mountainous rural district where he worked during the Cultural Revolution, 1,700 people out of a population of two million had been beaten to death or committed suicide. If his district was average for China, that would mean more like 850,000 deaths nationwide. In a speech in 1980, Deng Xiaoping stated that 2.9 million people had been rehabilitated since the end of the Cultural Revolution, and "many more whose cases were not put on file," he added ambiguously. In one article, the *People's Daily* declared that 60 percent of all those accused of being counterrevolutionaries were falsely charged.

The official 20,000-word indictment against Jiang Qing, her cohorts in the Gang of Four, and the generals who participated in the plot to kill Mao with Lin Biao charged that they were personally responsible for wrongfully persecuting 750,000 people, 34,380 of whom died as a result, including six men who were mayors or deputy mayors of Peking and Shanghai. In the biggest single case mentioned in the indictment, over 346,000 cadres and others were falsely accused of belonging to a secret party in Inner Mongolia; 16,222 of them were killed. During the trial of the Gang of Four, the New China News Agency disclosed that a former Minister of Public Security, Xie Fuzhi, had instigated a wave of terror in Peking during late August and September 1966. In a forty-day period, "1,700 people were beaten to death, 33,600 households were searched and ransacked, and 85,000 people were driven out of the capital."* The list could go on and on. The indictment against the Gang of Four also accused them of persecuting 142,000 cadres and teachers under the Ministry of Education, 53,000 scientists and technicians in the Academy of Sciences, and over 500 of the 674 professors in China's medical schools, some of whom died as a consequence.

The Gang's trial itself produced graphic testimony of the terror of the times. The prosecution in the special high court set up to hear the case played parts of twenty tape recordings made at the interrogation of a sixty-seven-year-old professor, Zhang Zhongyi. Professor Zhang, who was already suffering from liver cancer, had been arrested because before 1949 he had taught at the now defunct Catholic-run Furen University in Peking. Wang Guangmei, the wife of Liu Shaoqi, China's head of state and Mao's chief target in the Cultural Revolution, had been a student in the school. The professor didn't know Miss Wang, the prosecution said, but Jiang Qing had organized a "special group" to gather material to prove she was an American spy and demanded that the team "squeeze" evidence out of Professor Zhang. Although he was confined to a hospital bed and had to be fed intravenously to keep him alive, Professor Zhang was interrogated twenty-one times dur-

*NCNA, December 23, 1980.

ing the twenty-seven days he was held, the last session alone lasting fifteen hours. After that, he died.

"People in the public gallery reacted with shock at the wailing of the aged professor during the interrogation," the New China News Agency said in its account of the trial. (I had to depend on the official Chinese reports of the trial because foreign journalists were not permitted to attend.) There were "moans and groans as the patient struggled to get up from the bed and was forced down again," the press agency reported, "orders to Professor Zhang to take medicine, shouts of 'Speak up, quickly,' and the confused answers of the dying man." Based in part on the professor's confession, Jiang Qing drew up a report labeling Miss Wang an agent of the U.S. Office of Strategic Services during World War Two. It was used to arrest her and Liu.

Political persecution under the Communists did not begin with the Cultural Revolution. In the land-reform campaign in 1949–51, in which land was redistributed to poor peasants, as many as three million former landlords, Kuomintang officials, and army and police officers were executed, according to one of the best-informed foreigners in China.* Mao himself gave a somewhat lower figure in a 1957 speech, reportedly stating that 800,000 "enemies of the people" were "liquidated" up to 1954.** In the "Campaign Against Counterrevolutionaries" in 1955–56, another four million people were investigated, documents circulated by Red Guards during the Cultural Revolution indicate. Then in the Anti-Rightist campaign in 1957–58, which followed the Communists' abortive experiment with more open expression in the Hundred Flowers period, several million students, teachers, scientists, writers, lawyers, and doctors—China's intellectuals—were sent to work in the countryside or sentenced to labor camps. Only in 1978, two years after Mao's death and the downfall of the Gang of Four, were the last 110,000 of these rightists released from the camps, a former prisoner told me in Peking. Many more died in prison, the ex-inmate said.

But where these earlier campaigns were aimed at particular groups, in the Cultural Revolution everyone became a potential target as the Party itself came under attack by its Chairman and the country was thrown into a madcap civil war. The slightest misstep could lead to arrest, imprisonment, or disgrace. A worker in a Peking chemical plant I met aboard a bus said that his father had been awarded three years in jail when he wrote a wall poster attacking the ousted chief of state, Liu. His father, who had only three years of schooling, had thought he was following instructions from his Party secre-

*Jacques Guillermaz, *La Chine Populaire*, 3rd ed. (Paris: Presses Universitaires de France, 1964), p. 47. General Guillermaz was French military attaché in China between 1937 and 1949 and again from 1964 to 1966.
**Roderick MacFarquhar, *The Hundred Flowers Campaign and the Chinese Intellectuals* (New York: Frederick Praeger, 1960), p. 270.

tary. But he accidently got one character wrong, and an alert cadre accused him of secretly slandering Chairman Mao.

A scientist related what he thought might have been the most absurd miscarriage of justice of the whole Cultural Revolution. Because Mao and Jiang Qing banned almost all literature except the Chairman's own works, a series of underground novels sprang up as popular entertainment. Some were serious autobiographical accounts of the sufferings of the period; others were merely serialized detective stories or pornographic romances told as oral epics. One thriller, entitled *Tales of the Plum Flower Society,* recounted a twenty-year effort to crack a Kuomintang spy network inside the Academy of Sciences. The chief Nationalist agent was a scientist named Peng Jiamu.

By coincidence, my acquaintance said, there existed a real scientist with the same name in the Institute of Optics and Precision Instruments in Changchun, in the northeast. The institute, one of China's most prestigious, had produced the country's first electron microscope in the 1950s and was a center of research for the defense industry. But in the Cultural Revolution a fanatic radical named Shan Guizhang was put in charge of the institute. He believed the character in the story was not just fictional but the real live Peng. As a result, 166 scientists in the institute were arrested as spies along with local accountants, policemen, workers, and even nursery attendants. A later dispatch by the New China News Agency, without giving any of the background of the incident, said Shan had "enforced fascist dictatorship" over the institute—"some of the people arrested were beaten to death, while others committed suicide." The scientists were slandered as "pigs, dogs, and devils with black hearts and rotten guts." Shan's proof that someone was a secret agent was that the accused either had a radio or camera at home or could speak a foreign language. Shan was rewarded by promotion to the provincial Party committee.

What made the persecutions of the Cultural Revolution more nightmarish for many Chinese than the earlier campaigns was the totality of it—it engulfed not only individuals but whole families; it divided each office, factory, and school into factions which are still contentious fifteen years later, and as happened in my brush with the authorities in Shanghai, the truth was a futile defense. Zheng Peidi, an English teacher at Peking University, slight, with delicate hands and a warm, likable smile, ran headlong into all these troubles.

"As we say in China, I have a very complicated family background," she told me with a self-effacing laugh. One of her mother's brothers was a Minister of Defense on Taiwan; another relative had been a dashing Communist movie producer in Shanghai in the 1930s who had introduced Jiang Qing into the Party and had an affair with her. "He could do everything, dance, ride, hunt, and they lived together," Peidi recounted. When she was an undergraduate at Peking University, she had mentioned her family connection to Jiang Qing to her roommates as student gossip. She graduated in 1962, was appointed a teacher at the school, and the story seemed forgotten.

But after the outbreak of the Cultural Revolution, Peidi found herself in a faction opposed to the one headed by the most prominent campus ultraleftist, Nieh Yuanzi, a woman cadre in the philosophy department. Nieh had composed the first wall poster in the Cultural Revolution, criticizing the university administration as revisionist, and Mao had ordered it published in the *People's Daily*. The Red Guards were looking for any excuse to attack Peidi's group, she recalled, and one of her former roommates informed on her. To the radicals, the story of her relative's affair with Jiang Qing was a malicious insult to China's leadership. Peidi was arrested and taken to what was called a "cowshed," a makeshift prison, in reality an old, small single-story classroom building that the Red Guards surrounded with coils of wire.

"There were twenty prisoners in my room, about two hundred in the whole building," Peidi remembered. "Most of them were famous older professors and the Party secretaries of their departments. I felt quite out of place." Like Lo, the former Red Guard, Peidi told her story with modesty, understating the terror and repulsion she felt.

"Actually, I was lucky," she said. "I was beaten only the day I arrived. They told me to confess the story was only a rumor, but when I said it was a fact, they accused me of slander and beat me." After that, she spent most of her time memorizing quotations from Chairman Mao.

"Every morning they would come into the room and make us recite a quotation by number—number thirty-five, number thirteen. I was young and my memory was good. So I could do it. I was also careful to keep my head bowed. But some of the older professors had studied in the United States and their Chinese wasn't very good. They couldn't memorize well enough to please the Red Guards. So they got beaten, with rubber whips, boards, bicycle chains. One professor was beaten every day till he died."

When Peidi was arrested in 1967, she had given birth to a son only a month before and was still nursing him. "The Red Guards said I couldn't see him anymore and gave me shots to stop my milk."

Her brother, an agricultural engineer, tried to visit her and complained that she was being treated inhumanely. He was locked up, too, for his insolence.

Meantime, her mother didn't know what had happened to Peidi. When she received an invitation from the Red Guards to see her daughter, she arrived only to be incarcerated in the building's cellar. The radicals tricked her into writing out a confession about the family connection with Jiang Qing by telling her Peidi had already admitted everything. When her mother, a "proud, old-fashioned intellectual," in Peidi's words, was sent back to her own office, she was put under what was called "supervision by the masses" and made to sweep the floors and clean the toilets for a year.

Nor did Peidi's father escape the dragnet. A prominent construction engineer, he was placed under house arrest. His driver recalled that once in the car he had complained that foreign can openers were better than Chinese can openers.

Peidi's husband was far away and couldn't help. He had been drafted into the army to work in Tibet as an English-language interpreter with Indian prisoners after China's 1962 border war with New Delhi. Only two years after her arrest was he able to get home leave and try to see her.

"The Red Guards wouldn't let him into the compound where we were kept," she recalled. "But he put on his army uniform and walked in. At the time the army enjoyed high prestige with the radicals because of Lin Biao." He managed to find her, but when a Red Guard became suspicious he whipped out a new single volume of Mao's quotations which had just been published by the army and wasn't yet available to civilians. He gave it to Peidi and said in a loud voice, "Here, see that you study this."

Only in 1971 was Peidi finally released, though she was also placed under "supervision" and made to live with the family of a politically reliable professor. "It was a very strange time," she told me one day sitting in the cafeteria in the lobby of the Peking Hotel. "None of my friends knew what crime I was supposed to have committed because the Red Guards wouldn't let me say what had happened."

Today many of the teachers and cadres who were involved in imprisoning her are still at Peking University. She has to work with them every day, and Peidi has learned to hide her feelings. Her only revenge was small. When she and her husband had a daughter several years ago, they named her Na, meaning "Silent."

Foreigners visiting Chinese offices, factories, and schools are usually unaware of how these factional divisions have persisted and how great a role personal vendettas play in everyday life. I displayed my own ignorance on my first trip to China in 1977. After eating lunch in a restaurant in Canton, I asked for the bill using the standard phrase I had been taught in Chinese textbooks and had heard in Taiwan, *suan-zhang,* or "settle the account." The pigtailed waitress stared at me angrily for a moment, then rebuked me sharply.

"We don't say that anymore in China, it isn't polite," she said.

What she meant, I learned, was that settling accounts with your friends and colleagues has become a serious national problem and so the old term for asking for the check has become an embarrassment.

China's leaders were not spared the terror. When Deng Xiaoping was purged the first time in the Cultural Revolution as a capitalist roader, he was sent to a rural cadre school in Jiangsu province, in central China, where he worked as a waiter, Chinese say. Liu Shaoqi, the disgraced head of state, was dispatched secretly to Kaifeng, the capital of Henan province, where he was kept under guard until he died of pneumonia in 1969. Two of his sons died of injuries or paralysis after being imprisoned or taken to struggle sessions, the Chinese press has since reported. Liu's widow, Wang Guangmei, a sophisticated, Western-educated woman who had been Jiang Qing's rival for the title of China's first lady, was confined to China's most top-secret prison, Qin Cheng Number One. Located inconspicuously near a verdant hot-springs resort once favored by the Empress Dowager Ci Xi in a suburb of Peking, it held about five hundred of China's leaders purged in the Cultural Revolution, including several who are now once again on the Politburo. Each was confined to a small cell by himself and forbidden to talk to other inmates; some prisoners went a decade without conversation. Every effort was made to ensure that no information leaked out about Qin Cheng. Until Mao's death and the downfall of the radicals, virtually no prisoners were ever released from it; inmates' families were not notified where they were; no visits were allowed, and prisoners were known to the guards only by numbers, never by their names.

I first learned about Qin Cheng from an exposé written by Wei Jingsheng, a former Red Guard and son of a high cadre turned dissident. His article was smuggled out of China in early 1979 by the wife of a French diplomat who had become close friends with Wei. She offered it to *The New York Times* bureau chief in Paris, Flora Lewis, who in turn passed it on to me. At almost the same time I reported Wei's account of the prison, he was arrested. The Chinese media have still never mentioned Qin Cheng by name, but the New China News Agency did once admit that there was a special prison outside Peking where thirty-four senior leaders were tortured to death, twenty maimed, and sixty went insane during the Cultural Revolution.

According to Wei and others, Qin Cheng had a series of peculiar regulations. Prisoners were required to sleep facing the glass-paneled door to their cells so the guards could keep watch over them. If an inmate turned over in his sleep, the guards would wake him. The Panchen Lama, the secondmost holy figure in Tibetan Buddhism after the exiled Dalai Lama, developed a swollen infected ear after sleeping on one side for over ten years. Only after he went berserk and tried to strangle his jailers when they woke him in the middle of the night was he permitted to turn over. Physical beatings were common, Wei contended; prisoners were kept on near-starvation rations, and some recalcitrant inmates were punished by being chained and left unable to move for so long their limbs were paralyzed. When Miss Wang was finally released in 1978, an inexplicable two years after the Gang of Four was arrested, her hair had started falling out, her back was bent double, and her hands and legs were palsied, mutual friends said.

One prisoner in Qin Cheng was a very bright and innovative woman theatrical director named Sun Weishi. Sun's father, an early Communist activist in the Shanghai underground, was killed in the 1930s and she was adopted by Zhou Enlai, who had no children of his own. Precisely why she was arrested is unclear—perhaps it was professional jealousy on the part of Jiang Qing, who fancied herself China's leading authority on drama. But Sun was thrown into Qin Cheng in March 1968 and died the following October after prolonged torture. Zhou, a truly popular figure among Chinese for his supposed efforts to moderate Mao's wilder policies during the Cultural Revolution, was unable or unwilling to save her.* When he found out she had died, he requested an autopsy, but when the medical personnel he sent to the prison arrived, Sun's body had been cremated and they couldn't even find the ashes. All the guards responsible for her death had already been transferred elsewhere. The man who told me about the incident was a friend of Sun's and a prisoner in Qin Cheng, an American, Sidney Rittenberg. A gregarious, charming native of Charleston, South Carolina, Sid first went to China as a Chinese interpreter with the U.S. Army in 1945. Sid's strong left-wing sympathies—he had helped organize southern textile-mill workers in the United States during the Depression—persuaded him to stay on in China after 1949, one of only about a dozen Americans to do so. His remarkable fluency in Chinese, his natural warmth, and his shrewd appreciation of the role of *guan-xi* in China made him a valuable conduit between Communist officialdom and the small community of maverick foreigners. But in the Cultural Revolution, Sid's usual enthusiasm and radical leanings got him in trouble. He was accused of participating in a faction that attacked Prime Minister Zhou and was kept in prison from 1968 to 1978.**

Qin Cheng is still in existence, Chinese friends said. Its most prominent inmate today is Jiang Qing. In his account of the prison, Wei had written, "We might ask the high cadres who have come out of Qin Cheng, When you suppressed the rights of others to express freely their political views, did you secure your own? When you persecuted others using political pretexts, did you foresee yourselves being subjected to the same kind of persecution?"

When they emerged from years of exile or prison after Mao's death and returned to power, Peking's current leaders like Deng Xiaoping clearly had a personal stake in preventing a recurrence of the trauma of the Cultural

*Zhou's ineffectiveness in protecting his own adopted daughter, of whom he was said to be very fond, raises questions about his real role in the Cultural Revolution. Most Chinese gloss over his crucial actions in 1966 when his votes with Mao in narrowly divided Party meetings enabled the Chairman to purge Liu and Deng and carry out the Cultural Revolution. Zhou awaits a full biographical study.

**Sid, a gifted raconteur, has been at work on his own memoirs about life in Communist China and Qin Cheng prison.

Revolution. They also knew that the persecutions of the past decade had shattered popular confidence in the Communist Party. So one of their first priorities was.to create a more equitable system of justice, or restore "socialist legality," in their own term. Hence in 1979 the Communists promulgated China's first criminal code since 1949. It promised that trials would be public; it prohibited the courts from using forced confessions as evidence; it gave defendants the right to a lawyer—the legal profession had been abolished in 1958—and it fixed strict limits on the time the police could detain suspects before bringing them to trial. Ominously, however, the new criminal code and a revised constitution passed in 1978 made no provision for judicial independence. Instead, the constitution reaffirmed that "the Communist Party of China is the core of leadership of the whole Chinese people" and that "citizens must support the leadership of the Communist Party." In other words, the Party is the law. And while China's tiny group of 2,000 lawyers was allowed to come out of the closet, the National People's Congress in 1980 passed regulations declaring them to be "state legal workers" who must "protect the interests of the state" as much as their clients. They should not act like their counterparts in the West and get bogged down in arguing against the prosecution. China's chief prosecutor gave an indication of how Peking regarded the new legal system when he disclosed in 1980 that 95 percent of all those arrested in the past year had been convicted. In essence, for those people who have been arrested and undergone police examination, by the time they get to trial innocence is no longer an issue. The question is, were the proper procedures followed to prevent arbitrary arrests, frame-ups, and torture. That was what the Chinese people hoped.

The trial of Jiang Qing, her cohorts in the Gang of Four, and five senior generals who had been associated with Lin Biao was to be the showpiece of the new legal system. The trial carried high risks—it couldn't help but look like personal vengeance and it would give Miss Jiang a political platform she had not had since her arrest in October 1976. But, friends said, Deng believed the trial would demonstrate to Chinese that he would not stoop to the low road the radicals had taken in dealing with their adversaries and he wanted to win back popular support from many disillusioned Chinese.

A few weeks before the trial began in November 1980, I accidentally encountered the general appointed deputy president of the special thirty-five-judge high court set up to hear the case, the most sensational in China's legal history. We were both at a reception in the Great Hall of the People for China's national day. The general, Wu Xiuquan, was a deputy chief of staff of the army and was considered China's leading authority on the Soviet military. He had studied in Moscow in the 1920s and had accompanied the Long March in the 1930s. His appearance was unmistakable, with an unusu-ally capacious girth for a Chinese and a long jowly face that reminded me of an elderly basset hound. General Wu, who was seventy-one at the time, had no legal training, but he had been purged in 1967, another victim of the Cultural Revolution like most of the judges. When he spoke, I had noticed on previous occasions, he was cautious, with the circumspection of an old-fashioned mandarin, revealing as little as possible, often only chuckling at a questioner's probe.

But when I asked him if he thought Jiang Qing and the others were guilty of the charges against them—they were variously accused of persecuting large numbers of officials, plotting to seize state power, trying to kill Mao, and engineer an armed rebellion in Shanghai—he replied without hesitation, "They are guilty of terrible crimes."

Could they be sentenced to death then? I pressed him, conscious of a retinue of his aides in army green surrounding us. "They might be," General Wu said. "Ten years in prison is hardly enough punishment for such people."

It was an extraordinary moment. If the deputy chief judge was already convinced of the defendants' guilt, what kind of trial would it be? The answer came a few weeks later. It proved to be a trial disguised as Peking opera, a polished, professional performance complete with actors, costumes, court intrigues, and a well-written script, an utterly Chinese pageant. The signs of the trial as theater, as a morality play, were everywhere. The entire proceedings, a Chinese journalist told me, had actually gone through two rehearsals, the second reviewed on videotape by the Politburo. The Party wanted to be sure there would be no slips. The rehearsals explained why it took almost two months between the time the government announced the start of the trial and its commencement. Miss Jiang, the vitriolic, sixty-seven-year-old onetime movie actress, and Zhang Chunqiao, a former member of the Politburo Standing Committee and mayor of Shanghai, refused to confess as criminals are expected to. Instead, my journalist source informed me, Miss Jiang had tried to defend herself by saying she had only carried out the orders of her husband. "I was Chairman Mao's dog, whoever he told me to bite, I bit," she said in one of the dress rehearsals. Zhang simply remained silent, as he did later during the official trial. He evidently calculated he would not be allowed a legitimate chance to defend himself, that he had already been adjudged guilty, so the most honorable course was not to cooperate.

Otherwise the trial went as scheduled. In the large, converted auditorium at Number 1 Justice Road the other eight defendants pleaded guilty, some even adopting the language of the court and referring to themselves as counterrevolutionaries. Chen Boda, a frail, stooped seventy-six-year-old man who for many years had served as Mao's political secretary and ghost writer, admitted he had concocted an infamous editorial in the *People's Daily* entitled "Sweep Away All Monsters and Demons." "I don't oppose my own death by firing squad," said Chen, who had to hobble into the courtroom on crutches. "But that might be letting me off too lightly. Chopping off my head might be better." Wang Hongwen, the forty-five-year-old former Shanghai textile-mill security guard whom Mao catapulted to be third in the Party hierarchy behind only himself and Zhou Enlai, rushed to tell the court how he had collaborated with Miss Jiang in trying to block Deng's appointment in 1975 as first deputy prime minister.

The prosecutors and judges all sat together on a raised platform overlooking the defendants. The only visible difference between them was that the prosecutors were dressed in light-gray Mao suits, the judges in dark gray. At the end of each day's session, a prosecutor declared that the charge being heard had been proved, the presiding judge concurred, and the defendant involved was marched out with military precision by a blue-uniformed policeman. The defense attorneys for five of the ten defendants—the other five were said not to have requested counsel—were relegated to small tables in a corner of the room. At no point in the excerpts of the trial shown on the nightly television news—the footage was also edited by the Politburo—did a defense lawyer raise an objection, ask to cross-examine a government witness, or call a defense witness. Their only action was to plead for leniency because their clients had confessed.*

Enhancing the impression of a staged performance, the television cameras often showed the prosecutors, judges, and government witnesses reading from printed sheets. Private conversations and telephone calls between the accused that took place more than ten years in the past were quoted verbatim by the prosecutors, suggesting the Party has an elaborate tape-recording service that bugs its own leaders. Where witnesses were too old, or apparently uncooperative, and in two cases where they were actually already dead, their testimony was read for them by popular announcers from Peking Radio. One of the deceased was Mao's private secretary, Zhang Yufeng, a comely woman with whom he reportedly had a romantic involvement in his later years. She had committed suicide when she was arrested after Mao's death by Hua Guofeng, the new Party chairman, who feared she knew too much, Chinese said. It was as if ten years from now Richard Nixon was posthumously impeached for the Watergate scandal and Walter Cronkite read the testimony of the President's former aides like H. R. Haldeman and John Ehrlichman.

When the trial began, Chinese were excited by it the way Americans are by a presidential election. A dour middle-aged woman who ran the elevator in our apartment building and worked for the Ministry of Public Security

---

*Miss Jiang was originally assigned China's most prominent criminal lawyer, Ma Rongjie, on the order of the Ministry of Justice, I was told by a Chinese friend shortly before the trial began. But when I disclosed this in The Times, the party leadership was furious at the leak. Ma was taken off the case and placed under house arrest, he later told a mutual acquaintance. Miss Jiang ended up without an attorney.

asked if she could sneak in for a glimpse of the first night on television. But as Chinese watched the trial progress they rapidly grew skeptical and indifferent. On a Saturday evening during the middle of the six-week-long trial, we went to our friends the Wangs for dinner. At 7:30 P.M., when the daily coverage of the trial began, no one in the family moved to turn on their new television set which we had helped buy. Only at eight o'clock, when they expected an American-made series about the exploits of a squad of commandos during World War Two, *Garrison's Guerrillas,* did Li flick the switch. Father, mother, and daughter groaned loudly when they found the television station had delayed their program for extended news about the trial. To me, as a foreigner, it was a key day in the trial. A general was testifying how he had supposedly plotted in 1971 to blow up a train Mao was riding in with bombs, bazookas, and rockets.

"Everyone knows it was really Mao who gave the orders in the Cultural Revolution and it is he who should be on trial," Li explained when I asked about his lack of interest. Besides, he added, "the defendants look so pitiful, you almost begin to feel sorry for them." He personally detested Miss Jiang —she aroused a visceral distaste among many Chinese with her posturing, her arrogance, the dictatorship she had exercised over culture, and her own privileged life-style, complete with private villas, screenings of old Greta Garbo movies, and her wardrobe of Western dresses, all forbidden to the masses. But to Li and other Chinese the trial had come to look like another struggle session, the same unfair harassment which was all too familiar and which they wanted to see ended.

"No one can have illusions anymore about what socialist legality means," Li said sadly as we left that night. "It means more of the same, only more polite. They gave her a trial first. If Jiang Qing had won, she would have just thrown the others in prison." I thought about Li's comments as we drove home. With the trial the Communists had squandered an opportunity to show they were capable of dispensing justice and recoup some of the prestige they had forfeited with the persecutions of the Cultural Revolution.

When the verdict finally came—after a month's delay to allow the Politburo time to debate the sentence—it was almost an anticlimax. Jiang Qing and Zhang Chunqiao, the two who refused to confess, were sentenced to death, but with a two-year reprieve to see if they reformed. The two-year stay of execution is a Chinese Communist legal innovation. The other eight defendants were given prison terms ranging from sixteen years to life. Some Chinese considered the verdicts fair, since Mao was really to blame and it was time to exorcise the ghost of the Cultural Revolution. But other Chinese I knew grumbled; to them it was another example of the Communists' double standard—one set of rules for the masses, another for Party members. A thirty-year-old factory worker with a wispy mustache was especially bitter. "Punishments do not reach up to the lords," he said, quoting an ancient adage. His younger brother, who was still awaiting his job assignment after finishing high school two years before, had gotten into an altercation with some other neighborhood youths that led to a fight and the fatal stabbing of one of them. Exactly who was to blame was unclear, the worker contended. But his brother had been taken before a public rally in a sports stadium, with a howling crowd of 10,000 people as a jury, and convicted of murder. Then he was executed on the spot by a shot in the back of his head, the standard method of administering the death penalty in China.

It was one of about sixty executions I read about in the press or heard about from friends during 1980 and kept track of in a special file. The majority were for murder or rape, but some were for lesser offenses: a Peking bank cashier was executed for embezzling 125,000 yuan ($83,000); a nineteen-year-old in the northeast city of Harbin was sentenced to death for robbing a passenger on a bus and then assaulting a policeman who tried to arrest him. The real total of executions was undoubtedly much higher. During a visit to the coastal city of Xiamen, I spotted several printed posters announcing the execution of a man named Zhang Qingfu, a forty-one-year-old dock worker. Zhang had slashed a friend forty-three times with a vegetable cleaver when he refused to give Zhang a rowboat to escape to one of the small islands outside Xiamen harbor, still occupied by Nationalist troops from Taiwan.*

These executions are part of Peking's effort to stop what Chinese feel has been a growing crime wave since the Cultural Revolution. For years the Communists had boasted to visiting foreigners that they had virtually eliminated crime: reformed the prostitutes, rehabilitated the opium addicts, and improved society to the point where robbery, rape, and murder had disappeared. There was some truth to this—the Communists did put an end to the country's terrible drug addiction problem. But the credulous visitors never noticed that Chinese always carefully lock their bicycles, put broken shards of glass atop the walls around their buildings, and install iron bars in their first-floor windows. It would be equally misleading now to picture the increase in crime in recent years as being as serious as it is in some large American cities like New York, Atlanta, or Houston. But I was surprised by how daring some Chinese had become in defying the police. In quick succession in one winter month, a twenty-one-year-old unemployed man robbed Peking's largest department store of cameras, calculators, and cash worth 10,000 yuan ($6,670), two masked men stuck up a branch of the People's Bank in downtown Peking and shot a teller with a homemade zip gun, and another man tried to steal a fifteen-pound gold imperial seal dating from the

*The biggest island in the group is Quemoy.

sixteenth century from the hallowed Forbidden City before he triggered an electric alarm and was caught. The government has not published nationwide crime figures as it does for grain and steel production. But China's chief prosecutor did disclose that in the first half of 1980 the police had arrested 84,000 criminals, more than half of them for "grave crimes," probably murder and rape.

The prosecutor also confirmed that there has been an increase in white-collar crime. In the first six months of the year, he said, the police had uncovered 10,000 cases of corruption among officials. But, he admitted, "there is still great resistance in dealing with cases that involve state functionaries."

The problem, said a thoughtful historian in the Academy of Social Sciences, is the same as the problem with the Party as a whole. Since Liberation the Communists have gradually lost their revolutionary discipline and become more interested in their own comfort. But the Party also remains an elite—Party cadres run the police, the courts, and the prosecutors' offices. They form an old-boys network. Therefore, unless an official commits a political error like the Gang of Four and is purged, he enjoys a kind of diplomatic immunity from criminal punishment. As an example, he cited a scandal involving a senior army officer who was simultaneously deputy commander of the critical northeastern military region, responsible for China's main defense against the Soviet Union, and Party secretary of Luda, the naval port formerly known as Port Arthur. The officer, Liu Decai, misappropriated 34 million yuan ($23 million) by constructing a total of sixty-four unauthorized buildings for the pleasure of local cadres, including lavish clubs, theaters, guesthouses, and offices at a time when housing for the public was desperately short. Finally, after a series of complaints, the Cabinet and the Party Military Affairs Commission in Peking sent a special team to Luda to investigate. Liu was not arrested or taken to court, and his only punishment was to be removed from his official posts and have his salary cut. He was not even expelled from the Party. Only six lower-ranking cadres caught up in the scam were arrested, and their sentences were heavier the lower their rank. To the historian, it was merely another instance of the Communists' arbitrary justice.

But of all the stories I heard about arbitrary justice and unfair punishment, the most horrifying were those involving the Communists' system of labor camps. Western Sinologists have known about the existence of the camps for years, and a few former inmates, who were among the lucky ones to be released, have left chilling accounts.* But the Western press, Western intel-

*See, for example, Bao Ruo-wang, *Prisoner of Mao* (London: André Deutsch, 1975), and Lai Ying, *The Thirty-Sixth Way* (London: Constable, 1970).

lectuals—including specialists on China—and Western liberal political organizations have not displayed nearly as much interest in the workings of the Chinese labor camps as they have in the Soviet Gulag charted by Alexander Solzhenitsyn. If a Russian writer or artist is banished to Siberia, it is front-page news in Europe and the United States. This is particularly true if the victim is Jewish, given the sensitivities of the Jewish people to persecution and the number of Jews in the West who are descended from or related to the Jews in the Soviet Union. But if a Chinese dissident is exiled to Qinghai, Peking's equivalent of Siberia, the story is cut to a few paragraphs on an inside page or not printed at all. How many Westerners can name three imprisoned Chinese political activists? I sometimes felt there was a double standard—one for the Russians, who are Europeans, another for the Chinese, who are Asians and therefore not supposed to have the same feelings for human rights and life. Or perhaps we didn't want to believe that a country which had produced such a high level of civilization, with poetry and art that touched the sublime, could be so cruel.

Whatever the explanation, it was an old man of seventy, with snow-white hair and a bent back, who first gave me an eyewitness report of the Chinese Gulag. When I met him, through a relative, he was so emaciated that his skin was waxen, strangely transparent, as if you could see straight through to his bones and skull. His fingers were twisted and discolored, some of them reduced to stumpy digits, for he had just been released from a coal mine where he had worked scraping up chunks of black rock with his bare hands for the past twenty-one years. It was not an ordinary mine, but part of a large camp set behind barbed wire with 10,000 inmates, all sentenced to one form or another of what is called *laodong gaizhao,* or more commonly in its abbreviated form, *lao gai,* "reform through labor."

The mine where he worked is located near the city of Datong in Shanxi province, in the northwest. It is only one of hundreds of such labor-reform camps scattered throughout China that I gradually came to learn about from former prisoners like this old man. They are where most ordinary Chinese who fall afoul of the police are kept—plain criminals like thieves, political dissidents, former Kuomintang army officers, and religious leaders. There are regular jails in every city, juvenile reformatories, and a variety of detention centers for people not yet convicted. But 80 percent of all prisoners in China are assigned to the labor camps, the *People's Daily* disclosed in a rare article on the subject.

It is impossible to calculate the exact total of inmates in the camps. Estimates by former convicts range from several hundred thousand to several million. The government refuses to discuss the subject. Repeated requests for information I made to the Information Department of the Foreign Ministry, the Peking city government, the Public Security Ministry, and the Justice

Ministry were all turned down. An official of the Justice Ministry, which administers the courts, said his office had nothing to do with labor reform and it was handled entirely by the police. It was an inadvertent admission of what Chinese know—that many of the convicts sent to the labor camps are not tried at all in the Western sense but merely sentenced by the police. In 1979, despite the government's pledge to improve the legal system, the National People's Congress reissued a tough 1957 decree which gave the Public Security Ministry authority to sentence suspects to "reeducation through labor," or *lao jiao,* without having to go through the courts. On paper the government makes a distinction between this "reeducation through labor" and "reform through labor": the former is supposed to be lighter, noncriminal, with a maximum sentence of three or four years and the offenders convicted under it are to be kept separate from those prisoners given "reform through labor." But in practice, former inmates said, there is little difference.

Take the old man I met. His crime was that he was accused of being an American spy. In his student days he had attended a Presbyterian seminary in the United States, and in 1950, after the outbreak of the Korean War, he had returned to China. His motive was patriotism, he said sitting in his son's shoe-box-sized apartment. Then in 1957, at the time of the Hundred Flowers movement when Mao seemingly encouraged criticism of the Party, he suggested that Peking should improve its relations with the United States. Despite the Korean War, he argued at a political forum in his neighborhood, Americans liked China, and he asserted the United States would make a more dependable ally than the Soviet Union, then still regarded as China's "elder brother." But in a few months, as criticism of the Party grew out of control, Mao reversed directions and launched the Anti-Rightist campaign. The minister was arrested and confined to a cell four feet long, four feet wide, and about the same height. He could neither stand up nor lie down. It meant constant physical discomfort. His only activity over the next eighteen months was to write and rewrite his confession, or "autobiography," as his jailers called it. When the time finally came for what the police said was his trial, he was glad to at last have a sentence.

"The court was two policemen who had interrogated me and a woman in a police uniform whom they identified as the judge," the minister related. "I admitted I had spoken out in favor of better relations with America, but I denied I was a U.S. spy. I said they had no evidence for the charge. They just laughed contemptuously. There was no need for them to prove it, they said. I had been given my orders in America and they obviously couldn't go there to document it."

His sentence, read to him at the hearing, was ten years. He had the right to appeal, the judge told him, but when he did, the term was doubled. His appeal was proof that he still was not contrite, the police said. To a Westerner, the minister's trial and sentencing were a parody of the judicial process.

In the coal-mine camp where he was sent, the convicts worked from 6 A.M. to 6 P.M., seven days a week, with one day off every two weeks for political study sessions. In the early years he was there, the prisoners' rations were based on how many buckets of coal they chipped away each day. Beginners got only thirty-five pounds of food a month, barely enough to keep them alive. "We worked harder than anyone in a regular factory or mine in China," the minister recalled. "If you stopped even for a minute to smoke a cigarette or relieve yourself, you were in danger of failing to meet your daily quota. For the first few months, my hands were a bloody mess and my back and arms ached all the time, but there was no medical attention." The diet consisted of small pieces of steamed cornbread or cornmeal mush for breakfast, a watery soup or gruel with some vegetables for lunch, and more cornbread for dinner. The prisoners got meat only twice a month, little chunks of fat which they happily devoured since it was the only animal protein or oil they received. In the 1960s, the minister recalled, the guards assigned the prisoners themselves the task of calculating each man's output and food ration, a shrewd and sadistic tactic. It set each prisoner against the other. Later this was relaxed and every inmate except those sent to solitary confinement ate the same meager diet.

Despite these hardships, the minister told his story without rancor, almost with a sense of detachment which muted the monstrousness of the camps. "When I first arrived, the camp commandant gave us a lecture. He pointed to a group of coffins. 'The only way you will ever leave this place is in a box,' he warned us. For most of my friends, that was true, they died of starvation, disease, or exhaustion, or they committed suicide.

"What enabled me to survive was my faith in God and my easygoing nature. I tried not to feel sorry for myself."

Still, the minister's experience left its mark. When his son went to pick him up after he was released—he was too weak to travel on his own—the son brought his father a wristwatch as a present. Watches are still a luxury in China, but the minister wouldn't wear it. "He said it reminded him of the handcuffs he had to wear much of the time," his son said.

Several former inmates said that from what they had heard about conditions in the Russian Gulag, the Chinese police were less viciously brutal than their Soviet counterparts, more subtle, that they made more use of psychological controls like political study, confessions, and struggle sessions, and relied less on sheer physical terror. But the former prisoners also recalled moments of physical cruelty. A convict from Shanghai remembered being called out with his whole camp, 30,000 people, to watch the execution of a twenty-year-old woman. Her father had been arrested during the Cultural Revolution for remarks critical of Mao, but she loved her father deeply and was very hotheaded. She went to the police to protest. Eventually she, too, was sent to the labor camp for her "bad attitude." But she kept shouting at the guards that she and her father were innocent, and the authorities decreed she must be silenced. To make sure she wouldn't scream a reactionary slogan before her execution, two women guards held her down and cut out her tongue in front of the other prisoners. Then another policeman put a bullet through the back of her head, splattering blood and brains on the prisoners in the front row.

Each city and province maintains its own camp or set of camps. The Peking Public Security Bureau has a large labor farm east of the city called the Clear Stream Farm, with about 20,000 to 30,000 prisoners, and a group of labor-camp factories in the suburbs known as the New Capital Foundry, the New Capital Tile and Brick Works, the New Capital Steel Plant, and the New Capital Rubber Plant. The government is fussy about the nomenclature; it doesn't like to use the words "labor camp" or "prison."

The most extraordinary thing about these camps, several former prisoners said, was that unlike many regular civilian factories and farms, which are mismanaged and operate in the red, the labor-camp factories and farms all earn a profit. It is a tribute to the guards' ruthless exploitation of the convict laborers.

In addition, some of the biggest and most dreaded camps have been established in China's sparsely populated and rugged frontier regions, where, like their Russian equivalents, the convicts are put to work clearing the forests and swamps, planting the virgin land, or building roads and railways. The Peking police controlled one of these located in the far northeast on the Soviet border which was known for a nearby lake, Xing Kai Hu, or "The Lake of Emergent Enthusiasm." Temperatures at the camp, which once held 40,000 prisoners, fell to 40 degrees below zero fahrenheit in the winter and in summer the inmates were plagued with giant black flies and mosquitoes. The inmates' behavior in the frontier camps was less disciplined than in those around Peking, a former convict recalled, because the farther people were sent away from their homes, the less hope they had of returning and the less incentive they had to obey the rules. Being allowed to stay in the camps near the capital was regarded as a privilege, he said, and the inmates behaved better. At Xing Kai Hu, he added, some of the convicts tried to escape across the border to the Soviet Union. But the Russians didn't want them and sent them back alive in burlap bags.

West of Ningxia, in the far reaches of China, lies Qinghai province, an almost treeless, bitterly cold plateau of grasslands, salt lakes, and snow-covered mountains that was originally inhabited by Tibetans. What Chinese who have been there remember about Qinghai are the wind and the bleak loneliness, the howl of the wolves and the camel caravans of nomadic herdsmen, and, they say, one of the largest concentrations of labor camps. Until 1980 Qinghai was closed to foreigners. When a group of Australian journalists were finally taken to Xining, the provincial capital, they noticed a mud-walled prison that stretched for a mile on the drive in from the airport. That evening the deputy provincial governor hosted a press conference for the Australians, but when they quizzed him about the number of labor camps in his region, he terminated the meeting in embarrassment.

"No one goes to Qinghai voluntarily, you are sent," said Daniel Kelly, the son of an American missionary doctor and a Chinese nurse who spent twenty years in Chinese labor camps, three of them in Qinghai. "The whole province was built up as a penal colony, a Chinese Siberia, there were camps all over the place," Kelly recalled. He was arrested in 1958 as a seventeen-year-old for allegedly trying to escape to Macao, though he believes the government was angry at him because he refused to renounce his American citizenship and work for Chinese propaganda agencies. He was never tried or sentenced.

In Qinghai, Kelly was assigned to a camp southwest of Xining that was so large "you couldn't cover it in a day in a horse cart." He estimates that the camp, called by its Tibetan name of Tangemu, encompassed over five hundred square miles, with nine branch camps, each having its own substations scattered around the small mountain basins where farming was possible. "Each station had its own adobe walls," said Kelly, a slender serious-looking man with distinct Chinese features and prominent black eyebrows. "Some of the walls were huge, like medieval citadels, twenty feet high and ten feet thick at the bottom." Escape was hopeless. It was a three-hour drive to the nearest tiny town, and the surrounding region was a dry salt marsh. The only inhabitants were gophers. Occasionally an inmate would try to run away.

"After a few days a shepherd would come by and report a body in the bush," Kelly remembered. "Then the guards would go out on horseback and pick it up."

Kelly had been transported to Qinghai with a group of 1,800 other prisoners, all from Guangdong province, near Hong Kong, in 1959, the time of the Great Leap Forward.* But because of the terrible food shortages that followed the Great Leap, when his group was rounded up for transfer in 1962, only four hundred were still alive. The rest had starved to death, said Kelly, who because of his parents' medical background was assigned to work in the main camp hospital. It was a terrible survival ratio. From Qinghai, Kelly was later sent to four different camps near Peking and was released only in December 1978 after the normalization of Sino–U.S. relations. By

*His camp was run for prisoners from Guangdong and Jiangsu only. The other provinces had their own camps elsewhere in Qinghai.

366

chance I entered China from Hong Kong as he walked across the railroad bridge from the Chinese frontier post of Shenzhen in the other direction. He now lives in Plainfield, Indiana.

The overall number of prisoners in labor camps has probably fallen in the past few years, for two of the largest categories of convicts have either died off or were released in amnesties in the late 1970s—former Kuomintang army and police officers and the rightists arrested in 1957–58. But many of the camps are now being used to discipline the cynical generation of young people created by the Cultural Revolution, hoodlums, and dissidents. The *Peking Daily* reported while I was in Peking that a young woman who tricked passersby into paying for having their picture taken in front of the Gate of Heavenly Peace without any film in her camera had been sentenced to three years in the camps. The total of these new recruits is not small. A former teacher arrested as a rightist and sent to a labor camp in the remote desert in southern Xinjiang province, China's far west, recalled how all the 20,000 inmates there were rehabilitated together one day in 1978. As they left, they watched as another equally large group of younger prisoners were driven in to take their places in a convoy of trucks and jeeps guarded by soldiers with machine guns.

His group was an exception. Most inmates in the camps never return home, even after they have completed their sentences, Kelly and other Chinese said, for they stay on, or are kept on, as "long-term forced employees." The major difference is that they now are paid regular salaries and are permitted to marry and raise families.

"In our society, most of the prisoners can't face going back home," said the engineer who had been in Ningxia. "It would always be on your dossier. You couldn't get a decent job, and you'd have trouble finding a wife." In the camps, at least, he added, the men had friends and some had learned a trade so they could make a living. "For some other people, the guards just tell you that your wife has divorced you, or that they won't give you a residence permit to go back home. So you don't have a choice."

Many of the ethnic Chinese inhabitants of Qinghai now are former prisoners, said an ex-Red Guard who was banished there as servitude for his radical activities during the Cultural Revolution. All the workers in a shoe and hat factory in the ramshackle town of Gonghe, where he was sent, were freed prisoners.

"You could always tell who they were by their eyes," he explained. "You got the feeling they didn't have any confidence left. When they talked with you, they always bowed their heads."

Some former prisoners tell stories of great courage, sacrifice, or friendship among the inmates which helped sustain them. I heard of one incident from Yih Leefah, a quixotic, good-humored, sixty-six-year-old, Chinese-born

American citizen who served in the Marines in World War Two but was arrested when he returned to China to see his dying father in Shanghai in 1963. Yih, who had been a professor of fluid mechanics at the University of Iowa, was charged with being an American spy. As proof, the police cited his membership in Phi Beta Kappa. He was dispatched to White Grass Mountain, a camp in southern Anhui, in central China, where the Shanghai police kept 30,000 prisoners from China's largest city. Because he was an intellectual, the guards deliberately put him to tending the pigs, working in his bare feet in a brick pigsty. His job was to shovel out the excrement, mix it with straw, and then, after it had fermented into a rich stinking black mess of fertilizer, scoop it up into piles. Several times he contemplated suicide, Yih told me during a chance encounter in the Shanghai airport when he was on his way to the United States after he was released in 1979. But it was Monsignor Kong Pingmai, the Roman Catholic Bishop of Shanghai, who had been a prisoner since 1955, who dissuaded Yih, a Methodist.

"Bishop Kong kept on praying, morning and evening, while he was out working with the water buffaloes," recalled Yih, a matchstick of a man who talked at double speed. Some of the other prisoners informed on the bishop, a practice the guards encouraged, and he was taken before a struggle session.

"He stood calmly, his head down, showing no emotion while I had to insult him. I said, 'You old fool, why should you pray, if there is a god in heaven you would not be here.' Then he looked at me with very disappointed but loving eyes, like Jesus must have looked at Peter when Peter denied him three times after he had been arrested. I felt terrible."

A few days later, Yih chanced on Bishop Kong in the fields. The bishop said he forgave Yih and urged him not to give up his struggle for life. Bishop Kong, who is now in his late seventies, remains in prison, unrepentant by Communist standards, still swearing his allegiance to the Pope.

What struck me most in listening to the accounts of life in the labor camps, and all the struggle sessions and all the persecutions, was what a waste this suffering had been for China. Did the camps really make China any more revolutionary, Mao's goal, or more prosperous and modern, Deng's target?

An American diplomat I knew ran across a twenty-nine-year-old man in Chengdu, the capital of Sichuan, who had recently been released after spending eleven years in a labor camp in the hills in the northwest corner of the province. His crime had been to make a pun using Mao's name during the Cultural Revolution when he was a teen-ager. A friend tipped off the police, and he found himself bound hand and foot in a labor camp. For the first three years, the jailers had beaten him every day. The man extended his arms to show the diplomat the scars. Later he was allowed to take part in digging ditches, for which he was paid two yuan ($1.33) a month. He used the money to buy paper and stamps to write his family. During his entire eleven years in the camp, they were never permitted to visit him.

Then one day, as suddenly as he had been arrested, he was told he was free. The police gave him a certificate saying he was not guilty, but no money for the bus back to Chengdu, more than a day's ride. When he got home, the city labor office declined to help him find a job. It was not their responsibility that he had been mistakenly sent to labor reform. He met an attractive young woman, but when she discovered his past record, she stopped seeing him.

"There is no future for me," he said simply. "There is no future for China either when things like this can happen."

17. The American Agent

美 国 特 务

DR. BILL GAO

"A revolution is not the same as inviting people to dinner, or writing an essay, or painting a picture, or doing fancy needlework; it cannot be anything so restrained and magnanimous. A revolution is an uprising, an act of violence whereby one class overthrows another."

Mao Zedong

The first thing I noticed about Dr. Bill Gao was his flat, nasal American midwestern accent when he spoke English. We had been seated next to each other on an airplane flight from Peking to Shanghai by an unsuspecting CAAC ticket-counter clerk. As a matter of practice, I always tried to strike up conversations with Chinese near me in planes, trains, or restaurants, hoping to cross that invisible barrier of secrecy with which Chinese shield themselves from foreigners. Three times out of four I failed. Talk rarely went beyond the first few halting sentences.

But Bill—he liked to be called by his Americanized first name—needed no encouragement. He was a gentle, modest, and friendly man, tall and erect, with large hands like a lumberjack's, a strong square jaw, a shock of gray hair, and an avuncular manner. His eyes were warm and inviting. Without any prodding on my part, he disclosed that he had been born in Ann Arbor, Michigan, in 1923, while his father was studying engineering at the University of Michigan. The family had later returned to their home in Shanghai, where his father became a distinguished professor, and when Bill was twenty-three he had gone to medical school at Harvard, specializing in surgery. In 1949, with the Communists poised to conquer Shanghai, Bill had elected to return to his native country "to try to help build China up," he recalled. His background made him a member of that small pre-1949 Western-trained elite which staffed so many of China's hospitals, universities, and scientific

institutes and was crucial to its modernization. In their education and professional interests, they had little in common with the Communist peasant
revolutionaries who took charge of running the country, except their patriotism.

But Bill wasn't practicing surgery anymore, he said casually, without elaboration. There is no trace of rancor about him, no bitterness, so it took several
visits to his home in Shanghai over a period of months before I learned why.
I dropped by to see him whenever I was in the city, China's largest, with a
population the government estimates at 11.4 million people.

After the outbreak of the Cultural Revolution in 1966, he eventually
confided, Red Guards among the younger doctors and staff at his large city
hospital had put up wall posters accusing him of being an "American secret
agent." "They said I was a spy for you folks, it was ridiculous," Bill related,
somehow laughing at the memory. The Red Guards' only evidence was his
diploma from Harvard, which they confiscated during a search of his apartment, and several stickers on his old suitcases with the initials U.S.A. written
on them. "That was the only English they knew, the letters U.S.A.," Bill
added.

"I suppose I am too Western, too outspoken, but when they put up their
wall posters, I put up mine, too, in response. I challenged them to produce
real proof I was a spy."

It was a futile defense; it only deepened the suspicions against him. The
young leftist doctors and cadres, working with radicals in the city administration, soon gained control of the hospital and stripped Bill of his posts as head
of surgery and deputy hospital director. They also placed him under "supervision by the masses." It meant confinement in a hospital room, where he was
not permitted to communicate with his wife, a nurse, and had to perform a
daily round of chores, sweeping the floors and cleaning the toilets. He was
also forbidden to see any more patients. From this menial position, he
watched as more and more of his older colleagues, the best-trained and most
competent doctors, came under attack, too, as capitalist roaders, reactionaries, or "ghosts, demons, and freaks."

"We became very sensitive to every nuance of our treatment," Bill remembered. "As long as they didn't kill you, it was all right. We could tell by the
work they assigned you. If they just kept you sweeping the floors, you knew
you were safe. But if they changed your work frequently, for example, made
you a stevedore on the docks or put you to work cleaning windows on the
outside of the tall buildings, you knew you were in trouble."

During this period, though he was held largely incommunicado, he began
to pick up rumors about his parents. His father, he heard, had also been
arrested as an American spy because of his years in the United States, and
his mother was detained too. But no one would tell him precisely what had

happened. They avoided his questions. It was only ten years later, long after the Cultural Revolution was over and the Gang of Four arrested, that he found out. His father, who was seventy years old at the time, had been kept in the basement of a classroom building on his campus; there he was interrogated every day for five months by his former students and colleagues turned leftists, subjected to struggle sessions, and, when he refused to confess his alleged crimes, beaten. Finally the beatings grew too violent and he died. Bill's mother was also beaten to death, but he had never been able to find out who was responsible. Despite Mao's successors' pledges to rectify the wrongs of the Cultural Revolution, there had not been an investigation into the incident. Many of the same faculty members and cadres who were at the school then are still there. So Bill thinks it will always remain a mystery.

"I was lucky myself, I didn't suffer as much as others," he said with his customary lack of self-pity. "I am still alive." I felt shriveled by his account and unable to speak. In a way, like the victims of the holocaust, Bill, his father, and his mother had all been persecuted because of their backgrounds, because they had lived and studied in the United States, not because of any crime they committed against China.

In his own case, Bill continued, after two years of "supervision," he was finally informed the evidence against him was not sufficient to arrest and convict him. But he was too dangerous to be allowed to stay in Shanghai. Therefore it was decided to exile him to Xinjiang, the vast, remote region of desert and mountains in China's far northwest that is largely inhabited by Turkish-speaking Moslem minority peoples. He was to work as a barefoot doctor, or paramedic, attached to a commune of Uighur peasants. It was the lowest, least dignified work the radicals could find for him. He was to dispense aspirin, help deliver an occasional baby, and bind up broken arms and legs with splints.

"I was willing to go, I like the peasants and I thought I could help," Bill told me over a meal of smoked duck and eels fried with red peppers that he and his wife had prepared. "At least they let me take my wife and two children with me."

But the difficulties were daunting. Recent Chinese settlers brought in by the army as part of its large Production and Construction Corps had seized the most fertile land in the region and pushed the Uighurs out to the edge of the desert where there was less water. "The Uighurs were terribly poor, but they were also very proud and hated the Chinese," Bill recounted. "At first when I set up my little medical operation in the village, the peasants would hide in their houses." The Uighurs were also very sensitive about the Chinese using their remaining wells.

"In my village, they would not let a Chinese come near their well. They felt the Chinese were dirty and they themselves were clean. The Chinese just left their buckets on the ground while filling them, but the Uighurs kept all their buckets hanging from pegs on a wall, so they wouldn't get mud on them and dirty the water when they dipped them down.

"Of course, when the wind blew, all the sand from the desert would just blow into the well anyway. But when you went to their village, you had to wait till they drew some water for you or there would be a fight."

In his spare time, of which he had a lot, Bill volunteered to go from village to village giving talks on elementary hygiene. The action was typical of his generous nature. "It was very simple stuff, I showed them how to brush their teeth, taught them not to use other people's handkerchiefs to blow their noses, and not to wipe their eyes with dirty cloths." The latter precaution was to try to curb the spread of trachoma, a contagious inflammation of the eyes that can lead to blindness and was chronic in the area. "For me, a skilled surgeon, teaching primary-school public health, it was a waste, but at least I was contributing something."

One day he and his wife and all the people in the village, a ramshackle collection of mud-walled buildings, were called out to attend a mass trial. Several policemen marched out an *ah-hong,* a Moslem holy man, into the main square in front of the crowd, perhaps 1,000 people.

"One policeman read out a document that accused the *ah-hong* of leading a rebellion against the government," Bill said. "But it was not really a trial. They just read out the charges, then the verdict, then shot him in front of us. It was all over in a few minutes."

After that relations between the Chinese and Uighurs grew even more tense. But a few days later when Bill went to the well to get some water, the peasants said to him, "You may draw water whenever you wish." He had become a friend.

In 1972, after three years of serving as a barefoot doctor, the provincial government transferred Bill to a large new industrial town founded by Chinese immigrants. He was assigned to the local hospital; it had eighty beds and sixty doctors, Bill remembers, all highly trained physicians like himself exiled for political reasons from the big cities on the east coast, Peking, Tianjin, and Shanghai. "With so many doctors, I performed three or four operations a month, an appendectomy, a cleft lip, an arm crushed in a factory accident, and the rest of the time was loafing. It was a terrible waste for all of us, and China."

Bill was a talented violinist. He had first met his future wife when he performed Beethoven's Ninth Symphony with an orchestra in Shanghai and she sang in the choir. But when the Red Guards had ransacked his home in Shanghai, they smashed his American-made violin and broke his cherished collection of records, all Bach, Mozart, and Beethoven. In Xinjiang, there were no violins for sale, so Bill had bought an accordion. Unfortunately the local stores were so poorly stocked they didn't have a manual to teach him how to play it, and it took him several years of experimenting to learn by himself.

His son and daughter had now finished junior high school, as far as they could go in the local education system. There was no senior high school, for Xinjiang does not receive as much government support as Peking and Shanghai, part of the government's surprising failure to press for full equality among different regions of the country. His son was assigned to be a construction worker with a road-building gang in the mountains; his daughter was made a peasant. Bill was afraid they would not be able to continue the family tradition of being intellectuals, a severe blow to him. By government regulation, every Chinese family had the right to keep one child home with them. It was a rule designed to mitigate the worst effects of the rustication policy. But this legal protection didn't apply to a suspected counterrevolutionary like Bill, a pariah.

"They didn't take our children away, that would be too impolite a word," he said with his usual restraint. "They just kept them away. We were considered such a bad influence."

He saw his son only once a month, when he came home for a bath, a change of clothes, and a good meal. He was always too tired to talk; he just collapsed. Bill's daughter made it home even less often, only once a year for a two-week visit. Oddly, however, Bill continued to draw his original hospital salary the entire time he was in Xinjiang, 120 yuan a month ($80), more than three years' income for the Uighur peasants in his area. "The Chinese are very rank-conscious," Bill explained. "They may attack you as a reactionary, but they wouldn't touch your rank or your corresponding salary."

When Mao died and then Jiang Qing was arrested in 1976, Bill hoped to be able to return to Shanghai. He had wasted too many years and he wanted to "pick up the knife again." He got his first encouragement when the old Party secretary of his hospital in Shanghai came all the way out to Xinjiang to see him, a week's journey by train. The Party secretary was a former peasant and a veteran of the Long March with no medical training, but he was a kind person and knew what a good surgeon Bill was.

"He told me Deng Xiaoping had declared that the intellectuals are now really members of the proletariat, the working class, not bourgeois as Mao said, and therefore things would be better for me if I came back," Bill told me. "I was flattered by the promotion."

So Bill took a trip to Shanghai to see for himself. "It was like a bucket of ice water poured on my head," Bill said. He could see that his own personal friends in the hospital, the older men, wanted him back, but many of the young leftist doctors and cadres promoted during the Cultural Revolution were still in key posts and they didn't want him. They were afraid he would try to "settle accounts" with them; they also knew he was a better surgeon and they might lose their jobs. Some of them had gone through medical school in the Cultural Revolution when classes were devoted to politics and were hardly qualified for the title of doctor. "They were good at shouting slogans but not much else," Bill asserted. The Cultural Revolution was not really over—it never would be. The internecine wrangles would go on. And China had missed a generation of doctors, a serious blow to the Communists' plan to expand the availability of medical care.

Bill now faced a difficult decision. "I was very apprehensive about going back to work there. It would be nice to be a surgeon again, to have my own ward, but that would mean having other doctors working under me and a secretary. I would have to get to know all the factional alliances, all the personal connections between these people. There would be administrative decisions to make and lots of potential for conflict."

So with some imagination Bill created what he called a "second-line job, out of the firing line." He applied his unusual command of English by offering to translate the English-language medical journals and textbooks which had accumulated in the hospital library. For years they had gathered dust while the hospital engaged in political battles and the doctors fell behind the staggering advances in the outside world in microsurgery, heart transplants, the use of computers, and bioengineering. In the past, the older doctors like Bill all knew a foreign language and could read the journals themselves. But because of the breakdown in China's educational system, the younger physicians knew only Chinese.

"It is a very safe job," Bill explained of his decision. "This way I can say I didn't write anything wrong. It is all in the journals, and you are the ones who ordered them from abroad."

He was almost apologetic about it. He had tried to make a comeback as best he could—he had even spent six months applying, pleading, and finally using a back-door connection to get permission to leave Xinjiang, where it turned out the local authorities now regarded him as valuable property. But the obstacles to resuming his old practice as a surgeon were overwhelming. So he had opted for survival. In the Chinese context, it was not unheroic.

"I am already over fifty. [He was fifty-seven when we met.] This hospital is the place I am going to work for the rest of my life. I can't afford to make any more mistakes, no business like the last time. In China, you can't just change jobs."

This reluctance to accept responsibility, to expose oneself to the vicissitudes of politics, was hurting Chinese science and medicine, Bill recognized. Another able doctor he knew, also trained abroad and a victim of the Cultural

Revolution, had been offered the post of the director of his hospital. He turned it down. "In that job he would have to make decisions about people every day. Some of them would get angry and would be waiting for revenge. You never know when the next campaign is coming, but it will. It's in the genes of this Communist Party. They can't help it."

Bill contrasted the pettiness, the cynicism, and the conservatism he saw around him with the happier, more optimistic, and idealistic days of the early 1950s when the Communists were fresh in power.

"At the time, I wasn't a Communist myself, but I believed in them. I saw how rotten the Kuomintang had been and how when the Communists entered Shanghai they changed things. Overnight they ended corruption and prostitution; they gave people work and they helped the poor. They were clean in those days, they practiced equality, there was a lot of hope.

"You weren't here then," he said to me, "you can't imagine how poor China was and how some people suffered. I remember one morning going to school in a rickshaw. The puller was very sick and weak. When I went home in the afternoon, he was lying in the street dead. I felt nauseous. I never took a rickshaw again."

We were sitting in the tiny one-room apartment where Bill and his wife were living after they returned from Xinjiang. Finding housing had been a serious problem. Their own apartment had been confiscated years ago and the hospital had no new housing to assign them. But in good Chinese fashion, Mrs. Gao's brother, who lived in Shanghai, had invited them to stay with him and his wife. There was space for only one double bed in the ten-by-twelve-foot room, so the families took turns sleeping on it. One night Bill and his wife used it while their in-laws slept on straw mats on the concrete floor; the next day they reversed the process. To make it even more cramped, they had to share their kitchen and a squat toilet with another family next door—the only separation was a blue cloth curtain. Every word was audible on both sides of the flimsy divider. Bill's only luxury was a miniature Japanese refrigerator which a cousin who fled to America in 1949 had given him when he returned a few months before on a visit. Whenever I arrived, Bill always had a cold bottle of beer or some watery Chinese ice cream ready in the ice box. He remembered what Americans liked from his years in the United States, and he was determined to be the gracious host no matter how humble his circumstances.

Resuming his account, Bill said that his first premonition of trouble came in 1952 when the Communists put all the doctors in his hospital into a thought-reform class, "what you Americans call brainwashing." It was part of the Communists' ambitious program to win personal conversions from all of China's intellectuals. Each individual's reform, his remolding, was to be part of the overall transformation of Chinese society. Just as the social evils of the past had to be eradicated, so did intellectuals have to cleanse their own personal sins in order to take part in the great renaissance. For doctors and scientists like Bill, it was an urgent task; his talents were badly needed by "the masses," yet his class background had so polluted him that until he was reformed he couldn't serve them.

For Bill, his thought-reform class consumed six painful months. "The Communist cadre who led our small group always said our task was to help the older doctors, to help them confess and carry out self-criticism. They were supposed to be the most poisoned by the bad old bourgeois thoughts they had.

"It was very hard for me. I was still relatively young then and some of the older doctors were my friends and teachers. I had great respect for them. I was brought up as a sort of Confucian, we believed in older people and teachers."

The final part of the course was the worst. Bill had to write out his own confession, first analyzing his class origin, going back three generations, then denouncing his father. It was a symbolic test to see if he was truly converted to the new Communist faith.

Bill penned an attack on his father, criticizing him for his slavish devotion to the United States and his bourgeois habit of liking Western food. But it was all false, Bill insists, extorted from him under pressure. "Thought reform was a fraud, it didn't work," Bill observed. "You always ended up pretending, not really telling what you thought." This laid the basis for much of China's current troubles, he believed, the cynicism, the deceitfulness, the easy reliance on the back door to get everything done.

"Because of all the thought-reform and criticism meetings, you could never even tell your wife what was on your mind. For the next time a campaign came along, the first thing the cadres would do was to turn to her and ask her to help you confess. So we hid our true feelings."

While we were talking, a ten-year-old boy with large, floppy ears and a crew cut knocked on the door. There would be a street committee meeting that evening at 7:30 P.M. in the large courtyard below and every family had to send one representative, he announced. I was afraid I might have been spotted coming into the building and gotten the Gaos in trouble, but they laughed and told me to relax. At 7:30 no one had yet shown up, and a middle-aged woman stood in the courtyard yelling, "The street committee meeting is starting, everyone hurry."

Mrs. Gao, a dainty, quiet woman with nervous eyes, picked up a small wooden stool, no bigger than a child's toy chair, and carried it downstairs to the open-air meeting. But fifteen minutes later she was back. "No one has come yet, they'll be lucky to get going at eight thirty," she reported.

At 8:30 she went again. Peering out from their third-floor window, I could see more than five hundred people gathered below. A squat and expansive matron with glasses was reading a document. When Mrs. Gao returned I asked what it was about, hoping it might be a new Central Committee directive with important political news. "I don't know what it was," she replied. "There were so many kids running around playing and shouting, I couldn't hear."

Here again was the result of Communist overkill. People had been required to attend so many meetings for so many years, to feign so much activism and fake so many confessions, that they tuned out.

On my last trip to Shanghai, I broached a delicate question to Bill. Had all the campaigns and persecutions of the past thirty years, particularly the greatest of all, the Cultural Revolution, caused any measurable increase in anxiety, depression, and mental illness? How had Chinese withstood all the tension?

"It's a question we doctors talk about often among ourselves," Bill answered. "But there have not been any scientific studies done, it's too sensitive an issue. In 1957 they abolished the whole profession of psychology and said all you needed to do to clear up a mentally disturbed person was to have them study Mao's works. It was nonsense."

Bill had a theory, however, based on his own experience and observation. "Contrary to what you might expect, there was no rise in mental illness during the Cultural Revolution," he suggested. "People either snapped all the way and committed suicide or they survived. It was something like what I've heard about the Jews in the concentration camps. There was very little you could do about it when they started attacking you—it was all arranged. So the main thing was to try and stay alive.

"In China, you also have to consider your family," Bill went on, now speaking more intensely. "It was knowing that I had to take care of my family that kept me going."

Some of his fellow doctors chose suicide instead, Bill recalled—over twenty physicians in his hospital from a total staff of three hundred killed themselves during the Cultural Revolution. "But if a person committed suicide, it was worse for his family. Then the Communists automatically considered you guilty. It was terrible. They would hold a ceremony, not to mourn the person but to formally condemn them."

But the strange thing was what happened when the pressure was lifted, after Mao died and the Gang of Four was arrested, Bill added. "It was then that the stress showed." Several of his friends were so happy they went out and drank so much alcohol they suffered brain hemorrhages. Another laughed so hard he became hysterical and couldn't stop laughing for weeks.

Bill's wife wouldn't talk for a month; she couldn't believe the radicals had really been toppled.

Settled in Shanghai, Bill and his wife were trying to put their lives back together. All their family memorabilia—their photo albums, their letters, their college yearbooks—had been burned by the Red Guards. But their friends had a surprise present for them. They had collected old pictures they had managed to keep of Bill, his wife, and his father and mother and assembled them in a new binder. There was even a fading snapshot of Bill as an infant sitting on his father's lap outside a rambling Victorian house in Ann Arbor. His father was sitting ramrod-straight, his hair parted neatly in the center, with an old-fashioned stiff high collar thrusting up his chin.

Bill's cousin in Chicago had arranged to pay for his daughter to make a trip to the United States and study English in a special program for foreigners. Since Bill was now legitimately living in Shanghai and no longer under a political cloud, the commune where his daughter had been sent agreed to let her leave. I gave her a letter of introduction to the U.S. Consulate in Shanghai to help her get an American entry visa.

A few weeks after she arrived in Chicago, Bill got his first letter from her. He was ecstatic. The letter was in English. "When she left China, she didn't speak a word of English," he said. "The English in her letter is terrible, really atrocious, but it's English." Another generation of the Gao family had survived; his daughter was on her way to becoming an intellectual, in Chinese terms, master of a foreign language and a higher education, not a peasant. For Bill, that was success.

PART

5

MESSAGES

—

18. Little Road News

INFORMATION

"There are comrades without elementary notions of politics, and this brings them to entertain absurd ideas, such as the idea that we live in a time when critical journalism remains a necessity."

Mao Zedong

In early January 1980, Chinese cadres in offices attached to the Central Committee were called in to be briefed on an important document. There were elderly white-haired veterans of the Long March now in the Military Affairs Commission, cautious operatives from the public security apparatus, and the heads of China's media, the *People's Daily,* the New China News Agency, and Peking Radio and Television. The directive was classified "secret" and the officials were not permitted to take notes on the briefing, but what they heard startled them. It portended a watershed in Chinese politics. At the next session of the National People's Congress, more than half a year away, they were told, the then Party boss of Sichuan province, Zhao Ziyang, would be named Prime Minister. At the time the Prime Minister was Hua Guofeng, the man picked for the job by Mao Zedong himself, and the cadres who attended the briefing must have known Hua would not voluntarily surrender his post.

It was almost as if a select group of Americans in Washington had been told in the spring of 1980 that Jimmy Carter would step down as President in favor of Ronald Reagan the next November. In the United States, the news would have been banner headlines on the front pages of all the newspapers the next day, but not a word about the impending switch in Peking appeared in the Chinese press. Nevertheless, over the next eight months, news of the change was slowly and deliberately spread through similar briefings and documents, moving out from officials under the Central Committee to government ministries in the capital, then to provincial Party head-quarters, to army commands, and finally in ever-widening ripples to middle- and lower-level cadres.

I first heard about the possibility of Zhao becoming Prime Minister only a few days after the original briefing from a journalist acquaintance who worked as an aide to a senior figure in the Party Propaganda Department. He mentioned it casually, and I had no idea what the source of his information was, so I reported it only as a rumor in *The New York Times.* I did journey down to Sichuan to interview Zhao. He, of course, denied the story and said he had no desire to give up working in the provinces where he had spent his whole career. Little did I realize how the news was being fed to China's officials. By the time the National People's Congress eventu-ally met that September, there was hardly a Chinese with any interest in politics who didn't know. But the *People's Daily* and other papers did not mention it until the NPC had made Zhao's appointment official by a formal vote. The last place news appears in China is in the papers or on radio and television.

The episode offered me an insight into the vast hidden communications network in China. Westerners numbed by reading endless articles in the *People's Daily,* the Party's flagship paper, about heroic factory workers and stalwart peasants churning out more tons of steel and grain are inclined to dismiss China's media as mere propaganda tools. That is a misunderstanding of how the system functions, I came to learn. For there is a separate, semi-clandestine information belt that carries accurate news about the inner work-ings of the Politburo, the real state of China's economy, and international affairs which never shows up in the country's public press. In fact, Chinese are often at least as well informed about what is happening in Peking as Americans are about politics in Washington.

Peking's leaders prefer their classified approach to the news, rather than using newspapers and radio and television, because it fits into their belief that information is power, the power to shape people's minds. Having risen to success as guerrillas, operating for several decades before 1949 in an envi-ronment where secrecy was essential for survival, the Communists are chary about disclosing anything, no matter how trivial.

During the time that the news about Zhao's elevation was being spread around China, Mayor Ed Koch of New York arrived in Peking to establish a sister-city relationship with the Chinese capital. The visit was more of a chamber of commerce promotional gimmick than a serious diplomatic mis-sion, and Koch himself admitted he had come partly because he hadn't had a vacation in over a year and had always wanted to see China. But in keeping with the niceties of protocol, the Chinese arranged for Koch to be received in the Great Hall of the People, like other distinguished visitors, by Li

Xiannian, a vice chairman of the Party. What questions should I put to Li? Koch asked me and some of the other journalists accompanying him. There were strong rumors that an important meeting of the Central Committee was under way in Peking—several Chinese had told me about it and convoys of Red Flag limousines had been spotted outside the Great Hall. Why not ask Li what the gathering was about? I suggested. Good idea, Koch responded, and the next day, when he walked in the polished marble entryway to the Great Hall, Koch popped the question.

"There's no meeting," Li said curtly, stopping the discussion dead.

Three days later the *People's Daily* reported there had indeed been a week-long Central Committee meeting and it had voted on a series of key decisions. One was to rehabilitate Liu Shaoqi, the former head of state vilified and purged in the Cultural Revolution as China's main capitalist roader. Another was to promote Zhao to the Standing Committee of the Politburo, a clue to his rising star. Li's misleading response to Koch reflected the contrasting styles of American and Chinese politicians. Both recognize the value of news as a tool; but where American politicians dispense it, to keep themselves in the public eye, Chinese hoard it.

The government goes to extraordinary lengths to try to encase its workings in secrecy. In 1980, upset by a number of foreign press reports on developments inside the Politburo, Peking pointedly republished a draconian set of "Regulations on Guarding State Secrets" first issued in 1951. The law is a detailed document enumerating fifteen categories of information that must not be revealed: anything about the armed forces and national defense, about foreign affairs, the police and state economic planning, but also about culture, public health, the ethnic minorities, warehouses, and even weather forecasts. The law then lists a sixteenth article covering "all state affairs which have not yet been decided upon, or which have been decided upon but have not yet been made public." For good measure a seventeenth article specifies the law also includes "all other state affairs which should be kept secret." Newspapers and radio stations "are not permitted to touch on state secrets," the law warns, and it provides for a government censor. "Before publications are published, they must be examined by the personnel in charge of guarding state secrets." To ensure that no one misunderstood the decree's intent, the *People's Daily* printed an editorial to accompany the text of the regulations. "In a situation where class struggle still exists at home and abroad, our enemies have never ceased to steal secret information from us," the paper charged. "A small number of counterrevolutionaries and other bad people at home and the hegemonists and other reactionaries abroad are always prying about our secrets."

My friend Bing told me that, shortly after the law was reissued, her school called a political study session to go over the regulations. The cadre in charge of her group summarized the message by saying that people should feel free to discuss only that information which had already been published in the newspapers. That was the way they could be sure something was not a secret.

"But what about my name?" a student asked flippantly. "My name has never been in the press. Is it a state secret?"

This fetish for secrecy means that Chinese must do without some everyday information that Westerners take for granted. Whenever I arrive in a new city, one of the first things I do is purchase a map so I can learn my way around. In Peking I bought a copy of the standard three-color street and bus-route map which the government publishes in Chinese. But our friends the Wangs laughed at me. It is not really accurate, they confided. The angles and dimensions of the streets and the locations of some important buildings have been distorted to foil Western intelligence. That helped me make sense of an incident I remembered from the time in 1972 when I escorted the first group of Chinese journalists around the United States. On our first afternoon in the car, we had stopped for gas on the New Jersey Turnpike. The three Chinese sauntered into the gas station to look around. One of them spotted a rack of road maps. He carefully unfolded a map of New Jersey and, as casually as he could, asked whether it was for sale. I explained the maps were free; you could take as many as you like. The three Chinese hesitated for a minute, then pounced on the rack like hungry wolves. They took several copies of each state that were available, New Jersey, New York, and Pennsylvania. Every time after that when we stopped for gas, the journalists made a ritual of stuffing a satchel full of maps. I could envision the award they would receive on their return to China for this intelligence coup.

Even something as ordinary as a telephone directory presents a problem in China. When I first arrived in Peking in 1979, the only telephone book available to foreigners was a thin red-covered booklet published for $25 by Julie Munro, the wife of Ross Munro, a former correspondent for the Toronto *Globe and Mail* who had been expelled from China in late 1977 after a series of tough articles on human rights. She had painstakingly assembled the telephone numbers of foreign embassies, journalists, hotels, restaurants, and the main government foreign-trade corporations to meet the need of Western residents to communicate in Peking. It was only after I had been in China for half a year that a friend told me there was a Chinese telephone book but it was supposed to be kept secret from foreigners. It was 190 pages long, my friend said, and was issued to offices by special subscription through the post office. An individual could not just walk in and buy one. As a favor, my friend one day smuggled out her office's copy of the bright-orange-covered telephone book to show me. It had been published in 1975, four years before, and not updated since, I noticed. On the back were eleven important numbers in bold print, among them the police, the fire department, the long-distance operator, directory assistance, and time and weather information.

But the telephone book contained odd lacunae. All the listings were for offices, there were none for individuals. Not many Chinese have phones in their homes, it is true, but the omission helped me understand why Chinese are always nervous about losing the little pocket-size personal phone-number booklets they must carry with them. The government phone directory gave nine numbers for the tiny non-Communist "patriotic parties" that have been allowed to survive as a token of democracy—but there was no indication which number belonged to which party. My friend speculated it was a ploy to prevent people from getting in touch with these largely moribund organizations.

In 1980, as part of its effort to become more open, and perhaps to compete commercially with Julie Munro's successful directory, the government for the first time issued a public phone book. About thirty pages give the numbers of public telephone kiosks, but it still did not list private phone numbers or people's addresses. The first number in the book is that of the Standing Committee of the National People's Congress, followed by the Supreme People's Procurate, relatively powerless organizations. The Communist Party Central Committee is included under the heading "Partisan Organizations." But for the nation's most puissant and important body constituting a complete shadow government that matches the entire structure of government ministries, the directory gave only two numbers—one for the reception center for petitions from "the masses," the other the United Front Work Department.

The numbers of the other Central Committee departments are strictly confidential, as I discovered when reports began to circulate in late 1980 that Hua Guofeng had suddenly been forced to resign as Party Chairman. For several weeks the government itself was in confusion. When I called the Information Department of the Foreign Ministry, the official spokesman, and asked who was Party Chairman, the cadre who answered said, "I don't know." With this uncertainty, I tried to think of other official sources who might be better placed to know what had happened. China had close relations with Yugoslavia and presumably would want to keep the Yugoslav Communist Party informed about something as important as a switch in Party Chairman. So I asked Lao Wu, my assistant, to try calling the International Liaison Department of the Central Committee, which deals with foreign Communist parties. Lao Wu had worked in the Yugoslav Embassy before being transferred to *The Times* office, and I was sure he would know the number. But he refused to tell me. "That number is *bu-dui-wai*," he said, "not open to foreigners."

Communication is much easier for senior officials. Politburo members have their own special telephone exchange—all their phone numbers begin with the prefix 39, Bing told me. There is also a separate exchange for the army, with its own lines, operators, and switching equipment, she added. This is quite a privilege, because telephones are not only hard to get in Peking— there is an installation fee of 1,900 yuan ($1,267) and a year's waiting list —but service is erratic. Phones often emit strange buzzing and clicking noises, and it can take several minutes to get a dial tone, signs, most foreigners assume, that someone else is listening.

During the visit to China by the U.S. Secretary of Defense, Harold Brown, when he was being feted at the Great Hall of the People, he ordered an American diplomat to send an urgent message back to Washington for him. The diplomat was uncertain how to proceed and asked a liaison officer from the People's Liberation Army for help. He was immediately taken to a central communications room inside the bowels of the Great Hall that had a bank of red phones and a list of the numbers for members of the Politburo and editors of the *People's Daily* and the New China News Agency, the latter presumably so the leadership could check on important articles or editorials. When the American picked up the phone, he noticed the connection was marvelously clear, unlike anything he had ever heard in China before. (There is also a secret underground passageway wide enough for cars between the Great Hall and Zhongnanhai, where China's leaders have their offices, so they can attend meetings in the Great Hall without showing themselves in the streets, friends said.)

The special telephones are only the tip of the iceberg of China's huge inner communications network. Like everything else in China, information is not a matter of money, but of connections. The higher an official's rank, the better informed he can be, for information, like consumer goods, is rationed out by title. The principle is to keep the leaders well informed without contaminating the minds of the masses.

The heart of this hidden network is a system of classified documents. Each Party, government, and army unit distributes its own, including the State Council and the various ministries. But because of its source, the most important are those issued by the Central Committee. It was one of the keys to Mao's power that he commanded the right to read and approve each of these Central Committee papers before it was sent.* The Central Committee documents are used for a variety of purposes, Chinese told me. They can transmit authoritative directives which must be followed punctiliously. They may be designed to start discussions on a new experimental policy—the Communists

*For a detailed and perceptive description of this document system, see Kenneth Lieberthal, *Central Documents and Politburo Politics in China* (Ann Arbor: The University of Michigan Press, 1978).

often try out a program in a limited area of the country before instituting it nationwide. Or they might simply be to keep local cadres informed of events in Peking, like the document about Zhao's promotion. The Central Committee documents are not sent through the post office but are delivered by a special courier, and each paper is numbered to forestall leaks. Each document also contains one of three levels of security classification: secret, institutional secret, or absolutely secret. The latter must be returned by the reader. A notation at the top specifies how widely the document may be circulated within the receiving office or province. Despite the extraordinary shifts in power in Peking since 1949, the document system has remained largely unchanged.

Many high-level organizations in Peking have a document room where cadres with the proper clearance can peruse the directives. Central Committee directives are also read out at what are called "transmission" meetings. Usually the process is divided into steps. First the cadres are read the actual document; later, if the document is not too highly classified, "the masses" are informed about its content in general terms, without the text, at their weekly political study sessions in factories, schools, and offices. Only after this transmission has taken place will references to the document begin to surface in the newspapers. People who are under political suspicion are not allowed to attend these meetings. Nor are those Chinese who have regular contact with foreigners, like interpreters for the embassies and foreign correspondents or guides for the China Travel Service. That way, they can't accidentally let slip some state secret.

A pert, vibrant woman I knew who worked for the Central Broadcasting Station was told she could no longer listen to documents because she had become overly friendly with a European colleague hired by the station to help with some of its foreign-language broadcasts. She was disconsolate; she knew it meant she was in political trouble, and it cut her off from the most interesting source of news.

Complementing this classified stream of documents is a hierarchy of *neibu*, literally "internal," or restricted, publications which go far beyond what is available in the open media. There are four layers of these internal bulletins, Chinese told me: the narrower and more high-level the circulation, the more complete, candid, and interesting the contents. At the bottom comes a four-page tabloid-sized paper called *Reference News*, which reprints articles from the foreign press about international events and carries some dispatches by Western journalists in Peking about domestic Chinese developments. Its circulation of over 10 million is nearly double that of the Party paper, the *People's Daily*, an indication of the value Chinese readers place on the two papers, and Chinese claim it is the most widely read paper in the world.

Reference News, I found, enables Chinese to be more knowledgeable about the outside world than foreigners realize. The day the vote on China's seat was coming up at the United Nations in 1971, after Peking had been excluded by American opposition since 1949, the Chinese people knew about it from *Reference News,* though the story had not appeared in the *People's Daily.* During the Watergate crisis, when President Nixon was under daily assault, the *People's Daily* spared him embarrassment by not mentioning it, since he was considered a "friend" of China for reopening Sino–U.S. relations after more than two decades of hostility. But *Reference News* kept the Chinese public informed, friends recalled.

Any Chinese can subscribe to *Reference News* for only 50 cents a month ($0.33). But though its content is drawn exclusively from articles written by foreigners, foreigners in China may not legally buy or read it. Often when I stopped by the service counter on the third floor of the Peking Hotel to pick up my laundry or buy a cold drink, the room attendants would be glued to the day's edition of *Reference News.* But as soon as they realized my presence, they would quickly tuck it out of sight under a stack of other papers. One reason for this secrecy is that *Reference News,* which is put out by the New China News Agency, doesn't pay the Western and Japanese wire services and newspapers for the material of theirs it prints, violating international copyright laws. Another is that Peking's leaders occasionally use it to float stories they don't want to confirm officially by printing in the government press. When I reported in early 1980 that Zhao might replace Hua as Prime Minister, *Reference News* carried an excerpt from my story on its front page, my friend Weidong informed me, presenting me with a copy of the paper. Its appearance in *Reference News* was a clue to politically conscious Chinese. An editor at the New China News Agency jokingly told me later that Chinese newsmen referred to this practice of using Western correspondents' stories about China as "turning exports into imports."

At the next level above *Reference News* comes *Reference Material,* a much richer and more detailed digest of foreign news articles that is printed twice a day, averaging a hundred pages in the morning and fifty in the afternoon. It is available only to Party members and cadres through their *danwei,* not to individuals, and is printed in large characters to help the fading eyesight of elderly officials.

"It is too thick to read all the way through, if you did, you wouldn't do your job," Weidong remarked. Now that he had become a cadre himself, he often took a copy to his political study meetings to avert boredom.

At a still more rarefied level is a group of publications known as *nei-can,* "internal reference," which are distributed only to officials above grade 12 on the ladder of twenty-four ranks, equivalent to deputy cabinet ministers. Each ministry puts out its own *nei-can* bulletin, a compendium of unvarnished reports about its area of responsibility—agriculture, industry, the railways, crime. But the most widely read *nei-can* are those published by the *People's Daily* and the New China News Agency. Wandering through the long corridors of the *People's Daily* and the huge compound of the New China News Agency, I often wondered what their staffs did all day. The *People's Daily* has 600 reporters to put out an eight-page paper (*The New York Times* has an editorial staff of 475 people to publish a daily paper averaging over eighty pages), and the New China News Agency has 3,000 reporters and editors in its Peking office, a total of 6,000 nationwide, to put out a few thousand words of copy a day. The explanation, a reporter at the *People's Daily* told me, was that many of them are assigned to *Reference News* and *Reference Material*, while the most trusted newsmen are detailed to work on *nei-can.* Here they can actually employ their talents as reporters, for they are empowered to investigate sensitive problems that receive scant coverage in the open media: official corruption, labor strikes, friction between Chinese and the ethnic minorities, rural hunger, police brutality, and the unequal treatment of women.

"Before Liberation there was a saying in China that reporters are uncrowned kings," the journalist friend added. "It isn't quite true anymore, but when a correspondent from the *People's Daily* or the New China News Agency shows up at a factory, the plant Party secretary has to be very polite and helpful. Otherwise he knows he may get in trouble."

As an example of a story published by the *People's Daily* version of *nei-can,* titled "Current Information," he mentioned an incident in Henan province in which the county Party authorities had been lax in implementing the government's birth-control campaign. When the local cadres realized there were 3,000 more women pregnant than their quota for the year permitted, they suddenly ordered a "clean out the stomachs" movement. All 3,000 women were ordered to undergo immediate abortions, including one expectant mother almost nine months along. Some of the women fled into hiding; when the cadres came around to find them, children in the neighborhood organized themselves into an antigovernment militia to warn the pregnant women and help them escape. "It was a shocking story, just like during our war against the Nationalists and the Japanese, only now the Communists were the enemy," the reporter said.

Finally, I learned, there is a special digest called *Cable News,* only for members of the Central Committee and the commanders of the large military regions. It provides them with a highly informative bulletin of major Chinese and international news flashes, like the daily briefing the U.S. President gets each morning from his national security adviser.

But if the Communists have devised a careful system to ration information according to rank, what intrigued me even more was how ingeniously the Chinese people have tapped into this with their own widespread grapevine dubbed *Xiao-dao xiao-xi,* or "little road news." Just as the Chinese use their connections, or *guan-xi*, in back-door deals to arrange a better apartment or a coveted job, they can call on their circle of relatives, friends, and colleagues to learn about Central Committee documents or intrigues in the Politburo. With a sense of triumphant self-satisfaction, a balding bespectacled scholar in the Academy of Social Sciences recalled that he had first learned of the arrest of Jiang Qing and her cohorts in the Gang of Four on Thursday, October 7, 1976, less than twenty-four hours after they were detained in the greatest secrecy. He had a niece who worked in the special army hospital in Peking for senior generals, and as soon as she heard the astounding news from one of her patients, she had rushed to tell him. The government did not publicly confirm the arrests for a week. Whenever there were Central Committee meetings, the scholar added, he read daily bulletins of their activities, virtual transcripts, lent him by a friend whose father was a Politburo member.

With the breakdown of Party discipline after the Cultural Revolution, children of high cadres have become notorious gossips, and I noticed with amusement that the press often complained about their loquacity. "Influenced by liberalism, some people pose as well-informed sources and are fond of spreading rumors," the *Worker's Daily* charged in one outburst. "Some allow their family members and children to read secret documents at will and reveal secrets to them. These children of high cadres then pass on the secrets to their friends. Consequently, a strange phenomenon has recently occurred. Party secrets have come back to us from outside the Party and state secrets have come back from abroad."

In January 1980, when Deng Xiaoping gave a major speech in the Great Hall of the People to 20,000 officials calling for the abolition of the right to put up wall posters, I learned about it the next day from another young reporter at the *People's Daily*. His father had been in the select audience and had recounted the contents to him when he returned home. I had been in China only a half year at the time and was still wary about the quality of such information. From two years of reporting in South Vietnam during the war I had become distrustful of all street rumors. But in China, I came to realize, "little road news" was uncannily accurate. When excerpts of Deng's speech were later made public, they squared exactly with what I had been told. The reason the grapevine was so reliable, Chinese friends suggested, was precisely because it was based on the government's own secret communications network rather than the public media, which the people disdained as propaganda.

Most Chinese take it for granted that journalists are servants of their government. When the *People's Daily* and the New China News Agency sent their first correspondents to Washington in 1979, they traveled on official government passports and took up residence in the Chinese Embassy, like other officials. Chinese I met usually assumed I lived in the U.S. Embassy and were baffled when I told them I had a room in the Peking Hotel. "But why don't you live in the embassy where the facilities are better?" they asked, since they did not believe my explanation that *The New York Times* is not part of the American government.

A senior editor at the *People's Daily* made no effort to disguise the political purpose the regular press is expected to play in China. On a sun-dappled early fall morning, with the leaves just starting to turn from mottled green to russet, I went for a formal interview to the old, drab, five-story concrete headquarters of the *People's Daily* around the corner from the Peking Hotel.* A People's Liberation Army guard with a fixed bayonet stood athwart the stairs leading to the front door. Inside, the building was a stark contrast to an American newspaper—instead of a large central newsroom, crowded with desks, reporters, typewriters, and computer terminals, with a hum of activity and cries of "copy," the building was quiet, the pace slow, and the space divided into a series of separate and unmarked offices with closed doors.

"The *People's Daily* is the organ of the Chinese Communist Party," explained An Gang, a deputy editor in chief. Youthful-looking and cherubic, with a rosy complexion and a full head of black hair though he was a veteran of the Long March, An put the paper's main purpose succinctly. "It is to propagate Marxism–Leninism–Mao Zedong thought."

To a Western reader, that is a prescription for dullness. There are no racy inside stories about how the country's leaders live, no sensational murders, no features on the latest fashion in clothes or trends in sexual appetites, no photos of bathing beauties, no tips on how to decorate your home or cook a gourmet meal. Some embarrassing subjects are ignored entirely. When a devastating earthquake obliterated the industrial city of Tangshan in north China in 1976 and severely shook Peking and Tianjin, one of the greatest natural disasters of recent centuries, the press gave no details. Only more than two years later, in a small box at the bottom of page four, did the *People's Daily* disclose that the quake had killed 242,000 people and seriously injured another 164,000. Instead, the *People's Daily*'s prose tends to be bombastic and self-righteous, with endless long-winded stories about model workers in the Daqing oil field laboring in subzero temperatures or peasants in south China exceeding their rice production quota. The result is a picture of a China ceaselessly advancing toward a brighter future. But since most Chinese are keenly aware of problems like unemployment, inflation, and persecution, the *People's Daily* tends to increase popular cynicism, adding to the credibility gap rather than making converts to socialism.

*The paper has since moved to an elaborate, new, walled compound on the outskirts of the city which encompasses its editorial offices, printing plant, living quarters, and schools.

393

One of the young reporters I knew at the *People's Daily,* whose father was a cadre, complained privately that all the articles were written by committee. If he was assigned to cover, say, a meeting between Deng Xiaoping and an American senator, after he wrote a draft of the story, it would be passed to another reporter who checked the facts and often rewrote it to get the political nuances correct. Then it went to the editor of his section, from there to the editor in charge of domestic news, and then to the deputy editor in charge of putting out the paper that day. There was a progress sheet attached to the story, and every reporter and editor who worked on it had to sign his name before it could be printed. In theory, my friend said, that was to make sure everyone took responsibility; in fact, it was a way to finesse responsibility if anything went wrong. No one person could be blamed.

My friend was also frustrated by a lack of a sense of timeliness. "Most of the stories we write don't have a date on them," he told me during a long drive around Peking. "That way, we can store them up, and on a day when there is a political meeting in the office, we can dump them in the paper." Walking past the paper's office early in the evening, the time when Western papers are at their busiest on deadline, I was surprised to see all the lights turned off and the front door shut. "Everyone goes home very promptly at five thirty," my friend related. "We usually have the paper laid out early in the morning for the next day, since we don't print much spot news. Sometimes after an event happens, a leader gives a speech or makes an appearance, it takes us two or three days to get the story into the paper." This leisurely pace is accentuated by the paper's delivery system. Newspapers in China are not distributed by delivery boys—shades of private enterprise—but by the post office, which brings the *People's Daily* around after 10 A.M., too late for breakfast reading but just in time to be consumed in the office instead of working.

Another young reporter I met, who worked for the English-language monthly magazine *Women of China,* recounted the instructions given her by the editor, Shen Yier. A vigorous sixty-five-year-old woman with a plain face and short, trimmed hair who had worked in the Communists' wartime cave headquarters at Yanan, Shen took a strict view of a journalist's duties. "All clues for a story must come from official papers, magazines, government broadcasts, and speeches by Party leaders," Shen cautioned her employees. "We don't print anything the Party has not said."

Shen personally assigned each story for the magazine, which was designed to advertise the achievements of Chinese women under communism to readers abroad. Then after an article was drafted, she read it, made revisions, and forwarded it to the English-language section to be translated. When the English-language version came back, she again read and revised it and signed her name before sending it to the printers. The reporters jokingly referred to her as "Marxist Grandma," partly out of respect. For they knew she was a conscientious old-fashioned cadre: she declined to use the office car, always riding the crowded public bus, and she and her husband, the head of China's largest publishing house, had pledged to leave all their savings to the Party, not to their children. But her fussy editing annoyed the more energetic members of her staff. One time in a story about a Rumanian women's delegation that visited the Great Wall, she found the sentence "Once we are standing here on the Great Wall, we are like heroines." Shen was displeased and phoned the magazine's English-language specialist, a scholarly sixty-year-old who had graduated from the Columbia School of Journalism.

"You must omit the word 'like,' " she said sternly. "You should bear in mind that the Rumanian Party is our brother Party and their people are a great people. We shouldn't underestimate their heroism and cater to the likings of the bourgeoisie. So make it read, 'Once we are standing here on the Great Wall, we are heroines.' "

But in spite of its reputation for fustian prose and somnolent subject matter, the Chinese press bore careful reading and often contained valuable insights into Peking politics. They would usually be buried obscurely, like clues in a detective novel. In 1973, when Deng Xiaoping first returned to public view after being purged in the Cultural Revolution as China's number two capitalist roader, his rehabilitation was signaled by his appearance at a banquet for Prince Norodom Sihanouk of Cambodia. In reporting the festivities, the *People's Daily* merely included Deng's name in the middle of the guest list, without comment. It was as if the Cultural Revolution had never happened.

Oddly, I also noticed, in one of the most secretive societies in the world, China's leaders often argued their most private political quarrels out in the pages of the press. When Deng was trying to remove Hua as Party Chairman and Prime Minister from 1978 to 1981, he repeatedly assured visiting foreign heads of state that he and Hua had no differences. But the Chinese press, in a series of vague and menacing articles, spoke of a serious conflict between those conservative officials who still clung to "whatever" Mao had said and other more progressive types who followed Deng's motto of "practice is the sole criterion of truth." Chinese readers could draw the proper conclusion. Hua had been picked by Mao and was the target of the stories. The reason for the oblique approach was that Deng did not want to destroy China's prized unity by attacking Hua head on. Instead, these indirect forays effectively warned away Hua's supporters and undermined his position.

Contrary to what many people think in the West, the *People's Daily* also does provide a safety valve for minor popular grievances against the government—letters to the editor. These are a big business. The *People's Daily* gets an average of 2,000 letters a day from readers, An, the editor, said, and the paper maintains a staff of eighty employees, "the Masses Work Department," just to handle them. Some of the letters are printed in the paper itself, others are forwarded to the government ministries the readers are complaining about, and some are printed in a classified bulletin that is circulated to the Cabinet and Central Committee. The most common criticisms are about inflation and corruption, An said. But unlike papers such as *The New York Times,* which see their duty done when a letter is printed, An continued, the *People's Daily* often assigns a reporter to check out the complaint.

"For example, in yesterday's paper some local officials in Hebei province wrote a letter to criticize the provincial Party committee for waste on their public tree-planting day. The problem was, the provincial officials took part for only two hours, but they used a hundred cars. It was an extravagance. We got in touch with the provincial Bureau of Forestry, which had arranged the occasion, and gave them a chance to reply to the letter. They wrote that they had worked hard and planted two thousand *mou* [330 acres] of trees," An went on. "Actually, that would take that bunch of cadres a whole year to do, so their answer was bad, they were lying. We printed both letters and we'll continue to follow up the story."

Such letters clearly provide Peking with a useful barometer of popular opinion. But how much real influence they have is another question. At the time of my interview with An, I was having trouble getting a New China News Agency teleprinter for *The Times* office, as were several other newly arrived American correspondents. We had all made repeated applications to the press agency, to the Information Department, and to the Ministry of Telecommunications, but each disclaimed responsibility and said we should try the other agencies. Without the news ticker, we had to wait twenty-four hours to get a printed text of the previous day's report by the New China News Agency, putting us at a competitive disadvantage with the other resident correspondents. It was a daily frustration, but no one would give us an explanation why we couldn't have the machines. When I mentioned this to An, he suggested I write a letter to the *People's Daily* which he would ensure got printed in their special bulletin and sent to the Central Committee. It still took a year to get the teleprinter.

But since Mao's death and Deng's ascendancy, the Chinese press has taken a number of steps to improve its coverage and try to increase its credibility. Several times while I was in Peking the *People's Daily* confessed that it had published false and misleading stories, like a dispatch from a commune in the east China province of Jiangsu where the peasants supposedly had discovered a way to manufacture celluloid from wheat straw. In fact, the paper admitted, all they had done was perform a few tests in a bottle. Even more serious, another time the paper admitted in a major front-page story that it had contributed to the disastrous Great Leap Forward in 1958 by spreading a "premature Communist wind" and had helped perpetuate the Cultural Revolution by making many "false accusations" against good officials. Several of my Chinese friends gave the paper credit for its newfound candor, but they were skeptical that the *People's Daily* could avoid similar fabrications in the future.

In the past few years, Mao's successors have also allowed the Chinese press to print more investigative articles. Chinese reporters had been writing these kinds of stories all along, but in the past they had appeared only in the limited "internal reference" publications for high-level officials. Some of the most shocking revelations have been about industrial accidents, a subject the press previously ignored. For China is officially a workers' state, a dictatorship of the proletariat, and only capitalists are supposed to exploit their workers with dangerous factory conditions. But in one case reported in the *People's Daily,* the Party leaders of a coal mine in Jilin province, in the northeast, realized in late 1979 that they were still more than 100,000 tons short of their annual production quota. To make up the difference, they held a series of "oath-taking rallies" among the miners, offered them large bonuses, and began what they called a "high output battle" in an unexploited though dangerous pit. The mine's gas inspector and the deputy chief engineer soon protested that an excessive concentration of gas was developing. But their warnings were ignored and the engineer was criticized for shirking his duty. A few days later an explosion occurred in which fifty-two miners were killed and six badly injured.

These investigative stories usually follow a pattern. They focus only on individual factories, directors, or ministries, I noticed. There have been no articles about the incidence of black lung disease among China's coal miners nationwide, though a doctor I met who worked in a coal-mining town said the problem was endemic and crippled most of the older miners. The purpose of this investigative journalism is not to question the sagacity of the Communist leadership but to show that it cares and is on top of the situation. The discovery of a few minor blemishes only proves that the Party is doing its job and is, as the thousands of billboards around China proclaim, "Great, glorious, and always correct."

Even so, this kind of journalism has aroused resistance from more conservative cadres, Yuan Xianlu, the former foreign editor of the *People's Daily,* told me, and therefore the press must tread carefully. Yuan confided that before another paper, the *China Youth News,* ran a sensational story in which a youthful cook accused the Minister of Commerce, Wang Lei, of entertaining his friends in Peking's most expensive restaurant without paying his bills, the paper first sought clearance from the Party Propaganda Department. "On a story like that, we can't afford to be wrong," said Yuan, a thin, angular man with a soft voice and pleasant manner. But Yuan, who has since been made one of the *People's Daily*'s correspondents in Washington, believes the press's courage shows it is improving. "Where there is a little hope, there is a beginning, a start toward more democracy."

China established its first television station only in 1958 and until 1979 there were less than five million television sets in the whole country of a billion people. But now suddenly Chinese are becoming as addicted to television as Americans and Japanese, at least in urban areas where the ownership of sets is concentrated. When a Peking television station aired its first American program, a lightweight science-fiction series about a man who can swim like a fish, *The Man From Atlantis,* so many people stayed home to watch it on Saturday nights that the usual jammed movie theaters were empty and the number of crimes in Peking dropped, a journalist from the television studio told me with astonishment. I was curious why the Communists selected such an improbable program as their first regular foreign series. It had no redeeming social message, and it showed Americans in wealthy, glamorous, and adventuresome settings, nothing to discourage envy of the capitalist way of life. The reason, the journalist explained, was that the government television station operates on a small budget—it carries only minimal advertising—and *The Man From Atlantis* was the cheapest series China could buy from Hollywood.

Chinese television was full of surprises. In 1980 the government took the liberal step of adding ten minutes of international news, picked up by satellite from Viznews in Britain and ABC in the United States, to its regular half-hour evening national news broadcast. Before, the evening news had been largely a turgid rehash of stories from the *People's Daily,* plus some dreary homemade features on the latest improvement in machine tool production. But now, in living color, without censorship, Chinese could watch the Pope touring Africa, Ronald Reagan winning the U.S. presidential election, political terrorism in Italy, and even stock-car races in North Carolina and surfing in Hawaii. After thirty years of almost total isolation from the outside world, the Chinese were being fed a rich, confusing diet of exotic new images. Television, it seemed to me, was likely to have a number of unintended side effects on China. For the Communists it could be a useful new propaganda tool. But it also tended to break down the old stratified system of rationed information; it gave Chinese a much better appreciation of how wide a political and economic gap separated them from the United States, Western Europe, and Japan; and it bred a desire for more consumer goods, particularly television sets. In 1981, Chinese factories upped their production of television sets to 2.5 million and the government imported another one million sets from Japan, ten times the number sold only three years before.

Television has also spawned one of China's first celebrities, the petite, charming teacher of a three-mornings-a-week class in English on Peking's educational television station, one of three channels in the capital. There are no Nielsen ratings in China yet, but the language class is considered the most popular program in China. In a bizarre and happy twist of fate, the hostess is Zheng Peidi, the woman professor from Peking University who was incarcerated during the Cultural Revolution because one of her relatives had an affair with Jiang Qing during the 1930s.

"Now wherever I go, I am recognized," Zheng told me with embarrassment, folding her tiny hands in her lap. "When I get on the bus, even when it is horribly crowded, people stand up to give me their seats. Often people gather in crowds to ask for my autograph." She gets an average of thirty letters a week from fans, and her husband is kept busy hauling back the gifts she receives from the post office: a 100-pound sack of potatoes from Heilongjiang in the northeast, bags of rice from the south, a crate of oranges from Zhejiang, the best in China, and packets of expensive tea. "The people are so kind, they write notes saying, 'We know you can't get oranges in Peking.' " Unfortunately, she added with a laugh, "My butcher doesn't study English, he is always rude and gives me the fatty cuts of pork."

Zheng has also authored a best seller—an English textbook that has sold 1.6 million copies and would sell more except for the severe paper shortage in China which limits the printing of all books, papers, and magazines. In keeping with past egalitarian practice, she gets only 1.50 yuan ($1) an hour for her television broadcasts, in addition to her regular university salary of 60 yuan ($40) a month. And she gets no royalties from the book. But there are emotional rewards. After she sent an autographed copy of her book to a soldier on the Soviet border who couldn't find one for sale in his remote region, he wrote back in exultation, "Tomorrow at the riflery competition I'll fire in the air as a salute to you, Zheng Peidi." It was the kind of guileless comment that makes Chinese often seem so good-natured despite the decades of turmoil and privation they have had to endure.

If television threatens to break down the government's system of controlled access to information, China's libraries have preserved it in its pristine form. The library at Peking University is one of the newest and most impressive buildings on its tree-shaded campus, a modern concrete and glass structure guarded by a three-story-tall white-stone statue of Chairman Mao, one of the last surviving icons of the Cultural Revolution. Inside, the library houses three million volumes, the second largest collection of books in China, after the Peking National Library near the Forbidden City; but there is no central card catalogue. Instead, I learned on a tour of the building, each department has its own individual catalogue scattered among a labyrinth of corridors and small rooms, most without identifying signs. The division serves a purpose. A student may borrow books only in the field in which he or she is majoring. A math student cannot take out books from the English-language section, not even a volume of Shakespeare's plays or Mark Twain's stories; a history major is barred from the philosophy department, though he may need a book on Plato or Confucius. There are other quirks, too, to discourage inquisitiveness. When I looked up Trotsky in the history department catalogue, the card said see Lev Bronstein, his original name. When I checked Bronstein, the card recommended trying under Trotsky. The stratagem was deliberate, a thirty-year-old major in library science said later, because the Chinese Communists still admire Stalin and view Trotsky as an apostate.

After you have found the number of the book you want, you take it to the main charge-out counter, a clamorous room crowded with knots of students shouting to get the attention of the few clerks, who are dressed in long beige smocks to protect them against dust. The library stacks themselves are closed except to a few privileged professors and library science majors, so students are totally dependent on the clerks, like supplicants.

"At least half the time, they take your slip, walk into the stacks, go only a few steps, and without ever leaving the main aisle check off *mei-you* (we don't have it)," the student studying library science related. One problem, she added, is that most of the clerks are former peasants or factory workers with only a primary school education. During the Cultural Revolution when the university was closed, a factory was set up in some of its classroom buildings; but in 1972 when the school reopened, the factory was shut down and the workers were given the option of transferring to the library, a soft job.

Angela Zito, a brilliant American graduate student from the University of Chicago who was writing her doctoral dissertation on Chinese philosophy, recalled a run-in with one of these clerks. Zito had requested a copy of *The Book of Rites,* one of the ancient Chinese classics, like the Old Testament in the West. But the clerk, a young woman dressed in old patched blue trousers and a faded jacket with printer's oversleeves, said the library didn't have the book. It didn't exist. Zito was perturbed and asked if she knew what the book was. No, the clerk said grumpily, she didn't know and she didn't care. It was the kind of contempt for learning that Mao had fostered with his statements that the more books you read, the more stupid you become.

Still, Zito and other students told me, the Peking University library is one of the best in China. Undergraduates are given five cards to borrow books, meaning they can check out five books at any one time. At other colleges I visited, like Yunnan University in the southwest, the students were restricted to a total of three books a semester. At the Shanghai Teachers College the students can take out six books a semester, but two of them must be in

Marxism–Leninism. The Peking University library also has several reading rooms with seats for 1,000 people. The trouble is, there are 8,000 students on the campus. Because the students live in small crowded dormitory cubicles of four to twelve people stacked on bunk beds, it is almost impossible for them to study in their rooms and there is tremendous competition for the reading-room seats. Students often line up at 6:30 A.M. for the 7:30 A.M. opening.

To further limit access to information that might poison young minds, in all the libraries I visited the foreign-language periodicals, the dictionaries, and the encyclopedias were kept in reference rooms reserved for teachers and graduate students. Once during a tour of the Shanghai Teachers College library with an American governmental delegation, we were led into the reference room of the foreign-languages department. The scene looked like that in any American library—there were several dozen undergraduates busily examining copies of *Time* magazine, *The New Yorker, Le Monde,* and *The New York Times.* I was surprised to see them there and asked the short, rumpled-looking boy who was thumbing through *The Times* if he came there often.

"Oh, no," he answered in a whisper. "This room is only for our teachers. They let us in here today just because of your visit."

But the worst problem in many libraries, students told me, was the damage caused by the Cultural Revolution. With the universities closed and education under attack, most libraries had to stop buying books and periodicals from 1966 to the late 1970s. At some schools, like Fudan in Shanghai, Red Guards vandalized the stacks, burning books or scattering them all over the campus. "Our catalogue is intact," a librarian at Fudan said in sadness, "but we don't know where most of our books are." In 1980 the Peking Cultural Relics Bureau reported it had recently returned to their original private owners 2.1 million copies of ancient Chinese books, weighing 314 tons, confiscated during the Cultural Revolution. They were part of millions more volumes that had been labeled as "old culture" and were carted off to paper plants, garbage dumps, and warehouses around the city. In one paper plant alone, the Cultural Relics Bureau disclosed, it had found 2,000 tons of valuable books that were being turned into pulp, but it was too late to stop much of the destruction.

Chinese science has also had to pay the price for the Communists' mania for secrecy and the ignorance of some senior Party leaders. In only a few cases, Chinese scientists told me, have they really been able to put together the facilities and talent they need free from political interference, like the large rocket and jet-fighter center outside Xian where China's ICBM was developed. Even it faced difficulties. A physicist from the rocket center told an American diplomat that its staff had trouble learning about research elsewhere in China because the government did not allow scientists to publish their findings in journals, write to each other, or meet in conferences. "Some professor at Qinghua University may have just made an important discovery in metals technology that would allow us to build a higher-performance airframe for our fighters, but we'll be lucky to find out about it," the physicist lamented.

The most curious case is the hold a Chinese-American scientist, Dr. Niu Man-chang, has had over Chinese biology, much like the infamous Trofim Lysenko in the Soviet Union under Stalin and Khrushchev. Just as Lysenko asserted that characteristics acquired from the environment can be transmitted in the evolutionary process, reversing the findings of modern Mendelian genetics, so Niu has convinced China's leaders that he can alter characteristics through the use of RNA, ribonuclei acid, in a controversial form of bioengineering. Niu was a little-known professor at Temple University in Philadelphia whose experiments with goldfish were largely discredited by the American scientific community until he began coming to China in 1972 after Nixon's pioneering visit. But Niu carefully cultivated contacts with Peking's officials in the traditional Chinese way. He came back to work in Chinese laboratories for six-month stretches, winning a reputation as a patriot, and he helped secure a large grant from the Rockefeller Foundation in New York to build a new Institute of Developmental Biology in Peking. Soon he was on good terms with Deng and Fang Yi, the Politburo member who heads the State Science and Technology Commission, friends said. What added to Niu's appeal was that the leaders of China's Institute of Genetics had been trained by Russians in the early 1950s and were still under the influence of Lysenko, since they had been cut off from the outside scientific world in the 1960s and 1970s. Hence Niu's theory was politically welcome to them. In his experiments with goldfish, Niu contended that by injecting RNA into the fishes' eggs he could alter not only their characteristics but that of their descendants. Niu claimed he achieved this because the injected RNA affects the structure of the fishes' DNA, or deoxyribonucleic acid, containing the basic genetic code of life. As an example of what miracles his research may produce, other Chinese biologists working with him say they have created rice with the protein content of soybeans by injecting RNA from soybeans into the ovaries of rice. The Chinese press has trumpeted this as a possible cure for the world's food problems.

To publicize his findings, Niu helped organize an international conference on RNA in Peking in 1980. But American scientists I talked to afterward said they were shocked by the presentations of Niu and his followers. Walter Gilbert, a Nobel Prize laureate and professor of microbiology at Harvard, said Niu's work smacked of "alchemy."

"What we found when we looked at their papers was that their experiments were entirely uncontrolled and were not doing what the people claimed they were doing," Gilbert said. He speculated that either Niu and his followers were intentionally misinterpreting the data or the laboratory technicians were sloppy.

If Niu's work was correct, Gilbert added, it would overturn one of the most basic tenets of contemporary biology, which holds that it is DNA that determines the form of life, not RNA. DNA is synthesized into RNA before being in turn synthesized into protein. Gilbert said that several Chinese biologists he met, who had not been invited to the conference, came up to him to thank him and other American scientists for publicly challenging Niu. Because of Niu's political position, they didn't dare, they explained, and many Chinese biologists had been ordered by the Academy of Sciences to assist him.

Many times Americans, aware of Peking's hold over information, have asked me if the government censored my dispatches from China. The answer is no, the Information Department never made an overt attempt to influence what I wrote, and the clerks at the cable office and the international telephone operators were unfailingly cooperative in helping me file my stories, no matter how late the hour. I owe them deep gratitude.

But the answer is also no because censorship in China is both more subtle and more pervasive than merely tinkering with a foreign correspondent's copy. It is designed to be so all-encompassing that it blots out facts of life that Deng and the Politburo do not want to exist.

I was reminded of this when the Chinese press in 1980 suddenly discovered that the country's long-time model agricultural unit, Dazhai, was a fraud. Since Mao first sainted Dazhai in 1963, proclaiming with his ultimate wisdom, "In agriculture, learn from Dazhai," millions of Chinese pilgrims had trouped to the small production brigade of eighty-three families on 250 acres of stony, arid land in Shanxi province, in the northwest. All across the country, China's peasants had dutifully copied Mao's words in bold characters written on every available wall, "In agriculture, learn from Dazhai." Dazhai was to China what apple pie and motherhood are to America—the symbol of its most sacred virtues, in this case, hard work, self-reliance, and cooperative living. Dazhai's peasants had even voluntarily given up their private plots to devote themselves to the common good. Or so the *People's Daily* and China's other papers had said in thousands of panegyrics.

But that was Mao's version of Dazhai. Now Deng saw it differently. Hua Guofeng, his colorless but stubborn opponent, had embraced Dazhai and called for all of China to turn itself into imitations of the shrine. Further, one of Hua's few remaining supporters was the former Party secretary of Dazhai, a peasant turned Politburo member, Chen Yonggui. So for Deng, Dazhai became a totem of all that was wrong with the Maoist way and a handy target with which to dishonor Hua. The *People's Daily* confessed that Dazhai hadn't really relied on its own efforts to terrace its rocky hills and dig its irrigation ditches; the truth was that Dazhai had accepted millions of yuan in government subsidies and help from battalions of army laborers. Dazhai's ever-increasing grain production figures were fake, too, a lie by the local authorities; its output had actually gone down year by year. Not only that, Chen, the Politburo member who wore a peasant's checkered cloth around his head, had persecuted 141 people to death during the Cultural Revolution and his son was a "spoiled brat and good-for-nothing moral degenerate," the paper added. The son had divorced his wife to marry another man's fiancée and raped a number of farm workers. One conscientious peasant who wrote to Mao and Hua about all these misdoings was beaten and imprisoned. Now all those millions of signs, "In agriculture, learn from Dazhai," would have to be painted over.

This kind of comprehensive censorship, of "turning black into white and white into black," to use a popular Communist slogan, is tireless work, requiring endless attention to detail. At a photographic exhibition on the life of Zhou Enlai in the huge, Stalinesque, sandstone Museum of History, one of the pictures showed the Party leadership attending his funeral in January 1976. In the solemn rank of mourners there were four blank spaces, gaps in the line. Once, I guessed, these had been Jiang Qing and the Gang of Four. Chinese visitors had noticed the holes, you could tell, because the glass covering the photo was smudged with fingerprints where they had pointed out the missing faces to their friends.

Museums present a tricky problem in China, and they often tend to be closed. In Shanghai, each time I visited the city I tried to get into the elegant black-brick mansion where the Chinese Communist Party held its first congress in 1921 and the home of Lu Xun, China's greatest twentieth-century writer. Both were now public museums, but each time I went, they were shuttered. In Peking, courtesy of the visit by Harold Brown, the U.S. Defense Secretary, I managed to make it into the Military Museum, but only one of its two wings was open, that commemorating the Red Army before 1949. The other, covering the history of the People's Liberation Army since 1949, its fighting in the Korean War, and its border skirmishes with India and Vietnam, was off limits. Why the difference? I asked my guide, a stunningly handsome woman in green army fatigues with high cheekbones, large almond eyes, short thick braids, and a saucy turned-up nose.

"We have not yet come to a conclusion about certain things," she replied with a straight face. Translated, it meant that it was difficult to decide what to say about Lin Biao, the former Defense Minister and military hero who had tried to assassinate Mao in 1971.

Later, driving back to the hotel, I asked my driver, Lao Shi, what he thought about Marshal Lin. "I don't know what to think myself, I just know what the newspapers tell me," he answered.

What was striking about these incidents, the debunking of Dazhai and the closed museums, was that the Party's monopoly of the means of communications makes it very difficult for Chinese to know what to think about anything. Accustomed to an ever-shifting political line, people tend to become cynical and apathetic.

"We are a nation where the government controls not only the present, but the past," my friend Bing remarked sagely. She had been given an essay of George Orwell's by one of her foreign teachers, "Looking Back on the Spanish War," and she quoted a passage she thought applied to China: "If the leader says of such and such an event 'It never happened'—well, it never happened. If he says that two and two are five, well, two and two are five. This prospect frightens me much more than bombs."

19.　To Rebel Is Justified

造 反 有 理

DISSENT

"Some people have the following view: it is revolutionary if we act in accordance with the will of the leaders in power and counterrevolutionary to oppose the will of the people in power. I cannot agree with this debasing of the concept of revolution."

Wei Jingsheng

It seems an old story now—Peking's Democracy Wall is already covered with billboards advertising water pumps, fork lifts, and machine tools. But one bitterly cold winter evening, a few weeks before an irritated government ordered the posters ripped down from that two hundred-yard stretch of yellow-gray brick wall in front of a bus station on the Avenue of Eternal Tranquility, I remember setting out for the home of an activist, Liu Qing, a thirty-six-year-old factory technician. The previous afternoon, a Sunday, he had been at the wall distributing copies of the transcript of the trial of China's best-known dissident, Wei Jingsheng, when a phalanx of fifty policemen arrived and arrested several customers and a teen-ager helping Liu count change. Liu himself melted into the crowd and escaped. The Public Security Ministry was angry that Liu had gotten hold of the text of the trial and published it, even though the government officially described it as a public proceeding.

I had found Liu's address in the back of the underground magazine he helped edit, *The April Fifth Forum,* where he daringly printed it so people who shared his ideas could contact him. But that Monday night it was hard to locate his house down a labyrinth of narrow mud-paved alleys in an old quarter of the city. There were no streetlights and no numbers on the doors. As I walked in the pitch black, each compound of traditional tile-roofed courtyards looked the same. The darkness did serve a useful purpose—it was easier for me to escape notice as a foreigner, dressed in a fur cap and a borrowed Chinese long blue overcoat. At one corner I almost bumped into a man drawing water from an outdoor common spigot. The encounter did not lessen my anxiety. After a few wrong guesses, I finally stumbled into Liu's tiny one-room apartment. Three men and a woman, all in their twenties, were sitting on low stools and Liu's bed debating what had happened to him. In an act of idealism, he had gone to a police station after the arrests to plead for the release of the innocent bystanders and confess that he was the man the police really wanted. That was twenty-four hours before, and he still had not returned.

The four people in the apartment were startled when I took off my cap and coat to see I was a foreigner. I was the first Western journalist they had met, and I could have been a danger to them, given the rules about contact with foreigners; but being Chinese, they were hospitable and gave me a stool to sit on. The first thing I noticed was how cold it was in the room. There was a small cast-iron stove in the center of the concrete floor heating a tea kettle, but it did not radiate much warmth, and in a corner of the room was a basin of water frozen into a block of ice. When I took my hands out of my gloves, it was difficult to write notes. My breath showed in tiny puffs. A pile of trash had been swept, or pushed, under the bed; Liu was a man with a mission, too busy for housekeeping. The one bare fluorescent bulb, dangling from a wire in the ceiling, cast a dim light, adding to the conspiratorial atmosphere.

There was a knock at the door. One of the men moved to answer it and asked in a whisper, "Who is it?" "We are people from Yunnan," came the reply, a province 2,000 miles to the southwest. They had read Liu's journal and had come all the way by train to visit him. It was a remarkable feat. Travel is expensive in China, and they either had had to get permission from their *danwei* Party committee or, more likely, had forged travel orders, an act that could land them in jail. I was astonished by these visitors; it showed that dissent in China was not limited to a coterie of malcontents in Peking. Indeed, as I was to discover, dissent was spread throughout the country and took many forms.

As the evening wore on, more and more young people arrived to fill the cramped room, about eight feet by ten feet. Most were factory workers, young people in their twenties or early thirties. Few of them had more than a high school education. But in their spare time they had been laboriously using a primitive mimeograph machine to print *The April Fifth Forum* and then sell the copies at Democracy Wall. The old wooden-frame machine sat on a bench. Each page had to be copied by hand on a cloth matrix. Then a sheet of paper was placed beneath and an inked cylinder roller over the matrix, printing the magazine one page at a time. Still they had managed to churn out 1,000 copies a month of the fifty- to sixty-page journal. There was an intensity in their conversation, an earnestness, and an innocence which reminded me of my own college days.

"What we need is democracy and freedom of speech," said Lu Lin, a stocky twenty-four-year-old press operator in an electric machine factory whom I had met before. "We also need more science." The juxtaposition of democracy and science was striking, because those were precisely the slogans of China's great nationalistic revival of the early part of the century, the May Fourth movement. It was named after the date in 1919 of a student demonstration in Peking against Japanese colonial occupation of parts of China and warlord rule. The movement had led to an upsurge of political activity by intellectuals and indirectly to the founding of the Communist Party in 1921.

Over and over again in talking with the young activists who took part in writing posters or printing underground journals for Democracy Wall I heard these echoes of the May Fourth period—it was as if the intervening sixty years had never occurred. China's political discourse runs on a strong historical track, and the workers who were responsible for Democracy Wall saw themselves as the descendants of that earlier movement. To them as Chinese the connection was made even more explicit by a historical and linguistic coincidence. For the Chinese term for May Four is *Wu Si,* or "Five Four," the month and the day. But the activists in Liu's house had taken their name from another more recent popular demonstration, the commemoration of Zhou Enlai on April 5, 1976, by 100,000 people in the Square of the Gate of Heavenly Peace which turned into a protest against the radicals and Mao. In Chinese, April Five is written *Si Wu,* "Four Five."

In listening to Lu and the others talk that night, I sensed they were grappling with the same questions and using the same language their predecessors had six decades before: how to bring about more democracy in China and how to modernize their country. There was one fundamental difference. Where for the young people of the 1920s Marxism was new and exciting, the latest and best panacea, it was now old and tarnished.

"Before, I used to believe in Marxism," said Lu, a dark-skinned man with a mustache. "But that was forced on me and I was blind. I didn't understand what it meant. Now I can see Marxism has not brought China any benefits." He did not want outright capitalism either; capitalism exploits the working class, he was convinced. But China should borrow more of the techniques of capitalism which make the Western nations and Japan more advanced than China, like democracy.

Most important to Lu was his commitment to China. "I believe the Chinese people are great, that they are intelligent and hardworking and our country should not be in this backward and tragic state." Here again was a theme redolent of the May Fourth era and of all modern Chinese patriots, including Mao and Deng.

Lu spoke slowly, almost awkwardly, not with the style and polish of college-educated Chinese I knew. Both his father and mother were factory workers, and he had gone only through junior high school. As with many young Chinese, his first political interest came in the Cultural Revolution when he heard older students shouting one of Mao's dictums: "To rebel is justified." Mao the revolutionary had unintentionally fostered a spirit of skepticism among young people about the Communist Party and Marxism. But it was the demonstration on April 5, 1976, which the radicals crushed with the urban militia, that triggered Lu's own political activity. He had been in the square facing the Gate of Heavenly Peace that day and was infuriated when he saw the militiamen beat people who had come to honor Zhou Enlai. "The people are not masters of their own country, there is no democracy," he charged.

As we were talking, Liu Qing's younger brother arrived. He had been at the main public reception center of the Peking Public Security Bureau for seven hours trying to find out about Liu's fate. The police were not helpful. In a Kafkaesque scene, they had first met his questions with silence, then a police officer had asked him to register, and next they had escorted him to a dark empty room.

"We repeated the process each hour, each time with another policeman," the brother told the group gathered in the apartment. He was smoking cheap cigarettes, lighting one after another in his nervousness. "They would never say anything, just stare at me, then make me register and lead me to another room." Finally one policeman broke the silence.

"We have been ordered to detain your brother, he is a counterrevolutionary."

Why, the brother asked, is it counterrevolutionary to print transcripts of the trial of Wei Jingsheng when the government itself declared it a public trial? (Despite the government's pronouncement, only specially selected spectators had been invited to attend, and even Wei's family were excluded.) "The trial was public," the policeman replied, "but Wei was a counterrevolutionary and therefore the transcript is a state secret." His double-speak brought laughs from the audience in the apartment.

It was approaching midnight, and I needed to go back to the Peking Hotel to file a story about the day's events for the paper. If I stayed longer, I would be too tired to write and would miss my deadline. Liu's brother put on his coat and escorted me with a flashlight back through the alleyways to the main street where I had parked my car. It was a Chinese gesture of courtesy. But I knew that I and the other foreign correspondents in Peking also represented one of the few resources these young dissidents had. *The April Fifth Forum* had a core of at most twenty-five people who put it out. Chinese friends estimated there were no more than twenty similar underground publications in Peking and perhaps another dozen in other Chinese cities during the period from late 1978 to early 1980 while they were allowed to exist. On any given day a few thousand people who had the time and the nerve might read the posters on Democracy Wall. But my story about Liu's arrest, and that by Victoria Graham of the Associated Press, who had also stopped by the apartment that night, would be picked up by the BBC and the Voice of America and broadcast back to China. Since Mao's death, the government had allowed Chinese to listen to foreign radio broadcasts without interference. The new policy was designed partly to help Chinese improve their foreign-language skills after a decade of stunted education. But it was also a sign of a genuinely more liberal approach by Deng Xiaoping and his colleagues. So millions of Chinese would hear the next morning about Liu's detention from their shortwave sets. I knew how intently people listened. If a story of mine was mentioned on the Voice of America, the next day I often got calls congratulating me from Chinese friends. This made foreign journalists participants in what Chinese called the democracy movement and angered the government, which saw our actions as outside interference. We could argue, justifiably, that we were only doing reporting we would do in the United States or Europe. But I understood their complaint. In China, the press is supposed to play a different role.

There was a tragic denouement to Liu's story. In the fall of 1981, after I had left China, he managed to smuggle out a 196-page manuscript describing his nightmarish odyssey from his first day in the police station till he was sent to a labor-reform camp. That first afternoon at the Public Security Bureau station, Liu wrote, when the police had detained him, he had bravely challenged them: "Without legal procedures, to arrest people is against the law."

"But they replied simply, 'This is the office of the dictatorship.' "

For six months, Liu said, he was kept in solitary confinement in a small unheated cell in Peking's main detention center with only a single thin blanket against the winter cold. He began to realize the harsh conditions were affecting his health. "One day I saw a great pile of hairs on my blanket. I walked over to the mirror on the door and saw I was bald on top. My left side was swollen and painful, possibly because of the coldness and dampness of the room and my habit of curling up for long hours in a corner to try to keep warm. My already severe nearsightedness deteriorated even further."

Liu was repeatedly interrogated by a white-haired policeman about his contacts with other dissidents, and one day when he refused a guard's order to bow his head and cup his hands over his crotch, he was beaten until he was black and blue. The guards then handcuffed his hands behind his back and covered his face with a cloth mask that impaired his breathing.

On July 21, 1980, more than eight months after his original detention, two guards entered Liu's cell and ordered him to get ready to leave. He was to serve a three-year sentence of "reeducation through labor" at a camp in Shanxi province, in western China, known as the Lotus Flower Temple. He had never been formally indicted or tried. What happened to Liu after his manuscript reached the outside world can only be surmised.

Liu's arrest had come on November 11, 1979. The democracy movement did not have much more time. On December 1, the *Peking Daily* reported that the city government had decided to close Democracy Wall. Then on January 16, 1980, Deng gave an important speech in which he insisted that the right to put up wall posters be stripped from China's constitution. It was being abused by a "handful of reactionaries with ulterior motives" to undermine China's "stability and unity," two of Deng's favorite words, and threaten his plans for economic development. Deng's speech contrasted with the position he had espoused only a little over a year earlier, at the start of Democracy Wall in November 1978, when he told a visiting Japanese politician that the appearance of the wall posters "is a normal thing and shows the stable situation in our country. To write big character posters is allowed by our country's constitution. We have no right to deny this or criticize the masses for making use of democracy and putting up big character posters. If the masses feel some anger, we must let them express it."

What went wrong? Had Deng miscalculated, as Mao did in the Hundred Flowers period, and believed that if he allowed people to speak out they would support him? Or was it just a political maneuver? In November 1978 Deng was preparing for a key party conference, the Third Plenum of the Eleventh Central Committee, in Communist terminology, where he scored a significant victory over Hua Guofeng and other conservatives who wanted to hew closer to Mao's old policies. At the beginning the posters had been largely aimed at these conservatives and had been useful to Deng. But after the Third Plenum, Deng himself began to become a target of some of the writers who complained he was not going far enough in allowing freedom of speech. There was still a third possibility that some thoughtful Chinese suggested. Deng was genuinely concerned that Democracy Wall had gotten out of hand and might turn into another chaotic movement like the Cultural Revolution. He also had not yet really finished off the conservatives—Hua remained Party Chairman and Prime Minister—and he had to stage a tactical retreat to prevent many of the old hard liners in the middle and lower levels of the bureaucracy from siding with Hua.

I happened to arrive in China on a tourist visa in December 1978 near the beginning of the movement. The first posters I saw were in the People's Square in downtown Shanghai pasted over three sides of an empty building. A crowd of 10,000 people was surging excitedly, almost euphorically, around the building, like surf breaking on a sandy beach, carrying me from one spot to another. Every time I tried to get close enough to read a poster, I would be swept off in another direction. The emotion of the crowd was contagious, and I, too, felt a thrill at seeing all these pent-up sentiments suddenly and daringly displayed in public. Some of the posters were only small single sheets of paper torn from a school notebook, others were written on old newspaper pages, and some were on pink or yellow paper over ten feet high. The largest poster was assembled on twenty-nine pages of white paper, each fifteen feet tall, and was titled "Human Rights and Democracy." "Society without human rights is a fearful society," it began. "Only with respect for human rights can we achieve real modernization for the people."

Human rights was a new term for China; it was borrowed from the West. But contrary to what some Maoist sympathizers have written, while the Chinese tradition subordinated the individual to the group, it did contain strong injunctions about good morality. To Confucius, the most important virtue was benevolence, *ren,* sometimes translated as "human heartedness." It was an essential quality for any ruler. Human rights and respect for the individual might not be the same in China as in the West, but it is condescending and incorrect to conclude that China lacked a humanist tradition.

As I was scanning the giant poster, a man in his early twenties grabbed my arm and pulled me toward a later page of the broadside. "Are you an American?" he asked with a smile. When I replied yes, he pointed toward the page. "Then you should read that." The phrases seemed oddly familiar, as if I had heard them before, but it took me several minutes to translate the Chinese back into its original English. It was the Declaration of Independence:

"We hold these Truths to be self-evident, that all Men are created equal, that they are endowed by their Creator with certain unalienable Rights, that among these are Life, Liberty, and the Pursuit of Happiness . . ."

"In 1776 in the American Revolution," the poster went on, "the Declaration of Independence for the first time in the history of mankind spoke about people's right to live as human beings. We ought to have these rights too, not to be the emperor's slaves."

A few days later, when I reached Peking, diplomats and journalists in the capital were talking about a brilliant new poster by a man named Wei Jingsheng, "The Fifth Modernization." Wei was the most articulate, outspoken, and forceful of the new writers who had suddenly made their appearance in the past month. The Four Modernizations was Deng's catchphrase for his development program: they were agriculture, industry, science, and national defense. All involved the economy. But Wei argued that without a fifth modernization, democracy, China would not advance.

"People should have democracy. If they ask for democracy, they are only asking for something they rightfully own. Anyone refusing to give them democracy is a shameless bandit no better than a capitalist who robs workers of their money earned with their sweat and blood."

Wei attributed China's current backwardness to Mao's "autocracy" and "the socialist road." "We can see that victory for democracy has always brought along with it the most favorable conditions and the greatest speed for social development. On this point, American history has supplied the most forceful evidence."

I never met Wei. My tourist visa soon expired and I didn't return to Peking until June 1979 to open *The Times*'s bureau. Wei was arrested that March. But I learned more about him from Chinese acquaintances. If Lu Lin represented one ingredient of the democracy movement, the young factory workers from humble backgrounds, Wei represented its other source, disillusioned offspring of Communist Party officials. His father was a deputy director of the State Capital Construction Commission and a close aide to Chen Yun, a powerful Politburo member. When Wei was twelve years old, his father began to make him memorize Mao's writings. He had to learn a page a day or got no dinner. His mother, also a Party cadre, tried a softer approach. She recalled for him personal stories from before Liberation in which only the Communists had helped China's poor and oppressed. Wei often cited this upbringing to explain his development. His father's rigidity taught him to question Party dogma. His mother's kindness led him to concern for all those Chinese still poor or persecuted.

The Cultural Revolution was another formative influence on Wei. He was sixteen when the Cultural Revolution began in 1966 and soon joined a Red Guard faction composed of other children of high cadres. This gave him an unusual opportunity to travel to remote parts of the countryside, where, he later wrote, he witnessed a naked young woman begging for food at a railroad station and people his own age exiled for life to state farms in the far western parts of China. At one point he was arrested and spent four months in jail for his factional activities. His disillusionment with communism dated from this period, he told friends, when he concluded that the Cultural Revolution was not designed to end bureaucracy, as Mao had preached, but merely to help Mao get rid of his personal enemies. Wei had later enlisted in the army, and when he was demobilized was made an electrician at the Peking zoo, not an inspiring job for a man of his talent and energy.

At his one-day trial in October 1979, Wei acted as his own defense counsel. The prosecutor charged that articles Wei had written for the magazine *Tansuo,* or "Explorations," were counterrevolutionary because they "agitated for the overthrow of the dictatorship of the proletariat." But Wei took issue with the prosecutor's view of what constitutes being a revolutionary and a counterrevolutionary. He said he could not agree with the presumption that criticizing a government in power is automatically counterrevolutionary. That would "debase" the idea of revolution. And as for trying to overthrow the dictatorship of the proletariat, Wei boldly denounced the need for dictatorship.

"We find that governments organized under the form of dictatorship, . . . such as the Soviet Union, Vietnam, and China before the Gang of Four was smashed, have without exception degenerated into kinds of fascist governments with a minority of the leading class exercising dictatorship over the broad masses of the working people.

"The fate of Marxism," Wei continued, "is like that of many schools of thought. Its revolutionary essence was emasculated after its second and third generations. Some of its ideals have been used by rulers as the pretext for enslaving people."*

I was standing outside the modern two-story concrete courthouse while Wei's trial took place. The police had barred all his friends and foreign newsmen from entering. Conveniently, the court reached its verdict, without needing to take a break to deliberate, at 5:30 P.M., the end of the regular working day. Wei was sentenced to fifteen years in prison. By the time I got back to my office, the New China News Agency English-language ticker already had a full account of the trial. It was a record-breaking performance. Normally the agency requires several hours, sometimes even days, to report on a breaking news story to make sure all the political nuances are correct. To translate the story from Chinese into English alone takes several hours. The press agency's speed gave the strong impression that the trial and verdict had been rehearsed.

Not long afterward I went to see another editor of *The April Fifth Forum*, Xu Wenli. A calm, cheerful man of thirty-six with a receding hairline and a delicate build, Xu was deeply disturbed by the sentence.

"It is killing the chicken to scare the monkey," he remarked, using a Chinese adage for a warning. Most of the other underground journals which had sprouted with Democracy Wall had now stopped publishing, and Xu was in a quandary. He considered himself a moderate, not a firebrand like Wei. "The socialist system has many good points," he liked to say, and he had scrupulously given a copy of each issue of his magazine to his boss in the Railroad Ministry where he, too, worked as an electrician. In his small apartment there were pictures of Zhou and Mao on the walls. But he wasn't sure whether he should keep publishing. So he had gone to the Public Security Ministry to ask if it was acceptable. He got no reply.

"They have a policy, they know the limits, but they won't tell us," he said afterward. His nine-year-old daughter, who had painted her fingernails red

*It was these excerpts that Liu Qing's group had gotten hold of and printed that aroused the police.

to match the ribbon in her hair and her dress, wandered into the room and climbed into her father's lap.

"We can see which way the wind is blowing," Xu commented, and he, too, made the painful decision to stop printing in January 1980. I dropped in to check on Xu every few months after that, wondering if the police would move against him, hoping they wouldn't. The last time I saw him was in January 1981, shortly before I left China. A few of the former editors still gathered in his room once or twice a week to chat, and he corresponded with the editors of several defunct magazines in other cities. But otherwise he had abandoned his political activities and he was sad.

"As a Chinese, I don't want disorder," he said, sitting on a bamboo chair. "But the government should learn from the recent events in Poland that man does not live by material things alone. He needs more political freedom also."

Four months later, after I had returned to the United States, Xu was arrested on unspecified charges. I remembered his last words: "The democracy movement will go through a very difficult period now, a low tide. But it won't die. Among the intellectuals and young people the democratic idea has been started. It will continue to exist."

For all the resemblances between these young dissidents and their counterparts in the Soviet Union, there was one profound difference: they did not include any prominent writers, artists, or scientists, any members of China's intellectual establishment. There was no Chinese version of Solzhenitsyn, no Andrei Sakharov, the pioneer of the Soviet hydrogen bomb turned opponent, or Boris Pasternak, or Zhores Medvedev, the dissident biologist. China's intellectuals, who took such pride in their centuries of literacy and leadership, were disconcertingly quiet. It was not because of a lack of tradition of dissent. The Confucian code decreed that a good mandarin must speak out when the government deviated from proper ethical conduct. Unlike the West, this right to opposition was not guaranteed by law, but it was assumed to be part of an intellectual's responsibility.* So at first I was puzzled.

"We intellectuals don't bother to go to Democracy Wall," a Columbia-trained economist, Tan, told me when I asked about this reticence. "The educational level of those people putting up posters is very low, even Wei Jingsheng is not really interesting," Tan added. "They don't represent the mainstream of Chinese thinking. You journalists make too much fuss over Wei," he chided me, sounding like a government spokesman.

If I hadn't known Tan well, I would have interpreted his attitude as condescension or indifference. But Tan did care deeply about both democ-

*For an excellent discussion of the intellectuals' role in Communist China, see Merle Goldman, *China's Intellectuals, Advise and Dissent* (Cambridge: Harvard University Press, 1981).

racy and China, and he was not snobbish. He was a kindly man with graying hair, reserved and courtly in his demeanor, cautious in his choice of words, but warm and affectionate with his friends and family. He was so erudite that his colleagues, other professors, nicknamed him "Doctor." He had been at Columbia when the Korean War broke out in 1950 and elected to return to China rather than stay in the United States and accept an attractive teaching job. For this act of patriotism, he had been labeled a rightist in 1957 and was arrested again in the Cultural Revolution—the police regarded him as a security risk.

Why then did senior Chinese intellectuals not become involved in the democracy movement? Was it because they were afraid of being arrested again or losing their comfortable salaries and apartments? I pressed Tan. No, he replied slowly, it was that I didn't yet understand Chinese politics. In China intellectuals worked inside the system, not outside it; they aligned themselves with factional groups at the center of power in Peking, just as they had in the imperial court. Actually, he asserted, some intellectuals today were very influential, right at the top with Deng himself, and were guiding him toward more liberal political and economic policies. It was dissent from within.

"Deng has his own brain trust made up of some of the freest-thinking people in China," Tan said. It was these people who had helped Deng formulate three critical documents on reforming industry, science, and the Party in 1975 when he made his first comeback from political purgatory. The radicals had labeled the documents the "Three Poisonous Weeds" and used them to disgrace Deng a second time in 1976. But when Deng returned triumphantly after Mao's death, the documents formed the basis of his plans for shifting China's priority from class struggle to economic growth and putting consumer goods ahead of steel production.

Deng's brain trust, Tan continued, was not composed of professors at universities, purely academic types; instead they were Party intellectuals, men who occupied administrative jobs in Party institutes or organizations. That gave them a deceptive face to the outside world. When they gave public talks or received foreign delegations, they often took a conservative line, criticizing dissidents like Wei. They had to for tactical reasons, to protect themselves against attacks from hard-line bureaucrats. But in private they were far more liberal and democratic, Tan assured me. Foremost among these men was Hu Qiaomu, the son of a wealthy land-owning family who studied physics at Qinghua University and is the author of the only author-ized history of the Chinese Communist Party. Deng named Hu president of the newly created Academy of Social Sciences in 1978. Other key members of Deng's inner circle of intellectual advisers, Tan said, were Feng Wenbin, the Director of the Higher Party School, Wang Roshui, an editor of the

People's Daily, and Deng Liqun, a deputy president of the Academy of Social Sciences. Several of these men had actively encouraged their children to take part in the democracy movement, including Deng (no relation to Deng Xiaoping), whose daughter helped organize the first unofficial exhibit of photography in a Peking park in 1979, Tan disclosed.

These men had also grown skeptical of Marxism. They frequently took trips to the United States, Japan, Hungary, and Yugoslavia to study other models of development and, among themselves, discussed whether China should turn toward market socialism or capitalism. One of them, Li Shenzhi, the director of the newly established Institute of the United States, told another friend of mine, "Nothing still holds true now, not a single element of Marxist theory." It was a breathtaking statement. Li was a graduate of Yenching University, the prestigious American missionary-run school in Peking and a longtime ghost writer for Zhou Enlai.

Deng's brain trust played an important political role, too, helping him in his battle to oust Hua Guofeng as Party Chairman and Prime Minister. Since Hua had been Mao's choice as his successor, Deng had to move against him indirectly, in traditional style, disguising his attack as an abstract intellectual debate, using historical allegories and esoteric aphorisms, Tan explained. That preserved the appearance of amity and the legitimacy of the regime. In this contest, Deng's intellectual advisers provided the ammunition by publishing a series of articles criticizing unnamed conservatives who still held steadfastly to "whatever" Mao had said. To Chinese readers, attuned to reading between the lines, the message was clear.

Although Tan was not a member of the Party, the existence of relatively liberal intellectuals around Deng made him optimistic for the future. It also helped explain why he did not become a critic himself and why China was unlikely to produce a Solzhenitsyn or a Sakharov.

"I'm a patriot, not a dissident," Tan said one afternoon sitting on a couch in his spacious living room. He had his own telephone, a mark of high status and good *guan-xi.* "I can see many faults," Tan went on. "But I'm not a dissident because I believe the present system is the best we can have, there is no viable alternative to Deng." Patriotism and preserving China's unity were so important to him that he would not risk criticism of the government. "It would be traitorous of me to jeopardize our modernization."

Tan did admit, however, that the combination of tight government control and this tug of patriotism had combined to stifle most Chinese literary and artistic creativity. "It is true that our best writers did all their great work before 1949," he conceded, like Ding Ling, the woman writer known for her outspoken views on the need for artistic freedom, Cao Yu, the country's most famous playwright, and Ba Jin and Mao Dun, China's leading novelists. None of them had produced work after Liberation to match the quality and force and honesty of their writings in the 1930s; none certainly could be compared in stature to Pasternak or Solzhenitsyn. Some had gotten entangled in Party literary quarrels or the persecutions of the Cultural Revolution and had been sent to prison, but with Deng's ascendancy, they now drew comfortable salaries from the official writers' association, along with homes and cars, and they kept a discreet silence.

If China has not produced a Solzhenitsyn or a Sakharov, great writers and scientists turned dissidents, neither has it been plagued by a series of famous defectors like the Soviet Union, dancers like Mikhail Baryshnikov or diplomats like Arkady Shevchenko, the Soviet Under Secretary-General at the United Nations. Indeed, despite an explosion in the number of Chinese officials, scientists, and theatrical groups traveling abroad in the past few years, there have been only two or three minor incidents of defections involving younger and unknown people. This, too, puzzled me, for China's intellectuals, artists, and even many officials bore deep grudges at their treatment over the past three decades and had more than sufficient reason to seek exile abroad.

An accidental encounter helped explain this to me. One of the very few prominent Chinese to defect was Fou Tsong, a musical prodigy and China's top pianist who had sought refuge in England in 1957 during a concert tour. But in 1979 he quietly returned to China and was staying in the Peking Hotel, where my assistant Jan Wong spotted him. It would be hard to imagine Baryshnikov going back to dance in Moscow, but arrangements had been made for Fou to come back and give a series of concerts and teach master classes for young Chinese pianists. When I went to his room to try to interview him, he was practicing on an old Baldwin grand piano, the words Cincinnati, U.S.A., still faintly imprinted on it. It had been his piano as a boy in Shanghai, he said, and now after his absence of twenty years and much rancor on both sides, the Central Conservatory of Music had found the piano and brought it to him in Peking as a gesture of reconciliation.

"It was with anguish that I left," he said of his defection. "But if I hadn't, it would have been the end for both my father and me." His father had come under attack as a rightist, and Fou feared that when he returned from his tour abroad the Communists were going to pit the two men against each other. "I would have had to attack him and he would have had to attack me. They were going to squeeze us at each other like two tubes of toothpaste." His father was a professor and China's leading translator of French literature. Later, in the Cultural Revolution, both his father and mother committed suicide. Fou did not want to talk about it. "It's an old story, like many others. It's only the theme and variations that are different," he added in the clipped tones of Oxford English he had acquired in his home abroad. He was dressed in a black turtle-neck sweater and gray slacks, and with his long hair flopping over his ears and a pipe stuck in his mouth he looked much more the emigré artist than a native Chinese. Chopin scores were stacked on the piano, along with a bowl of tangerines some Chinese admirers had sent as a present.

Why had he come back? "I have too much feeling for China to stay away," Fou answered. It was that instinctive sense of patriotism that Chinese have, the inescapable pride at being a member of the world's oldest and largest and arguably greatest civilization. Defection was not a glorious act by a noble individual asserting his right to artistic freedom but a traitorous insult to China.

Still, Fou did not intend to settle down permanently in China; when his concert tour was up, he went back to London. "If I was here to stay, I couldn't do and say some of the things I have," Fou said. He was a realist who saw that the Party still exercised rigid control over culture. But he hoped to come back for future visits, if the authorities agreed.

"The ironic thing for me is that the Chinese people are very kind, they have a Mozartian quality, a natural charm," Fou said. "They still smile no matter how hard life is, no matter how oppressed they are. This fools foreigners who think China is different from the Soviet Union. I always have to argue with naïve foreigners about this."

Paradoxically, where nationalism may constrain older and more prominent Chinese from defecting, young Chinese—those who have known nothing but years of political campaigns and a sluggish economy—have regularly escaped in far greater numbers than East Germans or Russians. These escapes, largely unnoticed in the West, have been across the one accessible border, into Hong Kong.

From 1975 to 1980, 460,000 Chinese made it into Hong Kong, constituting almost 10 percent of the tiny British colony's 5.08 million people and straining its already overcrowded housing and schools. Some of these were legal immigrants—people with valid exit visas from China who were able to get out because they had relatives living in Hong Kong or elsewhere in Southeast Asia. But most have been illegals. To escape, the refugees must often walk for several days to get to the heavily guarded special border zone on the Chinese side. Then they must swim for several hours across shark-infested waters or climb over the double walls of barbed wire along the rugged, hilly twenty-five-mile land border. Each morning there are fresh scraps of bloodied clothing snagged in the coils of wire. Cardboard cartons flattened on top of the fences show where people have clambered over. Finally the refugees have to evade patrols of British and Gurkha mercenary soldiers on the Hong Kong side.

Despite the large number who have managed to flee, these escapes are risky. In 1979, 320 bodies of escapees were found in the ocean or on the beaches of Hong Kong's numerous islands. The rubber tires or inflated plastic bags they used to help them swim proved insufficient. I remember one poignant incident in which a man who had lost part of his leg to a shark was rounded up by a British patrol after finally making it ashore and shipped back to China. Because of these physical difficulties, the Hong Kong government estimates that 80 percent of those who escape are young men between 18 and 26 who live in the counties of Guangdong province adjacent to the colony, largely peasants or city school graduates sent down to the country-side.

When I interviewed a number of these refugees, they offered several reasons for leaving. For some it was simply the poverty of life on their commune and the much higher standard of living in Hong Kong. For others, it was the lack of individual choice over schooling, jobs, and housing. But for all of them, Hong Kong's streets looked paved with gold. One refugee, a sturdily built twenty-five-year-old man with a short neck and powerful arms like a boxer, said he had tried four times before escaping successfully—once he was caught by Chinese soldiers, twice by Hong Kong patrols. Each time he was taken to a detention center at the border town of Shenzhen and then to a prison in Canton that the refugees called "Eat Four Ounces" because of its meager diet.

"It was worth it," he said. "Now I send money back each month to my parents in our village and they have bought a television set." He himself had made a trip back, legally, protected by his new Hong Kong identity card. "The cadres were happy to see me," he related. To them he represented a valuable source of foreign currency earnings.

But finally in November 1980, after the number of illegal refugees rose to as high as five hundred a night, the Hong Kong government moved to turn off the flow. It declared an end to its liberal "touch base" policy under which any escapee who made it past the actual border or coastal area into urban Hong Kong was allowed to stay. The flood was reduced to a trickle. For Hong Kong the new restrictions were a matter of economic survival. But I wondered what would happen if the West German government refused to accept escapees from East Berlin or the United States turned down a request for asylum by a Russian scientist. Do we have a double standard, one for exiled Europeans, another for Chinese peasants?

Young Chinese in other parts of the country do not enjoy the geographical advantage of those in Guangdong, and escape for them is impossible. But I was surprised at how open young people could become about their criticism of the regime. The government itself unwittingly provided an opportunity for this dissent in 1980 when it began experimenting with the first free, if limited, elections in China since 1949. The move was part of Deng Xiaoping's plan to relax the Stalinist political controls of the past decade and try to rekindle popular enthusiasm for the Communists. Deng also envisioned the elections as a way to make incompetent, senile, or conservative cadres more accountable. The elections were held for district people's congresses in the cities and county people's congresses in the countryside. For the first time Peking required that the ballots be secret and that there be more than one candidate for each seat. In theory the winning candidates were to have some authority to oversee local government, though the Party remained the supreme organ of power. The local congresses were also to pick delegates to city and provincial congresses, and they in turn would select representatives to the National People's Congress. In the past, Chinese friends joked, delegates to the NPC had only two rights: to raise their hands to vote yes and to applaud the speeches of Communist leaders. But at a session of the NPC in September 1980 the official press gave prominent coverage to sharply framed questions by deputies who quizzed cabinet ministers about scandals like the expensive Baoshan Steel Mill in Shanghai and the offshore oil rig that sank, drowning seventy-two people. In most places the elections to the local people's congresses were lackluster affairs, guided carefully by Party cadres. But some university students were encouraged by the press accounts about the NPC and took their own elections seriously.

One evening I received a surprise telephone call from Judy Shapiro, an American woman teaching English at the Hunan Normal College in Changsha, in central southern China. A native of New York and a graduate of Princeton, Shapiro had married one of her students, Liang Heng, one of the first Americans to wed a Chinese since 1949. I didn't know Shapiro or her husband, but she wanted to report that eighty students at her college had gone on a hunger strike and another 5,000 had joined them in a sit-in demonstration at the provincial Party headquarters in Changsha. They were protesting Party interference in the election for deputies from the college to the local congress. Four of the students on the hunger strike had already fainted from lack of food, she related, her words rushing out faster than I could grasp the unusual situation. Many of the protestors were shouting "Down with bureaucracy, down with feudalism, long live democracy," Shapiro added. Students from several other schools in the city had joined the demonstration and they planned to start boycotting their classes the next day.

The conflict had begun when Liang, her husband, a non-Communist candidate, had gotten up to introduce himself and make an unplanned campaign speech before an outdoor movie show. He was afraid that otherwise the election would not attract any interest, like those held in many offices and factories. Liang had startled his fellow students and faculty members by admitting he did not believe in Marxism.

Not all the students supported Liang, Shapiro admitted. Some wall posters had appeared asking whether the college should pick a representative who didn't believe in socialism, and some students had snickered at her—"We don't need foreigners interfering in our affairs."

But in a preliminary election Liang was among the top vote getters and qualified for a run-off contest. It was then the local authorities tried to rig the election by putting pressure on Liang to withdraw and adding several new candidates of their own. The resulting student revolt was stopped only when the Central Committee in Peking agreed to investigate the students' complaints.

At Peking University, which has a long tradition of activism dating to the May Fourth movement, some of the student candidates were equally outspoken. An American graduate student I knew recounted attending a campaign rally by a twenty-six-year-old former Red Guard named Fang Zhiyuan. The meeting was held in a classroom with seats for two hundred, but over five hundred spectators had packed the hall, sitting on the floor and spilling out the double doors. One of the first questions put to Fang, passed up on a sheet of folded paper, was whether he considered China a socialist country.

No, he replied, holding a microphone and rummaging through a stack of other written questions. The written form provided the safety of anonymity. "I think, domestically speaking, Russia and China are similar and Russia isn't socialist either," Fang explained. His candor brought applause.

"I don't think that what we have now in China is what Marx called socialism," he went on. Public ownership of the means of production, or machines and factories, doesn't constitute socialism by itself, Fang said, taking issue with the government's usual definition of socialism. "To say something is truly publicly owned, we must see if the leaders represent the interests of the people.

"To have this, you need a system, and that system is democracy," Fang concluded. The audience exploded with approval.

For the students the election provided an outlet for their concern with China's direction, just as putting up posters on Democracy Wall did for the activists of the democracy movement. But some other Chinese have found expression for their discontent with the Communist regime in a quieter, more personal form—religion.

When Communist guerrillas took over Long Bow village in 1947 in Shanxi province, in western China, one of their major targets was the local Catholic church, a gothic brick structure built by Dutch Franciscan fathers at the turn of the century. It had a tall square tower that stood proudly, arrogantly some thought, high above the peasants' mud houses, and many of its parishioners were associated with the defeated Kuomintang. The Communists chased away the priest, closed the church, and persecuted the worshipers. William Hinton, the American writer who described the Communist victory in Long Bow in his classic book, *Fanshen,* thought the Church was on its way to extinction. "All the power of the Church and all its efforts to convert Long Bow to Catholicism failed in the end," Hinton wrote.* He calculated that most of the converts were only "rice Christians," Chinese who were attracted to the Church because of its wealth and privileged position, protected by the Western imperial powers.

But in 1980 when he returned to Long Bow, Hinton found many peasant homes had printed pictures of Mary and Jesus on their walls, along with the stock portraits of Marx and Mao. On Sundays a group of 150 families, about the same number of Catholics as in 1947, had also started to hold mass again. They gathered in the loft of the house of a carpenter, a man whose father had been a lay preacher before Liberation.

"There are so many people the crowd spills out into his courtyard," Hinton told me with incredulity. "I didn't want to ask them where they got the pictures of Mary and Jesus," since presumably they were either smuggled into China or printed illegally. "It is mighty quiet in the village on Sundays now," Hinton added, tossing back a lock of white hair that fell in his ruddy face. "The peasants would rather go to the service than out to the fields to work."

The reemergence of the villagers' Catholic faith is only part of a broad if cautious revival of religion in China in the years since Mao's death.** It has taken place not only among Catholics and Protestants, but also among China's other religions as well, Buddhism, Islam, and Taoism. Mao's more pragmatic successors have encouraged this rebirth by lifting some of the stifling restrictions placed on religion during the Cultural Revolution. Deng and his associates have recognized the need to mobilize all possible support for their modernization program. Some Chinese and diplomats I knew were skeptical at first that Peking's more tolerant policy was merely a well-contrived showpiece to attract foreign backing for China, particularly from the Arab states in the Middle East and the Buddhist countries in Southeast Asia. But as I traveled around China, I sensed that there were deeper forces at work, forces the government didn't control, and that this renaissance was an outpouring of profound human feelings, another form of dissent.

By chance, along with a group of other foreign correspondents escorted by the Information Department, I happened to be in the southern coastal port of Fuzhou on Good Friday. Fuzhou had been a center of American and

*William Hinton, *Fanshen, A Documentary of Revolution in a Chinese Village* (New York: Random House, 1966), p. 67.
**In 1949 there were roughly three million Catholics and 700,000 Protestants in all of China, a tiny minority of the population.

British Protestant missionary activity in the late nineteenth and early twentieth centuries when it was a treaty port, one of the Chinese cities where the foreign powers had arrogated extralegal powers for themselves from the weak Manchu, warlord, and Kuomintang regimes. There had been a total of twenty-four Protestant and four Roman Catholic churches in Fuzhou before 1949, most with small congregations of a few hundred people. In the 1950s the Protestant churches were gradually forced to close down and unify in one remaining "patriotic" nondenominational church guided by Peking. The Catholic cathedrals were also compelled to merge and forswear their allegiance to the Pope as a foreign power. Then in the Cultural Revolution all Christian churches in China were shuttered except for one Protestant and one Catholic church in Peking reserved largely for the foreign diplomatic community. But the officials in Fuzhou told us they had recently permitted a Protestant church to reopen in accord with the government's new more liberal policy and, after repeated entreaties, they let us visit it.

It proved to be an old gray-stone building down a narrow alley that had been built by American Methodist missionaries in 1938 and was known as the Flower Lane Church. The inside had been freshly painted a cool lime green and white by the parishioners to cover up the traces of vandalism by Red Guards. For the past dozen years, the church had served as a warehouse. At the front a tall, elderly man with thinning hair was practicing for the Easter service on an old tinny piano. In a full rich tenor voice that filled the hall, he intoned in Chinese, "Christ the Lord Is Risen Today." Our guides from the Information Department in Peking and local officials from Fuzhou were standing there with us, and I had to pinch myself to be sure the scene was real.

Upstairs in the vestry we met the chief pastor, Bishop Moses P. Xie, an Anglican. A warm, gentle man of seventy-seven, he spoke English with the high church accent he had acquired in his early training in Britain. He had already picked out the psalm with which he would begin his Easter sermon, from St. Matthew:

> And, behold, there was a great earthquake: for the angel of the Lord descended from heaven, and came and rolled back the stone from the door, and sat upon it. His countenance was like lightning, and his raiment white as snow. And for fear of him the keepers did shake, and became as dead men. And the angel answered and said unto the women, 'Fear not ye: for I know that ye seek Jesus, which was crucified. He is not here: for he is risen, as he said. Come, see the place where the Lord lay.'

Bishop Xie said he expected 2,000 worshipers for the morning service, another 2,000 in the afternoon. Since the church had reopened a few months before, people began coming for the nine o'clock service at 7 A.M.

"If you don't come early, you can't get a seat," the bishop said with a twinkle in his eye. "Then they stay after the service is over, to read the Bible and practice singing some more. After thirteen years, one service is not enough."

There are actually more Protestants in Fuzhou now than in 1949, he insisted. His claim was seconded by five other ministers sitting with us who had banded together, as required by the government, to open the one nondenominational "patriotic" church which had no links to foreign organizations.

How did he account for the increased number of parishioners after all the persecutions of the Cultural Revolution and the government's restrictions on religion? I asked.

"The people are thirsty for something spiritual," he explained. Then, as if to answer our doubts about his claims, he added, "Before Liberation, we used to have a half-hour sermon. Now, if you preach for only half an hour, the people wouldn't be satisfied." But the bishop was careful to add that he does not preach anything against the government. "We are very clear about that."

During the Cultural Revolution Bishop Xie had all his vestments and religious books burned by Red Guards, and he was sent to work first in a factory and then in a village. His superior, the former Anglican Bishop of Fuzhou, was tortured to death.

The Christian faith had survived by going underground, he recounted. "Quite a number of people had services in their families secretly. They would preach to their friends and relatives. I think they did an even better job than we did."

Although he and the other five ministers who now share duties in the church are older men, in their sixties and seventies, he said one third of the congregation is composed of young people with another third drawn from the middle-aged. There is no Sunday school, because the government has forbidden the pastors to try to convert people under eighteen. (The 1978 constitution guarantees that the people "enjoy freedom to believe in religion and freedom not to believe in religion," but a further clause adds that they may only "propagate atheism.") Yet the ministers said they can now baptize adults who wish to become Christians, they have officiated at some weddings and funerals, and they planned to send a few students to the newly reopened Protestant Theological Seminary in Nanjing, one of the most significant concessions by the government. Without it, the Protestant Church would eventually wither away.

As another indication of the Church's strength, the bishop said the congregation had raised enough money to pay its six ministers a monthly salary of 70 yuan ($47) apiece, better than average in China. Some of the funds come from rent on church properties which have been returned by the government, some from English classes the pastors teach in the church, and the rest from Sunday collections. At the back of the church was a blackboard that recorded that on the previous Sunday the worshipers had contributed 267 yuan ($180) to the collection box, a munificent sum of money given the low wages Chinese earn. They had also donated ration coupons for twelve pounds of rice which the church will give to the poor, the bishop said.

The church's main problem, Bishop Xie related, was that all their Bibles and hymnals had been destroyed by Red Guards. He was waiting for a shipment from Shanghai where the government had allowed a printing house to reissue copies of the Bible for the first time in over a decade. Some of these treasured books had already made their way into the hands of Chinese I knew. The *a-yi,* or maid, who worked for Hong and Weidong, had made a special trip to Shanghai to purchase one. A middle-aged woman with a stout figure, buck teeth, and short bowl-cut hair, she was always reading her Bible aloud around the house, Hong told me. Neither Hong nor Weidong had any religious predisposition, but their *a-yi* often tried to persuade them of the superiority of her faith.

"Do you know why there are so many rich Americans?" she asked Hong. "It's because they believe in Christianity."

China's own folk religion, an eclectic amalgam of Buddhism, Taoism, ancestor worship, and popular superstition, also has proved more resilient than outsiders realize. During the 1950s, and then particularly during the Cultural Revolution, most Buddhist and Taoist temples and monasteries were closed and their priests and nuns defrocked. But Susan Wilf, a Harvard graduate student who taught in Peking and married a Chinese, recalled what she saw when she spent her honeymoon climbing Mount Taishan in Shandong province, east of the capital. It is one of China's traditional five sacred peaks, like Mecca or Jerusalem to Moslems and Christians. As she walked, she encountered hundreds of peasant women making the trek to the top. They had come by train from villages throughout north China and climbed all night to reach the summit on the anniversary of the local goddess. Some of the women, whose feet had been bound as youngsters, burned paper offerings and incense or brought food and bowed before an image of the goddess in a temple atop the mountain. Until a few months before, such celebrations were illegal.

A Peking office worker who went home at New Year's to visit her family in the central province of Anhui said the peasants there had become excited by a prophesy about a miraculous stone animal. The animal, a Qilin, a Chinese mythical beast with the head of a lion, is one of several that stands guard outside the tomb of the mother of the founder of the Ming dynasty.

"The peasants believe the animal has come alive and is very powerful medicine," the woman said. So many peasants had chipped away at the animal's legs to get shavings to eat that the Qilin was toppling over.

Local officials made no move to stop the cannibalization of the stone animal. But Peking has become concerned that some forms of religious expression are going too far and either reviving what the Communists see as the evils of the old pre-1949 society or challenging their rule. In Jiangsu province, near the city of Nanjing in central China, the police arrested a witch and a warlock after they put two six-year-old boys to death during an exorcism, a provincial broadcast revealed. The witch beat the boys with branches, poured boiling water over them, and then set fire to one and strangled the other. The rites, which started with a dance of incantation, were supposed to heal a paralyzed woman by ridding her of ghosts that had come back to haunt her.

If religion has provided an outlet for long-pent-up and proscribed feelings among China's Christians, Buddhists, and Taoists, it is an even more volatile and important issue to many of the country's ethnic minorities who inhabit much of the vast western parts of the country. Sitting in Peking it is easy to forget that there are fifty-five identifiable separate minority peoples in China, making China a more heterogeneous society than the countries of Western Europe, Japan, or even the United States. They account for only 56 million people, 6 percent of the total population. But they occupy over half of China's land area, and their significance is magnified because they live along the critical inner Asian frontiers with the Soviet Union, Mongolia, Afghanistan, Pakistan, India, Burma, and Vietnam.

In theory the Communists have recognized the cultural, religious, and ethnic diversity of these non-Chinese peoples by declaring the areas where they live "autonomous regions" rather than regular provinces. Thus Xinjiang, 8 of whose 12 million inhabitants are Turkish-speaking Moslem peoples, including Uighurs, Kazakhs, and Kirghiz, closely related to the natives of the Soviet Central Asian republics across the border, is called the Xinjiang Autonomous Region. But in practice the Communists have kept political control tightly in the hands of Chinese officials and soldiers sent to settle the frontier areas. To the Chinese their presence is civilizing; to the ethnic minorities it is colonial.

In Urumqi, the nondescript modern capital of Xinjiang built on the north side of the snowcapped Mountains of Heaven, the sun does not rise in the summer till 8 A.M. and office hours don't start till 10 A.M.; the lunch break begins at 2 P.M. For though Urumqi is over 1,500 miles west of Peking, as far as Denver from New York or London from Moscow, the Communists have decreed that Urumqi must operate by Peking time, ignoring the meridians of the earth. All of China does.

"We tried to use local time, but it wasn't convenient," explained my guide, Wang Guorong, a Chinese, or Han, as they are called in Xinjiang, after the name of the early dynasty. I told Wang, an eager boyish man with crew-cut hair and a desire to please, that in the United States we overcome the problem of the 3,000-mile distance from New York to California by having four time zones. But he was dubious. "It would cause confusion with the railroad and airplane schedules," he insisted.

Wang had been assigned to Xinjiang from his home near Peking, one of four million Han settlers dispatched to the province in the past thirty years. In 1949, when the Communists marched into Xinjiang, only 6 percent of the population were Chinese; now the proportion is up to 42 percent. Despite Mao's successors' proclaimed policy of being more respectful of the minorities' rights and giving them greater political power, the Party boss of Xinjiang is a Chinese. So is the army commander and six of the eight provincial Party secretaries. Only 40 percent of the 400,000 Party members in Xinjiang are minorities, most of them working at the lowest village level.

The Chinese presence has brought prosperity to parts of Xinjiang, the Chinese proudly point out. Where there was only the terrible red rock desert of Central Asia, nomadic herdsmen and ranges of mountains over 20,000 feet, now there are oil wells, railroads, and dozens of factories. In Turfan, an oasis city on the ancient silk route where Marco Polo rested on his way to China, Wang and a local Chinese official took me to see Zora Han, a heavyset forty-year-old Uighur woman with a deeply wrinkled face and skin parched brown by the desert sun. She, her husband, and her grown daughter earn an average of 275 yuan ($183) a year apiece planting wheat and cotton for their commune, she said. That is more than three times the national average. The family makes another 525 yuan ($350) a year—a prodigious amount in China—by growing green seedless grapes in the shaded courtyard of their mud-walled home. She picked a large bunch from a trellis, washed them with water drawn from an irrigation ditch that flows gurgling by their house, and handed them to me. I had never tasted sweeter grapes, I admitted. Outside, men perched astride slow-footed donkeys trotted past on their way to the large free market where the authorities allow the Uighurs to sell their produce.

Conversation was awkward because Mrs. Han, who was dressed in a black skirt and stockings with a green scarf over her head, very distinct from the blue trousers of Chinese women, spoke only a few words of Chinese. My Chinese escorts, both of whom had been in Xinjiang for over ten years, spoke no Uighur at all. Finally a twelve-year-old neighbor, a Uighur girl who was watching from the doorway, helped translate. She was learning Chinese in school, she said. She had to—all her classes were in Chinese, for the benefit of the Han students.

This ready Chinese assumption of cultural superiority, not unlike Americans' treatment of the Indians, has kept relations between the Han immigrants and native Moslems tense. In 1980 several hundred civilians and soldiers were killed during a fight in Aksu, another oasis city west of Turfan. A Peking actor who was in the town at the time filming a movie said he and his colleagues had to hide for several days inside a building while angry Uighurs roamed the streets shouting death to all Chinese. To quell the disturbance, the government had to call in an army division, some of 300,000 troops Peking keeps stationed in Xinjiang, partly to defend against the Soviet Union and partly to assure local order. A Uighur student in Peking said the incident was only one of several that year, often involving gun battles and then the execution of the suspected rebel ringleaders. The situation grew so tense that Deng Xiaoping himself paid a quiet visit to Xinjiang to investigate.

Many of the disputes arise from the government's attempt to control religion. Virtually all the mosques in China were closed during the Cultural Revolution and Peking began to allow some of them to reopen only in 1980. At the main mosque in Urumqi, a simple edifice devoid of any religious decoration, the *ah-hong,* or "religious leader," Abdullah Haji Imam, said he had been kept under house arrest during the Cultural Revolution.

"The Red Guards burned my copies of the Koran and called me a monster and a demon," he related, speaking in heavily accented Chinese. A tall, proud man with a patriarchal gray beard, flashing dark eyes, and a strong aquiline nose, he was clad in a black clerical robe and a white turban. He could have been in Iran or Saudi Arabia. In fact, he said, he had been on a pilgrimage to Mecca in 1958; but then, aware of the Chinese officials with me, he hastily added that he had also met Mao. I wondered if the two events were of equal significance to him. He drew his salary not from the mosque but from the United Front Department of the Party, he related, the agency responsible for the Communists' ties with non-Communists. It was Friday, the Moslem holy day, and he asked to be excused to prepare himself for prayers. Old men and young boys with white-, green-, and red-embroidered skullcaps were drifting into the unlit mosque. There were few men between the ages of twenty and fifty, I noticed. It was because they are at work, the *ah-hong* explained. Friday is not a holiday in Xinjiang—only Sunday, the Chinese official day off.

As the Communists have sharply reduced the powers of the Moslem clergy in Xinjiang, so they have transformed the once-all-powerful Lamaist theocracy that long ruled neighboring Tibet into little more than a museum piece. Since the Chinese assumed full control over Tibet after an abortive Tibetan uprising in 1959, the number of Buddhist monasteries has been cut from 2,464 to 10, Chinese officials told me during a week's tour of "the roof of the world." Some, like the Gadan monastery, once the third largest in Tibet with nearly 10,000 monks, simply disappeared during the Cultural Revolution, the officials added without explanation. Their fate was suggested by what I found when I went to look for a famous temple on Medicine King Hill in the center of Lhasa, the capital. It had been razed and its site is now occupied by a company of the People's Liberation Army. The only traces were several red, green, and orange frescoes of Buddha in a cave partway up the rocky promontory; each had had its face gouged out, its stomach disemboweled, and was then smeared with lime. The damage was done by Red Guards who poured into Lhasa from China, a Tibetan teen-ager confided on an impromptu tour of the hillside. As recently as 1979, a Chinese archaeologist told me, large numbers of precious bronze statues looted from temples in Tibet had been transported to Peking by truck where they were melted down for copper. The practice was stopped only after a high-ranking Communist leader who liked antiques intervened. The remaining objects are being kept in a warehouse outside Peking by a so-called waste-collecting company, the archaeologist added. He said no decision had been made on what to do with them.

At the same time, the number of lamas, or monks, has shrunk from 110,000, about one fifth of Tibet's pre-1959 male population, to about 2,000, the Chinese officials who hosted me in Lhasa disclosed. They were "not too clear" about what had happened to the monks. Some, they said, were returned to being peasants and herdsmen. But others, according to Tibetans I met in Peking, had been executed or sent to labor-reform camps.

Several of the surviving monks professed they now believe socialism is a better faith than Tibetan Buddhism, a rich mixture of the benevolent teachings of Buddha and Tibet's own primitive nature worship cult, Bon.

"In the final analysis materialism will triumph over religion, because Marxism–Leninism–Mao Zedong thought is true and scientific," remarked Gandunjiacuo, a fragile, aging monk in a thick crimson wool robe in the Drepung monastery. Before the 1959 revolt when the Dalai Lama, the supreme pontiff of the Tibetan church and state, fled to India, the Drepung was the largest monastery in the land with up to 15,000 lamas and ownership of estates with 25,000 serfs. Now it is a ghost town, albeit a majestic layered complex of terraces, balconies, and tiled roofs built on a cliff overlooking the brown, sere Lhasa Valley, 11,800 feet above sea level. To reach its main halls, which the Chinese were now repainting in preparation for the arrival of foreign tourists, a visitor must walk up steep overgrown cobbled paths between old stone barracks where the monks once lived. Today most of them are vacant with the windows boarded. Before the advent of the Chinese, the monasteries, along with a small noble class, governed Tibet through a religious-secular hierarchy like Europe's political system in the Middle Ages.

It is a strange, lonely place, full of memories and not much future. Gandunjiacuo, who said he studied Mao's works every week, insisted Buddhism would die out. There have been no young men admitted to the church since 1959, he disclosed. To become a lama, an acolyte must study sutras with a living buddha, and the government does not permit anyone to hold that title anymore. "The masses have raised their consciousness and have not asked anyone to read scriptures," was the way another monk put it to me and a group of journalists from Peking.

Shortly before our arrival the government had reopened the Drepung and two other major holy places which had been closed since the start of the Cultural Revolution. They were the Potala, the magnificent 1,000-room palace upon a fortress upon a hill where the Dalai Lama resided, and the Jokhang, the golden-roofed temple built in 652 to commemorate the arrival of a Tang dynasty princess who brought Buddhism to Tibet. They had been placed under the Chinese-run Bureau for the Preservation of Cultural Relics, and stern-faced Chinese cadres in blue Mao tunics opened and closed the gates for our arrival and departure.

After a few days in Lhasa, I was inclined to accept a prophesy made in the fifth century B.C. by Sakyamuni, Buddha himself. He forecast that in 2,500 years, the present century, the faith he preached would die out. In Tibet, at first glance, that seemed to be coming true.

That was certainly the impression our Chinese hosts wanted to give. The Chinese presence is formidable. The First Party Secretary of Tibet is a Chinese, an army officer, and every few miles in the countryside there is a mud-walled Chinese fort with its garrison, looking like a French Foreign Legion outpost in *Beau Geste*. Only 120,000 of Tibet's 1.78 million people are Chinese, but they account for 53 percent of the cadres and many of the teachers, doctors, factory workers, and even bus and truck drivers. Although Lhasa is located eight hundred miles away from the nearest Chinese city, in Sichuan, separated by four mountain ranges each taller than the Rockies, the city awakens every morning to the strains of "The East Is Red" over loudspeakers in Chinese.

Tibetans and Chinese differ about the history of their relations. Tibetans argue that they were an independent nation with their own language, literature, and civilization and were never really occupied by China. Peking asserts Tibet "is an inalienable part of China." No effort is spared to reinforce this point.

In a fresco in the Potala honoring the thirteenth Dalai Lama, there is a scene that looks like His Holiness riding in a gold encrusted 1930s Packard sedan. The Dalai Lama, resplendent in an orange silk robe and high, yellow conical hat, is beaming graciously to a welcoming crowd. Our guide in the Potala, a pigtailed woman in her twenties, made a special point of showing us the mural. She said it depicted the thirteenth Dalai Lama's trip to Peking in 1908 to pay homage to the Chinese Empress Dowager, Ci Xi, and the boy emperor who was soon to be deposed by the Revolution of 1911.

The guide was not conscious of the drawing's anachronism. Indeed, it is a small point easily lost in the magnificence of the chamber, which also contains a fifty-foot-high stupa—a dome-shaped Buddhist shrine—coated with 270 pounds of gold and a miniature pagoda made from 250,000 pearls. The whole room, including the ceiling and pillars, is swathed in silk brocade.

But the guide used the fresco for a history lesson. It proved that Tibetans had always recognized China's suzerainty, she said. In the hall of the fifth Dalai Lama, she again pointed to a fresco showing a visit to Peking, this one in 1652. Score another point for China.

But did the Dalai Lama ever visit another country? a French newsman asked. No, the guide replied flatly. Then what, he pressed her, was a drawing that looked like the Dalai Lama on a pilgrimage to India, the homeland of the Buddha? "I don't know, I'm not a Buddhist," the guide responded, her temper rising.

But aren't you a Tibetan? she was asked. No, she confessed, she was a Chinese, from central China, and she didn't speak or read Tibetan. It was like having a German give the tour of the French forts at Verdun or a Japanese guide Americans around Pearl Harbor.

It was only after we had been in Lhasa for several days that I realized my mental picture of a moribund religion being inexorably squeezed out of existence was askew. The Jokhang, the most sacred of all the temples to Tibetans themselves, was open only three mornings a week to the public, and we had been taken there on a day when it was closed. So several of us decided to go back on our own when Tibetans could get in. To our surprise, the small square in an old section of the city around the temple was jammed with people; they formed a long line waiting to go inside. There were people from all over the high plateau of Chinese central Asia, pilgrims in grimy black robes, silver daggers at their belts, with high canvas boots and carrying chalices laden with yak butter for offerings. It looked like a picture in a medieval tapestry.

As the faithful entered the richly decorated inner chamber of the Jokhang, many fell to the floor, prostrating themselves before a statue of Guanyin, the goddess of mercy, or a gold-encrusted carving of Sakyamuni. One young man, with his face burned nearly black by the sun, which pierces the thin atmosphere at Tibet's altitude, kowtowed repeatedly for a full ten minutes. In an elaborate ritual, first he raised his hands over his head, then he folded them in a gesture of prayer before his face, dropped to his knees, and finally flung himself on the cement floor, hands and arms outstretched.

As he chanted an incantation, a boy about ten years old performed the same ritual beside him. Nearby an elderly woman, with a shaven head and a red blouse under her worn woolen robe, rubbed her wooden prayer beads before dropping to the floor. Along the walls of the temple other worshipers were pouring yak butter into open lamps. Some stuck coins or paper money at sacred spots with globs of melted butter.

It was a young Chinese cadre who helped me comprehend this fervor, the vitality of the Tibetan faith despite the government's destruction of the church organization. The cadre had been sent to Tibet from his home in Peking eight years before to work as an administrator in a small county seat. He and his wife, who was also from Peking, worried about the effect of the high altitude and the poor diet of wheat and barley on their children. So when his wife became pregnant, she went back to Peking to give birth and left her son and daughter with their grandparents. They saw their children only once every two years, when they got home leave. They yearned to be allowed to return to their home in the Chinese capital, but they had never been given any date for the end of their term of duty in Tibet. Yet the cadre said he felt more sorry for the Tibetans around him.

Despite government subsidies, grain production in his county had not increased since the Cultural Revolution; and the number of cattle, which produce milk for the butter that forms a mainstay of the Tibetan diet, had declined year after year. For the local Chinese officials had ordered the Tibetans to plant wheat, a Chinese crop, rather than barley, which the Tibetans eat. And the government had placed strict limits on the number of cattle the peasants could raise privately, equating prosperity with capitalism.

"The people's stomachs are never full," the cadre told me during a talk in Peking while he was on leave. "It is no wonder the Tibetans have no love for the Communist Party and put their faith in Lamaism." From the few Tibetans he had gotten to know, he learned that each family still selected one male member to secretly be a monk, in keeping with tradition, and that the Tibetans themselves still picked living buddhas.

When a delegation of exiled Tibetans, including the Dalai Lama's sister, visited his county town in 1980, the local people lined the streets to greet them. The visit had been arranged by Peking as a gesture of reconciliation to the Tibetans, with hopes it might entice the Dalai Lama himself to return from India. But the local people used it to make a point of their own. They prostrated themselves in front of the visitors and stuck out their tongues, the Tibetan sign of welcome.

"When the delegation passed, the people stuffed money into their pockets and begged to be rubbed on the head, which would ensure them a place in paradise," the cadre recalled. The people even deliberately jostled Chinese officials escorting the guests in the streets. It was a rude shock to the Chinese. The behavior of the Tibetans, like the activism of the young dissidents in

Peking and the Christians in Fuzhou, suggested there is still a range of deep human feelings in China, an inner center of resistance to political controls and enforced ideology, that even thirty years of Communist rule have not obliterated.

20. Serving the Workers and Peasants

为 工 农 服 务

WANG KEPING

"The statesman hates the writer because the writer sows the seeds of dissent. What the statesman dreams of is to be able to prevent people from thinking, and thus he always accuses the artists and writers of upsetting his orderly state."

Lu Xun

The floor of Wang Keping's fourth-floor walk-up apartment is littered with wood chips, the sign of his adopted trade, sculpture. To do his carving, he sits on a wood plank spread over two sawhorses—at night it doubles as his bed. He has only a few rough tools: a knife or two, and an awl he fashioned himself. It is always dark in Wang's six-by-ten-foot cubicle—the one small window doesn't seem to have the capacity for light—so when he works, he keeps on the single bare forty-watt bulb, suspended from the ceiling by a wire. Outside, on a tiny balcony, are several cabbages and a bowl with scraps of meat left over from a previous meal—Wang's refrigerator in Peking's long cold winter.

But clustered in rank upon rank on the walls above his head, jammed onto shelves, and stuck in corners around the room are the brooding, bitter, powerful works that have made Wang an important symbolic figure for many young Chinese. He is China's best-known dissident artist. On one shelf is a primitive, distorted gargoyle of a head titled "The Silence." One of its eyes is blinded, slashed in geometrical patterns, "so he gets only a one-sided view," Wang explained during a visit to his home. The nose has no nostrils with which to smell, and the mouth is plugged up with a cylinder, so he cannot speak. "This is our average bad cadre, he symbolizes our lack of freedom to speak what is in our hearts," Wang added. On another shelf is a satirical bust of Jiang Qing shaped from a toy wooden gun Wang found on the street. The stock is carved to look like a woman's skirt, the barrel is an extension of her arm, which she is using as a cudgel to beat people. "Mao always said, 'Political power grows out of the barrel of a gun,' " Wang added with a smirk.

Short, friendly, and ingratiating, with a soft, almost whispery voice and plain, homely features, Wang in person doesn't suggest the anger and brazen political challenge implicit in his carvings. I had to strain to hear his words.

Carefully concealed under his workbench-bed, hidden behind old rags, is his own favorite, a large totemic figure of Mao as Buddha, with one slanted eye closed in repose and the other slyly opened "to see who is praying and making their devotions to him." The resemblance to the late Chairman is striking; no one could miss the point. "It stands for the deification of the Communist Party and our worship of idols during the Cultural Revolution," Wang elaborated. His works are not subtle and sophisticated, at least by contemporary Western aesthetic standards; they are more crude and home-spun. Wang had only begun to sculpt in 1978, I later learned. But his carvings are provocative and moving, the invention of some minor form of genius.

Wang keeps the Mao icon secreted because he lives with uncertainty about how the police and the Party authorities who govern China's art world intend to deal with him. To compound the problem, Wang is not only irreverent and censorious in his sculpture, he is not, by the government's calculation, even an artist. By definition, artists in China must belong to one of the state art associations, an official *danwei,* like the Peking Art Academy or the Peking Creative Society. The older, more senior artists were accepted as members on the basis of their recognized work before 1949; the younger artists, with few exceptions, have had to go through a state art school, study formally, and pass academic exams. There is an advantage to this official sponsorship— these artists draw a regular salary and are provided with housing by the art associations, like other government employees. No airless garrets or worrying about where the next meal will come from for them. In return, these official artists are expected to teach in an art institute or commune or factory study class and to produce paintings to decorate hotels or perhaps sell in expensive shops to foreigners to earn hard currency.

They are also expected to conform to the Party's aesthetic canon. This was laid down, with breathtaking clarity, by Mao himself in 1942 in a series of talks on art and literature at Yanan. "Art for art's sake, art which transcends class or party, art which stands as a bystander to, or independent of, politics, does not in actual fact exist," Mao intoned. "In the world of today, all culture or literature and art belong to some one definite class, some one definite party." In China, Mao explained, that meant artists and writers must serve the workers and peasants. "Our literature and art are first and foremost for the workers, peasants, and soldiers." It also meant that artists would have to be reeducated. "The science of Marxism–Leninism is a required course, not excepting artists and writers." Mao was impatient with any art that did not glorify and idealize the workingman or that found fault with the Communist Party. "We cannot love our enemies or social evils; our aim is to eliminate both. How can our artists and writers fail to understand this commonsense view?"

The problem was, how should China's artists create the new national revolutionary art after 1949 that the Party wanted? The Communists were uncomfortable with China's traditional ink-wash landscapes, a relic of the feudal aristocracy, they thought. But they also condemned modern Western painting, virtually everything European and American since 1890, as "bourgeois formalism." Abstract art they abhorred as empty, form devoid of content, a morally neutral statement. Nudes were offensive to their revolutionary puritanism. One safe solution, China's post-Liberation artists found, was to churn out banal propaganda posters of clean, healthy, smiling pink-cheeked soldiers; another was to embellish an old landscape of mountains and mist and plum blossoms with a tractor cultivating the fields or a hydro-electric plant and high-tension power lines. China's great artistic tradition was muffled.

But Wang did not fit this mold. He had not attended an official art academy; he actually worked for Peking Central Television as a scriptwriter, and he had taken up sculpting as a hobby. In the fall of 1979, encouraged by Democracy Wall and the Party's temporarily more liberal line toward literature and art, he and a group of twenty-two other amateur artists decided to organize their own exhibition. It was a daring step. There had been very few art shows of any kind since the Cultural Revolution began in 1966. A few years before the radicals had taken works by China's most honored traditional painters and held an exhibit of "black art." Since 1949 no one had ever tried to open a display of his own work without clearance by the government art association. But when they could not get official permission, Wang and his friends went ahead anyway and set out 150 of their paintings and carvings on the sidewalk outside the Peking Fine Arts Museum for two sunny days in September. Each time the police broke up the exhibit and tried to confiscate their works, claiming they were "upsetting social order." But to their surprise, the group, who styled themselves "the Stars," had an unknown ally in the Art Museum who helped them take their paintings inside before the police could grab them.

Wang was never sure who authorized it—he speculated it must have been a sympathizer high in the Party—but after two months of negotiations with the Ministry of Culture, his group finally received permission to hold a formal show in the North Ocean Park behind the Forbidden City. Wang was ecstatic. The site lent for their exhibition was a lovely Qing dynasty courtyard, set around a frozen pond, which encompassed a series of small one-story pavilions decorated with flaming red, green, and blue prancing dragons and frolicking cats, all connected by covered walkways. It was late November and the temperature had already dropped close to zero, driven down by boreal gusts from Siberia, and none of the old buildings where the art was hung was heated. But that didn't discourage thousands of people from coming to see the show each day.

When I arrived, Wang was sitting on a balustrade over the pond, the reflected glare off the ice of the noonday sun in the azure sky giving the only warmth. He was also basking in the glow of sudden new glory. His fiercely provocative sculpture, though an unusual medium in China, had struck an instantaneous response. As I approached, a middle-aged man in a quilted black jacket and black scarf stopped to ask Wang for his autograph. As if in apology for the intrusion, he explained, "I used to be an artist, too, until they labeled me a counterrevolutionary for my sketches and locked me up for three years."

He came from the coal-mining city of Fushun in the northeast, the man said, where he and his friends had put out a private journal in which they published photographs of their paintings. There was no text, only the photographs and the titles of the works. The magazine circulated among a few art connoisseurs in the city. They had gotten through twelve issues before the "Counterattack the Right Deviationist Wind" campaign in early 1976 struck, the radical-inspired movement to dump Deng Xiaoping a second time. The amateur artist had been imprisoned and beaten. Now at last he had been freed and had come down to Peking to see Wang's show.

In traditional Chinese practice, the exhibitors had set out a large book and sheets of paper for comments by visitors at the gateway. The show included paintings in a variety of styles which had all been officially attacked as decadent—imitations of French Impressionists, haunting abstract canvases, and a sprinkling of nudes. But it was Wang's grotesque carvings that had stolen the show. A number of young Chinese stood beside them, tracing their blatantly political shapes in copy books.

"Wang Keping, we congratulate you on your daring," one visitor had written in an elegant calligraphic appreciation. "Compared with you, the professional sculptors of China are like walking corpses." Another guest commented, "Have the Chinese people gone numb? No, I have seen that the Chinese people's spirit is still alive. This is the best art exhibit since Liberation." The *People's Daily* and the other major government papers studiously ignored the exhibition.

One of the carvings on display, in dark brown wood that could almost have been African, was of a misshapen, mindless man with mouth agape, his two arms protruding to the side. In one hand is a little red piece of plastic, the infamous Little Red Book of Mao's quotations which millions of Red Guards memorized and embraced as their hymnal during the Cultural Revolution. In the other hand is a miniature knife, a symbol of the destruction the Red Guards wrought. The work is titled "Hold High," shorthand for the radicals' rallying cry, "Hold high the great banner of Chairman Mao."

The sculpture is an ironic personal indictment, for in 1967, fresh out of high school, Wang had been a self-righteous Red Guard and helped loot a Roman Catholic church in his home town of Tianjin. "I burned paintings like these and smashed statues," Wang recalled, still sitting on the balustrade, his long, unkempt hair protruding from beneath a gray worker's cap. "I believed Chairman Mao was our savior."

Wang was born in 1949, the same year the People's Republic was established, he recounted, and his father, a high-level Communist writer and army officer, had named him in commemoration of the Communists' triumph. His given name, Keping, means "Conquer Peking." His mother was a Party member, too, an actress in a military drama troupe, and his sister was in the navy. The sunny living room of their apartment—where Wang had his bedroom-studio—was decorated with pictures of his parents with Mao and Zhou Enlai. I was always amused that among the photos was one of his sister posed coquettishly on the bow of a rowboat, hand on her chin, with her legs showing under a short skirt, like some cheesecake snapshot from the 1940s.

Wang's transformation from fanatic votary to disillusioned skeptic had followed the path of so many young Chinese. Watching the endless factional wars among his Red Guard colleagues, the beatings, burnings, and arrests, he had come to question the purpose of the Cultural Revolution. Then at a critical juncture in his thinking, he had been shipped off to a state farm in Heilongjiang province, in the frozen northeast, part of Mao's rustication program to continue the Red Guards' revolutionary education at the hands of the peasants.

"It was terrible, worse than hell," Wang remembered. "Ten of us slept in one tiny room, all piled next to each other on one bed like dried persimmons, all squashed flat and wrinkled. And the lice, whew," he added, pursing his lips. He reached under his blue ski parka to squeeze an imaginary louse. It was an ignoble end to Wang's vision of revolution.

He had come to sculpture accidentally. Bored with his job as a writer, one day he picked up a piece of wood that had broken off a chair. "I didn't know how to carve, but as a scriptwriter I had been influenced by the French theater of the absurd, especially Beckett's *Waiting for Godot* and Ionesco's *The Bald Soprano.* So I decided to try to carve a kind of theater of the absurd in wood."

Finding wood to sculpt was a tough problem. China has such a huge population and its forests have been depleted for so many centuries that there is a chronic shortage of timber. In Peking lumber is not for sale to individuals, not even by ration coupons. But in China there is always the back door. Wang began dropping by a small factory that supplied kindling to people with wood-burning stoves.

"They are supposed to break up old pieces of wood into kindling, but sometimes the wood is too hard, or too big, or they are too lazy, and they don't chop it up," Wang recounted. "I made friends with them, chatted them up. Whenever I stopped in, I gave them a few presents—liquor, cigarettes, movie tickets. They began giving me wood." It was a modest supply, and the wood was knotted, gnarled, and rough, but that served to make his heretical carvings all the more disfigured.

His parents were originally opposed to his sculpting; good Party members, they were shocked by his unorthodox art. "They said I was wasting my time and would get in trouble," Wang told me. Only after his exhibit, when they read all the flattering comments, did they realize Wang wasn't mad. "They didn't say it, but they were secretly proud of me, I think."

Despite the exhibition, Wang lived in a kind of political minefield—he could never be certain when one misstep might lead to a confrontation with the authorities. So we arranged to rendezvous with conspiratorial precaution. I had recently come back from Hong Kong with two thick books on modern sculpture for Wang. At the show he had surprised me by saying he had never heard of Henry Moore, Brancusi, or Giacometti; the most recent Western sculptor he knew was Rodin, whose safe "realistic" works are reproduced in Chinese art books. Like other Chinese writers and artists, he lived isolated from the rest of the twentieth century. To meet Wang to deliver the books, I had to first drop him a note—he didn't have a telephone. Then, when he called from a public phone booth, without identifying himself, we agreed on the spot where we had last seen each other, the pavilion in the park, not mentioning the place over the phone for security reasons.

To be as inconspicuous as possible, we made our way from the pavilion to a quiet enclosure of artificial hills, rock gardens, and a covered promenade around a small pond. In imperial times, the emperor and his consorts must have played there, imagining the earth mounds to be mountains and the pond an ocean. In the distance skaters glided over the frozen surface of the park's main lake in the pale gray light of a Peking winter afternoon.

Wang was the first to notice something was wrong. "Police," he said simply, twisting his head slightly to the right. There they were, standing on one of the little man-made peaks, two men in bright-blue uniforms with high fur caps decorated with red stars. Did he want to leave? I asked. No, he replied.

"As the saying goes, a dead pig doesn't care about being scalded." He had already been spotted, it was too late.

From their perch on the hill, the two policemen, one tall and thin, the other short and round, descended to the stone bench where we were sitting, Wang, myself, and Jan Wong. I was half frozen by the bitter cold and a raging wind, but the sight of the police made me even chillier. They walked directly up in front of us, eyed the three of us, and I felt certain we were about to be arrested as spies. I had the two books in an Air France airlines bag at my feet, what must have looked to their suspicious eyes like proof of our evil intent. But instead of detaining us, the two officers sat down on our bench, one on either side of us, close enough so our legs and shoulders were touching and I could smell the garlic on their breaths.

I felt intimidated, but Wang kept his courage, he had lived with the system and still chose to challenge it. Wang generated a steady conversation about modern art, the virtues of form as content, the integrity of the artist, the names of famous museums in Europe and America. Finally, after fifteen minutes, the two policemen got up and left, walking away without a word.

On our way out of the park, I saw they had stopped at the little booth near the entrance where a middle-aged woman bundled in layers of padded clothing sold penny admission tickets. So she had tipped the police off that a Chinese and a foreigner were together in the park, I realized.

I offered Wang a ride in our car. The police didn't seem to have a vehicle, and we could drop him off where they couldn't follow him. But he declined.

"If they want to get you, they will," he said.

What reason would they give? I asked.

"They don't need a reason. After they arrest you, they will make up a reason. Reasons are very easy to come by. Besides, in our society, to have contact with a foreigner is one of the worst crimes." Wang knew, because after his show several agents from the Public Security Ministry had come to see him to ask why he had talked to foreign journalists. "They told me not to do it again, if I knew what was good for me."

Wang's hope, what kept him going, was a belief that Mao's successors hadn't yet entirely made up their minds about what kind of art was acceptable.

"Our new leaders have made their ideas about economics clear, but they have not yet decided about art and culture," he said during another encounter. "Many of them are still afraid of Western influences, thinking they are bad for China and immoral. The leaders have been isolated for such a long time that many of them are not very cultivated. But as living standards go up, there will be an effect on art and culture too. The best way to develop art is not to pay official attention to it at all."

I wondered if he was too sanguine. Deng's program for China is the Four Modernizations, four and no more: agriculture, industry, science, and defense. All are material. There are none for politics, social life, leisure-time recreation, or culture. That is not accidental. The term "the Four Modernizations" reflects Deng's own interests.

During his triumphal tour of the United States in early 1979, Deng was escorted one evening in Washington to a gala reception at the soaring new wing of the National Gallery of Art. It was designed by I. M. Pei, the Shanghai-born architect who is the best-known contemporary Chinese artistic figure in the world. (Why has China itself not produced contemporary artists of international stature? Wang once asked rhetorically, suggesting the reason lay with the government, not the race.) Pei, short, bouncy, and gracious, was eager to show Deng around the building. But Deng staggered his hosts by skipping the tour and leaving abruptly after he gave a prepared speech. I was standing next to an official of the Information Department, Yao Wei, a crew-cut, boyish-looking man in his fifties who had been educated at a school run by American missionaries and spoke English with a deceptively American accent. He always impressed foreigners who met him as being thoroughly Westernized. What did he think of Pei's creation? I asked.

At first Yao didn't respond. He hadn't really looked around, he confessed. Then when I pressed him further, he finally said, "What a queer building. If this is modern art, it is one modernization we don't need."

The Communists' selective interest in the West is not new. It goes back to the nineteenth century when the first Chinese reformers, seeking to modernize the old Central Kingdom in the face of incursions by the industrialized Western powers, pondered over what course to adopt. They hit on a formula that translates as "Western learning for practical use, Chinese learning for the essence." It meant China should copy the West's science and technology, its machines and gunboats, but somehow preserve its own philosophy and culture intact. China's leaders today, like their forebears, still have difficulty grasping that industrialization carries its own new values.

But Peking has fought to insulate itself against the contagion of most of the cultural developments of the twentieth century: atonal music, modern dance, stream-of-consciousness prose, abstract art. Several American and European orchestras visiting China have been asked not to perform any twentieth-century music. In 1981 the Communists vigorously sought to remove thirteen abstract paintings from the first show of American art in China since 1949. They backed down only at the last minute when U.S. officials threatened to cancel the whole exhibition if the paintings were taken out and scrap a Sino–U.S. cultural exchange agreement for the year. Even then, as a face-saving protest, the Chinese delayed the opening ceremony for an hour, holding up a speech by the U.S. Chief Justice, Warren E. Burger, who had flown to China in part to dedicate the exhibit. Among the canvases the Chinese objected to were Jackson Pollock's "Abstract Number 10" and works by Franz Kline and Helen Frankenthaler.

Wang himself had been subjected to this kind of dogmatism. He had once talked with officials from the Peking Art Academy about becoming a member; they said they could accept him only if he gave up his heretical work.

"They told me the workers, peasants, and soldiers can't understand my art, so it doesn't serve the masses," Wang related. "They accused me of being a slave of the West. I answered that they aren't workers, peasants, or soldiers themselves, so how do they know what the masses want."

Wang was not alone in playing this cat-and-mouse game with the authorities, searching for new modes of cultural expression before being suppressed. Many other artists and writers labor in silence and obscurity. Wang introduced me to one, a tall, reticent painter with a high forehead and finely chiseled features. He was a factory worker by trade but took up painting in his spare time. For several years he had lived in the far southwest of China, on the border with Laos, a region of tropical rain forests, towering jungle-covered mountains, and verdant valleys inhabited by the Dai ethnic minority, cousins of the Thais. For him, it was like Gauguin's journey to Tahiti. He came away with a mystical vision of this primitive land that he transformed into shimmering silvery-blue canvases, the colors of the rain forest. In his scroll paintings, which he unrolled for me, the people were engaged in some ancient ritual, the women eloquently slender, with bare breasts, long black hair cascading to their waists, and their narrow hips outlined in batik wrap skirts. His figures were all seated amid the forest, along with giant cranes whose own elongated legs and narrow frames mirrored those of the women.

His work was a blend of Chinese and Western sensibilities, of Chinese ink-wash colors and Western perspective, and I was enraptured. I asked if he had ever tried to sell any of his paintings. He had taken one, he said, to Rong Bao Zhai, the fancy shop on Wangfujing Street near the Peking Hotel which sells contemporary Chinese art to foreigners at inflated prices. They turned him down. "No one would understand it," the shop clerks told him. "Try sticking to landscape painting."

Another time I met an industrial designer who wanted to be a poet. From somewhere he had acquired an old leather jacket and he had let his hair grow long over his collar, still a rebellious act in China. It gave him the desired Bohemian effect. But his verse was too blasphemous, in subject matter and its free-wheeling style, to be accepted by the Party's cultural czars and win him a job as an established writer. So he had to settle for his factory post. He belonged to an informal group who called themselves the *tui-fei-pai,* literally the "decadent school," China's Beat poets. One evening he recited a verse he had titled "Mad Dog":

"After enduring cruelties,
I don't think of myself as a human being.
It is as if I had become a mad dog,
wandering around without purpose in the human world.
I am not yet really a mad dog;
if I were, I could jump over a wall when I am desperate.
Now all I can do is bear things in silence.
If I was really a mad dog,
Then I could free myself from this invisible chain and lock.
Then I would not hesitate
To give up my so-called human life."

Despite all his artistic trials, Wang considered himself better off than some Western artists, for he had a regular job that paid him an average wage, by Chinese standards. It was even better than that, Wang said, because he didn't have to go to work. The only time he reported to his office in the Central Broadcasting Station was on the fifth of each month to pick up his salary.

But didn't his absenteeism get him in trouble? I asked.

"It doesn't matter," Wang replied with a sly smile. "Under socialism, they can't fire you, that's one of the virtues of our system."

Of the five writers in his section, who were supposed to produce two-hour plays for evening television, none reported for work. "I'm actually considered the most productive," Wang went on. "At least last year I wrote one play. Some of them in twenty years haven't turned in a single manuscript for radio or television. They have good relations with the leaders of the office, so it doesn't matter.

"They don't use our plays anyway, they're not politically safe," he added. "The leaders prefer to use stories from the *People's Daily* or government magazines, that way they can't get in trouble. They have never used a single word I have written. When I submit a manuscript, about ten cadres have to read it. First one reads it, he gives it to another, who gives it to another, and so on."

It was beginning to sound as if Wang's idea for a theater of the absurd in wood grew out of his experience in the office. Here was a government that prided itself on ensuring that every worker had a job—how different from the evil ways of capitalism. But then in a mad burlesque of policy-making, the regime didn't care what happened in the office.

Wang laughed at my consternation. He had saved the choicest morsel for last. "Anyhow, even if I did go to work, I couldn't work, because there isn't an office anymore," he said with delectation. "The broadcasting station ran out of housing for the staff a long time ago, so they converted our office into a dorm. My leader even told me to stay home."

444

Wang's situation was not much different from that of workers assigned to factories that had never opened because of delays in construction or that had been closed down by Peking because of shortages of electricity and raw materials. They all still drew their pay. No one complained. It was the government's way of keeping people happy.

In the fall of 1980, not long before I left China, the country's most beloved movie actor died, Zhao Dan. He had starred in more than sixty films since the 1930s, and Chinese liked to compare him with Clark Gable. Zhao Dan was also a Communist, and as an indication of the esteem even the Party leadership held for him, he was visited in the hospital by no less than Deng, the new Prime Minister, Zhao Ziyang, and the then still Party Chairman, Hua Guofeng. Perhaps emboldened by these callers, Zhao Dan penned a deathbed appeal to the Party to relax its grip over literature and art.

"The Party can lead in formulating national economic planning and implementing agricultural and industrial policy," he wrote. "However, why should the Party tell us how to farm, how to make a stool, how to cut trousers or how to fry vegetables? Why should they instruct writers how to write, or actors how to act? Literature and art are the business of writers and artists. If the Party controls literature and art too tightly, there will be no hope for literature and art, they will be finished."

It was intoxicating language for China. What made it even more astonishing was that the *People's Daily* printed the text; that seemed to give it the Party's imprimatur. A few weeks later I paid a final call on Wang. I suggested he might have been encouraged by the movie star's plea and the *People's Daily*'s action. Wang eyed me with disdain, like a teacher chastising a schoolboy who forgot his lesson. Didn't I know what had happened? Wang asked. The Politburo was furious about the article. The *People's Daily* had acted on its own authority, without checking with the Party leadership. Now the paper's liberal editors had been forced to make a self-criticism. Things were getting tighter again, Wang sensed; Deng had told a Party meeting that there had been too much "bourgeois liberalism" in culture. Wang was desolate. He knew he would have to draw his carapace around him again, like an armadillo's hide, to toughen himself for the harder Party line.

Before I left, Wang had a present to give me. It was an old Qing dynasty vase, in yellow and famille rose, emblazoned with dragons and flowers. But the gaudy glaze was chipped and there was a jagged piece missing from the vessel's narrow mouth. Wang had scavenged it in the Cultural Revolution.

"It is broken, I know," he said, handing it to me with both hands, a Chinese gesture of politeness. "Consider it a symbol of our broken culture."

China, the West, and the Future

EPILOGUE

"The present of the Soviet Union is the future of China."
Zhou Enlai, 1959

During Deng Xiaoping's historic journey to the United States in 1979, the first by a senior Chinese Communist leader since 1949, a group of high-ranking officials and army officers in Peking were attending a banquet. There were the usual cold plates of crispy jellyfish in mustard sauce followed by sliced giant prawns with green peppers and roast Peking duck served with sesame-seed buns and flat wheat pancakes. The cadres had drunk several bottles of *maotai,* the clear, fiery liquor brewed in the mountains of southwest China, and they grew unusually candid. There was a television set in an anteroom of the private government guesthouse where they were dining, and after their meal they adjourned to watch scenes of Deng's tour broadcast by satellite from the United States. The screen showed Deng visiting a highly automated Ford automobile assembly plant in Georgia that turns out fifty cars an hour and the gleaming seventy-three-story Peachtree Plaza Hotel with its glass elevators in Atlanta, where Deng was staying.

The officials had been congratulating themselves on China's recent break-through in relations with the United States—normalization had taken place only a month before—but as they watched the images on the color tube, their composure was shaken. China had been cut off from the West for so many years by Mao's insistence on self-reliance and the endless round of political campaigns, culminating in the Cultural Revolution, that they didn't know how great a gap now existed between them and the industrialized world.

Finally, when the day's television footage of Deng's tour was over, one of the cadres turned to the others. "What have we done?" he asked. "Have we wasted thirty years?"

A son of one of the men at the banquet, Weidong, told me about it later. It had been an extraordinary moment, he said, for these were all veterans of the Communists' early days in Yanan in the 1930s, and some had been on the Long March. They were proud men—they had thrashed the Nationalists, beaten the Japanese in World War Two, in their view, fought the world's greatest power, the United States, to a standstill in Korea, and then stood up to the Soviet Union when it suddenly withdrew its aid and advisers and turned from friend to foe in 1960. They had initiated China's industrialization in the 1950s, exploded a hydrogen bomb, and launched an ICBM. But had they really succeeded?

This was a question I found many Chinese asking about the Communists in 1979 and 1980, several years after Mao's death and the overthrow of the radicals. There was a mood of introspection and self-doubt. Some senior Chinese officials and foreign sympathizers inevitably answered that things of course were much better under the Communists than they were under the warlords, the Japanese, or the corrupt Nationalists. But that response ignored the reality that 65 percent of China's one billion people—650 million of them—have been born since Liberation and don't remember the bad old days. They are concerned only with what the Communists have done in recent years, when all they can remember is tumultuous political campaigns and a sluggish economy. The comparison with pre-1949 China also seemed to me to be condescending and insulting. It suggests that China could not do as well economically as its neighbors Taiwan and South Korea, or achieve both the political democracy and the economic growth of Japan. Some foreign apologists for China point to the improvements in health care, literacy, life expectancy, and cleanliness and contrast China with India. But India, except for the Gandhi coup, has maintained its political freedoms; there have been no unchecked Public Security Ministry, no street committees, no network of forced-labor camps, no persecution of whole groups of people because they were intellectuals or had relatives who had once been landlords, no destruction of libraries and universities. And India, in any case, belongs to a different culture. It should be measured against Pakistan, Burma, Bangladesh, and Sri Lanka, just as China should be weighed with Korea, Japan, Taiwan, Hong Kong, and Singapore, countries that share similar cultural values and social organization.

It was the model of Taiwan which most troubled my Chinese friends. Taiwan's 18 million people had all come from China, and it was run by a government which had failed miserably on the mainland. But with China's greater openness after Mao's death, my acquaintances now knew that Taiwan's per capita income had reached $2,000 a year, that 95 percent of the island's families had television sets, and that an increasing number of people had their own cars. Taiwan is no bastion of democracy—the Nationalists have their own formidable secret police. But Taiwan now does have hotly contested local elections and its citizens are largely free to travel abroad as tourists or students.

"What young people like me want to know is why China can't do as well as Taiwan," Weidong said one evening when he and his wife, Hong, came over to our apartment for dinner.

But for all the disaffection and cynicism of China's young people, the demoralization in the Party, and the rise of problems like crime, unemployment, and inflation, I had no sense that the Communists' hold on China is in danger.* For one thing, their control apparatus, with its police, the *danwei* organization, the street committees, and political study, remains intact. For another, China is such a vast country that it took even the Communists thirty years to succeed in their revolution despite having a nation that was torn raw by foreign invasion, famine, banditry, and total economic collapse.

But most important, despite all the discontent, the Chinese are in no mood for more disruption. To borrow Richard Nixon's phrase, there is a silent majority of Chinese who want nothing more than the political stability and economic prosperity that Deng himself yearns for. People may grumble in private about the shabby, inadequate housing, the higher prices, the constricted opportunities for education and jobs, and the political harassment. But they still accept the current system as the best they can hope for. Almost no one wants a return to the Maoist style of mass movements and organized enthusiasm which they are afraid is the alternative to Deng and his program.

"What every Chinese hopes for," said a thirty-year-old college English teacher in Shanghai, "is that there will never be a political campaign again. I don't think that even if the radicals somehow managed to make a comeback they could get a movement started. People are too tired." The teacher, a lithe, very pretty woman with large almond eyes, permed hair, and a penchant for well-tailored clothes, summarized her feelings in one phrase: "For me and my friends, politics is dead." Although she doesn't feel she has benefited by Communist rule, she said she will go along with the government, hoping that Deng can improve the standard of living. For her, any further revolution in China will have to be economic, not political.

How well China's economy does may depend on four factors. First, can Peking really brake the increase in population? Even if all Chinese follow the government's plan of one child per family, the population will still mount to 1.2 billion by the end of the century. That raises the second question: can a nation with 1.2 billion people, roughly a billion of them peasants, with a land area only about the size of the United States and only one tenth of that

*Prices rose from 6 to 15 percent in both 1979 and 1980, depending on whose estimates you accept, not an astronomically high inflation rate by world standards. But it shocked the Chinese, who had enjoyed years of virtual total price stability.

cultivable, hope to do more than just feed itself? If Peking is to make an economic breakthrough, it will have to shift vastly greater resources to agriculture than it has been willing to do so far, giving the peasants a better price for their produce and stop charging them exorbitant costs for tractors and chemical fertilizer. Third, the Communists will have to tackle their own bureaucracy and the Chinese traditional love of hierarchy which sprouted it. Deng started a progressive program to reform industrial management in 1979 and 1980, but then, faced with opposition within the Party, suspended it. He will have to go further. Fourth, Peking will have to win back the confidence of the young people, since, after all, those under thirty make up the great bulk of the population. That means much more government investment in education, faster promotion for younger people, higher wages, and more production of consumer goods like television sets and tape recorders. Unless Peking can overcome the lassitude of many young people and give them new incentive, productivity in factories will remain low and crime and social discipline will remain problems.

What kind of country will China be a decade from now? Will it be a giant version of Taiwan or South Korea with its own economic miracle as Deng and his colleagues hope? The more likely course, an economist attached to the Academy of Social Sciences suggested, is a continued pattern of uneven development. Some cities, like Peking and Shanghai, with their strong industrial bases and large numbers of educated people, will shoot ahead; similarly, some rural areas, particularly those close to the cities with fertile land and plentiful rainfall, will grow rapidly. But other less-favored cities and more remote villages will lag behind, pockets of poverty.

It is easy for foreigners to be overwhelmed by China, to see China as one vast uniform country and miss the vital differences between regions. But already the per capita gross national product of Shanghai is $1,600, according to government figures, more than six times the national average and close to that of Taiwan. Shanghai's factories account for one eighth of the nation's industrial output; they contribute one fourth of all China's exports; and they provide the government in Peking with one sixth of its national revenue.

That is all the more astounding because after 1949 the new Communist regime deliberately set out to shift Chinese industry from the vulnerable and, in its view, decadent cities along the east coast, where it was then concentrated, to the undeveloped interior. In the First Five-Year Plan, which began in 1953, of the 156 major industrial projects, none went to Shanghai. From 1949 to 1979, Shanghai's factories got $10.6 billion less government investment than those in Hubei province, in central China. But Shanghai's industries, with their more experienced management and educated workers, prospered while Hubei's remained weak. In 1980 the total assets of Hubei's factories amounted to $933 million more than those of Shanghai's factories, but their output was only one third of Shanghai's industry. Shanghai's success is also remarkable because in three decades it has gone from being a city of 5 million people to 11.4 million, with a suffocating population density of 100,000 people per square mile in the downtown area, more than four times that of Tokyo and ten times that of New York. For thirty-one years, a Shanghai city official told me, there was never an overall plan for its urban development. Housing and sewerage and transportation in parts of the city are a disaster.

But like New York and Tokyo, Shanghai exudes a vitality, a sophistication, a grasping will to succeed born of its crowded, competitive circumstances. Unlike Peking and other cities, some of Shanghai's restaurants stay open twenty-four hours a day, and Shanghai women have the reputation for being the best dressed in China, an impression easily confirmed during a stroll down Nanking Road, the city's main shopping thoroughfare.

"We pay more attention to what we look like," said a spirited young guide from the China Travel Service who escorted me during during my first tour of the metropolis. She had on pink-tinted sunglasses, a pair of tightly cut gray wool slacks, and a dash of lipstick. "In Peking, all they care about is their cabbages and dumplings."

During another visit I remember watching a basketball game at the domed 18,000-seat Shanghai Sports Stadium between a team of visiting U.S. college all-stars and the Sichuan provincial team. At the outset the crowd cheered for the Chinese team to win, but as the Americans pulled ahead 61 to 30 at half time, the spectators began to jeer at the Sichuan players. "They're only from Sichuan, what do you expect?" cursed a pudgy middle-aged man in an army uniform in the row behind me. When a Sichuan forward missed an easy lay-up shot, another man yelled derisively, "For Sichuan, nothing works, they're country bumpkins." It was Chinese provincialism at its best, or worst.

If these differences were pronounced in the past three decades, they are likely to become even more important in the future because Mao's successors have announced they now want to concentrate their scarce investment resources on fast-growing areas that will produce the quickest return, like Shanghai. The theory is that economic progress in the advanced regions will trickle down to the more backward cities and villages, which will grow more slowly whatever is done.

"We tried all getting rich together, eating from the same pot," the economist from the Academy of Social Sciences related. "But egalitarianism dampened enthusiasm and efficiency. Now some people will get rich quicker and we think they will pull the others along."

Despite Deng's interest in raising the standard of living as fast as possible and avoiding Maoist political brawls, I left China pessimistic about whether

Deng would really prove more liberal than Mao in his approach to cultural and political freedom. My skepticism was unhappily confirmed a few months after I returned to the United States when the *Liberation Army Daily,* the army newspaper, bitterly assailed a new screenplay titled *Unrequited Love* written by a well-known author and army major, Bai Hua. Although Bai Hua was a veteran of the People's Liberation Army since the 1940s, he had been an outspoken advocate of greater freedom of expression for artists and writers. His film script told the story of a painter who returned to China after 1949, filled with patriotism and a desire to take part in the building of a new China. But during the Cultural Revolution he is harshly persecuted for his suspected foreign connections, and he finally takes refuge in a reed marsh, subsisting on raw fish. After the downfall of the radicals in 1976, he collapses in a snow-covered field and dies. His body leaves an imprint in the shape of a huge question mark. The painter makes clear his point before dying when he says, "I love the motherland, but the motherland does not love me." His predicament is familiar to many Chinese, like my friend Dr. Bill Gao. But the army paper was outraged by the story, accusing Bai Hua of attacking the leadership of the Communist Party. He was forced to make a self-criticism, and no less a person than the new Party Chairman, Hu Yaobang, delivered a major speech in September 1981 indicating the Communists had decided to retract much of their experiment with a more liberal policy toward the arts during 1978 through 1980. Hu proclaimed that the Party would no longer tolerate the kind of "bourgeois liberalism" and "pernicious writing" that he said cast doubt on the supreme virtues of socialism or exposed flaws in Communist society.

"We should all come forward to criticize and resist works of this kind as well as those who thrust them on the public, especially on young readers with little experience of life," Hu muttered. "Some comrades have done well and written many good works" glorifying socialism, Hu continued. But, he warned, the Party was furious with those writers "who have an ingrained hatred for New China, socialism, and our Party."

"We must punish them by law for their counterrevolutionary activities," Hu demanded. The new One Hundred Flowers, which Deng had said should blossom after the toppling of the radicals in 1976, had wilted.

I recalled a remark my friend Bing had made that now seemed prophetic. "You foreigners don't understand China," she said to me. "You take our political squabbles too seriously. There really isn't any difference between Deng and Hua Guofeng, or between Hu Yaobang and Mao. They are all authoritarians. They don't believe in democracy, only in Party leadership. They are all out of touch with what young Chinese are thinking." It was a somber assessment, but Bing carried her thought further. "China really isn't that different from the Soviet Union. We just smile more than the Russians, so the Chinese people seem nicer." In her view the difference between Chinese communism and the Russian brand had only been Mao's rhetoric about revolution and egalitarianism, but much of that was a fraud and now Deng had abandoned it.

But there is one crucial difference between China and the Soviet Union. Despite having a 4.5 million-man army, nuclear weapons, and intercontinental ballistic missiles, China is not a superpower. Peking's ability to affect international events, to project its authority beyond its borders, is limited. China looms larger in our imaginations because of the sheer size of its population than it does in military or diplomatic terms. For the weapons of China's army, navy, and air force are largely antiquated versions of thirty-year-old Soviet designs, and Chinese strategic doctrine still calls for defense by a people's war fought on Chinese territory rather than any aggressive pre-emptive strikes outside the country's borders. Surprisingly, Deng has not moved swiftly to improve the military's arsenal. In his Four Modernizations program, defense conspicuously ranks last, and Peking has actually cut defense spending by almost 33 percent from a high of $14.7 billion in 1979 to an estimated $10 billion in 1981. Taken together, these constraints have made Peking more a regional than a global power.

China's limited outreach has been underscored by its frustration in stopping recent Soviet interventions, ranging from Angola in 1975 to Ethiopia and Afghanistan. Since China's foreign policy is built on one fundamental objective, as it has been for a decade, countering what it sees as the world-wide threat of Soviet expansion, China's inability to respond to Moscow's moves has been painful to Peking's leaders. The Chinese were particularly disconcerted by their failure to prevent Vietnam from realizing its dream of dominating Laos and Cambodia, thanks to Moscow's backing. As for Europe, Chinese power and influence seem even more modest. As Zhou Enlai once remarked to a Yugoslav journalist, "Faraway water cannot put out fires."

But for the United States, China remains an important ongoing foreign policy issue. President Nixon's trip to China in 1972 and then President Carter's normalization of relations with Peking at the end of 1978 laid the basis for new ties between Peking and Washington, ending decades of hostility. These ties have been filled out by a series of subsequent bilateral agreements on the thorny frozen claims and assets problem, on aviation, shipping, grain sales, and most-favored-nation tariff status for China. But despite these advances, there are still real choices before both the Chinese and the Americans over whether they want to be adversaries, friends, or military allies. There are still two basic unresolved questions—Taiwan and Sino–U.S. defense cooperation. These unanswered questions give Chinese–American relations a fragile, tentative quality that most Westerners don't realize.

The normalization process of the 1970s worked only because of a brilliant tactical agreement by both Peking and Washington to set aside the Taiwan problem. On the U.S. side, Washington acceded to Peking's position by recognizing that there is only one China and that Taiwan is part of China; but at the same time, America reserved the right to "maintain cultural, commercial, and other unofficial relations with the people of Taiwan" and said it would continue to sell "arms of a defensive character" to Taipei. Parallel with this, Peking dropped its long-standing belligerent stance toward the Nationalists. China stopped referring to "liberating" Taiwan and instead offered a number of proposals that would lead to gradual unification between the mainland and Taiwan, theoretically allowing Taiwan, as a region of China, to keep its own capitalist economy, its political system, and even its army. The Communists also invited President Chiang Ching-kuo, Chiang Kai-shek's son, to visit the mainland and take part in unification talks.

But none of these conciliatory moves by Peking and Washington have solved the impasse over Taiwan. On the island itself, virtually none of the 18 million inhabitants—15 percent of whom fled to Taiwan with the Nationalists in 1949 and 85 percent of whom are descended from earlier immigrants from Fujian province—want to be placed under Communist rule. There is a real fear that Taiwan would lose its high standard of living. And for the native Taiwanese, there is deep-seated hatred and distrust of all mainland governments. Given the Nationalists' superior economic record, they might have taken the initiative by inviting the Communists to come and inspect their model of development. But instead, each of Peking's overtures has only made President Chiang more defensive. Although his power is unquestioned, he is seventy-two years old, he is a diabetic, and it seems unlikely he will last through another decade. He has intentionally prevented any strong man from emerging as a possible successor, so his death could touch off a period of uncertainty. This in turn makes Peking nervous, because the Communists fear a native Taiwanese might emerge in control and try to set up a government that would make Taiwan permanently independent of the mainland.

Taiwan poses a delicate continuing problem for President Reagan, particularly the issue of U.S. arms sales to the Nationalists. The Communists were annoyed by Reagan's pro-Taiwan rhetoric during the presidential campaign, and their suspicions about him have led to a hardening of China's attitude toward the United States. Peking was outraged by the Reagan Administration's decision in January 1982 to allow Taiwan to buy more F-5-E jet fighters, claiming it constituted interference in China's internal affairs, even though the Nationalists were disappointed that Washington turned down their request for a new, more advanced aircraft. Senior Communist officials have now warned that the United States should clear any weapons sales in advance with Peking or face a possible downgrading of regular diplomatic relations.

In the long run, there is no clear solution to the Taiwan problem. It is impractical for either the United States or any other country, including Japan, which maintains close ties with both Peking and Taipei, to act as mediator. There is a growing indirect trade between Taiwan and the mainland, routed through Hong Kong and Japan, that may amount to as much as $200 million a year. But unless the people on Taiwan have a real change of mind, the political impasse will remain. And since Taiwan represents an emotional, nationalistic issue to Peking, and a matter of loyalty to an old ally of Americans, it may be a potential time bomb to Chinese–American relations.

The other unresolved issue in Sino–U.S. relations is how far the two sides wish to move toward transforming their current entente into a military alliance. From the beginning, in the late 1960s, with the Russian invasion of Czechoslovakia and then the Sino–Soviet border war of 1969, China has looked to improved relations with the United States primarily for strategic and security reasons. But while the Chinese have recently expressed interest in buying U.S. weapons—such as antiaircraft and antitank missiles that would give them a quick improvement in their defense capability against a Russian attack—Peking has not actually made any purchases. Part of the problem is money; China's foreign exchange earnings are too small. The other problem is that Peking is afraid that if it buys American weapons it will be trapped into accepting the sale of more U.S. arms to Taiwan. There are also reservations on the American side. Would the sale of lethal arms to China provoke the Soviet Union more than it would increase Peking's and therefore America's defense against the Russians? Would the Chinese someday turn their American weapons on Taiwan or the United States? But if China wants to buy American arms, can Washington now refuse without relations slipping backward? Part of Peking's quarrel with Moscow was over what the Chinese saw as the Soviets' failure to meet the expectations of aid they had created.

For ordinary Chinese, however, their interest in the West has little to do with these questions of strategy and diplomacy. Instead, many of the Chinese I met, rightly or wrongly, were enthrall to a dream of going abroad to study or live, even older people whose lives were already fixed in narrow grooves. A few days before I left China, I had a last dinner with our friends the Wangs, Miao and Li. Miao was fidgety during the meal, as if there was something on her mind. Finally, after the dishes had been cleared and the small table folded up and stashed in the corner, she said she had something private she wanted to discuss and asked me into their other room, their daughter Yuanyuan's bedroom. In the dim light of a twenty-watt bulb and the bone-chilling cold of an unheated room in January, she announced she had a plan.

"I want to go to America, I would like to learn something more," she said, looking me straight in the eye. Miao was forty, only a year younger than I, and I marveled at her ambition, her energy.

"I will bring Yuanyuan so she can go to school in America and get a better education than she could here in China. I am willing to do anything, even be a maid," Miao went on, her words rushing out in a torrent. "I am not afraid of hard work. I am not proud. My health is good. I can *chi-ku*" (eat bitterness).

What about her husband, wouldn't he object? I asked. Li had quietly entered the room and sat down on Yuanyuan's bed.

"He doesn't mind," Miao answered. Li nodded in assent. "I have done a lot for him already. Later I will bring him too if he wants to come. I want to expand. There is no chance for that in China. The future is too uncertain, too dangerous. There are too many campaigns. What happens if Deng dies?" she asked, presupposing the answer would be chaos. Miao had become very emotional; her eyes were moist, and there were tears on her cheeks.

Would I help arrange it? Miao asked. Could I find an American family where she could work as a maid? I stumbled, hesitant in reply. I would try, I said. As I left their house that night, I drove out past the gleaming-white statue of Chairman Mao in front of their apartment building, his regal visage staring into the distance, and I remembered that both Miao and her husband were Communist Party members.

But perhaps this wasn't as strange as it seemed. Mao had turned to communism in the early 1920s because, after the victory of the Russian Revolution in 1917, it had seemed the latest and best panacea from the West. Now Chinese were searching again. They were looking for a new solution to make China "rich and strong," and for many Chinese, the United States seemed the richest and strongest nation, or at least the most attractive place to live. When the Party hierarchy ordered the giant portraits of its Communist ancestors, Marx, Engels, Lenin, and Stalin, taken down from the Square of the Gate of Heavenly Peace in 1980, where they had hung in honor for two decades, it was a significant signal. Marx and Engels, with their bushy whiskers and prominent noses, had always looked out of place in China, like the pictures on the Smith Brothers cough drops. I wondered if China was on its way to absorbing and transforming communism the way it had swallowed Buddhism centuries before. Deng himself had declared that all communism really meant was "seek truth from facts."

On my final departure from China I had what seemed a small augury of things to come. When I had entered China the first time, in April 1976, it was by train from Hong Kong. Like other visitors, I had to get off the British train at Lo Wu and walk with my baggage across the railroad bridge to the Chinese border checkpoint of Shenzhen. The cavernous, dank hall where we passed through immigration and customs—the proceedings took over an hour—was decked with red flags and large portraits of Chairman Mao and it resounded with the piercing strains of "The East Is Red" played over dozens of loudspeakers. The only diversion was racks filled with back copies of the *Peking Review* and *China Pictorial,* China's English-language propaganda magazines. At the time, because the Chinese couldn't or wouldn't coordinate their train and plane schedules, it took two days to get from Hong Kong to Peking, with an overnight stop in Canton. The journey is only about the same distance as from Puerto Rico to New York and could be accomplished in a three-hour plane ride.

But on my last exit from Peking, to return to the United States in 1981, both CAAC and Pan American had established direct flights from the Chinese capital to San Francisco and New York. Clearing immigration and customs at the Peking airport was a brief formality, and then on the other side of the official barrier, to my consternation, was an area of gleaming, new, white Formica counters set up by Duty Free Shoppers, the worldwide American-owned chain of airport shops. There were stalls with French perfume, shelves of Scotch whisky, display cases full of Swiss watches and gold pens, and boxes of chocolate-covered macadamia nuts from Hawaii, a passion among Japanese travelers. And there were no propaganda broadcasts. It was only a five-year difference in time, but a century in ideology and economic change, or so it seemed.

Yet was China progressing fast enough to make up for all the years that had been squandered, all the dreams and lives that had been shattered? When I sat down in my seat in the CAAC Boeing 747 for the trip across the Pacific, I noticed that the passenger assigned the seat next to me was a serious-looking rosy-cheeked woman in her late twenties with a broad face and short pigtails. She was dressed in rumpled, loose brown wool pants and had a green plaid shirt under her regulation blue Mao jacket. Her feet were resting on a pile of straw baskets, part of her luggage. She had evidently not been on a plane before, because when the stewardess announced that it was time for everyone to fasten their seat belts, she did not react. That gave me an opportunity to strike up a conversation with her, demonstrating how to put the two ends of the belt together, but aside from a perfunctory "Thank you," she kept her silence.

As soon as the plane cleared the runway, however, her demeanor abruptly changed. She turned to me with a warm smile. "I'm going to the United States," she said, "to Chicago, to study, where my aunt lives." Then as she watched the flat, brown parched earth of north China retreat and grow smaller beneath us, she added, "And I'm not coming back." She seemed to be talking to the country spread out below as much as to me, and I was curious why she would make such a decisive utterance.

"It's because of my father," the woman explained, adding that her name was Ping. He had earned his doctorate in engineering at the Massachusetts Institute of Technology, she related, and had elected to come back to China in 1949 out of strong feelings of patriotism. Her story was starting to sound ominously familiar.

"The 1950s and early 1960s were a good time for our family," Ping went on. "My father earned a very high salary, three hundred twenty-five yuan [$217], way above average. We lived in a very comfortable house of our own provided by the Academy of Sciences, and my father made a number of trips abroad to the Soviet Union and East Germany. He was recognized as a leading authority.

"But then in the Cultural Revolution they dredged up his background as a student in the United States and accused him of being a counterrevolutionary. They threw him in jail until his health was broken and he had a heart attack. They dragged my mother off to a cowshed," a makeshift prison in the institute where both her parents worked. The radicals also seized their house, throwing the family out on the street, and forced Ping out of school. She was only in the sixth grade. Instead of continuing her education, she was assigned to work in a textile factory, where she had been for the past ten years. The terrible agglomeration of events had destroyed her faith in the Communists, though not her love for China.

"I have been raised in the motherland for twenty-six years, I will always be a Chinese no matter what," Ping said. But if she was going to stay permanently in the United States, would she consider marrying an American? I asked. "No, I will never marry an American, I am a Chinese," she said.

"But even though I love my country very much, I will not make the same mistake my father did," Ping said, looking at me directly. "He wasted his life."

To me, Ping's story summarized the tragedy of China in the past three decades, all the hope, the energy, the talent, the idealism that were wasted, blighted by misguided political passions. Now it was up to the Communists to try to win back popular confidence or face a steady hemorrhage of China's human resources as people lost interest in their work or actually left the country, like Ping.

"If China ever opened its doors," Ping said as we caught sight of the muddy waters of the Yellow Sea, "everybody would go. To the United States."

Index

children (continued)
  sale of, 255
  See also education; youth
China, People's Republic of:
  as "Chinese" vs. "Communist,"
    61–62, 69–70, 87, 175, 217, 273,
    330
  constitution of, 165, 324, 356
  demography of, 14, 15, 16, 141,
    181, 196, 197, 220, 237–239,
    247, 270, 327, 448
  egalitarian rhetoric and practice in,
    64–88, 100, 101, 164–165, 168,
    176–177, 199, 244, 276–277,
    450, 452
  fate of revolution in, 6, 8, 19–20,
    70, 88, 181, 201–202, 225, 298,
    309, 448
  geography of, 14, 239
  historical national character of,
    12–13, 24–26, 41–42, 44, 48–49,
    52, 56–57, 61–63, 69, 72,
    133–134, 164, 196, 207–208,
    217, 252, 281, 284–286, 289,
    298, 329, 408, 412, 415
  minority peoples in, 240, 372–373,
    427–434, 443
  prospects for future of, 446–456
  Westerner's view of, 6–7, 26, 447,
    449
  Western influences and, 37–38,
    441–443, 446, 453–454
  xenophobia in, 24–25, 289
China Democratic League, 163
China Reconstructs, 179
China Travel Service, 3, 66
China Youth League, 201
China Youth News, 142–143, 157, 397
Chinese Music Association, 186–187
Chinese People's Association for
    Friendship with Foreign Countries,
    175
Chin Shi Huang, 12
Cho Lin, 169
Chong Wen Men market, 103
chop (seal), 62, 99
Christianity, 7–8, 202, 422–426
Church, Frank, 53–54
cigarettes, 81, 86, 95, 153
Clark, Marsh, 281–282
Classic for Girls, 164
Coale, Ansley J., 242n
Coming Alive, China After Mao
    (Garside), 34

communes, 27–28, 116, 165–166,
    170, 219, 238, 240–252
communications system, 383–405
  classified documents in, 388–392
  libraries and, 399–401
  museums and, 404–405
  public vs. semi-clandestine, 384,
    388, 389, 391
  shortwave broadcasts and, 410
  television and, 398–399
  Xiao-dao xiao-xi in, 391–392
  See also newspapers and journals;
    specific publications
Communist Party, 7, 181, 200, 356
  artistic conformity and, 186–187,
    436–437, 445, 451
  bureaucracy and, 286–292
  Central Investigation Department of,
    335
  contemporary attitudes toward,
    448–452
  control by, 122–123, 124, 249, 308,
    322, 328, 329, 334, 344, 364,
    376–377
  corruption in, 11, 361
  cult of Mao and, 301–304
  disaffection from, 138, 181–182,
    201, 295–301, 310–312
  educational levels in, 290–292
  factions in, 292–294
  foreigners as viewed by, 26
  headquarters of, 62
  intellectuals in, 416–418
  loyal supporters of, 218, 228
  marriage policy in, 154–155
  Marxism and, 62, 68, 69, 164, 299,
    300–301, 327, 408, 414, 417,
    421–422, 455
  Military Affairs Commission of, 169
  military personnel in, 76–77, 297
  news stories on, 383–385, 387, 390,
    393
  peasants in, 248, 287, 288–290,
    292, 297
  persecutions by. *See* political
    persecutions and repression
  prerogatives of officials of, 8–9, 67,
    70–78, 83–87, 155–158, 189,
    288, 296–297, 359, 361, 392
  Propaganda Department of, 187, 384
  secrecy imposed by, 383–391, 392,
    405
  self-evaluation in, 299, 302
  United Front Department of, 429